Two v

To my husband on
Valentine's Day
February 14th 2013
All my love, Wifey xxx

Stephen W Follows

Stephen W Follows

Published March 2011 by Stephen W Follows

Authors note

Although some actual locations and titles are used, this is a work of fiction.
Any resemblance to actual events, organisations, or persons, living or dead, is entirely coincidental.

ISBN 978-0-9566 109-5-9

Published by Stephen W Follows
Jericho Road
Newark
NG24 3GT

Printed by Berforts Group
Stevenage, Herts SG1 2BH

Cover design by Aimee Fry

Stephenwfollows.co.uk

Comments on the works of Stephen W Follows

'Great; polished and well written'

'A clever and complex story'

'Nice professional writing style'
Leigh Ferrani, Author

'Unputdownable'
Elaine Hunt, Peterborough

'Thrillers should have a good strong ending and this doesn't disappoint'
Oxford Literary Consultancy

'Very clever; it certainly kept me guessing'
Andrea De Ville, Queniborough

'Had me guessing right up until the end; looking forward to the next one'
Rachel Allsworth, Oxford

1

The red roofed buildings of Abrego in North East Colombia, started to take in the heat of the sun as it came up over the mountains to the east. The light shone on the white walls, shutters were being opened and dogs started to bark. One of those buildings was an old farmhouse, not far from Highway 74. In a small back room of that house, seven Rebel Guerrilla soldiers were sitting around a large wooden table next to a wide cast iron fireplace. The fire was burning well, taking the chill off the early morning damp. At one end of the table, Column Commander Antonio Compito was tapping the table with his fingers. He looked at the other six men in turn. Their ages ranged from 18 to 50; some tidy and clean, some unwashed and tired. 'Somebody in this room has failed.'

The soldier to his left; the elder of the six, took a cigarette from his mouth and spoke knowingly. 'Someone has, but we can deal with that later; we have to get to that European agent before he gets to his pick up point.'

'So where is his pick up point?' asked Compito.

'We think he is heading north, towards the coast, possibly to be picked up by boat.'

'But that is 500 kilometres or more; and he would have to stay on the main roads. Why have we not been more successful in finding him?'

A small man with a dark beard and yellow teeth sitting at the other end of the table finished slurping his coffee and looked at Compito. 'This agent has been able to mix with the community,' he said. 'He even looks Colombian. We were told he was driving north in a Nissan, but it was found abandoned about fifty kilometres from here. He could be anywhere; in any type of vehicle.'

'So!' shouted Compito. 'We do not give up! This man has stolen vital information about who does what in our drugs operations; he must be stopped. He must not leave Colombia!'

The small man spat on the floor and looked at Compito with contempt. He looked around the table in search of other comments. They all stayed quiet and did not look up. Compito shouted again. 'Get two jeeps fuelled up and ready to go, now! We head north towards the coast. Everyone will get changed out of their uniforms, check their weapons and be ready in five minutes. I will not have failure. Move, now, all of you!'

As everyone got to their feet, the small man hesitated and looked at Compito. 'But where are we going? This is crazy without a plan.'

'We head for the northern coast,' said Compito. 'He is probably heading for Barranquilla where it would be easy to rendezvous with a boat.'

'Huh, a wild guess,' said the man. He remained in his seat.

Compito pulled his handgun out of his belt and aimed it at the man's chest.. The other men looked at him and moved further away from the table. 'Are you disobeying me?' asked Compito.

'I don't like you, Compito; I don't trust you.'

'It is most important we maintain discipline. Our Commander in Chief demands it. We have a hierarchy within our ranks; as you know. You have now questioned that hierarchy.' He fired twice; the force threw the man back onto the fire, blood coming from his chest and mouth. Two men rushed over to drag him off; his dead eyes were open and his jacket had started to burn. The others watched as Compito replenished his magazine and put his gun back into his belt. 'Throw some water over him,' he said.

One man tried to grab the dying body by the arm and pull it off the fire, but the heat got the better of him. The older man quickly grabbed a bowl, filled it at the sink and threw water over the bloody, burning body. He looked at Compito. 'Well; now we are one man down.'

'We do not tolerate that sort of attitude, as you all know,' said Compito. 'Now move; we need to catch this foreign agent before he succeeds in his mission.'

Belgian Interpol Officer, Peter Giers was making good time. The Guerrillas back in Abrego had underestimated his skills. They had found him downloading files onto a laptop computer in the office next to Compito's. After a long drawn out fight, they had eventually overpowered him and put him into an old meat freezer that was barely working. Two hours later, expecting to find him almost dead, two guards opened the door to see him standing there looking at them; not realising he was holding two meat hanger hooks behind his back. He swung both arms around and hooked the men simultaneously, one in the neck, the other in the shoulder. The unexpected assault and pain had them both crying out in agony and it was not difficult for Giers to push them over, withdraw the hooks, and sink them in again. As the two men struggled to get up and pull the hooks from their bodies, he kicked one of them sideways and grabbed the handgun from the belt holster. The two shots rang out loud against the metal walls.

He waited for a while to listen for some sort of response, but the freezers were in a basement, a long way from the main rooms. The Guerrillas lack of forethought was again demonstrated to him when he found the laptop he had been using, on a desk a few metres away from the freezer rooms. He grabbed a canvas bag, pushed the laptop into it and the two guns he had acquired from the incompetent guards. A window allowed him to access a small side street and it did not take long for a local teenager to be persuaded to give up his Nissan; not with a gun held to his belly.

When he was about 300 kilometres from Barranquilla, he stopped the car near a wide, slow moving rivulet and put the canvas bag into a plastic shopping bag he had found in the Nissan. He checked the compartments in the car and found some loose change that he stuffed into his pocket. A cheap plastic cigarette lighter was lying on the back seat; he put it in his shirt pocket and then drove the Nissan down the shallow embankment towards the water. He got out of the vehicle, opened the engine cover and pulled out some wires from around the engine. He threw the wires as far as he could and pushed the Nissan into the flowing water.

After walking for an hour; keeping parallel with the road but 30 metres from it, he approached an old wooden bus stop shelter. With his dark looks, unshaven face and locals clothes, he did not look out of place. A young girl waiting at the bus stop glanced at him momentarily without comment. He smiled and sat down cross legged, on the curb, a few metres away from her.

Twelve minutes later a small blue bus approached and stopped in a cloud of dust. Giers followed the girl on to the bus and shoved a good amount of the loose change into the drivers hand without speaking. He sat near the door and looked up at the digital clock above the driver. 11.28. He estimated they were about one hour away from Barranquilla. He would need to stay low and wait for a few hours for the boat that was due to collect him.

A Belgian Navy frigate had left Port au Prince seven hours earlier to make its way across the Caribbean Sea to the northern coast of Colombia. As it approached the shallower waters of the coastline it slowed and dropped anchor. The captain ordered the deployment of the two-man, high speed assault launch. Frigates were equipped with two such boats; always ready for action; their on board equipment consisting of high velocity rifles and grenade launchers. The two-man crew was a steersman, who piloted the craft from the rear, and a boatman, responsible for the armaments. Both men needed to be highly trained and experienced before they were accepted as 'Assault Men'. The steersman guided the boat towards the shore and pulled up about 200 metres from the beach. He kept the engines running and held the craft in a steady position as his boatman checked their rifles and grenade launchers. They waited and watched.

The bus station at Barranquilla was busy and it was easy for Giers to lose himself in the crowds. He waited for one hour before asking a taxi driver to take him to the coast. Twenty minutes later he had paid the taxi driver and was walking alongside a large estuary towards the shore. He stopped every two minutes to kneel and look around; carefully checking the contents of the bag. The laptop was still in good order and the two handguns he had wrenched from the incompetent guards were loaded and ready. The area seemed deserted. As he got closer to the beach, he noticed some kind of craft in the water, not far away with at least two figures that were visible, and his taught mind slackened in relief.

Suddenly there was the roar of a vehicle coming up behind him; he turned and dropped on to one knee. A jeep was racing towards him, with three men in it. He turned to look seaward; the powerful assault launch had started racing towards the shore. He ran towards the sea, grabbing both guns from the bag. There was the sound of machine gun fire and he dropped to the sand. He looked back to see the jeep bearing down on him; he fired two shots, both missed. As he turned towards the sea, he saw a flash from the small launch followed by a muffled thud. He dropped down again; the grenade went over his head and landed nine feet in front of the jeep, sending it sideways; it turned over and came to rest upside down, two men trapped underneath it. Its third passenger had been thrown out and by now was getting to his feet. He pulled a large Machete from a trouser leg pocket and charged at Giers. A shot rang out and the man was stopped in his tracks, falling backwards onto the soft sand.

By now the boatman was in the water, striding through it to get to the beach. Then a second jeep came flying over a patch of dune grass and was airborne for twenty feet until it came to rest. Two men jumped from the vehicle, rifles in hand, and raced towards Giers. The third man, Antonio Compito, stood up from the driver's seat and shouted after them. 'Do not kill him! Get the bag! You are not to kill him!'

They did not hear him as they fired their rifles at Giers and at the boat. Giers took two bullets in a shoulder that rolled him around and he dropped into the shallow surf. He held the bag firmly in his hand, swung it round and hurled it towards the boatman, who was now himself in the shallow water. Another muffled thud came from the boat and a grenade landed inches away from one of the chasing soldiers, throwing him into the air, his legs severed from his body. The other soldier stopped, knelt and took careful aim. Two or three bullets hit Giers as he lay in the water. The boatman grabbed Giers' bag and stuffed it into his jacket. A shout came from behind him and he knelt, holding his hands around his jacket, making sure the bag was kept dry. The steersman's shot was perfect; it downed the soldier as he was just two metres away from the boatman.

Giers' looked up from where he was lying in the water to see the boatman looking at him. He shook his head as he tried to speak, as though he was telling the boatman to leave him. Then he collapsed completely, his last breath stifled by the sand and the surf.

Compito was now racing towards the sea in the jeep. The boatman turned and trudged his way through the water towards the launch that was nearly with him. He threw himself into it as the steersman turned it seaward and pressed the throttle forward.

The jeep halted near the water's edge. Compito switched off the engine. He walked back to the overturned jeep. One man was dead, almost decapitated by the roll bar. The other man made a slight sound. Compito knelt down to see that he was still alive. He took his gun from his belt and shot the man in the head. Then he walked to where Giers and the other man were; their blood turning

10

the sea red. He looked over to where another soldier lay, without his legs; the blooded sea water was filling the hole left by the grenade.

He spun quickly as he heard a voice; the soldier who had shot Giers was crawling towards him. 'Co...Commander...we... we got him.' He only managed a few metres before he had to stop, rolling himself on his side so he would not suffocate in the soft white sand. Compito looked at his closed eyes and said, 'sorry my friend.' Then he raised his gun and shot the soldier twice.

He looked all around him at the blood, water, sand and bodies. 'How do I explain this to my superiors?' he said to himself. Getting back into the jeep, he looked seaward. The boat was now a tiny speck on the horizon.

2

As she climbed out of bed, Ellie Shanks thought that she was feeling alright, given what she had gone through over the last few weeks. The coffee tasted good and the day ahead would be much less fraught. The hair dryer made her feel warm and she opened a window to let in some fresh air. The sun was peeping through in between buildings.

She had worked in Antwerp for 12 months since her successful transfer from London; and now today, finally, she was going to move to a house in the suburbs, away from the concrete apartment blocks and their damp underground car parks. She brushed her long brown hair and sprayed Eden underneath her ears. Casual clothes for a change, she thought, and reached for some jeans and her favourite old Benetton T-shirt.

Breakfast would be different this morning; she decided she deserved it. The yoghurt stayed in the fridge and the cereal bar stayed in its wrapper. She cut open a pack of bacon and placed three rashers in a pan, adding some olive oil. Two eggs went into the pan a moment later and she was soon easing the contents of the pan onto a slice of toast. As she ate her 'naughty' breakfast – which she indulged in once a month – she thought how nice it was to feel more relaxed.

Since her placement at Interpol, she had worked on some intriguing cases and the last 48 hours – which had got her close to one of the main criminals in Belgium – had been very rewarding. She and her colleagues were getting ever closer and the previous evening her boss had congratulated her on her achievements. They were looking forward to what was surely going to be a good result.

A strong coffee finished off the breakfast nicely. She put the dishes into the sink and picked up a piece of paper with an address on it; the new house would be very different to the present surroundings, she thought, and she realised that her next 'naughty' breakfast would be in a new kitchen. She picked up her phone and car keys as she headed for her front door, humming a tune that had been in her head for days.

As usual, the basement car park was dark and wet. The old building had had some bad leaks for a few years and the night rain had been brought in by vehicles coming in out of the overnight downpour. Outside of the car park it was a bright morning and she walked to her car in anticipation of getting out into the fresh air and driving to the new house to meet her friend.

Her attacker came from behind, very quietly and professionally. She didn't hear anything. He grabbed her long hair and pushed her head forward as he plunged a heavy knife twice into the top of her back. He felt it hit her spine. The second stab was into the side of her neck. He moved away as she turned; her wide eyes staring at him. Then she dropped; her body lying against the wheel of her car. It was all over in six seconds. Two minutes later she was dead. Her attacker, by that time, was about 200 metres away walking slowly down a quiet street, having discarded the knife in a small waste bin.

3

Like any other government organisations, or departments, the Home and Foreign Offices were, from time to time, subject to a reshuffle.

Tom Delaney had expected it to happen soon. The usual pre-shuffle rumours had been going around for some time so it was no surprise to him when he was asked to attend a meeting to meet his new boss. But Delaney was the Managing Director of TOLA – The Overseas Liaison Agency – not, officially a civil servant. Having spent some years in the army, reaching the rank of captain, he had joined the metropolitan police and had been fast tracked through the ranks due to his experience and maturity. His calm phlegmatic manner gave him an edge on other recruits during the training programmes; keeping a mild, level-headed disposition enabled him to think properly while others around him panicked. He was soon spotted as someone who could diffuse hostile - or potentially hostile - situations and make good decisions.

He had been put in charge of an overseas department, working with other police forces from overseas, on serious international cases. But the Home and Foreign Offices had a problem; there was only so much they could do 'by the book'. Sometimes they needed to stretch protocol rules and be more offensive than 'agreements' would allow. So it was, that TOLA was created. A private company; registered as an international provider of 'diplomatic and mediating services'. It would be run as a business by Managing Director Tom Delaney and a staff of five. They would receive instruction from various government departments – Foreign Office, MI6, MI5, CI5 - and carry out their duties, for which they would be paid.

14

The risks for TOLA were high; carrying out clandestine work in overseas locations and against some pretty ruthless criminals, but the rewards were good; the government had to pay them the going rate for diplomatic services.

When he arrived at the Whitehall headquarters the atmosphere seemed different. People were talking in corridors and more doors than usual were closed. As he walked towards the main meeting room he met an old colleague, Sir Adrian Lusher, Head of MI5. Delaney spoke first as they shook hands. 'Adrian, I thought you would have retired by now.'

'Not yet, Tom, what about you?'

'Oh a few years yet; about ten if I'm lucky, I don't want to start vegetating too soon. Anyway what's going on with all these reshuffles, any idea?'

'Well I've just been told that I'm staying with MI5; no change. Are you off for your meeting now?'

'Yeah, not sure who with though.'

'Probably the new boss.'

'New boss?'

'Mm, as from today we don't report to the home secretary anymore.'

'Really? So who is it then?'

'Oh you'll see,' said Lusher, smirking. 'Well good luck, Tom; we must catch up with each other sometime, we're long overdue for a pint.'

Delaney sensed something that made him uncomfortable. He walked along to the meeting room expecting to be told something that he would not like.

The home secretary John Hunter was waiting for him in the main meeting room. Coffees were poured and the two men sat opposite each other at a table by the window. There were the usual photos of various well known civil servants on the dark wood panelled walls and the green leather chairs held together by brass fixings.

'Well, Tom, yet another reshuffle eh?' said Hunter in his normal casual manner.

'Mm, we wouldn't know what to do without a bloody reshuffle every few years.' Delaney replied.

'Err, yes, quite, Tom, quite. Anyway your overseas liaison team will be staying as it is you'll be pleased to hear.'

'Right, well that'll save me some work then. I thought maybe I would have to jiggle things around. What about budgets; will they be staying the same? Will my invoices still be paid?'

'Yes, I would think so, Tom, although it may not be my decision.'

'Oh; go on,' queried Delaney.

'Well, my responsibilities remain the same, but we're bringing in a new person who will have specific responsibility for a few departments. MI6 and CI5 will still report to the Foreign Secretary; your TOLA and Lusher's MI5 will report to a new person now.'

'Right, who's that then?'

'A new title has been created; International Liaison Chief.'

'No, Mr Hunter, I said *who's* that then.'

Hunter had only been in his position for a few months following a fiasco in which his predecessor had been jailed for crimes against the state. He was easy for experienced people like Delaney to handle. Delaney knew when something else was about to be said. So he waited. Hunter leaned forward, raised his eyebrows briefly and took a deep breath; then lifted himself from his chair. Just then, as though rehearsed, there was a knock on the door and it opened.

A woman came through and closed the door behind her. Delaney knew her. She was in her late forties by now he thought, black straight hair, brown eyes and a well formed attractive face. The thin stylish spectacles complimented her already intelligent look. She was slim and shapely too, as Delaney had often noticed in the past.

Hunter beckoned the woman towards them and looked at Delaney. 'I think you've met before, Tom; this is Lady Stonehaven; Shirley Stonehaven.'

'We have yes,' Stonehaven said as she looked at Delaney in a gentle yet confident way. 'A few times I think, for various reasons, how are you, Tom?' Delaney stood up and moved forward to shake her hand. 'Hello there, nice to see you again.'

Hunter asked them to be seated and offered Stonehaven a drink. She refused and it was about half a minute before Hunter spoke again, looking at both of them in turn. 'Well Tom, Lady Stonehaven...'

'Shirley,' interrupted Stonehaven, 'look both of you, it's Shirley, please.'

'Okay; Shirley,' Hunter continued, 'has joined us from the CIA. You may remember she went across to the States to take up a position in their overseas office for a while.'

Delaney looked at Stonehaven and acknowledged, 'Yes I do I think. I believe the last time we met was at a coroner's court just before you left us.'

'Right,' she said, 'yes, err, it was at Manchester Coroners Court, the Jasmin case I believe.'

'Yes, that's it, the Jasmin case.' confirmed Delaney.

Hunter enjoyed seeing the banter but he had other things to do and his announcement came next. 'Well, Tom; you'll be reporting to Shirley from now on, she joined us yesterday and this completes the reshuffle. Your team will remain the same but Shirley here will take overall responsibility for the Operations of TOLA and MI5. Of course, *specific* responsibility for TOLA remains with you.'

Delaney looked surprised but not disturbed at the news. 'I thought maybe that would be the case.' He looked at Shirley Stonehaven. 'Welcome along anyway, Shirley, I guess you'll be letting me know of any changes you want made.'

'Yes, but in due course, Tom, I don't want to change things unnecessarily or rock any boats. Not in the early stages anyway. Let's get used to each other first. I'll let you know when I would like to have our first meeting, if that's okay with you.'

Delaney said nothing and nodded gracefully.

'Good, well, thank you, Tom' said Hunter 'if you'll excuse us, there are a few things Shirley and I need to go through.'

'That was quick,' said Delaney. 'No questions or proposals?'

'Not right now Tom; as Shirley said; she'll contact you when she has a meeting planned.'

Delaney felt like staying and getting a few things straight, but he decided to play things politely; for now. 'Of course, I'll err, leave you to it then.' Then looking at Stonehaven, 'and hope to hear from you soon, Shirley?'

'Yes, and, thanks again, Tom.'

He left the room and walked back down the corridor towards the car park. He was not disappointed. He knew he was too anti-establishment to get any more promotion himself and he somehow had always expected someone like Shirley Stonehaven, or a male equivalent to get the job. The people they wanted at the top these days had to be good with the press and PR. He had seven or eight years left before retirement and he would be relatively happy working at his job until then; as long as they left him alone to get on with it without interfering. This had been Hunter's style since he had become Home Secretary and it had worked well.

The meeting between Hunter and Stonehaven lasted another 30 minutes. They swapped notes on current and future jobs, not only for the The Overseas Liaison Agency, but for MI5 and the UK Drugs department, which would also be reporting to her.

It was a cold and wet night as Shirley Stonehaven was being driven home from London to the estate she and her husband had recently bought near Buckingham. The thought provoking rain

18

was lashing down on the car windows and she subconsciously drifted into thinking of how things had changed.

She had been born with her twin sister, Siobhan, in Winchester. Her mother was a meteorologist and her father had worked for the old National Coal Board before moving to the Home Office as a private secretary. After finishing at Cheltenham Ladies College, she worked as an administrator for a law firm before moving to the Home Office as a junior negotiator. She was always quick to point out that her father did not get her the job because of his contacts. She had persevered to get the job on her own merits.

Her natural aptitude for negotiating and diffusing difficult situations soon lead to more prospects and after some time in the field with MI5 operatives, she was asked to take up a post at MI6. It was there that she met Simon Stonehaven; Lord Simon Stonehaven. He had got his title from his father before hereditary peers had been looked on less favourably by the government of the day. His father had also worked for the government as a foreign diplomat.

Simon Stonehaven was MI6's chief negotiator, and it was on a job in Tel Aviv that they had met. They were fond of each other right from the start and a marriage was announced one year later, just as Shirley was offered a post with the CIA. Her two years in the States passed very quickly and she returned to the joint committee of the MI5 and MI6 as a Commander, in charge of drug and fraud cases. It was there that she and Tom Delaney had met from time to time.

The Stonehavens moved to their new home a couple of years later. They were happy there; most of the time. Her life had seemed so 'planned' or set out for her and even in marriage, she felt the same. The social gatherings and the high profile life put a strain on their time together. Simon would always put her, and their life, second to everything else. And although she too was a workaholic, she now wanted more life and less work. But 'plans' had been made and she would stick with them.

She had not asked for the new post with British Intelligence, she had been offered it. The Home Secretary had apparently asked for her to have the position after speaking to a number of her former mentors, and like any other job she had been given, she would get on with it and try her best. She had always liked Tom Delaney. He had always seemed so easy going and yet forthright when the decisions were needed. On the few times she had had to liaise with him on cases, they had worked well together and their standards of what they expected from their people had been the same. She was sure things would work well. This was good, she thought, especially bearing in mind some cases that were imminent.

Angela Casey arrived home at 8pm. She had lived with Tom Delaney for two years and they both understood each other's jobs and how to work around schedules and unsociable hours. Their dog Rocky – a cast-off German shepherd police dog who 'didn't quite make the grade' - was waiting near the front door ready to greet her. 'Hello Rocky boy! How are you?' Rocky wagged his tail and ran around in circles. Mrs. Chappell, a good neighbour who had retired a few years ago, had walked him and cleaned up a few items in the kitchen. Angela always told her not to and Mrs. Chappell always did.

Delaney arrived home a few minutes later and joined Angela in the kitchen where she was she looking through some cookery books. He kissed her on the cheek and went to the fridge. 'Wine?'

'Mm please. Just looking at this new book; what do you fancy for supper?'

'You.'

'Well you can't have me, you're so trite sometimes,' she answered jokingly.

'Perhaps, but you love it really don't you, and...'

They looked at each other with disappointment as Delaney's phone rang.

'Hello?'

'Tom, its Shirley Stonehaven, sorry to bother you.'

Delaney held his phone away from his mouth and mimed the words 'my new boss' to Angela.

'Hello, Lady Stonehaven, not at all; how can I help?'

'It's Shirley, please Tom, I'm sorry to have to call you at this time but I phoned your man Taffy Burton and he said you would be able to help me. I asked him about someone called Ellie Shanks and he didn't know too much about her because she was only with you for short period of time before she left to go work for Belgian Intelligence.'

Delaney knew Ellie Shanks. She was a good operative and had been one of his key people before she left to work in Belgium so she could be closer to her boyfriend. He answered as briefly as he could as he reached for his glass of wine. 'Yes that's right; I know her, she's good.'

'Did you ever hear from her after she had left?'

'Only once I think; a phone call on a quiet afternoon. Why, does she want her old job back?'

'No, Tom, sorry. She's dead.'

Delaney did not speak for a while. On a recent case he had lost two good men and now there was this news about someone who was rather special. How are we going to survive and how do we deal with the sort of people that commit these sins, he thought to himself. He began to get angry.

Stonehaven spoke again. 'Tom? You okay?'

'Yeah, yeah, I'm still here; and I'm okay. What were the circumstances; do you mean dead because of operational tasks?'

'Must be; she was stabbed in the back and neck. She had an apartment near the centre of Antwerp and was attacked as she walked to her car in the underground car park this morning. She was working for the Belgian division of Interpol; did you know?'

'Yes I knew,' said Delaney. 'She worked for me for about a year before she went over there; she was good.'

'I'm sure she was, Tom, if she worked for you. Our counterparts in Belgium want to come over here and talk to us. They believe it's a possibility that the people who killed her, did so because of what she knew about an Anglo-Belgian crime gang doing work for some Colombian Rebel Guerrillas.'

'Really, I thought they just operated in Southern America?'

'Not any more it seems; anyway, they'll be here tomorrow so I told them that I would meet them and bring them to your office at about ten. Your department deals with overseas liaison better than any other. Hope you don't mind; are you okay with that?'

Delaney was impressed with the way Stonehaven had asked politely, even though she did not need to. 'Of course, see you then,' he said.

Delaney put his phone down and strolled around as he thought; it always seemed to be the younger agents that got killed these days. Ellie Shanks had joined his team a couple of years ago and had left after just one year to go to work in Belgium. She had been very cautious and a terrible time keeper, he thought, but a good operative and quite tough. She met a Belgian Intelligence officer when he had been working in London and had got a job working in Antwerp because she could speak Belgian and German.

Angela pushed a glass of wine in front of his nose. 'Here, you left it in the kitchen.'

'Thank you, sorry, I was distracted; more bad news.'

'I guessed. I'm still not sure what I fancy for supper.'

Delaney sat down heavily and took a deep breath. 'Don't bother cooking for me; I'm not hungry. Sorry.'

Angela knew him well enough to know when something bad had happened. 'Who was it this time?' She asked.

'A woman who worked for me a while ago; she left to go and work in Belgium. She was murdered this morning.'

4

Ben Wyatt was the first to get to the office the following morning. Delaney arrived not long after him. They sat down around the large, low central table.

Wyatt was the undisciplined member of TOLA; Delaney had said that every team needs an undisciplined member when rule books were not always followed. Wyatt's CV had impressed him; Organised Crime Squad, Close Quarter Battle, top marks; Weapons and Tactics, first in class; Multi-skilled adaptability, second in class; Defensive driving, top marks; punctuality, *not* usually on time. Delaney had almost terminated the interview at the outset when Wyatt turned up in Chinos and a sweatshirt with about three day's stubble covering his chin. 'Sorry guv; just got off a very long stake-out in Plymouth,' Wyatt had said. 'We got the bastards though.' When Delaney had asked him why he wanted to join TOLA, Wyatt ran his hands through his thick brown hair, leaned back and said, 'I just hate the bad guys gov, and maybe being part of your outfit will give me job satisfaction.'

Delaney had sent him the formal job offer the following day.

'Taffy said you would have some news for me this morning,' said Wyatt. 'Something about a new boss?'

'That's right; they've brought a new person in to be responsible for us and MI5.'

'Anyone I know?'

'Shirley Stonehaven.'

Wyatt stopped sipping his coffee and put the cup down. 'You mean Lady Stonehaven, formerly of MI6 and CIA?'

'Yep.'

24

'Well well, were you surprised, gov?'

'I stopped being surprised years ago, Ben.'

Taffy Burton walked into the office, poured a coffee and sat down. He looked at Delaney. 'Have you told him sir?'

'Yeah he's told me,' said Wyatt.

'I've told you about Stonehaven, Ben,' said Delaney, 'but there's something else; do you remember Ellie Shanks?'

'Yeah, course I do, great gal. Went to Belgium, right?'

'That's right. She was murdered yesterday.'

Wyatt clenched his mouth and put his hands behind his head. 'On a job?'

'Probably *because* of a job, yes.'

Wyatt was getting into his angry mono-syllabic mood. 'How?'

'Doesn't matter how, she's...'

'How?'

Delaney forgave Wyatt for interrupting him and paused before answering. 'She was stabbed in the back and neck.'

Burton leaned forward. 'Anything we can do to help, sir?'

'I'm sure there is; Stonehaven is on her way here now with someone from the Belgian Interpol office that Ellie worked for.'

Burton had been Delaney's second-in-command for a number of years. They worked well together and he knew Delaney well enough to know when to keep his questions short and straight forward. 'So they're probably looking for us to get involved, sir; if they're coming here.'

'Highly likely, Taffy.'

Wyatt was not as good at reading what other people were thinking. He leaned forward and looked at Delaney. 'This is bad news, guv; we always seem to end up helping other people from other countries because of their shortcomings.'

'Yeah, Ben, that's what we're called; The *Overseas* Liaison Agency. Live with it.'

They discussed a few cases they were working on for a while; an hour later, a knock on the door interrupted their thinking. 'That'll be them,' said Delaney.

Shirley Stonehaven walked into the room followed by a short overweight man. Delaney was first to his feet. 'Shirley, come in.'

'Thank you, can I introduce you to Chief Inspector Baart, Belgian Intelligence.'

Delaney shook the man's hand and offered him a seat. Inspector Baart sat down as he looked around; taking in everything in a quick and experienced way. Delaney introduced Burton and Wyatt to the visitors and they settled around the table.

'Well, perhaps first,' said Stonehaven, 'we should spare a moment for Ellie Shanks.'

'Indeed,' said Baart, 'she was a fine operator; for you too, I believe?' He looked at Delaney.

'Yes, I was sorry to lose her. Tragic.'

Baart continued. 'Obviously, we are keen to get the people who did this and it was a coincidence that she worked for you for a period as we may need your help.'

Delaney and Burton started to speak at the same time. Delaney let his second-in-command carry on. 'Go on, Taffy.'

'So was Ellie working on an international case?' asked Burton.

'Yes,' continued Baart. 'For the last nine months there has been a group working in Belgium that call themselves the Revolutionary Armed Forces. They have attacked right wing establishments and they were very nearly successful in killing a prominent business leader who has links with the United States and Australia. They are very mobile and we can never pin them down to one location.'

Stonehaven leaned forward to speak. 'This is where we come in, gentlemen; the Chief Inspector believes they now have a cell in the UK, possibly Scotland as well as England.'

Delaney looked at Stonehaven. 'When we spoke last night, you said something about the Colombian rebels.'

'Mm, the inspector has every reason to believe that this Belgian group is led by a member of FARC that was sent to Europe to recruit sympathisers and set up an active offensive cell.'

'Why Europe?' asked Wyatt.

'FARC have followers in Eastern Europe,' said Baart, 'they are after all, an organisation that admits to being Leninist; against capitalism.'

Wyatt nodded in acknowledgement. Burton sat back and sighed. 'So what do we do?'

'You help Chief Inspector Baart and his men track down the cell that is operating in the UK,' said Stonehaven. She looked at Baart and gestured with her hand towards Delaney. 'I'll leave you in the capable hands of Delaney's department Chief Inspector Baart.'

'Very well, Lady Stonehaven, my thanks to you for welcoming me.'

'Not at all,' she replied, turning to Delaney. 'Keep me informed please, Tom; and good luck with it. I'll let MI5 know what you're doing. What else are you handling at the moment?'

'Ben's looking after some Norwegian state police officers; they're over here looking for criminals wanted for paedophilia.'

'Not anymore,' said Wyatt. 'The trail went cold so they gave up.'

'Right, well I'll let you decide who does what, Tom, but this is important.'

'I know.'

She shook hands with Baart and left quickly.

Delaney closed the door behind her and sat back down. He offered Baart another coffee and asked him where they should start. The inspector had obviously already thought about how to approach things. 'I can give you a full briefing on what we know and about some of the members of this group. It would be helpful meanwhile, if one of your men could go to Antwerp, to meet my right hand man, Sergeant Brun; he can explain where we are with things over there. I can remain here to work with you as you would wish.'

Wyatt looked around and made a sarcastic saluting gesture. 'That'll do, Ben, thank you,' said Delaney. Baart smiled as he looked at Delaney. 'It's fine, I'm used to it. There is perhaps one more thing to mention at this early stage; I may need to go to Colombia in the next few days.'

'Why?' asked Burton.

'Lady Stonehaven did not mention that I have a man in Colombia now; working undercover, he will need my help to get to Europe; passports and visas etc.'

'Very well,' said Delaney, 'we can arrange flights for you.'

'Do you want me to go to Belgium, sir; to meet Sergeant Brun?' asked Burton.

'I think so Taffy, how did you know?'

'Well, a job like this needs a real professional doesn't it,' said Burton as he looked at Wyatt with a smirk.

Wyatt swayed his head from side to side. Yeah, yeah, very funny.'

'Right,' said Delaney, 'Taffy; get yourself a flight booked to Antwerp. Chief Inspector Baart can brief me and Ben on the details; let's get on with it.'

5

The flight to Antwerp was quick and easy and Taffy Burton took some time out to have a beer at the airport until it was time to get a taxi. The bar was quiet; a couple were sitting in the corner whispering and a man sat nearby reading a newspaper.

Burton had been with Delaney since day one of TOLA, after nine years working for Special Branch in London. He still had his Cardiff accent. His factual monosyllabic answers suited Delaney's usual style of questioning down to the ground and they had always got on well, while maintaining the discipline between boss and employee. His clothes never really suited him. The cheap suits and the dirty shoes were something that Delaney had got used to over time; although in the early days he had often dropped a hint. Burton's ruddy face and unkempt hair gave him a rough look and the scarred nose – courtesy of a gang of youths in Swansea – gave him the 'experienced' look that so many of the younger men lacked.

When it was 6 p.m. he finished his beer and walked out to get a taxi. The driver was an old man. Too old, Burton thought, to be driving around a busy city for a living. He took the folded paper from his jacket pocket and read out the address to the driver. Museum Mayer van den Bergh please, Lange Gasthuisstraat?' He always tried to have a go at the local pronunciations. It made him feel as though he was doing his bit for international relations. The taxi driver smiled and nodded politely. As the taxi pulled away Burton looked over his shoulder to his right, back towards the airport entrance. He noticed a man standing at the entrance, looking at the taxi, or at him. It was the same man that had been sitting a few tables away from him in the airport bar. As the taxi moved quickly in the direction of the exit road, he turned again to see what was happening and just before the taxi turned a corner, he could see the man on his mobile phone, still looking in his direction.

Some 40 minutes later, the taxi was approaching the museum. Burton leaned forward and spoke to the driver. 'Excuse me, will you go past the museum please and drop me just around the corner. It's the side entrance I need'.

Again, the driver smiled and nodded politely. The taxi turned the corner and dropped him off. He walked along the street and turned left at the next street, to go around the block. After a couple of more short streets he was entering into Lange Gasthuisstraat again. He paused for a while before moving on towards the museum. It was quiet and a church bell somewhere chimed seven times.

As his notes had instructed, he knocked four times on the museum door and it was answered just a few seconds later. A tall elegant looking man stood before him and as Taffy looked him up and down quickly, he could see that he was wearing a shoulder holster. The man put his hand out and spoke quietly. 'Mr Burton?'

'Yes, hello.'

'Please, come in.'

Burton showed the man his ID card and the man reciprocated.

'Welcome to Antwerp. My name is Brun, Sergeant Brun. Inspector Hubert is expecting you, please come with me'.

Brun led the way through a few large rooms that were displaying paintings and tapestries. He opened a large oak door and gestured to Burton. 'After you'.

Burton walked through into the room to see a man with a moustache sitting at an oak desk. The man stood and offered his hand. 'Welcome, Mr Burton, Delaney speaks very highly of you. Please, have a seat'.

'Hello Inspector Hubert, good to meet you'.

30

'Can I offer you a drink? Hot, cold, something?'

'No I'm fine thank you'.

Inspector Hubert sat down and Brun rested on the edge of another table nearby. Burton settled in a large arm chair in front of the oak desk.

The Inspector stroked his moustache and spoke solemnly. 'Now, I know you would like to know more about the death of Ellie Shanks. A tragic loss. Such an intelligent young lady, and tough with it. We were all devastated when we heard. To be killed in such a way'.

'Mm, stabbed wasn't she?' Burton asked.

'Yes; in a car park. She wasn't officially on duty at the time. Perhaps this is why her guard was down'.

'Perhaps. What was she working on?'

'You are aware of the group that call themselves the Revolutionary Armed Forces; I believe Chief Inspector Baart has given you a brief history since his arrival in London.'

'Yes, I'm aware, but not about too many details; Chief Inspector Baart is briefing my colleagues back in the UK.'

'Well, they have been operating in Belgium for about one year,' said Hubert. 'We believe a man called Stait is running things. We have done a lot of leg work to find out what we can; Ellie Shanks was involved in that. From what we know so far, it seems Stait worked in Colombia for a while and married a Colombian girl who was the daughter of a rebel leader.'

'Hence the name,' said Burton, 'FARC also stands for Revolutionary Armed Forces; or something like that.'

'Correct, Mr. Burton. Stait returned to Belgium when his young wife was killed; some unknown forces attacked one of the FARC villages and 40 or 50 people were killed; she was one of them. We think it was an elite American unit going after a major player in drugs, but we can't be sure.'

'And you think that Ellie Shanks was murdered by one of Stait's men?'

'Yes we do, and the intelligence seems to be pointing to someone he has used before'.

Brun took a small book from his pocket and looked at some notes as he spoke. 'Yes, we believe a man called Hawkwell killed Ellie; he has killed others the same way, from behind, with a knife. According to our sources, he has been working for Stait for a number of months, part time. He also works for another man called Sondhiem, but Stait is his main employer.'

'Any idea of his whereabouts now?'

'No, he moves around too much,' said Hubert.

'We have more than that,' said Brun, as he took two photographs out of his top pocket and handed them to Burton. 'The black and white photo is Stait; you can keep those.'

'Thanks very much, I'll study them later.'

'Now then Mr. Burton,' said Hubert, 'we have arranged some accommodation for you; Sergeant Brun will look after you, he is a bit moody, but a good chap never the less'.

Brun smiled faintly and said nothing.

Hubert continued. 'With your permission then, Mr. Burton, he will also accompany you back to London to work with you.'

Burton hesitated to consider proceedings. 'I suppose that's alright, but Chief Inspector Baart is already there.'

'I know but an old colleague of mine has said it might be a good idea to have someone else with you also.'

'Right, can I ask who that colleague is?'

'Lady Stonehaven; your new boss I believe.'

'Okay, I'm on the 10 o'clock flight in the morning so you'd better check there are seats available'.

This time it was the Inspector's turn to smile faintly. 'There is a seat already booked for him Mr Burton and I have changed your seat to a first class so you can sit together. We tend to get what seats we want on flights you see. My department also provides the Air Marshalls for the flights out of Antwerp'.

'That's fine Inspector', said Burton 'we don't get many perks these days so I'll take this one while I can'.

The meeting over, Brun escorted Burton back through the corridors to a side door. A car was waiting and Brun gave instruction to the driver, before opening the door for Burton. 'This man will get you to the hotel Mr. Burton.'

'Thanks very much, see you in the morning.'

Burton arrived at the small hotel on Hoogstraat in the Old Town area some twenty minutes later. He was quite pleased with the way things had gone. Brun seemed like a good reliable sort of man and was obviously very experienced. It was evident, he thought that Brun's elegant looks and his well cut suit were hiding a pretty tough cookie.

He had a small meal in the tiny hotel bar and went to his room to think about things and study the two photographs Brun had given to him. The black and white photo of Stait looked like it had been taken with a long distance lens. The subject was standing in front of a bar in a busy street somewhere. He was about 50 with straggly black hair and large bushy eyebrows. Judging by the people in the background, Burton guessed him to be about five foot ten tall. He looked intelligent but lacked presence.

The colour photo of Hawkwell was a head and shoulder shot. He looked very young and attentive; his smooth skinned face and well groomed hair did not give him the look of someone who murders people by stabbing them.

Burton paused then to think. He thought about the man at the airport who he thought was watching him. Was he being paranoid? No, he thought; he was too experienced for that. Then he picked up the photo of Stait and studied it again. After a few seconds, he realised why something had come to his mind. One of the people in the background on Stait's photo was standing about five feet away from Stait, looking to one side as though he was checking out who was around him. It was the man Burton had seen at the airport.

A few minutes later, as he was unpacking his travel case, a knock on the door took him by surprise and brought him out of his deep thinking. There was no fish eye lens in the door to see who was on the other side. He called out clearly. 'Who is it?' There was no reply. He moved back away from the door and to one side. He waited; innocent people said who they were. He waited one more minute. There was the sound of a creaking floor board and he could see the shadow cast by someone's feet under the door. Then he heard the sound of a gun being cocked. The door handle started to turn slowly.

A few seconds later a single gunshot rang out. A few more seconds and there was the sound of movement of some kind and another knock at the door.

Burton didn't need to enquire this time. The voice on the other side of the door was clear to him.

'Burton, open the door. It's me, Sergeant Brun'.

'Put your ID card under the door, Sergeant,' said Burton.

The card appeared; it was genuine. Burton opened the door. Brun was standing next to the body of the man he had just shot, holstering his gun. The man on the floor was the one that Burton had seen at the airport. Brun turned to tell the watching maid to call the police and then looked at Burton. 'Bernard Lissett; one of Stait's men. He followed you from the museum.'

Burton was pleased at that moment; it was clear that the man who would be working with him back in the UK was no amateur. 'Right,' he said, 'well. Err, thank you'.

Brun shrugged his shoulders and replied. 'Okay. It was nothing. He was an amateur compared to us my friend'.

'Perhaps. Anyway what's your name? I can't keep calling you Sergeant or Brun'.

'Why not? Everyone else does. My first name I think is not so good anyway'.

'Okay. Brun it is then; I'm known as Taffy by the way.'

'That is Welsh I think.'

'Yes it is, haven't been back there for years though.'

Their conversation was interrupted by a groan coming from the man on the floor.

Burton looked down. 'He's still alive.'

Brun took his gun from his holster again and fired another shot into the man's chest. 'No he's not.'

'Sergeant Brun, you're not supposed to do that.'

'No, Taffy, I'm not. But he was dying anyway. Now he is dead; like Ellie Shanks. Do not grieve for him.'

The following morning their flight was on time and Wyatt met them at Heathrow. Burton did the introductions and they were soon on their way to Delaney's office. Brun sat in the back of the car and Wyatt kept looking at him in the mirror. 'I'm sure we've met before Sergeant Brun.'

'I do not think so,' answered Brun.

'Have you worked in the UK before?'

'Yes; two years ago, but only for about one week.'

'I must be thinking of someone else then,' said Wyatt as he continued to concentrate on his driving. Then Brun leaned forward. 'But I have seen a picture of you and Mr Burton here; Ellie Shanks had a photo of both of you and Delaney in her office. She thought a lot of you all.'

They arrived at the office to find Delaney and Chief Inspector Baart going through some documents. Baart and Brun said hello to each other in their native tongue before Burton introduced Delaney to Brun. 'Welcome Sergeant Brun,' said Delaney. 'The Chief Inspector tells me you are one of his best officers.'

Brun did not say anything as he nodded in polite acknowledgement.

'Well,' said Burton, 'I've known him for less than a day and he's already possibly saved my life.'

Delaney looked at Burton for an explanation.

'Someone followed me in Antwerp; someone linked to the person that had Ellie Shanks killed. Sergeant Brun here, err, how can I put it, took them out of the picture?'

Delaney asked everyone to sit down and Baart started to update them all on the latest situation. His briefing was interrupted when his phone rang. He excused himself and moved across to the other side of the room to take the call.

Burton established that Delaney and Wyatt also knew about Stait and his main man, Hawkwell, and their links with the FARC in Colombia. Delaney was explaining to Brun how they had dealt with a similar case a few years ago involving the global contacts of a Spanish terrorist group, when Wyatt interrupted. 'That's it,' he said looking at Brun. 'That's where I remember you from; the Spanish case two years ago, you were the one who had his picture in the Spanish newspapers.'

'Ah yes, that is so,' said Brun.

Delaney remembered the case and pointed at Brun. 'Yes, you were the one who rescued a local politician, killing three of the terrorists in the process.'

Brun did not speak as he got up to help himself to another coffee. Wyatt looked at the other two and smiled as his head moved sideways in the direction of Brun. 'He's obviously going to be useful then.'

Baart came back to join them having finished his call. He had a forlorn look to him.

'Chief Inspector?' said Delaney.

'The man I was going to help get out of Colombia; he is dead.'

Brun turned to look at Baart as he finished filling his coffee cup. 'Giers, Chief Inspector?'

'Yes, Peter Giers; he was shot as he tried to rendezvous with his connection on the coast. Apparently he could not wait for help because they discovered who he was. He managed to download some important information though before he was killed and the navy retrieved the laptop computer. They are sending it to me now.'

'I'm sorry.' said Delaney. 'What information would he have downloaded?'

'Hopefully information about the top men who are involved in the drugs trade; that's where they get their money from. The US state department will be interested in that information also.'

'Where is the computer now?'

'On a plane flying from Port au Prince; that's where the frigate is based that was responsible for connecting with Giers.'

Burton was on his feet within seconds. 'I know sir, I'll go.'

Delaney explained to the others that Burton would make contact with the flight and arrange a special escort for the package when it arrived.

'So what now, sir?' asked Wyatt.

'We wait for the information; but in the meantime we can start to get what information is already out there.'

'Excellent,' said Baart.

Brun stood up and held his shoulders back. 'I can help; tell me what you want me to do.'

'Stay with Wyatt please, Sergeant, for the next couple of days. By the way his name is Ben; what's yours?'

'Just Brun, sir.'

'Okay, Ben; take him with you, find out what you can about any FARC links the big gangs in the UK may have.'

Wyatt nodded. 'Will do.' He looked at Brun who was already waiting in anticipation for instruction. 'Come on then big man, stay close.'

Baart smiled as they left the room. He waited until the door had closed before speaking. 'Your boys do realise how serious this could get don't they?'

Delaney raised his eyebrows and took a deep breath. 'Yes they do Chief Inspector; they're very experienced. And so am I.'

'Of course; let us pray we can keep casualties to a minimum.'

Delaney thought about the last big case they had dealt with and the three good men that had died. 'Indeed, I want a nil body count on this one, so let's make sure we get it right.'

6

It was earlier than usual when Delaney got home. He had decided to leave things to the others for a few hours and get some exercise. Angela had left a note on the coffee table to say that she would be late. She always left a note. There had been an occasion when she had not contacted him for 17 hours; he had read the rule book to her, and ever since that day she had always let him know where she would be and for how long. The ubiquitous notes got on his nerves sometimes, but he always reminded himself that it was better to know too much, than not enough.

He got the exercise he wanted; Rocky was eager and they walked about 7 miles around two different parks and a disused railway track. They both settled down when they returned home; Delaney on his favourite chair in the conservatory reading George Orwell's Burmese Days, and Rocky on the sofa; eyes on the front door, waiting for Angela.

It was the ringing of the home phone that woke them both up at midnight. Delaney walked to the front hallway to answer it. 'Hello?'

'Have you seen the breaking news on the telly, sir?'

'Hello, Taffy. No I haven't, what is it?'

'A bomb has gone off in a night club on Cobham Street. First guess is about 12 dead.'

'Suicide bomber?'

'Too soon to say.'

'Right well, thanks, Taffy. This is for the Met and Special Branch though, not us.'

'I know, but they've just announced that the club is owned by a Norwegian businessman that the authorities are trying to track down. Apparently some of the emergency exits were blocked.'

'Taffy, this is a tragic event, but I'm trying to figure out why you've phoned me at this hour to discuss it.'

'The Norwegian business man's called Sondheim. When I was in Antwerp, Inspector Hubert mentioned him; he employs Frank Hawkwell sometimes on a temporary basis.'

'Blimey, that's all we need,' said Delaney. 'Find out what you can, Taffy; I'll be in the office about nine.'

It was nearly 3 a.m. when he looked at the clock to the side of his bed. Angela was coming up the stairs with Rocky close by her side. 'Seen the news?' she asked quietly.

'No, but Taffy told me about; those poor kids.'

'Mm, they say its 17 dead now.'

She undressed and got into bed, pulling the duvet over her. Rocky took advantage of the space between them and claimed it for himself. Three hours later, Delaney was getting dressed as silently as he could. Too many things were on his mind; he needed to be at work.

He arrived at his office at seven. The 24 hour news channel on the small television in the corner was still covering the bombing. He rested for a while and decided to put one of his jazz CD's on that he kept at the office. After spending some time contemplating, he chose Nina Simone - Live at Caesars' Palace. He switched on his computer and started to look into the database. TOLA had access to the entire police database, as well as MI5 and some of the MI6 records.

The name Sondheim did not come up at all. He thought it must be wrong, or not up to date. Would there be a code needed? No, it would have told him if that was the case. Had he spelt it right? He tried a few more ways of spelling it. Nothing came up. After a few more tries he abandoned the search and went about reading some of the latest information that had been left on his desk or e-mailed to him.

The time soon passed and Nina Simone had long since stopped singing as Burton entered the room. Delaney looked surprised; as surprised as his phlegmatic nature would allow.

'You're early, Taffy.''

'Yeah, wasn't really sleeping anyway.'

'Join the club.'

'Anyway, there's lots to go through.'

'Fine, sit down and let's see what we have. Ben should be with us soon. Did you get the computer safely off the flight from Port au Prince?'

'Yes I did, it's in the lab now, the technician said he would get it all burnt onto the system and send us a copy before he puts it in the secure data bank.'

'Good. Anything else on the night club bombing?'

'Yeah, Ben went along to have a look; he should have some news when he gets here.'

A voice came from the corridor. 'Ben's here and he *has* got news.'

Wyatt walked in and sat down opposite Delaney. He nodded to both of them and took a deep breath.

'Right, well; bear with me, there's quite a bit here. A man called Micky Sondheim *does* own the night club. He was born in Oslo in 1960, his father was a well known local criminal – small stuff sir, mainly robbery and prostitution – his mother died when he was 20 and he left his father to go to live with his girlfriend soon after. Using what he had learned from his father, he soon built up his own little gang and started to take over nightclubs by just frightening the owners away with stories of drugs scams and protection rackets. He owned his first night club in Oslo by the time he was 25, funded mainly by drugs money. Over the next 20 years he got involved with some pretty serious gangsters in

41

Sweden, Spain, Portugal, where he has a villa, and Colombia and Venezuela. He...'

'But what is he doing right now, Ben?' Delaney interrupted.

'Ah well, here's the interesting bit, sir; nothing.'

'Nothing?'

'Well, as he built up all of these businesses he passed them over to his managers who later became business partners. He still owns these places but doesn't do anything with them; he leaves it all to his managers and brothel keepers to sort out. Our man from Norway says he's in his villa in Portugal and has been there for a while. And something else, five years ago he had a car accident and is now disabled and will be for the rest of his life. He can walk but not far and usually needs crutches. His latest girlfriend is more of a companion; he calls her Michelle. There's even a suggestion that he's started to give money to charities. There now; I told you there was quite a bit to it.'

'Well there's a first, Ben,' said Delaney. 'You ever investigated someone who's disabled and living in Portugal before?'

'No, can't say I have.'

'Good work, Ben,' said Burton. 'I phoned the Inspector who was investigating the bombing to tell him to get everything he could for me ASAP; we should hear from him in a couple of hours.'

Wyatt nodded in acknowledgement and made his way towards the door. He paused for a while and turned back to face Delaney. 'Thing is,' he said with a furrowed brow, 'this bloke is sort of semi retired, disabled, owns nightclubs and brothels, quite small establishments by all accounts and he hasn't been very active with drugs or dirty money for a while apparently.'

'So you're thinking why a bomb eh, Ben? And why in a nightclub that would kill other people?'

'Yes guv, that's exactly what I'm thinking.'

'Me too, Ben, me too.'

'And,' Burton joined in. 'He has links with Colombia.'

'Interesting gentlemen, isn't it? Anyway; had you both forgotten we have a young man coming to see us this morning? He could be joining us if we think he's up to it.'

'Can I leave it to you and Ben, sir?' asked Burton. 'I need to start looking at the contents of the laptop.'

'Go ahead, Taffy. We'll catch up with you when you have some news.'

Delaney's phone rang. 'Hello...Good, yes....send him up now.'

'I hope this new boy is ready to be thrown in at the deep end,' said Wyatt.

'Well, in about 30 minutes time we'll know. By the way where's Brun; I thought he was shadowing you.'

'I left him to sort out his accommodation while I tracked down this information. I told him I would be in touch again tomorrow.'

'Right, we'll see. Now, let's see what we make of this new applicant.'

When the newcomer knocked on Delaney's half open door and walked in, Wyatt noticed how fit he looked. You look fine physically young man, he thought to himself, I wonder how the mind is.

Delaney and Wyatt shook hands with him and offered him a seat. There was a few minutes silence as Delaney went through the papers that the young man had brought with him. Wyatt took the opportunity to ask the first question. 'So, Detective Sergeant Pitt, what's your first name anyway?' Delaney looked at Wyatt over his reading glasses and then put the papers on his desk. Pitt looked confidently at Wyatt and spoke with a well educated voice. 'Ajit; It's Ajit Pitt.'

'And is that an Indian name, Ajit?' asked Delaney.

'Yes Sir; my mother is from Mumbai and my father is Scottish.'

'I see, interesting; where did they meet?'

'In Goa, sir; my father was stationed there with the Air Force and my mother was a civilian clerical officer.'

'And you've been a policeman for 10 years?'

'Yes sir, Constable, Sergeant and now Detective Sergeant.'

Delaney hesitated and sat back. 'That's quite a quick rise; in ten years.'

'Perhaps sir, maybe it's other people who are too slow.'

'Well,' continued Delaney. 'You must know what we do; why do you want to join TOLA?'

There was a pause. Pitt looked at Delaney and then at Wyatt. 'Mm, well,' he said, 'not to promote world peace and save starving children.'

Wyatt smirked. 'A sense of humour, good; you're half way there.'

Delaney thought it was funny also but he was not about to show it. 'But could you save your own skin and mine if it came to it?'

'Sir?'

'Are you hard enough for this position, Mr. Pitt?'

The young man suddenly started to look nervous. He held up his hands in a gesture of apology. 'I'm sorry, sir, my last remark was flippant. But I believe I am ready, yes sir. Please take a look at page five.' He pointed to the papers in front of Delaney. After reading some of page five, Delaney passed the papers to Wyatt. The young man did not speak while Wyatt was reading the documents, which impressed Delaney; normally, nervous people could not go for long periods without speaking.

Wyatt looked up after a few minutes. 'Impressive; the two men that you shot; how good were they?'

'I don't know; I never met them.'

'And the two hoodlums in Birmingham; chasing them could have led you into a planned ambush.'

'But they didn't, and my back-up was only a few metres behind me.'

'According to this, you didn't need your back-up though.'

'No, the hoodlums, as you call them, were to slow and too fat.'

Delaney raised his eyebrows. 'Okay, DS Pitt; we'll be in touch, thank you for coming.'

Pitt was taken by surprise at the way Delaney had brought the meeting to a close so quickly. He stood up, shook Delaney's hand and nodded to Wyatt.

As he walked towards the door, Wyatt looked at Delaney with a questioning face that Delaney had seen before. He nodded once at Wyatt who quickly drew out his gun from his shoulder holster and threw it towards Pitt as he called to him. 'Hey Pitt!'

Pitt turned in a millisecond, grabbed the gun that was sailing towards him and held it down, pointing towards the ground in the 'safe' position.

'Could you kill me from there Detective Sergeant?' asked Wyatt.

'No, not with this anyway; there are no bullets in it; it's too light.'

He threw the gun back to Wyatt as he turned to leave the room.

Delaney got up from his desk and closed the door as he looked at Wyatt. 'What do you think?'

Wyatt shrugged his shoulders. 'I think he'll be okay, as long as he doesn't work alone for the first few months.'

'I agree, I'll phone him later and tell him to report to you in the morning. Teach him right, Ben; he could end up being thrown in at the deep end.'

'I will; as you said yesterday, we want a nil body count on this one.'

Delaney sat down again and held his head in one hand. 'We'll be lucky.'

7

The Villa Miranda stood in seven acres full of olive and orange trees. Micky Sondheim had owned it for five years. From the front balcony you could see the Atlantic Ocean and the town of Cascais. From the rear garden you could look towards Sintra in the mountains.

Lisbon is in easy reach and it was there that Frank Hawkwell touched down at the airport after the two hour flight from London.

Frank Hawkwell had worked for Sondheim for fifteen years and had become known as a 'fixer'. They had met in Sweden when Hawkwell had been involved in a bar room brawl in one of Sondheim's clubs. A rival of Sondheim had gotten drunk and the usual bodyguards were not on hand when a punch was thrown at Sondheim as he tried to calm the man down. Hawkwell had been observing from his table and could see what was coming. He not only knocked the man out cold but also diffused the situation and settled everyone back down again. Sondheim told him he admired how he worked and a few drinks later, Hawkwell was employed as his 'problem solver'.

Hawkwell grew up in Portsmouth in the sixties. After 12 years in the Parachute Regiment he was demobbed for 'unprofessional conduct' involving an incident in the Falklands that never made the news. He had built up a good business as a security advisor and sometime bodyguard/driver for wealthy businessmen. But Sondheim had given him something different; the chance to travel, to earn serious money, to have beautiful women of his choice and to be able to spend a week at his boss's villa while house staff brought him drinks by the pool.

The villa looked the same to Hawkwell as the car pulled in to the drive. The gardens were still being looked after and everything was neat and tidy just as the occupier always wanted it. Sondheim was just being wheeled out onto the driveway as the car came to a stop. Hawkwell looked at him and thought how this big strong man with red hair and a strong, forceful face had changed since the car accident. He had become quieter and more thoughtful and yet somehow, he still commanded respect and his employees probably were still in awe of him. Michelle was the one pushing the chair. She had joined Sondheim just after the accident as his PA and companion and was one of the best things that had happened to him. There was no sex between them but she had an altruism toward him that was admirable. She was still a sexy lady, Hawkwell thought, as he stepped out of the car and she moved to the side of the wheelchair revealing her long, tanned legs.

The handshake was the usual strong one as Sondheim spoke first.

'Frank, my friend, how are you?'

'Great, Micky, fine thank you, good to be here again, I've missed it.'

'Well after you have filled me in with the London situation you can relax and enjoy a few days off, come now, let us go through to the garden.'

Michelle was beckoned to turn the chair around and she smiled at Hawkwell as they made their way. 'How was the flight, Frank?' she said.

'Okay Michelle, okay. You're looking good.'

'Thank you, Frank.' She said as she lowered her sunglasses and walked in front of him in a way she knew he would like.

The patio garden was clean, warm and inviting. Drinks were served by the house maid Connie who had suffered Sondheim for nearly two years. She knew how to serve the drinks and leave quickly. Michelle excused herself. Sondheim wheeled his chair closer to Hawkwell.

'Okay, Frank, let's have it.'

Hawkwell leaned forward in his chair and put his glass down. 'It was nasty Micky, very nasty. The police are saying that 17 are now dead and more on the critical list in hospital. The news this morning said that a bomb went off just after midnight and it was probably about 30 or 40 kilos. So far they haven't mentioned your name as the owner, but that's probably because they're not sure, so they won't say in case they're wrong. They haven't said yet how it was detonated either.'

'Who the hell in London dislikes me so much to do this Frank?'

'What makes you think it's you they're after?'

'Well who else?'

'Could be a terrorist bomber, they pick anywhere that's easy, although seeing what I have seen on the television and in the papers, I don't think so. I've got some contacts snooping around in the police HQ and they'll let me know if they find anything. And in case you're wondering, Jeanette wasn't killed, it was her night off.'

'Who is Jeanette?'

'Bloody hell, Micky, she's the one that manages the place, Jeanette Fleming? She was on the game in the Chelsea house when you gave her the job, years ago now.'

'Ah yes, Jeanette. So Frank; if it wasn't a terrorist and they weren't after me or my business, then what?'

'Been thinking about that on the plane. This has put your London nightclub out of business, you won't be able to start up again what with all the new regulations and licences needed these days, so who would want you out of business?'

'How about Aaron Stait?'

'He wouldn't do it that way.'

'Hey come on, Frank, pick any two out of a hundred. You know how much rival owners and keepers dislike me, they're jealous of my success right?'

'Jealous enough to kill innocent people with a bomb? Don't think so Micky.'

'Well someone put a bomb in my night club, and I want to know who, and I want them dead.'

'I know boss, I know, I'll sort it, believe me I'll sort it. I know a good snout who should have some information for me, I'll be starting there.'

'Okay, Frank, Just keep me informed. By the way, are you still doing work for Stait?'

'Now and again, yes.'

'You should forget him; come and work for me full time.'

'You said that before Micky, and I ended up not earning money for two months.'

'Mm, I guess you're right. Is Stait still buying from the Colombian boys?'

'Yes, he's getting even more involved now.'

'How sure are you that Stait didn't arrange the bombing?'

'Sure enough; I know him too well.'

Sondheim nodded his head in quiet acknowledgement. He picked up his glass, emptied it and threw it to the ground, hard. As it smashed it sent tiny pieces of glass flying in all directions. He turned in his chair, his face almost purple, and called for the maid. 'Connie! Get out here and clean this mess up!' He hesitated for a while before looking at Hawkwell again. 'Sorry, Frank; but the whole of the Colombian connection used to be mine; now I only have part of it.'

Hawkwell did not respond. He knew when to stay quiet.

In the evening, Sondheim, Michelle and Hawkwell sat out in the garden for dinner. Connie had made a seafood salad and roasted a large lamb shank. Good wine was always available – imported from France and Chile – and they enjoyed a few bottles of it.

Slamming his empty glass down on the table, Sondheim raised his hand to beckon Michelle. 'Come my dear, wheel me back into the house, the breeze is chilling my dead legs.'

Michelle took up her position behind his chair and wheeled him backwards. She spoke to Sondheim but was looking and smiling at Hawkwell. 'Of course Micky, let's get you inside and maybe you will doze as you do these days after so much wine.'

Hawkwell let them go inside and left it for a few minutes before reaching for another bottle of wine. This bomb is getting to me, he thought. Who the hell did it? He wondered if his boss knew more than he was letting on. Even a bad old bastard like Stait wouldn't kill all those people; it had to be a rival gang or an individual who wants to get at Micky. He decided he would cut his stay at the villa short and return to London within a couple of days to get on with finding out more and getting to the answer.

He stood up to stretch out and admire the view down the hill toward Cascais. It was still warm, but so was his wine so he made his way to the kitchen. Connie had been dismissed for the day a while ago and he searched through the fridges for ice cubes. 'Ah ha, gotya!' he said as he found a large tray of ice and turned to make his way back to the garden.

But he couldn't because Michelle was standing in front of him.

'Hello,' he said 'I thought you'd be tucking Micky in.'

'I have 'tucked him in' as you say, another silly British thing.'

'Err, I suppose so yes. Anyway fancy another wine? I've just got some ice, the Chardonnay is getting a little warm.'

'Why not,' she replied.

They settled again at the table and Hawkwell poured some more wine, over ice.

Michelle looked at him in a questioning style. 'So, Mr Frank Hawkwell what are you going to do about this bomb? You know Micky is quite upset about it.'

'Yes I know, I've had a few ideas, but you will be the second person to know about it my love, not the first.'

'Okay, okay, just asking Mr big strong problem solver! What else are you working on?'

'Nothing much,' said Hawkwell as he frowned, wondering why she asked.

She moved her chair away from the table in order be able to face him better. He was looking at her purposefully because he knew she wanted him to. She crossed her legs and tossed her hair to one side in a teasing manner. He was annoyed with her. 'Who did you think you're dealing with?' he said 'a schoolboy on his first date?'

'Why whatever do you mean Mr big strong English man?'

He put down his wine glass and stood up in front of her chair. He grabbed one of her arms and pulled her from her chair and towards him. He held her around her waist and kissed her. His hands moved up her legs but she pulled away. They kissed again and she bit him on the neck. He jolted and moved back.

'Michelle? Where are you? Are you there?'

They moved away from each other to see Micky sitting on the porch.

'Yes of course I'm here darling,' she shouted back, 'how come you're out of bed again?'

'Oh I could not sleep, now get your pretty little arse over here. Is Frank out here still?'

The darkness and a couple of olive trees were just enough to block the view to where Michelle and Hawkwell were.

'No, I think he went for a walk in the moonlight, you know, these crazy English men.'

She made her way towards the porch as Hawkwell walked quietly away in the other direction. Sondheim looked at her closely as she approached him.

'Are you alright my dear,' he said, 'you look, err, well, you look bothered?'

'Don't be silly, I'm fine, it's been a hot day, I need my beauty sleep.'

The following day Connie did not turn up for work and Sondheim was angry.

'That is it Michelle, I want her fired! All I have done for that woman. She must be the best paid Portuguese peasant in the whole of Portugal! God damned Portuguese!'

'Very well, my darling,' Michelle replied 'I will fire her and you will never see her again. Now come on, have your coffee and relax, it's decaf as you asked for.'

Hawkwell came into the room when he heard the shouting. 'Alright boss? What is it?'

'What it is Frank,' said Sondheim, now in quieter voice, 'it is peasants, peasants who are incapable of proper work, incapable of communicating and incapable of realising how lucky they are to have the sort of money only a man like me can pay them.'

'Well you know what the answer is boss, you need a good English butler.'

'A butler? Are you serious?'

'Yes I am. You can afford it. They would never let you down and would serve you much better than any 'peasant' as you call them.'

'And I suppose you know where to find me a good one eh, Frank? Your cousin or something?'

'No no, I'm just advising you, that's what you pay me for.'

'Well, I'll think about it. Yes. I will think about it.'

When things had calmed down, Hawkwell told his boss that he was off back to London early to continue his work.

'Your choice, Frank,' Sondheim said, 'you know what you're doing.'

The, with a look of suspicion on his face, he turned to Michelle. 'Michelle will be disappointed won't you my dear? I think she was looking forward to showing you around Cascais. Isn't that so my dear?'

'Oh it was just a casual idea, you know.' Michelle said.

Hawkwell looked at her when he knew Sondheim wasn't looking, and smirked. She turned away to serve the coffee.

Two hours later, the taxi arrived to take Hawkwell back to the airport. Sondheim looked at Hawkwell as he got into the car. 'Work hard, Frank; get me these bastards and I'll look after you.'

Hawkwell nodded. 'Will do boss, leave it to me. Chow.'

'Chow, Frank.' Michelle said as she smiled at him from behind the wheel chair.

The Mercedes made its way down the drive onto the small country road. The driver started to talk about his family and the weather and Hawkwell told him to shut up as he looked out over the scenery on both sides. A few hundred metres away from the villa, the car slowed down to let two small children ride by on their bicycles. Just as the car was about to accelerate again, Hawkwell caught site of something in the long dry grass, 20 metres away from the road, that didn't quite look right. It was a lump, like a dead sheep or a goat; but some of it looked blue in colour.

'Pull over and stop, driver.'

The driver pulled up about 30 metres past the object and Hawkwell walked back to see what it was.

It was a body of a woman; the blue he had seen was a head scarf. He rolled it over with his foot. It was Connie; Sondheim's maid. She had been shot in the head.

8

Taffy Burton arrived at the King Street Laboratory early to find a new receptionist sitting at the desk in the main entrance hall. She looked at him with an over helpful false look. 'Can I help?'

Burton showed his ID card. 'Burton, Overseas Liaison, you must be new.'

'Started this morning.'

'Right, I dropped off a laptop computer with the IT technician yesterday; I'm here to speak to him again.'

'Very well,' said the receptionist in an officious voice. She dialled a number and waited for a while. 'No answer; I'll try the other lab.'

She dialled again and waited again. 'No answer, oh where are they all?'

'Could they be having a break?' asked Burton.

'No, too early, I've been told that they have an early lunch because they start at seven in the morning. Perhaps they're having a cigarette outside.'

'Outside?'

'Yes, you know, out the back. When I was shown around this morning on my induction, they explained where people were allowed to smoke; there's a shelter, just outside the back door.'

'What else is out there?' asked Burton.

'Nothing, just an old shed and a dirt track next to a field.'

Burton moved quickly and pointed to the woman. 'Stay here.' He ran towards the corridor that led to the labs; on the wall he noticed a break-glass fire alarm and he hit it hard. The sirens sounded instantly. He ran into the first lab to find an empty room, the tables and desks had been swiped clean and everything that would have been on them was on the floor. But the equipment on the floor was scientific; tubes, test beds, pipettes, samplers. He turned and ran next door, that room too was empty, but spread out around the desks and work stations were hundreds of computers. A rear door was open and he took his gun from his jacket before walking slowly towards it. As he was half way through the door, a smell caught his attention. It was the smell of two-stroke petrol, like the petrol they use for scrambler bikes.

He put his gun away as he looked down to the ground realising what had happened. Two men were lying on the ground in their white lab coats. But their coats were covered in blood. One was on his back, blood streaming from his chest, the other was face down in some rubble; two bullet holes in his back. He felt for pulses on both men. It was too late. He went back inside the lab and looked for the small green and brown case that he had delivered there the day before. It was nowhere to be found. Computers were everywhere and he searched desperately. There were numerous laptops, PC's and monitors. But the small laptop was not there.

He sat down and reached for his phone. Delaney answered quickly. 'Taffy?'

'They've got the computer, sir, killed two lab technicians and got away through a back door, on a scrambler bike across a field, I reckon only a few minutes ago, I can still smell the exhaust fumes.'

'They?'

'Must be the Colombians; that's who it was taken from.'

'Right, I'll get the local boys and forensics down there, make sure all the staff stay away and then get back here as soon as you can.'

'Will do' Burton finished the call and made his way back to the reception area. The new receptionist was not there but an older lady was trying to switch off the fire alarms and a security guard was ushering people out of the door. As the alarms were silenced, Burton waited by the reception desk for the arrival of the emergency crews. The older lady looked at him with concern. 'Oh my goodness, what's happened now?'

'Someone's taken a computer.'

'Is that all?'

'Mm, that's all. Where's the other lady?'

'What other lady?'

'The younger one that started work here this morning.'

The woman looked down at her switchboard and was pre-occupied as she answered Burton. 'I've run this reception for three years and probably will do for many more to come, no one else started here this morning.'

Delaney was with Chief Inspector Baart when Burton arrived back at the office a couple of hours later.

'Is the computer definitely gone, Taffy?' asked Delaney.

'Yes it's gone. I think we can use this as confirmation of Chief Inspector Baart's assumption that these people have a cell in the UK.'

'Too easy wasn't it?' asked Baart.

'Yes, sir, I'm afraid so. A young woman turned up at the lab this morning before anyone else. She told the security man that she was the new receptionist starting work there today. He phoned the number on the card that she gave him; they confirmed that she was a new starter. The security guard was a bit wet behind the ears. She settled herself behind the desk and when the guard went to check something that was happening out front, she went through to the lab, grabbed the computer and opened the back door. There's a chain link fence around the premises and she threw the computer over the fence. An hour later when the technicians turned up, they didn't realise that the computer was missing, but one of them went outside for a cigarette just as someone on a motorcycle scrambler turned up to pick the computer from where the woman had thrown it. The rider shot the technician as he challenged him; that brought the other technician running out to see what was happening. As soon as he saw what the situation was, he turned to run back inside but the rider shot him in the back. It's all on CCTV.'

Delaney held his hands out. 'So where was the security guard?'

'*Not* looking at the CCTV monitors, sir, because he was out the front of the building helping someone who had been knocked down by a passing car just outside of the entrance; presumably a diversion to free up the young woman's time.'

Baart shook his head. 'All that information; gone.'

'Not gone,' said Delaney, 'just in the wrong hands for a while.'

'Very optimistic of you.'

'Perhaps Chief Inspector. Well it seems that they do have a cell working here; any suggestions?'

'Yes,' replied Baart. 'We must try to track down Stait. I think he would not come to the UK. He would issue instructions from Belgium. I suggest that I send Sergeant Brun back to Antwerp with one of your men to track him down. Meanwhile I will stay here and work with you; we can start with the CCTV footage.'

Delaney stood up and reached for the phone. 'Sounds alright to me, Chief Inspector; I'll phone Ben and tell him to arrange it. But I think there should be two people helping Sergeant Brun; my new recruit can go with them as well.'

'You took on that Ajit Pitt then, Sir?' asked Burton.

'Yes I did, Taffy; he seems capable enough, and working with Ben for his first few weeks will give him a good grounding.'

Delaney held up a hand as he heard Wyatt answer the phone. 'Ben, go and get your Sergeant Brun will you; you're both going back to Antwerp; the computer with all the information on it has been taken. We need to find Stait; he's the only one that can lead us to the cell that's working here.'

Wyatt's voice sounded relaxed. 'Sure no problem, I'll arrange it all; I could do with a change.'

'Good; and get hold of Pitt. Tell him his first job is with you. Take him with you to Antwerp.'

'So you meant it then, guv?'

'Meant what?'

'After we'd seen him, you said he might end up in the deep end.'

'Yes, so I did, but he's got a good instructor.'

9

Hours later, Delaney was sitting back in his chair at home. Angela had gone to her yoga class and Rocky was lying near the front door waiting for her return. As Delaney ran his fingers along the row of CDs, Ella Fitzgerald took his eye. Her voice was always good at helping him to relax, he thought. The music on, he reached for his wine and started to think about this latest case.

So, he thought, what was it about this case that was bothering him so much? A number of things went through his mind. Sondheim was obviously quite a ruthless businessman and his links to some previous crimes made him quite dangerous too. A nightclub owned by Sondheim had been bombed and it had been bombed by a professional. So, if someone wanted Sondheim dead they wouldn't have bombed a nightclub knowing he wasn't there. If someone is out to ruin his business empire, that was a good start, but why do something that would kill so many people? Then there were the links with Stait and the Colombians; too many coincidences, he thought. This was going to be interesting. He sat thinking for another 30 minutes before he was interrupted by a knock on the door.

'That was quick, Taffy; come in.'

'Thanks.'

'Drink?'

'Why not, just one.'

Delaney poured him a small brandy and they went through to the conservatory.

'Well,' said Burton, 'this man Hawkwell is actually on the police databank.'

'Okay, tell me.'

'Frank John Hawkwell, born in Portsmouth 1958. Served in the Parachute Regiment for 12 years, did Northern Ireland, Belize and the Falklands before he was discharged for unprofessional conduct, whatever that is. The information on the databank seems patchy to say the least, but basically he set up his security and bodyguard business before meeting Sondheim at some point about 15 years ago, give or take a year. Sondheim calls him his 'problem solver' according to my sources.. He seems to travel all over the place sorting out problems for Sondheim and dealing with some of his businesses for him. But here's the interesting bit; he only works for Sondheim part time, whenever he's needed. The rest of his time he works for Stait, that Belgian man that Chief Inspector Baart told us about.'

'There's the link then, Taffy. Organise a trip to Portugal for us will you.'

'I err, I already have, sir.'

'What?'

'Portugal; I've arranged it, we fly out this afternoon.'

'Very organised, Taffy, but what if I didn't want to go?'

'But you do, sir.'

'Well, I know, but if I...ah forget it. What time is the flight?'

'15.00 hours.'

'Right, pick me up about twelve then will you?'

'Will do, sir.'

Delaney shook his head as he closed the door behind Burton, with a smile on his face.

At 9 a.m. the following morning, Delaney and Burton were sitting near the pool at the Vila Gale hotel in Cascais near Lisbon. Their flight had been on time and Burton had taken the opportunity to brief Delaney on the details of all the relevant information. He had arranged for the local Portuguese police to meet them at the hotel to explain what they knew and how they could help.

Delaney enjoyed his breakfast of croissant and coffee and Burton had regretted having his sausage and eggs, saying that he did not realise the little sausages would have garlic in them. 'Not ideal for breakfast when you're meeting people.'

'Not to worry,' Delaney replied. 'It's good for the heart apparently.'

After some time the two men were joined by a small tanned man, casually dressed but still looking business-like. Burton stood up to greet him. 'Ah, Senore Segressa, good to see you again, can I introduce you to Tom Delaney, Head of TOLA.' Burton then turned to Delaney. 'This is Senore Segressa, sir, Portuguese Police.'

'You two have met before then?' asked Delaney.

'Indeed,' replied Segressa, 'I had the good fortune of training in Cardiff many years ago when I was on secondment; Mr Burton here looked after me when I was off duty.'

'Right,' said Delaney, raising his eyebrows, 'you'll know where the best pubs are then.'

'Of course,' said Segressa, smiling.

The formal handshakes over, the three men sat again while Segressa explained what information he had. It took half an hour for Burton to brief Segressa on what they knew about Sondheim. Delaney listened and took notes as he heard of a man who had been a nasty character for most of his life. Drugs, fraud, prostitution and almost 'legitimate' businesses had made him rich and he had moved to his Villa near Cascais some five years ago and was starting to wind down his involvement in many of his operations leaving it to his managers and Frank Hawkwell to look after things.

When Burton had finished, Segressa leaned forward, taking up his large espresso. 'Well gentlemen, I have some new and interesting news which I will come on to in a moment, but let me tell you what we have. Sondheim is still living at the Villa Miranda, it's about 4 kilometres from here; I will show you soon.

He has few visitors – sometimes foreigners, sometimes Portuguese or Spanish and sometimes from the UK, I believe you already know of a Mr Hawkwell?'

'Yes we do,' said Burton.

'Well, the only other people that we ever see visiting his villa are delivery drivers and utility workers and usually these are given instruction from his present girlfriend, Michelle Depout. She lives with him all the time apart from taking the odd break in, I believe, London or Paris. She leaves the villa alone to go shopping in Lisbon and sometimes to here in Cascais where she will shop and sometimes have lunch. She always returns to the villa before 4pm. But the new bit of news I have for you gentlemen is that Sondheim had one other person working for him as cook and maid. Her name was Connie...'

'Was?' interrupted Burton.

'Yes, was. She had worked there for some time. She was well known to the locals and err, she was found dead, about 300 metres from the villa; she had been shot in the head.'

'Who found her?' enquired Delaney.

'A local farmer, simply out on his bike on his way to check some livestock. She was by the side of the road; apparently she would walk home from the villa as it is just about 2 kilometres. Other people had seen her many times on that road.'

Delaney continued his questioning. 'So I presume that Sondheim has been interviewed about it.'

'No, not yet, other people have, but not Sondheim. But I was going to speak to him today and thought you might like to be with me.'

Burton seemed surprised. 'Are you sure? He may know we're looking at him.'

'I doubt it, you do not have to say anything, as far as he is concerned you will be my colleagues, you need say nothing, but perhaps if one of you waited in the car?'

'Of course, I will', said Delaney, turning to Burton, 'You go ahead if you want to, Taffy; I'll wait in the car and perhaps have snoop around.'

Segressa stood as if to conclude the decision. 'Well then let us go. I can drive through the town to show you around and then we shall go on to the villa. We have all day, relax, you are in Portugal now.'

Segressa's relaxed manner suited Delaney. They had a good conversation in the rear of the car while Burton joined the driver up front. The police driver had already been briefed on the route to take. They took the main road past the old military establishment, the harbour and the marina. The sun was hot and the car wheels squealed as they slowly turned corners on the shiny white sandstone cobbled streets.

Pointing to his right, Segressa looked at his two guests. 'Now, if you look through there you can see the fish market and beyond that in the Rua das Flores you can see the Restaurante Sagres. This is where Michelle Depout often has lunch with a friend who runs a boutique here in Cascais.'

'How often does she go there?' asked Delaney.

'About twice a week, she has not been for a while so maybe a visit is due.'

'Why do you watch her so closely?' Burton asked.

''Mm, because she lives with a known criminal and err, maybe because it is more interesting for the local police than watching out for drunken tourists and our fishermen who are not licensed, you know? Anyway they keep me informed so if you would like to witness a meeting, I will tell you when she is there next.'

The car left Cascais and headed up towards Sintra on the main carriageway. After about 4 kilometres they turned on to a smaller road which went through some barren looking fields and Orange tree groves before arriving at the long straight narrow road that lead to the Villa Miranda.

As instructed the driver sounded the car horn and an attractive brunette appeared on the front porch. She made her way down the driveway and beckoned the car to come closer.

'Gentlemen; that is Michelle Depout.' Segressa said.

They pulled up near the porch and Segressa and Burton got out of the car to meet her. Delaney stayed in the car. Segressa walked forward, his hand outstretched. 'Miss Depout?'

'Yes, and you must be Senore Segressa.'

'Indeed and can I introduce my colleague Sergeant Colmia.'

Michelle Depout nodded at Burton and he returned the acknowledgement before looking at Segressa with a frown.

'My driver and the other officer will wait in the car for me out here.' said Segressa.

'Very well, but they must let me know if they want a drink,' she replied. Her French accent was unmistakable. She led them through some doorways towards the back of the house. Sondheim was in a chair in the back room where it was cooler. He smiled at the two men as they entered the room behind Michelle.

'Well gentlemen, Michelle will get us some drinks, as err, I believe you know, my maid Connie cannot do that for us now.'

'No sir,' said Segressa, 'that is why we are here as I think you were told?'

'Yes of course. A terrible thing, do you have any idea who did it yet?'

'No, sir we do not. But I need to ask you some things, okay?'

'Sure, sure you go ahead, go ahead and ask.'

Segressa asked the usual questions as Burton looked on. Sondheim swore he knew nothing of Connie's death until he was told by the person from Segressa's office who phoned to make the appointment. Connie had left the villa at about 5 o'clock after she had been told she could leave early. Neither he nor Michelle had heard any shots that night and none of the locals had been to see them. Connie had seemed in a normal state of mind when she left.

Outside in the car Delaney was getting restless. 'I'm going have a walk around driver, you stay here, okay?'

The driver was nervous. 'But, sir I think maybe, Senore Segressa would prefer that…'

'I'll be Okay, I won't be long.'

Delaney walked slowly around the side of the house in a casual manner as though to show he was just stretching his legs. It was very quiet. No motor vehicles could be seen and apart from the odd bird singing, there was not much life at all. There was a small brown trunk on the floor near a side door and he thought of how it looked out of place, as it did not match any of the older surroundings. He moved closer to it out of curiosity and looked around to see if anyone else was about.

It was the smell of perfume that made him look twice in one direction. A figure moved out of a shadow and stood watching him. It was Michelle Depout.

'Hello, officer.' She said.

'Hello; nice perfume if you don't mind me saying.'

'No, of course not. You are not Portuguese.'

Delaney panicked a little. He didn't want her to know where he was from. He put on his dubious Dutch accent. 'No, I am being from Amsterdam on err, how do they call us? Secondment?' He was thankful for the word that Segressa had used earlier.

'Ah yes I know this word, it is French.'

'Are you French?'

'Yes I am.'

'Okay, well err, I was just looking for a drink actually, perhaps you can help I didn't want to disturb anyone.'

'Okay then, if you go back to your automobile I will bring some to you and your friend.'

'Right. Zank you.'

They both turned slowly away from each other. Delaney afforded himself a little smile. Eat your heart out, Lawrence Olivier, he thought.

Back at the car he waited, leaning against the door. Depout appeared a few minutes later with a tray of cold drinks for them. Delaney looked at her closely to make sure he would recognise her again, although, he thought, it wouldn't be difficult. She was about 40, slender and stylish and her womanly figure and shapely legs could be seen through the lightweight summer dress against the sunlight. Her hair was brunette, shiny and long and her eyes were sad yet beautiful.

'So, here we are, Mr policemen,' she said as she handed the tray to Delaney.

'Zank you Ma'am.' He said, conscious of not over doing the accent.

She turned and made her way back to the house just as the other three men were emerging on to the porch. Delaney saw them shake hands and they said goodbye.

As the car made its way back toward Cascais, Burton explained to Delaney what had happened. 'Senore Segressa here has a hard job finding the maid's killer, I think.'

Delaney looked at Segressa. 'What about a gun or bullet?'

'The bullet,' replied Segressa, 'is still in her. We are perhaps not so fast with our pathology here. Now then, gentlemen, I have some more information back at my office about Mr Sondheim's operations here in Portugal and Spain, perhaps I could show you both what we have, after all that is the main reason you are here, no? We will go and see what we have.'

Delaney excused himself. 'Not me. You two go back to the office and I'll have a walk around Cascais.'

'Sure thing, I will drop you in the town centre and take Mr Burton to my office. Okay with you, Mr Burton?'

'Yes of course; and it's Taffy,' said Burton. Then, turning to Delaney, 'I'll see you later, sir; perhaps for dinner?'

'Sure; you can let me know what you learn this afternoon.'

Delaney strolled around Cascais admiring the old scenic streets and buildings. The fishermen were finished for the day now and their cigarettes hung heavily in their mouths as their eyes watched the tourists pass by and their street dogs lay in the shade.

The restaurant that Senore Segressa had pointed out to him was just in front of him as he walked down Rua das Flores and he decided to have a beer. The waiter brought him a large cold lager and enquired, in his excellent English, as to whether his guest was on vacation.

'Yes just a short break for a few days.'

'You have some friends here?' asked the waiter.

'Yes a few, you know, and business colleagues.'

'So you please must bring your friends here for dinner one evening.'

'Yes of course why not, I like the look of your menu. Actually I believe one of my friends comes here anyway, Miss Depout?'

'Ah yes I think so. Just one moment please.'

The waiter left the table for some time and Delaney started to wonder. He had just finished his beer when the waiter returned.

'Yes sir, I thought so, I was just checking; your friend Miss Depout; she has reserved a table with us for tonight.'

'Ah excellent, well I must telephone her and see if I can join her.'

'Good, okay, sir, and now I will get you the bill?'

'Yes thank you.'

Burton was reading up on the information he had been given when there was a knock on his hotel room door. It was Delaney. 'Fancy a meal in town tonight, Taffy?'

'Sure why not.'

'Good, because I've booked a table at that restaurant that Segressa showed us.'

'You mean the one that Sondheim's girlfriend goes to?'

'Yep. And she'll be there. Worth a look don't you think?'

'Absolutely, what time?'

'About 8.30.'

'Okay thanks, sir, I'll meet you in the lobby.'

Cascais was busy and warm that night. The Restaurante Sagres was quite full with tourists and local families as the two men sat down at one of the outside tables. They had their backs to the building and were facing other tables on the busy esplanade as tourists, shoppers and fishermen strolled past.

They ordered drinks and chose from the menu. Burton had a good look around. 'No sign of her yet,' he said as he caressed his cold beer.

'No, well it's early yet for a place like this.'

Both men were halfway through their first dish of prawns and scallops when Delaney gave Burton a nudge. 'There you go,' he said as he motioned toward Michelle Depout who was approaching the restaurant from the busy end of the esplanade. She was with a man. He was about 40, smartly dressed with northern European looks, a small grey moustache and narrow, modern spectacles. They were greeted by the restaurant owner and ushered to a table had that had obviously been reserved for them.

'Should we say hello?' asked Burton, smirking and nudging Delaney's arm.

'Well if she sees us we can wave I guess, nothing wrong with two policemen having a meal. But if she doesn't, no, we'll stay here and watch for anything unusual. Who do you suppose that is with her then?'

'A boyfriend? A friend? A body guard even?'

'Mm, difficult to guess isn't it. I wonder if Sondheim knows she's with someone else.'

Burton shrugged his shoulders as they were interrupted by the waiter who had served Delaney earlier in the day. 'Good evening sir, I see your friend is also here tonight, and err, yes Miss Depout also, you want I should take a message to her table?'

'No, thank you, I'll catch up with her later.'

'As you wish, sir, please, let me clear the table for your next course.'

As the two men observed Michelle Depout and her dinner partner, they noticed that she seemed angry. The man had handed her a couple of pieces of folded paper which she had unfolded, read and put in her handbag. On more than one occasion she had raised an arm in the air as though to complain about what he was telling her. The man made two phone calls during their meal, during which he was doing more listening than talking, and when each call had finished, he had looked at her as if to give an answer.

Their meal seemed quick and hurried but they were smiling when they got up to leave. Depout did not see Delaney and Burton as she said goodbye to the man, with a handshake, not a kiss, and made her way past the other tables and down the esplanade toward the taxi rank.

The man walked the other way and was looking around as though to check if he was being followed. He was about 50 metres away from the restaurant, walking toward the main street when a small car pulled up next to him.

'Could be interesting,' Burton said as the two men's eyes were pinned on the situation.

'Yeah, he looks very nervous.'

Just as Delaney had finished his sentence, two men got out of the car and went over to the man. One of them pulled his arm but he moved away and started to run.

Delaney got up quickly from his seat. 'Come on Taffy, this is turning bad.'

They both walked quickly toward the scene as the waiters looked on with fright. At the same time the two men from the car had caught up with the man. One grabbed him around the shoulders and held him tight, spinning him to face his colleague. His colleague plunged a knife into the man's stomach, withdrew it, and plunged it in again, this time, into his throat. They let the man fall to the ground as they ran back toward their car. Delaney and Burton were almost upon them by now but they were very quick and the first one jumped into the driver's seat and started to move away as he opened the passenger door for his friend to jump in. But his friend missed the step and he didn't jump in but instead, rolled along the pavement as the car drove off towards the sea front. The man dragged himself up from the floor as Delaney approached him. Burton ran after the car. The man lunged at Delaney with a knife and managed to cut Delaney's hand as he jumped to one side. Another lunge was on its way and Delaney picked up a chair from one of the esplanade tables and held it out like a lion tamer. The man tried again and he managed to stick the knife into Delaney's hand forcing him to drop the chair. Damn it, thought Delaney when will I ever bloody learn. The noise of a gun and the man being thrown to the ground with blood coming out of his head were simultaneous. Delaney looked at him for a while lying on the ground before he turned to see who was approaching him.

'Mr Delaney, I knew you would need me some time or another.' It was Segressa, with two men behind him. He moved closer to Delaney as he put his gun back into his shoulder holster. A police car rushed by, heading in the direction of the sea front.

Segressa shook his head as he looked at the body of the man he had shot. 'Well, it seems this case of yours is more serious than I thought.'

'Maybe,' replied Delaney 'Taffy went after the car in the direction of the seafront, can your men help him?'

'They'll sort it out.'

Segressa moved over to the body of the man who had been with Michelle Depout. He knelt down to look at him closely. 'Do you know who this is?'

'No I don't, but don't tell me, you do.'

'Yes. It is Peter Sondheim, Micky's brother.'

A police car pulled up near the scene and the driver moved toward Segressa. He spoke in Portuguese for two or three minutes as he gestured toward the sea front.

Segressa explained to Delaney. 'Taffy is okay and on his way back to us, Mr Delaney. The driver of the car got away on foot, but we will get him.'

A few minutes later, Burton arrived back, having been driven from where they had lost the second man. He was taken aback when Delaney spoke to him, holding his bandaged hand. 'Taffy, why the hell wasn't I told that Sondheim has a brother?'

'Because he hasn't, sir.'

'Yes he bloody has and we've just seen him get killed.'

'Sir, honestly, all the dossiers we had and all the information did not mention a brother.'

Delaney's voice quietened. 'Well he *had* a brother, Taffy; could have been a different father or mother, but he had a brother.'

'Right Sir, I'll check the files again and see what I can find.'

They were both sitting by the hotel pool the following morning. They had 'helped' Segressa with his enquiries and were trying to put together events of the last two days. Burton looked at the dressing around Delaney's hand. 'You were lucky last night.' Delaney nodded slowly before replying, 'Mm, well it wasn't the first time and I doubt it will be the last.'

The two men exchanged thoughts about what had happened and why. The nightclub bomb in London had killed many people but was that the intention? Why would someone want Sondheim's maid, Connie, killed and why in the open, in daylight? Why didn't they know about Sondheim's brother?' Sondheim had been winding down his operations for some time and all the signs were that he was beginning to retire and that people knew he was, so why all this now?

They decided to make their way back to London. Hawkwell was still there and hopefully someone was watching him. Maybe by the time they got back, they would have something new to work on.

The following day a driver met them at Heathrow. The traffic was heavy and slow as they made their way towards the city. Delaney was anxious to hear if there was anything new. The driver had been well briefed. 'We've got someone watching Hawkwell, sir; rumour has it that he wants to find out who was behind the nightclub bombing. Chief Inspector Baart is still talking to his people back in Belgium to find out what he can but as yet we haven't heard from Antwerp.'

'Thanks, let's get back to the office, said Delaney. 'If I'm any judge, Hawkwell didn't come to London for a holiday.'

10

Phil Layton was worried. He was worried because Frank Hawkwell was coming to see him. As he sat at the corner table in the Dog and Whistle he knew that Frank had some questions and that he would want some good answers.

He had just turned forty seven and a person did not need to be a doctor to see that years of drinking and smoking had taken its toll. His pushed his greasy greying hair back across his head as he put down his copy of the Racing Times to finish his third scotch of the morning. He had known Hawkwell for some time now, he thought, ever since the McKay brothers had done the bullion job in Glasgow for Micky Sondheim. Josh McKay had forced him to drive the car from Glasgow to London with half a tonne of gold bars in the boot. 'You owe me a favour wee boy,' Layton remembered him saying 'and you get it wrong again, you won't be here to try for a third time.'

But he did not get it wrong. He would never be the bravest of criminals or the richest but he knew how to drive and how to get things delivered. His other talent was snouting and he had built up quite a clientele list including police officers, politicians, and prostitutes, and of course, Frank Hawkwell. But Hawkwell had worked for Sondheim for years now and Sondheim hadn't done any 'jobs' in the UK for a long time.

Layton choked as he was taken by surprise when suddenly he realised Frank Hawkwell was standing by him. 'Phil, you old rascal, how are you?'

'M, M, Mr Hawkwell, please don't do that.'

'Sorry, Phil, let me get that topped up for you, still on the scotch?'

'Yeah er, yeah thanks, Mr Hawkwell.'

Layton watched Hawkwell as he went to the bar and returned with the drinks. He could feel his face getting warmer and his knee started to twitch.

'There you go, Phil, so how are you? Long time no see.'

'Indeed it is guvner.'

Silence followed as they both took a drink and Hawkwell stared at Layton until he cracked. 'So er, Mr Hawkwell, I can't possibly think what you might want with me after all these years, I mean you was always okay with things and er, I don't think any jobs av…'

'Shut up, Phil.' Hawkwell interrupted. He paused for a while before asking his first question. 'What do you know about the Graphic Night club that was bombed last week?'

'The Graphic? Well, not a lot of word out about that one yet Mr Hawkwell, bomb wasn't it?'

'Yes it was, Phil. A good bomb. Someone was paid an awful lot of money to arrange that one and I would like to know who.'

'Not for me Mr Hawkwell, no no sir, that question's not for me, I don't know any bombers me.'

Hawkwell leaned forward with his elbow on the table. 'Phil, you know everyone in this city who does wrong. You may not know the bomber, but I bet you know the man who paid him. Now, I was thinking of going to the cinema this afternoon Phil, and I need to be leaving here by about one o'clock. That gives you 30 minutes. I'll get you another drink.'

Hawkwell returned to the table and put the drinks down before taking a sip from his own glass and looking again at Layton without saying anything. Layton started the negotiations. 'I might know some news, Mr Hawkwell. A big bomb like that must involve some nasty people. Must be worth a bit, that sort of information.'

Hawkwell smirked. 'How much, Phil?'

'Ooh, I'd say about five thousand Mr Hawkwell, how does that sound?'

'It depends what you know.'

Layton looked around the pub and pulled his chair closer to the table. 'Thing is guvner, word is that the bombers weren't even from the UK; some foreign mob. No one knows for sure but word is that they were from France. Someone imported them for the job. Big money by all accounts.'

'Who?'

'Don't know that one guvner.'

'Who, Phil?'

Layton paused for a while. He may have been scared, but he knew a serious question when he heard one. The sort of question that was worth money. 'Well now, Mr Hawkwell, we're talking money now aren't we?'

'Phil, my dear boy, you tell me who imported and paid those bombers and I'll give you ten thousand.'

'Blimey guvner, you want these boys don't you; Why?'

'Didn't you know that the Graphic Club was owned by Micky Sondheim?'

'Maybe, guvner.'

'Well you know now. So, who was it?'

Layton took a deep breath. 'Ready for this? It was Stevie Packman.'

'Stevie Packman? Are you taking the piss?'

'Knew you'd be surprised Mr Hawkwell.'

Stevie Packman was a small time villain from Wimbledon. Frank Hawkwell knew something about him. He had been in jail a few times for small stuff and had roughed up a few people for money, mainly debt collection jobs. He knew the night club scene in London because he provided some doormen for some of them. He decided Layton was telling the truth.

Layton interrupted his chain of thought. 'Okay, Mr Hawkwell; payment in the usual way then eh?'

'When I know you're right, Phil, when I know you're right, but yes payment in the usual way. Still living in that flat near the Golden Goose?'

'That's it, Mr Hawkwell, that's it.'

It was 6 p.m. when Delaney looked at Burton across the office. They had been discussing the Portugal trip and Burton had been trying to get hold of Wyatt and Pitt in Belgium. 'Still nothing, Taffy?'

'Nothing, sir; I don't know why Ben would not answer his phone.'

'Have you tried to get hold of Pitt, the new man?'

'Mm, no answer there either.'

'Well, I'll give them another 12 hours before I press the button. What about Brun?'

'Baart has tried to contact him as well, but apparently he often switches his phone off anyway.'

As they were about to leave, Burton's phone rang again. He picked it up and shook his head as a sign to Delaney that the call was not from Wyatt. After a few minutes, he replaced the phone and referred to his notes.

'What have you got, Taffy?' asked Delaney.

'Well, sir, that was our man watching Hawkwell. He's just been to meet Phil Layton.'

'Surprised old Phil is still busy.'

'Yeah me to, but he is, anyway; after Hawkwell's meeting with Layton he went to a house in Hammersmith. Someone let him in but he was only there for a few moments.

'And who lives at the house?'

'Stevie Packman.'

'Stevie Packman? The Stevie Packman that nicks motors and beats up people for a few bob?

'Yep' it's all been confirmed.'

76

'Okay Taffy, I'm not messing about too long with people like Packman. Go and bring him in.'

'Now?'

'Yes please.'

'Will do, sir, oh and there's a message for you to ring MI6, they wouldn't say why.'

'Right, I'll phone them.'

Stevie Packman was a small slim man with a scarred face. He had never really grasped that fashions change and he didn't seem to realise why people smirked at him with his shirt collar over his jacket and his greasy, combed back hair. He looked nervous as he entered Delaney's office, accompanied by Burton. They both sat down in front of Delaney's desk as he leaned forward to speak. 'Well Stevie, long time no see.'

Packman said nothing and looked around the room. Delaney stood up and looked out of the window, before turning to face Packman again. 'Okay Stevie, as you're in a quiet mood, let me tell you what I know and what I want. I know you have met someone called Frank Hawkwell. I know who Frank Hawkwell works for. I know you would do anything for money if the price was right and I know you've been doing a little dealing in explosives.'

Packman said nothing. His knee started to twitch as he looked at Burton and then at Delaney.

'Now; that's what I *know*,' continued Delaney, 'this is what I *want*. I want to know where you got the explosives from and where you used them or who you sold them on to. Let's start there.'

Packman remained quiet as though he knew this issue was bigger and wider than he had realised. Delaney waited for two minutes. Burton knew to be quiet also. After the two minutes, Delaney spoke again as Burton got to his feet.

'Taffy, take him down to the holding cells and call the duty solicitor, I want his place fingerprinted and his girlfriend brought in for...'

'Wo, wo, wo!' Packman broke his silence. 'What the bloody hell is all this for? I said I would come in for a chat, your bloke here never said anything about...'

'Just take him down, Taffy!' interrupted Delaney, 'I'm not messing about.'

Burton took Packman by the arm and led him towards the door. As the door was opened Packman turned around. He and Burton stood still for a while in the doorway before Packman spoke to the ceiling and then to Delaney. 'Right, right, Hang on, I'll tell you what I know, but I want this putting down as being co-operative.'

Burton looked at Delaney for an answer. Delaney nodded and Packman was led back to his chair. Both knees were twitching now as he addressed Delaney.

'Look, I don't know why you're involved in this, but it looks like it might be getting out of my league. Okay, I didn't *buy* any explosives, I was *given* some explosives. I got a phone call from a foreign sounding bloke and I had to collect the explosives from Paris. All they said was that I had to deliver them to Hyde Park and leave them in a bag next to a waste bin, and that's all I did, honest.'

'And you don't know who it was that gave you the job?' asked Burton.

'No, all he said was that I would be paid in cash.'

'How much and how?' asked Delaney.

'Oh come on man...'

'How much and how?'

'Alright, alright. It was ten grand, in Euros. They left it in a van near where I dropped off the explosives.'

'What sort of explosive was it, Stevie?'

'D'know.'

78

'Come on Stevie, you may be a little silly, but you're not totally stupid, you wouldn't have handled it if you didn't know what you were dealing with.'

'Err, I think it was Gelmeck.'

Delaney shuffled position in his chair. 'Thanks for that, Stevie. Now tell me what Frank Hawkwell wanted when he came to see you.'

'Same as you, Delaney; difference is, he's going to pay me.'

'*Is* going to pay you, you mean he hasn't yet?'

'No, said he'd come to the house later with the cash.'

'And you believed him?'

Packman didn't say anything else. Delaney looked at Burton before nodding towards the door. 'Okay Stevie, you can go, and if I ever find out that you're getting involved in explosives again, I'll have you inside before you can say bang.'

Packman left the building and made his way out to a taxi rank. That wasn't too bad, he thought to himself; Delaney had always been straight with him and he knew he would have to let him go; hard evidence was needed. And anyway, in a few hours time he would have the five grand from Hawkwell. The taxi pulled up outside his house as the night grew dark and damp.

Hawkwell moved in behind him with quiet stealth. The knife went into Packman's spine before he felt it. His scream was muffled by the big arm smothering his face. Hawkwell turned him around and looked at him. 'You shouldn't have messed with big stuff like this Stevie; you're out of your league, matey, and Mr Sondheim wants people to pay for what happened to his nightclub. You're the first of many, you poor bastard.' Hawkwell's knife then went into Packman's stomach. He twisted the knife, pulled it out, and then repeated the action three times.

11

Ben Wyatt managed to get a signal on his mobile phone just as he, Brun and Pitt were driving out of a forest near Herbeumont 200 kilometres south of Antwerp. As soon as they had landed at Antwerp International Airport, Brun had received a call from Inspector Hubert, who was still working out of the office in the museum where Burton had met him a few days earlier. An intelligence officer in the Belgian forces had found out about a small farm near Herbeumont in a quiet forested area and there had been some reported sightings of a man who matched Stait's description. Sergeant Brun had driven them to the area some four hours later. They had found nothing at the farm but a moody gentleman who had lived there for forty years and didn't have a clue what they were talking about. They had been driving around the area for some time when Wyatt noticed he had a signal on his phone.

'I need to phone the boss; I've finally got a signal,' said Wyatt. He left Brun and Pitt to have a good look around as they drove from copse to copse, in the Belgian police unmarked Range Rover, along small roads, farm tracks and byways.

Delaney answered his phone in a manner that told Wyatt to be quick. 'Ben; how come I couldn't reach you and where have you been?'

'In a bloody forest, sir, 200 clicks south of Antwerp. Some of the intelligence boys over here had some information about Stait; they thought he and some of his men were using an old farm as a base but we've found nothing. We're just about to pack it in for the day.'

'Right,' answered Delaney. 'How's Ajit doing?'

'Alright, he's seems quite observant and he's still young enough to have the stamina for these long days.'

'Good, I'll let you carry on then; keep me informed yeh?'

'Yes, sir.'

New recruit Ajit Pitt looked at Wyatt. 'Was he asking about me?'

'Of course he was; he needs to know.'

'Sure, I know, I just wondered.'

Brun suddenly told them both to be quiet. He stopped the car and switched off the engine. Pitt was about to speak but Wyatt held up his hand to stop him. Brun pointed to a small piece of woodland on the top of a large shallow hill to their left, about 600 metres from where they were. A narrow band of smoke was rising from the woodland.

Wyatt spoke quietly. 'If they're in the area and have heard we might be looking for them, they could have decided to wait it out. From up there they have good all-round line of sight.'

'So why the fire?' asked Pitt.

'Barbecue?' suggested Brun.

Wyatt looked at him with still eyes; he did not know if he was joking or not. Brun shrugged his shoulders and spoke again. 'Why not? They could have bought something to eat from a local shop or farm and be cooking it to have with a beer or wine.'

Pitt had already begun to understand Wyatt and he decided to make a suggestion when he saw the look on his face. 'Well either way, we should get out of sight shouldn't we?'

'Quite right young man,' said Wyatt as he tapped Brun on the shoulder. Brun drove the vehicle slowly and quietly for 100 metres and parked it next to a yew hedge out of sight of the hilltop woodland. He looked at his watch and turned to Wyatt. 'It will be getting dark soon, perhaps we should wait until the morning.'

'No; we have a look now,' said Wyatt. 'I'm not sitting around all night to find out that we've been waiting to grab a couple of innocent campers.'

'Good point; I'm up for it,' said Pitt.

'Shame; because you're staying here to look after the vehicle,' said Wyatt.

'But you'll need...'

'You're staying here I said.'

Brun and Wyatt checked their guns, got out of the vehicle and started to walk slowly towards the hill. There was no cover at all and although they had moved stealthily and stopped every few metres, Wyatt was surprised they hadn't been challenged as they approached the woodland's edge. They lay on the dry grass for five minutes, not speaking. Brun whispered as he kept looking ahead. 'The smoke; it has finished.'

Wyatt looked back down the hill to make sure there was no movement behind them and then edged himself closer to Brun to speak. 'I think if they had seen us they would have said something by now, or shouted something; even if they *are* just campers.'

'Perhaps, we should try to get a little closer so we can...'

The roar of the engines seemed to be almost instantaneous with the sight of the helicopter rising from the woodland. The dark blue Bell Jet Ranger soared into the air with its nose pointing towards the ground. Three or four people could clearly be seen inside it as it turned and gathered speed, racing towards the spot where Wyatt and Brun were lying. One of its side doors was open and the barrel of a weapon could be clearly seen. 'Run at it!' shouted Wyatt. 'To the woods; there's no cover here!'

Both men ran as fast as they could and dived into the bushes on the periphery of the woodland as a hail of bullets hit the ground all around them. They kept running deeper into the woodland and then jumped into a small crater as another hail of bullets came at them through the tree tops. They froze and waited for a while, then prepared their guns in readiness to have a pot shot at the airborne attackers. The helicopter circled around for a minute; someone on board was taking wild shots at anything that moved. There was just the noise of the engine and the propellers as it hovered for a moment and then turned away and flew in the direction of the road. Brun suddenly jumped to his feet and ran in the same direction. 'What the hell!' shouted Wyatt as he ran after him. As they reached the edge of the wood, Brun threw his gun down and reached into his pocket. He pulled out a small camera, aimed it at the helicopter and kept taking photos until it was out of sight.

'Nice one,' said Wyatt.

'I always carry it with me,' said Brun. 'Come; we must get back to the vehicle.'

As they approached the vehicle, they realised that Pitt was not waiting behind the wheel in readiness as Wyatt had instructed. 'Perhaps he went for cover,' said Brun.

Pitt then appeared out of nowhere. 'Damn right I did; I heard and saw all the action and I wasn't going to stay in there to get blown up. I took a couple of shots at them but they were too far away.'

Wyatt was impressed with the new recruit's decision; it showed quick thinking and self preservation, two requisites for the job. Two minutes later, they were driving back to Antwerp. Wyatt phoned Delaney to explain what had happened. After an hour's driving, Pitt noticed how quiet the other two were as they headed north and he waited for a while before asking a question. 'Was that Stait in the helicopter then?'

There was a moments silence before Brun answered. 'No, he would not get involved in front line action like that. But they must be linked somehow to Stait and they must have known that we were looking for them and who we were or they wouldn't have gone to the extremes of trying to kill us.'

'So, with that helicopter and that fire power, how come they didn't persevere and finish us all off?' asked Pitt.

'A helicopter has one disadvantage,' said Brun. 'It has to hover or turn slowly when it is searching for people. One good shot from us in the engine or the fuel tank could have brought it down; that's why they did not wait around.'

'And that's not the most important question,' said Wyatt.

'What is then?' asked Pitt.

Wyatt pondered for a while and scratched his forehead before answering. 'What were they doing there; in a clearing in a wood; with a helicopter in the middle of nowhere?'

'I will make a phone call and get some people to search the area for clues,' said Brun.

'Fascinating,' said Pitt.

Wyatt sunk down into his seat and folded his arms. 'That's one way of looking at it I suppose.'

It was 7 a.m. when Delaney and Burton sat down in the office to discuss the killing of Stevie Packman. Delaney had received a call a few hours after Packman had left them the night before.

'Has to be Hawkwell doesn't it?' asked Burton. 'Not surprised our boys lost him; he's good.'

'Highly likely; but if Chief Inspector Baart is right and Hawkwell has two or more employers, which employer was he working for on this occasion?'

There was a knock on the door that interrupted the conversation. Shirley Stonehaven walked in and looked at Delaney. 'Good morning, Tom, can I have a word please?'

Burton stood up, said good morning to Stonehaven and left the room closing the door behind him. Delaney sat forward at his desk as Stonehaven took a seat in front of him. 'You're early, can I get you a coffee, Shirley?'

'No thank you, Tom, but you can answer a question for me.'

'Certainly.'

'Why haven't I been told about everything that has happened since the time I introduced you to Chief Inspector Baart?'

'With the cases I deal with, I wouldn't call any of what has happened, *significant.* I would normally only report any significant changes or problems.'

'And you don't think stabbings, shootings and you going off to Portugal are significant?'

'But these are regular activities in our line of work.'

'Right, well let me redefine the word *significant* for you. From now on, you keep me informed on a daily basis about what's happening. *Anything* on a case like this is *significant.*'

Delaney nodded thoughtfully. 'Very well; it's I suppose, easy for people like me to forget that others need to *know* but you need to trust me to get on with things.'

'I will trust you, as and when I wish; I'm not going to let you just 'get on with it' without involving me. This is a serious case; the Colombian FARC *and* Interpol for god's sake, and who knows what else. When people in the cabinet ask me for an update, I need to have answers.'

'As I say; these are regular activities; people don't realise it, but they are.'

Stonehaven curled her mouth downwards. 'Right, well from now on, you report these 'activities' to me on a regular basis.'

Delaney raised his eyebrows. 'Okay, but you'll be getting a lot of phone calls.'

'So be it. Oh don't you see, Tom; I get phone calls from some top people and I need to able to give them up to date correct answers. I know you know what you're doing, but not everyone does.'

'Sure I know, you have my apologies,' Delaney answered. He was not happy about her new involvement and the way she wanted to know everything, but he decided to go with the flow. It had not been the first time he had been criticised for his lack of communication.

After a big sigh Stonehaven finished her coffee and passed the empty cup to Delaney. 'Right, thank you, I'll have that coffee now please, and then Taffy can rejoin us and we'll see where we are.' She had more than enough strength of character to handle Delaney, but she was able to switch to a calmed atmosphere and put things behind her in a stealthy kind of way. Delaney poured more coffee and called for Burton to come back and join them. They sat around Delaney's desk and were soon discussing things sensibly, almost as though the argument had not happened.

Stonehaven listened with interest as Burton did most of the talking. He had almost concluded the story so far when she interrupted him.

'So we know Stait is the FARC contact in Europe and that Hawkwell works for Stait as well as Sondheim. And although Sondheim is not involved with FARC any longer, he is involved – or was involved – with drugs and that's where the connection between him and Stait lies.'

'Mm,' muttered Delaney, 'And Sondheim owns the club that was bombed, using Gelmeck explosive that has previously been used by the FARC in Colombia. That last part, I suppose could always be a coincidence.'

'I doubt it, sir,' said Burton.

'And this man Hawkwell,' continued Stonehaven, 'we think he killed Ellie Shanks and Stevie Packman?'

'I'd be surprised if he didn't,' said Delaney.

Stonehaven moved in her chair to cross her legs and Delaney was reminded of how she had always looked attractive to him. She looked into his eyes; 'Well Tom, with those men that you currently have in Belgium and all the work you and Taffy have ahead of you, I'll leave you to do your work.' She stood up and walked towards the door. As she turned to say goodbye, she noted Delaney looking at her legs. Then their eyes met and she smiled. 'Bye for now for gentlemen, good luck.'

Burton noticed the smirk on Delaney's face. 'Quite a woman, sir; attractive as well as intelligent.'

'Yes, Taffy. Yes she is.'

A few hours later, Chief Inspector Baart joined Delaney and Burton for lunch. They settled down around a small table in a public house not far from the office. Burton brought him up to date with what had happened in London and Belgium but Delaney was keen to find out what Baart had been up to for the last two days.

'I have been in contact with Inspector Hubert in Antwerp,' said Baart. 'He told me about sending Brun and your men to the south of the country, but that they had found nothing.'

Burton noticed the poker face on Delaney when Baart did not mention the helicopter and their close shave that Wyatt and the others had had. 'Go on,' said Delaney.

Baart continued, sensing he was being judged. 'Inspector Hubert also confirmed that Stait does have two men working in the UK.'

'Only two?' asked Burton.

'Yes, one in England, one in Wales. It seems they have had instruction to infiltrate the UK arm of the International Leninist Rebels to recruit new members who would be willing to work for the FARC on various money raising initiatives in Europe.'

Delaney put his glass down on the table with a huff. 'You mean making money from illegal drugs.'

'Perhaps,' said Baart, far too diplomatically for Delaney's liking.

A young girl cleared their table of the empty lunch plates and Burton sat forward. 'How come Hubert knows so much about Stait then Chief Inspector?'

Baart replied with an arrogant air. 'He is very good, Mr. Burton; are you questioning our professionalism?'

'No, not all, it's just that this is good information and I wonder why, if he knows so much about Stait and his men, he doesn't apprehend them.'

'Inspector Hubert has many informants, as do I; but you will know that informants will normally stop short of telling you where people actually are.'

'He's right, Taffy,' said Delaney who then looked at Baart. 'I hope you're not offended Chief Inspector, I thought it was a valid question.'

Baart held up a hand in an understanding gesture. 'Of course, let us proceed. Now, these two men; if you could help us to find them, it is thought that there is a meeting of the

International Leninist Rebels every two months.'

'One in Wales and one in England then,' said Burton.

'Yes, in Puttawyth, a small village in mid Wales, and Shiphampton in Essex.'

'I know Shiphampton; it's not far from the coast,' said Delaney.

'And I know Puttawyth,' said Burton, 'it's in Ceredigion about 10 miles from Aberystwyth.'

'In that case gentlemen,' continued Baart. 'Can I suggest that we observe who goes to these meetings.'

'You know when they are then?' asked Burton.

'Yes, that is why I am here at this time; they hold their meetings on the first Saturday of alternate months. In two days time, they will be having their September meetings.'

Delaney nodded his head in quiet acknowledgement as he wondered how Belgian Intelligence knew about this but he did not. He tapped his fingers on the table. 'Organise it will you, Taffy; you and the Chief Inspector here can look at Puttawyth, I'll drive up to Shiphampton.'

'I can get more men if you wish,' said Baart.

'Not necessary thank you,' said Delaney, 'we're only observing at this stage.'

He looked at Burton again. 'Well I suppose I had better go and tell Lady Stonehaven; I don't want to get into trouble.'

As Delaney walked out, Burton smiled at the bemused look on Baart's face.

Jane Westwood answered the phone in her usual polite manner. 'Westwood's Boatyard, how can I help?'

You can help by leaving that husband of yours to run away with me.'

'Tom Delaney, you old devil!'

'How are you, Jane?'

'I'm fine, it's great to hear from you, how are you?'

'Yes I'm fine thanks.'

Delaney had phoned the boatyard as he was walking back to his office. Tim and Jane Westwood had had a business on the coast of Essex for ten or more years. They hired out yachts and boats and ran a sailing school and chandlery shop. Delaney met them both some nine years ago when he had been on holiday and they had kept in touch, visiting him and Angela in London occasionally.

'So, are you coming to hire a boat again?' asked Jane.

'I wish I was Jane, too busy right now, truth is, I have a question for you.'

'If it's something technical, I'll go and fetch Tim.'

'Well it's about boat hire actually; you look after that side of things don't you?'

'Yes I do, what is it?'

Delaney knew he would find it difficult to make his story short and easy. 'I remember you once said that you hired boats to people who sailed to the continent.'

'Mm, yes we do.'

'And by law, they have to say where they're going don't they?'

'Err, yes.'

'Do you get many people going to Holland or Belgium?'

'Yes we do; I hope you're not going to ask me to divulge client information, Tom.'

Delaney did not answer her question as he realised that later, that was *exactly* what he could be asking her to do. 'And you would keep a log of those people?'

'Yes. I'm not giving you names, Tom; unless that is; you're calling in a professional capacity.'

'I wouldn't ask you to do anything against your wishes, Jane.'

'Good, because I wouldn't.'

Delaney hesitated for a while before continuing. 'Of course not, sorry. By the way, am I right in saying that you're about seven or eight miles from Shiphampton?'

'No; we're only about 4 miles from Shiphampton.'

Bingo, thought Delaney. He cleared his throat. 'I fully understand about not giving out peoples' names Jane, but perhaps I could have a quick look through your records.' There was a pause. He realised he needed to try harder. 'Of course I mean in return for taking you and Tim out for an expensive meal and a few top class wines.'

Another pause; then she spoke cautiously. 'Oh alright then; it'll be nice to see you again. When?'

'Tonight, see you about eight, be ready; and tell Tim he's not wearing his jeans.'

12

It was a warm evening in Belgium. Thirty kilometres west of Antwerp the sun shone on to the grounds of a large house on the outskirts of Eeklo.

Aaron Stait was feeling restless as he walked around the tennis court. His racket had been thrown to the floor in anger and he was near to shouting as he spoke on his telephone. 'No no, that is not what I said. I want to know why the helicopter was not at the farm out of harm's way; it is the only one we have here.'

He had thrown his racket to the floor because his opponent, bodyguard Freddie Ludic, had served an ace which had put him out of the game. Stait was a fit man and a good player, but Freddie Ludic was younger and leaner with reflexes twice as quick. Stait ran a hand through his black straggly hair as he finished his phone call and pointed to his racket on the floor. 'Pick it up for me Freddie and don't beat me as decisively as that again.'

Ludic knew he was joking. He picked up the racket and joined Stait on the bench at the courtside. They both reached for their drinks and paused to take breath for a moment. Stait's dark eyes looked upwards through his bushy eyebrows at Ludic. 'That was your brother on the phone; he nearly went and got himself caught.'

Ludic's older brother Henry also worked for Stait. He had gone to the south of the country with another man to arrange a pickup up of some drugs from across the border in Luxembourg. Henry was a risk taking man with little forethought, but a good helicopter pilot. 'Why, what did he do?' asked Freddie.

'Some landowner came back to the farm when they were there; but instead of bluffing their way out of it, your brother shot him. Then they panicked, left the farm and parked the helicopter in a clearing in a nearby wood until things calmed down again.'

Ludic shook his head. 'Did they get the drugs?'

'Yes, but just as they were about to leave from their little hideaway, two men approached them, so they tried to gun them down as they flew away from the scene. They're on their way back now.'

'Do you want me to take care of transhipping the goods?'

'Yes, I think so; take them to the usual place on the coast. Henry can stay here for a few days.'

Thirty minutes later they were sharing herbal tea in the dining room when they heard the unmistakeable sound of a helicopter. As they looked out, the Bell Jet Ranger descended slowly; it turned and landed a hundred metres away from the house near the tennis court. Henry Ludic and his helper Tommy made their way up to the house. Stait opened the door for them as they got closer. 'We got it all,' said Henry. 'It can stay in the helicopter until the morning.'

Stait looked at them both and then moved closer to Henry. His left fist moved swiftly and buried itself into Henry's stomach; the right fist then came down on to the face and Henry was on the floor, almost unconscious. 'You got it all,' Stait mimicked, 'at a cost; why kill an innocent landowner. All you had to do was give him a few thousand to stay quiet.'

Freddie Ludic helped his brother off the floor and led him to a chair. 'There you go big brother, I'll get you a beer.'

'He can get his own beer,' said Stait.

Henry's young helper, Tommy, sat down and ran his hands across his eyebrows. 'In Henry's defence, Mr. Stait, I don't think the landowner would have taken money. He looked like he was from the old school.'

Stait ignored the remark and turned to Freddie as he left the room. 'Sort it out Freddie; take this young apprentice with you.'

When Stait had left, Henry asked his younger brother what was happening as he sipped at his beer and wiped the blood from his mouth. Freddie sat down in front of both of them to explain. 'The drugs are being taken to England. I'm getting them to the coast tonight; Tommy you're coming with me.' He looked closer at his elder brother. 'And you my brother are staying here for a while to rest. There is something big happening in a few days and Mr. Stait wants his star pilot fighting fit.'

Henry nodded without saying anything. Tommy anticipated Freddie's instruction. 'Shall I start to unload the goods, Freddie?'

'Yes please, quick as you can; I'll bring the car around to you.'

The young man finished his beer and made his way back to the helicopter. Freddie took two rifles from a corner cupboard and nodded at his brother as he made his way to the door. Henry moved the blood stained cloth away from his face to speak. 'What's this *big* thing then little brother, that I have to be fit for?'

Mr. Stait is not saying yet, all I know is that it involves some of the richest criminals in Europe.'

The Restaurant Planalto was busy as Tom Delaney and his friends, Tim and Jane Westwood, sat down near a window to enjoy some good Mediterranean food. Having eaten their way through copious amounts of seafood and sampled some excellent Bordeaux, they sat back, and it was Jane Westwood who first broached the subject of Delaney's 'blackmail'.

'Well, Tom; this little lot will cost you a fortune, but it's lovely to see you again. Now, how can we help?'

Tim Westwood was more relaxed at divulging client's information than his wife was and he offered Delaney a lift to the boatyard.

'Not likely,' said Delaney, 'none of us is driving tonight, I'll order a cab to take us to the boatyard and then to your place; you have still got that spare room have you?'

'Yes we have, Tom,' said Tim Westwood, 'and you ca...'

'Hang on you two,' said Jane, 'I run the boat hire side of the business and I haven't said yet that you can see the log book; even if you did treat us to all of this, Tom, it's still a big ask.'

Delaney put his serious face on. 'This information you have Jane, could be of vital importance.'

'How?'

'You're the only boat yard that hires out boats for miles; I think you may be leasing boats to some serious criminals.'

The Westwoods were clearly shaken by this remark. 'Right,' said Tim, 'That settles it. Let's get a taxi and go to the yard. The sooner we give Tom what he needs, the sooner we can find out what it's all about and stay out of trouble.'

The taxi journey was just 30 minutes and it was nearly midnight when Tim Westwood unlocked the gate to the boatyard. The office was small with two desks, both cluttered with papers and books. The stained wooden walls looked old and damp and photos of people standing next to boats were pinned up everywhere.

Jane Westwood made her way to a metal filing cabinet in one of the corners. On top of it were two photos of the Westwoods sitting on the deck of a large yacht. On the front of the top drawer, someone had written BOAT HIRE in large letters. She opened the drawer, pulled out two folders, and put them in front of Delaney who had sat down at one of the desks. 'There you go, Tom, that's the last two months, help yourself, and don't be too long; that taxi outside still has the clock running.'

'Thank you,' said Delaney, 'and don't worry about the taxi, I'll pay.' He opened the first folder. The records were nothing too technical and he was surprised that all the information was in the folders and not on a computer. The papers were in date order, with columns running across the page; date, name, name of boat, indemnity signed, deposit paid, balance. He took a piece of paper from the desk and wrote down the names of the people who had hired the boats and on what date. None of the names rang any bells with him and none of them sounded Belgian or foreign; Baker, Dring, Worthington, Main, Fowler, Norfolk, Porter.

After writing down the names and looking for something unusual which he could not find, he closed the folders and handed them back to Jane Westwood. She put them back into the filing cabinet and sat on the desk next to Delaney. 'See anything useful then?' she asked.

'Not sure; I've made a few notes. Would any of these be regulars?' He handed her the list of names he had made. After a few seconds, she handed the names back to him. 'Mr. Porter is a regular; he goes out about four or five miles to do a bit of fishing. Mr Dring hires one of the larger motor boats now and again; he brings friends with him and they go down the coast towards Southend on Sea for a jolly. Most of those names would be regulars though. Apart from those they would all be one-off hires; a lot of people think they would like to have a go on a boat, but once they're out there in the big sea swells, they soon change their mind.'

'I'm sure they do,' said Delaney. 'Okay thanks very much; we'd better get back to your place before the taxi driver gets impatient.'

Tim Westwood came back into the office looking tired. 'I've just been checking the cat food,' he said, 'alright Tom? Find anything?'

'I've taken a few notes that may be useful but I'm not sure; come on, let's get going, I've used up enough of your time.' They got back into the waiting taxi and headed for the Westwood's home. Thirty minutes later, they were enjoying a glass of brandy and remembering some good times.

The following morning, Tim Westwood drove Delaney back to his car that had been left at the Restaurant Planalto. They shook hands as good friends do. 'Thanks very much for all your help, Tim. Sorry to have been a bother.'

'Not at all, you know Jane and I enjoy your company, you look after yourself and come and see us again soon.'

'I will, I promise.'

As Delaney drove back to London, he started to think about the intricacies of this latest case and all the people involved. 'Another blasted mess to sort out' he said to himself.

As he was approaching north London, his phone rang. 'Hello, Taffy, what have you got to tell me?'

'Not a lot, sir.'

'Why's that?'

'I'm on my way back to London now with Chief Inspector Baart. We got to the meeting place these people use in Wales at about seven last night.'

'Nothing to see then?'

'Only a burnt out building; the place was torched yesterday. I spoke to the local Fire Station Commander; he said it was arson and that a body had been found inside. It will be a while before they ID the body.'

Delaney shook his head. 'I don't suppose it was coincidence or an accident?'

Burton huffed. 'Err, no sir; the dead person had been tied to a chair.'

13

Antonio Compito was restless as he stepped out of the shower in the back room of the house he shared with his partner, Christina, in Colombia. It was 9 a.m. He had been summoned to a meeting with the FARC's Central High Command at a temporary location in the northern state of Cordoba. He was the Column Commander who had been responsible for holding the Belgian Intelligence agent, Peter Giers, in captivity. He had not only failed to do this, but had also allowed Giers to escape with some vital information. It was of little consequence to the Central High Command that Giers had been killed; the information had fallen into the hands of the European capitalists.

Christina was ironing his uniform as he walked into the room naked having taken his early morning shower. She admired his lean bronze body and the dark hairs on his chest. They had been living together for two years and the lust between them was as vigorous now as it had been on the night they met.

'The uniform is getting old now,' he said as he pulled on his pants.

'It is old,' she replied, 'but I will make it look good.'

The FARC rebels didn't really have an official uniform but some of the high ranking officers had taken to wearing old light green army uniforms. Many of them had personalised their own uniforms with cloth badges showing symbols of animals and mottos. – Some of the Columns, Companies and Squads were named after animals; Tiger, Buffalo, Eagle, Wolf. Naming their groups after strong dominant animals gave them a feeling of victory and command.

Compito's uniform was not bedecked with badges or stripes but the two stars on the shoulder pads reminded his colleagues that he was a Column Commander. He looked at Christina as she finished off ironing the shirt with a graceful movement over the crease in the sleeve. She passed the shirt to him and its warmth made him feel comfortable as he pulled it on and buttoned it up carefully

Christina could see that he was not feeling comfortable. 'You are a good man Antonio,' she said, 'you try your very best for the revolution and your superiors.'

Compito smiled at her and nodded his head in an effort to appear agreeable but he was worried. The Deputy Commander at Central High Command had told him to be at their office at 11 a.m. When this happened, it usually meant that they were going to reprimand you and then send you straight away to somewhere on the same day where you would work for a month in poor conditions, more often than not to the camps in the isolated areas of Vichada in the south where they trained new recruits and ate rice and bread for a month and slept with the new recruits in old tents to show how strong they were and lead by example.

But he could not be sure. The decisions taken by the Central High Command had, for some time, been inconsistent and this had led to criticism and descent in other ranks. He had packed two bags of clothes and equipment just in case.

He finished dressing and pulled on his thick beige boots. As he leaned forward in the chair to tie his laces, Christina wrapped her arms around his shoulders and rubbed herself up against his head. He put his arms around her buttocks and squeezed them softly as he lifted his head to kiss her breasts underneath the thin yellow blouse. She took his head in her hands and drew him towards her to kiss him. He moved his hands gently around her thighs until they were between her legs. She pulled away. 'You must go now,' she said, 'you must not be late.'

He did not answer because he knew that she realised this may be the last time she saw him for a few weeks. He finished tying his laces and stood up to kiss her. 'Of course I will be careful. Everything will be alright and I will be back soon and you and I will have a good future because the revolution will look after us and one day we will be rich and I will be one of the deputies in the Central High Command.'

Christina kissed him and opened the front door of their small farmhouse. He picked up the two bags he had packed earlier, loaded them into his jeep and smiled at her as he drove away.

He was soon approaching the town of Planeta Rica on route 25. When he saw a large white house on his right, he turned left and drove down a smaller road towards an old open-cast mine. The quarry had not been mined for years and shrubs had grown through the hard surfaces. A small track then led him down into the quarry where he could see the office buildings and the rusting diggers and conveyor belts. He had been here twice before and had always been surprised at the choice of the place as a meeting venue; no trees, no cover, easily seen from the air. He parked the jeep outside the main office and walked towards the two men standing on the veranda. He recognised their lapel badges as those of Deputies. The Central High Command had five deputies who acted as aides and who were the personal bodyguard of the Commander in Chief. The smaller of the two men walked towards Compito and held out his hand. 'Antonio, my friend.'

Compito then realised that it was Manuel Tolima. He had fought alongside Tolima on two occasions and had heard that he had gained promotion but not to this level. 'Manuel, I see you have done well,' he said as he looked at Tolima briefly and then at the other man.

'Yes Antonio, but it has been hard.'

'I'm sure.'

Tolima introduced the other man and opened the door to the office. 'Come with me Antonio; I'll show you where to wait.'

Inside the office, there were two desks, each with four chairs around them. On one of the desks there was a small folder with an elastic band around it. Tolima pulled out a chair at that desk and gestured for Compito to sit down. 'Please wait here Antonio; you have the honour of meeting the Commander this morning.'

The Commander was the second highest rank in the entire FARC organisation, second only to the Commander in Chief. Compito felt his stomach turn; a meeting with the Commander was serious. Tolima left the room and closed the door behind him. The early morning sunshine was beaming through a broken window and Compito stood up, tapping the table nervously. He walked around the room slowly, his keen thin eyes taking in everything. He paused as he saw a picture of Jacobo Arenas, one of the first idealogical leaders of the FARC. The picture was not quite straight and Compito levelled it out gently. As he turned around, he was shocked to see a man standing in the open doorway; he had heard nothing which was unusual for him. As soon as he saw the man's face, he knew it was Commander Carnas; second-in-command of the entire FARC movement.

Compito straightened himself up and saluted. Carnas looked at him and returned the salute as he made his way to the table with the folder on it. 'Please Column Commander Compito, sit here with me.'

Compito tried a half smile and failed as he sat down opposite the big man. Another man appeared in the doorway and Carnas sent him away with instruction to bring two coffees. Compito sat upright in his chair and looked at Carnas, but Carnas was looking down and opening the folder on the table. He took out two pieces of paper and put them on the table face down. Then he looked up and nodded knowingly as he spoke. 'I have heard some good things about you, Compito. I was surprised that you let the Belgian intelligence man get that information.' He paused for a while to remove his hat and wipe his eyes before he continued.

'Well, at least he is dead and we now have the information back in our hands.'

'Yes sir,' said Compito. 'But I did not know we had recovered the laptop.'

'Yes we have,' confirmed Carnas. 'It was recovered from a laboratory in London by one of our allies based in England, but we do not know if they managed to access the information before we retrieved it.'

Carnas picked up the two papers in front of him and turned them face up. Compito kept his eyes on Carnas and purposefully did not look at the papers. As Carnas began to study the first paper, Compito noticed a tattoo on the back of Carnas's right hand. The dark hairs almost obscured it but Compito could make out an eagle clasping what looked like a human head in its talons. Carnas lifted his head and brushed his bushy grey hair backwards with his hands. He held his strong roman nose and his large chin in his hands for a while before resting his hands on the table in front of him. Compito had no idea what was coming as the old grey eyes looked at him.

'And so, Compito; your name is Antonio?'

'Yes, sir.'

'So, Antonio, the mistake you made was a bad mistake.'

'Yes, sir,'

'Well I am sure you will learn from that mistake. But you will not learn any more in a training camp. Sending you to a training camp would not help us. You are too experienced, I believe, to waste time with new recruits; the less experienced younger officers can do that.'

'Yes, sir.'

So, Compito thought, he's not sending me to a training camp, but is that good or bad? Carnas handed the first piece of paper to Compito and asked, 'Do you know who this man is?'

The top half of the sheet of paper was covered in addresses and phone numbers. At the bottom of the page was a photo of a man.

He was wearing a suit and sitting in the window of what looked like a restaurant opposite another man and a woman. He looked to be in his late fifties with silver grey hair and a presence to match. Compito could not make out the colour of his eyes but they looked experienced and cunning.

'Well?' said Carnas.

Compito handed the paper back to him as he spoke. 'No, sir, I do not know. I am sorry if I should know.'

'Perhaps I should not expect you to know,' said Carnas. 'We have a limited amount of information that we can send to everyone in the revolution. That is something we must improve upon.' He handed the second piece of paper to Compito. It was another photo of the same man, but the photo had been blown up to show a close up of the man's face. He was holding a menu that had the words *Restaurant Planalto* on the cover. 'You can keep these photos and the rest of the information in this folder,' said Carnas. 'I am not sending you to a training camp Antonio; I am sending you to England.'

Compito was scared; many of their soldiers had been sent to England or Europe and many had not returned. He looked Carnas in the eye. 'If that is your order, sir; what am I to do?'

Carnas tapped his tattooed hand on the large photo. 'You are to kill this man.'

'Who is he?'

'His name is Delaney and he is in charge of an organisation called The Overseas Liaison Agency; TOLA. He has four or five people who work for him. They work for the British government and they are, as I believe they say, a thorn in our side.'

'But I have very little experience of such work sir and I have not been trained to work on such missions.'

'No you have not, but you are experienced and disciplined; you need to learn, and I am confident that you will do well on such tasks.'

Compito could see the serious look on the face of Carnas and he decided not to say anything else. Carnas pushed the folder towards him and stood up. 'In there, you will find everything you need, tickets, money, passport, information. Your flight leaves at two o'clock this afternoon from Bogota. You will fly to Mexico City and from there to Paris where you will be met by one of our senior European people. Good luck Antonio.'

14

Shirley Stonehaven was waiting for Delaney in his office. As he walked in, he could see that she was not just 'popping in' for a coffee.

'Thank you very much,' she said sarcastically.

Delaney did not answer; he picked up a jug from a corner table. 'Coffee? Water?'

'No thank you. Why didn't you tell me about the meeting places in Wales and Essex?'

'I was going to, of course, but things happened quicker than I thought they would. By the time I thought of letting you know they were already...'

'They were already on their way to Puttawyth where they found the cabin that was *allegedly* used for meetings of the International Leninist Rebels, but it had been razed to the ground by fire and there was a charred body that had been tied to a chair. But I had to hear this from Chief Inspector Baart when I should have heard it from you.'

'I was going to tell you this afternoon; Burton and Baart are still driving back from Wales and I've just got back from Essex where I've been looking into another issue. You would have been told all of this by me in five minutes time.'

Stonehaven sat down, pursed her lips and shook her head before she looked at him again. 'Coffee, black, no sugar.'

As he poured out another coffee, he watched her looking into her handbag. She had crossed her legs and he allowed himself a quick glance. He put the coffee down at the side of her chair and decided not to apologise unless he was forced to. He took out a piece of paper from his jacket pocket, unfolded it and put it in front of her. 'Recognise any of these names?' She looked at the list of names from the boat yard that Delaney had written down and considered them carefully, one after the other. 'Baker; no, Dring; I think so, Worthington; maybe, there's a Worthington who works for the Foreign Office. Main; not sure, Fowler; no, Norfolk; no, Porter; Porter rings a bell, but I'm not sure, why?' She handed the piece of paper back at him.

'Porter,' he said. 'Jethro Porter; also known as John Pedro or Jasper Potter, real name Freddie Ludic.'

'Ludic the hit man?'

'Has to be; he hires a boat now and again for a few days at a time from a boat yard on the Essex coast. My guess is that he does return journeys to Belgium and back.'

Stonehaven caressed her coffee cup in two hands and looked at the floor thoughtfully. 'Could be anyone; there must be a thousand or more Porters in England.'

Delaney handed the piece of paper back to her. 'Have another look at the names.' She looked down the list again carefully. After a couple of minutes she placed the piece of paper on the desk and looked at Delaney. 'You mean Worthington of the foreign office or the Fowler Family?'

'No, Dring. One of the names is Dring; think hard.'

'It would be quicker if you explained, Tom, I'm busy.'

Tom? He thought to himself, maybe her initial outburst was not meant to be as harsh as it sounded. He moved his chair closer to her and spoke quietly. 'Remember the Jasmin case we worked on together in Manchester before you joined the CIA?'

'Yes; Helen and Sarah Jasmin. They were put away for trafficking: just. The jury was targeted by the...' she hesitated. 'The jury were targeted by the Belgian gang who the Jasmins were working for. MI5 raided a house near the court and arrested two men, but a third man got away. Their false papers and passports were found in the house and the man that escaped had called himself Dring.'

'Spot on, and now it's all coming back to you, do remember what MI5 told us about Dring?'

Stonehaven nodded slowly. 'Damn; of course, they knew the name Dring from other cases, he was better known as Hawkwell, Frank Hawkwell.'

'Yep, the same Frank Hawkwell that we believe is working for Stait and Sondheim.'

Stonehaven picked up the list again. 'So where did you get these names from?'

'Some friends of mine run a boat yard and boat hire business in Essex; they're the names of their regular boat hire customers. I visited them last night. They're innocent enough; I didn't mention that I recognised two names.'

'But why would Porter and Dring use their real names? It's one hell of a coincidence that they're using the same boat yard.'

'Not if they both have the same boss. Hawkwell, aka Dring, is trusted by Stait and he also does some work for Sondheim. Ludic, aka Porter, has just started work for Stait. Why wouldn't they both be able to do boat trips between here and Belgium, and why wouldn't they both use the same boat yard once they had gotten used to it and not been challenged for months?'

Stonehaven sipped her coffee. Delaney could see that she was thinking hard. After a couple of minutes, she put down her cup and walked over to the window. She turned and looked at him as she leant back against the window ledge. 'And what about the International Leninist Rebels? Who burnt down their meeting place in Puttawyth? I assume the charred body will be their UK operative?'

'I'd bet on it,' said Delaney. 'And my guess is that it was Hawkwell who did it.'

'Sure?'

'Yeah, I know people like Hawkwell, that's just about his style.'

Stonehaven frowned. 'So why would Hawkwell kill someone on his own side?'

'Good question; probably because he'd kill anyone if the price was right. He was just doing as he was told. He wouldn't have known what those meeting places were for.'

'And what about the other meeting place in Essex?'

'It's near Shiphampton, not far from a boat yard I know of, but they won't use it now. They must have torched the place in Puttawyth because they thought we were getting close. They won't take a risk that we don't know about Shiphampton.'

Stonehaven's phone rang. She looked at it and said, 'for god's sake' before she answered. 'Simon, I'm busy; I said we could talk later...so...and that makes it my fault does it...really, well screw you, Simon!'

She clicked the phone shut and gripped it in her hand. Delaney guessed it was her husband, Simon Stonehaven. He had been a top negotiator in MI6 for a few years, which wasn't easy for either of them and there had been some gossip about their relationship for some time. Delaney had met him at a couple of social gatherings and they had never seen eye to eye on issues. Simon Stonehaven had always done everything by the book and had always been squeaky clean; Delaney had not.

'Sorry, Tom, that was unprofessional of me.' Stonehaven said as she sat down again.

'Not at all,' said Delaney, 'we all have our personal lives to sort out as well as our jobs.'

Stonehaven smiled gently at him and put her phone on the table. 'By the way,' she said, 'I didn't just come here to ask you about those meeting places; I need you to know something.'

'Okay,' said Delaney, 'tell me.'

'Do you know what a P.O.O. is?'

'You're insulting my intelligence as well as my experience,' Delaney said quietly. 'Presumably you mean Paramilitary Operations Officer. The CIA has a few of them around the world.'

'Sorry, yes I do. Well we should have one of them joining us soon, as a sort of back-up to what we're doing.'

'When?'

'I'll let you know as soon as I can. It's all to do with the Americans and the United Nations. If the FARC are present in Europe they want to be involved.'

Delaney raised his hands slightly in a gesture of acceptance. 'Fine; some of those guys can be pretty useful. Anyone you know from your days in the CIA?'

'I met him once I think, not sure; they don't exactly get around socially.'

He nodded and offered her more coffee. As he poured the coffee, she looked at him from behind. A well built handsome man, she thought; broad shoulders and a bum to be proud of for a man of his age. Why didn't we have more men like Tom Delaney these days, instead of all the skinny pretty boys that people go on about? She checked herself and brought her mind off the matter as he turned around. 'Thanks,' she said as he placed the fresh coffee in front of her. He looked at her as she sipped her drink. He needed to get on with his work but he did not want to be rude and end the meeting abruptly.

'I need to phone and Ben and Ajit; see how they're getting on over in Belgium with Sergeant Brun,' he said.

'How is the new man getting on? She asked.

'Alright I think: Ben would soon let me know if he wasn't performing, but its early days yet.'

'Did the Belgians find out the address of Aaron Stait's latest hideaway?'

'I believe so, but I haven't had confirmation yet; that's why I need to speak to Ben.'

Stonehaven put down her cup and stood, picked up her phone and walked towards the door. 'Well, I'll let you get on with things then. And Tom; keep me informed, yes?'

He smiled, remembering their conversation a few minutes earlier. 'Of course.'

She hesitated in the doorway and turned to face him again. Delaney looked at her in anticipation of another question. 'We have a lot to discuss,' she said, 'how about dinner one evening? My treat.'

Delaney tried to hide his surprise at the invitation. This is new, he thought, what was going on here? Then he remembered the phone call from her husband. When most people argued like that with their partners, they craved another's attention. 'Sure,' he said. 'Tell me where and when and I'll be there.'

'How about that new Indian restaurant on Hawton Lane? Say, eight tomorrow night?'

'Okay, thanks, look forward to it.'

'Good.'

She turned and closed the door behind her. Delaney took a deep breath, in and out. 'Well well.'

Wyatt sounded despondent as he answered the phone. 'Yes, Wyatt speaking.'

'How are things, Ben?' asked Delaney.

'Oh sorry, guv, I didn't realise it was you. Things could be better to be honest.'

'Ajit alright?'

'Yeah he's fine, doing well.'

'Good; and Sergeant Brun?'

'He's good too, but we haven't made much progress.'

'Tell me about it then. I already know about your trip to the south. Inspector Hubert was in touch with Baart.'

'We're back in Antwerp now,' continued Wyatt. Brun has spoken to a lot of contacts in the underworld out here but he says that everyone is keeping quiet, even if he offers them more money than usual. He said the last time people went quiet on him was because something big was about to happen.'

'Big?' asked Delaney. 'Did he say what happened?'

'Not in detail, but it involved gangs from four countries and 17 people got killed.'

'Right, big enough then.'

'Exactly; anyway, Brun has taken Ajit with him to see a woman. Apparently she's related to someone who works at an airfield. We think Stait has a helicopter and this airfield is where he gets it serviced.'

'Every little bit helps,' said Delaney.

'Yeah, I'm expecting them back soon sir, so I'll...wait...speak of the devils, I think that's them.'

Delaney waited for a while. He heard the sound of men talking and doors closing. Wyatt came back on the phone and told Delaney he was putting it on speaker. Sergeant Brun and Ajit Pitt acknowledged their presence for Delaney who held his phone closer to his mouth so they could hear him clearly. 'Ben tells me that you may have some information Sergeant Brun.'

Brun spoke slowly and clearly. 'It may be something that is good; it may not.'

'I have a feeling it'll be useful,' said Pitt.

Brun continued. 'There is a small airfield near Eeklo.'

'Eeklo?'Interrupted Delaney.

'A town that is to the south west of Antwerp commander; about an hour from here.'

'Thanks, go on.'

'My friend had mentioned that the airfield is well known for having a specialist helicopter maintenance service. When we were there, she left us for a while to look after some customers. Your man Mr Pitt here, is very quick at looking through files. Within a minute he had found a file in the name of Porter. That name does not mean anything to us I know, but each file has a photo of the helicopter in question and the photo in that file was the one that took a shot at us in the south, no doubt about it. A dark blue 206B3 Bell Jet Ranger.'

Wyatt looked at Pitt. 'Did you get anything else?'

'The address,' said Pitt. 'It said Mr Porter, Eeklo, but that was all.'

'It's enough,' said Delaney, before any of the others had time to speak.

There was a pause before Wyatt spoke. 'Enough, guv?'

'Porter is another name that Freddie Ludic uses. How far is Eeklo from the coast?'

'About one hour,' answered Brun. 'Belgium is not a big country.'

Wyatt started to speak but Delaney interrupted him. 'Sergeant Brun, can you or Inspector Hubert authorise a helicopter?'

'Yes, but it will be in the morning now.'

'Will you do that please. For a pilot and three passengers; you three. Ben, make sure you get well armed, just in case. How big is Eeklo sergeant?'

'Not too big for a good aerial sweep, if that is what you mean.'

'Good, thanks gents, keep in touch.' Delaney ended the call.

Pitt looked at Wyatt. 'Is that it?'

'That's it,' said Wyatt.' The boss won't waste time on chatting once he's given his instructions. No point; he'll just expect us to get on with it.'

Brun smiled as he made his way to the door. 'I like your Mr Delaney; he is straight forward; black and white, I think you say.'

Wyatt got up to join Brun and beckoned to Pitt. 'He certainly is; come on you two, I'll get the beers.'

Burton and Baart listened as Delaney explained what had just been said in his 'conference' call to Belgium.

Baart seemed restless as he trudged around the office, unable to settle. Burton poured himself a coffee and took out his note book. 'Right sir, Puttawyth; this is what we know.'

Delaney leaned forward and rested his head on his hands. Burton read slowly as he turned the pages. 'The cabin was next to an old barn on some farm land about five miles east of Aberystwyth. Some of the locals knew that meetings were held there now and again. A woman who runs a village shop nearby said that a few cars had pulled up outside her shop a few days ago and quite a few people, women as well as men, had bought a lot of food from her. When they had stocked up, they got back into their cars and turned around to head in the direction of the cabin. The interesting bit is that only one or two spoke English; they translated for the others.'

'Anything new about the ID of the corpse?' asked Delaney.

Burton turned back to another page to look again. 'Err, yeah, the local investigators phoned me not long after we spoke to you, sir.' He looked through his notes and paused. 'Here we are; the fire was started by petrol and naked flame, the petrol was probably spread across the whole floor. The man tied to the chair has not been identified but there was something on the floor that they thought had maybe been in his pocket.'

Delaney raised an eyebrow. 'Mm?'

'A small knife sir, like a small flick knife, with some wording on the handle.'

Baart joined in. 'The wording is not in English commander. They are faxing the wording to us here; any moment now hopefully.'

Burton closed his notebook and wrapped his hands around the back of his neck. 'I'll wait for the fax sir if you want me to; no need for all three of us to wait.'

'Right, Taffy, let me know what it says will you; I'll be at home.'

Baart stopped pacing up and down and took up a seat next to Burton. 'I will stay also.'

'Of course, if you want to Chief Inspector,' said Delaney.

On his drive home, Delaney was thinking about Shirley Stonehaven. He remembered the first time they met at a conference in Bristol. He had been living alone for some months after a break up of a relationship involving a woman he had met in Paris. They had lived together for eight months before she realised that the phone calls at two in the morning and the interruptions at dining tables were not temporary, but more a way of life for people like Delaney.

Shirley Stonehaven and her husband Simon had been introduced to Delaney by a woman who worked in the foreign office. The conference – 'Better International Policing' – had been a sober affair and people were starting to leave as Shirley Stonehaven took Delaney's hand. 'Tom Delaney, eh? I've heard so many good things about you.'

'Oh dear,' Delaney had replied, 'how embarrassing, you obviously don't know *everything* then.'

He could tell she had had a few drinks as she took him by the arm and led him away towards the bar. 'Come,' she said, looking at her husband and the foreign office woman. 'Come and tell me about your adventures and leave those two to talk about international policing.'

The conversation at the bar had not lasted. After just two minutes, Simon Stonehaven had interrupted them and pulled his wife rudely away and escorted her to another couple who were very officious looking as they eyed Shirley Stonehaven with a look of disappointment.

Then he remembered the Jasmin case in Manchester. He had been sent there to help out with interviews of the main suspects; Helen and Sarah Jasmin, drug traffickers. Shirley Stonehaven had also been asked to spend a few days there before she was due to go to the states to join the CIA. They had worked closely on interview techniques and had been so thorough that a guilty verdict was thought to be inevitable. When Dring had been the only one to escape a raid on a house, it was left to Delaney to try to close the case, as Stonehaven flew off to Washington.

There was then, and there is now, he thought, something about her that he liked. The dinner tomorrow night was going to be interesting.

Angela was coming down the stairs as he opened the door of their home some 30 minutes later. She slowed down her descent as she saw him close the door and walk towards her. He loosened his tie and held her around her thighs as she paused on the last step. She was wearing Rive Gauche again. He kissed her nape and moved his hands up to her waist to draw her closer to him. 'That'll do,' she said. 'Get me a wine, or we won't be eating tonight. I'm doing grilled salmon; okay?'

'Yeah fine,' he said, 'I'll go and get changed.'

Rocky stopped wagging his tail after Delaney had fussed him and settled himself down near the kitchen door.

When dinner was over, Delaney told her to go and sit down as he loaded the dish washer. 'I'll tidy up in here and come and join you. Anything worth watching on the TV?'

He could hear the sound of a newspaper being flipped through before she answered him. 'CSI Miami or David Attenborough?'

He called back to her. 'Well, I'm sure they'll both feature killing of some kind, so neither thanks.' He finished tidying up, replenished his wine glass and went through to join her. She had put down the newspaper and was reading something that looked like work.

'I'll be late tomorrow night; one of the girls is 40 and we're taking her for a drink.'

'I won't be in anyway, he said, 'I'm being taken out for dinner.'

'Oh yeah, who by?'

'Lady Shirley Stonehaven, no less.'

Angela looked interested, but not surprised. 'What's that all about then?'

'Not sure: we had a meeting today and she just came out with the invitation. Mind you, I've always thought that she fancied me a bit.'

Angela laughed out loud as she put her papers down and picked up her wine. 'Oh you men!' she said. 'You are funny sometimes.'

Delaney looked at her and smiled. 'I'm serious actually, and I actually fancy her as well, if you must know.'

She laughed again. 'Yeah right! Since when did you ever have time for anyone that you worked with?'

'Go ahead and laugh,' Delaney said jokingly, 'you're only jealous.'

The jovial mood lasted a few minutes longer before they settled down; Delaney reading a book on gardening and Angela preparing for tomorrows meetings. Rocky was laid out at Delaney's feet, asleep, dreaming and twitching.

As he looked up from his book some twenty minutes later, he noticed Angela starting to fall asleep. Her pen had fallen to the floor and loose papers were sliding off their pile on the sofa one by one. He closed his book and thought about Shirley Stonehaven. Had she invited him to dinner for friendship? Did she want to have an affair? Or was it to talk about work and find out more about him and how he operated? Either way, it was all perfectly innocent, as far as he was concerned; but very intriguing.

115

15

Micky Sondheim woke up at 8 a.m. The rain was pounding against the bedroom window. The sun had been hot every day for the last 12 days in central Portugal and in some way, it was good to have everything dampened and cooled down by the fresh rain coming in from the west.

He eased himself out of bed and reached for his crutches. Today he was going to get around without any help. He was determined. Michelle opened the door as he was sitting on his bed pulling his trousers up. She put a hand on his shoulder and spoke to him quietly. 'Are you alright, my baby, I can help if you wish.' Sondheim swiped her hand away and looked down as he reached for his shoes. 'Don't talk to me like that, you condescending bitch. Get me a coffee.'

She left him alone and made her way to the kitchen to make fresh coffee. Sometimes he spoke to her like that. She put up with it because she had to. The last two years had been fraught, but it would not be long now before she would be able to return to France.

At the breakfast table, Michelle was spooning out her grapefruit segments and Sondheim was chewing on an over cooked omelette when the phone rang. Sondheim tapped the loudspeaker button hard and then the answer key as he swept away his plate to one side with a look of dissatisfaction. 'Frank, what have you got?'

Frank Hawkwell's voice sounded cool and controlled. 'The man who planted the bomb at your Graphic Night Club was Stevie

Packman. He fetched the explosives from someone in Paris. It was 30 kilos of Gelmeck. That's why it did so much damage.'

Sondheim's eyes narrowed as he looked at the phone. 'Gelmeck? That's what the mafia use isn't it?'

'Yes, as well as some Colombian drugs gangs.'

Michelle continued to eat without looking up. Sondheim looked at her and then at the phone again. 'Do you think the bomb could have been arranged by Aaron Stait, Frank?'

'No I don't, Micky. I work for Stait sometimes remember. It's not his style.'

'But he might have thought I was there on the night or that I had an office there. You know he doesn't like me getting involved with the Colombians. He could have been trying to warn me off.'

'Sorry, I don't buy it.'

There was a pause as Sondheim nodded his head slowly and looked at Michelle again. She averted her eyes and sipped at some coffee. 'Right,' Sondheim continued, 'what about this Stevie Packman? Did you deal with it?'

'I dealt with it.'

'Good; thank you, Frank.'

Michelle looked at Sondheim and smiled. When he did not respond, she cleared the table and left the room. Sondheim spoke to the phone again. 'Listen, Frank; you're welcome to come back here and stay for a few days; just in case people are looking for you.'

'Thanks, Micky, I'll join you, but in a couple of days. I have some other work to attend to.'

'Anyone I know?'

'I'm freelance, you know that. If you want me on your books full time it will cost you.'

Sondheim hesitated before he answered. 'Maybe sometime, Frank, maybe sometime. Look after yourself.'

Michelle came back into the room a few moments later and stood by the window. She started to make a list in preparation for her trip to Cascais and the fish market. 'I will get you some more fresh sea bass and the octopus that you like,' she said, without looking up. He looked at her perfect figure and admired her. 'I want to go away for a few days,' he said.

She looked up from her writing. 'You mean on business?'

'No, for a vacation; with you.'

'But a while ago you called me a condescending bitch.'

'I know. I am sorry. Where shall we go?'

She paused to think before answering. If he was leaving the choice to her, she would make the most of it. 'Monte Carlo.'

He raised his eyebrows. 'Very well, Monte Carlo it is my dear. Arrange it. Somewhere nice; perhaps a yacht in the marina or the best hotel.'

She tilted her head to one side and smiled. 'Very well, and I will buy some new clothes that will be stylish enough.'

'You are always stylish, that's why I wanted you.'

Thirty minutes later as she was driving towards Cascais, she started to think about Frank Hawkwell. Sondheim would want a minder if he was going to Monte Carlo with god knows how much cash, she thought. Perhaps I ought to suggest that Frank Hawkwell comes with us to look after us.

Hawkwell immediately phoned another number when he had finished talking to Sondheim. When Aaron Stait answered, he sounded anxious. 'I thought you were going to phone last night, Frank.'

'Sorry, I was busy dealing with something.'

There was the sound of Stait drinking from a glass as he paused before continuing. 'I want you to be with me when I meet someone.'

'Who?'

'You'll find out soon enough. Can you be at Charles de Gaulle airport tomorrow afternoon?'

'If that's what you want. Is that where the meet is?'

There was another pause and another gulp. 'Yes, be in the arrivals lounge at 2 p.m. We're meeting someone on a flight from Mexico City.'

Hawkwell waited for a moment, but no further information was forthcoming. 'Is it just one man, Aaron?'

'Yes. He is being sent to help us to...'

'To what?'

'Never mind,' said Stait curtly, 'just be there. I want you to get him into England.'

Hawkwell laughed quietly. 'Must be someone important then eh?'

'Why must it?'

'There are plenty of direct flights from Mexico City to London, Aaron. I take it this person is not welcome in England.'

'Perhaps, but that is for him and me to be concerned about, not you. Do not worry Frank; you will be paid well, as usual.'

'Alright, Aaron, see you tomorrow. I'd better go and book a flight.'

16

The Belgian Police helicopter was flying slowly around the farmlands of Eeklo. Next to the pilot was Sergeant Brun, his gaze alternating between the landscape beneath him and a map. Behind the pilot, Ajit Pitt was looking down to his right. Wyatt was on the left, scanning the countryside with binoculars.

After getting the go ahead from Delaney, they had secured a ride with Peter Lorette, one of the best police helicopter pilots in Belgium; based at the Antwerp headquarters.

Lorette pointed to a built up area ahead of them. 'That is Eeklo. I will circle the town and then widen my sweep. We have one hour's worth of fuel left.'

Brun gave him the thumbs up. A moment later, Pitt tapped Wyatt on the arm and pointed downwards. 'There; an airfield. That must be the one with the specialist helicopter services; I can see at least five or six.'

Lorette used the intercom to reply. 'You are right I think, there will not be many more airfields around here.'

Brun asked Lorette to go lower so they could have a closer look, but Wyatt interrupted. 'No, we need to spend our time looking for Stait's residence. An airfield is an airfield. Start a peripheral sweep around the area please, Peter.'

Brun looked back at Wyatt and nodded. 'I agree.' And he gestured to Lorette to start the sweep. 'It will be a large home with room enough to land a helicopter,' Brun said. 'And probably surrounded by trees for privacy.'

Lorette flew the helicopter with consummate ease; climbing as they got close to some possible places, so as not to arouse suspicion, sweeping left and right, only back tracking when absolutely necessary.

Henry Ludic was awakened by a noise that was familiar to him. He had been sleeping heavily in one of the small bedrooms in Stait's home near Eeklo. As he pulled on a bathrobe and walked out to the living room, he remembered that his brother Freddie and the young man Tommy had left for the coast with the drugs they had transhipped from his helicopter.

He stood very still to see if he could hear that sound again, but the sound had gone for now. He walked through to the kitchen to find a note on the table. It was straight forward and to the point, written by Stait. *Gone to Paris for meeting. See that you have the helicopter checked over and ready for my return. Do not touch the alcohol.*

As he finished reading the note, he heard the sound again, and then realised why it was familiar to him. He listened intensely. It was the sound of a Bell Jet Ranger helicopter; probably the same class and model as his. He walked over to the window where he could see the large garden, the tennis court and the helipad, where his own helicopter was parked.

Then he saw it; flying at about two thousand feet. A white and green Jet Ranger. It was flying from right to left as he looked at it. There was a moment when it went out of sight and then appeared again moving in the opposite direction, now flying lower. He could not make out the markings on its side, but he could only think of one organisation that had white and green helicopters.

'See it?' asked Wyatt, over the intercom.

'I see it,' said Brun.

'Me too,' said Pitt, 'how come they don't try to camouflage it?'

121

'Waste of time,' said Wyatt. 'It would take a lot of camouflage to hide a helicopter, and besides, they would want it ready for a quick take-off.'

Lorette interrupted. 'I do not think that is it; you may be wasting your time and we will have to make our way back soon.'

Wyatt tapped Brun on the shoulder. 'Can you log the coordinates, Sergeant?'

'I've already started,' said Brun as he looked at two gauges in front of him and began writing.

'Right,' continued Wyatt, as he looked at Lorette, 'thanks Peter, you might be right but we'll check anyway. On your way then; we need to get back and organise some vehicles and a few more men. We can't risk this being shot down with all of us in it.'

'A wise decision, Mr Wyatt,' said Lorette. A second later, Brun made a circle with his thumb and first finger as he looked at everyone. 'I have what I need, over to you, Peter. Lorette heaved his stick to the right and the aircraft fled away towards Antwerp.

Henry Ludic got dressed quickly and phoned his younger brother. 'Freddie, it's me, I think the police have been flying around here.'

'Shit,' said Freddie, 'where's Aaron?'

'Gone to Paris; he left when I was still asleep.'

There was a moment of silence.

'Freddie?'

'Wait, Henry, I'm thinking.'

'There is not a lot I can do, Freddie. If I leave now they will think we...'

'I know, I know. But there is very little I can do. I have to stay here with the shipment and Tommy. We have a deadline to meet and Aaron will not let us postpone this one.'

'I will stay here, I can...'

'You must phone Aaron and keep him informed.'

'But he's on his way to an important meeting.'

'And if you don't let him know that the police have found his home, then what do you think he will say, Henry?'

The phone went dead and Henry Ludic started to sweat as he dialled Stait's number.

'Aaron, it is me.'

'Make it quick, Henry, I'm just about to board a train for Paris.'

Ludic wiped his brow as he looked at a bottle of scotch on the bureau. 'Aaron, I think the police know where we are.'

Stait hesitated before he answered, wondering if Ludic had ignored his instruction to leave the alcohol alone. 'Why do you think that?'

'There was a helicopter, white and green; police colours, a Jet Ranger like ours. It passed by here a few times and varied its height. Then it hovered for a while before moving off.'

'Not all police helicopters are white and green.'

'No, but most of them are, and why would they take a good look around here if they weren't police?'

'Good point, Henry. I suppose we have to assume that they saw our helicopter?'

'Difficult to miss.'

There was silence for a moment. Ludic could hear the sound of people in the background and waited for Stait to speak again. The background noise got quieter and Stait continued in a low voice. 'Right, listen; get the helicopter back to the airfield. Tell them you want it in a hangar. Then get back to the house, empty the safe and the weapons cupboard and go to the farmhouse. Use the Lexus.'

'The code for the safe, Aaron; I don't know the code.'

'Two, Nine, Nine, Two, Nine, Two, now get on with it; if it was the police, they'll be making plans to raid the place. I'll keep in touch.'

'Right.' Ludic put the phone down and immediately started to take off his bathrobe as he headed for his room to get changed. He paused as his eye caught the whisky bottle again. He wiped the sweat from his forehead, poured himself a large glass and drank it down in one. Then he took the bottle into his room and continued to drink as he packed and got changed. By the time he was emptying the safe, he had almost finished the whisky. Then he spotted something at the back of the safe. He should have left it there, but any level headedness he had was now consumed by alcohol. He began to smile as he dragged the box towards him.

Lorette had flown the helicopter smoothly and quickly away from where they had seen Stait's house insisting they were wasting their time. They were back in Antwerp an hour later. Wyatt phoned Delaney to give him the news.

'We've got them, sir, a house near Eeklo. The dark blue helicopter was there; the one they used to take a shot at us a few days ago. We're back in Antwerp now. We'll go in on foot when it gets dark.'

'Right,' Delaney said, 'be careful. How many of you will there be?'

'Me, Pitt, Brun and a couple of extra officers that Brun knows; he says they're good.'

'What time?'

'By the time we get things arranged and get there, it will be about eleven.'

'Okay, I'll let Chief Inspector Baart know. Presumably you have permission for this from Inspector Hubert?'

'Brun's with him now; shouldn't think it will be a problem. I'll let you know how we get on.'

'That's very good of you, Ben,' Delaney replied sarcastically. 'I'll be on the mobile.'

'Right, I've got your home number anyway.'

'I may not be at home; Lady Stonehaven has invited me to dinner.'

'Really? Well if you get chance to mention it, we're overdue for a pay rise; all this extra work and...'

'Get lost, Wyatt.' Delaney finished the call. Yet again, he found himself wondering how Wyatt kept himself so relaxed and matter-of-fact as he went about his duty dealing with some of the hardest people on the planet.

Sergeant Brun had related the account of events to Inspector Hubert. Brun was surprised when Hubert left the room and asked Brun to wait there. Brun looked at his watch as Hubert came back; he had been gone for twenty minutes.

'I have just spoken to the head of section nine,' said Hubert, as he settled back down behind his desk. 'They are in agreement and you are authorised.'

Section nine was the Belgian equivalent of MI5. It was perhaps understandable that they should be kept informed, but Brun was curious as to why Hubert would want to leave the room; he could have phoned them. 'Anything else, Sergeant?' Hubert continued.

'Only to let you know that I am taking two more officers with me.'

'But you have the British operatives don't you?'

'Yes, but I think we need five, not just three.'

Hubert paused and then nodded. 'Very well, I wish you good luck with it. Who are you taking?'

'Maes and De Vos.'

'They are both quite young, look after them.'

'Of course.'

An hour later, Brun had confirmed to Wyatt that they had permission and that two more officers would be with them. They took two cars; Brun driving one, with Pitt as his passenger, and Maes driving the other with Wyatt at his side and De Vos behind them.

It would take over an hour to get to the house near Eeklo. Once there, they would wait until the time was right.

17

Frank Hawkwell had managed to get to Paris that afternoon to meet Stait. The rain was lashing down on to Charles de Gaulle airport as the flight from Mexico City landed and came to a halt at gate 17.

Stait and Hawkwell waited in the arrivals area. After nearly an hour of sitting together, Stait had still not offered any information on his expected guest.

'So you want me to get your visitor to England, is that right?' asked Hawkwell.

'Yes, how do you propose to do that?'

'Have you a got a new passport for him?'

'Yes; he is Tony Fowler, an engineer.'

Hawkwell considered for a moment. 'In that case via Eurostar, it should be easy.'

'Good,' said Stait, 'he is important to us.'

'Us?'

Stait looked annoyed, but answered anyway. 'Okay, important to me.'

Hawkwell sighed. People like Stait did not scare him or unsettle him. He leaned forward in his chair. 'Aaron, you ask me to do these things for you because you know that I'm good. But one of the things that makes me good, is knowing who I'm dealing with. Now, you tell me who your visitor is, or I'll be walking towards that taxi rank in one minute.'

Stait knew he had no choice. He could not afford to lose an ally like Hawkwell.

He put down his coffee cup, looked around to make sure no one else was within hearing distance and spoke to Hawkwell as he kept one eye on the arrivals gate. 'His name is Antonio Compito. He is a FARC Column Commander. There was a Belgian special agent working undercover in Colombia. When the agent was found out, he was given to Compito's column for safe keeping. But he got away; they shot him dead, but not before he managed to get a laptop to his colleagues out in a naval assault boat offshore. The FARC recovered the laptop from London. But Compito has been given a job to do by way of making up for his mistakes; that's what the FARC does.'

'So why are you helping him and the FARC?'

'Because more than half of my drugs come from, shall we say, sources, in Colombia.'

Hawkwell sensed there was something else. 'And what else?' he asked.

Stait leaned forward. 'He's been given the job of killing someone. If he succeeds our lives will be easier; it's a kind of good will gesture from them.'

'Who has he got to kill?'

'Someone who has many contacts in Europe; Interpol, MI5, MI6 and various other state police forces in Europe. His department has put many of my friends behind bars.'

Hawkwell raised his eyebrows. 'British Intelligence then?'

'Yes; kind of; Delaney.'

Hawkwell looked up and then nodded his head knowingly.

'Do you know him?' asked Stait.

'Yes, I know him; overseas liaison. Not *officially* an intelligence department. He's good. He was involved in a case in Manchester. We never actually met, so to speak, but it was close.'

Stait stood up as he looked in the direction of the arrivals gate. 'Well, this man is good too. Let's go and meet him.'

Antonio Compito walked out of the throng of tourists and stood for a moment, looking for his host. When he spotted Stait, holding up a sign that said FOWLER, he walked towards him. Hawkwell stayed back from Stait to allow them to meet, and to allow himself some time to take a measure of the visitor. He was pleased to see a man that looked capable, lean and fit. He noticed how the man looked around quickly to take things in without making it obvious. His black hair was neatly combed and held back with some sort of gel, his nose was roman. He carried a large bag under each arm and Hawkwell could see his hands. Workers hands; hard, gnarled and ready. He let the visitor say hello to Stait before he moved forward.

'Mr Fowler,' said Stait as he turned, 'this is Mr Hawkwell; he will be helping you with the project.'

Compito shook the hand of Hawkwell. It was a good hand shake; the sort that Hawkwell liked. 'Pleased to meet you, sir,' said Compito. His accent was Colombian Spanish but his English was almost perfect.

'Hello,' said Hawkwell, 'let me take one of those bags for you.'

Compito handed over one of the bags, Stait gestured towards the exit and they made their way out to a taxi rank. A waiting driver helped them with the two bags and when they were seated, he asked where they would like to go. 'Hotel Toulet, in the Latin quarter,' said Stait.

An hour later, they were sitting in a room that Stait had reserved for the evening. The room next door had also been booked, for Hawkwell.

'I take it,' said Compito, as he was unpacking some clothes, 'that you will now tell me how I get to England.'

'Correct,' said Stait. 'Mr Hawkwell here will get you to England.'

Compito looked at Hawkwell. 'I am in your hands then, Mr Hawkwell, for now.'

'Yes, and its Frank, by the way.'

Okay, err, Frank, what happens now?'

'You rest here for the night; you'll have some jet-lag. Then we get the Eurostar from Gare du Nord to Lille. We'll get off at Lille and then back on again, on the following train. Once through the tunnel, we'll get off at Ashford; I can have someone arrange a car for me. You're Mr Fowler, an engineer. I'm Mr Forbes, a contract manager. Here's your passport.'

Compito looked at Hawkwell and then at Stait. 'Frank knows what he is talking about by the sounds of it.' He then turned his eyes to Hawkwell. 'I will have to trust you, Frank, I think we will be okay together.'

'Perhaps,' replied Hawkwell cautiously.

'Only perhaps, Frank? Will you trust me also?'

'I trust no one; get used to it.'

Stait interjected. 'Please gentlemen let's not get into an argument over trust. You are both professionals, I'm sure it will all be alright.'

Hawkwell nodded, Compito said, 'sure.'

Stait reached into his jacket pocket and pulled out an envelope. He placed it on the bed next to Compito. 'There Antonio, that is for you. A few thousand Euros and a few thousand sterling; call it my contribution.'

'Very kind,' said Compito. 'However, I do not do this for money. My superiors in the revolution have given me an order; money will not make a difference to my strategy.'

'I have to go now,' said Stait, ignoring Compito's remarks. 'I will leave you in Frank's capable hands.' He then looked at Hawkwell. 'Frank?'

'It's fine, Aaron, I'll look after him. We'll be at the London hotel tomorrow.'

'What about weapons?' asked Compito.

'Don't you worry about that; they'll be with the car in Ashford,' said Hawkwell.

Stait shook hands with both men, without talking again, and left.

Hawkwell kept the door open and smiled at Compito as he turned to leave. 'I'll knock on your door at 9 a.m. Be ready.'

'Of course I will be ready, thank you.'

When the door was closed, Compito looked at the mobile phone that Stait had given him in the taxi. He tossed it to one side, reached into his trouser pocket and pulled out another mobile phone. He pressed a short-dial key and waited for it to be answered as he moved into the bathroom, turned on the shower and closed the door.

Delaney arrived at the Indian Tiger on Lawton Lane just before eight. The new restaurant was well appointed, with dark red carpets and lighting levels that were perfect. It was ten past eight when Shirley Stonehaven walked in. As soon as he saw her, he knew that the purpose of this meeting was not to talk about cases or criminals. Everything about her looked classy.

She was wearing a tight fitting dark blue dress that followed every line of her body as she walked towards him, her high heels accentuating her elegant feminine gait. Wow, Delaney thought to himself, good job I put a tie on.

The waiter pulled out the chair for Stonehaven and she sat down as she glanced at Delaney who had stood to greet her. 'Hello Tom, you found the place alright then?'

'Yes, of course. How did you find out about it?'

'Oh, a friend of a friend, or something like that. Have you ordered some wine?'

'Yes, dry white Okay?'

'Mm fine.'

Delaney was always professional with work colleagues, but he found himself unable to resist a remark. He looked at her as she was reading the menu. 'If you don't mind me saying so,' he said. She looked up at him. He continued. 'You, err, you look a bit err, special, tonight.'

'Thank you, Tom. One tries ones best. I'm not getting any younger.'

During the meal, they spoke of many things. They swapped stories about a few cases, and places they had worked in and people they had worked with. Stonehaven seemed keen to remind him of all the experience she had gained in MI6 and the CIA and he acknowledged gracefully. They spoke for a while about the current situation with the Belgian gangs and their Colombian link. Stonehaven was dubious about a link with the FARC. She had dealt with some people linked to them during her time in the CIA. She recalled how one of her superiors had said, 'They make enough money working out of Colombia, why go elsewhere?'

'I agree with that,' said Delaney. 'I reckon Stait, and other people, just think of them as another supplier.'

Stonehaven suddenly looked uncharacteristically melancholy. 'Let's not forget poor Ellie Shanks.'

'No, indeed,' said Delaney.

'Are we certain it was Hawkwell who killed her?' asked Stonehaven.

'All the signs point to him. Something big is about happen; I'm sure of it. I think Ellie found out about it, so Stait put Hawkwell on the job to make sure.'

'Mm, he made sure alright; killing someone like that, it seems...'

'Killing someone like that means nothing to people like Hawkwell; he's probably killed dozens of people in brutal ways. I should really try harder to get closer to him.'

Stonehaven could see the look of anger on his face. She changed the subject. Delaney was surprised when the conversation turned to relationships and married life.

'By the way,' she said, 'sorry about my little outburst on the telephone earlier in your office.'

'No problem, I take it, it was your husband?'

132

'Yes, he's been quite indifferent just lately. I know both of our jobs mean that we don't see each other very much, but that should mean that when we do see one another, we should pay attention to each other and care about what the other one has to say.'

'Either way it's not easy. Divorce is ever present in our line of business.'

'I suppose; anyway, Tom, I shouldn't burden you with such things.'

'That's fine, people tell me I'm a good listener.'

'Well,' she said, leaning forward with her chin on the back of her hands. 'I think your partner is a lucky woman; Angela isn't it?'

'Yes that's right, we've been together now for two years.'

Delaney found himself feeling uncomfortable. Stonehaven was looking at him; almost staring, but in a loving way. He looked away for a moment. When he looked back at her, her eyes were still fixed on him. Much to his relief, the waiter placed two coffees in front of them, which made her sit back. In some way, he was disappointed at what he was about to say. 'Shirley.'

'Yes?' she replied in provocative way.

'You said earlier, you weren't getting any younger. Well, neither am I. So, can we leave the personal stuff there and move on, please.'

'Why, Tom; afraid you might start to like me?'

'Yes. As you ask, yes I am.'

Stonehaven looked flattered. Somehow, Delaney managed to turn the conversation back to work and he reminded her that Wyatt, Brun and Pitt had an operation to deal with in Belgium that very evening.

'How is young Pitt getting on?' she asked.

'He seems to be doing well.' He checked his watch and continued. 'Hopefully, Ben will be calling me later to let me know how they got on.'

'We are keeping the Belgian authorities informed of all this, aren't we?' Stonehaven asked.

'Of course; two of their operatives are helping out tonight.'

'Excellent,' said Stonehaven. She moved her head to one side and flicked her earrings in her fingers as she looked around. Delaney took the lead, in an effort to draw the evening to a close. 'Well, thank you very much for the invitation tonight,' he said, 'I enjoyed it.'

'Oh me too, I've enjoyed your company. Let me pay, I'll claim it back as a business meeting anyway.'

Outside the restaurant, Delaney waited with her until a taxi arrived. She kissed him on the cheek as he opened the taxi door for her. She slid gracefully in; he was not sure, but he thought that she purposefully took her time to position herself on the seat, so that her dress rode up and showed her legs before she pulled her coat around her. 'Bye, Tom, keep me informed won't you,' she said, as the taxi pulled away.

Delaney looked at his watch. It was 10.55pm.

Brun had led the two-car convoy to Stait's house near Eeklo without too much trouble. It was nearly 11 o'clock when they pulled up a few hundred metres away from the main gate. With very little talking between them, the five professionals double-checked their weapons and protective clothing.

'We go in two minutes,' said Brun. 'I will go across that small wooded area to the left of the main gate and make my way to the side of the house. Ben, you go with De Vos and make your way around the back via the stables. Ajit, please stay here with Maes and be ready if anyone tries to race out of here in a car.' He pointed to a large four door garage. 'There will be some fast cars in there, I am sure of it.'

Ajit Pitt started to speak but Wyatt cut him off. 'Do as you're told Ajit. And get our cars turned around and ready.'

'I was only going to ask if anyone had noticed that the helicopter is not there, and there are no lights on in the house.'

Brun looked at Wyatt, raised his eyebrows and turned his mouth downwards in a gesture of being impressed. Wyatt nodded slowly and looked at Pitt. 'Good call, Sherlock.'

Pitt glanced at both of them. 'Ah shucks, ain't nothin', he said jokingly. Wyatt slapped his head softly and Pitt's green ski cap fell to the floor.

A moment's silence followed as Brun held up a hand. He checked his watch and pointed to the house. 'Now; we go.'

Aaron Stait had arrived back in Belgium a few hours earlier. He booked himself into a small hotel near Eeklo so he could stay out of the way until it was safe to return to his home. It did not disturb him too much that his home could be raided by police. He had another home near Antwerp and a yacht moored at Bruges.

He phoned Henry Ludic. 'Did you get everything out of the safe and cupboards?'

'Yes of course I did,' said Ludic. 'I always do as you say don't I, Aaron?'

Stait knew Henry Ludic too well. 'You've been drinking again haven't you?'

'Yes I have.'

'You fool. What if I told you now that I wanted the helicopter?'

'Well, sorry Aaron, you would have to find another pilot. I have done what you said. Everything is safe here with me.' Stait was grateful for that, at least.

'Well, nearly everything,' continued Ludic.

'What do you mean?' asked Stait.

'I left something at the house for the visitors.'

'What, Henry? What did you leave?'

'A few sticks of Gelmeck; attached to trip wires at the entrance doors.'

'You drunken moron!'

Stait put the phone down. He paused for a while before speaking to himself. 'That will be the last thing you ever do for me, Henry Ludic.'

18

Brun was the first in place. He waited for two minutes to give Wyatt and De Vos time to get around the back. He checked his watch and moved forward towards the side door of the house. As he got closer, he noticed that a small lamp had been left on in the kitchen. Through the window, he could see the table and chairs, some dirty pots and pans and a large mirror. Looking into the mirror, he could see the back of the door and an old coat hanging on a hook. Then something caught his eye. Something was shining. He peered into the mirror again and studied as much of the reflection as he could. Then he saw it.

The glimmer was coming from a trip wire just inside the door. If it had been in the dark or fully illuminated, it would have been lost against the background. But the gentle glow from the lamp made it stand out as it caught a small amount of reflecting light.

Brun was sure no one was in, so he elbowed the window and broke the glass just above the catch. He gently opened the window and climbed, his big frame struggling with the confined space. Once inside, he shone his torch on the trip wire and followed it along to a small device on the shelving that was adjacent to the door. He could clearly make out two sticks of what looked like explosive and a pin attached to the wire via a detonator. He moved to the door and carefully removed the wire from the handle. With the wire loose, he was able to reel it up and lay it to rest near the explosives. The detonator was removed easily enough and he let out a big sigh of relief. But wait, he thought to himself, chances are that other doors had devices rigged on them as well. Maybe the back door; that Wyatt and De Vos were about to go through.

He ran as fast as he could across the floor, through a door, into a hallway, through another door and there it was; a trip wire linked to the rear patio door. He could just make out the silhouette of De Vos on the other side of the lace curtains. Then the door handle started to turn. 'No! Stay ba...'

The explosion ripped through the room like a tornado, throwing Brun backwards against the doorway he had just come through. There was the sound of ornaments and glasses being smashed and then falling to the floor. Then silence. After about 20 seconds, Brun was pulling himself up off the floor. He gazed towards the hole in the wall where seconds earlier there had been a door and windows. He moved slowly towards De Vos who was lying face up just outside the blast area. His face was burnt beyond recognition. He was dead. A small fire had started, setting alight carpets and curtains. Then he heard another sound. It was Wyatt, staggering towards the scene from the garden. He had stayed back while De Vos approached the house, but the blast had still been strong enough to knock him off his feet. He looked down at De Vos and then at Brun. 'We need to get him away from here before the fire takes hold, 'he said.

'Yes, drag him onto the lawn out of the way,' replied Brun.

Hearing the blast, Pitt and Maes had sprinted to the scene in double quick time. As they rounded the corner they froze to take in the scene. Wyatt shouted instruction. 'Ajit, get the car round here now!'

Pitt sprinted back to the car and was reversing it onto the lawn two minutes later. All three men lifted De Vos into the back seat. Pitt and Maes drove away as Brun was calling to them. 'Get straight back to Antwerp! Get his body to the mortuary and tell Hubert!' Maes waved a hand out of the window in acknowledgement as the car raced away.

Brun turned to see Wyatt standing near the flames that had spread outwards; covering the side of the house and the entire room where he had been moments earlier. 'Come! We must go now!'

Wyatt looked at Brun with a look of despair. 'Sorry, I shouldn't have let him go in first.'

'No time for guilt my friend, we need to go.'

It was nearing midnight when Aaron Stait got to the farmhouse that Henry Ludic had also gone to. He had left his hotel in Paris as soon as Ludic had phoned him. Ludic opened the door as Stait approached. Stait turned to his left just as he was nearing the door and beckoned to Ludic to join him. 'Follow me, Henry, now.' Ludic left the door open and walked fast to catch up with him as they rounded the corner of the building. To the rear of the property there was a raised lawn area and Stait walked to the middle of it, Ludic at his side by now. The full moon shone on the newly cut lawn and some garden furniture.

Stait turned to face Ludic without saying anything. Ludic put his hands in his pockets. His breath smelt of whisky. He noticed the cold look on Stait's face. 'Aaron? What is it?'

'What have you done, Henry? With the explosives that were at the back of the safe; what have you done?'

'Well, I just left a little surprise in case it was the police that were snooping around; teach them a lesson.'

Stait looked down at the floor and shook his head. 'You're a fool, Henry.' He turned to his right and looked out on the dark horizon. Then he raised his head quickly. 'Look over there.'

Ludic turned and looked in the same direction. The land was sloping away from the farmhouse. Small hills and wooded areas to the left and right, concentrated the eyes on the middle ground. About three miles away the sky had an orange tint to it and as Ludic's eyes lowered, he could see a large fire. Smoke was ascending in a straight line. To the right of the flames, red flashing lights could be seen.

Stait let Ludic take in the scene. 'You know, now, what that is don't you Henry,' he said, his gaze still on the flames in the distance.

Ludic said nothing. The flames had to be coming from Aaron Stait's home. Within seconds, he realised that someone had touched the trip wires at the home that he had set. But he had not thought about what the explosion could have done. He continued looking at the flames, too scared to look back at Stait. He heard a muffled sound and then a click. As he turned to face Stait, he saw that he was looking down the barrel of 9mm Smith and Wesson.

'No. Please, Aaron, no. I can...no, please...no!'

The bullet entered his head just below the nose. As it passed through, it severed the top of his spinal cord and threw him back a few feet. He came to rest, face up, his dead eyes staring at the full moon.

Four men stood in front of Inspector Hubert's desk, in his office in Antwerp. Wyatt spoke first. 'Sorry, Inspector, I should have looked after De Vos. It's my fault.'

'Partly your fault, Mr Wyatt.' Then he looked at Brun. 'But Sergeant Brun's also I think.'

Brun nodded slowly without speaking. Ajit Pitt looked across at Brun and Wyatt and then said to Hubert, 'Sir, they tried their best and Mr Wyatt was...'

'And Mr Wyatt's best was not good enough! And when I want you to speak young man, I will tell you!'

After a few seconds silence, Hubert looked at Maes. 'Have you anything to say Maes?'

'No, sir.'

Hubert looked at each of them in turn. 'De Vos got married two months ago. Which of you wants to break the news to his wife?'

'I will do it; I was leading the operation,' said Brun.

Another few seconds silence.

Very well,' continued Hubert. 'It is now 3 a.m. I suggest you try to get some rest. Mr Wyatt, I want you and Mr Pitt here to return to England. I will phone Delaney to let him know. Things have not been successful.' He turned to Brun. 'Sergeant; you will stay in Belgium and I will be talking to Chief Inspector Baart in London also. No one has brought me anything at all that I can use about this alleged drugs boss, and now we have a dead policeman. We clearly need to regroup in our own forces and then meet again when we have reviewed things in a more considered way.'

Brun nodded and led the other three out of the room. As they made their way to Brun's office, Pitt tapped Wyatt on the shoulder. 'Can he do that, Ben? I mean, just tell us to go back to England?'

'Course he can lad, it's his country. We're guests.'

'Delaney will not be happy.'

'Correct.'

Brun looked back at Wyatt and smirked. Wyatt held Brun's arm for a moment. 'Do you want me to come with you? To tell De Vos's wife?'

'No thank you,' said Brun, 'you get back to England; perhaps we will meet up again sometime.'

Wyatt shook his hand. 'Hope so my friend; it's been a pleasure working with you.'

19

Angela Casey looked at the clock next to the bed. She was surprised Delaney was still lying next her. It was 6 a.m. She prodded him in the arm, just enough to wake him. 'It's six o'clock.'

He opened his eyes. 'I know, I've been awake for hours.'

'I thought you would have slept, you didn't get in until about midnight did you?'

'Just after midnight, I left the restaurant at eleven. Did you hear me get up earlier?'

'No, when was that?'

'About three; my phone went and I took it downstairs so I didn't disturb you.'

'Who was it?'

'Inspector Hubert in Antwerp, to say that he was sending Ben and Ajit back home. Bad news all round really.'

'Oh no, what have they done?'

'A young Belgian officer was killed last night. Hubert described it as a failed operation with no forethought applied. Sounds like he might be right.'

Within the hour, they were both downstairs. Angela waited until Delaney had finished his scrambled eggs before she asked him about his dinner date with Stonehaven. 'Did you enjoy your dinner date last night then?'

'It wasn't a date,' he replied, 'and you know it.'

'Ah, but did she realise that?' Angela asked, trying not to smirk.

142

Delaney hesitated before answering. 'Well, my darling, if you must know, I don't think she did, going by the way she was dressed. And as you're probably about ask; she was wearing a nice sexy dress and she looked rather good.'

Angela smiled. 'Trying to make me jealous?'

'You started it. Look, it was just a meeting okay?'

'Did she kiss you when she left?'

Delaney smiled and lifted his head in a proud manner. 'Yes she did actually, on the cheek.'

'You old silver haired charmer,' she said, smiling, and looking at him with a sense of pleasure. Delaney stood up, cleared his plates away, and reached for his jacket. 'Got to go,' he said, 'I'm picking Ben and Ajit up from Gatwick.'

As he turned in the doorway, he saw her sipping her tea and looking down into the cup. He walked back over to her, kissed her on the neck from behind and moved his hands down until they were caressing her breasts. When she responded by moving her head around, he kissed her hard on the lips. She was just beginning to feel aroused when he straightened himself up and made for the door. 'I shouldn't be going anywhere today,' he said, 'so I'll see you later.' After a pause he added, 'well, unless another woman wants to take me out.'

He heard the sound of something hitting the door as he closed it.

Angela was smiling as she finished her tea.

The traffic on the main roads was almost at a standstill, as Delaney endeavoured to get to Gatwick on time. His phone rang when he was doing about five miles per hour, approaching the M25. He recognised the caller's voice instantly. 'Hope you enjoyed last night, Tom?'

He hoped Stonehaven was not calling just to ask him that. 'Indeed I did. It was very enjoyable.'

'Good,' she replied, 'we must do it again sometime.'

Delaney raised his eyebrows and pursed his lips as he thought about her kissing him and his conversation with Angela a little earlier. 'Of course, why not.'

Stonehaven's tone changed without warning as she continued. 'Right, to business. I have had a phone call from Inspector Hubert in Amsterdam. He has explained what happened last night in Belgium. We need to decide where we go from here.'

'I think you're right,' said Delaney, 'I'm on my way to pick up Wyatt and Pitt now; I'll be back in my office later.'

'Okay, it may be worthwhile having Burton with you as well as Wyatt and Pitt. My diary is full today but we could have a conference call. I've got something else to tell you as well.'

'Right, I'll let you know when we're all there.'

'Thanks, Tom.'

As the phone went silent, Delaney thought about how she had sounded. She had said 'thanks Tom' even though things were not good and a young Belgian officer had been killed. A few days ago she would have spoken to him in a positively harsh manner after such events.

The traffic started to flow again and he was well on his way to the airport, when his phone rang again. He looked down to see the name, Burton.

'Hello, Taffy.'

'Hello, Sir, I've just heard.'

'Who told you?'

'Chief Inspector Baart; he got a call from Inspector Hubert early this morning. Hubert has asked him to go back to Antwerp today or tomorrow to help with other things.'

'Listen, Taffy, we'll talk later. I'm just about to pick up Ben and young Ajit from Gatwick. You and Baart get to my office. I'm having a talk over the phone to Lady Stonehaven later. I think we should all be there.'

'Right, will do.'

144

Wyatt and Pitt did not say much on the journey from the airport to Delaney's office. When they arrived, Burton and Baart were already there. Delaney took Wyatt to one side for a 'chat' and Wyatt explained to him what had happened in Antwerp and at Stait's home near Eeklo. Delaney was surprised at Wyatt's decision to send De Vos forward before himself, but he did not pursue the issue. For every bad decision that Wyatt had ever made, there had been a hundred good ones.

The five men sat around Delaney's desk with note pads, coffees and teas. After a few frustrating conversations with secretaries and receptionists, they were connected to Stonehaven. Her voice, on the speaker phone, sounded anxious.

'Who's there with you?'

'Burton, Wyatt and Pitt. And Chief Inspector Baart.'

'I thought you would be on your way back to Antwerp by now Chief Inspector,' Stonehaven questioned.

'I think tomorrow I will be back there, Lady Stonehaven. There are some more cases that I need to be involved in.'

'Very well. Gentlemen, it seems we have another problem.'

'Another problem?' asked Delaney. 'So this is not just about Stait and the Colombians then.'

'It's connected in a way. When you and Burton visited Sondheim in Portugal, it was because of Sondheim's links to Colombian drugs suppliers, remember?'

'Yes, Stait doesn't like Sondheim because he's taking some of the drugs that are destined for Belgium. Sondheim pays the Colombians more to get what he wants for his Norwegian buyers.'

'Mm, well he won't be doing that for much longer.'

'Why, is Stait challenging him?'

'I doubt it. Sondheim is losing interest in drugs money, because he has another source of income.'

Delaney nodded slowly and shrugged his shoulders. When Burton could see that Delaney was not going to respond, he leaned forward to the speakerphone. 'And do we know what this other source of income is, Ma'am?'

'Child smuggling; probably for slavery and paedophilia.'

The four men looked at Delaney for a response. But he remained quiet and shook his head. Wyatt guessed what his boss might be thinking and leaned forward himself to speak. 'So, we leave this to the specialists, right Ma'am? Interpol have plenty of specialist teams out there who are well versed in these matters.'

'The so called *specialists* were already there,' said Stonehaven. Interpol had a woman who had been with Sondheim for two years. She was working undercover as a housemaid.'

Delaney interjected. 'Connie, the housemaid. When Segressa from the Portuguese police questioned Sondheim, he said he had no idea who might have killed her. She was found near the villa a few days earlier, shot in the head.'

'That's her,' said Stonehaven. 'She was Interpol.'

'So are we going in after Sondheim then?' asked Wyatt, 'with Interpol?'

There was a pause. Delaney put a finger to his mouth as an instruction to the others not to offer an answer to Wyatt's question. After a while, Stonehaven responded. 'We have been asked to go in and get him, yes,' she said. 'Interpol and the Portuguese police will work with us. But they're only asking us. If we say no, they'll understand. What do you think, Tom?'

'I suppose it will take one man out of action. That will enable us to concentrate on another man; Stait.'

Burton nodded in agreement. Wyatt put his thumb up and Pitt said nothing. Chief Inspector Baart raised a finger as a request to speak and Delaney put out his hand. 'I assume you may need some Belgian operatives for this?' asked Baart.

'Not at this point Chief Inspector,' said Stonehaven. 'But I'm sure we will be working together again when we go after Stait.

Are we in agreement then gentlemen? We help out with Sondheim's arrest?'

Delaney looked around the table and then answered her. 'They're all nodding, Lady Stonehaven, so that's a yes.'

'Right, I'll let people know. Now, could I have a quick word with just you and Burton please, Tom?'

Delaney shrugged and waved his hand in the direction of the door. Baart, Wyatt and Pitt left the room. 'Okay, Lady Stonehaven,' said Delaney, 'just me and Taffy here now.'

'Thank you. We have received some intelligence from a reliable party in the States. Apparently someone has been ordered to kill you; at whatever cost.'

This did not set Delaney or Burton back as much as Stonehaven may have been imagining. 'Wouldn't be the first time,' said Delaney.

'Perhaps not, but it would be the first time the threat came from armed guerrillas.'

'Right, I'll be careful,' said Delaney. 'Who is this *reliable party*?'

'Someone who's been listening to some radio communication. They work for the CIA; they're based in Chile. I think this threat is real. There is also a possibility that the man sent to kill you may be getting help from someone local.'

'Okay, thank you. Anything else, Lady Stonehaven?'

'No, let me know how you get on with the Sondheim job.'

'Of course.'

Burton waited until he was sure the phone call had finished before he spoke. 'Do you want me to do anything, sir?'

'Yes, please, Taffy. Go and draw my Walter from the armoury; and a couple of boxes of rounds.'

'You might need practice, you haven't used that for a good few months now.'

'You're probably right. I'll book myself a slot on the range.'

Burton tidied up a few chairs and left the room.

147

For a reason he could not think of, Delaney found himself ringing Angela to ask if she was alright.

20

Micky Sondheim looked out from a hotel balcony in Monte Carlo. Michelle Depout was standing behind him. 'You see, my dear,' he said. 'Didn't I tell you that we would come here if that's what you wanted; and to one of the best hotels in Europe.'

'Yes you did, and thank you.'

'Ah, this is nice. Would you get me another glass please, my dearest.'

She slipped her hand off his shoulder and walked back to where the room service waiter had left the champagne. Sondheim looked out to the night sky. It was warm and pleasant. The lights in the harbour and marina shone brightly and a helicopter came in low from the west, heading for the helipad on top of their hotel. Depout returned with his replenished glass and sat next to him. Sondheim sighed heavily. 'This is where I belong,' he said. 'Perhaps we should move here; leave Portugal.'

'Perhaps,' said Depout, sounding indifferent.

'Well,' he continued. 'I think my guest has just arrived on the helipad, and if all goes well, I should be able to *buy* this place, let alone stay here.'

Depout turned to look at him. This was the first time he had mentioned a 'guest'.

'Who's this guest, Micky? We are supposed to be on holiday.'

'Oh he won't be here long; he is a busy man; and an extremely rich one.'

Ten minutes later there was a knock on the door and Depout answered it. A small, slim man, wearing tinted spectacles stood in the doorway and smiled. Behind him, a large, well built man wearing a short leather jacket stared at her. 'Good evening,' said the small man as he leered at her. 'My name is Pollitt; I am here to see Mr Sondheim.'

Sondheim shouted from the balcony. 'Let them in my dear and get them a drink.'

Pollitt walked slowly towards the balcony, followed by the other man. Sondheim shook hands with both men and they settled in chairs opposite him. 'This is Borg,' said Pollitt, pointing to the other man. 'He is my friend and my pilot. He runs a helicopter charter business with a colleague, employing some of the best pilots in the world.'

Sondheim nodded once in acknowledgement. Depout brought through two glasses of champagne on a tray and placed them on a small table in front of Borg. There was silence for a moment as Pollitt looked at Depout and then at Sondheim.

'Would you mind leaving us for a moment, my dear?' asked Sondheim, as he looked apologetically at Depout.

'Of course,' she said. 'Call me if you need more drinks.' She left them and made her way to the spacious dining area in the room. She turned as she heard a sound. Borg was closing the door to the balcony so she could not hear.

How dare you, Micky Sondheim, she thought. This was planned all along. It is no holiday. You are here to do business with those low lifes, who look like they would kill their own family if they had to. What is it this time?

Sondheim's two visitors were drinking their champagne as she glanced back and looked through the glass door. Borg saw her looking and he smiled at her, but turned his attention back to Sondheim when he started speaking. Thinking of how the luxury apartment was laid out, Depout walked casually towards the main bedroom and looked back. From where the men were sitting, they could not see the bedroom entrance. The bedroom had a sliding door that led out onto another balcony. There was only a small partition separating this balcony from the other one where the men

150

were talking and she could hear what they were saying quite clearly. She stood quietly in the doorway and listened.

'And so; to business,' said Pollitt. 'I understand you have what I want?'

'I do,' said Sondheim. 'But they are still in Colombia, Venezuela and Cuba. If you intend to make your deposit now, I can have them shipped over within days.'

'And how many are there?'

'Eleven.'

'What ages?'

'Four to seventeen.'

Borg's lower, rougher voice interjected. 'What do you mean *shipped*? It will take more than a few days by sea.'

'Perhaps,' said Sondheim. 'But how else do you think I can get them here? In a private jet, with passports?'

'Be calm, my friend,' said Pollitt, looking at his colleague. 'I am sure Mr Sondheim knows what he is doing.'

'I do,' retorted Sondheim, sounding put out. 'Do you two want these kids or not. I have some customers waiting in Switzerland if you don't.'

'I think we will have them, Mr Sondheim,' said Pollitt. 'We have customers waiting also. Good slaves are hard to come by, you know. And Mr Borg here has certain appetites that I need to keep feeding.'

Depout's eyes were wide and unblinking. She wanted to sit down and absorb the shock of what she had just heard. She moved slowly away from the open door and sat on the bed for a moment. She could still hear the three men talking, so after a few seconds, she walked back to the main room where Borg could see her and pretended to look busy at the drinks cabinet. Pollitt stood and opened the balcony door. He held up his empty glass. 'Forgive me. Please may I have some more of this?' As she went to wipe a fresh glass, she realised she was shaking and tears were coming from her eyes.

151

She pretended to be wiping her nose and acknowledged the request with a smile. Borg was leering at her and Sondheim was smirking. She felt a surge of something go through her body. It was a surge of bile, nausea, fright and abhorrence. As she finished pouring more champagne, she could still hear them talking. They had lowered their voices since the door had been opened but she thought she heard Pollitt say 'Five million; as agreed.'

She managed to compose herself just enough to walk confidently back towards the balcony. She put the fresh glass down in front of Pollitt and looked at Borg. 'Not for me, thank you,' he said, as he held a hand over his empty glass. 'I have an aircraft to fly.'

Sondheim smiled at her and she excused herself again and made her way to the bathroom. As she knelt, the vomit rushed from her mouth. The three men continued talking for a few more minutes and then she heard them moving around. The sound of a door closing was followed by Sondheim's voice. 'My guests have gone, my dear. Are you okay?'

She flushed the toilet and turned on a tap. 'Of course, I think I will have a bath now.'

There was a pause before Sondheim answered. 'Very well; and then we will dine somewhere expensive I think. In fact, I will insist that the hotel manager gets us a table at the best restaurant in Monte Carlo.'

As the bath was filling with water, Depout was struggling to hold back more tears.

21

The small beach hut on the Belgian coast near Knokke was cold and damp. It's green and yellow timbers were too weathered now to shine in the moonlight. A light coming from a window shone on the small adjacent jetty where a boat swayed gently on the quiet sea. Freddie Ludic and his young helper Tommy had been there for long enough. 'When do we get going?' asked Tommy as he looked at Ludic and exaggerated a cold shiver.

'When Aaron says so, and not before.'

They had been there for two days awaiting instruction. The drugs had been loaded into their vehicle from the helicopter. Stait had told them to get to the usual coastal point where they had a high speed touring motor boat. He would tell them when the time was right and they would make for England, where they would be met by a contact on the Essex coast.

The inquisitive Tommy stirred again. 'Do you think he will phone tonight?'

'Perhaps,' said Ludic, 'be patient; Aaron knows what he's doing.'

He cleaned his boots and checked the rifles again, as Tommy began to fall asleep. With everything in order and ready to go, Ludic reached into his small canvas bag. Good, he thought, better that young Tommy does not know of my extra insurance. He checked four magazines and the handgun before he lay them on top of the six grenades that were wrapped individually. His phone vibrated in his top pocket. The blue wording said, *Aaron calling.* He answered the phone and spoke softly, trying not to disturb Tommy as he was dozing off. 'Aaron; go ahead.'

'How are you, Freddie?'

'I'm am alright thank you; do we go now?'

'Yes; but first, I have to tell you something.'

Freddie Ludic had listened to Stait speak for many years; he knew when something was amiss. 'What is it, Aaron?'

'Last night, Freddie, 24 hours ago, someone raided my home. Your brother Henry was there. I told him to get out of the house, get the helicopter back to the airfield and get to the farmhouse. But he made a mistake.'

'Let me guess, he started drinking again.'

'Yes he did. When he emptied the safe he found some explosives and decided to leave a little surprise for the visitors. He booby trapped two doors.'

Ludic remained quiet, expecting Stait to say that Henry had blown himself up. 'I was on my way back from a meeting in Paris,' continued Stait. 'I got to the farmhouse a couple of hours behind Henry. The explosives had worked; but they started a fire and my home was razed to the ground. We could see it burning from the farmhouse. Henry was drunk; god knows how he got the helicopter out of there.'

'Aaron, you must be very angry with my brother, he is so stupid when he drinks.'

'He is not stupid anymore Freddie, he is dead.'

Ludic hesitated and looked at Tommy, who was still dozing. 'Dead, Aaron? What happened?'

'I shot him, Freddie. I shot your brother dead. Forgive me.'

Freddie Ludic, regardless of how indifferent he had become, was shocked by the news. He held the phone away from him for a while. After a few seconds, he brought the handset to his ear again and spoke softly. 'Well, Aaron; you must have been very disappointed with him. I suppose you thought it was necessary. I know my brother was a fool sometimes.'

'He became a liability. I am sorry.'

154

'He was my brother; but I trust your judgement. I only hope you never think of me as a liability.'

'I doubt that will ever be the case. Rest now; I will phone again when it gets light, with the rendezvous details. Be ready to leave at 08.00 hours tomorrow please.'

'Alright, and err, Aaron?'

'Yes, Freddie.'

'Thank you for being honest with me.'

Tommy was young, but he was not stupid. He had not been dozing and had heard Freddie's part of the conversation. So Henry had been drinking again, he thought. When Freddie had said *dead*, did he mean Henry? And then Freddie had said, it *was necessary* and he was *a fool*. He kept his eyes closed and rolled over. Perhaps it would be better to say nothing. If Freddie wanted to tell him something, he would probably do so in the morning.

Frank Hawkwell answered the phone in his hotel room in London when it rang at 7 a.m. He and Compito had arrived without incident; picking up more ID cards and weapons on the way from Hawkwell's contact in Ashford. He waited for the caller to speak. 'Mr Forbes?'

'Yes.'

'I have a call for you, sir.' The phone played some old jazz music for a few seconds and then he heard a distinctive voice. 'Frank, it's me.'

'Hello, Aaron, what's happening?'

'Are you okay, and is Compito alright?'

'Of course; he's is in the next room. Why are you calling so soon?'

'Delaney; I want you to bring his demise forward.'

'Forward by how much?'

'About 48 hours.'

'What! That makes it today; not much time to plan, my friend. What on earth has happened?'

'The Belgian police are getting close to me, Frank, my snout has confirmed it. And they've been helped by Delaney and his crew. I had to kill someone the night before last, and I've lost my home near Eeklo. I want some people taken care off, so when I leave here and set up somewhere else, there will be no one to follow me. No one that is any good anyway. And besides, I need you to get this job finished. I have another job for you.'

'Ah okay,' said Hawkwell hesitantly. 'Are you sure taking Delaney out will help?'

'No, not a hundred percent sure. There is someone else here in Belgium, but I will take care of him.'

Hawkwell waited for a moment. He looked at his watch. The phone call had lasted two minutes; long enough. 'Alright then,' he said, 'you had better leave me to get on with things. I will let you know how things go.'

He put the phone down, knocked on the adjoining bedroom door and shouted, 'Mr Fowler; it's today. Be ready to leave in one hour.'

Stait's next phone call was at 7.30 to Freddie Ludic. Freddie answered quickly and confirmed that he and Tommy were ready.

'Well done, Freddie,' said Stait. 'If you leave at eight, you should be nearing the coast in about three hours; about eleven o'clock.. Head for Blackwater Estuary again; the small red boat will be upside down on the sand bank. Put the bags under it and return to your motor boat. Stay off shore, just enough to keep the red boat in sight. A woman will lift the bags from underneath the boat and throw a red towel down on the sand. When that happens, head further west and moor up at Tollesbury Pier; on the north side of the estuary.'

'Understood,' said Ludic. 'I remember; we did this about two years ago.'

156

'Correct; the payment will be made in the same way as it was then.'

Hawkwell and Compito had moved quickly after Stait's phone call. Hawkwell got in touch with his vehicle provider with instruction to have it ready early and Compito checked the false papers in preparation for the assignment. A taxi dropped them at their first destination an hour later. In the small back street garage in Stanmore, two men were waiting for them; a small older man with the look of a heavy smoker and a younger man with scruffy auburn hair. A small commercial vehicle had *Hockwell Maintenance* on the side of it. Frank Hawkwell looked at the two men who had prepared the vehicle for him. 'Are you being funny?'

The younger of the two men looked at the name and then at Hawkwell. 'We just thought it would be a good idea, Frank; no one would ever make the connection.'

'No one of your intelligence would; you're correct.' He walked over to the vehicle to see that the letters were just stick-ons. Very carefully and one at a time, he removed the last four letters of the first name until it read *Hock Maintenance.* 'There, that's better. Where are the guns?'

'In the back,' the young man said, 'all tested and ready.'

Compito opened the rear doors to find a short barrel shotgun, a 9mm handgun and cartridges. He tossed the handgun to Hawkwell and reached for the cartridges. Hawkwell moved the gun from one hand to another, checked that the magazine was full, and placed it at the side of the driver's seat. Compito put four cartridges into his pocket, loaded two into the shotgun and placed it carefully inside his long jacket that had *MAINTENANCE* written on the back of it.

'So who said you get to have the shotgun?' asked Hawkwell.

'I do,' said Compito. 'If Stait wants Delaney dead, he'll get him dead. I'm not taking chances.'

'Fair enough,' said Hawkwell with a look of appreciation on his face. A few minutes later, they were driving out of the garage towards the city.

They were lucky. When they arrived at the office tower where Delaney's office was, at least three other maintenance vehicles were parked outside. Hawkwell smiled as he glanced at Compito. 'The difference is, those vehicles are genuine.'

The security man at the entrance to the underground car park frowned as Hawkwell lowered his window and showed his pass. 'If you're here about the gas leak as well'' the man said, 'you'll have to park outside with the others.'

'Take another look at the card matey,' said Hawkwell, 'and the only thing that's going to fix the leak is in the back of this van.' The man looked more carefully at Hawkwell's card. It was the usual government properties maintenance pass, but on the reverse were the words *Special access – emergency staff only* and it was signed by a BG Hooper, head of security. The security man had an impressed look on his face as he handed the card back. 'Okay, park down there to the left; walk from there, up the stairs. I think the leak is on the third floor.'

As Hawkwell reversed the vehicle into a parking bay, Compito said, 'I cannot believe how easy that was.' Hawkwell smirked as he reached for the handgun.

They approached the stairway. Compito was carrying a small box with the words EMERGENCY PARTS on it. The shot gun in his coat was well hidden. Hawkwell unbuttoned his short jacket and put the handgun in his belt at the small of his back.

As they walked quickly up the second flight of stairs; a smartly dressed man coming down, trying to read his Blackberry at the same time, glanced at them. Hawkwell smiled. 'Excuse me, we've got these emergency parts for the leak; we're looking for a Mr Delaney's office.'

'Next floor,' said the man, concentrating on his text message, 'second door on the right.'

Hawkwell and Compito said nothing. They entered the second floor corridor and walked calmly to the second door on the right. They could see two figures through the frosted glass. Hawkwell tapped on the door and walked in slowly. Compito followed, carrying the box.

The well dressed man on the staircase had been wrong. The second door on the right was the office used by Taffy Burton.

Burton was standing in the middle of the office with Chief Inspector Baart to his left. 'What is it?' asked Burton as he eyed the visitors. When Hawkwell remained silent, Compito placed the box on the desk. They both realised that neither of the men standing in front of them was Delaney. 'We have come to do emergency work,' said Compito.

Hawkwell shut the door behind him and stared at Baart and Burton as he spoke to Compito. 'Forget it, my friend.' His gaze fell on Baart. 'As soon as this gentleman looked at me, he knew who I was. And I know him. I forget your name, sir, but you're Belgian Intelligence; correct?'

Baart nodded. 'Yes; and you are Mr Hawkwell, the man that killed Ellie Shanks.'

'I only do what my paymasters tell me to do,' said Hawkwell. 'Who is he?' He gestured towards Burton.

Burton stood still and started to unbutton his jacket. 'Never mind who I am. Both of you pu...'

In one quick movement, as though without thought, Hawkwell reached for the hand gun from the small his back. He aimed it at Burton. 'Be quiet my friend or I'll have to kill you as well.'

'As well as who?' said Burton.

Hawkwell's aim moved to Baart. Without flinching or saying anything else, he shot Baart in the chest. As Baart was thrown to the ground with the force of the bullet, Hawkwell fired a second shot that entered Baart's head from below his chin.

Burton went to pull his pistol from his shoulder holster, but it was only halfway out when Hawkwell shouted 'Don't!'

Compito yanked the shotgun from his coat and held it still, pointing it at Burton, who let his pistol drop back into the holster and moved his hand slowly away from his jacket.

Hawkwell tilted his head in the direction of Compito as he spoke to Burton. 'This man to my right is going kill Delaney. You will not stop him. The trouble is, for me to be sure of that, I need to kill you as well don't I? Your friend on the floor was working out of his league. He should have been given a desk job long ago. But you strike me as being a bit more useful. Where's Delaney?'

'He's not here,' said Burton.

'Wrong answer,' said Hawkwell.

Hawkwell's aim moved from Burton's face and he lowered his gun to his side. He sat down on a chair and looked at Compito. 'Perhaps you'd like to finish him off my friend.'

Compito, still holding the shotgun on Burton said, 'why not, it will give me chance to test my new weapon.'

Hawkwell leant forward to put his hand gun back in his belt and then sat back. He had a smirk on his face as he spoke to Compito again. 'Go on then; I haven't really seen what you're made of yet.'

'No you haven't I suppose,' said Compito.

Burton looked at Compito. 'Killing me will only make things worse for you. With two or three of us dead, you will be hunted down for the rest of your life.'

'Don't give him time to talk,' said Hawkwell, 'just do it and let's get to Delaney. This place will be swarming with armed cops soon.'

'Very well,' said Compito. He moved the shotgun in a gesture to Burton for him to move back. 'Back against the wall, away from your dead colleague, I want more room.'

Burton stepped back a few feet until his back was against the wall. Compito moved forward; the shotgun was raised and pointing at Burton's face. Burton was surprised that he got so close; close enough for him to attempt to snatch the shotgun away from his grip. He was a millisecond away from trying just that when Compito turned around and aimed the gun at Hawkwell. In another millisecond, Hawkwell realised what was about to happen and started to reach for his handgun. His hand moved only slightly, when Compito shouted, 'Don't!'

He stared into Compito's eyes. Compito raised the shotgun to one side and brought it down across Hawkwell's face, sending him reeling sideways, blood pouring from his face. Hawkwell went to grab his gun again as he was getting to his feet. Compito's swung the shotgun around again and hit Hawkwell once more, this time on the other side of his head and Hawkwell collapsed, unconscious.

There was the sound of a door being smashed in and Compito threw the gun to the ground and raised his hands, shouting, 'Unarmed, unarmed!'

Two officers in black uniform burst into the room, their assault rifles pointed at Compito; one red laser light was on the back of his head, the other on his legs. The first officer shouted as he moved forward. 'On the ground now! On the ground now!'

Compito was down quickly, staying perfectly still. The second officer looked at Burton. 'Leave the room now, go.' Burton left quickly. Whoever these men were, they had been properly trained, he thought. Outside in the corridor, Delaney was walking towards Burton. 'With a noise like that, Taffy, I take it we have a dead body.'

'Yes we do. Chief Inspector Baart.'

Delaney stood still and wrapped a hand around his head in anguish. 'Shit!' He let his arm drop down to his waist. 'Who else is in there?'

There were two of them; something's not right though.'

'What?'

161

'One of them shot Baart. They said they were here to get you, then the other one turned around and floored his mate; instead of shooting me.'

Delaney frowned and moved past Burton to enter the room. One of the special officers looked around when they heard him and said, 'stay there.'

'Shut up,' said Delaney. He moved past the officer and looked down at the man on the floor. He ordered the other officer to turn him over. Compito looked up at Delaney; his face said nothing. He was indifferent and silent. Delaney stared at him for a while and then turned to the officer. 'Take him to my office and stay with him.'

'We can't sir, we need to...'

'Get him to my office! If your superior has a problem with that, tell him to come and see me. How come you were here so quickly?'

'We got a call from the security man; he said he was suspicious, so we checked the CCTV. Two of us recognised Hawkwell.'

'Frank Hawkwell?'

'Yes, sir.'

Hawkwell started to stir and Delaney told the officers to stay with him until the ambulance arrived. The first officer told Delaney where they would be taking Hawkwell and that two of them would be with him at all times. As Delaney walked out of the room, he could see Burton resting against a wall wiping the sweat from his face. 'Come on, Taffy, I'll get you a drink. These guys are going to bring that man to my office.'

'Yeah, I heard.'

They made their way to Delaney's office. Burton sat down in the comfortable armchair. 'I'll send out for a bottle, Taffy.'

'No. don't sir, I need good strong tea, not alcohol.'

'Okay, tea it is then.'

162

'Anyway,' continued Burton, 'I thought people like you always kept a bottle of scotch in a filing cabinet.'

'Only in the films, Taffy, and on TV.'

Burton allowed himself a small chuckle and then his mood suddenly changed. 'The Chief Inspector, sir, poor bastard, he had no chance.'

Delaney pulled a chair around in front of his desk in readiness for the two officers and Compito. A minute later, Compito was brought into Delaney's office by two of the Special Forces team. They had handcuffed his hands behind his back and put a leg tie on that gave him just enough room to shuffle. They sat him on a chair in front of Delaney and Burton.

Delaney told the two men to wait outside and leave the door open a few inches. Compito kept looking at the floor. Burton stood up, moved forward and knelt in front of him. 'Did you do that to your accomplice to shut him up or to try to get in our good books knowing your colleague had killed the other man?'

Delaney remained quite. Burton continued. 'Who sent you both here?'

Compito raised his head. He looked at Burton with respect and then at Delaney as he spoke. 'Stonehaven; get Lady Stonehaven here, now.'

Burton turned to look at Delaney for instruction. Delaney took a long hard look at Compito and then picked up the phone. 'Get me Lady Stonehaven, straight away.'

An hour later, there was a quiet knock on the door. One of the Special officers opened it and stood back. Lady Shirley Stonehaven walked in, dressed in her no-nonsense trouser suit, with a file under her arm. Compito looked at her as she walked around him and settled on a chair next to Delaney. She opened the file, studied it carefully and then handed it to Delaney. Burton

163

watched as Delaney took a photograph from the file, looked at it for a few seconds and then handed the file back to Stonehaven.

Compito sighed heavily and looked at Delaney. 'Can someone please get these handcuffs off me and cut the leg tie?'

Burton looked at Delaney and held out two hands in a pleading motion. 'What is it, sir?'

Delaney looked at Stonehaven and then tilted his head towards Burton. 'Tell him.'

'Of course,' said Stonehaven as she looked at Burton and then held out a hand towards Compito. 'Mr Burton, this is Michael Riego, Paramilitary Operations Officer, CIA.'

22

The midday sun was settling on the balconies in Monte Carlo. Micky Sondheim looked out over the harbour as he smiled contently and swirled his wine around the glass. Michelle Depout reached for the bottle of Chablis to top him up. He drank some more and put the glass down on a small table. 'Ah; you know Michelle; I think when I have done this latest deal, we will move and live here.'

'Why here,' she asked trying to make conversation. She did not want to speak to him. She hated him.

'Well, why not.' He moved his arm around in a sweeping motion over the panorama. 'Look at it: sunshine, money, millionaires. We could buy a villa up in the hills and then an apartment that overlooks the Formula One circuit.'

Depout did not say anything else. Dinner the previous evening had been torture for her. After she had listened to the conversation between Sondheim, Pollitt and Borg, she had never really recomposed herself properly and it was all she could do to keep down the meal that was served to her. Sondheim had chatted all night, not realising that she hated every minute of it. She knew he had some pretty ugly, nasty friends, but learning about the child smuggling had knocked her back completely. As she was sitting listening to him and watching him eat his lobster, she knew it had to end.

She had a job to do. Her employers were expecting her to plan everything meticulously, so Sondheim could be brought to justice along with some of his most important allies. But yesterday's events somehow made all the major objectives look secondary.

This man could not be allowed to go any further. Her thoughts were interrupted by the sound of Sondheim trying to get up. 'What are you doing?' she asked.

'I am determined to spend some time on my feet again today. Help me.'

His legs had been getting stronger just lately. Depout kept two crutches to hand so he could use them whenever he wished. Holding himself carefully, he walked slowly to the balcony door. 'Perhaps we should go somewhere this afternoon,' he said. 'Gambling maybe?'

He turned in the doorway to look at her. She was not expecting this and she certainly did not intend to spend another half day in the company of this man that was staring at her with a combined look of lechery and disdain.

As he was looking at her, she walked slowly over to the balcony rail and looked down at the cafeterias bar eight storeys below. When she turned, he was about six feet away, walking towards her. She put out her arm towards him and glanced at his unsteady feet. 'Come,' she said, 'enjoy the view with me for a while.'

He smiled and walked closer to her. What she had been taught about balance and the element of surprise, suddenly all came to her mind. When he was within two feet of her she reached for his hand. He let go of one of the crutches and grabbed her hand thankfully. In one swift but very calculated movement, she jerked him towards her, put one leg out in front of him and turned sideways. She brought him onto her hip and continued to pull with all her might. Having been knocked completely off balance, Sondheim was helpless. As he rolled over her bent body, she grabbed the rail with her free hand and jerked to a stop. The momentum of his body that she had started could be not stopped. As he rolled over the railings his grip tightened on her hand, but it was too late. He continued rolling as he fell. He did not scream or shout out. She looked down at his rolling flailing body as it descended and hit the concrete below. Within seconds, a dark red pool was forming around his upper body and head. Screams could be heard from the cafeteria and people started to look up to where Michelle was standing.

She walked slowly away from the rails and moved into the main room. Lifting the telephone, she took a deep breath and dialled reception. 'Get me the manager, straight away; and the police.'

She finished the call, hesitated, and checked her watch as she dialled another number When a young man answered, she spoke clearly and quickly. 'This is euro five, two, nine, zero. I have a dead X-ray.'

23

It was getting dark as Taffy Burton reached for the light switch in Delaney's office. He sat back down to the side of Delaney's desk and looked at Michael Riego again. Shirley Stonehaven sat with a look of tiredness on her face next to Riego. They had given him plenty of time to clean himself up and take a shower and had provided him with a change of clothes. He sat opposite Delaney waiting for the next question.

'How are you feeling now?' asked Delaney.

'Tired,' said Riego in a mid-west American accent. 'But I'll live, I guess.'

'I guess you're right,' quipped Delaney. 'You'll probably out live a lot of other people you come across.'

Stonehaven glanced at Delaney with an expression that said *get on with it*. Noticing the situation, Burton continued the questioning. 'If we're going to be working together,' he said, 'we need to understand your character and your objectives. We need details. How did you end up in Colombia in the first place?'

Riego straightened himself up in his chair and drew a hand across his mouth. 'You may not be aware, but the CIA has had undercover people in place there for years, not just weeks and months. I went to Colombia two years ago to infiltrate the FARC.' He looked at Burton and then towards Delaney. 'You know about the FARC, right?'

Delaney nodded, looking impatient as he answered Riego's question. 'The Revolutionary Armed Forces of Colombia; established in the 1960's out of the Colombian Communist Party. They deal in cocaine, kidnapping, bombings, armed raids on the

Colombian army and guerrilla warfare. We don't recognise them; neither do you, and quite a few others as well, including the United Nations.'

'Right; I was sent there to join up with the movement after 11 deputy lawmakers were killed in 2007. My parents are both Spanish and I speak the language fluently. I did my time in their training camps and worked my way up through the ranks to be a Column Commander, in charge of two companies, about 90 combatants.'

'Two years undercover like that, must have taken its toll,' said Burton.

'It did. I was about to be shipped out when something went wrong. A Belgian Intelligence man was caught when he was trying to steal some information from them about people and places. I was given the responsibility of guarding him and I purposefully made it easy for him to escape. He made it to the Coast to try to meet up with the navy; one of my men shot him. But he had already managed to get the laptop containing the information to the Belgian navy assault boat. I was summoned to the FARC high command. They blamed me for the mistake, so I was dispatched to Europe.'

'To kill me,' said Delaney wryly.

'Yes, to kill you. Sorry.'

'Did you know the laptop arrived in London?' asked Stonehaven.

'Yes,' said Riego, 'but I believe they retrieved it.'

'They did,' confirmed Delaney, 'killing two lab technicians in the process. Did you know they had people working for them in Europe?'

'Oh yeah; I was sent to meet one of their Belgian contacts in Paris. An Aaron Stait; do you know him?'

'We know of him; so do our colleagues in Belgium. So where did Frank Hawkwell come in?'

'He was with Stait in Paris. It was he who got me here and into this building.'

There was silence for a moment as everyone seemed to be digesting what had been said. Burton poured another coffee for Riego and looked at him thoughtfully. 'Well, thanks for saving my life back there by the way.'

Riego put out a hand. 'Not at all.'

'One thing though,' said Burton. Delaney and Stonehaven looked at Burton as he continued. 'Why nearly kill him? You could've disarmed him and waited.'

'I needed to be sure,' said Riego. 'He could have lunged for me or pulled the gun. He deserved a good beating anyway; did you know it was him who killed Ellie Shanks?'

Delaney raised an eyebrow. 'We did; how did you know?'

'Please,' said Riego, 'Don't make the same mistake that a lot of other intelligence agencies do.' Delaney tilted his head, waiting for the next sentence. Riego picked up his coffee, took a couple of sips and continued. 'Don't underestimate the CIA.'

Burton joined in. 'We won't; as long as you don't underestimate us.'

'Sure, I mean I...'

'That will be quite enough gentlemen,' interrupted Stonehaven. 'You have to work together from now on. I'm sure your skills will compliment each other's.'

It was approaching 9pm when Delaney called it a day. Ben Wyatt and Ajit Pitt had joined Delaney, Burton and Riego to discuss how they were going to get to Stait and his gang. Shirley Stonehaven had left them to it, with instructions for them to give her a daily update.

As they all left Delaney's office, Burton confirmed that he had arranged accommodation for Riego and that he would take him to the apartment near Hyde Park. Riego thanked Burton, but asked if it was possible to have a one-to-one with Delaney before they left. Burton looked at Delaney who nodded and Riego stood near the door after Burton had closed it.

'What is it?' asked Delaney.

Riego looked worried. 'Have you heard of someone called Sondheim?'

'Yes, he's been linked to Stait. Taffy and I had the pleasure of visiting his villa in Portugal with someone from the Portuguese police. It's a long story.'

Riego seemed on edge. 'I need to tell you something. I haven't told anyone else, including Lady Stonehaven.'

'Okay,' said Delaney, 'sit down; Taffy will wait for you.' Riego scratched his chin nervously and hesitated for a few seconds before fixing his dark eyes on Delaney. 'You may not be aware of this, but you're quite well known in international crime fighting circles and you have a reputation for being a doer.'

'Maybe; where is this going? It's late and I'm tired.'

'There are two women; one I need to tell you about and one that needs rescuing.'

'Are they both involved with what we're doing?'

'Yes, very much so. The woman you need to know about is called Julie Greaves. She works for the CIA's European division and for the last two years she's been working for their clandestine section, posing as a helper and companion to Micky Sondheim. The last I heard she was getting close to finding out about all the people that Sondheim deals with. She'll know about Aaron Stait by now, I'm sure of it.'

'But that's good isn't it?'

'Yes it's good; but her work is done.'

'Is she about five eight, dark hair, dark eyes, French accent?'

'Yes, that's her, although the last time I saw her she was blonde.'

'Well right now, she's dark; I met her when I visited Sondheim; goes by the name of Michelle Depout.'

'That's her; and of course it's good she knows. But now is the time to get her out, before Sondheim and his colleagues start fighting each other.'

'I probably agree, so why me? Why not tell your boss back in Washington. They send the instruction and she gets out. Or is there something else to this?'

Riego sat back and sighed before continuing. 'It's kind of political I guess. Washington is not in control of the European operations anymore. A year back, they realised that the local knowledge was missing, so they handed over control to London. All the CIA people in the European theatre now report to London.'

'When you say, London, you mean the CIA office here.'

'No, I mean MI6. For the past 12 months the European operations have been handled by them. The head of MI6 meets with the Washington boys every two months to update them, but Julie Greaves and the other 14 CIA Operations Officers in Europe report to MI6.'

Delaney paused for a moment before continuing the conversation. 'So, in some way it's like the CIA franchising out their European operations to MI6.'

'I guess it is, yes.'

'And you want me to talk to MI6 about getting Julie Greaves out of Sondheim's way.'

'That's what I had in mind, yes.'

'Okay, let me think about it. Now, you mentioned two women; who's the other?'

'The woman I've been living with in Colombia for the last two years. Her name is Christina Marez.'

Delaney raised his eyebrows and huffed. 'You don't ask for much do you Mr Riego.'

'She deserves it; she has helped me for the past two years without question.'

'Does she know you're CIA?'

172

'No. But I would tell her as soon as we can arrange to make contact again.'

A long pause followed; Delaney looking at Riego for something else. Riego gave way. 'Are you going to ask me if there is another reason to get her out?'

'Yes,' said Delaney, 'I think I am.'

'Because we've fallen in love with each other. And there's another reason: I don't think I could do it on my own.'

Another pause was followed by another huff from Delaney. 'I'll have to tell Lady Stonehaven of course; you realise that. I would also need her permission.'

'Of course, I understand the protocol and I don't want to step on anyone's toes. But your Overseas Liaison team has what is probably the best track record in the world for getting results.'

'Perhaps; sadly sometimes, at great cost, Mr Riego.'

'And you have all my sympathy and empathy sir. But these people we are after are killers. They murder hundreds, maybe thousands of innocent people to get what they want. It's nothing less than international enmity, bordering on savagery. We may lose some of our people sometimes, but we must always consider the big picture and what would happen if we were not out there doing our best to combat all of this wickedness.'

Delaney looked at his watch and stood up. 'Well, you've made your request; and your point. I need to speak to my superiors and my boys. We should call it a night now; Taffy will be getting impatient and you should get some sleep. Now, let me ask you another question; do you know about Interpol's involvement with Sondheim?'

'No, I thought it was just our guys.'

'Well it isn't; your Julie Greaves was working with another undercover operator. She was working as a housemaid and she was shot in the head a few days ago.'

173

Riego seemed to be struggling to say something. 'Jesus. Err, right, I'll need to contact Washington tomorrow. Can we speak again soon?'

Delaney nodded as he turned out the lights on their way out.

The house was quiet and Angela was in bed when Delaney got home. Rocky jumped off the sofa to greet him. He poured himself a small Merlot and sat down. Rocky sat next to him for a fuss and Delaney obliged. 'Something doesn't fit, Rocky.' The dog looked at him, wondering whether to stay there or go upstairs. 'Why did he come direct to me and bypass Stonehaven? How come he knew all about Julie Greaves but nothing about the Interpol girl?'

A few minutes later they were both making their way upstairs and Riego was still on Delaney's mind. I can understand him wanting to get the woman out of Colombia, he thought, that's just love, or infatuation. But he's been undercover in Colombia for two years; why the interest in a European operative, and how come he knows so much about her anyway? Perhaps Shirley Stonehaven could help. She still had useful contacts in Washington.

24

Michelle Depout had been questioned by the Monte Carlo police for almost ten hours when Harry Mitchell, head of MI6 in Europe, arrived to collect her. Her phone call had gone through to the MI6 office in Paris and Mitchell's people had verified the facts of Sondheim's death before passing on the information to him.

A young, thin Monte Carlo detective sitting next to Depout asked Mitchell to sit down and poured out another glass of water. Mitchell took a drink and stared at the young man. 'I'm not waiting here for any longer than a few minutes detective; these are the papers that you need to clarify the situation.' He pushed a folder across the table and the young man opened it. Two minutes later, he nodded, closed the folder and handed it back to Mitchell.

'Thank you, Mr Mitchell,' said the detective. He then turned to look again at Depout. 'I am sorry we have kept you so long. Am I correct in saying that from now on we call you Julie Greaves?'

'No,' said Greaves. 'You and your people must always refer to me as Michelle Depout. When the press asks about Sondheim's death and the hotel guests and staff ask questions, it was Michelle Depout. She was on holiday with Sondheim when he fell from the balcony and she has gone home to be with her mother.'

Mitchell realised that he did not need to add anything to what she had said. The detective took a note book from his pocket. 'Very well,' he said. 'Now, you asked me to find out about a helicopter that landed on the hotel's helipad yesterday.'

'Sondheim had two visitors yesterday,' she said. 'They arrived by helicopter to do business with him. Their names were

175

Pollitt and Borg; Borg was the pilot, but that's all I've got, for now.'

Mitchell nodded. He knew that the '*for now*' meant that she had something else to tell him once they were out of Monte Carlo.

Mitchell checked his notes. 'The helicopter is owned by Pollitt Air Services. Apparently they operate charter flights for the rich and famous from two bases; one in Trieste, the other in Nice. Do you need me to find out more?'

'No, thank you,' said Mitchell, 'my people will enquire further. We should be on our way now.' He stood up and Greaves and the detective followed his lead. An hour later, they were sitting in a private jet, heading for Paris.

Harry Mitchell had been in charge of MI6 European operations for 3 years. He had been summoned to London 12 months ago to attend a meeting with some top cabinet ministers, various heads of intelligence departments and the CIA. The British government had agreed to oversee the activities of the CIA's European Paramilitary Operations Officers and to help them whenever they could. He looked across at Julie Greaves who was sitting opposite him in the second of the two booths on board the Boeing jet. The voice of the captain came over the intercom. 'Paris in about 15 minutes Mr, Mitchell.'

Greaves was looking out of the window and she came out of her concentration when the captain spoke. Mitchell smiled at her. 'I told my people to find you somewhere nice to stay; they should be waiting for us when we land.'

'Thanks,' said Greaves, 'there are details I need to discuss with you though; perhaps we should go straight to your office first.'

'It'll wait until the morning. By then I'll have more information on Sondheim and the visitors he had yesterday.'

'Okay; they were talking about importing children for slavery and paedophilia. When I heard them talk it made me throw up.

176

Pollitt said that good slaves were hard to come by and that his friend Borg had certain appetites. They were talking about kids from four to seventeen years old for Christ's sake.'

Mitchell leaned across the table and put a hand on hers. 'Well, Julie, you've started off on the right track by getting rid of Sondheim.'

'What do you mean?'

'You threw him over the balcony rail didn't you?'

'He fell, he was unsteady on his feet, you know? What's all this about?'

'Julie, it's okay; he deserved it. He was scum.' Greaves was about speak again but Mitchell held up a hand to stop her. 'Would you believe me,' he continued, 'if I said that we keep a close eye on all of you, when you're out in the field?'

'I guess so,' Greaves said quietly.

'So would you believe me if I told you that we followed your tracks to Monte Carlo and that we were watching the hotel you and Sondheim were staying in?' Greaves nodded, Mitchell continued. 'We had an observer positioned out on a yacht. He could see every balcony that overlooked Monte Carlo Marina. When I got the phone call just after you phoned it in, I was opening an e-mail with a video attachment. It showed you heaving Sondheim over the balcony to his death.'

The captain came over the intercom again. 'And seat belts on please, I'm starting our descent to Charles de Gaulle airport.' Greaves turned down her mouth as she fastened her belt. 'Jesus, Harry; you guys are good.'

'We have our moments, but we need people like you. We call it Accumulative Force.'

'So only you, me and the observer will know what I did, right?'

'Right,' said Mitchell, giving another tug on his seatbelt.

'You're smirking,' she said, 'is there something else?'

'Oh I was just thinking; I could use another dozen like you.'

25

Freddie Ludic and young Tommy made good time on their journey from Knokke to the Essex coast. The motor boat ploughed through the North Sea with ease; its twin engines working hard. Ludic steered it carefully towards the Blackwater estuary. It was 10.45 and he slowed down to a crawl when he realised he was 15 minutes early. Five minutes later, he cut the engines and let the boat drift; it didn't wander far in the calm seas and still air.

From where they were, they could see the red upturned boat on the narrow sand bank to the south. Tommy started to chat about insignificant issues and Ludic told him to shut up. At 11.10 Ludic kicked Tommy in the legs where he lay. 'She's here, get ready.'

Through his binoculars, Ludic could see a young woman, slim, no more than 5' 2". She was wearing a baseball cap, jeans and a baggy cardigan over a shirt. He watched as she lit a cigarette, took a couple of sucks on it and threw it away. After a pause, she did the same again, throwing the cigarette in the opposite direction. Then she sat down about 50 metres from the upturned boat. 'That's the signal,' said Ludic, 'get on with it.'

Tommy took up the two bags they had carried with them. He handed them to Ludic and lowered himself over the side to stand in the shallow water that came up to just below his waist. Ludic handed the bags over the side to him; they were heavy and Tommy struggled as he waded towards the beach. When he was on dry sand he paused to take his breath, before walking to the boat. He placed the bags underneath it without pushing them all the way out of site.

Ludic watched the woman as she looked around her carefully and walked slowly towards the boat. Tommy was making his way back to Ludic as she reached the upturned boat. She pulled the two bags out from underneath the boat and carefully opened one of them. Then she took some sort of implement from a pocket. Ludic could not quite see exactly what she was doing, but five minutes later she walked around the far side of the boat and re-emerged holding what looked like a red towel. She put the red towel down on the sand next to where she was standing.

'That's it,' said Ludic. 'Come on, boy; we're off to get the payment and dump this boat.' As Ludic was bringing the engines to life, he looked back to the beach. A motorcyclist was riding slowly towards the woman. He pulled up near her, they put the two bags into the panniers and rode off.

It was only a short journey to the northern side of the estuary; ten minutes later Ludic was pointing to a sign that said TOLLESBURY PIER, FREE MOORING. They moored the motor boat up next to a small cruiser. 'Get the kitbag,' Ludic told Tommy. 'I'll bring the weapons.'

'Where to now?' asked Tommy.

'We put this stuff in the cabin and then take the motor boat back to the boatyard when it's starting to get dark.'

'How?'

'A river; just around that headland.' He pointed westwards. 'It goes straight to the boatyard, only a couple of miles away.'

They were just a short distance from a cabin that Ludic had used before. The door was open. A single plastic beach table was in the middle of the single roomed cabin with two fold-up garden chairs near it. On the table there was a plastic food container with some bread and cakes in it. Two bottles of beer were at the side of it with a note that read, *Dusk – about 19.00.*

Ludic put his bag down containing their firearms and snapped the top off one of the bottles with his teeth. 'Help yourself boy; we'll leave about six thirty.'

'What about payment for what we've just dropped off?'

'We'll get paid when we get to the boatyard.'

It was 5 p.m. when Aaron Stait phoned Ludic. 'You okay, Freddie?'

'Yes, I'm good.'

'And the boy?'

'He's okay too. We take the boat back and collect payment at about seven.'

'Good.'

'Then we will take the normal route back; I have the tickets with me.'

'Not this time, Freddie.'

'Not this time?'

'No; I want you and Tommy to stay in England for a while. Use some of the payment to get yourselves some hotel rooms and stay low until I contact you again.'

Ludic had worked for Stait long enough to know when something was not quite right. 'Something gone wrong, Aaron?'

'Frank's been taken.'

Ludic froze; his mouth open. It took a moment for him to digest what he had heard. 'You mean our Frank; Frank Hawkwell?'

'That's why I want you to stay there, Freddie; do you realise that this could mean you get a promotion?'

'Promotion?'

'Frank was my number one fixer Freddie; *someone* will have to take his place.'

'Yes, yes, but, Frank; I mean how and who?'

'He and our friend from Colombia went in to hit Delaney; they failed.'

'Have they both been taken?'

'I've only had confirmation about Frank. But I haven't heard from the Colombian, and he hasn't contacted me. That's one of the reasons I want you to stay there; he may need help. Let me know when you are settled somewhere, and be careful with all of that money.'

Ludic was still shocked as Stait ended the call. His thoughts were darting between the thought of Hawkwell getting caught and the opportunity that lay ahead for him. *Frank Hawkwell taken. He lost a fight. He failed.*

Tommy had heard everything. 'Mr Hawkwell been taken then?'

'Mm, he has, Tommy. We have to stay in England; Mr Stait needs us here now.'

'This will mean that you become Mr Stait's right-hand man?'

Ludic did not answer.

Tommy stayed away from him and remained quiet. This could mean I am now second-in-command to Aaron Stait's number one man, he thought to himself. If Hawkwell does not come back; if he stays in jail. I could be as notorious as any of them one day, and very rich. He decided he would stick to Ludic like glue; learning, helping, protecting him when he could. I will prove to them that I am not the *young* Tommy anymore or the *boy*. One day, when they are old, I might even take over their business.

26

Julie Greaves was surprised to find that the MI6 European Headquarters in Paris were old and dark, with limited workspaces and small meeting rooms. The windows, with brown Venetian blinds had not had a good clean for a while and the grey plastered walls had cracks and unpainted repairs.

Harry Mitchell tried to lift one the blinds at the window behind him, but failed. He left it halfway raised at an angle, returned to his seat and poured coffee. 'I called Washington last night; they suggested you remain here for a while to rest. How was the hotel?'

Greaves shrugged her shoulders. 'It's okay.'

'Well, sorry, but 'okay' isn't good enough for what you've just been through; I'll find you somewhere special.'

'Oh it's fine; I don't want to be here too long anyway. Have Washington given you any indication of what happens next?'

'No, but they gave me a number for you to ring.' He pushed a piece of paper across the desk to her. 'It's a mobile; by the way, I've ordered a new phone for you, it should be with us today.'

'Thanks.' Greaves left the piece of paper on the desk, ran her hands through her dark hair and yawned. She knew that Mitchell was not telling her everything and that he was probably aware of who the phone number belonged to. 'I'll phone the number now then; might be important.'

'Go ahead, use this phone.' Mitchell turned his desk phone around so it was facing her. She looked at him as she picked up the handset and paused before she dialled. 'I'm staying here,' he said. 'So don't look at me like that.'

She smiled faintly and dialled the number. She knew the voice of the person she was calling immediately. 'Yes yes.'

She hesitated for a couple of seconds and swallowed. 'Well, what sort of a way is that to answer a phone Michael Riego?'

'Julie! Where are you?'

'Sitting in the MI6 office in Paris, enjoying a coffee.'

'You're safe! Christ, thank god your safe.'

'I'm okay; now anyway. It's good to be out after two years.' *Out* was the phrase they used for coming off undercover work.

'Yeah, tell me about it,' said Riego, 'I've been out myself just over a day.'

'Right, so where are you?'

'London.'

'London! So Colombia is over?'

'For now, but we can go through the details when we meet. Will you be resting up for a while?'

Greaves looked up at Mitchell, who was looking back at her. 'I guess so, but not for too long; you know I don't like being inactive.' Mitchell looked impressed, which was just what Greaves wanted.

'Listen,' continued Riego, 'I'm going to be working with some Brits for a while; I'll get the head honcho to talk to Paris; see if we can get you back here with me.'

Again Greaves looked at Mitchell. 'Okay, I'd better go now.'

'Yeah, sure; Jesus, Julie, if you knew how much I worried about your situation with Sondheim; boy, am I glad you're okay.'

'Thanks, Michael, see you soon.' She finished the call and Mitchell turned the phone around to its original position. 'Don't worry about another hotel,' she said, 'I don't think I'll be here long enough.'

'Okay; but remember, I have a say in where you go and what you do as well.'

She paused and nodded in acknowledgement. Mitchell took a bundle of money out of his desk drawer and handed it to her. 'Here, go and shop for whatever you need and then rest for a while; when you're new phone arrives, I'll have it delivered to you at the hotel.'

She was glad to get out of the old fashioned dark offices. As she walked to her hotel she decided what she needed; a few hours in the Paris shops followed by dinner and wine would do nicely.

After his call from Greaves, Riego made his way to the offices of TOLA. He was to meet Delaney, Burton, Wyatt and Pitt for a strategy meeting. TOLA, he thought to himself as he got into a taxi, The Overseas Liaison Agency; not even an official government department. *'Diplomatic services'*. Huh, yeah sure. They probably had more clout than MI6 and MI5. Being able to be offensive as well as defensive when they wanted to be; only the Brits would come up with something like that. Genius really; little wonder they were headed up by one of the most respected guys in the business and a someone like Stonehaven, with an intelligence pedigree to match anyone's.

Ben Wyatt and Ajit Pitt were in the office when he got there. 'Good to see you both again,' said Riego, as he put his phone down onto the low centre table and sat back. 'Sure is good to be working with you guys.'

Wyatt looked up from his newspaper; right, cut the crap, he thought to himself. But he answered. 'Morning.'

Riego looked over to where Pitt was standing near Delaney's desk. 'Any chance of a coffee?' Pitt looked at him and smiled. 'Help yourself it's over on the corner table.'

Riego looked put out; as though the younger one in the room should get the coffee. He poured himself a coffee and sat down again. Wyatt put his paper down to finish his own coffee and Pitt joined them with his orange juice. 'So,' said Riego, 'you guys been doing this for long?'

'Quite a few years now,' said Wyatt, 'you?'

184

'Mm, me too. The CIA don't pay the best salaries in the world, but they look after me and mission pay can soon add up.'

'What about the risks?'

'I probably just get used to accepting them; like you do maybe.'

'Probably,' said Wyatt, 'but being undercover for two years must be a hell of strain.'

'Some exciting situations as well though.' Pitt joined in.

Riego looked at him thoughtfully. 'Guess you're new to the game eh?'

'Yes, quite new.'

Wyatt stood up to get more coffee and patted Pitt on the shoulder as he passed. 'What he means, Michael, is that he's worked for us for two weeks.'

'Two weeks?' said Riego, 'I thought you both just got back from a tricky job in Belgium?'

'We have.' said Pitt, looking at Riego as if to say, *do you have a problem?*

'How did you get on over there?'

'We did okay.'

Wyatt let out a quiet laugh. 'What he means is, we didn't get anyone, we got one of their police officers killed and we got sent back to London with a telling off.'

Riego looked at Wyatt and smiled, understanding the humour. He was about to wish Pitt good luck in his career, but Pitt was getting to his feet as the door opened.

'Morning,' said Delaney, not looking at anyone as he made his way to his desk.

Wyatt nodded, Riego offered a quick 'hi there, how are you?' which Delaney didn't answer, and Pitt said, 'good morning, sir' as he poured a coffee the way Delaney liked it.

'Right,' said Delaney, 'as soon as Taffy gets here, we'll get on with it. I spoke to Lady Stonehaven and someone else on my way here this morning; they've approved my ideas, so I'll take you all through it.'

'Your ideas?' asked Riego.

Delaney looked at him. 'Yes, Michael, my ideas.'

'So who was the *someone else* you spoke to?'

'Harry Mitchell; until further notice, you'll be reporting to me.'

Riego did not offer another question. He nodded slowly and sighed.

Pitt hovered near Delaney's desk. 'Excuse me sir, could I ask who Harry Mitchell is?' Delaney looked displeased that Pitt didn't know as he sipped his hot coffee. Wyatt called over to Pitt. 'Come and sit down mate; let the boss have his coffee.'

Pitt sat down and Wyatt leaned forward to speak to him. 'Harry Mitchell is Head of MI6 in Europe mate. They have a kind of franchise for the CIA. Michael here,' he tilted his head towards Riego, 'will have to report to him unless Washington override the agreement for special circumstances.'

Delaney smirked. 'Very good, Ben, couldn't have explained it better myself.'

'Sorry, I should have known,' said Pitt.

'Yes; you should have,' said Delaney.

Twenty minutes later, the door opened again. Wyatt looked around and smiled. 'Taffy, my old Welsh mate; nice of you to join us.'

'Bollocks,' said Burton, as he took of his coat. 'And remember who you're talking to. Ajit, get me a coffee.'

Riego seemed bewildered. 'Jeez, you guys don't waste time with salutations do you?'

Delaney smirked again and told them all to gather around the centre table.

'Okay,' he said, 'first of all; who.' He handed out a photograph. 'Photo One, Aaron Stait; about 50, Belgian, very elusive, does drugs mainly, a bit of diamond smuggling, did a few deals with Micky Sondheim, buys drugs from FARC in Colombia, and, as we know, recently lost his part-time right hand man, Frank Hawkwell.' The photo showed Stait drinking beer in a bar. His black straggly hair was combed back and his eyes were deep set and dark. The broad neck and solid shoulders were evidence of someone who kept himself fit and strong.

Burton was going to say something, but Delaney held up a hand to stop him and handed out another photo. 'Photo two, Freddie Ludic; 30, younger brother of Henry Ludic who was found shot dead on a property near Stait's home in Belgium that Ben and Ajit here found. Now that we have Hawkwell, it's very likely that Stait will have to rely on Freddie.' Freddie Ludic's photo looked like it had been taken in the same bar. He was holding an orange juice. He was medium height with a stocky build and auburn hair and well trimmed, short beard. His complexion looked healthy and he looked sober and fit.

Delaney continued. 'Two more, then you can ask questions. Photo Three, Tommy; no surname, just known as Tommy. Only about twenty, Belgian police think he joined Stait a year ago when he left jail; he was in for beating up his father and trying to drown his mother when he was high on god knows what after a rave. Previous to that, he stabbed a man in the stomach when he was getting away from a policeman following a ram-raid. He was just sixteen. Word is, he's become Ludic's protégé.' The photo had not been taken in the bar. It showed a farmhouse in the background and it was a full length photo. He was about 5' 10" and thin, hands in his pockets and a shaved head. His shoulders were stooped and his chin was low, almost touching his sunken chest. The pale, narrow face suited the eyes, which were lifeless and indifferent.

'Photo Four; Julie Greaves.' Riego looked up at Delaney who held up his forefinger and shook his head. Only Burton noticed this from the corner of his eye. Delaney continued. 'Julie Greaves, also known as, Michelle Depout; 33, CIA paramilitary operations officer, like Michael here. She's been undercover for two years working as a companion to Micky Sondheim, who is now dead. She will be joining us shortly.' The picture showed an official photo, probably taken for ID purposes. Greaves long dark hair was tied back tightly which made her dark brown eyes stand out more. The top lip was raised slightly in the middle, giving her a mouth an attractive shape.

'When exactly do you mean, when you say *shortly*?' asked Wyatt.

Delaney looked at his watch. 'About an hour.'

'And what happens then?'

'I'm just about to come on to that; before I do, any questions about the photos?' When he didn't get any response, he continued. 'Okay, so they're the people; this is the idea. Aaron Stait has been buying drugs from Colombia, although we can't be sure they're from the FARC. Sondheim was also buying from Colombia, so there was a little competition there. Now Stait will be able to buy Sondheim's share, which means he could end up being the richest drugs baron in Europe; but there's a catch.'

'Thought so,' said Wyatt.

Delaney continued. 'MI6 tells me that the reason Stait gets away with so much, is that someone in Europe is helping him.'

'One of us you mean,' said Burton.

'It's likely to be an agent or police officer, yes.'

'But this shouldn't be too difficult,' said Riego, 'if we get all the European guys and Interpol onto it.'

Delaney looked around at all of them. 'We can't; there's us five and Julie Greaves, that's it. The British Government and the Americans have agreed that they don't want the FARC to get a foothold in Europe. To achieve that, we have to go on the offensive, and probably not by the book. We need to trap Stait and his FARC contact; the person that's helping him. They need to be removed indefinitely.'

'When you say, indefinitely you mean, put away for good, right?' asked Riego.

'Something like that.'

Wyatt got to his feet. 'Well, I'll say one thing for you gov; you certainly keep it interesting.'

'Mm, not always my decision though, Ben; this directive came from the top.'

'So, what's your *idea* that you mentioned?' asked Riego.

'We invent a new rival for Stait.'

Burton joined Wyatt at the corner table for more coffee. When they both sat down again, Burton raised his eyebrows. 'We?'

'Yes, Taffy, as in one of us,' said Delaney.

'Who?' asked Wyatt.

'That's what we're here for, right?' said Riego, 'to decide.'

'I suppose so; when Julie gets here, I'll go through the details,' said Delaney. 'So you have about 50 minutes to think about it and maybe come up with some good ideas.' Then he looked directly at Pitt. 'Ajit; I'm giving you a choice, now. You're still very new to this, if you wanted to sit this one out, I would understand. It's going to be risky.'

Pitt noticed everyone looking at him. He stood up, replenished his orange juice, sat back down and nodded once, looking at Wyatt. 'I'll be fine; with my mentor here looking after me.'

Wyatt scratched his chin. 'No pressure then.'

Julie Greaves arrived an hour later. Riego hugged her and took the lead on the introductions. She was offered a seat next to Pitt, who seemed to be infatuated with her. 'So you were really undercover for two years?'

'Two years, yes.'

Pitt shook his head in amazement, his knees, bobbing up and down. Burton could see Delaney wanted to get on with things, so

189

he tapped the table with his pen. 'Right; can I start sir,' he said. Delaney held out a hand as a *go ahead* signal.

'I think it should be me,' said Burton.

'What should be you?' asked Wyatt.

'I should pose as Stait's Rival.'

Greaves asked what was meant by 'rival' and Delaney gave her a brief history of the previous conversation.

'Well, it can't be me, the FARC know my face too well,' said Riego.

Delaney nodded. 'I agree.' Then he looked at Burton. 'Why you Taffy?'

'I'm the most experienced, aside from you sir, and we can't risk you.'

'Very noble of you, Taffy. Any other suggestions?' He looked at Wyatt and Pitt. They both remained silent. Greaves shuffled in her chair. 'What about me? I'm capable; Michael can vouch for that.'

'No way, Julie,' said Riego, 'you're just out of a two year stint.'

Delaney realised that all of them were probably right. He sat forward. 'Okay, well, as Ben will need to stay close to Ajit; it looks like you're right Taffy.'

'Good,' said Burton, 'I'll start practising my *hard man* face straight away.'

'Can't be any scarier than the one you've got,' said Wyatt.

Delaney huffed, opened a folder in front of him and began to lay out his plans to them.

27

On the outskirts of Antwerp, in a small house with pink walls, green window shutters and a grey tiled roof, Aaron Stait was pacing up and down in the white tiled kitchen holding a glass of brandy. It was midnight; 5 p.m. in Colombia.

Freddie Ludic had phoned him a few hours earlier to confirm that he had made the connection at the boatyard and received the money. He and Tommy had found a small, quiet hotel near Tilbury. They had booked in as Mr Long and Mr Waters, working at Tilbury docks on a temporary contract. 'The money?' Stait had asked.

'Under the back seat of my hire car, Aaron; I'll look after it.'

'Okay; I'll call you tomorrow.'

Stait poured himself another brandy. It was past midnight. The phone call he was waiting for would not be long now. He looked around the old kitchen; the white tiles were cracked, some were missing. The pine cupboard would have some tinned food in it, but he didn't bother to look. The house was one of two he had as his boltholes as well as a motor yacht; all empty, all stocked with some kind of non-perishables. One of the houses he would need to abandon; it was where he had shot Henry Ludic. The other was near Antwerp. He wondered what he was doing sitting in a place like that when he was worth about 180 million Euros.

His phone rang. He picked it up, pressed the answer key, then turned it off again. He opened up a small laptop that was on the table, turned on the webcam and pressed the receive key. His caller was a big man wearing a military jacket. He flipped his large nose with a finger and brushed back his grey bushy hair with both of his large weathered hands. Stait knew by the vexed look in his green eyes that the conversation was not going to be pleasant.

'Commander Carnas; how are you?' said Stait, reaching for his brandy.

'I am alright, Mr Stait; but I am troubled.'

'About what?'

'Your man, Mr Hawkwell.'

'Yes.'

'And it was he who was to accompany our man, Compito, to London, to kill Delaney.'

'Yes; but I have not heard from Compito.'

'He has not been taken, Mr Stait.'

'How do you know?'

'We know, Mr Stait. Do you think we in the FARC just potter about in our own little Colombia, not knowing what goes on around the world?'

'So you have men in London?'

Carnas hesitated as someone out of shot passed him a glass of water. He leaned forward as though he was actually sitting at the table with Stait. 'How do you think we retrieved the laptop with your name and Sondheim's name on it? Of course we have men in London, in Glasgow, in Antwerp. Compito is not captured, and his name is not Compito.'

Stait remained quiet, almost speechless; not sure of what to say. Carnas continued. 'We do not have his name yet, but he is a CIA operative.'

Stait sat back. 'But you said he was a Column Commander.'

'He was; he joined the FARC two years ago. The CIA are not stupid Mr Stait.'

The two men sat looking at each other's webcams. Carnas took a drink of water and wiped his forehead. Stait sipped at his brandy and sighed. 'So what happens now? I can still buy bulk from you; I have the cash. Delaney and his men will not be able to penetrate our procedures.'

'I think,' said Carnas, rubbing his hands through his hair again, 'If Mr Hawkwell failed to get to Delaney, other people will. Did you hear about Mr Sondheim?'

'What about him? Has he offered you more money than me for the next big shipment?'

Carnas shook his head. 'He is dead; he fell from a balcony to his death in Monte Carlo. That makes you our number one buyer.'

Stait tried not to look pleased. 'That is something that I can handle, Commander Carnas.'

'Perhaps. Now we have about one minute left before we have to stop transmitting to avoid tracking devices; have you any other questions?'

'No Commander Carnas, thank you.'

'Very well; I will be in touch with regards to the next transaction.' Carnas sat back as someone slid the laptop away from him, closing the lid.

The room from where Carnas had called was a large meeting room with a cold slate floor and thick red curtains. As the laptop was being removed from the oak table, two other soldiers walked into the room. One of them stayed near the door, the other, who had chevrons on his sleeves, walked forward to Carnas. 'We have the woman, Commander.'

'Bring her in.'

'The soldier near the door turned around and left the room. A minute later, he returned, holding a woman by the arm. She was about 30 with a slim figure and ample breasts. Her black hair shone in the dim lights and her flawless, olive skin creased slightly as she smiled nervously. She was shaking with fright. The soldier led her to the table and gestured for her to sit down, facing Commander Carnas. The chair was an old high-backed carver and she looked small as she settled herself and put her hands on her knees.

There was a moment's silence, before Carnas put his large hands on the table in front of him and looked at her. 'You are Christina Marez?'

'Yes, I am, sir.'

'The lover of Antonio Compito; Column Commander in the Eastern section.'

She stopped smiling and nodded.

'You have been with him for two years' continued Carnas.

'Yes; has something happened to him?'

'Yes, he has returned to the CIA.'

'CIA?'

Carnas slammed both hands down on the table. 'Do not take me for an idiot!'

She straightened herself up, shocked and scared. 'But I do not know of this.'

'Liar!'

'Please, please! To me he is my lover my friend. What is this CIA?'

'You have been helping him! You could be CIA also!'

'No, no! He is Antonio, my husband. I am Christina; I was born and raised in Colombia, like Antonio, What is this!' She began to cry, but it had no effect on Carnas who leaned forward and stood up.

'Liar! We have seen papers in your house; you are his accomplice!'

She put her head in her hands and sobbed. Carnas reached for the gun in his belt. She looked up at him and held her breath, completely motionless. He fired once; the bullet hit her in the neck, passing straight through it, and hit the back of her chair. He fired again as she was falling backwards.

The two soldiers stood together. The look on both of their faces was one of horror. Carnas had not told them what to expect. The sergeant knelt down, to look at the still body. 'But sir, she may have been telling the truth; or she could have been useful to us if she was a foreign agent.'

'Be quiet! Get her out of here, now'

'We will have to tell the...'

'Just get her out!'

28

A couple of days passed before Burton was asked to go for his 'fit-out'. The equipment specialists were based on the seventh floor of an old office block near Heathrow. The home office occupied just two floors, although they owned the entire building; as far as the public were concerned, it was empty. He turned up at the 'technical office' of the department to find three people waiting for him. A small man with glasses and a moustache welcomed him and did the introductions.

'Mr Burton, I'm Dodd; head of department.' He gestured towards the other two. 'This is Sam; he'll be taking care of ID; and this is Maria; she's our sound expert.'

Sam was about 50; scruffy, with a look of experience. The younger Maria was wearing a white lab coat, looking officious.

They offered Burton a coffee and settled him down on an upright chair. He looked at Maria as she wheeled over a trolley towards him with various small instruments on it. 'I hope you're not just thinking of old fashioned wires and jewellery; I'm going to be dealing with some hardened, knowledgeable people.'

Maria shook her head. 'We're a bit more advanced these days.'

'Right, what have you got then?'

'An implant; do you want a local anaesthetic?'

'What?'

'Do you want a local anaesthetic? It can be painful.'

Burton hesitated and sensed the others looking at him. 'Err, no, I need to drive after this, get on with it.'

'Very well, tilt your head back please and open your mouth just a little.'

He did as she asked. 'Thank you,' she continued. 'Now, I'm going to pass a small wire up through your nose, it'll hurt when it gets towards your Eustachian Tube; let me know if you want me to stop. Then I'm going to release a tiny microphone and transmitter from the end of it; we call it a micro. It will stay there until it's removed. After a few minutes, you won't know it's there. We'll give it ten minutes to settle and then a magnet stick will be placed gently into your ear. This will draw the micro out towards the eardrum. Then we can test it. Easy really.'

Burton did as he was asked and she went about her work. It did not hurt as much as he had expected. Twenty minutes later she passed him a book. 'I will be outside. I want you to wait for two minutes and then start reading from this please.'

He took the book and opened it at the first page as she left the room. He waited as she had asked before reading. 'When the quick brown fox did not manage to get over gate, he thought about what to do next, so he counted, one, two, three, seven, thirty, and then he sat in silence and ate a mushroom. The...'

'That's fine, thank you.' He could hear Maria's voice in his ear. 'Can you hear me clearly?' she asked.

'Yes, perfect.'

'Not too loud?'

'No.'

She came back into the room and smiled at him. 'Thank you, that's all done then. Range is about one mile.'

'The little tale I read out, by the way, was wrong; it should have said...'

'It was not wrong, Mr Burton; you needed to say certain words because of different frequencies.'

She tidied a few things on her trolley and left the room.

Burton turned to Dodd. 'Doesn't mess about does she?'

Dodd did not answer, but Sam did. 'No, unfortunately.'

The remark was ignored by Dodd. Burton stood up to move around. 'So, am I right in saying that I can now speak to people and hear people that are up to a mile away?'

'Of course,' said Dodd, 'but only if they have the right frequencies on their handsets; you can take three handsets with you. Now then, ID. First of all, Sam will take your photo.'

They led Burton to a small room filled with chairs, cameras and lights. When the photo was taken, Sam sat down at a desk while Dodd offered Burton a seat opposite him.

'Do you like the designer stubble?' asked Burton. 'I stopped shaving two days ago.'

'Good,' said Dodd, 'you probably shouldn't look too clean.'

'I just wanted to look different for the passport.'

'That's fine. Now; listen carefully please. We have given you the name of James Padley. You're 42 and you were born in Swansea. If anyone checks they won't find out anything. James Padley was a real person and any registry office will confirm that. What no one knows is that he was shot dead last week by an armed police officer. His body will be on ice until further notice.'

'I won't ask for the details.'

'Good. You work alone. You started in business ten years ago and have assets of 56 million pounds sterling. An account has been set up in your name at the Standard Bank of Antwerp. These are all the cards you should need.' Dodd handed him a card holder with seven cards in it. 'Each one has a spending limit of ten thousand.'

Burton paused as he carefully went through the cards checking names and numbers. He looked up at Dodd as he put the cards in his pocket. 'One question; just what sort of business am I in?'

'Diamonds.'

'Not drugs?'

'No, too obvious. We have something you can take with you for collateral.'

The two men talked for another ten minutes; Burton listening intently. He had always had a good memory, which was just as well, he thought. They had finished the briefing just as Sam approached holding a passport in one hand and a briefcase in the other. He handed the passport to Burton. 'There you go, Mr Padley.'

Burton studied it. They had even stamped it with various customs logos and made it look old. Apparently, Mr Padley had been to France, Belgium, Chile, Brazil and Cape Town.

'Amazing,' he said.

'That's not all, Mr Padley,' said Dodd. He gestured to Sam to put the briefcase on the table in front of Burton.

'Please be very careful with this,' said Sam. 'It is expendable, but getting it back would be nice. Think of the tax payer.'

Burton opened the briefcase slowly, wondering what they meant. All he could see was a dozen dark blue velvet bags that almost filled it. Dodd took one bag out, untied a string bow and emptied some of the contents onto the table. Burton could see they were diamonds but he was surprised at how unique they looked.

'Diamonds, Mr Burton. All about 1.01 carat, oval cut and shaped. Colour D; that actually means colourless. Worth about eleven hundred dollars each.'

Burton looked at Sam. 'I thought you said it was expendable.'

'It is; we're actually way under budget this year.'

Burton then looked at Dodd. 'How many are there?'

'About four million dollars worth.'

'And this is my 'in' to Stait is it?'

'That's correct,' said Dodd. 'Approximately forty percent of the world's diamond trading is done in Antwerp. You just tell Stait that they're S12, GIA graded; he'll know what they're worth.'

'But, how can they be expendable; you're joking, right?'

'As Sam said, it would be nice to get them back, but put your life first won't you.'

'Mm, I will. Is four million enough? Stait will deal with much bigger numbers than that.'

'It's enough to get you in; especially this quality.'

Burton put the few diamonds back into the bag and closed the briefcase. 'Right, are we done here?'

Dodd acknowledged. 'We're done. Try and bring us back a profit; no one else has.'

'I'll be lucky to be bringing myself back. Thank you, gentlemen.'

'Don't forget the handsets,' said Sam, as he passed a small bag to Burton.

As Burton drove to Delaney's office, he kept looking at the briefcase on the seat next to him. The bag containing the handsets was next to it. 'I hope this bloody micro keeps working,' he said to himself. 'The boys are going to love this.'

29

Aaron Stait had stayed at his small house near Antwerp for a couple of days after getting his phone call from Commander Carnas. He knew he needed to keep moving around to avoid staying in one place too long; there were rumours going around that the Belgian Interpol were getting close to him and his man on the inside had confirmed his suspicions. His motor yacht was moored at Terneuzen and he decided to make it his base for a few days. The 50ft vessel had cost him half a million so perhaps it was time to use it more.

The journey to Terneuzen was just a couple of hours. He left his car in a locked garage near the marina which he had bought when he had acquired the motor yacht and his mooring. He stood for a while on the raised gangway to look over the marina. There was only one yacht that looked more impressive than his, he thought, and he wondered if the owner was a business tycoon or a criminal. Although he had not been on the vessel for some time, it was well looked after and cleaned inside and out by the marina's services department, for which he paid them a retainer.

He had named the yacht *Adinerado*. It was a Birchwood 500, with long flowing lines and windows that matched the shape of the design. The brilliant white colour had not faded and the fly bridge and rear swim platform were still very clean. Once on board he unpacked and poured himself a beer. A neighbour at the marina had once told him that he should really have someone with him rather than try to navigate on the open sea on his own, but he had done it before and he would do it again. But before he decided where he was going, he needed to check the guns.

The cover to the engine department that housed the high-tech twin engines was accessed easily via the crew cabin. A quick stock take of his Heckler & Koch equipment revealed that everything was in order; two HK416 rifles, 3 P10 handguns and ten boxes of ammunition. He hoped he wouldn't need to use them, but it was nice to know they were there. Back on the upper deck he scanned over his charts and maps. After a few minutes he phoned Freddie Ludic in England.

'Freddie; everything is good?'

'Yes it is, Aaron. Tommy and I are staying low as you requested.'

'Right; I want both of you to drive to Salcombe in the morning; it's in Devon. Make sure to bring all the money from the last payment. I'm leaving Belgium for a few days. By about six tomorrow morning I'll be moored up at there; I'll let you know exactly where tomorrow,'

'Okay, we'll leave early in the morning. Is there any news about Frank?'

'No, not yet. See you tomorrow.'

As Stait was checking the instruments and setting the coordinates of the automatic navigation, three hundred metres away in the raised observation room of the harbour master's office, Inspector Hubert of the Antwerp police headquarters was watching the *Adinerado* through binoculars. He put the binoculars down and turned to the man on his right.

'He's taking to sea, Sergeant Brun.'

'Shall I notify the people in England?'

'No; I'll do that later, there's no hurry for now.'

In Delaney's office, Wyatt, Pitt, Riego and Greaves were waiting for Delaney and Burton to arrive. It was approaching midday when Burton turned up and put the briefcase and handsets in front of them.

'What's in the case?' asked Pitt.

'Something pretty interesting,' said Burton. 'Have a look if you like.'

Pitt swung the case around to face him and flipped the catches. 'What's in the bags?'

Riego looked at the blue bags and raised his eyebrows as he glanced at Burton. 'Diamonds, right?'

'Diamonds,' confirmed Burton.

Wyatt whistled and leaned forward. 'Are we going halves then, Taffy; early retirement?'

'No you're not.' The voice from the door was familiar. Delaney walked in and stood in front of them all. 'We need to bring our plans forward; Stait's on his way to England.'

They all looked surprised at what he had said. 'How do you know?' asked Wyatt.

'I've just had a phone call from your mate Sergeant Brun. He said that Stait left the marina in Terneuzen an hour ago, heading west towards the English Channel.'

'Why on earth don't they just arrest him, if they know where he is?' asked Pitt.

'Not sure, apparently Hubert told Brun to wait until later to tell us but Brun phoned anyway.'

'How did they suddenly discover where he was then?' asked Burton, frowning. 'The last time we dealt with Hubert, he didn't have a clue where Stait was.'

'Not sure, Taffy; I wondered that myself. Anyway; Stait's on his way here, so you need to meet him sooner than we anticipated.' Delaney looked down at the briefcase. 'I see you have the diamonds; what about the handsets?'

'They're here.'

'Handsets for what?' asked Greaves.

Delaney made sure they were all listening as he explained. 'Taffy has had a micro fitted. The only things on the same frequency are these handsets.'

'What's a *micro*?' said Pitt.

Riego jumped in. 'A transmitter and receiver; placed in the ear. You can hear, and speak and be heard; right, Taffy?'

'Right; the handsets are pre-set. You don't need to fiddle with them. The technical lady who fitted the micro said it was good for up to a mile.'

'As soon as we know where Stait's heading,' continued Delaney, 'we'll get you there, Taffy. I'll be with you, so will Michael and Ajit.' He turned to Wyatt. 'Ben; I want you to visit Hawkwell at the prison. Take Julie with you and find out what you can. We can get a...'

'Hey, wait a minute,' said Greaves. 'Don't we get a choice or a say in this?'

'No you don't. If we get this wrong, the people at the top will come to *me*. That's why you have to afford *me* the decision making.'

Riego sat up. 'Yeah, sure but we should be able to...'

'That'll do, thank you,' said Delaney as his gaze switched between Riego and Greaves. 'You have both been told that until further notice, you report to me. You need to do as I ask and work with us or you'll both be on the next flight back to Washington. Your choice.'

Riego got the message. 'Okay, okay; you're the boss.'

Greaves said nothing and turned away from Delaney's gaze.

'Good,' said Delaney, 'thank you.'

Burton cleverly changed the subject. 'So I suppose there's not much we can do until we find out where Stait is heading then, sir?'

'No, not really; the coast guard can track where he is, as long as he stays in the Channel. Presumably he's heading for somewhere on the south coast.'

'Could be northern France, sir,' said Pitt.

'Possibly, Ajit, but we can get there as well if we need to.'

Wyatt stood up, sniffed and clapped his hands together. 'Well, Julie, if the boss wants to visit Hawkwell; we may as well do it now. Err, if that's okay with you.' Only Burton noticed Wyatt's sarcasm.

'Why not,' said Greaves. 'I'd quite like to see the look on his face when I tell him who I really am and that Sondheim is dead.'

'Good, let's go then.' He turned to the others. 'Good luck, guys.'

'You too, Ben; don't lose your temper with him will you?' said Burton.

Wyatt smiled as he followed Greaves out of the room who did not acknowledge anyone.

The Longworth High Security Prison had only been open for two years. It was surrounded by open fields in the middle of Wiltshire. The landscape and roads had been designed from scratch; guards had a clear field of view that stretched for half a mile on all sides. It was approaching 4 p.m. when Wyatt and Greaves pulled up outside the main gate. Wyatt had phoned ahead and they were fast-tracked through the security procedures.

They were led through to an interview room adjacent to the medical centre. Hawkwell was wearing handcuffs, sitting on a bright aluminium chair in front of an oval wooden table. His face had been stitched in a few places to mend the damage done by Riego and his shotgun. He sat up with a proud straight back; his muscular hands on the table. His demeanour seemed intelligent and strong; the short cut brown hair was greying slightly at the sides and his piercing dark eyes glanced at Wyatt only momentarily, because he did not know him, and his eyes were soon fixed on Greaves.

'Michelle? What the hell is all this.'

Greaves did not answer; she sat down in front of the table, facing him. Wyatt walked around the table and looked at him. 'Is that as painful as it looks?' he asked, pointing to the stitches on Hawkwell's face.

'I'll get over it,' said Hawkwell. Wyatt sat down to the side of table.

'Do you want me to do the introductions?' asked Wyatt, looking at Greaves.

'Mm, why not.'

'My name is Wyatt, Mr Hawkwell; I work for the government, in a round about sort of way. Security and crime and all that.' He gestured to Greaves. 'This is...'

'This is Michelle Depout,' said Hawkwell. What the hell is happening?'

'No,' continued Wyatt. 'This is Julie Greaves; Julie works for the CIA.'

Hawkwell nodded slowly, hesitated and stood up. 'Sit down please,' said Wyatt.

'Sure,' said Hawkwell, 'in a second.' He leaned forward across the table and spat into Greaves face. She wiped her sleeve across her face and then drew a tissue from a pocket to clean herself properly. Hawkwell sat down and stared at her. 'You bitch. You're a dead woman. Wait until Micky finds out about this one.'

'Micky Sondheim is dead, Frank,' she said.

After another hesitation, Hawkwell sighed and crossed his arms. 'When and where?'

'Monte Carlo; an accident. He fell from a hotel balcony.'

'Were you with him?'

'No, I was taking a shower when it happened.'

'Right, well; keep looking over your shoulder, because when I get out of here, you're the first one I'm coming for.'

'You won't be getting out of here,' said Wyatt. 'We'll be charging you for murdering Ellie Shanks at least; maybe a few more too.'

'Who's Ellie Shanks?' asked Hawkwell.

Wyatt huffed and spoke quietly. 'The woman you stabbed in Antwerp. What a man; kills a woman by stabbing her in the back, and can't even look at her when he does it.'

Hawkwell's expression changed to one of indifference.

'Now,' said Wyatt. 'What can you tell us about Aaron Stait?'

Hawkwell remained quiet. 'Come on,' continued Wyatt, 'you're in here for a while; giving us information could be worthwhile to you.'

Still nothing from Hawkwell. 'Okay, try this,' said Greaves. 'If you're not going to speak and remain silent from now on, nod your head.'

Hawkwell nodded his head slowly and smiled at her. She got up to leave. Come on, Ben; he's not going to say anything. Let him rot in here.'

Wyatt stood up and went around the corner of the table to where Hawkwell was sitting. 'I think you're right, Julie, we're wasting our time.' Then he looked at Hawkwell. 'On the way out, Frank, I'll get the medic to come back in with the guard.'

Hawkwell glanced at him. 'What for?'

Wyatt's right fist came round fast and landed on the side of Hawkwell's face. The force was enough to knock him off his chair. Wyatt spoke again on his way out. 'To stitch your face up again.'

As they made their way out, the prison officer stood by the door and looked into the room. 'What is it with you people?' he said. 'Don't tell me; he tripped and fell over, right?'

Wyatt stared back at the officer. 'No, funny bastard; I hit him.'

On the drive back to London, Greaves was thinking about Wyatt as he drove without saying anything. Looks like this guy next to me could be good to work with, she thought.

30

It was 7 p.m. in Antwerp and Sergeant Brun was just about to leave his office when the phone rang. He recognised the voice immediately. 'Mr Delaney; good to hear from you.'

'How are you sergeant?'

'Fine, yes thank you; and how are Ben and Ajit?'

'They're doing well thanks. Is Inspector Hubert with you?'

'Yes, he will be back shortly if you would like to wait.'

'Please; by the way, I understand it was you two who found Stait's motor yacht.'

'Not both of us, just the Inspector. He said he had a tip-off from someone, but I didn't get to know the details.'

There was a pause before Delaney spoke again. 'Right, and then you both went to stake it out.'

'No, no, Inspector Hubert was already there; he phoned me later to ask me to join him.'

'I see. Well, a good result eh?'

'Indeed, here is the Inspector now.'

Inspector Hubert entered the room and Brun passed his phone to him as he explained who it was. 'Ah good,' said Hubert, 'I have news for him. Hello Mr Delaney.'

'Hello, Inspector, I was just saying what a good result it was; you finding Stait's boat.'

'Yes. However, firstly let me tell you that we are sending a plane to pick up Chief Inspector Baart's body tomorrow. Can you make sure any of his belongings are sorted out please?'

'Of course, I'll get someone onto it straight away.'

'Thank you. Now, presumably you are phoning to see what information we have about Stait's boat.'

'Yes, I am.'

Brun passed Hubert a sheet of paper. 'I have the details here, Mr Delaney. It is a 50ft motor yacht called the *Adinerado* not very old, colour, white; as most of them are. It has a high level fly bridge and a swim platform at the rear.'

'Great, thank you,' said Delaney.

'Have you heard from your coastguard yet?' asked Hubert.

'No, but I'm confident we will; they're very good at such things.'

'As are ours, Mr Delaney; having that narrow strip of sea between our two countries is an advantage, I think. As soon as the vessel leaves our radar area, it enters yours.'

'Mm, well I won't keep you, Inspector, and thank you.'

'Not at all; let me know how you get on.'

Brun looked at Hubert as he put the phone down. 'They have not heard of the boats whereabouts yet then, sir?'

'No, but I'll bet they're well prepared for it when they do.'

Angela was watching television when Delaney got home a couple of hours later. 'What's on?' he asked.

'Nothing much; unless you want to know about the history of Russian Tsars or houses that people are buying in France.'

'No, not really.' He leaned over and kissed her. 'You smell nice.'

'Thank you; it's a new one I bought today.'

'Have you eaten?'

'No, I thought I'd wait for you; fancy a pie? It's in the oven.'

'Sure; and a glass of Merlot.'

Angela turned off the television and went to the kitchen. Delaney joined her and set the table as she was serving up the food. They sat and discussed their daily work duties as usual, and again, Angela got the feeling that something was about to happen. She knew him very well now; he never seemed to relax fully when something troublesome was just around the corner. She was right. He explained to her what was about to happen and that he was expecting a phone call at any time that evening from the coastguard.

A few hours later, Delaney was the first to feel tired. 'Right, I'm off to bed.'

'I won't be far behind you,' said Angela.

Delaney undressed and sat on the bed rubbing his hands over his face and eyes. He knew he would not sleep much, knowing a call could come through at any moment. A few minutes later, he was still sitting on the edge of the bed, thinking, when Angela joined him. She undressed, sat beside him and put her arm around his wide shoulders. 'I do like that new perfume,' he said.

'Good, because I think about you when I buy things like that.'

Delaney looked down at his groin. 'I got a twinge then.'

'So did I, anyway lets get some slee...'

'Shut up,' he said as he pushed her gently backwards and kissed her breasts. Within seconds they were enjoying each other and it was not long before they lay back, exhausted, and went to sleep.

As if by telepathy, Delaney awoke to look at his bedside clock, just before his phone rang. It was 4 a.m. 'Hello.'

'Mr Delaney?'

'Yes.'

'Devon Coastguard here, sir. I was told to phone you when we had definite information about the motor yacht *Adinerado*.'

'Yes, thank you, what have you got?'

As he was on the phone, Angela woke up and climbed out of bed. She had to be at work early anyway, so she went downstairs to make tea. The Coastguard Pilot told Delaney what had happened over the last hour and how to get to the right location. Twenty minutes later he was kissing Angela, as she sat in her dressing gown caressing her mug of tea. 'Got to go, now; see you later.'

As soon as he was on the road, he phoned Burton. 'Taffy, its Salcombe, Devon. Phone Ajit will you and tell him to pick up Riego and head down that way. I'll pick you up in about 40 minutes. Tell Ajit I'll phone him in a couple of hours.'

The *Adinerado* was moored up at the end of the last jetty near the Salcombe lifeboat station. It was much larger than any of the craft around it and Stait had decided to chance the conspicuousness; he would only be there for a few hours. Delaney and Burton were sitting in their car looking at it from a cafe car park that overlooked the harbour and marina. Pitt had parked up at the side of them and he and Riego had taken the back seat behind them. As Burton looked through the binoculars, Riego leaned forward. 'See anything?'

'No, probably too early; he may not surface 'til later if he was late getting here last night.'

'He was,' said Delaney, 'it was about three this morning when he got here.'

Pitt seemed anxious. 'Do you want me to get closer, sir?'

'No, I bloody don't. Did you make that call to the coastguard that I told you make on your way here?'

'Yes, I did. They confirmed that Stait is on the radio and is acknowledging as a Mr Howe.'

'Right; get back in your car, Ajit, drive to the coastguard station and ask them to say that a Mr Padley will be boarding the yacht in an hour's time to inspect the charts and safety equipment. Nothing to worry about; just a routine visit for new craft arriving in Salcombe.'

Pitt put his thumb in the air and made his way without further questions. Delaney looked at Burton. 'Okay with that, Taffy?'

'Yeah, that's fine; it'll get me in.'

Riego looked at them both in turn. 'So, err, you're going to tell me what's going to happen, right?'

'You have one of the handsets, Michael,' said Delaney. 'I'll let you listen to Taffy do his stuff. When you've heard him, you'll want to send in an Oscar nomination.'

When Riego had finished shaking his head, Burton confirmed the communications. 'Right; I'll sniff once if everything is okay. If I start to cough a lot, you come in.'

'Sounds good to me, Taffy. We'll get as close as we can. Take this car, so Stait or anyone else will see you arriving alone.'

Burton arrived at the marina an hour later. All of the moorings were occupied; a few people were working on their yachts or speed boats, but it was generally quiet with very little sign of any of the vessels being occupied permanently.

Stait's motor yacht was on the end of the last jetty, two hundred metres from the harbour entrance. The 50ft craft was brilliant white all over and the name, ADINERADO, was displayed on the bow in a flowing blue style to match the design of the yacht's windows.

Stait was sitting just inside the rear of the yacht under the canopy looking towards the gangway as Burton approached. 'Mr Padley, I presume,' he said as he stood up and emptied half a cup of coffee over the side.

'Correct,' said Burton. 'Are you alone?'

'I am; come aboard.'

'I thought under the circumstances, you would have some men with you.'

'What circumstances; I was told it was just a routine check,' said Stait, with a worried voice.

'It's not a routine visit Mr Howe; or can I call you Mr Stait now I'm on board?'

'I see,' said Stait. 'You are not the Coastguard.'

'No, but don't worry, I'm on your side. Now, you do have someone watching me I take it.'

'I have,' said Stait, 'they're watching from a distance.'

Burton made sure to repeat what Stait had said, so Delaney and Riego could hear it. 'Watching from a distance? You mean they're somewhere out there with a rifle trained on me.'

'That's exactly what I mean, Mr Padley. Now; I can offer you coffee, wine, champagne or Belgian beer.'

'A beer would be nice, thank you.'

Stait gestured towards a dark wood oval table with a cushioned bench seat around it. Burton sat down, facing the gangway with his briefcase next to him. Stait took the top off a bottle, handed it to Burton and sat down opposite him.

'Well, Mr Padley, you have five minutes. Then you will be leaving this vessel; dead or alive.'

'I understand,' said Burton. 'I realise that I'm dealing with a professional; as long as you realise it too. My people have been watching you, Mr Stait and I know what makes you tick. I'm not interested in drugs from Colombia, by the way. My mate, Micky Sondhiem, told me all about that. I'm interested in selling something else to you.' He flicked the catches on the briefcase and turned it around to face Stait. 'Help yourself, have a look.'

Stait opened the case slowly. As soon as he saw the blue bags, he knew what would be in them. Burton waited until Stait had opened one of the bags. 'And before you ask, they're all S12, GIA graded, about four million dollars worth. You can have them for two.'

Stait emptied one of the bags onto the table and closed the case. He sat back and reached for his beer. 'Let's just wait a minute, Mr Padley. Before we go any further let me establish a few things.'

'Go ahead.'

'How do you know about me?'

'Micky Sondhiem. At one point, he nearly hired me to kill you.'

Stait did not look as impressed as Burton hoped he would. Stait continued. 'And how did you know I was here?'

'A certain Belgian policeman I have on my payroll and our beloved Coastguard. One of their senior people has a nice big house in Florida, thanks to me.'

There was a pause for a moment. Burton heard a voice in his ear. 'All okay, Taffy?' He sniffed once.

'Mm, and finally,' said Stait. 'Why don't I just tell my man out there to shoot you now and take the briefcase with me when I leave here in an hour's time?'

Burton paused, took a drink of his beer and then leaned forward to stare at Stait. 'Two reasons; you're probably as greedy as me and there's lots more where this came from, and if your man kills me now, my man kills you. You don't seriously think that I would come to you without cover.'

Stait looked around him and into the distance. Burton could see the doubt on his face.

'Alright, Mr Padley; but before I give you two million, I want to know where you work from. Next time, I will come to you.'

'That's fine, I'll write down my details for you.'

'Good, and while you do that, I will take one these rocks below and test it.'

Again, Burton heard a voice. 'Taffy, tell me.' He sniffed once, as he took out a piece of paper from his pocket and wrote down; *Padley Aggregates, Horseman Quarry, Nanpath, Surrey.*

Delaney's voice came again. 'What's that you're writing down? A number?' Burton shook his head. 'An address?' Burton nodded.

A few more minutes passed and Stait came back up from the lower cabin. 'They are good, Mr Padley. But I am not paying you today. Take them away with you; I will arrange for collection and payment. Do you have your address?'

Burton passed him the piece of paper. 'Yes, there we are, and that's fine by me, but I want them collected within one week.'

'That can be arranged. But please, before you go, I want some identification; something that I can photocopy, and I also want you to take off your shirt.'

'You can have my driver's licence, but nothing else.'

'Very well.'

Burton took his driver's licence from his jacket pocket and handed it to Stait. He took off his jacket and then his shirt and turned around so Stait could see all of his upper body. 'A few years ago,' said Burton, 'I would have dropped my trousers for you as well; but not now. Get my licence copied and I'll leave, before you start to annoy me.'

Stait looked impressed. He left Burton to put his shirt back on and went below again. A few minutes later, he re-emerged and handed Burton's licence back to him. 'Thank you, Mr Padley, goodbye.'

Delaney wound down his window as Burton parked at the side of them. 'Good work, Taffy; could you hear me alright?'

'Yes, clear enough.'

Riego scratched his chin. 'Mm, too easy.'

'Possibly,' said Delaney. 'But we'll know for sure when he collects the goods.'

'If he *does* collect the goods,' said Burton. 'I'll need to be at the quarry from now on; I hope it's still kitted out.'

'It is; and Ajit can be with you,' said Delaney. Pitt looked up and acknowledged but looked at Delaney with raised eyebrows. 'The quarry?'

Burton explained. 'It's an old abandoned quarry in Surrey; hasn't been used for years. We've done a couple of meetings there and carried out a few stings there as well. It's kitted out with food and drink, comms, a few guns and some transport.' He looked at

Delaney briefly and then back again at Pitt. 'I think you'll like the transport.'

'Right; you'd better get there then, Taffy; Stait will probably start checking things out straight away.' He looked at Pitt. 'Stay close to him, Ajit, and do exactly as he tells you.'

'I still say it's too easy,' said Riego. 'Something's not right; a man like Stait wouldn't expose himself so easily like this.'

'Maybe,' said Burton. 'By the way, someone was out there with a gun on me, so I think Stait will have company with him soon; probably at least two men I'd say.'

'He won't stay here too long either,' replied Riego, 'A few hours maximum.'

Delaney nodded as he looked down again towards the jetty. 'I agree, which is why I want you to stay here and watch him. Let me know when he leaves.'

'Sure; I'll watch him. Can I keep this car?'

'Yes, I'll go with Taffy and Ajit to the quarry and then take the other car back to London.'

Riego settled down in the car to watch over the harbour area and the jetty as the other three men drove off in the direction of Surrey.

Aaron Stait looked out from his motor yacht as he took his phone from his pocket. 'Is that you, Freddie?'

'Yes, it is; can we come down now?'

'Yes you can; both of you. Did you see anyone else up there?'

'No, I think he was alone.'

'Right, well get down here then and I'll tell you what happens next; I'm heading for somewhere else in a couple of days; you're staying here, I've got a job for you.' He finished the call and dialled another number. 'Good morning, James; it's Aaron Stait.'

'Aaron; long time no speak, how are you?'

'Not too bad thank you. Are you still working?'

'Of course I am; for the usual fee. How can I help?'

'Do you remember Frank Hawkwell?'

'Of course I do; is he still working for you?'

'Err; well he will be, after you've got him out of jail for me.'

'How the hell did Frank end up in jail?'

'It's a long story. Have you still got Louis and Rick working for you?'

'Mm, where's Frank being held then?'

'Longworth.'

'The new place in Wiltshire; I know it. High security. I'll have to use a hostage or something like that, but I'll sort it. Give me a few days.'

'Sure; and I want you to get him to Belgium.'

'Not a problem, Aaron; usual payment?'

'Yes; one million.'

As Stait was finishing the call, Freddie Ludic and Tommy were climbing onto the swim platform of the yacht. Ludic asked where the beers were. 'You haven't got time for beers, just leave the money with me, get changed and freshened up and be ready to leave in an hour.'

'What's happening now?' asked Ludic.

'I want you to watch a quarry for a couple of days; then I'll be joining you.'

'Wow, how exciting,' said Tommy. Stait was close to him and he lifted his hand and slapped him on the face hard. 'Get funny with me, boy and I'll kill you where you stand,' said Stait as he turned to look at Ludic. 'Come and see me when you're ready Freddie; I'll give you the details of where to go.'

Ludic nodded quickly and he and Tommy went below to get changed. After a few minutes, Ludic shouted up to Stait. 'Any news on Frank, by the way?'

'Yes; with any luck he'll be back with us soon.'

31

It had been almost a year since Delaney and Burton had seen the Horseman Quarry. Most of the wild vegetation had grown another few feet and the cabins still looked suitably abandoned. As Delaney drove slowly down the narrow access road, Pitt leaned forward from the back seat. 'A normal looking quarry then, sir; not much security.'

'That's the idea, Ajit; it's supposed to look like a *normal* quarry. You'll see why we use it though, when we get inside.' Delaney pointed to the group of wooden buildings and portable cabins up ahead. 'I'll drop you two off and then get back to the office; I need to keep Lady Stonehaven informed. Taffy will show you around.'

'Right, sir.'

The narrow road was the only road in and out of the quarry. To the left, the right and straight ahead, the quarry walls were vertical and almost 700 feet high. The horizontal layers of rock and sandstone were interspersed with weeds and bushes growing out of the cracks. There were five buildings; two wooden huts in the centre of the quarry, that looked like they may have been rest rooms or canteens, two portable cabins about 40 feet away with wired windows and doors and a large sheet tin shed set back behind the cabins, probably used for the quarry vehicles and maintenance. As they approached the cabins, Burton pointed towards one of the front doors. 'See that?' he said.

Delaney pulled up about forty feet from the cabin. 'I see it, Taffy; I can't see any vehicles though.'

'What is it?' asked Pitt.

'That door,' said Burton, 'it's open; the wire mesh and security catch have been taken off.'

218

'Interesting,' said Delaney. 'Ajit; go to the left, just walk nice and slow. Taffy; to the right. Probably just a tramp or kids; I'll go to the door.'

The aluminium door was half open and Delaney pushed it slowly. He recognised the perfume straight away. A woman was sitting in one of the four chairs around the old Formica topped table. It was Shirley Stonehaven. Delaney smiled politely and looked around the room. 'I see you're wearing that nice perfume again. Are you alone?'

'Hello, Tom. No, I'm not alone. My driver is with the car out the back.'

'How did you know I was coming here?'

'Riego phoned me.'

'Ah, right. So; how can I help?' It surprised him that Stonehaven did not start voicing her displeasure again at him not keeping in touch. She sat quietly and nodded towards the door. Burton walked in with Stonehaven's driver, followed by Pitt.

'We met up out the back, sir,' said Burton. 'Everything's fine.'

'Good, give me a minute will you, lads. Wait outside for a while.'

They turned to leave and Stonehaven pointed a finger to the door as a signal for her driver to go with them. Delaney walked around checking things and looked into the fridge. 'I see our logistics people are still doing a great job; food, drink, fresh towels. They make it easier for us sometimes.'

'They've always kept this place and a few others well stocked,' said Stonehaven. 'They get told to check regularly.'

'I wonder if they've checked over the transport as well.'

'They have.'

'Good. Did Riego tell you about Taffy's meeting with Stait?'

'Yes, he brought me up to speed. I just wanted to see that everything here was okay; this is a big risk you're taking, Tom.'

'So what else is new? We'll be alright; Taffy knows what he's doing and they'll be four of us as a back-up.'

'Yes, I was forgetting about Ben and Julie Greaves. Where are they?'

'Probably back in London now; they went to see Hawkwell, but I doubt if they got anything out of him or I would have heard by now.'

Stonehaven stood up to leave and Delaney looked at her enquiringly. 'What, no reprimand for not keeping in touch and telling you about this?'

'What's the point, Tom? And besides, I'm fed up of asking. Like I said, I just wanted to see that everything was okay.' She put a hand on his arm as she walked slowly past him. 'Be careful won't you? Stait and some of his international cronies are pretty bad people.'

'Of course we'll be careful, and er, thanks for seeing that things are okay.'

'Not at all, Tom. I'm off to Belgium tomorrow by the way, so I'll catch up with you in a few days for a progress report.'

'Of course, take care.' Delaney sat down. He could hear the sound of Stonehaven's car being started up and driven away. Yet again, she had left him wondering. If Riego had phoned her from Salcombe, she must have come straight to the quarry. She must have stopped what she was doing and told her driver to get her here now. And was it a coincidence she was going to Belgium, or was she going to see Inspector Hubert? He looked out the window to see Burton and Pitt walking towards the shed where the transport was kept. He opened the fridge again and poured himself a lemonade.

Pitt was keeping close to Burton as they approached the large shed. 'So, do those logistics people look after everything then; including the vehicles?' he asked.

'Pretty much, yes. Like I said to you earlier; you'll like the transport we have here.'

Pitt had wondered why they had referred to it as *transport* rather than *vehicles*. As Burton opened the two sliding doors he began to realise why. There were four 'vehicles' under large brown dust covers. Yesterday's date had been written on the covers in felt-tipped pen to show when they were last serviced and checked. Pitt stood back as Burton went to the first cover and pulled it backwards slowly until it rested at the back of the vehicle. 'Audi R8 pursuit vehicle; full roll cage and twice the normal capacity fuel tanks.'

There was another car next to it; much larger. Burton pulled the cover off. 'Lexus RS 450; with special rough terrain tyres and suspension.'

'Crikey,' said Pitt. 'It's just as well they haven't capped our budget this year.' Then he looked at the other two dust covers as Burton walked over to them. The shapes below the covers were much smaller than the other two.

'I'll just take off one cover,' said Burton, 'they're both the same. I'll need to give you a quick lesson.' He was very careful to remove the cover slowly, so as not to snag it on any of the protruding parts. 'Kawasaki ZZR 1400; both with radio intercom helmets and luggage panniers removed to make way for the rifle racks.'

'And both with the RAM air engines,' said Pitt, 'four stroke and digital ignition.'

Burton's gaze left the motorcycle as he raised his eyebrows at Pitt. 'Do you know about these things then?'

'I know about this one, yes; they don't come much better. I've done a bit of club racing.'

'Right, so you probably won't need that lesson then.'

'Probably not, can I take it for a test?'

'No, not yet. Come on; we'll let the boss know that you can ride before he leaves for London. Oh and over there,' Burton pointed to a metal cupboard. 'There's four 9mm Brownings and two HK rifles.'

221

Delaney was sitting at the desk finishing his lemonade when they walked back into the cabin. He noticed the pleased look on Pitt's face. 'So, has Taffy shown you our transport?'

'Yes, sir.'

'And he can ride,' said Burton. 'Used to do a bit of racing or something.'

'Really,' said Delaney, looking at Pitt. 'Right, I'll remember that. Okay I'm off back to London to see how Ben and Julie got on.' He looked at Burton. 'I doubt if anything will happen for a couple of days, Taffy; I'll probably be back with Ben in a couple of days. Keep in touch, yeah?'

'Will do; we'll be fine.'

As Delaney reached the main road, he reached down and pressed a short dial number on his phone. Riego answered straight away. 'Hi there.'

'Any movement, Michael?'

'He's still on the yacht; but two men joined him about two hours ago.'

'Right, keep in touch please.'

'Of course; are Taffy and the kid at the quarry?'

'Yes, speak to you later maybe.'

Two men have joined Stait then, thought Delaney; must be Ludic and the young Tommy. 'What happens now then, eh, Mr Stait?' he said to himself.

32

Maggie Timms was the first out of bed again. The Timms household was a happy place and now the children were getting older, she found it easier to let them help themselves at the breakfast table.

Jason Timms worked as a Prison Officer at Longworth Prison in Wiltshire. He had been there for a number of years after being transferred from Manchester. Now, as part of the supervisory staff, things had gotten a little easier and the early morning shifts were behind him.

'Making you lazy, all these late starts are,' said Maggie. 'I wish you were on the early shifts again, at least I'd get my tea in bed.'

Jason smiled as he pulled on his coat and kissed her on the cheek. 'Nonsense,' he said, 'you love getting up early anyway, you know you do.'

A voice came from the hallway. 'No she doesn't, neither do I; getting up early is for daft people.' It was Janie, their 12 year old daughter. She ambled into the kitchen, school tie not tied properly, and flopped herself down in front of the plate of toast.

'And leave some toast for your little brother today,' said Maggie.

'You see,' said Janie. 'Little brother knows better; he doesn't get up early.'

Maggie looked at Jason. 'Now see what you've started.

Janie's ten year old brother, Jack, came into the kitchen, took a slice of toast from the plate and went into the living room to sit in front of the television. 'Make me some more toast, Mum, I'll hav...'

'You'll have nothing young man, without a please or thank you.'

'Go on; do him a bit more,' said Jason, 'he's a growing lad aren't you mate.'

'He eats too much anyway,' said Janie.

'Whatever; I'll let you discuss it; see you later,' said Jason as he closed the door. He checked his watch once he was in the car; perfect timing as usual. Seven minutes to the shop for his newspaper and chocolate bar, twelve minutes to the prison and ten minutes to get changed and sign in for duty.

James and Louis were waiting for Jason Timms to arrive at the shop. They had watched him for three days and like many commuters, his trip to work was regimental; never altering.

As Jason pulled up outside the shop, they drove slowly forward and parked behind him. They watched as he got from his car and went into the shop. They had stolen many a car, this way; thousands of people every morning left their cars unlocked as they 'nipped in' for a newspaper.

Louis stayed in his driver's seat as James quickly left the vehicle and walked to Jason's car. He opened the back door and laid flat behind the driver's seat as low as he could. A minute later, Jason was getting back into his car. He reached for his seatbelt and clipped it in place.

James rose slowly, grabbed Jason's hair with his right hand and pushed the barrel of a revolver into his cheek with his left hand. 'You will do exactly as I tell you, Mr Timms; do you understand?'

Jason moved slightly. 'I have to ge...'

'Do you understand?'

'Yes.'

'Very well, drive on. I have a friend who is following us. I will tell you to stop somewhere in a few minutes.'

They made their way to a main road, Louis following closely behind. After about two miles, James told Jason to pull into a farm entrance and park up. Louis pulled up behind and came over to them. 'No problems,' said Louis 'He's at the house and has his phone on; he's sending the pictures now.'

James took the phone from Louis and put it in front of Jason's face. 'Watch, Mr Timms.' A video was showing on the telephone. The sender was scanning his phone camera around the living room at the Timms house. Maggie was sitting on the sofa next to Janie. Thick tape was covering their mouths and their hands appeared to be tied behind them. Janie was sobbing and leaning against her mother, who had blood coming from her nose. In the chair next to them, Jack was also gagged with tape. His hands were taped together in front of him. He was staring at the phone being scanned around the room, his face ashen with fright.

James pushed the barrel of the revolver harder into Jason's cheek. Now Mr Timms, as you can see, your wife and children have been hurt a little bit. If you don't want any more harm to come to them, you will do what I tell you to do. If you want to see them dead, you just ignore what I tell you. Do you understand?'

'If you...'

'No, Mr Timms; I said, do you understand?'

'Yes, I understand.'

'Good, now, me and my colleague here are going to go to the prison with you; I'll give you your instructions on the way. Meanwhile, that man back at your home is going to wait for a phone call from me. If you do well, he will leave without harming them further. If you *do* choose to ignore me, he'll kill them. And he will, Mr Timms, he's done it before.'

'Alright, alright, I'll do as you say,' said Jason. James moved the phone away from Jason's face and handed it back to Louis. 'Good, now Louis here is going to follow us to the prison and he'll be checking in with me every couple of minutes. When I inform him that you've done what I ask, he'll let our man at your house know and your wife and kids will be left alone. So, drive down the road and towards the main gate and I'll tell you what to do when we get closer.'

Ben Wyatt and Julie Greaves had been looking through some information held by TOLA for a couple days and had spoken to some informants that Wyatt knew. They came up with very little that could help; two informants had given false information, one had said he needed more time, and some documents and records they had looked at did not really tell them anything new.

Delaney had spent some time at home, keeping in touch with Burton at the quarry and writing up reports and invoices for Shirley Stonehaven. When he got to his office, there was a few days worth of reports to look at and an in-tray that was high enough.

It was early afternoon and Wyatt and Greaves were just coming back from lunch.

'How did you get on with Mr Hawkwell?' asked Delaney.

'Not very well at all,' said Wyatt. 'You could be getting a call from the prison governor, sir.'

Delaney looked at both them. 'Go on.' Greaves sat down, crossed her legs and folded her arms. 'He hit Hawkwell; knocked him to the ground,' she said. 'But hey, if he hadn't, I might have done.'

'Right, well if there's a complaint, we'll deal with it,' said Delaney, looking at Wyatt. 'I take it you got nothing from him.'

'Nothing,' said Wyatt. 'He had no idea about Julie's cover as Michelle Depout and he denied any knowledge of Ellie Shanks; after that he said nothing.'

'Except that he was going to kill me,' said Greaves.

'He'll be lucky, Julie,' said Wyatt, 'he's not going anywhere for a while.'

226

Delaney sighed as he continued going through his in-tray. 'Okay; time to concentrate on Stait then. Taffy and Ajit are still at the quarry; no news yet. If I haven't heard anything by tomorrow, we'll drive down to see them. You can take over from Ajit, Ben. Michael is watching Stait on his yacht, so if he leaves it, we should hear from him.'

Wyatt and Greaves explained what little they had found out and Delaney briefed them fully on the diamond story and about Burton's Oscar winning performance. Greaves seemed concerned for Riego; 'But Michael's working on his own right now and everyone else has a partner; is that right?'

'It'll have to be,' said Delaney. 'Michael will be back with us soon, I'm sure of it. I'm not expecting Stait to stay here much longer; that's why I'm hoping he'll make his way to the quarry soon, to buy the diamonds.'

Greaves said, 'okay, I hope you're right,' as she turned to look at some documents on a desk. Wyatt made coffee and helped out with Delaney's in-tray.

Jason Timms stopped just short of the prison gates as James had instructed. James got out of the car and leaned down to Timms' window. 'So you know what to do; any questions?' Timms shook his head. 'Good,' continued James, 'Get on with it then; the sooner you start, the sooner you'll be back with your family.' He made his way over to the other side of the road and got into the car that Louis had driven behind them.

Timms parked his car in his usual spot and signed in for duty. He had ten officers that reported to him and two of those were trained for special escort duties. One of them, Jack Ridd, was eating his breakfast as Timms entered the staff canteen. 'Don't eat too much, Jack; I've got a special job for you today.'

'Bloody hell, not again.'

'Yes, again; special escort to London.'

'Who?'

'That Hawkwell bloke, that came in a few days ago. I've just been to see the Governor; he asked me to get to him to London by midday, using the low profile method.'

Ridd took a mouthful of tea and stood. 'Right then, I'll get a car; I'll drive.'

'Fine; I take it that means you're going to get the bullet proof Audi before anyone else signs it out.'

'That's exactly what I mean. You know they'll have to be three of us don't you, if it's high risk, low profile.'

'Not on this occasion; the Governor said just you and me; I'll get the prisoner and see you in the pick-up bay.'

Ridd hesitated for a moment as though he was about to challenge what had been said, but carried on towards the door and the pool car office. Timms made his way to A wing and his peer, Al Coates, led him to Hawkwell's cell. 'How come you got this job, Jason? I thought the police would come for this one; he's a nasty piece of work.'

'Exactly; that's what the Governor said, and that anyone looking to spring him would be looking for a police escort.'

'Good thinking, I suppose; he's here in cell three.' Coates opened the door and went into the cell followed by Timms. 'This is Senior Officer Timms, Hawkwell; he's taking you out for a few hours.'

'What for?' asked Hawkwell.

'Just a quick visit to a law court and then back again,' said Timms. 'They still haven't decided whether or not you're going to stay in here 'til you die.'

Hawkwell did not respond. He stood up and looked at Timms as he held his hands out in front of him in readiness for the handcuffs. As Timms looked into his eyes, he thought about his wife and children back at the house. Hundreds of ideas seemed to flash across his mind as he thought of any possible way out of this. But there was not a way out of it. All he could would be to get Hawkwell out and then make sure that the third man had left his home before raising the alarm. At least then, he would be able to tell his people where he left Hawkwell and in which direction he fled.

Coates led the way out of the cell followed by Hawkwell and then Timms. They got to the wing exit gate and Coates handed over the handcuff keys. 'There we are Jason, be careful.' Then Coates looked at Hawkwell. 'And you, Hawkwell; behave yourself. Remember you're coming back to me and I don't like people like you, especially if they misbehave.' Hawkwell almost smiled. 'Yes, sir.'

Jack Ridd was waiting with the Audi in the pick-up bay. When he saw the two men approach, he opened the back door and Hawkwell and Timms occupied the back seat. Timms took Hawkwell's hands and attached another short chain to the handcuffs. The chain was then attached to the built-in holding bar behind the driver's seat, meaning that Hawkwell would have to lean forward slightly for the duration of the trip. Ridd settled himself in the driver's seat and made his way to the side gate. Once the gate man had seen the papers that Timms handed to him – the papers that Timms had falsified – the gate was opened and Ridd made his way North. 'I'll go up to the M4 then; it shouldn't take us long on the motorway this time of day.'

Timms was sweating; he had to keep moving his hands so Hawkwell wouldn't notice them shaking. When he saw the landmark that he had been told to watch for, he leaned forward and tapped Ridd on the shoulder. 'Sorry mate, I forgot to visit the gents before we left, you're going to have to pull over for a second or I'll we'll stopping on the motorway.'

'Bloody hell, Jason; you should know better.'

'Sorry, Jack; just down here will do, near that old bus shelter.'

Ridd pulled into an old gravel car park. An old wooden bus shelter was set back in front of a high hedge. There was a farm track that made a gap in the hedge and some milk churns lay abandoned. As Timms got from the car, the experienced Ridd left the engine running and pulled out a gun from the compartment in front of him. Hawkwell sat perfectly still. A minute had gone when Ridd noticed a man walking towards the car from the rear. He was carrying a petrol can. He blew a couple of short blasts on the car horn as a warning for Timms and wound his window up. The man came up to the car and knocked on the window. He was holding his petrol can aloft in a gesture of need. Ridd looked around for signs of other people and when he could see no one else, he lowered his window. The man smiled. 'Sorry to trouble you, only, I ran out of petrol back there. If you're going in that direction it'll save me a lot of time if...'

'Sorry, forget it; I'm not allowed to take passengers,' said Ridd. The man looked down and saw the gun on Ridd's lap. As he turned slightly, he kept the petrol can between himself and Ridd.

Then his other hand came from behind him and Ridd saw the gun. 'You don't need to take passengers,' said the man. Before Ridd could react, the man shot him in the side of head; his body was thrown sideways onto the passenger seat and the man fired again, the bullet piercing Ridd's chest, then again, the bullet burying itself into Ridd's backside. Timms came running back through the gap in the hedge. 'No! You didn't need to kill him you bastard!'

James turned around and put the gun back in his belt. 'Shut your mouth and give me the keys.'

'Oh Jesus, you bastard! Why?'

'He had a gun; now give me the keys, Mr Timms.'

Timms reached into his pocket and undid the key chain from his belt. He tossed the keys to James. Without saying anything else, James opened the back door of the car and looked hard at the man in the back seat. 'Mr Hawkwell, I presume; come with me please.' He unlocked the handcuffs holding Hawkwell. Another car appeared and pulled up at the side of the Audi. James opened a rear door. 'In here please, Mr Hawkwell.'

'Who are you?' asked Hawkwell.

'Let's just say Mr Stait sent us.'

'Good enough for me.'

Hawkwell got in the car and moved over to allow James to sit next to him. Timms moved closer to the car and looked at James. 'My family; your man leaves my house now, as agreed.'

Hawkwell interrupted. 'What's this all about? Isn't he bent then?'

'No,' said James, 'we're holding his wife and kids.'

Hawkwell got out of the car and walked around to the Audi. He leaned through into the front window and grabbed Ridd's handgun. 'What are doing?' asked James.

'You don't leave people like this,' said Hawkwell. 'Able to talk about me, you, your car, descriptions. This man knows it all.' He walked close up to Timms who stood, frozen. 'Sorry, officer, at least your family will be okay.' He fired once into Timms stomach. The bullet passed through his body and gouged out a piece of his back as it exited the other side.

Hawkwell threw the gun back into the Audi and went back to sit with James. 'Get on with it then, driver; I'm not pissing about. Let's see what this car can do.'

James breathed out heavily. 'Well, Mr Hawkwell; I'm not sure you needed us to get you out. It looks like you've got the balls to have done it on your own.' Hawkwell did not respond. As he drove towards the motorway, Louis made a phone call. 'Rick, it's me; you can let them go and leave the house.'

'All okay then?' asked Rick.

'Er, yeah, sort off.'

Jason Timms was trying, in vain, to somehow hold the blood in his stomach. He was crawling towards the Audi using every last bit of life he had left in him. His intestines were starting to work their way out of his body as he inched along the ground. He yelled out in agony as he reached up and opened the passenger door. The radio-phone was underneath the passenger seat, now covered in Ridd's blood. He managed to grab it just as he fell away onto the ground again. Lying on his side, still clutching his stomach with one hand, he pressed the transmit button with the other and spoke as clearly as his tortured voice would allow. 'Timms, Jason Timms, Hawkwell gone, my family, check my family, Timms, Jason Timms, Ridd dead, Hawkwell...' He kept his finger on the button and kept talking for as long as he could, until his voice was no longer there and the last ounce of strength was spent.

33

It was raining at Antwerp International Airport, when Shirley Stonehaven's plane touched down. Inspector Hubert had arranged a car for her and had decided to ask Sergeant Brun to do the driving. As she settled in the car, she looked at Brun in the mirror. 'Sergeant Brun isn't it?'

'Yes, Ma'am.'

'You were with us in London for a while.'

'Yes, Ma'am.'

'I'm very sorry about the loss of Chief Inspector Baart.'

'So am I; I wish more people were.'

'Sorry?'

'What I mean to say is, his death has been forgotten about very quickly.'

'I see.' She decided not to ask questions. He was clearly not happy about Baart being forgotten. But forgotten by whom? She thought. Brun pulled up outside the Antwerp headquarters thirty minutes later and escorted Stonehaven to Hubert's office. When the introductions were out of the way, Hubert asked Brun to leave them. Stonehaven thought that Hubert looked nervous as she opened the conversation. 'Well, Inspector, you asked to see me, so I'll let you start.'

Hubert sipped at his frothy coffee and wiped his mouth. 'Have you heard of a man called James?'

'James who?'

'Just James; that's the only name he goes by.'

'In that case, no, I haven't.'

'He is based somewhere in Belgium; although, we don't know where. He specialises in doing tricky work for criminals; if anyone wants a difficult job doing, they go to him. They pay him extortionate amounts of money, but word is, he never fails. He works with two other men; they're called Louis and Rick. They never use a last name; ever.'

'And?'

'And one of our top undercover people, have had word from an informant that they left Belgium yesterday to go and do a job in England.'

'Right; and I suppose you're going to tell me it's linked to Stait et al.'

'I'm afraid so; we have good reason to believe that their paymaster this time, was indeed, Stait.'

Stonehaven knew this was good information, but it was information that he could have passed on by telephone or secure E-mail. 'If you don't mind me asking, Inspector; if you know so much about these men, why don't you apprehend them? And why not tell me this over the phone?'

'Because I was asked not to.'

'By whom?'

'Belgian Interpol, they left this package for you.' He handed her an envelope that was marked confidential. There was just one photograph in the envelope and a short letter. The photograph was a picture of Delaney; it was the same photograph that Commander Carnas had shown Antonio Compito in Colombia' before he knew Antonio Compito was a CIA operative. It showed Delaney sitting at a table with two other people, in a restaurant called Planalto. She studied the letter; it was from the office of the Belgian Minister for Foreign Affairs, but had been written on Interpol paper.

Dear Lady Stonehaven,

It is of the utmost importance that only your most senior people are aware of this communiqué. Following a recent meeting of the Joint European Intelligence Group, it was decided that no further operations or involvement will take place with, or within, the Colombian Armed Rebels Group, FARC.

The American Central Intelligence Agency is not in agreement and their operations within Colombia will continue.

You are required to cease any operations that may be linked, directly or indirectly, with FARC with immediate effect. Your British Foreign Secretary has already been informed.

There were two signatures on the letter; that of the Belgian Foreign Minister and Joseph Croisse, Head of Interpol. The seal and water mark at the bottom of the page, told Stonehaven that the letter was genuine. She folded it and put it in her handbag with the photo of Delaney. 'Thank you, Inspector; very hush-hush, but I fail to see why I was asked to come here, to be told this.'

Hubert looked as though he was unable to answer that question. 'I am sorry for any inconvenience, but I was of course, simply obeying orders.'

'Very well, was there anything else?'

'No, Lady Stonehaven, thank you.'

'In that case, I have a request for you. Do you mind?

'Please,' answered Hubert, subserviently, 'I'll do what I can; as long as I have the authority.'

On her flight to Belgium, Stonehaven had been thinking of ways to speed up the process of getting Stait. The letter she had just read was actually good news; it meant that she could tell Delaney and his people to get on with it. Without the Colombian connection, they could go for Stait, and Stait alone; if only for just his European operations.

'I think that Stait will be heading back to Belgium soon in his motor yacht,' she said. 'I would like you and Sergeant Brun to seize the yacht, wherever it moors, and inform us when that is done.'

'You mean to arrest Stait as well?'

'Of course I do.'

'I believe it could be arranged, Lady Stonehaven, but you understand that I would have to get permission from our Federal Chief of Police.'

'And why would he not agree?'

Hubert hesitated and then stood up. 'Why indeed; now, let me see you to your car, unless there was something else?'

'No, thank you, Inspector.'

Sergeant Brun was waiting outside the office and he took over from Hubert in escorting her to the car. On the return journey to the airport, she remained quiet and it was Brun who spoke to her as they approached the departures terminal. 'How are my friends Ben and Ajit?' he asked.

'They're fine; working very hard.'

'It would be good to work with them again.'

'That opportunity may come sooner than you think.'

The flight to Heathrow gave her chance to think. She understood the reasons why Interpol would want to cease operations in Colombia; they had never been very good at it. And her time in the CIA, gave her enough knowledge to understand why they *would* want to stay involved; a vast amount of narcotics used in America originated in Colombia. This directive was a good thing; the operation to get Stait should be shortened. As the plane taxied to its designated gate, she reached for her phone. 'Tom, it's Shirley. Can we meet up straight away please; I have some news for you.'

'Yes, we need to,' said Delaney. 'I was just about to call you.'

'Oh? About what?'

'About Frank Hawkwell; I'll be at your office in an hour.'

34

After three days of waiting at the Horseman quarry, Taffy Burton was starting to get suspicious. Although he and Ajit Pitt had agreed that it was a welcome break – doing virtually nothing except test driving the 'transport' now and again – they were starting to wonder if it had all been worthwhile and whether or not Stait was going to turn up. During the evenings they had chatted about their work and Burton had told Pitt a few tales and handed over some useful tips. There was one thing that Burton said one evening that made Pitt think, and he had the feeling that if ever there was piece of advice he was not going to forget, it was what Burton had said when he was talking about survival tactics; 'Always persevere and try your damndest; but stop when your life is at risk.'

On the evening of the third day, Pitt was, yet again, beating Burton at Scrabble when they heard a noise. Burton looked out of the main window to see a car approaching. 'This is it, young man; get out the back and wait in the transport shed.'

'Right,' said Pitt. 'Do you want to check the micro?'

'Good idea, switch your handset on.' Burton said a few words and the signal went to Pitt's handset. 'Loud and clear,' said Pitt. 'I'll contact the boss from the shed.'

'Good, go.'

Burton opened the main door to see two men standing there; a fit looking younger one with the air of a hooligan, holding a shotgun, and a taller man in his thirties with a hard but professional look about him. The taller man did not waste any time. 'Mr Padley, I take it; my name is Freddie and I have come to collect some diamonds. I have two million dollars for you.'

Burton stood back and pointed to the table. 'Put the money on there; I'll get the diamonds. How come Mr Stait isn't with you?'

'He said he trusted you,' said Freddie Ludic, 'and that we would not have any trouble from you and that he wanted to do more business with you in future.'

Burton said, 'Okay,' as he turned to a cupboard. The case of diamonds was in the cupboard; but so was his 9mm Browning. He hesitated to consider his actions. Stait not being there meant that he couldn't 'close' the situation. Shit, he thought to himself, as he reached for the case.

Once inside the shed, Pitt's first job was to phone Delaney. He suddenly started to feel hot and sweaty when a voice said, *'this number is temporarily unavailable.'* He quickly dialled Wyatt's number, *'this number is temporarily unavailable.'* 'What the...' he said to himself as he dialled the office number. A woman answered the phone. He didn't give her chance to complete the salutation. 'This Ajit Pitt, code 12, is Delaney there?'

'No, no one is; except Maggie Phelps.'

'Thank god for that, put her on.'

'But I need...'

'Put her on!'

After a few seconds, much to Pitt's relief, Maggie Phelps was there. 'Ajit, hello.'

'Hello, Maggie, boy am I glad you're working late tonight.'

Phelps was experienced enough to know when to be quick. 'Tell me.'

'I can't get hold of the boss or Ben; where the hell are they?'

'In a meeting at Lady Stonehavens office; you won't get them on their mobiles. Her office is in the MI5 building; no mobile signals get through to the inner meeting rooms.'

Pitt thought quickly; 'right, listen, I need you to get to the boss. I'm not bothered how, Maggie, just do it. Tell them to interrupt the blasted meeting and tell them it's a call from the quarry.'

'Of course, Ajit. Finish the call and let me get on with it.' Pitt clicked his phone shut and opened the shed door slightly to watch. There was no sign of any movement from the cabin.

When Burton had checked the money in the case that Ludic had put on the table, he slid the briefcase containing the diamonds across the table. 'Okay, here we are then; take them and enjoy them.'

Tommy moved forward and lifted the briefcase from the table. 'Take it to the car, Tommy, and then come back and help me with the body.'

'Body?' said Burton.

'Yes; body,' said Ludic. He grabbed a gun from inside his jacket, pointed it at Burton's right arm, and fired. Then he pointed it at Burton's left arm and fired again. Burton was spun round by the force of the bullets, but he soon realised they were not bullets; they were tranquiliser darts, heavy duty and strong. Within seconds he was falling to the floor, the room spinning around him.

Pitt started to run for the cabin. He had heard what Burton had said on his handset. But Tommy was on his way back to the cabin after dropping the case off and he spotted Pitt. He pulled his shotgun up to waist height and fired at Pitt, who dived behind an old digger bucket for cover. Tommy ran to the cabin and stopped at the door so he could keep an eye on where Pitt was. 'There's another one, Freddie!'

'I gathered that when I heard your shotgun, reload, then help me with him.'

Tommy reloaded and Ludic put the dart gun back in his jacket and drew out a pistol from his belt. He grabbed one of Burton's arms and Tommy grabbed the other. They dragged him to the door; Pitt was running towards them and Tommy fired again. Pitt hit the ground, rolled over and fired twice, but his shot was way off mark. Ludic let off a shot in Pitt's direction as they pulled Burton closer to the car. 'Get him!' shouted Tommy, 'I can handle this.' Ludic let go of Burton and Tommy started to haul him into the back seat of the car. Pitt felt useless as he rolled back behind the digger bucket. Tommy ran back into the cabin to grab the diamonds and sprinted back to the car as Ludic continued firing at the digger bucket to keep Pitt at bay. As Tommy started the car, he opened the front passenger door and Ludic jumped in. Within 20 seconds they were racing up the road that led out of the quarry.

Pitt ran back to the shed and pulled the cover off the Kawasaki. He grabbed one of the HK rifles from the cupboard and stuffed it into the specially adapted carrier on the bike. He quickly checked that the ammunition was already in the bags as Burton had said it would be and pulled one the helmets over his head. The bike started up faultlessly and he was soon leaving a trail of dust behind him as he raced up the same gravel road that Ludic and Tommy had taken seconds earlier. At the exit gate, he turned right. The road headed west; the same direction as Salcombe and Stait's yacht.

Shirley Stonehaven was de-briefing Delaney, Wyatt and Greaves in sound proof meeting room number eight at MI5 when the head of communications walked in without knocking. The overweight middle-aged woman looked at Stonehaven immediately and explained herself. 'Sorry, Ma'am; we've received a phone call from Mr Delaney's office, and a message has come through from GCHQ; a short distance handset signal has been picked up. It seems someone has left it on transmit permanently.'

'Who was the phone call from?' asked Delaney.

'A Maggie Phelps; it was from an Ajit Pi...'

Delaney got to his feet straight away and headed for the door; Wyatt and Greaves followed him. He looked back to Stonehaven as they left. 'The quarry; Stait and his men must be there. I'll let you know what happens.'

Delaney switched on the blues and twos as he raced the unmarked car out of London towards the M23. 'It'll be midnight by the time we get there.' said Greaves.

Delaney handed Wyatt his handset from the seat at the side of him. 'Take this, Ben. As soon as you get a signal from Taffy's micro let me know. It should work when we're about a mile away from him. But it did not work. Wyatt kept trying it as they got closer and closer to the quarry. Fifty minutes later, they were about half a mile from the quarry and there was still no signal. 'Nothing, guv,' said Wyatt. 'Does that mean it's not working?'

'No, it means Taffy isn't here.'

They could see the cabin light on as they approached. Delaney and Greaves checked out the cabin and Wyatt went straight to the transport shed. When Wyatt got back to the cabin, Delaney was pacing up and down. 'Nothing then?' asked Wyatt.

'Nothing,' said Delaney. 'No money, no diamonds, and no Taffy or Ajit. Is all the transport still there?'

'No; the Kawasaki's gone, and one of the HK's.'

Greaves was also walking around the room with her hands in her jacket pockets. 'So, either one of them left in another vehicle, or they're both on the Kawasaki, right?'

'No,' said Wyatt, 'the bikes for one rider only; they were modified to make room for the rifle racks. We need to get...'

Wyatt paused as Greaves phone rang. She looked at the phone and then Delaney. 'It's Michael...Hi Michael; have you got something?..when...okay...wait.' She moved the phone away from her. 'He's just seen two men get back to the yacht and they had someone with them who they had to almost carry on board; he's not sure but he thinks the third man may be Taffy.'

'Tell him we're on our way; and tell him not to go in alone,' said Delaney.

'And tell him to look out for Ajit; probably on a bike,' said Wyatt.

As Greaves relayed the messages to Riego, all three made their way back out to the car. 'We're not dealing with idiots, are we,?' said Wyatt. Delaney just shook his head as he drove out of the quarry.

Stait sat opposite Burton in the lower crew cabin of his motor yacht. Ludic and Tommy stood behind Burton as he started to come round. 'Can you see me, Mr Padley?' asked Stait. Burton felt himself swaying slightly and his vision was blurred, but he was able to read the situation. He remembered Ludic shooting him in the arms; he assumed they had left Pitt back at the quarry. 'I can't see you yet, no,' he said, 'I take it I'm talking to you, Mr Stait.'

'Yes, you are. You are on my yacht, as you will find out soon enough. I will give you another few minutes; you should be much more lucid by then.'

As he started to feel capable again, Burton took his time letting them know. He tried to look around him as much as he could without appearing too conscious. He could see Stait in front of him and just make out the legs of the two men standing behind him. There was nobody else in the cabin. Is Ajit out of the picture, he thought, or is he out there somewhere looking out for me?

It was about three more minutes before Stait made a move. He walked around to Burton, and grabbed hold of his chin, holding his face up to look in to his eyes. 'I think we can get on with things now, Mr Padley; you look okay to me.' He let go of Burton's chin with one hand, as the other hand came up and thumped his face, sending his head sideways with a brutal jolt. Stait sat down again and opened a small container on the table as

242

he looked at Burton. 'And that, Mr Padley, was just to show you who you're dealing with.'

The contents of the small container were poured out into a small shallow dish. It was some form of powder and Burton guessed it might be a drug of some kind.

Burton tried to clear his eyes as he shook his head. His hands were tied behind him. He glanced at the dish and then at Stait. 'If that powder is a drug, it doesn't look very clean.' He looked at Stait for an answer but there wasn't one so he continued. 'If you're going to force something into me you shit head, let's get on with can we, I've got lots to do.'

Stait laughed out loud. 'Okay my friend, we will!' His voice then went quiet as he pulled his chair closer to the table and moved the dish towards Burton. 'I am not going to inject anything into you. It could kill you; and then where would that leave me? Besides; it's a powder, not a liquid. Your friends are angry enough as it is, and I know my limitations.'

'My friends?'

'Whoever it is you're working for, Mr Padley; you are no more a diamond dealer than the two men standing behind you. No, I am not going to inject you; I just wanted to teach you a lesson and leave you something to remember me by. You will be taken from here soon and dumped somewhere out of the way. But you will be alive; for a few years anyway.'

Burton nodded his head slowly and looked at all three of them in turn. 'Right, you've made your point. But all I want is my money for the diamonds. You're reading the situation wrongly.'

Stait did not answer. Ludic and Tommy held Burton by his shoulder and pushed his head forward until his face was about six inches from the dish. Stait said, 'hold him tight,' as he pulled on a latex glove. He picked up some of the powder and shoved into Burton's nose. Then he picked up some more and rubbed it into Burton's face. The two men were holding Burton too firmly for him to react. All he could was to take it, so it would be over

243

quickly. He tried to smell the powder but it seemed odourless. He was struggling for breath and tried to blow some of the powder out, but Stait kept pushing more and more of it into his face and nose. Then Stait stopped what he was doing and simply said, 'okay,' to the two men. Ludic and Tommy forced Burton's face hard into the dish until he was struggling for breath. They lifted his head and then slammed it down again. Fine dust from the powder was starting to fill the air. 'That's enough,' said Stait. Let's get out into the fresh air; leave him here for a while and we'll clean up later.'

As they left the cabin, Burton tried to relax to recover his breathing pattern. What the hell is it? He thought. No smell, probably not fine enough or white enough for a drug, but you could never be sure. He tried to work his hands loose but they had done a good job and he realised that all he could do was to wait. Hopefully, Stait meant what he had said and they would dump him somewhere, without doing any more harm.

Ten minutes later, the three men came back down to the cabin. Ludic and Tommy lifted him from his chair and led him up the steep stairs to the outside. As he was climbing the stairs, Burton looked behind him to see that Stait was carefully lifting the dish and putting it into a plastic bag. 'At least wipe my face for me,' said Burton. Ludic huffed as he forced Burton down onto his knees on the swim platform. 'Get the car, Tommy, be quick. I'll wait for a minute and then bring him out.'

Tommy ran down the jetty towards the car park, not realising he was being watched.

Riego, from his high position, was keeping an eye on proceedings and he was on his phone to Wyatt as he kept looking through his binoculars. 'They've brought Taffy out; his hands are tied behind him. It looks like one of them is going for the car. Where are you?'

'About ten minutes away,' said Wyatt, 'hold your position. Have you spotted Ajit anywhere?'

'No; the only action here is what's happening on that jetty. Why don't we just go in and get them all?'

'Because the boss says not to; something about instruction from Stonehaven and Inspector Hubert.'

Riego felt helpless as he watched Tommy get into a car and reverse it to the exit gangway of the jetty. He knew he had to wait; Delaney was his boss now and for the foreseeable future and he had accepted that. He wanted to stay on this case and he knew that if he went against orders, they could have him back in the States in 48 hours. He watched intently. He looked at his watch; only two minutes had gone since Wyatt had said they were ten minutes away and a lot could happen in the next eight minutes.

Ajit Pitt had not had any trouble catching up with Ludic and Tommy, as they drove to Devon with Burton. He had kept them in sight but stayed far enough back not to be seen. Their car was no match for the Kawasaki and on the odd occasion when Tommy had put his foot down, Pitt had kept with him without difficulty. He could have gone right up to the back of the car or overtaken it at any time, but he needed to be sure not to put Burton in danger. As they had approached Salcombe, Pitt had watched as they had parked near the jetty and taken Burton on board Stait's yacht.

Now, as he watched Tommy open the back door of the car and Ludic bring Burton along the jetty, he felt as though it was all down to him. No communication from the boss, he thought, and none from Riego either. Why? He moved the bike backwards into a small yard at the side of a hotel as Tommy – driving like a drunken racing driver – fled past him; Ludic and Burton in the back. He eased the bike out onto the road and followed at a sensible distance.

About four miles out of town, Tommy pulled off the road near a junction and drove through an open gate that led to a single track dirt road. Pitt stopped where the dirt track started; he could see the car clearly. A back door opened; Burton was pushed out. Ludic moved into the front passenger seat next to Tommy. As the car swung round, creating a dust trail on the dry earth, Pitt moved the Kawasaki behind the hedgerow. He pushed the open gate and it closed across the track making a loud clunk as its heavy duty catch locked. He took the HK rifle from the holder on the bike and loaded a magazine onto it. Then he waited behind the hedgerow.

'What the bloody hell!' said Tommy as he drove towards the closed gate.

Ludic had not noticed; he was dialling Stait's number to report back to him. 'What's the matter?' he asked.

'Someone's closed the gate, Tommy; I'll ram it.'

'Don't be stupid. It's solid metal; pull up just short of it, it'll only take me a second.'

Ludic's door was already fully open as Tommy slowed down. Pitt lowered himself to the floor and took aim through the hedge. He fired twice; the two front tyres were blown apart. 'Shit!' said Ludic as dived to the ground. 'Get out of the car, Tommy! Throw me a gun!' Tommy rolled out of his door, tossed a gun to Ludic and ran to the back of the car. Ludic grabbed the gun and stayed on the floor at the side. Pitt had stood up by now and he was aiming the rifle at the car. 'Both of you stand up!' he called. 'I have a clear shot; I will use it if I have to.'

Tommy whispered, 'who's that?'

'I don't know,' said Ludic, 'could be the other man who was back at the quarry? Can you see anyone else?'

'No.'

Pitt was keen not to give them thinking time. 'One more minute,' said Pitt.

'Who are you?' shouted Ludic.

'All you need to know,' said Pitt, 'is that I can legally arrest you for taking a hostage. That would be the preferred action.'

Tommy, not thinking to check with Ludic first, squatted by the corner of the car and aimed his gun at the hedge where he thought Pitt's voice from coming from. Ludic spotted what he was doing as he looked underneath the car. 'Stay where you...'

The three shots that Tommy fired off were aimed at a point about four feet from where Pitt actually was. When his fire was not returned, Tommy stood up to take aim again. Pitt squeezed his trigger for a second and three or four rounds left the HK rifle and buried themselves into Tommy's chest. He hit the ground backwards about six feet from where he had been standing. Ludic started to run back to where they had thrown Burton out of the car; Pitt realised he would try to use Burton as a hostage or a shield. He hesitated. 'Bollocks!' he said to himself; he could not shoot anyone in the back. Then he heard Burton call out. 'Take him Ajit!' Burton had seen what had happened and he shouted again. 'Take him Ajit! You have t...'

Then Burton dived to the ground as Ludic fired two shots at him. Pitt aimed carefully again, keeping his cool; Ludic was brought down by three bullets that hit his legs just below the knees. Burton moved towards Ludic as he started to scream with pain. Pitt ran to them, holding his gun on Ludic. When he could see that Ludic was helpless, he nodded to Taffy. 'You okay?'

'Yeah; you gambled; shooting him in the legs.'

'I knew I could bring him down; I'm not shooting anyone in the back.'

'Okay you bastards; you've got me!' shouted Ludic. 'Get me an ambulance before I bleed to death!'

Burton kneeled down to look at Ludic's legs. 'You'll live,' he said. 'So shut up or I'll give you a thumping.' Then he turned to Pitt. 'Now, get back on your bike, Ajit; get back to the yacht; I'm betting that Stait would have left by now, but you might get there in time. If you do le...' Burton stopped talking and held up a hand

247

as a request for silence. There was a voice coming through to his micro implant. 'Too late, Taffy; Stait left in his motor yacht about five minutes ago.' It was Delaney.

'Where are you then, sir?'

'Obviously less than a mile away if we hear each other at last.'

'But I only left the yacht twenty minutes ago; how do you know?'

'Riego's there; he's phoned us to confirm. It's okay; we've told the coast guard and they'll track him.' Burton could hear the sound of a transmitter being switched off. He looked up to see Delaney parking at the gate that Pitt had closed. Wyatt and Greaves got out of the car, opened the gate and walked towards them. Wyatt looked down at Tommy's body as he passed it and smirked at Pitt. 'Your handy work, I take it.'

'Yes,' said Pitt. He pointed to Ludic. 'This one needs an ambulance; I just brought him down to stop him.'

Wyatt took his handgun from his shoulder holster and aimed at Ludic. 'Sod the ambulance, let me kill him; save a lot of trouble.' Ludic looked in horror as Wyatt stared at him. Delaney was walking towards them by now and he left it until the last second to speak. 'Let him live, Ben.'

'I was only joking,' said Wyatt as kept staring at Ludic. 'There's as much sweat coming from his face now as there is blood from his legs.' Ludic made an attempt to spit at Wyatt but he failed.

'Well,' said Burton, 'just Stait now then.'

'Stait and Hawkwell, Taffy,' said Greaves. 'Frank Hawkwell was sprung from jail earlier today.'

'Marvellous; that probably means he's on his way to join Stait somewhere.'

'Yes,' said Delaney. 'And my guess is that Stait's on his way back to Belgium.'

An hour later, Ludic was being escorted into a hospital by two armed police officers. The paramedics had arrived just in time.

Delaney, Burton and Pitt were driving back to the quarry and Riego – who had joined them after leaving the jetty - was following close behind. Wyatt and Greaves drove into Salcombe to confirm that Stait *had* left the area and had not returned.

It was getting light as the two cars approached the quarry an hour later. Delaney had things on his mind, as usual. Especially Taffy; who had been coughing for most of the journey.

35

At Horseman quarry, it took about an hour for Pitt and Riego to get things back in place. They had always been told to 'leave things as you find them' but they also knew that the logistics boys would check things out anyway. The quarry was used by MI6 now and again as well, so it was well looked after. The 'transport' was covered up again.

'Don't suppose the boss would let me keep the bike for a while?' said Pitt.

'I doubt it,' said Riego.

When they had checked to see that both cases had indeed been taken, Delaney told Burton to take a seat at the side of him. 'Stait will have both of them then, Taffy; the money *and* the diamonds.'

'Yes, of course he will.'

'Okay, well, we'll make our way back to London, get some rest and get after him then. But what about you? What did they do to you on that yacht?'

'Sir?'

'You've been coughing nearly all of the time; did they give you something?'

'Oh it's alright; I think they tried to scare me by shoving my face in a bowl of powder. I'm pretty sure it wasn't drugs or anything too bad or I would have realised it by now. I'm fine.'

'You always say you're fine, Taffy. When we get back we'll get you checked over; they'll be some residue somewhere left on you.'

'Yeah, okay. There's probably some of whatever it was in my hair; they could take a sample from there.'

The following day, all four men and Greaves were sitting around the desk of Lady Shirley Stonehaven in her large modern office. Wyatt and Greaves had driven back to join everyone after establishing that Stait had gone. They agreed it had been good to take Ludic and Tommy out of the picture, even though Stait was still out there. Stonehaven told Riego that he could go back to Washington when he wanted to; the CIA had been in touch with her and they desperately needed more officers back there to help out on an imminent nationwide sting operation. Riego asked if he could stay for a few more days and she agreed. Greaves remained silent. Pitt was given the job of staying in touch with the UK and Belgian coastguards to find out where Stait was heading.

When each of them had been questioned about the events of the last few days, Stonehaven asked all but Delaney to leave the room. As they left, she pulled her chair forward and spun her computer monitor around so Delaney could read an e-mail that was on the screen. 'Read that, Tom; quite interesting.' Delaney leaned forward and read slowly and carefully. It was from Harry Mitchell.

Lady Stonehaven,

You asked me to confirm things in writing following our conversation.

The CIA have received a message from Commander Carnas of the Colombian Rebels, via a website, saying that they wish to disassociate themselves from the dealings of certain people who are – and were – based in Belgium and Portugal respectively.

The message states that they have no wish to deal with any party in relation to the trafficking of children from Colombia. They may not be recognised by most Western states, but they have some honour and would never get involved in such things. This will have an impact on your quest to nail Stait and his international colleagues, I'm sure. But it should mean that you

*can deploy your people accordingly to get a quicker result. Let me
know if you require my help.*

*The CIA also confirmed that Julie Greaves, aka Michelle
Depout, is wanted back in Washington within 48 hours. – I trust
you can make arrangements.*

Regards,

Harry Mitchell

Head of MI6 Europe.

'You were told in Antwerp to cease any links with the
Colombians anyway, weren't you?' asked Delaney.

'Yes; and we can do. I'm quite pleased really. But what about
Julie Greaves, being wanted back in Washington? Where did that
come from? And why her and not Riego?'

'But you said a minute ago they desperately needed officers
back there.'

'Exactly, so why not both of them?'

Delaney shrugged his shoulders. 'Why don't we ask Julie
herself?'

Stonehaven nodded and Greaves was asked to come back into
the room. Delaney told the four men to have a few hours off and
be at his office at lunchtime. When Greaves had settled back into
a chair, Stonehaven told her about the E-mail from Mitchell.

'But, I don't want to go back yet,' said Greaves.

'Sorry, but you'll have to,' said Stonehaven. 'But we were
wondering why they hadn't asked for Michael to return? They
need as many people as they can get right now; why would they
not want both of you back, knowing that we're handling things
here anyway?'

'Probably Michael; he's done this before.'

'Done what before?' asked Delaney.

'If Washington wants to phone someone about an important
job, they'll bypass Harry Mitchell and phone the officer direct. If

Michael had taken such a call, he would have talked them into asking for me instead of him. He's good at stuff like that.'

Stonehaven felt some sympathy for her. She had experienced the male dominated security services for herself. It was still an unfair truth that the male officers were favoured; as in other organisations. 'Would you like me to say that I'm keeping you here for a while longer?' asked Stonehaven. 'I could say you're indispensable at the moment; I do have some authority.'

Greaves looked surprised, but not as surprised as Delaney. 'Yes, that would be good of you, if you could try,' said Greaves.

'Not at all; we'll leave it there then.' Stonehaven glanced at the door as Greaves left. 'You look surprised, Tom.'

'Oh, I just think we can handle things now, without a CIA contingent.'

'Don't be so proud, Tom; and don't start upsetting me again. I was just about to ask you out to dinner.'

'Again? People will talk.'

'Perhaps; did you hear about me and Simon?'

'No.'

'We separated last week. He's living at our apartment in Westminster now. We're divorcing.'

Delaney tilted his head. 'I'm sorry.'

'Don't be; I'm not. Anyway, I'll let you get on with things. Will you be in touch with Hubert in Antwerp?'

'Probably; I think Stait will go back there; I'll keep you informed.'

'Thanks, Tom, and er, dinner?'

'Maybe another time, if you don't mind.'

As he left room, he realised why, perhaps, Stonehaven had been so amiable to him at the quarry. That would have been about the same time as they separated. He wondered if it was just a plea for company while she was on the rebound. I doubt it, he thought to himself; she's made of sturdier stuff.

Greaves was waiting for him outside and they drove back to his office to meet the others. 'They won't be there yet,' said Greaves. 'Do you mind if I take a few hours off while I wait for lady Stonehaven to get back to me?'

'No, you go ahead; Let me know when you've heard from her.'

'Sure, thanks.'

He dropped her near a tube station and she made her way to her flat in Chelsea that the logistics people had acquired for her.

Delaney arrived at his office late morning and settled at his desk with a coffee. As he often did, when he had things to think about, he started scribbling down notes and lists. After an hour, he looked again at the list he had written;

Stait – was he back in Belgium by now?

Hawkwell – where was he?

Riego – why did he want Greaves back in Washington?

Taffy – test results for powder residue left on him?

Hubert & Brun – what can they do for me?

Then he realised he had missed someone off the list; his beloved partner, Angela. How was she? He picked up his phone and sent a text.

Dinner tonight, 8, be ready, I love you.

36

The motor yacht, *Adinerado*, was anchored one kilometre off the coast of France near Le Conquet in Brittany. Aaron Stait had steered it there with expertise. The journey had only taken a few days, zigzagging to evade radars and back tracking a few times, and he had slept for a while as the yacht steadied itself on the calm waters. As the sun came up, he prepared himself some coffee and defrosted some hams and cheeses from the freezer.

The UK Coastguard had tracked the yacht from Salcombe to Jersey and the Channel Islands authorities kept an eye on it as it passed into French waters. The French Coastguard had reported that it had anchored near Le Conquet and the Gendarmerie had despatched one the their marine units to the area. Shirley Stonehaven had given specific instructions to her French counterpart that Stait should not be approached until Delaney and The Overseas Liaison Agency had been informed and that any instruction to go in would come from the Belgians only.

Stait picked up his mobile phone to dial a number. Then he paused and looked around as he thought about tracking devices and radio signals. He switched the phone off and tossed it into the ocean. He made his way to the lower cabin and switched on the computer. There were four E-mails showing in the in box; two from James, one from a company trying to sell him chandlery, and one from Commander Carnas. He opened Carnas's E-mail:

I am severing all ties with you, Mr Stait; with immediate effect. The shipment that was due to be delivered to you next week will not be arriving; I have diverted it to another customer. I am withholding any payments you have made as 'severance payments'.

Stait pressed the reply button; he hurriedly typed in a message to ask what this was all about and pressed the *send* key. He hit the desk with his fist as he read the screen again: *message undeliverable; addressee not recognised.* The coffee was thrown onto the floor and documents, ham and cheeses flew into the air as he swiped a hand across the desk and shouted. 'Aah! You cannot do this!' Thoughts flashed though his mind as he stood up and kicked out at some furniture, breaking a glass cupboard door that had fine crystal glasses behind it. 'My money,' he said to himself. 'The drugs; they must not do this, it could ruin me, the investment, the customers, they'll kill me.'

As he sat down again to think, a new message popped up in the in-box: It was from James:

Aaron,
Hawkwell out as planned. But he wouldn't come with us. He says he will be with you in 24 hours if you text him your location. Please make final payment in usual way by midnight tonight.
Until the next job,
James.

He growled, took off his shirt, and went up onto the fly bridge, and sat on his rowing machine as the sun got higher and hotter. He rowed solidly for one hour; until the sweat was gathering in pools around him, and he had expended every last idea in his mind. As he leaned over the side to get his breath, a dolphin surfaced momentarily and then disappeared. He reached for one of the P10 handguns and slammed a full magazine into it. A few seconds later, the dolphin appeared again and looked up as though it knew something was wrong. Stait kept his finger on the trigger and emptied the entire magazine into the dolphin. It spun around, up and down, backwards and forwards until the blood coloured the sea, and it floated away from the yacht; lifeless.

Seagulls screeched as Stait growled out loud again.

Julie Greaves had slept well; Shirley Stonehaven had phoned her just before midnight to confirm that the CIA had been spoken to and that she could stay with Delaney and his team for another two weeks. It was 7 a.m. when she woke; late for her, for she had always been an early bird and the later she slept in, the worse she felt. Delaney had been in contact with them all to tell them to meet him at the St. Pancras Eurostar terminal at 10 a.m.

She showered and made tea. She would miss the British cuppa, she thought, when she was back in the States. Still in her dressing gown, she found her handgun was in its usual place under the sofa and she checked it, loaded it, and laid it in its shoulder holster on the coffee table while she went to get dressed and packed.

The flat she had been given was not a modern one, but it was large and clean. The door to the flat was reinforced steel and the small balcony that looked out over a busy back street, had solid walls and handrails. She stood for a while on the balcony finishing her tea; it seemed a long way away from Washington, as she looked down at all of the people. They always looked busy, she thought, like the whole of London.

Checking her watch, she turned to leave, closed the balcony doors and went to pick up her belongings and shoulder holster.

The holster was not there.

She looked up as she heard a sound. Frank Hawkwell was standing in the kitchen doorway about ten feet away from her. The holster was in his left hand; he was holding her gun with his right hand, pointing it at her. She stood perfectly still as he stared at her without saying anything. The look on his face was one of disdain. His narrow dark eyes and his unshaven, lean face looked hungry and tired. He threw the holster onto a chair and ran his hand through his dark greasy hair. Greaves thought about what was all around her without looking; trying to think of anything that she could use as a weapon if the opportunity arose. Then Hawkwell moved a step closer to her. 'Put your hands in your pockets,' he said. She did so, and kept her eyes on him all the time.

'I heard someone had sprung you out; they must be good,' she said. 'How did you get in he...'

He shot her in her right knee; she went down but did not cry out in pain. He was not going to get that satisfaction, she thought. Holding her agony within herself, she looked at him again. 'That'll do, Hawkwell; quit while you're ahead.'

'That was for Micky Sondhiem you bitch. This is from me.' He shot her in the other knee. This time she could not hold back the scream. It echoed around the room as she lay on her side looking down at her shattered legs. When her screams subsided, he moved closer. The look of defiance on her face made him feel even more determined. He fired again; the bullet went into her left shoulder; then he fired once more; at her right shoulder. She laid still in shock and horror; her arms and legs bleeding out onto the floor. Even then, when she was within seconds of passing out, she stared at him as a final act of resistance. He threw the gun to one side as he made his way to the door. Then he turned to look at her again. She was still staring at him. 'I'll leave you to die slowly then,' he said. 'It should only take about half an hour.' She was still staring at him as he closed the door.

Two young people were in the corridor, looking shocked. He smiled at them. 'It's okay; I'm a police officer, get back in your rooms please.' They did, quickly. At the bottom of the stairs, the caretaker was holding a bunch of keys tightly. 'Thanks again,' said Hawkwell as he pushed £200 into the man's shirt pocket and left.

A woman, holding a towel around her, came running down the stairs and shouted at the caretaker. 'You have to phone the police! Didn't you hear that noise; I think it was a gun being fired.' The caretaker turned to go to his room. 'Will do,' he said, 'here; it's key number three.' He tossed the keys to the woman who grabbed them and ran back upstairs. She unlocked the door to Greaves' room and went in cautiously. 'Hello? Are you okay?' As she went into the main room she saw Greaves lying there. 'Oh my God!' She turned to face the door. 'Help! Somebody please!'

Greaves managed to open her eyes when she heard the woman shout. In a strained voice that was fading, she spoke to the woman as she pointed to her phone on the table. 'Dial four...just say...Greaves code one...Hawkwell.'

The woman did exactly as Greaves asked. Then she looked at Greaves. 'Nothing; there's no response.'

'Okay,' said Greaves. 'Okay...they got it...alright...now get me a...' She passed out. The woman said 'Oh my God,' again and ran to the corridor. 'Quick, someone! Please!'

It was 20 agonising minutes before an ambulance arrived, followed closely by a police car. They would have been there sooner but the caretaker had waited about ten minutes before phoning, as he had been instructed by Hawkwell. The first paramedic ran upstairs with her bags. The woman with the towel around her was standing on the corridor pointing into Greaves room; the paramedic went in and knelt down at the side of Greaves. She looked back at the woman. 'Do you know her name?'

'No; she's only been here for a few days.'

'Okay, keep all the corridors clear for me and keep people back.' She looked into Greaves eyes. 'Can you hear me?' She tapped her gently on the cheek. 'Can you hear me? I'm Jane.'

There was no response from Greaves. The second paramedic came in and knelt at the side of his colleague. He looked down at Greaves legs and the blood on the floor. 'Looks like both femoral arteries have been hit. I'll pack her legs, you sort out a drip; two bags. We'll have to call it in so they can have a surgeon standing by.'

The Eurostar terminal at St. Pancras was quieter than usual; Ben Wyatt and Ajit Pitt managed to find a vacant table at a coffee bar. 'The boss said 10 o'clock,' said Wyatt, looking at a schedule displayed on a screen, 'So we're probably going for that departure at 10.40.'

'We're early anyway,' said Pitt. It was 09.40 when Burton arrived and Riego five minutes after him.

'Well, we're all here,' said Riego, 'except the man that told us to be.'

'He said ten,' said Wyatt. 'That makes him better at utilising his time than us doesn't it?'

Burton's phone rang. 'That's him now,' he said. The others looked at Burton as he listened to Delaney. He did not say anything, apart from the odd, 'I see' or 'okay' now and again. He was looking at the floor throughout the conversation and when the call was over; he closed his phone shut and put it into his pocket slowly and thoughtfully.

'What is it, Taffy?' asked Wyatt.

'He won't be here. He wants us to get the train to Brussels; he's texting through the ticket numbers.'

'Okay, big man,' said Wyatt, 'that puts you in charge; let's get on with it.'

'Wait a minute,' said Riego. 'Why isn't he coming?'

Burton had a worried look on his face as he glanced at Riego. 'He's err, he's staying for a while to sort something out.'

'Sort what out?'

'It's Julie, Michael; she's been shot.'

'What?'

'Someone shot her in her flat; she died on the way to the hospital, massive blood loss. She'd been shot in the legs and shoulders.'

They all stood motionless; Riego kicked a chair that was near him. It narrowly missed a passerby. Pitt picked it up and

260

apologised to the woman who was looking at them all. Pitt and Riego walked slowly towards the platform; Riego with his hands around the back of his neck. Burton followed and Wyatt nudged him on the arm. 'Hawkwell?'

'Has to be, Ben. Who else?'

'So what's happening in Brussels?'

'We go on to Antwerp; the boss has set up a meeting with Inspector Hubert. Stait's disappeared off his yacht. They think he's headed back to Antwerp to meet Hawkwell.'

None of the four men spoke during the three hour trip to Antwerp; except to ask for a drink in the bar, where they spent most of the journey. It was 1 p.m. when Wyatt knocked on Inspector Hubert's door. The same door he had been shown out of a couple of weeks earlier.

37

Inspector Hubert's office was large and modern. Wyatt – tongue in cheek - re-introduced himself and Pitt. 'Ben Wyatt, Inspector; and this is Ajit Pitt. You may remember asking us to leave Antwerp a couple of weeks ago.'

'Of course I remember, Mr Wyatt; I hope this time your trip to Belgium will be more fruitful.'

Wyatt tried to ignore that remark as politely as he could and introduced the others. 'I believe you have met Mr Burton, and this is Michael Riego of the CIA.'

Hubert looked at Burton and smiled. 'Of course; you came to see us when we were in the museum office, Mr Burton.'

'I did, sir; is Sergeant Brun still with you?'

'Yes, yes; he will be along shortly; please everyone, take a seat.'

The four men took up chairs around the room and Hubert moved from behind his desk to sit with them. Burton noticed that Hubert was looking at Riego most of the time. Sergeant Brun came into the office, shook hands with all of the visitors and sat down. Wyatt was pleased to be getting another chance of working with him. He sat forward as he remembered their last job together at Stait's house near Eeklo. 'So, Brun; how is Maes?' asked Wyatt. 'And how has Mrs De Vos been?'

The big Sergeant tilted his head. 'Mm, they're okay, thank you, Ben.' He looked at Pitt then. 'And you two are alright? It is good to see you again...'

'Okay that's the introductions done,' said Hubert. 'Where is Delaney, Mr Burton?'

'He's had to stay in England for another day, sir; he'll join us tomorrow, possibly the day after.'

Hubert wiped a finger and a thumb across his moustache a few times. 'Very well; let me tell you all the situation. Delaney knows most of it anyway; he was going to brief you on your journey here.' He tapped his chin and checked his tie. 'Aaron Stait's motor yacht is still anchored off the west coast of France; it seems a local resident saw him shoot something and he told the Gendarmerie, just in case it was human. It turned out to be a dolphin that was washed up a few miles away. When the French Coastguard boarded the vessel it was empty; the outboard boat had gone so they assume he took off and landed somewhere quiet on the coast. We have good reason to believe that he is on his way back to Belgium; Lady Stonehaven may have told you that the Colombian gangs have stopped dealing with him, so he has to be coming back here to collect what he can of his wealth so he can flee and retire somewhere; possibly Brazil or Argentina.'

'Did you know about Frank Hawkwell?' asked Burton.

'Yes; I was told last night. And yes to your next question; I think he will be on his way here to join Stait.' He looked at Pitt. 'You, of course, did good work, getting rid of Ludic and Tommy; and that means that Stait and Hawkwell will be working alone. They will be a formidable couple to deal with. And we have no knowledge of other credible gang members that Stait can call upon on.'

'So how will we find out where Stait is heading for?' asked Wyatt.

'All border crossings, airlines and train companies have been sent a photo of Stait; I'm confident someone will spot him.'

'Assuming you're right about him coming back to Belgium,' said Burton. Hubert looked at him as though he was displeased with the remark. 'Yes, Mr Burton; assuming I'm right.' He sighed heavily and looked around at all of them. 'I take it you are aware that someone in England paid for the last shipment that Stait sent out; we think it was delivered to the Essex coast by Ludic and Tommy, before they joined Stait again in Devon.'

'How much?' asked Wyatt.

'Seven million.'

'Seven million what?'

'Pounds sterling.'

Wyatt raised his eyebrows as he looked at Burton. 'So he's got the seven million, the diamonds, and the two million he was going to pay for the diamonds.'

'Looks like it,' said Burton.

Hubert folded his arms. 'Diamonds?'

'It's a long story, Inspector,' said Burton.

'Okay, but don't forget gentlemen; these amounts of money are petty cash to Stait. We estimate that somewhere, he has about 200 million Euros put away, from various rackets and deals he has run over the years; that's why he has to come back to Belgium, to retrieve the money.'

When there was silence for a few seconds, Hubert nodded to Brun who took car keys from his pockets and tossed them to Wyatt and Burton. 'We have arranged accommodation for you,' he said. 'You will follow me please; I will take you to the cars and then to the house where you will staying.'

'That will be all,' said Hubert. 'You will be contacted as soon as we hear anything.'

An hour later, Brun was approaching the suburb of Linkeroever to the west of the centre of Antwerp. Burton and Riego followed him closely and Wyatt and Pitt were close behind in a third car as he pulled onto the driveway of a large three storey house. An automatic garage door opened and the three cars parked up in an area that big enough to take six cars. Brun got out of his car and pointed towards a side door. The four men followed him, carrying what little luggage they had.

There was a room for each of them, a swimming pool, a gymnasium and copious amounts of food and drink in a kitchen that was 'large enough to play football in' according to Pitt. Later, they settled around the table in the main dining room to share some food and a few beers. Wyatt was already getting impatient, Pitt was just happy to be there and Riego was extraordinarily quiet. Burton was feeling uncomfortable; something wasn't quite right, he thought, but what? He wandered around the house looking out of numerous windows as the early dusk arrived.

A few hours earlier, in a quiet cove, on the coast of Brittany, Aaron Stait had looked at his watch. It was midnight. Realising his shouting and the shooting of the dolphin would have aroused some suspicion, he had launched the small out board boat from the motor yacht, placed all the weaponry and some food into it and made his way to the shoreline. Finding the small cove had been a bonus and neither the French Coastguard nor the Gendarmerie had succeeded in finding him or even contemplating that he may still be in the vicinity.

He pulled the small boat back to the water and started its engine. Keeping the speed low and the engine noise to a minimum, he made for the *Adinerado*. There was no sign of any night patrols, nor of anyone being left on board in case he should return. Manoeuvring the boat around the yacht, he looked for the marks on the sides and the bow. Satisfied he could remember what he had been taught, he started to peel away the markings. At the left hand tip of the word *Adinerado,* he felt for the tiny flap that was sticking out. Pulling gently, he peeled back the name. When it was completely off - -revealing another name; *Juliet,* in black – he moved his hand lower down and reached for a tab that was sticking out just below the water line. He pulled the tab slowly outwards until it became three feet wide and he could see two holes in it. Turning the small boat around, he put a rope through both of the holes and tied it off. The other end of the rope was fastened to the rear of the boat. As he accelerated very slowly, the entire side of the yacht was revealed in another colour ,as the massive transfer was peeled off. He carefully put the heavy duty transfers into a bag and switched off the engine. A few minutes later, satisfied that no one had heard anything and that the new look yacht was to his liking, he started the engine again, took the boat to the other side of the yacht and repeated the exercise.

Within 15 minutes, he had the boat hooked back onto the rear swim platform of the yacht and the bagged rubbish and weapons safely locked away. The twin engines of the motor yacht started up faultlessly. As he was waiting for the engines to warm up and the anchor to retract, he went into the main cabin and lifted a panel below each window. When he had unclipped four fastenings, the specially designed and shaped windows of the yacht fell away and sunk into the ocean; helped by the metal weights bolted to them.

And now the *Adinerado* was the *Juliet*; in blue, with square windows; not white with shaped windows. The conversion option had cost him £90,000 and he decided it had been worth it.

Although he was still angry, he allowed himself a faint smile when he pushed the control handle forward and the motor yacht powered its way out to sea. He set course for Jersey and flipped open the new phone he had commissioned earlier. 'Frank, it's Aaron; if James got you the phone I told him to, and you get this message, make your way to Jersey. Look out for Juliet.'

Frank Hawkwell picked up Stait's message about an hour later. It was 1 a.m. and he had been sitting in the soup kitchen for the homeless for 13 hours. After killing Julie Greaves, he had torn some of his clothes, bought an old bag and rubbed dirt onto his face. There had always been one place that the police, Special Branch and MI5 had never searched for a gunman; soup kitchens.

He waved to a drunken man that had been shouting at people for some time and then to the lady at the reception table. 'Thanks, bye,' he said in a weak voice. The lady smiled and said 'Be careful; you know where we are.' When he was round a corner and out of sight, he cleaned himself as best he could with a towel he had dampened in the soup kitchen, and waved down a taxi and after many short journeys, the driver was only too pleased to take him to Dover.

As they approached Dover, Hawkwell told the driver to carry on and go through the town, heading west. A few miles out, they turned down a dirt track that led to an old farm building. Behind the farm, the land opened out to reveal an old airfield and a hangar with the words, Jewel Crop Sprayers, on the side of it. He paid the taxi driver and told him to keep his mouth shut. The doors to the hangar opened easily. A single engine Cessna aircraft was parked up and a night light illuminated a corner of the hangar where an old war time telephone was screwed to the wall. He picked up the handset and dialled a number. 'This is Frank; is that you, Bingo?'

The voice on the other end sounded shocked. 'Yes, this is Bingo. Do you mean it's Frank as in Frank Hawkwell?'

'Course I do you old tosser. Are you still in business?'

Bingo had actually noticed on his phone, where the call was coming from. 'You know I am, as you're stood in front of my aeroplane.'

'Good, only I wasn't sure; I heard you had a close shave a while back doing a job for Alan Farrah.'

'That's all over; and Alan's dead, poor bastard. But I get by; where do you need to go?'

'Jersey.'

'When?'

'Now.'

'Bloody hell, that'll cost you.'

'Whatever, Bingo; just get here before I'm tempted to fly the frigging thing myself.'

It was 5 a.m. when the Cessna took off, heading west.

38

The pathologist's lab next to the Coroner's office was, as they all were, bright, light and clinical. Shirley Stonehaven was standing next to Delaney. The body of Julie Greaves was lying on the cold aluminium table. The young attractive pathologist looked at both them over the top of her stylish spectacles. She had explained the injuries that Greaves had suffered and how she had died. 'Any questions?'

'No,' said Delaney, 'it's about what I would expect from Hawkwell; he knew that she would die if he shot out her femoral arteries.'

'The shots to the shoulders didn't help either,' said the pathologist. 'They probably hit the subclavian arteries.'

'Are you sure it was Hawkwell?' asked Stonehaven,

'Yes, I'm sure; it's just his style,' answered Delaney. He looked up at the pathologist. 'Okay; thank you, she can be put away now. We won't get anything else from cutting her open. Do you want me to tell her family?'

'You could do,' said the young lady, 'but we would normally leave that to a Minister when overseas people are involved.'

Stonehaven held up a hand. 'It's alright, I've already spoken to human resources at CIA; they're probably on their way now to the next of kin.'

They thanked the pathologist and her assistant again and made their way to Stonehaven's car. Her driver opened the door for her as she turned to face Delaney. 'Can I offer you a lift, Tom?'

'No, thank you; I walked here, I'll walk back. It helps me to think.'

'Okay; are you off to join your boys in Belgium?'

'Eventually; but I'm looking at a few things first. If it's okay with you, I'll be in touch if we get closer to Stait.'

'Which you may not; I take it you heard about Stait disappearing from his yacht?'

'Mm, I heard; Taffy will let me know what's happening, I'm sure.'

As she was being driven away, Stonehaven looked back to watch Delaney walking away with his hands in his pockets looking at the ground.

It was well into the afternoon when Delaney arrived at Shiphampton. He had thought of many things on his walk back to his office and he only stayed there long enough to change a shirt and get his car keys.

The Westwood's boat yard was still open when he arrived at five thirty, and Tim Westwood was reversing a small cabin cruiser into a land bay with the tractor. When he saw Delaney he stopped at once and came over to him. 'Tom, my old friend; what a surprise.'

'Yeah, sorry to turn up unannounced.'

'That's fine; Jane's in her office; go and say hello and I'll join you in a moment.'

Delaney parked his car in the customer area and wandered over to the office marked BOAT HIRE where they had been two weeks earlier. Through the window he could see Jane Westwood talking on the phone so he paused for a while to look around and let her finish her call. There were about 30 boats in the yard, ranging from small sailing dinghies to a 40ft cruiser. He watched as Tim Westwood expertly backed the small cruiser into its place. Jane opened the door to call out to her husband and then she noticed Delaney. 'Tom! What are you doing here?'

'I was in the area so I thought I'd call in,' he lied.

'Good, good; come on. I'll put the kettle on.' She kissed him on the cheek and he followed her into the office. 'So, how are you?' she said, as she poured the hot water.

'I'm alright, thanks; you two?'

'Fine; business could be better, but we're okay.'

'Actually,' said Delaney, thinking he would ask about things before Tim came in to the office, 'you might be able to help with something.'

'Oh; what?'

'It's probably nothing, but just in case; have you heard anything from other boatyards, closer to the coast maybe, that have had a boat back from a Belgian trip at all?'

'No, I don't think so; something wrong?'

'No, it's just that we've been looking for a motor boat of some kind that was used to do a drugs drop somewhere near here. Word is that the payment for the drugs was made around here somewhere. And there would have been two men with it, who probably stayed in England.'

She looked at Delaney and put her cup down on the table. 'You weren't in the area at all, were you Tom?'

'Err, no.'

'You don't suspect us of any malpractice, I hope.'

He avoided answering. 'Jane, do you remember when I visited last time and you showed me your hire records?'

'Yes?'

'Well, two of the people who hired your boats were called Porter and Dring.'

'Right; I think so. Go on.'

Porter's real name is Freddie Ludic. Dring's real name is Frank Hawkwell. They're both criminals; nasty criminals. One of them is out of the picture now, but Hawkwell is at large and that's why I'm here; I need to look at your records again.'

Tim Westwood walked in and immediately noticed the look on Jane's face. 'What's wrong?'

'Tom here is on official business; apparently I've been hiring out boats to criminals.'

'Well that wouldn't surprise me,' said Tim jokingly, 'I've always told you to get more ID when they sign the forms.'

'Oh shut up, Tim! Tom's serious.'

Delaney held up both hands in a calming gesture. 'Look, honestly, it's just coincidence, I'm sure. If you'll let me take a brief look again through your records I'll be out of the way and we can meet again soon; still as friends, I hope.'

'Why not,' said Tim. He looked at Jane. 'Darling?' Jane nodded her head but did not look at either of them. 'Alright.'

Delaney remembered which filing cabinet he had looked in on his first visit and he put down his cup and opened it gently. He did not waste time looking at the Porter file; Ludic was dead. He pulled out the Dring file and moved to the table to lay it out in front of him. 'Mind if I...'

'No, just get on with it,' said Jane.

The file contained limited information as he had remembered. After turning over both pages, he turned to Jane. You've put here that Mr Dring hired out a motor boat and that he says he goes to Southend and all around there.'

'Yes.'

'How long did he hire the boats for?'

'Usually a few days.'

'Long enough to go to Belgium and back then.'

'Yes; but he'd have to take extra fuel cans with him and we don't supply extra fuel.'

There was a pause as Delaney looked at the front page again. 'Do you ask for ID when they give their address?'

'Only a driver's licence; we ask them for an address and see if it matches what it says on the licence.'

Delaney took out a pen and scribbled the address that Hawkwell had given on a piece of paper. 'Okay, thanks, now all

I'm going to do is check out this address, that's all. Honestly, I doubt it will go any further.'

Jane was still looking angry and upset. Tim put his arm around her. 'Come on, darling; Tom's a good friend, he means well and he's only doing his job.'

'Okay,' she said, 'but you've got what you want, Tom, so please leave now. Perhaps you're right; we'll meet again under nicer circumstances.'

Delaney shook Tim's hand and turned to Jane who shunned him. 'Listen, both of you; I'm sorry, and thanks very much, I'll be in touch. How about a meal at the Planalto again sometime? My shout.'

Tim looked at him and smiled as Jane refused to look up. Delaney acknowledged and left quietly.

When he was a few miles away, he pulled into a lay-by and phoned Maggie Phelps. 'Glad you're working late again, Maggie; check out this address for me will you?' he relayed the address to her and finished the call. It was half an hour later when she phoned him back as he was waiting in a traffic queue on the A12. 'Thanks, Maggie; go ahead.'

'It's complicated, Tom; this address is registered as a business address. This Staleybridge House; it's a stately home near Hertford. It was bought freehold at an auction four years ago. The buyer was registered as Adinerado Enterprises. They rented out offices and apartments to small businesses and domestic tenants. Mr Hawkwell lived in one of the apartments for two years. The Managing Directors of Adinerado Enterprises were registered as a Mr Aaron Stait and a Mr Henry Hubert.'

'*Were* registered?'

'Yes; the holding company; Sondheim Holdings, went bankrupt a year ago; the house has been empty ever since.' Delaney was silent as he took it all in.

272

'Tom? You still there?'

'Yes, sorry. Good, thanks Maggie. Get on to forensics will you; ask them if we can borrow a team and ask them to meet me at Staleybridge House in the morning, 7 a.m. Oh, and err, get a message to Lady Stonehaven; just tell her about this conversation.'

'Will do, Tom; you drive carefully.'

As stately homes go, Staleybridge House wasn't a particularly attractive one. The forensic team and a police patrol had already cut the chain and locks that secured the big iron gates; Delaney drove towards the house looking either side of him. There was a mixture of oak and birch trees, heathers, pampas grasses and a few statues in need of a good wash. He guessed the house to be about 300 hundred years old. The front doors had been replaced at some point by someone with little taste; they were double glazed UPVC with a sticker that said *beware of the dog* on them.

One of the forensic team handed the ubiquitous blue overall and slip-over shoes to Delaney as he got out of his car. 'You must be Delaney; I'm Hale. Can you wear these all the time that you're inside please?'

'Of course, thanks.' He put on the overalls and made his way to the doorway. Hale walked at his side; he was a tall man in his fifties and Delaney guessed he was in charge of the team. 'Am I to take it that you're as experienced as you look, Mr Delaney,' he said.

'Err, yes, I suppose so.'

'Good; you're not squeamish then?'

'Probably not, why? All I wanted to do was look for some documents and evidence.'

'Right,' said Hale, as he led the way into a back kitchen. The whole area was filthy; cobwebs and dust covered everything. Rat faeces were lying around in most corners and two old bird's nests

273

were perched on the cupboards. Hale noticed when Delaney had spotted the bird's nests and he pointed to some broken windows. 'They came in through there; the whole place was probably crawling with animal life at one time. Judging by the dirt and cobwebs around the doors, I'd say the place has been uninhabited for about a year.'

'Mm, I've seen worse,' said Delaney.

'Ah but I haven't shown you down here yet.' Hale pointed towards a door; it led into a large timber-clad room that smelt of charcoal. 'I think it was a big smoking room,' said Hale, 'used to smoke fish and meat many years ago.' Large meat hooks hung down from the low ceiling and the floor was covered in ants and flies. 'The interesting thing is,' said Hale, 'those flies are probably from maggots that were not very old; look.' He switched on a torch and pointed it at the floor on the other side of the room. Then he raised the torch so it's light settled on one of the meat hooks.

Delaney frowned as he realised why Hale had asked him if he was squeamish. On the floor was a human skeleton; bent and twisted as though the person had died in agony. Ants were hurrying around all over the bones and all around the floor, feeding on rat faeces. On the meat hook, a naked man hung; partly grey, partly purple. He had been a large, well built man and the bar supporting the hooks was bending under the weight. The hook came through his chest and the point of it was sticking out of his rib cage. Flies buzzed around his face, settling now and then to feed on his lips and the flesh inside his mouth.

Hale switched off the torch, as someone behind turned on a large floodlight. 'First thing we do is kill off all of the insects; then we can inspect what's on the floor. Move away now please, Delaney, while they spray the room.'

They both moved back into the kitchen. Two men with face masks shut the door and the sound of some sort of sprayer could be heard. Delaney tilted his head towards the closed door. 'How old do you reckon?'

'The one on the floor I'd say died about a year ago; the one on the hook, about a week ago. But that's your lot for now; you can have a look around the rest of the house if you want to.'

'Thanks, I will.'

As Delaney walked around the house, it became more and more evident to him that whoever the occupiers were; they left in a hurry. Clothes were still in wardrobes and a shaving kit had been left in one of the five bathrooms. In the main living room, cups had been left half empty and a fire had been made up in the huge iron hearth, ready to light.

He heard someone shout out and made his way back to the kitchen. Hale stopped him as he approached and pointed to another door. 'This way; we've found another body.'

In a smaller room, not far from the main hallway, the body of a man was slumped in a chair. Cheese wire had been tied around his neck and the back of the chair. He was naked from the waist down. Unlike the man on the meat hook, this one had been short and thin. Blood lay around the chair; dried and blackened. 'Stabbed in the scrotum, I'd say,' said Hale. 'The stabbing made him lunge forward, and the cheese wire cut his throat.'

'Nasty,' said Delaney. 'Would that be about a week ago as well?'

'Yes; and whoever did it hated them pretty badly,' said Hale, 'the word 'savagery' comes to mind. And look over there.' He pointed to a table under a window that was covered in magazines. When Delaney got close to the table, he could see what type of magazines they were.

'Don't touch please,' said Hale.

'No, I won't; I don't have to; I can see what they are.' Delaney only had to glance at some of the pictures before he got an idea of what the house had been used for.

'Poor helpless kids,' said Hale. 'Any ideas?'

'Possibly, but I'll need an ID of the dead bodies first; how long will that take?'

'Not long; there's still hair, skin and teeth, so I'll have something for you in a couple of days. The killer made the mistake of not removing the watches and rings as well.'

'Thank you. Shitty job, eh?'

'Mm, we get used to it.'

Once outside the building again, Delaney removed the blue plastic overall and shoe covers. He was about to get in his car when another car pulled up alongside him; it was Shirley Stonehaven. 'I got the message from your lady, Tom; anything?'

'Yes, but I'll explain later; best if you don't go in there.'

'Really; have you forgotten who you're talking to? I've seen a lot.'

'Okay, be my guest, but put these on.'

She pulled on the protective garments and walked into the house. A forensics man was near the door and he led her in. Delaney waited for ten minutes. When she re-emerged, she did not say anything. Her face was white and he noticed how she held on to the concrete balustrade to steady herself on her way down the steps. She removed the overall and looked at Delaney. 'Remember me telling you about Sondhiem being involved in child slavery and paedophilia?'

'I remember.'

'And this house was bought by Sondheim; and used by Stait and Hubert. Henry Hubert. It has to be same man doesn't it?'

'Probably.'

Stonehaven raised her fist in the air and brought it down on the roof of his car. Delaney reached for a bottle of mineral water from beside his seat and passed it to her. 'Here, drink some of this.' She took it and drank.

'Your boys are out there, Tom; with Hubert and Brun. We need to get them on to this ASAP.'

'I know; I'm flying out there today; I'll leave it 'til I get there. I'll take charge; Hubert is mine.'

'What about Stait and Hawkwell?'

'Not sure, everyone out there seems to think they're heading back to Belgium so Stait can get his money and lose himself, but I'm just not sure.'

'Right, well I'll keep hounding these boys until we get an ID for the bodies; I'll let you know as soon as I hear anything if you want to get over to Antwerp. The PM wants to see me this afternoon; the CIA want an explanation of how Greaves got killed.'

'Rather you than me.'

'Quite.'

By mid afternoon, Delaney was on a flight to Belgium. He had told Burton to pick him up from the airport and to come alone. He needed to make sure that the news about Hubert was kept quiet until he was sure.

39

The sun was getting lower and the sky was red as the dusk started to take hold on the west coast of Jersey. Aaron Stait had anchored up about a mile from the beach in St. Ouen's Bay. The journey from Le Conquet had been uneventful; he had not seen any coastguard vessels and hardly any other craft, save for a few early morning shrimp boats.

Frank Hawkwell's flight from near Dover was a little more hazardous; the pilot – nick name, Bingo – had radioed the air traffic control at Jersey to say he was on a trip from Spain to Southampton and that he was in trouble. The astute air traffic controller asked several questions; some of them tricky, before he would let them land. At 7 a.m. there was only one customs person on duty and Hawkwell - having handed over his new driver's licence supplied by James – was allowed through to the arrivals lounge. The Cessna was allowed a flight path to Southampton and Bingo was on his way before the first commercial flight of the day arrived.

After a short taxi ride to the coast, Hawkwell spent some time on the beach looking around. A young couple with a speed boat did not take much persuading to give him a lift to a motor yacht that was anchored not far away; not after Hawkwell had pushed £200 into the man's hand.

The westerly breeze picked up slightly and Stait reached for his jacket as Hawkwell poured him a drink. They had both spent an hour checking the rifles and handguns that Stait kept on the yacht. At Stait's request, Hawkwell had re-checked the cash, that had been acquired over the last few weeks; it totalled seven million Euro's, four million dollars and the briefcase of diamonds that had been taken from Burton. Hawkwell poured himself a drink and sat down next to Stait; the various bags of cases and money were in front of them. 'Ah, not bad, Aaron, all things considered.'

'Not bad, Frank? It's peanuts. That bastard in Colombia has kept all my deposit money; the contacts in England say they don't want to buy anymore, and my partner in Antwerp is sitting on my fortune, locked away in a property somewhere, to which, only he has a key. As soon as we get to Antwerp, I'm taking the lot, packing it all in, and heading off to Brazil. You can have a couple of million, Frank.'

'Thanks,' said Hawkwell, not knowing what else to say.

'I'd like to hang around and personally kill Delaney,' continued Stait, 'for what his men did to Freddie and Tommy; but it could jeopardise my getting away from Europe.'

'Yeah, they were pretty good; why not consider recruiting James and his guys full time? They would be even better; they're all experienced; Tommy had a lot to learn.'

'Mm, but he was a quick learner. Damned shame.'

'They had quite a long time in England, by the way; I mean, between dropping off the last delivery and getting to you in Devon.'

'I sent them to do a job somewhere.'

'Where, and what?'

Stait did not answer straight away; he paused and took a drink. 'Getting a bit nosey, Frank. Okay; I just sent them to that old house in Hertfordshire. You know the one where you had the big apartment for a while when you needed to lie low?'

'Yes, I remember it well; big damp old place.'

'Mm, well I just wanted them to get rid of a couple of people that were living there for a while, doing pretty terrible things.'

'Right; let's leave it there; I wish I'd never asked.'

'I should have given the job to you, Frank; Freddie and Tommy went a bit over the top.'

279

Hawkwell nodded slowly in acknowledgement, poured a couple more drinks for both of them and sat forward. 'So, Aaron; what's the plan? Am I right in saying you need me to help you get your cash out of Belgium?'

'Of course I do, Frank; it won't be easy, but we can do it. Then we can go our separate ways. I'll set a course for Terneuzen and we'll get on our way. I want to be there by the early hours of the morning.'

'Okay; Terneuzen?'

'On the water near Antwerp; I've got a mooring there.'

Hawkwell sat back and enjoyed his drink as he watched Stait expertly prepare for the journey. He was thinking about Stait's words that he could have 'a couple of million'. Not bad, he thought, but I could probably take it all. What does another dead body matter? Just because it would be Aaron Stait's? Whoever his 'partner' is in Antwerp, they obviously have a big stake in it all as well. He decided he would make a decision en route to Terneuzen: help them out and take a couple of million; or kill them both and take the lot.

Taffy Burton knew Delaney well enough to know when he was going to be told something serious. He had walked towards Delaney in the arrivals lounge with a smile, ready to greet his boss. But as soon as he saw the look on Delaney's face, it was clear to him that some bad news was on its way.

On the car journey to the house that they were all using, Delaney told Burton about his trip back to the boatyard and the stately home used by Hawkwell and Stait, the two dead bodies and the skeleton. When he told Burton about Hubert being a joint managing director of the company that used the house and of Sondheim being the owner, Burton realised why he had been asked to come alone. He was not comfortable.

'We're The Overseas Liaison Agency, sir; we're supposed to help other law enforcement agencies when they work in Britain and Europe. This is turning into a hunt for a crime boss and we're the only ones in it, if you discount Riego. Shouldn't we be giving this to MI6 or Interpol now?'

'I nearly said exactly the same thing to Lady Stonehaven, Taffy, but I didn't.'

'Why?'

'Because. err, because of Ellie Shanks, because of Chief Inspector Baart, because of Julie Greaves, and let's not forget Peter Giers, the Belgian, who died in Colombia when all this shit probably kicked off.'

'You're making it personal, sir; you don't usually do that.'

'No, but I suppose the last straw on this back of mine was Hubert.'

'Right, well you're here now, sir, so you can take charge; what happens now?'

'We go to the house; you don't tell the others 'til I've been to see Hubert, which I'll do first thing in the morning.'

'Right; I'll come with you.'

'Okay.'

Wyatt, Pitt and Riego were playing cards and sharing a few beers when Burton and Delaney got to the house. Burton explained to them all that he and the boss were going back to see Hubert because there were a few more things to iron out before they went for Stait.

Riego was the restless one. 'Hubert said he would let us know as soon as he heard anything,' he said. 'But that could take days; I say we call in more men. Put more people out there.'

'To do what?' asked Delaney.

'To look for Stait and Hawkwell.'

'Where?'

'Any god damned where! He has to cross borders for Christ's sake!'

'You raise your voice to me, Michael, you had better have good reason; and as far as I can see, you haven't.'

'Yeah, well how about Julie Greaves lying dead on a slab; how's that for a reason?'

Wyatt tried to cut in and calm things down. 'Hey, Yank; get me another beer while you're up.' He was expecting Riego to tell him to piss off, but he did not. He went to the fridge, took out two beers and opened them. He passed one to Wyatt and then took one to Delaney. 'Sorry.'

Delaney nodded. 'Forget it, I suppose Julie is a reason; maybe you're right to be angry.' Then he turned to the others. 'Not much more alcohol please, gentlemen; I need you fit and able tomorrow. I'm going to get some sleep. Taffy; we'll leave at nine in the morning.'

They were all up early the following morning; Riego and Pitt went for a good run and were back to join the others before breakfast. Pitt looked like he'd been for a stroll but Riego was panting. 'Did he keep up with you, Ajit?' asked Delaney.

'Only just, sir.'

Riego looked put out. 'Hey there's about 15 years between us; I did okay.'

'Load of old bollocks,' said Wyatt, as he ate some toast and sipped at his coffee. Burton came into the room; he was coughing loudly.

'I heard you coughing last night, Taffy, 'said Delaney. 'Are you okay?'

'I'm fine.'

'All the same, if I haven't heard from someone about the powder sample they took from your hair by tonight, I'll chase them up.'

282

'As I said, sir; if it was something bad they shoved into my face I'm sure I would have smelt it or had some sort of bad feeling by now.'

Delaney's phone rang. 'That could be them now,' he said. 'Hello.'

He recognised the voice; 'Mr Delaney, it's George Hale from the forensics lab in Stevenage; we've been looking at the bodies from Staleybridge House?'

'Hello there; that didn't take too long.'

'No, if you remember; I did say it wouldn't be too difficult.'

'What about the skeleton?'

'Nothing much for you there, I'm afraid; other than it was 14 months old.'

'Right; and the two dead bodies?'

'Oh that was much easier. I won't bore you with how we find out these things; but the small man on the meat hook was an Aldo Pollitt. He was Austrian; 52 years old, ran a helicopter business for rich business people and officials.'

'I'll bet he ran another kind of business as well.'

'You mean the magazines and the photos?'

'Mm.'

'I think you'll be hearing from someone else about that; not long after you left the house, Interpol arrived. They took everything we didn't need.'

Delaney waited for a while but Hale did not offer any more information. 'Okay,' he said, 'I'll wait for their call; what about the big man in the room next to the hallway?'

'He was Mark Borg; from Denmark, 51 years old, pilot and business man; had a criminal record.'

'Anything else?'

'Not from me, no; but at least you have the ID's.'

'Sure, thanks very much; bye for now'

He explained the phone call to the others. Burton frowned when he mentioned his findings in the house, but Delaney nodded to him and explained to the others about the dead bodies in the house, but not about Hubert being a co-owner. Riego left the boiled egg he was preparing and sat down. 'Julie told me about Pollitt and Borg; they were the ones that visited Sondheim in Monte Carlo. I think she said it was Pollitt who wanted kids shipped over from Colombia, but Borg was the one into paedophilia.'

'Makes sense,' said Delaney. 'I think they used that house for their sick little games; Stait found out and he got someone to kill them. He was dealing with Sondheim on drugs. Sondheim probably agreed with Stait that they could use the house, just thinking it was as a business base or something.'

'Do you think it was Hawkwell that killed them?' asked Pitt.

Delaney stood up to leave as he answered. 'No; Hawkwell's a pro. He would have killed them quickly and cleanly and gotten out of there. I think it might have been Ludic and Tommy; on Stait's orders.'

It was only a ten minute drive to Hubert's office. When Burton and Delaney arrived, Sergeant Brun showed them through. They both took water when offered a drink; Hubert stayed at his desk and Brun remained standing. Delaney took a notebook from his pocket as Brun and Burton acknowledged each other with a nod, remembering their last encounter together, when Brun had killed the man outside Burton's hotel room.

'Where are your other men, Mr Delaney?' asked Hubert.

'I've got them doing some finding out; I thought we could discuss tactics before we brief them all.'

'Certainly.'

'Have you heard anything of Stait?'

'No; his yacht has gone missing also.'

284

Hubert did not offer any more, and Burton glanced at Brun, who also remained quiet. Delaney pressed on. 'How long have you been trying to collar Stait, Inspector?'

'Quite a while unfortunately; he seems to have access to a lot of money which means he can pay well for silence and services.'

'You are aware that we took out Freddie Ludic and Tommy?'

'Yes; we got a communiqué from Lady Stonehaven; that was good work.'

'Mm, but I'm afraid we let the side down a bit; Hawkwell is back out there again. You do know it was Hawkwell that killed Chief Inspector Baart?'

'Yes,' said Hubert as he wiped a hand across his face and fiddled with his moustache. 'I would think that he is far away by now, looking for somewhere to live on the other side of the world if he knows what's good for him.'

Delaney stared at Hubert. You lying bastard, he thought to himself; you know that Hawkwell is on his way to help Stait, or he's already with him. And you probably know where they are.

'Now then,' continued Hubert, 'why not let Sergeant Brun here show you where Stait used to moor his yacht; it's not far away. That could be a starting point. You may be able to speak to some of the locals in case Stait dealt with any of them; you may get a few clues.'

'Okay, thank you; lead on Sergeant.'

Brun left the room and Delaney and Burton followed. Hubert raised a hand as cheerio.

Brun was to take them to Terneuzen; where Stait's mooring was. On the journey, he chatted with Burton about the events of the last two weeks as Delaney gazed out of the window, deep in thought. He had noticed how Brun had frowned when Hubert suggested the trip. If there was anything to find around the area, it would have been found by now. If Stait and Hawkwell were on their way back to Terneuzen, Hubert would have kept people away.

The jetty was full when they arrived; they spent some time walking up and down looking for signs of the *Adinerado* but there was nothing that resembled it. A couple of motor yachts were the same size but most were older and smaller. 'I will check in to base, and then we will have pastries and coffee, yes?' said Brun.

'Sure,' said Delaney, 'somewhere where we have a good view though, if you see what I mean.'

Brun smirked. 'Naturally, and then...'

'Wait,' said Burton. They all paused. Delaney could see the concentration on his face. 'What is it, Taffy?'

'Can we walk back along that second jetty again?'

'You sure?'

'I'm sure, sir.'

That was enough for Delaney; he let Burton lead the way and asked Brun to stay back and keep them both in sight. They walked slowly around the area again. Now and then Burton hesitated to look at things without making it obvious. Ten minutes later he looked at Delaney and then led the way back to Brun. 'Don't make it too obvious gentlemen,' he said. 'But the yacht with the outboard boat and the square windows; the *Juliet*, see it?'

Brun and Delaney took their time to have a look while casually moving around. 'I see it,' said Brun.

'It's the *Adinerado*. The rear swim platform has lots of marks on the timber deck A couple of the marks are diagonal and someone tried to varnish over them but the colour is nothing like the rest of the deck. I was forced onto my knees by Ludic to wait while Tommy fetched the car; I was staring at that deck for a minute or more. That's the deck; it's the *Adinerado*.'

Delaney walked on slowly and they both followed. 'Right, let's find somewhere to sit and watch for a while.'

'I will take you to the harbour master's office and the raised observation room; we will have a good vantage point from there.

It's where the Inspector and I observed the yacht from before it left for England.' A few minutes later Sergeant Brun was explaining to the assistant harbour master why they were there and which boat they were interested in.

As they watched, Delaney took the opportunity to sound out Brun. 'Have you worked with Inspector Hubert for long, Sergeant?'

'About four years.'

'Do you get on well together?'

'I suppose we get on okay; as we should do; sometimes he can be too officious but I've worked for worse bosses.'

'Do you think he will get Chief Inspector Baart's job now it is vacant?'

'It has been mentioned but I think he may be looking to retire early.'

'Really?'

'Yes, he has mentioned it once to me. He has changed over the last two years; I think the job does not interest him as much as it used to.'

'Oh, right.' Delaney left it there. Burton cleverly changed the subject and asked Brun if he would accompany him to get some more coffees. As Delaney was looking through binoculars in the direction of the marina, he started to piece a few things together. If Hubert started to lose interest two years ago, that was a hell of a coincidence. Ellie Shanks had joined Belgian Interpol two years ago; they had asked for British and French operatives because their internal affairs people were concerned about corruption. According to Stonehaven, the Colombian rebels started dealing with Stait and Sondheim about two years ago. That would have been when the big money started to change hands. And it would have been when Stait was earning big money; enough money to hand out a few million to people that could be corrupted.

When Burton and Brun came back, he gave the binoculars to Burton and sat down near Brun without saying anything. 'How long shall we keep watching?' asked Brun.

'Not much longer,' said Delaney. 'I hope you don't mind me asking you those questions about you and Inspector Hubert.'

'No, Mr Delaney, that is okay.'

'Well I'm sure the Inspector...what is his first name anyway, Sergeant; I can't keep calling him Inspector Hubert.'

'It is Henry, but he hardly uses it. Most people just call him Inspector.'

'I see; well I will as well then.'

That confirms it then, thought Delaney; he was *Henry* Hubert; the same Henry Hubert that was joint Managing Director of Adinerado Enterprises that was registered at Staleybridge House. He was about to suggest that they get some more people to watch the yacht, when Brun spoke quietly with him. 'Mr Delaney; I feel I want to mention something to you.'

'Please do, Sergeant.'

'You will remember when Ben and Ajit were working over here with me?'

'Yes.'

'It's just...well...when we were all in agreement, I went to see the Inspector to ask permission for the raid at the house near Eeklo.'

'Right.'

'Well, the Inspector asked me to wait and he left the room; he said he had to ask Section Nine. I think at the time, Ben was on the phone to you.'

'Go on.'

'I wondered why he left the room to speak to Section Nine; he could have phoned them; as he had done in my presence on many occasions before. And their office is next door to his, but he was gone for twenty minutes.'

'Mm, why are you telling me this, Sergeant?'

'Because I have doubts about the Inspector, sir; and I think you do too. This is why you ask me questions I think?'

Delaney knew when to be straight and get on with things. 'Yes it is; and yes, I do have doubts.'

'I was going to mention it to Chief Inspector Baart before he was killed.'

'Before he was killed by Frank Hawkwell.'

'Yes.'

'Do you know who Frank Hawkwell works for, Sergeant?'

'No,'

'Aaron Stait; joint MD of Adinerado Enterprises; the other joint MD is a Mr Henry Hubert. That boat down there, now called the *Juliet,* was called the *Adinerado*; it's Spanish for wealth.'

'But the Inspector stood with me in this very office as we watched the yacht.'

'Yes, and when you phoned me to say that Stait had left here, you said that Hubert had found this place on his own and then asked you to join him. He found this place on his own because he already knew where it was. It wouldn't surprise me if he shared a glass with Stait on the yacht and then came here to phone you.'

'Why, sir?'

'So you – and the harbourmaster – were witnesses in seeing him observing, supposedly secretly.'

Burton had heard all of the conversation; he put own the binoculars and looked at Brun. 'We need you to help us, Brun.'

'Yes, I think so.'

'We need to somehow get Hubert to go to Stait.' He looked at Delaney. 'Am I right, sir?'

'Of course you are, Taffy. Let's get back to the car and I can tell you both what I have in mind.'

40

The motor yacht, *Juliet*, had been vacated some time ago. Stait and Hawkwell had arrived at Terneuzen at 3 a.m. They loaded the car that Stait kept near the marina with some belongings, the firearms and the money and diamonds and headed for a farm on the outskirts of Antwerp. Two large barns had been converted into homes; when Stait had gone to buy one two years ago, he ended up buying both of them *and* the farm.

They settled down to rest for while, taking it in turn to sleep and be on the lookout. It was 11 a.m. when their visitor arrived. Hawkwell watched as Stait opened the door to a smartly dressed man with a moustache. The man settled in an armchair and was quiet until Stait introduced him. 'Frank; this is Henry.'

Hawkwell said 'Hello, Inspector,' as he looked at the man. Stait offered the visitor a drink and he accepted. It was after a few sips of tea that the man spoke as he looked at Hawkwell. 'How are you, Frank?'

'I'm okay.'

'You two know each other?' asked Stait.

'Oh yes,' said Hawkwell; I've done a couple of jobs for Henry here.'

Stait seemed displeased that they were acquainted; Hawkwell explained. 'You don't really think I killed Baart just for the hell of it do you, Aaron? When I was with Compito, or whatever his bloody name is, I couldn't believe my luck when we walked into the wrong office and saw Baart standing there. Henry had asked me to get rid of him a while back, hadn't you, Henry?'

'Yes, I thought he was getting suspicious.'

'So I just took the opportunity to do what I had been paid for,' continued Hawkwell. 'Then that undercover bastard turned round and swiped me one; what's his name?'

'Riego,' said Hubert, he's CIA.'

Stait stood up quickly and walked around them both. 'Hang on, you two; are you saying, Frank, that I was paying you to help get Delaney and at the same time Henry was paying you to kill Baart?'

'Yeah, that's right; don't forget I'm freelance.'

Stait turned to Hubert. 'And you, Henry; you never thought that it would be a good idea to tell me that you had employed Frank, when you knew I was employing him as well?'

'Why would I; I did not know that you had sent him to kill Delaney or that Baart would be there. It was lucky coincidence.'

'Not that lucky; Delaney's still alive.'

There was silence for a minute; Stait poured himself and Hubert some more tea. Hawkwell gulped on his coffee and smiled. 'Something funny, Frank?' asked Stait.

'Yeah, you two are; a couple of the most dishonest men in Europe and you get annoyed at each other for not being up front about things.'

'Dishonesty is in all of us at some point,' said Hubert. 'When I first joined the police, I...'

'Oh shut your mouth, you hypocrite,' said Hawkwell, 'before I knock your bloody head off your shoulders for you. You're greedy.' He looked at Stait; 'so is he, we all are, so let's cut the self righteous shit and get on with things can we?'

After a few seconds, Stait sat down again and looked at Hubert as he tilted his head towards Hawkwell. 'He's right; we need to get moving. Is everything where we left it?'

'Yes; follow me,' said Hubert.

They made their way out of the converted barn and Hubert led them to a garage. It had been the stable block of the original building and two double doors opened automatically when Hubert pressed a remote control. Inside the garage there was an old Citreon that had not been cleaned for some time. 'Very clever,' said Hawkwell. The other two knew what he meant; the last thing they wanted now was a conspicuous large car or a sports car that would turn heads. Hubert led them to the rear of the car and unlocked two metal cabinets that had hazardous chemical warning logos on them. There were four shelves in each cabinet; all full of briefcases and holdalls. Most of the cases were black; some of them were brown. The holdalls were also in two colours; blue and red. 'I thought you said it was all safe,' said Stait, 'anyone could have got in here.'

'No they couldn't,' said Hubert. He held up the remote control in his hand. 'As soon as I pressed this, it de-activated a trigger on the cabinet doors as well. If anyone had tried to open these cupboards they would be dead; look.' He pointed to a narrow strip of plastic explosive on each door hinge; designed to blow outwards causing minimum harm to the cases and the holdalls. 'Now listen,' he continued. 'The six brown cases hold dollars; about two million in each. The 15 black cases hold Euros; about five million in each. In each of the two red holdalls, there are nine million dollars worth of bearer bonds and gilt certificates. The certificates are guaranteed by the Belgian Treasury.' He looked at the other two for a response.

'And the blue holdalls?' said Hawkwell.

'That's your department more than mine.'

Hawkwell took one of the holdalls off the lower shelf and opened it. He let out a whistle as he reached into the bag. 'Holy shit; I thought we were just getting away with a lot of money. You should have said we were waging war on Europe.'

'Yes, well,' said Hubert, 'you can examine it all later. Everything will fit into the boot of the car; I've tried it, so come on let's move.'

As they loaded the car, Stait nudged Hawkwell on the shoulder. 'Too much fire power, even for you, eh, Frank.'

'I'll try to live with it.'

When the car was loaded, Hubert gave the keys to Stait. 'You two take this car and head for Brussels; there are three seats reserved on the Eurostar leaving for London at 4 p.m. You'll find new passports on the passenger seat. I must return to my office to attend a meeting; there is no way I can get out of it; it involves Interpol and I don't want them getting suspicious. I will meet you in Brussels.'

'So you're letting us take all this lot?' asked Stait.

'You won't leave me out of it, Aaron; I could have half the Belgian police force come down on both of you whenever I wanted.'

'Why London; back into the lion's den isn't it?'

'Exactly,' said Hawkwell, 'No one will expect it. Right, Henry?'

'Right; so move; and when we get to London, we change vehicles and stay at Heltern Manor for a while.'

When Stait noticed the frown on Hawkwell's face, he explained. 'Another property owned by Adinerado Enterprises, Frank; tucked away nicely in the Pennines; we fly from Manchester to Mexico, the day after tomorrow.'

'I'm impressed, said Hawkwell. 'Perhaps at this point, I should tell you that Eurostar is for passengers; not vehicles.'

'I am aware,' said Hubert. 'I have made arrangements for a large goods compartment and a porter; when you arrive, you say you have the luggage for Inspector Hubert and they will assign a porter to you.'

'Risky,' said Stait.

'Yes, so I hope people won't be expecting it; now go.'

Hubert watched the Citreon drive away. He closed the garage doors and locked the house doors and windows. When he was sure that everything looked normal, he threw all the keys and the remote control into some long grass to the side of the house. He was pleased that things were finally coming to an end and that he would be able to live the sort of life he had always wanted to. But as he drove back towards Antwerp, his hands were sticking to the steering wheel and sweat was oozing from every pore on his face.

Just outside the main police building in Antwerp, Brun sat behind the wheel of his car. To his right was Delaney; Burton was sitting behind them. In another car, to the rear of the building, Wyatt occupied the driver's seat and Riego and Pitt were sitting in the back.

It was Pitt who saw Hubert first. He tapped Wyatt on the shoulder and pointed. 'I see him,' said Wyatt as he reached for his radio. 'He's here, boss; he'll be going in the back entrance in about two minutes.'

In the other car, Delaney acknowledged the message and turned to Brun. 'Remember, Sergeant; you need to burst into that meeting with conviction. Don't let anyone stop you.'

'I will not,' said Brun. He left Delaney and Burton and made his way to the meeting rooms. He walked slowly past room number two and listened to the voices inside. When he heard Hubert's voice, he took a deep breath, opened the door quickly and walked in. All the delegates looked up. Hubert stopped talking and stared at Brun. 'Sergeant? What...'

'I had to interrupt, Inspector. It's Stait; he's been spotted, with another man; you must come, Inspector. Quickly we need authority for more men and armed squads.'

Hubert did not get a chance to question Brun; one of the high ranking Interpol officers stood up. 'You must go, Inspector, at once; we can go through the rest of your presentation ourselves.'

'We must go now,' said Brun.

Hubert gathered up a few things from the table and followed Brun out of the room. 'I have the authorisation form for you to sign, Inspector,' said Brun. He passed two forms to Hubert who signed them hurriedly as they made their way to the car park.

294

'Have you told Delaney and his people, Sergeant?'

'No; I wanted to check with you first.'

'Very well, leave them out of it for now. Where has Stait been seen?'

'Not far from here, heading west; the traffic police are going to send me the location any moment.'

'Right; I'll make my way out towards that area, call me as soon as soon as you hear something.'

Hubert did not have time to notice that Brun had not challenged what he had said. Brun , like everyone else, did not know where Stait was. It was a gamble, as Delaney had said it would be; but so far the gamble had been worth it. He contacted Delaney. 'He's leaving now; via the rear gate.'

Delaney put his radio on *share*. 'Did you get that, Ben?'

'Yes.'

'Good, don't get too close. Sergeant Brun, you know what to do.'

Before rejoining Delaney and Burton again, Brun made his way to his office and made a phone call. An hour earlier, a stand-by call had been made to an old friend. The phone was answered sharply. 'Peter Lorette .'

'It's on, Peter; he has just left the rear entrance in a blue Peugeot station wagon' heading west.'

'Okay, Brun; tell your following car to stay well back.'

'He has already been told; his car has S37 on the roof, mine has M37.'

'Right; I'll be in touch.'

Lorette pulled back gently on the control lever of the Bell Jet Ranger and the helicopter rose into the air, turned towards the west, and stayed at a thousand feet as it picked up the main road heading west.

As soon as Hubert was out of the city traffic, he phoned Stait. 'Aaron, someone has spotted you; I'm leaving Antwerp now. Get to the Eurostar terminal as quick as you can and change cars; a hire car or something. If you think you're being followed and they get close, you may have to get rid of them. I should be with you in an hour or so.'

'Who the hell could have seen us? They don't even know we're back in Belgium.'

'One of my sergeants had the information and he's good; believe me, someone has seen you. He wouldn't have interrupted a top meeting unless he was sure.' He heard Hawkwell talking in the background to Stait. After a few seconds, Stait acknowledged. 'Okay, we'll keep an eye out for anyone getting close. I'll change the car in Brussels; what about the number plates and the tickets?'

'Just tell them the other car broke down; I've done it before.'

Wyatt and Delaney; driving the two cars that were unmarked except for the roof ID numbers, heard Lorette simultaneously as he sent his first message. 'I have the blue Peugeot station wagon; it is heading south on the A12 towards Brussels.'

Brussels, thought Delaney; not west to the coast, but south, to Brussels. He kept looking straight ahead as he spoke to Brun and Burton. 'What do you think gents?'

'A long haul flight that he couldn't get from Antwerp; or the Eurostar terminal,' said Brun. 'I know a road down here; we can soon be on the A12.'

'My money's on Eurostar,' said Burton, 'then Paris or London; good places to get lost in.'

Wyatt pulled over to let Brun overtake and lead the way. Both cars used their blues and twos to help them get a move on. Delaney decided to use the time to get in touch with two important people; he sent a text to Angela. *Are you and Rocky ok? Hope to be back in a day or two. XX.* Then he phoned Shirley

Stonehaven. He was put through straight away. 'Have you got news, Tom?'

'Hello, Shirley; yes we might be getting close to a result.' He told her what had happened since their last meeting at Staleybridge House and how he had managed to recruit Brun and Peter Lorette and his helicopter. She seemed pleased and she also agreed with Burton that it must be the Eurostar that Hubert was heading for.

'Thanks for letting me know, Tom; I'm going to Companies House later to see if I can find out any more about Aaron Stait's business empire and his Adinerado Enterprises. Stay in touch, yes?'

'Yes, I will. If Hubert *is* meeting Stait and Hawkwell at Brussels, we'll let them get on the train; if it's London, we can handle it and if it's Paris, Harry Mitchell can help us.'

Brun slowed down as he came to a junction. Peter Lorette told him which way to go and confirmed that he had them both in sight. By now, Hubert had parked up, a couple of miles to the north of Brussels. Lorette checked his fuel gauge as he hovered again, keeping his distance. He told them he had one hour's worth of fuel left; if Hubert did not meet up with Stait soon, he would have to leave it to the people on the ground.

41

Stait and Hawkwell produced their tickets and new passports to the check-in desk when they arrived at Eurostar, Brussels. 'We have special luggage for Inspector Hubert of the State Police; we were told to tell you as soon as we arrived.' The experienced looking man behind the desk asked for their passports. As he handed his over, Stait noticed his new title; Chief Inspector Moiret.

The check-in man looked at him for a moment. 'The Head Porter will see to the luggage, Chief Inspector. Please wait near your vehicle.' They went back to the car and waited; five minutes later, a large well dressed man came to them. He was followed by two younger men in uniform. 'Chief Inspector Moiret?'

'That's me,' said Stait.

'These men will take all of the cases and luggage and stay with it throughout the journey; Inspector Hubert gave us specific instructions.'

Hawkwell looked at Stait and shrugged his shoulders. 'Looks like it'll be well looked after then.'

Twenty minutes later, Stait and Hawkwell were sitting in a private passenger compartment, waiting for departure. Stait answered his phone when it played a tune. 'Henry; where are you?'

'About twenty minutes away; the train departs in half an hour.'

'Good, get on with it then.'

Peter Lorette had seen it all from his position a thousand feet up. He guided Delaney and Wyatt in their cars, to the Eurostar check-in building. Both cars were parked in disabled bays; Delaney made for the check-in desk, swiftly followed by Brun, Burton, Wyatt, Riego and Pitt. Brun showed his warrant card to the man at the desk. 'Two men just booked in; which carriage are they on?'

'Many men book in, sir.'

'Any police officers?'

'Only a Chief Inspector Moiret; are you travelling with him and his colleague?'

Brun turned to look at Delaney. 'I do not know a 'Moiret'; what do you think?'

Delaney moved forward to speak to the check-in man. 'Was his colleague well built, in his forties with dark hair and some fresh looking scars?'

'Yes, yes he was; do you want me to get the duty manager?'

'First, I want you to delay the departure of the train.'

'But I need authorisation from the head of...'

'You've got authorisation; from me,' said Brun. 'And what about the luggage; they would have a lot of luggage.'

'Yes they did; we were told to put it into a special secure luggage department on the train.'

'Have you done so?'

'No, not yet.'

'Right, hold the luggage as well as the train.'

The man turned around and made for an office at the back of the check-in area. A smartly dressed woman was sitting in the office. 'Tell her to contact Commander Torres,' said Brun, 'tell him Sergeant Brun says it is a code seven.'

Delaney tapped Brun on the shoulder as he turned and headed for the departure gates. 'Come on. Ben; you come with us. Taffy, stay here with Michael and Ajit; you both know what Hubert looks like, call me if you see him.'

The three men walked to the departure gates and forced their way past the various officials and staff. 'Have a quick look along the train,' said Delaney, 'and I mean *quick;* they know us, remember.'

Frank Hawkwell put his cup down slowly as soon as he spotted Wyatt walking along the platform. He thought about Wyatt and Greaves visiting him in jail and how Wyatt had hit him. For an instant, he thought about not telling Stait; he could find a way out of the situation, leaving Stait on his own. But he needed Stait; *Chief Inspector Moiret*, to get to the luggage; and he still had not made his mind up about whether or not he was going to get rid of Stait and Hubert and take it all for himself.

'Don't look out of the window, Aaron; we've got company.'

'Who?'

'One of Delaney's men, so it probably means he's not alone.'

'Any sign of Henry?'

'No.'

'Okay, Frank, earn your money; get me out of here.'

'And what about the contents of our luggage?'

'*They* don't know about the luggage; if we can get away, I can have a London contact meet the train.'

'You ask a lot, Aaron.'

'And I pay a lot.'

Hawkwell sighed and reached into his jacket to undo the retaining strap on his shoulder holster. 'Right, they haven't seen us yet; come with me.' They moved towards the rear of the train and got out on the opposite side, away from the platform. Some work men had left their high visibility orange waistcoats hung over some shovels and Hawkwell grabbed two of them. 'Here; put that on, and walk casually.' Stait did as he was told. They walked away from the main platform towards a freight train that was moving very slowly; as the train moved heavily away at walking pace, they both walked alongside it pretending to be ushering it along. Hawkwell looked back for a moment to see Wyatt looking around the platform, having completed his stroll past the carriages.

As Delaney and Brun were hovering around the platform and the entrance gate, a man walked past them, raising his voice to another man that was with him. Delaney frowned. 'What is he saying, Sergeant?'

'He must be a maintenance man; he's moaning that someone has taken his safety jacket.'

'Oh right, lets...'

'Wait' said Brun. He stopped the maintenance man and spoke to him for a few seconds before turning to speak to Delaney again. 'Two jackets, sir; he says two jackets have been taken.'

They both scoured the surroundings; a group of five men were working on a signal post and another group of four men were manoeuvring a sign into place further down the track. As Brun looked farther away, across the tracks and down the line, he saw two men walking slowly alongside a freight train. Another train was coming the opposite way on a nearby track and blew its warning signal. But the two men did not acknowledge. Brun knew that when a warning signal was sent, maintenance workers had to acknowledge they had heard the warning and raise a hand in the air. Then he saw one of the men look back furtively. 'There! They're there! The two men with that freight train!'

Delaney did not wait to question anything; he started running. 'Come on then!' As they ran towards the end of the platform, he shouted again. 'Ben! There; by the freight train!'

When they heard the shouting, Stait and Hawkwell ran at full pace to overtake the train and get on the other side of it. Realising they were too far back to do the same, Delaney, Brun and Wyatt waited until the freight had passed. They could still see the two men running to the opposite goods platform and loading bays. Delaney told Brun to go to the left and Wyatt to the right. Stait and Hawkwell reached the road on the other side of the goods building and stopped a car in its tracks. Stait opened the driver's door to see a young man with a defiant look on his face. 'Get out now! I'm a police officer.' The young man shouted back at him. 'You can't do...'

Hawkwell shot him in the chest and dragged the body out of the car as he shouted to Stait. 'We don't have time for shit like that! Get in!'

Wyatt was rounding the right hand corner of the building as the car sped away. He fired three times at the vehicle, smashing the back window and most of the tail lights. Brun was running towards him and slowed down as he saw the car disappear around a corner. Delaney was on the scene by then, talking on his radio. 'Two men, Taffy, in a car without a back window, get hold of a local officer and get the traffic police on to it.'

The three men were still catching their breath when a police car pulled up in front of them. Brun raised his warrant card aloft. 'Police!' The driver nodded and his passenger got from the car and put his handgun away. 'You are Sergeant Brun?'

'Yes.'

'We got a message from Commander Torres in Antwerp; he says to help you.'

'Err, thank you,' said Brun, looking at the other two. 'But I fear it may be too late.'

42

A car without a back window and lights was too conspicuous and Frank Hawkwell knew he had to get rid of it. When they were out of sight of the goods building and Brun and Wyatt, he headed for a large multi-storey car park. He reversed into a corner so the back of the car could not be seen and they looked around for another vehicle that would not draw attention. 'Do you know how to start a car without a key??' said Stait.

'Don't be so bloody stupid,' said Hawkwell. 'We wait for someone to collect their car.'

It was not long before a woman carrying shopping bags stepped out of a lift and made her way to a Ford parked nearby. When she had unlocked the car with the remote control as she approached it, Hawkwell went up to her, punched her in the face and grabbed the keys. She fell to the floor, unconscious. 'Let's hope she paid at the machine,' said Hawkwell, 'I haven't got any change.

The woman *had* paid at the machine and they were soon heading out of Brussels on a quiet rural road.

When Delaney, Brun and Wyatt got back to Burton and the others, there was another piece of news that Delaney did not really want to hear. 'We've lost contact with the helicopter,' said Riego.

'He might have needed fuel,' said Pitt, 'but we er...'

'But we what?' asked Delaney.

Burton interrupted. 'He's trying to tell you that we haven't seen Hubert either. The last message we got from the helicopter, said that Hubert had left his car nearby and was walking to the station. But we haven't seen him anywhere.'

'So why didn't the pilot follow him when he was on foot?' asked Brun

'Like I say, probably fuel,' repeated Pitt.

Brun frowned. 'No; he would have told you if it was fuel.' He reached for his radio and spoke clearly as he looked skywards. 'Peter, this is Brun; do you hear me. This is Brun; come in Lorette.' There was no reply.

'Well, let's just hope he's okay,' said Delaney, 'come on you lot; let's scan the area for a while and check the other carriages.' The train due to depart was still being held by the senior station officer. They walked the length of it, checking every carriage and compartment; there was no sign of Hubert. Delaney asked Brun to get in touch with Commander Torres in Antwerp, in case some news had gone through to him. Brun left for a while to make a call and returned, looking disappointed. Torres confirmed that he had heard nothing, that no one had reported a sighting of Hubert or the helicopter and that Brun was to return to Antwerp immediately; he would send a car. 'I have to go to Antwerp,' said Brun. 'I fear I may be in trouble for staying with you.'

'Well then,' said Delaney, 'don't make things worse; get yourself back there, Sergeant, and thank you very much.'

Brun looked at Wyatt and then at Pitt. 'This is the second time we have failed and I do not get the chance to carry on working with you.'

'They'll be other times, mate; good luck,' said Wyatt.

'Yeah, take care,' Pitt said, as he shook Brun's hand. Brun walked slowly out of sight and they all looked at one another. Burton could only think of one option. 'Back home, sir?'

'Back home, Taffy; what the frigging hell else?'

It only took about a hour to arrange a flight; Delaney got in touch with Shirley Stonehaven and she redirected a charter flight that was on its way from Vienna to London with some diplomats on board. Very little was said during the flight. Riego started to drink too much and Delaney told him to pack it in. Burton joined the crew to have a look around the cockpit and Wyatt discussed things that had been learnt over the last few days with Pitt; whether Pitt wanted to or not.

43

Frank Hawkwell threw another cigar butt out of the car window as he sat with Stait. Stait had told him to head north out of Brussels, but when he had received a phone call, he told Hawkwell to go west towards Ninove. After another call, Stait told him to turn right into an airfield entrance and park up near the apron.

Hawkwell was losing his patience. 'So who was that on the phone, Aaron?'

'Henry; he's on his way to meet us here.'

'So they didn't get him either.'

'No. But do we need him, Frank?'

'Probably not.'

'That's just what I was thinking. Are you still carrying that gun?' Hawkwell opened his jacket slightly to reveal the hand gun. Stait smiled. 'Can I have the honour, Frank?'

'Be my guest.' He handed the gun to Stait and put a finger out. 'And do it properly; I don't want to have to clean up after you.'

Stait put the gun in his belt and got out of the car; the sound of a helicopter could be heard and Hawkwell looked. 'That's him now,' said Stait, 'come on; we're going to join him.' Hawkwell stayed in the car; he was too wise to let someone have the upper hand. He switched on the ignition and started the car.

'What are you doing?' asked Stait.

'Being ready, just in case; you do realise that it's a police helicopter do you?'

Stait did not answer. The Bell Jet Ranger landed smoothly as it faced them. The left hand door opened and Hubert jumped out. As he was walking towards them, the pilot cut the engine and jumped down from the other side. Stait turned as Hubert joined him and they settled against the car. The pilot shook hands with Stait and started to unbutton his shirt. 'Good to see you again, Aaron; I'll just get out of this uniform and we'll get on our way, if that's okay with you?'

'Sure, go ahead.'

Hawkwell leaned out of the car window and eyed the pilot. 'And who the hell are you?'

'Allow me to introduce you, Mr Hawkwell,' said Hubert. 'This is Peter Lorette; probably the best police chopper pilot in Europe.'

Hawkwell moved his head around slowly and curled his mouth down. 'And don't tell me; now he's an *ex*-police chopper pilot and a lot richer.'

'That's about it, Frank,' said Stait.

Lorette changed his shirt and shoes. 'Can someone help me with the luggage; I'll need to re-arrange things so we can all sit comfortably on the flight.'

'Would you mind, Frank?' asked Stait.

'Okay, but not until you explain what's happening.'

'Allow me,' said Hubert. 'The luggage porters at the station had been given instructions by me. I had told them that your luggage was not to go on the train, but was to be left in my car, which was in the staff car park. I drove out of Brussels to a disused power station site. Peter flew the chopper to meet me; we transferred the luggage to the helicopter and here we are. Peter cut off all radio transmissions to the people on the ground, after dropping a hint that he was short of fuel; he wasn't.'

'But we were on the train, ready to go; the luggage, you bastard, you were going to take it all.'

'No, no, Mr Hawkwell. You and Stait were to get off the train just before it left and come to me. Then Aaron noticed that you had seen one of Delaney's men; if you had tried to get off the train, they would have jumped you. As soon as Aaron saw the situation, he let you take over knowing that you were best placed to get the pair of you out of there; right, Aaron?'

'Right.' Stait looked at Hawkwell. 'I didn't want you to be concerned about the luggage, Frank; I knew Henry would find another way of meeting up with us.'

'So all the luggage is in there,' said Hawkwell, pointing to the helicopter.

Hubert and Lorette nodded.

'All the money, the diamonds, the bonds?'

They nodded again.

There was silence for a moment. Hawkwell thought again of the ideas that had gone through his mind earlier. They were all here, he thought; Stait *and* the bent bastards. He could kill the lot and take everything. Then Stait interrupted his thoughts. 'So if you don't mind, Frank,' he said, 'if you help Peter, I'll dump this car.'

Lorette was already near the helicopter. As Hawkwell walked towards him, Stait nodded to Hubert who acknowledged the signal. Stait caught up with Hawkwell as he approached the helicopter. He took the hand gun out of his belt and aimed it at the back of Hawkwell's head. 'Sorry, Frank.'

Hawkwell did not have time to turn around; Stait fired twice into his neck. As Hawkwell hit the ground and twisted around, Stait fired again, putting two bullets into his chest. He was horrified to see that Hawkwell's eyes were still awake, in defiance. He was almost decapitated and his lungs were shot to pieces, but his dark calculating eyes still stared at Stait. 'Sorry, Frank; I had to do it to you, before you did it to me.' An artery burst open out of Hawkwell's neck, the side of the helicopter was showered in blood, and Hawkwell died; his eyes wide open.

'Jesus, Aaron!' said Lorette, 'you could have given him a couple of million and told him to get lost, you animal!'

Stait threw the gun away and got on board. 'Maybe; you won't need to re-arrange the luggage now, will you? There'll be enough room.' Hubert got on board and Lorette made preparation for the flight. 'Now just get this thing airborne,' continued Stait, 'and get us out of here, or you'll be next. Have you arranged the route?'

'Yes,' said Lorette. 'There's a seaplane waiting for me at Blankenberge. And a commercial vehicle marked up as a Royal Mail van, waiting at Dunwich on the Suffolk coast. From there we drive to Heltern Manor.'

44

The wind and rain lashed against the window as Angela Casey looked out into the back garden. She had received a text from Delaney 24 hours earlier saying that he should be with her soon and she had taken a couple of days of work to be at home. As she looked out, seeing only the wetness and occasional blackbird, she started to feel like the weather; downcast.

'You have no idea, Tom Delaney,' she said to herself. 'You have no idea how much I love you and how I don't sleep with worry for you. Where are you for heaven's sake?'

She picked up her phone and dialled his number. There was no answer. She sent him a text message; *got your message yesterday, are you coming back today? Xx.* She felt Rocky licking her hand and looked down at him. 'Oh where is your master, eh, lad?' Rocky might have cared where his master was, but he did not show it; not when he was due for a walk. She put him on his lead and they walked to the local park. As Rocky was enjoying chasing a ball and running around with other dogs, a gust of wind forced Angela's umbrella to fold itself inside out. It was almost blown from her grip; the rain got heavier and she was drenched as she called out to Rocky. 'Come on then! Let's go home!' She pushed the broken umbrella into a rubbish bin and they both ran back to the house.

As she opened the door, all the work she had done recently, all the bad weather, and all of the loneliness seemed to hit her at once. She took off her coat, sat down at the foot of the stairs and started to cry.

The front door opened; it was Delaney. He looked at her for a moment and she wiped her eyes and stood up to greet him. They held each other tightly. He kissed her gently and caressed her face in his hands. 'Are you okay? What is it?'

'It's nothing,' she said, 'I'm fine; I'm just tired and cold, blasted weather, I'm soaking.'

Delaney knew there was more to it than that, but he did not labour the occasion. 'You go and have one of your special baths,' he said, 'and I'll nip and get us our favourite fresh bread and some croissants; how does that sound?'

She held him around his buttocks and kissed his chest through his shirt. 'You're not going anywhere. We've got some good wine in the fridge; that'll do.'

'What, at ten in the morning?'

'Yes, at ten in the morning, Tom Delaney, by order.'

'Right then, I'll cook us both up a nice meal,' he said. 'How about an omelette?'

'Perfect; that special one you do with crème fraiche.'

'Okay.'

An hour later they were settled in front of the fire, sipping wine and picking at the leftovers of Delaney's omelette. Rocky was determined not to be left out and he lay down at their feet as Angela stretched her legs over Delaney's thighs. 'I do so worry for you, you know?' she said.

'Well you shouldn't, I may not be as quick as I used to be, but don't forget; I've got some good men around me.' He sensed his answer was not good enough for her. She held his arm.

'When are you off again?' she asked. 'Have you got a few days off now?'

'I don't know. Sorry. We're hoping for some intelligence news so we can find out where people are. How is work anyway?'

'Very busy,' she said, 'Maggie from your office was in touch yesterday. She just phoned to say hello; she said you were in Belgium.'

'Mm, I bloody well was, another cock-up; we don't seem to get any consistent advice, dealing with other law enforcers. People

311

just went missing out of thin air; police officers as well as the bloody criminals.'

By lunch time, Delaney was ready to do some work; he needed to get a change of clothes, check his messages and see how Shirley Stonehaven was getting on. But he did not move. Angela had fallen asleep; he was pinned down by her legs, unable to move, and he decided to sit still and let her sleep rather than disturb her.

At about the same time, Lady Shirley Stonehaven was being driven towards Maindy in Cardiff. The Head of the Registry at Companies House, Jim Moor, had received a phone call from her three hours earlier to say that she was coming to see him, she wanted his undivided attention, and every bit of information they had about Adinerado Enterprises.

Moor's office was modern, with glass and chrome furniture and a cold clinical feel to it. Stonehaven did not waste time with salutations; she took the coffee that was offered to her and got straight down to business. A couple of folders were in front of Moor on his desk.

'Is that information on Adinerado?' she asked.

Moor was a fit looking man with a confident air to him and he spoke without hesitation or nervousness. 'Yes, it is; but I have to say, it may not be entirely up to date.'

'Why not?'

'The information we hold and collate is based on the information that is sent to us. When I was looking through this lot briefly, in preparation for your visit, the first thing I noticed is that we haven't had correspondence of any changes to names or addresses for two years.'

'Is that unusual?'

'It is in this case; because *we have* received something from the land registry about property and deed changes.' He pushed the

312

folders across the table towards Stonehaven. 'Would I be correct in saying that you would like to go through the files yourself?'

Stonehaven looked pleased that he had judged her correctly. 'Yes, thank you,' she said. 'Can I use your office?'

'Of course, I have other people to see in various departments, so I'll leave you to it; an hour okay?'

'Yes, thanks.'

By the time she was half way through the second folder, it all started to fall into place and she was angry that no one - including her - had picked up on certain things sooner. Adinerado was Spanish for wealth or wealthy; Aaron Stait had used a Spanish word at the request of his business partner; his wife, Juliet, who was the daughter of a Colombian man who was involved with Colombian rebels. Not long after Adinerado Enterprises was formed, five new names had been added to the list of directors; Sondheim, Pollitt, Borg, Hubert and Lorette. Sondheim was named as the Financial Director, Pollitt as the Sales Director, and the other three as non-executive directors.

There was a cross reference document that had details of another company, because the director's names were the same. Henry Hubert ran a company that specialised in security guarding and 'diplomatic information' services. The names of Pollitt and Borg were down as running a subsidiary of Adinerado Enterprises called Business Security and Flight Services; the directors in charge of high level security flights by helicopter were Borg and Lorette; both highly skilled pilots.

The activities of Adinerado were listed as 'international couriers', ' importers', 'security services' and 'head hunters'. So that was it, thought Stonehaven, the courier and importers would have been the drugs; the security was so Hubert could divert people away from any imports into Belgium if they became suspicious, and the head hunters would be a front for the child trafficking. Stait and Sondheim would have registered the business in the UK to be sure of a proper legal standing if

313

challenged by the authorities; they would not have been allowed to register in Belgium or Portugal because of their criminal records there.

She checked the last few pages which were address and contact details. Three properties were registered to the business; Staleybridge House, a manor house in west Derbyshire and a small ship yard in Essex. She made a note of the addresses and some contacts and closed the folders.

The hour had gone quickly and Moor came back into the room to ask if everything was okay. She thanked him for being so helpful at such short notice and left as quickly as she had arrived. When they had travelled a few miles back along the M4, her driver asked for confirmation that they were going back to London. 'No, I don't think so, Jim; take me home please. I want to get changed; by then I'll know where I want to go.'

He looked at her in the mirror. She had that expression on her face that he had seen before; a countenance that was one of anger and determination.

45

Taffy Burton was standing at the bar in the Fox & Hounds with Ben Wyatt. There was just the two of them; Michael Riego had opted out and gone to his temporary home and Ajit Pitt had gone to the office to see if he could find out anything else about Stait and co.

Wyatt put his empty glass down on the bar. 'Boy, I needed that.'

'Yeah, me too,' said Burton, 'another?'

'Damn right.'

As they were waiting for their drinks, Burton's phone rang. He didn't recognise the number because Shirley Stonehaven was calling from her home. 'It's Shirley Stonehaven, Taffy.' Burton got Wyatt's attention and pointed to the phone as he mouthed *Stonehaven*. 'Hello Ma'am,' he said as he frowned at Wyatt.

'Taffy, I need you to treat this call as very confidential; are you on your own?'

'Yes, Ma'am.'

'Right, do you know anything about a ship yard in Essex that Tom visited not long ago?'

'Yes; it's more of a *boat* yard though. It's in Shiphampton.'

'Mm, and I believe Tom visited it because he knows the people who run it and it's not far away from the coast.'

'That's right.'

'Okay, listen, Taffy; if Tom phones you I want you to ignore his call. I want you to go to Shiphampton and question the owners; I think their name is Westwood. They could be involved in the Stait case.'

'How?'

315

'It would appear that the boat yard is owned by Adinerado Enterprises.'

Burton raised his eyebrows. 'So why wouldn't I tell Tom?'

'He may be involved; he knows the Westwoods and I just want you to talk to them as an independent party as it were.'

'Right, Ma'am; if you're sure.'

'I'm not a hundred percent sure; that's the trouble, and that's why I don't want you to involve Tom at this stage. Can you leave now?'

'Yes, I should be there by mid afternoon.'

'Okay; take someone with you if you wish.' The phone went dead; Burton hesitated and shook his head before he told Wyatt what had been said.

'So you tell the boss, right?'Said Wyatt.

'Yes; there's no way I'm going behind his back, regardless of what she said.'

They decided to leave their drinks and get on their way. Wyatt drove, Burton phoned Delaney. When he had explained what Stonehaven had said, Delaney's response was predictable. 'Okay, Taffy, if she wants to play those sorts of games, we will as well; I'll meet you at Shiphampton. If you get there before me, wait.'

'Right, sir; What about Michael and Ajit?'

'Leave them out of it for now.'

A couple of hours later, Delaney pulled up outside the Westwood's boat yard, to see Burton and Wyatt already there, parked away from the entrance. he pulled up behind them and gave his instructions as he passed Burton's window. 'Wait here, but get closer to the gate and don't let anyone leave.

Jane and Tim Westwood were both in the main office as he walked in without knocking. They both looked up at him with surprise. 'Tom? Hello,' said Tim.

'Hello both of you, sorry to turn up unannounced.'

316

'And without knocking,' said Jane. Delaney sensed she was still annoyed about their last meeting when he had found out about Staleybridge House. They both had a worried look on their faces. He sat down opposite them and got straight to the point. 'When I came back to get that address from you, why didn't you tell me that you rented this yard and that it was owned by Adinerado Enterprises?'

'What?' said Tim.

'You heard.'

'Hey wait a minute,' said Jane, 'whether this is ren...'

'I'm sorry, I won't wait a minute,' interrupted Delaney. 'Tell me why you didn't tell me.'

Jane sat back and folded her arms tightly. Tim stood and started pacing around as he answered Delaney. 'We didn't want any trouble, Tom; we were afraid of being harassed again.'

'Harassed? Carry on.'

'When we first rented the yard a few years ago, everything seemed fine; it was a good rent for a property like this. Then, when we had been here for a few months, a man came to see us; he said that he represented Adinerado and that the rent had to be doubled. I said we simply couldn't afford it and that business was very bad anyway; so he offered an alternative solution. He said that Adinerado would let us occupy the yard rent-free as long as we helped them in another way.'

'What did this man look like?'

'He had a foreign accent, early forties.'

'Black straggly hair and big eyebrows, a couple of inches shorter than me?'

'Yes.'

'Go on.'

'I mean we suspected it might not have been strictly legal, but he said that if we kept a couple of fast sea-going motor boats and always had them available, they would not charge us any rent. Then he said that sometimes we would be required to hold a

317

package or two here that would be collected by some friends of the company.'

'And who collected the packages?'

'A couple on a motor bike; a man and a woman. The woman always wore a baseball cap.'

'What else? There's something else missing.'

'I converted both of the boats; bigger fuel tanks and more luggage space by taking out some seats.'

Delaney sighed and shook his head slowly as he looked at both of them. 'If you knew something was not quite right, you should have told me. You've been my friends for 15 years for heaven's sake. What about the money you had to start up the business? Your father left you a small fortune, Tim.'

Tim Westwood remained quiet. Jane stared at him. 'Tell him.'

'What does it matter, that's history,' said Tim.

'Tell him.'

Delaney waited for a while. When neither of them said anything else, he stood up and moved towards the filing cabinets. 'Well; while you're deciding whether or not to tell me, I'll have another look in your files.' He opened the first drawer and Jane raised her voice at him. 'Be my guest! Don't bother asking will you.'

'No, sorry; not this time.' He found the folder marked *Dring*. He remembered the details that he had seen before; there was little else. Then, as he went to put the folder back, he noticed a small coloured brochure in the bottom of the drop-down file. It showed a large home on the front cover set amongst a hilly background. Inside the brochure, there was information on the facilities offered; weddings, clay pigeon shoots, conferences. On the back page, a small text box said, *for one summer only*. He looked at the front again; at the bottom of the page, in old style font, were the words Heltern Manor, in beautiful West Derbyshire. He turned to look at Jane. 'What's this?'

'It's all out of date now; the same company that rented us this yard also owned that place as well. We were given it to look at; they said it wasn't used anymore as a tourist place, but if we ever wanted to stay there, they would arrange it for us, as a sort of perk, or payment in kind for helping them.'

'Okay, I'm taking this with me.'

'So what happens to us now?' asked Tim.

'I don't know yet,' said Delaney. 'It would be hard for a court to decide that you knew you were dealing with criminals; beyond all reasonable doubt. But you knew deep down, didn't you?'

'Yes, I suppose we did,' said Tim.

'Oh shut up, you fool,' said Jane. She looked at Delaney. 'We were innocent people in all of this, Tom.'

'No you weren't; don't give me bollocks like that. You suspected you were helping people do something illegal and you told no one.' He turned to leave. 'Someone will be in touch with you. And if I were you I'd get rid of certain files, but I didn't say that.'

Nothing more was said by the Westwoods. As Delaney opened the door, he looked back towards Tim. 'So, err, your inheritance? Are you sure you don't want to tell me?'

Tim shook his head, but Jane leaned forward and huffed. 'He lost it all, Tom. He lost it all gambling. Every blasted penny. That's why we got into trouble when we first set the business up and that's why we took the offer of a rent-free boat yard.' She paused to look at her husband. 'He's pathetic.'

Tim looked at Delaney and shrugged his shoulders. As Delaney went to close the door, he looked back again, tilted his head and pursed his lips. 'Well; I'm sorry for both of you, if that's the case. Bye; and expect a phone call from someone from the forensics team. They may want to go over the boats that were used by Messieurs Porter and Dring.'

When Wyatt saw Delaney leaving the yard, he sat up and nudged Burton. 'That didn't take long.'

319

'No, maybe everything's alright. They're his friends anyway, did you know?'

'No. So why are three of us here?'

'As contingency?'

'Mm, he does like to cover his bases.'

As Burton opened the car window, Delaney knelt down and supported himself on the door. 'Taffy, transfer everything to my car; you drive, we'll leave this one here.'

'Right, sir.'

'Ben, get in touch with Ajit and Michael; tell Ajit I want him here to look after the two owners until further notice. And tell Michael to get in touch with Lady Stonehaven. Tell him to tell her I've been to Shiphampton and its sorted.'

'She'll know I told you, sir, 'said Burton,' against her wishes.'

'Yeah, well; can't win 'em all, Taffy.'

Fifteen minutes later, Burton was adjusting the driver's seat in Delaney's car as Delaney reached his seatbelt. Wyatt slid onto the back seat having made his phone calls.

'Where to?' asked Burton.

'Looks to me like you're on one of your gut feelings, boss,' said Wyatt.

'Yeah, I suppose I am, Ben.'

'So where to then?' repeated Burton.

Delaney ran both hands through his hair and then slapped them down on to his thighs. 'Err, Derbyshire.'

Burton looked in his rear view mirror to see Wyatt smirking back at him, thinking exactly the same.

46

Michael Riego eventually managed to track down Shirley Stonehaven. Maggie Phelps was not going to give out phone numbers to a CIA operative, without getting what she called 'double clarification'. She sent a text to Delaney to ask him to confirm that Riego's orders had come from Ben Wyatt. Riego had gotten impatient. 'Oh come on! Who the hell do you think you're dealing with?'

'A CIA operative, Mr Riego; not a TOLA operative, so you see, I check things first. However, I can confir...'

'However, I can confirm? Where are you from lady?'

Riego regretted challenging her, because the pause was excruciating.

'As I said; I can confirm that you may have Lady Stonehaven's phone number, if you would like to make a note of it now.'

'Well, thanks a lot, go ahead.' He made a note of the number and put the phone down without speaking again.

Stonehaven sounded hesitant when she answered, because she did not recognise the caller's number. 'Hello?'

'Lady Stonehaven, it's Michael Riego.'

'Hello, Mr Riego; how did you get my number?'

'It's a long story. I have a message for you from Delaney, via Ben Wyatt.'

'Go on.'

'He says he has been to Shiphampton and everything's sorted.'

'Everything's sorted?'

'That's all there was, yeah.'

'Okay, thank you. Where is he now?'

'I don't know, but I have an idea that he may be playing things close to his chest; you know, not saying where he is in case there's another double agent amongst us.'

'Double agent? We're not still in the cold war Mr Riego.'

'Okay, okay, undercover operatives, but whatever he and Wyatt are up to, they're not involving me.'

'And what about Taffy Burton?'

'I don't know Ma'am, Wyatt said *he* was with Delaney but he didn't mention Taffy.'

'Okay, Michael, Thank you.'

'So what do *I* do?' asked Riego impatiently.

'Stay in London please; we should keep someone in London.'

Before he had time to ask why, she ended the call. Riego phoned Pitt to ask him if he had received any messages; Pitt told him he was already on his way to Shiphampton. Riego was not fully aware of the involvement of the boat yard and Pitt told him the small amount of information he knew himself.

'Okay,' said Riego, 'do you mind if I join you?'

'You can if you want to,' said Pitt. 'But I think it's just a sitting job.'

Pitt was only a few miles into his journey so he turned around and picked up Riego. They were heading into Essex as the afternoon became cloudy and an early dusk descended.

The seaplane that had been made ready at Blankenberge was piloted by Peter Lorette as professionally as he had piloted the helicopter. As it touched down on the Suffolk coast, Stait tapped Lorette on the shoulder. 'You and Henry take the Royal Mail van to Heltern Manor, the flight to Mexico is at eight in the morning. Henry has the new passports and the visas. I'll see you at the airport about two hours before the flight leaves.'

Hubert looked surprised. 'What's all this, Aaron? Where are you going?'

'I'm going to Essex; the boat yard.'

'Why?'

'There could be some evidence there that we have overlooked; and I don't want anyone blabbing to the police.'

'How will you get there?'

'I'll get a car from somewhere. It's not far from here so I'll only be about two or three hours behind you.'

Stait's contact in Suffolk, Jack Baines, was ready with the van and he drove it to the pier when he saw the seaplane approaching. Stait and Baines left Hubert and Lorette to transfer the luggage into the Royal Mail van. By the time they were driving out of Dunwich, Baines had already spoken to a friend about another vehicle and Stait was on his way to Shiphampton within thirty minutes.

It was 7 p.m. when Pitt and Riego got to the boat yard. The Westwoods were still there; Riego hesitated at the window before Pitt knocked on the door. 'They're arguing about something, Ajit; let them cool down before we say hello.'

They waited for a few minutes; when Tim Westwood moved to open the door, Pitt blocked his way. Jane Westwood stopped shouting when she saw Pitt standing there. Tim moved backwards as though he was afraid the visitors were criminals.

'Sorry, but you can't leave just yet,' said Pitt. 'My name is Ajit Pitt and I work for Tom Delaney; I've been asked to keep an eye out for you.'

'Let's see some ID,' said Tim.

Pitt produced his ID as Riego entered the office. 'Two of you?' said Tim.

'Afraid so, I'm Michael; Michael Riego.'

The Westwoods seemed shocked. They both sat down closer to each other. Jane held her head in her hands. 'We're just a couple business people for heaven's sake,' she said.

Pitt was the first to react. 'I know Ma'am, but Mr Delaney told me to look after you both; it's for your own good.'

'We'd be better at home,' said Tim.

'Yes, sir; we'll escort you there shortly. Has anyone else visited between Mr Delaney leaving and us arriving?'

'No; we were about to go home.'

Riego was impressed with Pitt's mature manner and confident questioning but it had been about three hours since Delaney and Wyatt had left. He knew they needed to get the Westwoods out of there before too much longer. He smiled at both of them. 'My friend here is right, folks; it's for your own good.' He looked at Pitt. 'We should get them home now.'

'Agreed.'

Riego motioned to the Westwoods. 'Okay, folks, grab anything you need and we'll drive you home; you can come with us and leave your car here.'

Riego left first, followed by the Westwoods. As Pitt closed the door behind them, he heard a dull thud. Within that millisecond, he knew it was the sound of silenced rifle. He spun round to see Tim Westwood falling to the floor; a small hole in his forehead. 'Down!' shouted Riego as he grabbed Jane Westwood and hurled her onto the ground. There was the sound of two more dull thuds; two bullets hit the ground a foot in front of where Jane Westwood lay still, screaming. Pitt fired three shots in the direction from where the bullets were coming. He ran to the left and dived behind an upturned boat, knowing that Riego would stay with Jane. But the concealed rifleman knew what he was doing; his fire was not drawn towards Pitt and two more bullets hit the ground near where Riego was, lying as a shield on the ground in front of Jane.

Pitt ran further to the left, stopped behind another small boat and fired again. Then there was silence for a few seconds. Riego took Jane by the hand and made sure she was looking at him. 'When I say *go*, you go, straight for the door, I'll be right behind you.'

Jane nodded as she shook with fear. Pitt guessed right that Riego would try to get back to the office and he let off two more shots to keep the rifleman's head down.

Riego took a deep breath. 'Go!' he stayed as close as he could to her as she ran for the door, then she tripped over her husband's body and fell, screaming again. As Riego went to grab her, one of his legs was shot from under him; he went down and another bullet hit him in his arm as he tried to raise his gun. Westwood threw herself into the office and ran to curl up in a corner. As she looked out, she could see Riego lying there motionless, but he was alive; he was breathing heavily and holding his arm. Then she held her breath; the man with the rifle was walking towards the office. He climbed the couple of steps, kicked the gun out of Riego's hand and stared down at him. 'Well, Mr Antonio Compito; or should I use your real name?'

'Use whatever name you want to, Stait. It doesn't matter either way, 'cus it's the last word you'll speak.'

'Well, anyway, Antonio; goodbye.' Stait aimed his rifle at Riego's face.

'Surprised you didn't send Hawkwell to kill me.'

'He's dead Antonio; and I only came here to kill the Westwoods, it's your fault you got in the way.'

Jane Westwood moved slightly and Stait's attention was diverted. He turned and walked into the office. She stayed in the corner and held her hands over her head. As she started to cry, Stait shot her. She was pushed back into the corner with the force of the bullet and then her body collapsed, still with her head in her hands. After a few seconds, her hands fell. She was gurgling blood, trying to breathe. He left her to die, knowing she could not be saved.

Riego had managed to roll away to one side and grab his handgun again. As Stait came out, he pointed it at him. A pain shot through his arm and he could not summon up the strength to pull the trigger. 'Sorry; where were we,' said Stait. 'Oh yes; I was just about to kill you.'

'Turn around, Stait! I don't shoot people in the back.' Pitt was about twenty metres away, his handgun pointed at Stait, gripped steadily with both hands.

Keeping his rifle trained on Riego, Stait turned his head and looked at Pitt.

'That's better,' said Pitt. His first shot tore through Stait's neck, severing the nerves, stopping any signal to his trigger finger. The second shot was at his chest; it threw him backwards and he landed about two metres away from Riego. Pitt ran up to him to make sure he was dead. He wasn't. From somewhere he had gathered up all of the few seconds of life left in him and he looked up at Pitt.

In his weakening voice, Riego spoke to Pitt. 'Let me have the deciding shot, Ajit.'

'Two wrongs don't make a right, Michael.'

'It's too late for that.'

Pitt nodded. Riego raised his gun and shot Stait in the face.

When Pitt noticed that Riego's breathing was still quite strong, he turned to check on the Westwoods; Tim was dead. He ran to where Jane was slumped in the corner. Blood was coming from her chest, but not in a way that made him think her heart or an artery had been hit. He held three fingers on her neck for a moment. She was still alive.

Forty minutes later he was sitting on the steps to the office. A paramedic had thrown a blanket over his shoulders. He watched as Riego was carried away into an ambulance. The paramedic saw him watching and shouted back to him. 'He'll be okay!'

Jane Westwood was being stretchered out of the office; two people holding bags above her. That had to be a good sign, Pitt thought. They carefully loaded her into another ambulance and as

326

it drove away, Pitt looked around to see two people looking down at Stait's body. One of them said, 'What a way to go; I'm sure he didn't deserve such a brutal ending.'

Pitt looked away and shook his head. Then he realised he hadn't reported in. He reached for his phone to find it was still undamaged; there was no reply from Delaney's phone. He dialled Wyatt's number. 'Ajit; how are you? Did you get to the Westwood's?'

'Yes, I did, is the boss there?'

'He's on the phone to somewhere in Derbyshire.'

'Taffy?'

'He's driving; so it's just me old mate; what's the matter, you sound quieter than usual.'

Pitt paused as he wiped his eyes. 'Well, Ben; remember when I first came to see you and the boss; you said I had a sense of humour, and that it would help?'

'Yes, I remember, mate; what's the matter?'

'Well, if I *had* a sense of humour; I think I've just lost it. The boss isn't going to like what I'm about to tell you.'

47

Burton was driving steadily through west Derbyshire; they were about 20 minutes away from Heltern Manor. He had been looking at Wyatt through the rear view mirror when he had been speaking to Pitt and he knew there was something bad about to be said.

Wyatt clicked his phone shut. Delaney kept looking forward as he spoke. 'Was that Ajit, Ben?'

'Yes, guv.'

'And?'

Wyatt paused, leaned forward and told them both exactly what Pitt had told him. Then he sat back and stayed quiet, as did Burton. After another mile, Delaney undid his seat belt . 'Stop the car, Taffy.'

'There's traffic behind me and...'

'Stop the fucking car!'

Burton pulled over and switched on the hazard lights. A few seconds later, Delaney got out and walked forward on the grass verge.

'He's walking it off,' said Wyatt, 'drive slowly and keep up with him, Taffy.'

Half a mile further on, Delaney stopped and Burton drove up alongside him, ignoring the other cars blowing their horns. Delaney got back into the car. 'Thanks lads.'

Neither of them spoke.

It was close to midnight when they approached Heltern Manor. Burton turned onto a dirt track adjacent to the grounds of the manor and turned off the engine.

'Well, with Stait dead,' said Delaney, 'my guess is that it's just Hubert we're after now.'

'Could he do all this on his own?' asked Wyatt.

'Not sure; but if Stait was telling the truth when he told Michael that Hawkwell was dead, who else is there?'

'Well, why don't we find out?' said Burton.

Fair enough, Taffy. We'll stay away from the front door. Ben, you go around the left of the building; use the handset to stay in touch. I'll take the other handset. Taffy, you go to the right. Is your micro still working?'

'I think so, I'll check it when we're out of the car.'

'Right, both of you go in about five minutes; by then I'll be round the back.'

The grounds of the manor house were in darkness. A large, heavy cast iron gate was open at the main entrance, it's hinges set firmly into the walls. All the curtains and blinds were closed; from one of the front windows a faint light could be seen through a small gap where the curtains came together.

The large oak entrance doors had a light fitting above them and the bulb had been taken out. In one of the second floor windows, a yellow light was visible, as though a lamp in a corner had been left on.

As Burton moved to the right, he kept a lawn and some conifers between himself and house. When he saw two double garages set back near the rear right hand corner of the main building, he spoke quietly to activate his micro. 'Garage, on the right, one of the doors is open a couple of inches.'

Delaney answered on his handset. 'Have a look, Taffy.'

Burton walked slowly over towards the garage, being as quiet as the gravel drive would allow. When he heard nothing for a few minutes, he eased the door open slowly. He whispered again. 'Two vehicles; a Royal Mail van and a Volkswagen estate. Back doors of the van are open. It's empty. Keys are in both vehicles.'

Delaney answered again. 'Take the keys out and stay near the garage, Taffy. Did you get that, Ben?'

'Got it.'

As Wyatt came slowly around the left hand side of the house, he saw Delaney, crouching behind a compost box and he ran to join him. 'No doors on the left, guv.'

'Okay; Taffy, any doors to the right of the house?'

'Just one, opposite the garage; I can see it clearly.'

Delaney paused, wiped the sweat from his brow and looked around once more. 'Right; Taffy, stay there. Ben, go to the front door, I'll go in the back, radio silence.'

He gave Wyatt a few minutes to get to the front. As he walked slowly towards the rear door, he thought how quiet it all was. Either the occupants were asleep or they had seen everything and were just waiting.

He tried the brass handle to the door; it was open. When he had pushed the door fully open as quiet as he could, he hesitated to listen for any sounds. Nothing.

The kitchen was warm. He held a hand on the electric kettle; it too was warm. Suddenly, there was the sound of breaking glass. He crouched down near a big square table in the middle of the room. Then he recognised Hubert's voice; 'It's okay, you fell asleep.'

Then another voice that seemed familiar to him. 'Sorry, it's been a long few days, I'll clear it up.'

'No, leave it. We'll be heading for the airport soon.'

Delaney realised that the other person had dropped a glass of something onto the floor. Then he heard Hubert's voice again. 'Why don't we load up the Volkswagen while we're waiting to hear from Aaron? I thought he would have confirmed he was on his way by now.'

'Mm, me too, I hope he's okay.' said the other man.

Moving quickly and quietly, Delaney went back outside and whispered into his handset. 'They're on their way to the garage, Taffy. Ben, move to the right.'

'Who's *they*?' asked Wyatt.

'Hubert and one other.'

Burton moved away from the garage and waited behind a conifer hedge. He recognised Hubert's gait straight away. Even now, he was still stroking his moustache. The other man, he did not know.

But Wyatt did. As soon as he saw the two men walking towards the garage, he hid near a dustbin and held his handset close to his mouth. 'It's Peter Lorette, what the fuck is going on?'

'Are you sure?' said Delaney.

'Positive.'

'The Peter Lorette that flew you and Brun to the house near Eeklo and who Brun called in to help track them to Brussels?'

'Yes, it's both of them; Hubert and Lorette. *Both* of them were in with Stait.'

'Did you get that, Taffy?'

'Got it. They're in the garage now, making a lot of noise.'

When Hubert and Lorette had arrived at the manor, they had unloaded the different coloured holdalls and briefcases from the Royal Mail van and left them in a pile under a cover at the rear of the Volkswagen estate. Burton had not noticed this in the dark. Nor had he noticed the small door at the back of the garage that led out onto a footpath towards the lawns and the conifers.

As they were loading the bags into the Volkswagen, Lorette heard his mobile phone make a Bluetooth connection sound.

'What's that?' asked Hubert.

'Another phone is nearby trying to make a Bluetooth connection. Where's your phone?'

'In the house, switched off.'

Lorette glared at Hubert and put a finger to his mouth. They stood very still for a while and then Lorette whispered. 'Carry on loading the van, I'm going out this back door to take a look.' He moved quietly through the doorway and peered around the corner. In the full moon, he could see a man standing behind a hedge holding a handgun at the ready. Then Hubert came out of the back and spoke at full volume, forgetting the situation they were in. 'The keys are not in the car.'

Everyone heard Hubert. Lorette let off a shot at Burton who dived to the ground as the bullet hit a tree behind him. 'Get out of the way!' shouted Lorette as he pushed past Hubert and knelt down next to the open door of the Volkswagen. He pulled out some wires from below the steering column. 'A knife, get me a knife or something like that.'

Hubert looked around, reached for an old chisel on a bench and passed it to Lorette, who tried to strip a few wires with it, getting it wrong and burning his fingers until he found the contact he needed. 'Open the doors, then get ready to jump in.'

Delaney moved closer to Wyatt. With the shot being fired and the garage doors being opened, he decided the time for the handsets was over. 'You okay, Taffy?' he said loudly.

'Yeah, they're making a move.'

'We can see.'

As Hubert opened the doors, Delaney and Wyatt could see Lorette in the car reaching over to open the passenger door. Wyatt aimed carefully. 'Got a good shot, guv; do I take him?'

'Yes.'

Hubert's legs were shot from under him and he fell to the ground crying out in pain. He had not quite opened the garage doors fully and Lorette accelerated hard, slamming the doors back against the walls. He raced towards the main gateway with the headlights on full beam, and made a slight detour, heading for the bins that Delaney and Wyatt were standing behind. Burton ran quickly to the edge of the lawn, kneeled and shot twice at the car from behind; one bullet missed, another hit a rear tyre. The car wavered for a second but kept going; it hit the waste bins and narrowly missed Delaney and Wyatt as they dived to one side. Burton fired again; the back window smashed but Lorette kept going towards the gateway.

Suddenly the car stopped. The big iron gates had been closed and Lorette knew the car would not be able to go on if he tried to ram them. As Burton moved slowly down the gravel driveway with his gun pointing at the car, Delaney and Wyatt approached from the right, staying well apart from each other. Lorette got out of the car holding a shotgun. Wyatt was about to crouch down and let off a shot, when a figure appeared at the other side of the gate. As Lorette raised his shotgun in the direction of Burton, the figure at the gate fired a barrage of bullets into the front of the car, bursting the two front tyres and smashing the headlights and the windscreen. Lorette turned and looked towards the gate to see two people now, aiming at him. He threw the shotgun to the floor. 'Okay, okay! Now I am unarmed!'

One of the people at the gate, moved to one side out of sight. A minute later a car was pulled across the driveway and the gates were opened. Delaney moved towards Lorette. 'Take off your jacket, turn around.'

Lorette did as he was told. Wyatt was the only one he had come across before, so he found himself looking at him rather than the other two. 'Hello, Mr Wyatt.'

'Hello, Peter; you do surprise me.'

'Well, you people had better be quick because there is someone on his way to Manchester airport you need to get if you want us all.'

'Stait is dead, Peter; we have got you all.'

333

The person who had fired the shots from the gate moved forward and Delaney was the first to recognise the face in the full moonlight. 'Nice shooting, Shirley.'

'Thank you, Tom.'

'This is Peter Lorette,' said Wyatt, 'Belgian police helicopter pilot.'

'And one of the directors of Adinerado Enterprises,' said Stonehaven. 'And I suppose the man on the floor back there is Inspector Hubert.'

'Yes it is,' said Burton. 'I'll call it in.'

'That's already been done,' said Stonehaven, 'I called for an ambulance and the local police a few minutes ago.'

Delaney walked up close to Lorette. 'So you weren't getting short of fuel near Brussels then? I thought those things had a greater range than that.'

'No comment,' said Lorette looking at the ground.

'You and Hubert; you had it planned all along; there wasn't going to be a train journey was there?'

'No comment.'

Hubert's life was spared, but only just; the paramedics were getting him into an ambulance twenty minutes later. One of them told Delaney that he'd lose both legs. Lorette stayed silent throughout the proceedings until Stonehaven opened the rear door of the estate car. 'I take it all of these bags contain the fortune, in some form or another, that you were all going to take with you.'

Lorette said, 'I don't know what's in them, I was only employed as a pilot and a driver; It was Hubert and Stait who masterminded it all.'

'Yeah, right,' said Delaney. He turned to Burton and Wyatt. 'Open them up lads.'

Burton passed a couple of holdalls to Wyatt and started to unlock some of the briefcases. 'I wonder which one has *my* diamonds in it,' said Burton.

Then they all looked towards Wyatt as he stood up, laughing, and emptied the contents of one of the holdalls onto the ground. 'Old clothes and a few newspapers.' He emptied another one. 'Old clothes again and a few paperbacks.'

Delaney looked at Stonehaven and then went to the car himself to open some of the other holdalls and briefcases. He opened two holdalls and threw them to the ground. 'Same again.' Then he opened a briefcase. 'And again.'

Lorette ran forward, grabbed some more of the holdalls and ripped them open. Every briefcase and every holdall had old clothes, old newspapers and old paperbacks in them. There was nothing of value at all.

When Stonehaven saw the look on Lorette's face she shook her head. 'I take it you didn't know.'

'No, I did not,' said Lorette.

'What *was* in the bags?' asked Delaney.

'Money, diamonds, bearer bonds.'

'Who had control of the bags when they were packed?'

'Hubert; he had put everything together and stored them at a house near Antwerp.'

'Then what?'

'Then they loaded the bags for Brussels, I picked them up in the helicopter and we transferred the bags. They weren't touched on the journey; I did most of the handling myself. Shit!'

'Right, well we'll have a think about that when we interview Lorette and Hubert formally,' said Stonehaven. A few minutes later, Lorette was being taken away by a local Special Branch team as Stonehaven's driver opened the car door for her. 'See you at your office, Tom; find out what you can about the money etc and we'll go through it in detail.'

As the car pulled away, Delaney turned to Burton and Wyatt. 'Anyone feel like sleeping?' They both shook their heads. 'Back to London then,' he continued, 'you two can split the driving; I *do* feel like sleeping.'

48

Thirty six hours later, Ajit Pitt was making coffee for everyone as they sat in Delaney's office around the central table. None of them had said much as they arrived and it was Burton who started to ask the questions when the coffee cups were full. 'Have we heard how Michael is?'

'He's okay,' said Pitt. 'I saw him last night; he'll be in hospital for a few weeks but he'll survive.' He looked at Delaney. 'Harry Mitchell phoned yesterday, sir; the CIA want Michael back in Washington as soon as he's fit to travel.'

Delaney just nodded and curled his mouth down.

'What about Jane Westwood?' asked Burton.

'She's okay too,' said Delaney. 'I phoned the hospital this morning; she needed a couple of risky operations but she's recovering well.'

'Well you were right, guv,' said Wyatt.

'Was I?'

'When you said we'd be lucky to get through this with a nil body count.'

'Mm, *we* have; but Interpol have lost Ellie Shanks and the undercover woman in Portugal, the CIA has lost Julie Greaves and the Belgians have lost Chief Inspector Baart and Peter Giers.'

'Let's not forget the money, diamonds and bearer bonds,' said Burton.

'Yeah, where the hell did they get to?' asked Wyatt.

Pitt leaned forward. 'I've been thinking about it, but I can't see any gaps, and the whole thing doesn't make sense anyway.'

'Mm,' said Delaney, 'but it's been a success, don't forget. Some pretty serious criminal scum are dead or behind bars.'

'At least we can leave the Colombians to the CIA,' said Wyatt.

Delaney's mind drifted as the others started to discuss the last few weeks. He left them to talk and went to his desk. As he was sifting through his in-tray, his subconscious mind went through what had happened.

Ellie Shanks was murdered by Hawkwell because she was getting too close to Stait and his Colombian connection. Riego had done an amazing feat, working undercover as Compito for two years only to find out that the Belgians had Peter Giers in there trying to get the same information that he had been after. For whatever reason – probably just greed – Hubert and Lorette had gotten involved with Stait and Sondhiem and they used their powers of privilege to help them get away with things. But when the Colombians pulled out, not wanting to get involved with child trafficking, that left Stait and Sondhiem without supplies and without serious income. It must have been one of Stait's men that killed Sondhiem; so he would be the only one in contact with their big customers. According to Lorette, Hubert controlled all of the takings when Stait was left without his Colombian contract.

Wyatt said something that caught Delaney's attention and he looked up. 'What was that, Ben?'

'I was just saying that if Hubert packed all the bags at the house, there was only him, Stait and Hawkwell who could have swapped the contents, but why would they? And, where could they have put it all?'

'What about Lorette?' asked Burton.

'No way; he was as surprised as us at what was in the bags,' said Delaney.

'So they put the bags into the Peugeot; Stait and Hawkwell drove to Brussels and Hubert followed when we got Sergeant Brun to say that they had been seen.'

'Yep.'

'We followed them to Brussels, with the help of Peter Lorette in the helicopter. At some point then; Lorette – maybe when he told us he needed fuel – diverted to somewhere to pick up Stait, Hubert and Hawkwell.'

'Yes.' said Delaney, 'so what about all of those bags that were supposedly loaded onto the train?'

There was silence for a moment. Wyatt stood up and scratched his chin, put a finger in the air and turned to look at them all. 'The bags didn't go on the train. All Hubert had to do was to arrange for the bags to be put into another car or even a taxi and driven out to somewhere where Lorette could land and tranship the bags into his helicopter.'

'Yes, but Hubert went missing at the station,' said Burton.

'Exactly, Taffy; he drove the car with the bags in it to meet Lorette.'

'Hang on, lads,' said Delaney from his desk. 'Sergeant Brun told the station master to stop the luggage being loaded as well as the train departing. But Hubert probably had the car loaded by then; there wouldn't have been any luggage to stop.'

'Right,' said Wyatt, 'so Hubert could have swapped the contents of the bags before he met Lorette.'

'So if he did, where are the diamonds, the money and the bonds; he wouldn't have left them in Belgium knowing he was going to England,' said Pitt.

'It has to be Hubert,' said Delaney. 'There would be nothing stopping him going back to Belgium instead of flying out with Stait and Lorette. We'll see what he has to say when we question him tomorrow.'

A gentle knock on the door interrupted the conversation. Shirley Stonehaven stood in the doorway. 'I'm not stopping, Tom. I have a meeting in one of the rooms upstairs with the technical people.'

'Right, do you want a quick coffee?'

'No, I just wanted to pass a message on to you all from the Home and Foreign Offices; they send their congratulations and their thanks. The PM also left a message.'

'Oh?'

'Yes; he said that yet again, it was The Overseas Liaison Agency who got the job done and he wants you to have more men.'

Delaney raised his eyebrows. 'Err, right, thank you.'

Wyatt sat back down and smiled. 'We don't need more men, Ma'am. We'll do it all, just pay us more.'

'That's enough, Ben, thank you,' said Delaney.

'Well,' continued Stonehaven, 'I just thought I'd let you know.' She smiled and left the room.

Delaney could see them all getting restless. 'Right, gentlemen, I'm sure you all have some sort of paperwork to sort, so let's get on with things shall we. If I don't get some invoices written up, you won't be getting *any* pay, Ben.'

As soon as Delaney got home and walked in the front door, he reminded himself why he would not like to go back to living on his own again. He opened the kitchen door to see Angela standing against the worktop with a glass of wine in her hand. He raised his eyebrows and smiled at her.

'What?' she said.

'I was just admiring two of my favourite smells.'

'And what would they be?'

'Lasagne; and you.'

'Charming, I come after the Lasagne do you I?'

'No; not right now. Rive Gauche?'

'Rive Gauche.'

They kissed and held each other around their backsides. 'You've got a few days off now,' she said.

'Says who?'

'Says me; I phoned Maggie Phelps today. She said you had two weeks holiday left to take this year and I told her to book you off from tonight for a week.'

340

'I might have an important case on.'

'You haven't; not now this one is all but over. I checked that with her as well.'

'Fine by me. Are *you* off then?'

'Mm, and I've booked us into a posh hotel on Jersey for a few days.'

Delaney took off his tie and hung it over the back of a chair. Angela turned off the oven and reached for the square dish. 'Here we are then, let's enjoy this and relax for the evening, I got you a bottle of your favourite Chilean.'

'Thank you, that'll do nicely,' he said. 'Just what the doctor ordered.'

49

Matthias Brun had been born in Leuven, east of Brussels. He was the second child of Louis and Martha Brun. Their first child, Mariella, was two years older than Matthias. Both children got on well with each other; Matthias, being - according to his mother at any rate - 'a monster of a boy with the strength of an ox', looked out for the demure Mariella and protected her from harm, throughout their years growing up together.

They were 16 and 18 respectively when their mother was killed in a car accident. Louis Brun tried his best to help them when they left school and embarked on their careers, and his sisters would attend to matters if he needed them to; he ran a small farm on his own, Matthias often helping him when he could.

Mariella started work as an office junior when she was 19, soon rising to be an 'indispensible' secretary for a firm of lawyers. Matthias joined the police force as a trainee cadet soon after; he too did well and by the time he was 22 it was clear he had a good career ahead of him.

It was a cold December night when they both told their father that they were moving out. Mariella wanted to be closer to her work in Brussels. Matthias and a colleague were about to be transferred from Brussels to Antwerp and they were to share a house close to their new office.

A couple of weeks later, some of their friends and relatives gathered at the small farmhouse and enjoyed a good night as they wished Mariella and Matthias well. As everyone slotted into the jovial atmosphere and enjoyed the drinks, Mariella took the lead, introducing those that did not know each other and making sure glasses and plates were full. She was setting out some more cheeses and pastries when her brother tapped her on the shoulder.

'You haven't said hello to my friend from the force, sister; not properly anyway.'

'No, I haven't,' she said, as she looked at Matthias's friend.

Matthias smiled as he pointed to his friend and looked at Mariella. 'Well, here he is, the scoundrel!' Then he looked at his friend. 'Peter; meet Mariella.'

A few metres away in a corner, Louis Brun noticed the look on his daughters face. Her eyes were moist and her smile was warm.

It was no surprise to him then, that a year later, Mariella and Peter announced their engagement; Matthias's friend, Peter Giers, was to become his brother-in-law. Mariella gave up her job in Brussels to be with Peter; they set up home near Antwerp and Matthias stayed in the home that he and Peter had shared.

Almost ten years later, Matthias Brun was a Sergeant; reporting to Inspector Henry Hubert. He had passed all of his promotion exams and he was only days away from being promoted to Inspector himself when things were put on hold. Belgian Interpol had been involved with a serious international case for some time and one of their new people, Ellie Shanks, had been murdered in Antwerp. The orders from on high were to hold all promotions and any departmental changes until further notice. Brun was not happy; he had never seen eye to eye with Inspector Hubert and he had been ready for a new challenge.

His brother-in-law had been somewhat luckier; in Brun's eyes anyway. He had been accepted by Belgian Intelligence as an Overseas Operative. After just one year with them, he was assigned to retrieve a laptop containing vital information, from a 'dangerous situation' in Colombia. Mariella did not like her husband being exposed to such dangers, but she would never stand in his way or argue with him; she loved him, he was a good provider and a good father to their new son, Aldo.

When Peter Giers was killed, trying to get away from the Colombian Rebels, Brun was told before his sister was; he accompanied the two people that went to her house to tell her of her husband's death. The day after, Ellie Shanks was murdered and the British – The Overseas Liaison Agency – were asked to get involved. It was when Taffy Burton visited Brun and Hubert at the museum in Antwerp, that Brun realised the international scale of the case and the amounts of money involved. And it was then, that he vowed to see that his sister and her son would never be without anything and that he himself would leave the police force *and* Belgium, to live somewhere remote and quiet; perhaps taking his father with him.

He first started to suspect Hubert's involvement with criminals on the night that he asked for permission for he, Wyatt and Pitt to raid Stait's home near Eeklo, with the help of De Vos and Maes. The Inspector had left the room to 'talk to Section Nine'. He had never done this before. Two days later, Brun checked all outgoing telephone calls to find that a call had been made from a phone in the corridor to a number near Eeklo; presumably to Stait, to warn him. He had also followed Hubert on two occasions; once to a converted barn near Antwerp and once to a cafe.

At the converted barn, another car had arrived and he could see Hubert telling the driver to back the car, an old Citreon, into the double garage; they left the house and Hubert dropped the man off at a bus stop. In the cafe, Hubert had waited for quite a while before he was joined by a well built man in his forties with dark, well trimmed hair. The package that Hubert handed to the man was big enough to hold a substantial amount of money.

Throughout all of the days that followed, Matthias Brun was always one step away from going to the Chief Police Officer, Commander Torres, to tell him of what he had seen and of his suspicions about Inspector Hubert. But something always stopped him. He was never sure exactly what; but something always stopped him. And it was only when he was accompanying

344

Delaney and his men to Brussels in pursuit of Hubert and Stait, that he realised what *had* stopped him; money. He surprised himself and he almost cried when he thought of what his father would have said if he knew what his son was doing. But a temptation of such magnitude changed the most honest of men.

It was at the Brussels Eurostar terminal that he took his opportunity. When he had told the man at the check-in desk to 'hold the luggage' Delaney had not questioned it, but when he was asked to go with Delaney and Wyatt in place of Burton and Pitt, his plans were put on hold for a few minutes. When Stait and Hawkwell had got away in the car, he also realised that Hubert was nowhere to be seen. They were told that Hubert had gone, but his car was still there.

Brun knew that Lorette's helicopter would not be out of fuel; he had accompanied him before on journeys that were twice as long. Then, when Delaney asked him to get in touch with Commander Torres, he took up another opportunity. He moved away from the others and pretended to make a call; but he did not. He returned to tell them that Commander Torres wanted him back in Antwerp and after a few 'good luck's he walked slowly away from them.

He identified Hubert's car straight away. A station attendant was standing next to it and Brun produced some ID. 'Where is Inspector Hubert?'

'We do not know, sir, but he said he would be back in thirty minutes.'

Brun acted fast. 'Very well, I am his driver, give me the keys.' The attendant did as he was told; Brun drove the car around a corner and parked outside a laundry room. He took all of the holdalls and briefcases from the car and emptied the money, diamonds and bearer bonds into a wheeled laundry basket. Two more baskets were nearby and he grabbed some old laundry and shoved it into the holdalls and cases. Some old books had been thrown on the floor and he took them and put a few in each bag to add to the weight before putting them back in the Citreon. The car was back in its original parking bay of the staff car park 15 minutes later.

Hubert had left the car and walked away from the station to make a phone call to Lorette, but had been forced to wait for an answer because Lorette could not confirm that he had found the old power station where they were to meet up. Just five minutes after Brun had parked the car back in the same place, Hubert got into it and drove away. The watching Brun was astounded that he had not noticed the absence of the station attendant and the fact that he had left the car keys in the ignition. But Hubert had actually told the attendant to leave the keys in; the attendant had removed them when he had seen Brun approaching.

An hour later, Brun had loaded the 'luggage' from the laundry baskets into police car number M37 and was driving towards Leuven.

Mariella was waiting for him, as instructed. He took the holdalls containing the cash and loaded them into her car. Then he transferred the diamonds and bearer bonds into police *scene of crime* evidence bags with 'Interpol' labels on them. Mariella kissed him as he went to get back into the police car and said, 'Be careful, I will contact you next year.'

'Yes, and not before; have you got the tickets?'

'Yes, I'm picking Aldo up from school soon; the flight is at 6 p.m.'

'Okay, try to enjoy the rest of your life and remember; you deserve it. No wife should have to lose a husband, the way you lost Peter.'

Brun's drive to the marina at Terneuzen was uneventful. He made a phone call on his way, telling Commander Torres that Hubert, Stait and Hawkwell had gotten away and that Delaney and his men were on their way back to England. Torres told to him to be at the office at eight in the morning. Brun said 'yes, sir,' and smiled. The *Juliet's* engines started easily enough; he piloted it successfully out of the marina and made his way towards Sweden.

The Air Canada flight from Gothenburg to Vancouver was on time. His new passport, courtesy of one his snouts, presented no problems; he was Mr Vanhoult, attending the diamond trader's conference on Vancouver Island. Four days later, he was Mr Johnson; moving into the old converted prairie shed on the outskirts of Medicine Hat, Alberta.

A year later his father, Louis, was looking out across the huge prairie lands they owned as he sat next to his son on their small veranda sipping brandy. 'We may have to buy a new harvester soon, Matthias; this is much larger than our small farm in Leuven, eh? And we'd still be there if you hadn't won all that money in the Euro lottery'

'Well, we all deserve a bit of luck now and again, Father.'

'Yes, I suppose we do. And now you have a beautiful fiancé as well; have you and Janie decided on a date for the wedding yet?'

'Yes; in about six month's time we think. We've been looking at...' Brun stopped talking when he saw a car approaching from the road. It moved slowly along the dry dirt track leaving a trail of dust to catch the moonlight. Louis frowned and looked at his son. 'Is that Janie? I thought she was on business in Toronto?'

'Hm, no,' said Brun, 'her car is smaller than that.'

The car stopped in front of them. Brun put his drink down on the table and shook his head as the two men in the car opened their doors and walked towards the veranda. Louis noticed the look on his son's face. 'Matthias; what is it?'

'Let me introduce you, Father,' said Brun. He started to sweat. Then he saw another car approaching the house; a police car. He looked at the man on the left. 'This is Taffy Burton.'

Burton remained quiet and still as he removed his handgun from his shoulder holster and held it down against his side. Then Brun gestured to the other man. 'And this is Tom Delaney.'

Delaney walked slowly forward, hesitated and then leant against the veranda railings and sighed. After a few seconds he raised his head to look at Brun. 'Hello, Sergeant Brun; how are you?'

Look out for the next fast paced novel from
Stephen W Follows; due out early 2012.

And don't forget to check out other books that are
available now –

Ruthless

Delaney *and* his adversary have to deal with death,
betrayal and treason.

ISBN 9780956610904 £7.99

Coffee break stories

Five short stories of intrigue to enjoy with your
cuppa.

ISBN 9780956610911 £2.99

E books also available
Stephenwfollows.co.uk

LOCAL GIRL MISSING

J. A. BAKER

B
Boldwood

First published in Great Britain in 2022 by Boldwood Books Ltd. This paperback edition first published in 2023.

1

Cover Design by Head Design

Cover Photography: Shutterstock

The moral right of J A Baker to be identified as the author of this work has been asserted in accordance with the Copyright, Designs and Patents Act 1988.

Every effort has been made to obtain the necessary permissions with reference to copyright material, both illustrative and quoted. We apologise for any omissions in this respect and will be pleased to make the appropriate acknowledgements in any future edition.

A CIP catalogue record for this book is available from the British Library.

Paperback ISBN: 978-1-83518-808-8

Hardback ISBN: 978-1-80415-354-3

Ebook ISBN: 978-1-80415-352-9

Kindle ISBN: 978-1-80415-353-6

Audio CD ISBN: 978-1-80415-360-4

MP3 CD ISBN: 978-1-80415-357-4

Digital audio download ISBN: 978-1-80415-351-2

Digital audio MP3 ISBN: 978-1-80415-358-1

Large Print ISBN: 978-1-80415-355-0

Boldwood Books Ltd.

23 Bowerdean Street, London, SW6 3TN

www.boldwoodbooks.com

To my three lovely little ones. You brighten up our world.

Walking with a friend in the dark is better than walking alone in the light.

— HELEN KELLER

1

DEBORAH

I'm not alone. Not any more. I heard her bringing them up here, this other person who is now lying across the floor from me. I heard the shush of fabric against fabric, felt the movement of air flowing past me as she forced them into the room after dragging them up the stairs, the clatter of their body as they fell against the floorboards, their grunt of pain as she kicked them into the corner, pushing at them with her foot. Enjoying the control she wields. Savouring every second of it. She must feel very powerful, doing what she does. She isn't. What she is, is a psychopath who happens to have an advantage over me. I'm shackled. Gagged and bound. She isn't. That's her only superior trait. Other than that, she is weak, depraved and pathetic, lacking all the usual identifiable traits that make us human – empathy, compassion, the ability to form positive relationships with others. She has none of those characteristics. She is a monster and I hate her.

I don't know who this other person is or why they're here; why they have been dragged into this hellhole and subjected to this ongoing torture. I don't suppose she needs a reason to do what she does. Her mind operates on a different level to normal people. She's unfathomable, has an alien sense of logic. I've long since given up trying to see inside her head. Truth be told, it isn't somewhere I would ever want to visit. I imagine it to be a dark, shadowy place, an infected, festering wound, damaged beyond repair. I've tried reasoning with her, pleading, crying. Begging. It doesn't work. She's impervious to it all; every human emotion – anger, fear, outrage – they don't seem to touch her in any way, shape or form, gliding over her like liquid mercury. I fear that they possibly energise her even, that she feeds off my terror and misery like a predator feasting on its latest kill.

I try to think about what day it is, whether it's morning, afternoon or evening. Maybe it's the early hours. How would I know, stuck here in the darkness? Time has lost all meaning. I'm not even sure how long I've been here. Days, definitely. Weeks, probably. Months, very possibly. I wish I'd kept a more accurate count. I didn't know it would go on for this long. I expected it to last a matter of days, my imprisonment here. I thought I would either escape or die. What I didn't expect was this – to still be here and have somebody join me. Another captive. Another prisoner. One more poor, enslaved soul at her mercy.

Tears prick at my eyes. I swallow, fight them off. All this time, sitting here in the darkness with no end in sight. It feels like hell. Scratch that. It *is* hell. In the beginning, I tried marking off the hours, shuffling my body about, scoring into the soft pine flooring, noting each day that passed with a small, splintered line to remind myself of how long it had been since I had seen daylight, been allowed to walk free. I tried to keep a note of it, not lose all sense of what day it was and how long I had been here, in this dark, dank place, but it didn't take long for my nails to tear, for my skin to split and bleed. So, I stopped.

Why make life harder for myself? I now focus all my energy on simply surviving, not caving in to her imposing manner and draconian rules. Her constantly shifting moods and demands. But it's so damn hard, like building on sand, the foundations of her character fluctuating from second to second, minute to minute. There is nothing steady or reliable about her presence, the drag of her ever-changing temperament as powerful as any riptide or raging current. I fear that one day in the not-too-distant future, it will pull me under, that I will drown in this place, choking on the toxic air around me, flailing and gasping my last in this miserable hovel while she stands by and watches, my demise feeding her warped urges.

The discomfort in my shoulder is a relentless dull ache interspersed with flashes of burning pain that spreads up my arm as I squirm and shift about, attempting to get into a more comfortable position. A few days ago, I asked for a cushion to try to alleviate the throbbing, nagging line of pain that is ever-present, but she refused, seemingly enthused by my agony, and yet there are other days when she spoon-feeds me, gently placing the cutlery on my lips, singing and whistling as food is shovelled into my parched, blistered mouth.

I would love to be able to talk right now, to ask what is going on and why this other person is here, but the gag makes it difficult to breathe, let alone speak. Even if I could, it would probably result in a beating. I'm a grown woman and yet like a small child, I fear her wrath if I say the wrong thing. What can be right one day is considered a serious breach of rules the next. There are no set guidelines here, nothing to help keep me safe. Nothing to keep me sane.

So I wait. I wait until I hear the clump of her feet on the stairs, listening intently as she fades into the distance. Then I open my eyes, my act of feigning sleep no longer required now she isn't around to gloat over my predicament. My helplessness and vulnerability. It strengthens her resolve, seeing the desperation in my eyes, helping to fuel her tenacity. She thrives on it which is why I now choose to look at her rarely, turning away or pretending to be asleep. A docile prisoner. Dead to her demands. She has her power. This is mine. It's all I have, a refusal to let her see my fear.

The figure on the floor twitches, their limbs gradually springing to life, a twisting backbone that arches and bends. They attempt to scramble themselves into a sitting position, hands and ankles bound tightly. It's futile, so instead they lie there, energy spent, gasping and grunting as their gaze adjusts to the dimness around us, to the swirling dust motes and stark surroundings. The bare walls, the dusty floor. The darkness and unutterable horror of it all.

I shuffle over to where they lie sprawled out, trying to get a glimpse of them; to see who they are, work out their gender, what they look like. What sort of person I am going to be sharing this room with. They turn to look at me, head angled to one side, and that's when I hear the sharp intake of breath. It's a simultaneous act, a collective gasp of disbelief from both of us. My breath balloons in my chest, my head thuds as I stare down at this person before me. The woman lying on the floor in this makeshift prison cell.

This woman who looks exactly like me.

2

ADRIAN

Everything is shit. I throw my phone down on my desk, then slide it out of view. Away from the prying eyes of the rest of the staff. They're all too keen to point the finger around this place. It's not like we don't have anything else to do. We're up to our eyes in work, and yet at the first sign of somebody nipping off for another cup of tea or slyly glancing at their phone, they're all so quick to jump. Like they don't all pop off for a sneaky fag whenever they can, or spend ages in the bloody toilet applying more lipstick or powdering their noses or doing whatever it is women do when they're in there. No wonder the ladies' loos in bars and restaurants always have a massive frigging queue outside with the amount of time they take just to have a piss and wash their hands.

Beneath the manila folder, I see my mobile phone light up again, its fluorescent glow making my pulse race. Jesus Christ, why can't she just leave me alone? I cannot be with her every minute of every day, solving her problems, making sure her life is as smooth and as easy as it can be. I just can't. At some point, she has got to start helping herself. I've got my own problems, my own issues and demons. Nobody helps me with those. God helps those that help themselves. Jesus, what a fucking stupid saying that is. God gave up on lots of us a long time ago, including me. Especially me.

'Everything okay, Ade?' Ruth is standing by my desk, her eyes flicking between my face and the fucking folder that is currently vibrating and lit up like Blackpool illuminations. Ruth is the only person in this place who calls me Ade. I don't mind. She's not that bad. Better than many of the other people in this office. She's not the best but she definitely isn't the worst.

'Yeah, fine. Just about to go through these quotes, see if we can tweak them and get some of the prices down to be in with a chance of getting the order.'

'Ah, good luck with that. Rather you than me.'

She hesitates, her feet shuffling on the tiled floor. Ruth wants to ask. She's HR manager. It's not strictly part of her remit to make sure we're all okay, that our home lives don't interfere with our work output, but she's a personable woman, always keen to listen, to offer solutions to problems that aren't necessarily anything to do with our job. I'm not sure she can help with this one. In fact, I know she can't, so I give her a meek smile and turn back to my computer, trying to look busy, my fingers hitting the keyboard with more force than is necessary. My fury is managing to leak out and it shouldn't. I try to stay alert; my ears are attuned to every little sound, my skin prickling as I wait for her to say or do something. She doesn't. Instead, she clears her throat and moves back off to her office at the far end of our main working area, the *tap tap* of her heels fading into the distance.

My phone continues to beep and vibrate, reminding me of how shit my life can be at times. How shit she makes it. I'll answer it at lunchtime, speak to her then. Or maybe I won't.

Maybe, like everyone else, I will sit in the staffroom, eat my sandwiches and give myself a fucking well-deserved break from customers, buyers and the woman who thinks she has the right to control my life every minute of every fucking day with her incessant phone calls and demands, and a constant and overwhelming need for reassurance.

Over the other side of the office, Allison is standing chatting to Yvonne. I can hear snippets of their conversation. They're talking about Deborah, Allison going on and on about it. As if we haven't been over this subject time and time again. And here I was worrying about being caught out on a sneaky phone call while wading through a mountain of quotes that need adjusting. Sometimes, the people in this place piss me right off, with their superior attitudes and gossipy fucking mouths. Deborah is gone; yes, it's sad, but it's time to shut up about it and move on, to let the police do their work without muddying the waters with supposition and idle bloody chit-chat. Anything could have happened to her, anything at all. She could have decided that enough was enough and has taken herself off somewhere. Somewhere far away from this office, this town, these people. Then again, maybe something bad has happened to her. Maybe somebody made something bad happen. I stare at my phone, Beth still lingering at the back of my mind, and shiver.

Merriel mentioned about us going back to the pub again after work on a Friday. I'm up for it. We need some laughs around this place. I'm not one for all that bullshit *come on, team, let's all pull together towards a common goal* nonsense, but I do think we need to start smiling and maybe even laughing and having a bit of banter again, not spending every day raking over Deborah's disappearance. It's become like a bloody morgue in this place since she went missing and I've just about had enough of it.

More buzzing from under that folder as I punch in new prices and readjust the quotes before sending them off to Roger, our chief engineer. He can't complain at them. The margins are tight but they're competitive and we'll at least be in with a chance of getting the order. And it's a big one too – £40,000. That should put a smile on the miserable old fart's face.

The incessant flashing and buzzing is enough to make me want to throw my phone against the nearest wall. My chest tightens as I slide it back out, stand up and slip it into my arse pocket. It's time for a break anyway. I need a coffee and maybe even a KitKat, that is if the vending machine decides to work and not swallow my money, giving me nothing in return like it did yesterday.

I heave a sigh and run my fingers through my hair, remembering yesterday and what Beth told me she had done. My skin burns at the memory, electric pulses firing and misfiring just beneath the surface of my flesh. Every day brings a new low. Just when I think things cannot possibly get any worse, she throws something else at me and I have to limbo my way under her latest trauma or misdemeanour. It's exhausting and I am truly fucking sick of it.

Coffee is needed before I speak to her. I need something to fortify me so I can deal with whatever it is she is about to tell me. Because there will be something. There is *always* something.

It's quiet out on the landing. Just me and the big, ancient vending machine, the pair of us locked in permanent battle as it eats my money, giving me nothing in return. Not today, however.

I shove my fingers in my pocket, bring out a handful of loose change and push two coins into the slot, watching as a bar of chocolate clunks its way into the tray at the bottom. Thank fuck for that. I need caffeine and I need sugar and I need them now.

The staffroom is empty. Something else to be thankful for. It's rare that things usually go my way. I'm always grateful when they do. I'm accustomed to hiccups and failure and rejection. I'm not being pitiful or acting like the victim. It's just how it is. I'm used to it, expect it even.

I make a strong coffee, almost black, and sit at the table that overlooks the main car park. It's quiet down there. Not like last week and the week before that and the week before that when the police were swarming all over the place. Just seeing them there made me jittery, with their dark uniforms and even darker expressions. At least things are getting back to something resembling normal. Until Allison opens her mouth that is, and brings it all back up again. She seems determined to keep going on and on about it to the point where I want to shout in her face to fucking stop it and just get on with her job and her life. Instead, I sit hunched over my computer screen, getting more work done than the rest of them put together while they all mope about, droning on and on and on about how terrible and scary it is and how they wish the police would hurry up and find her.

They enjoy feeding off somebody else's misery, that's what it is. They fucking thrive on it. It makes them feel better about their own lives. Not that they've got anything going on at home that is enough to drag them down. They all have easy little numbers with nice houses and cars, and husbands who have good jobs that can supplement their income. What do they know about trauma and neglect and terror so real it keeps you awake at night? Maybe they should all open their eyes, take a good look around, see how easy they have it, how fortunate they are. Not all of us are that lucky. Not all of us were born into caring, compassionate families who knew how to love, families whose natural instinct is to nurture and care for their offspring.

The KitKat makes a snapping sound, echoing around the room as I break it in half and bite into it, the sugar relaxing me as the chunks melt in my mouth. Two slurps of my coffee and the world begins to take on a different hue – lighter, brighter, marginally easier to bear.

I pull out my phone and stare at the screen. Four missed calls and two texts. Jesus. I'm really not in the mood for this. No amount of chocolate or coffee is ever enough to face Beth and the barrage of problems she regularly throws my way. Still, at least she has stopped following me to work, waiting outside the main doors for hours like some sort of stalker. That was embarrassing, the way she would try to talk to people she didn't know as they made their way to their cars or into town to catch a bus or a train, running alongside them at a lick, chatting as if they were old friends. The way she tried to befriend Deborah as she headed out of the office on an evening. I close my eyes and swallow, batting away that particular memory.

The past couple of weeks she has eased up from hanging around me and my colleagues, staying in her house instead. I say house – it's more of a derelict building, somewhere the local authority and social services put her to keep her safe from the rest of the world. To keep her safe from herself. God knows what she gets up to when I'm at work and she is left to her own devices. What I do know is that she has stopped following me and it feels like a small victory. I try not to think about it. It's down to her social worker and mental health team to take care of that part of her life. I have enough to be getting on with.

She picks up after just one ring when I call her, her voice husky and breathless. I visualise her crouched in the corner of her bedroom, fending off invisible faceless enemies who don't exist.

'You took your time,' she says, her anger evident, her latent terror a tangible force, always present, never giving her any respite from its nasty little clutches.

'Beth, I'm at work. You know that. We spoke about this, didn't we – how I have to put my phone on silent during the day when I'm in the office?'

She doesn't reply, knowing we have indeed spoken about it many, many times. Too many to count. It doesn't stop her calling me. When Beth has things on her mind, a barrier the thickness of a submarine door wouldn't be enough to halt her in her tracks. She is relentless. A force to be reckoned with.

'Anyway,' she says, blatantly ignoring my requests to be left alone during the day so I can get on with my job, 'I need to talk to you about my new friend.'

I roll my eyes, suppressing a deep sigh. In the past I have actually bitten at the inside of my mouth so hard I ended up drawing blood to stop myself from shouting at her. I don't do that now. I simply let her talk. It's what her doctor told me to do. Sometimes it works and sometimes it doesn't. I never can tell. When it comes to Beth, there are no rules. She is her own mistress and I am forced to dance to her tune.

'Right,' I reply, knowing she doesn't have any friends, aside from the imaginary one she has recently taken to talking about. 'Fire away. I'm all ears.'

3

YVONNE

It's quiet. The office feels eerie, the weight of silence a heavy, cumbersome thing. The usual repartee that keeps us going throughout the long and often arduous days of paperwork and invoicing, and the stream of endless emails from irate customers demanding their parts be delivered immediately despite a backlog at customs, is absent.

I gaze around the place, and apart from Allison wandering about, see nothing but a sea of dipped heads as people tap away at their keyboards, eyes focused on their computer screens, everyone too anxious, too despairing, to communicate with each other. There seems little point in making idle chatter. Nothing any of them can say will ever make this situation any better. They know it. I know it. Nobody can magically make Deborah reappear at her desk. She is missing, has been gone for weeks now. Weeks and weeks and weeks. How many is it? Three perhaps? Or is it four? Perhaps longer. I should know this. Our desks are next to one another. I should be keeping count. One day feels as if it is blending into another. Seconds, minutes, hours all bleeding into a vast pit of nothingness. Time has no meaning. There seems little point in counting if nothing changes and Deborah remains missing. That's what everybody is saying. It's what Ruth keeps on saying, her bottom lip quivering every time Deborah's name is brought up in conversation. Every day that passes gives her disappearance another strand of finality, bolting it firmly into everyone's minds that she isn't coming back. That she won't be found alive. Each extra week of her being gone nudges her farther away from people's consciousness. Soon they will forget about her altogether. She will be another story pushed off the front page, replaced by bickering politicians, climate change stories, rapes, rising knife crime. Anything but Deborah. She is an adult. They don't lodge in people's heads the way missing children do. Helplessness, vulnerability. That's what drives the interests of the masses. That's what keeps them hooked into the story. And Deborah is neither of those things. She is a woman who left the office one evening and never arrived home.

Perhaps, with the passing of time, her name will be mentioned once in a while, the investigation into her disappearance re-examined, given air space on a prime news slot, the grainy picture of her smiling face filling our screens for the briefest of minutes before vanishing again.

A ribbon of discomfort sits across my forehead, tight and unforgiving as I clear my head before wringing my hands and cracking my knuckles. I should really get these invoices sorted. I need to clear my inbox and answer unopened emails. Do something. Anything at all to occupy my mind. There are so many tasks I could be pressing on with but I am not in the mood to think about tackling any of them. My bones are aching, my muscles knotted, threads of discomfort running through my veins, weighting me to the ground as I think about Deborah's absence. I feel heavily anchored to this place, to this moment in time, to the ambience around me now Deborah is no longer here working alongside us. Everything has changed, her absence altering the dynamics of our working relationships with one another, everyone treading carefully, colleagues feeling on edge for fear of saying the wrong thing.

It's too hot in here. Too hot to work, to think clearly. Deborah's empty desk shifts in and out of my focus, obscuring my peripheral vision. Conspicuous. Wieldy. An oversized piece of furniture, reminding me and everyone around me that she is no longer in the office. I begin to wonder if and when they will replace her. When is the right time to move on after somebody vanishes? A month, a year, a decade?

'It's weird, isn't it?' Allison is standing behind me, her eyes also sweeping over the person-sized space where Deborah used to sit, her voice a sharp crack as it cuts through the silence. 'So strange how it can happen, how people can simply disappear. Just like that. Poof. A magic act. Here one minute, gone the next. Now you see her, now you don't.'

I blink, unsure what to say, how to react to her glib statement. I remain silent and manage a smile. Allison nods, carries on walking, her figure silhouetted against the light that is streaming in through the full-length office windows. My fists are clenched in my lap. I don't remember doing that, curling them up into tight balls until my nails dug into my palms. Sometimes that happens, my mood determining and driving my actions without me even realising it.

I stand up, turn down the thermostat, waiting for the screams and protests from the others that it's too cold, and am prepared, for once, to fight my corner, to tell them to shut up, that I need some clean, cool air to help me breathe, help me think, not the muggy recirculated wafts of oxygen that are pumped my way every single day, filling my lungs, coating them with the bacteria and foulness of others. I need to feel free of the toxicity I am forced to inhale in this modern yet remarkably stuffy little office.

My thoughts turn back once again, to Deborah, to her soft laughter, the ease with which she would wade through a mountainous stack of invoices, her fingers tapping away at the keyboard, her eyes flicking between the screen and her notepad as she cleared the backlog and scribbled off her to-do list, smiling before heading off to the kitchen area and returning, coffee in hand.

It's like a mist in my mind, the memory of her as she sat there, her image dissipating and swirling, a kaleidoscope of muted colours. The others in this office will eventually forget about her. That's the sort of people that they are. Once the novelty of her disappearance has worn off, they will all go back to their humdrum little lives and speak her name only once in a while, half closing their eyes as they cast their minds back to that day, that evening, when she left this office and vanished into thin air. But I won't. I won't forget what her voice is like, how we would spend our lunchtimes together, sitting on the ancient wooden bench in the park, shooing away pigeons that hung around as we ate, hoping for scraps of food, their beady eyes watching. Waiting.

'Bastard pigeons,' Deborah had once shouted at them, stamping her feet and clapping her hands before relenting and throwing a half-eaten sandwich their way.

I smile at the memory. Always the soft one. Full of false bravado before eventually capitulating. We have had many conversations about her in the office, how she went missing, colleagues and friends voicing their thoughts.

Was the fact that people warmed to her, her undoing?

Did some wicked person see through her chattiness and easy-

*going manner, spotting her vulnerable softer side beneath before
taking advantage?*

Becoming embroiled in that sort of dialogue isn't my thing. I
prefer to switch off from it all. It seems that some people get a
kick out of visualising Deborah in an unimaginably horrible
situation: distressed, frightened. Fighting for her life. But not
me. I will not get drawn into any of that dreadful talk. I blot it
out, get on with my day. Easier to push it back into its locked
box in the farthest reaches of my mind. To turn the key and
throw it away. I keep my thoughts to myself, revealing them
only when I'm alone, away from this office, away from these
people. They are private, my innermost thoughts, and will
remain that way.

At the desk beyond Deborah's, Merriel stands up, her tall,
willowy frame eclipsing the light from the nearby window. I
half shift away, too tired, too weary to become engaged in
conversation with this woman. Talking to Merriel is always an
ordeal, like wading through treacle or scaling a mountain with
one arm tied behind your back – possible but utterly pointless
and, at the same time, downright bloody painful.

'No news yet?' I can feel the heat of Merriel's curiosity, like a
missile seeking its target. If there was any news, we would all
know by now. The police would be crawling all over this office;
reporters would be waiting outside, their vehicles and photog-
raphers clogging up the car park. Merriel is aware of this fact
but has decided to press ahead with her pointless question
anyway. I am the one they come to, to chat about Deborah.
Always me.

I shake my head, too drained to reply. Merriel knows the
answer to this question. They all do. She is picking at scabs,
hoping they bleed. The people in this office go over and over it
until they have exhausted every possible scenario. It's unneces-

sary and undignified. They're not interested in Deborah's welfare. All they care about is churning over the remnants of it all, picking at the bones of the story. Gossip, that's all they care about. Idle chit-chat and gossip.

'I wonder if the police have any more leads? I saw them in Ruth's office last week. I suppose they'll be visiting her family again, going through her belongings, looking for clues.'

A sensation shifts between us, a tacit moment of understanding that I am unwilling to talk about this subject. Not here. Not now. And not with this woman. This woman who barely knew Deborah, the same woman who would brush past her in the canteen without giving her the time of day. And now so much interest from her about Deborah's whereabouts. So much faux compassion. It's sickening. Sickening, ghoulish and macabre. That's what it is. A woman clinging to the vestiges of a sensationalistic story, something she can dine out on for months to come. I suppress an almost overwhelming urge to tell her to fuck off, to mind her own business and get herself a fucking life. Preferably one that doesn't involve missing colleagues and poking her nose into other people's business.

Rather than answer, I turn away, the top half of my body twisted to face the window. Outside, a fat white seagull is perched on the windowsill, its unseeing beady eyes scanning the immediate vicinity. Clouds gather overhead, grey and heavy, their bellies loaded with rain. Fitting, I think, for such a dim and depressing moment. Wouldn't we all like to shelter from the imminent storm? Be a big, docile old seagull and do nothing but sit and wait until the darkness has passed and sunlight once again shows its face.

'Anyway. I'm here if you need me or fancy a chat.'

Only when I hear Merriel's footsteps fade away do I turn around. I see her figure slip round a corner out of sight and squeeze my eyes closed, suppressing a sigh that always seems to want to emerge when Merriel stops by my desk to chat. We are very different people, Merriel and I, she a confident individual who likes to talk whereas I prefer my own company these days.

When Deborah first went missing, some of the office staff suggested we all go out looking for her, convinced she could be easily found. So one evening after work, they piled in my car and I drove around the area, stopping every couple of minutes, all of us carefully scanning each and every dark doorway, every back alley, every lonely and desperate-looking part of town and seeing nothing but piles of rubbish and the occasional homeless person huddled in a shop doorway, their gaunt faces staring up at us, eyes searching ours for a glimmer of hope and assistance: all the things we couldn't give.

By the time I dropped everybody off and got home, I felt exhausted, my stomach empty and hollowed out, my mind numb. I had known it would be a pointless endeavour, tried even to talk them out of it but was outnumbered so went along with their plans, a silent, unwilling accomplice.

'I felt dirty,' Allison said the following day. 'All that grime and those poor people living on the streets. I spent the evening lying in a hot bath, eyes shut against the unfairness of it all.'

Everyone murmured their agreement, heads angled away, eyes lowered, frustration biting at them.

'We're powerless,' she continued. 'I feel like a useless friend. Deborah could be out there right now, helpless, possibly even dying as we speak. I have no idea how police officers do it – waking up and going into work every day to face a mountain of crime. I mean, I'll bet there are literally hundreds of unsolved cases. The sheer scale of it is unthinkable. Or maybe they become hardened to it, inured, developing a second skin to all the destruction and hurt out there.'

More murmuring. More flickering eyes, sighing, rapid breathing. A suggestion was made that perhaps Deborah went missing voluntarily, took herself off somewhere because she was depressed or had problems at home.

'That's nonsense,' Merriel chipped in. 'She was happy. No reason to disappear. No reason at all. Unless you count her useless boyfriend who isn't capable of keeping it in his trousers.'

A silence descended. He had already been questioned by the police, had an alibi, had been ruled out of the inquiry, although, as Merriel had pointed out, how visiting his mother the night Deborah disappeared was considered a solid alibi was laughable.

'Perhaps it's because his mum is a police officer and her word is considered irrefutable. It's a flimsy story, easily picked apart. Spending the night with your mother, eating a takeaway and watching a film hardly constitutes a rock-solid explanation of your whereabouts. It's weak and fragile and is almost certainly a lie.' Another silence as people started filtering away back to their desks, having nothing else to offer the conversation that would lighten our worry and anxiety.

Everyone knew that Deborah's boyfriend, Brett, has a weakness for other women. As many as he can gather. Like a predator storing up his kills to display to the watching world. I'm guessing that even Deborah knew.

'So, if Brett is ruled out of the inquiry, then where is Deborah? Did a complete stranger snatch her off the street? Bundle her into a car and do unspeakable things to her before disposing of her body?' Allison refused to move, standing instead next to my desk, her voice loaded with curiosity.

Stop it, stop it, stop it!

I wanted to reach up and slap her. She and Deborah weren't

close. Not really. Why she had felt the need to say such a thing was beyond me. I did my best to ignore her words, switching on my computer and flicking through my diary, a pen held so tightly between my fingers, the plastic casing began to crack and splinter.

I snap back to the present and stare at my watch, wishing away the hours, wishing it was time to leave this place with its gossipmongers and wild, uninformed theories and endless rounds of guessing games as to where Deborah is and what has happened to her. It's depressing, disheartening and disrespectful. Deborah wouldn't want her name bandied about like this. She would tell everyone to get on with their day, to leave the police to do their job without any interventions from uninformed bystanders.

Behind me, the phone rings, people chatter, the photocopier begins to whirr. All the usual sounds of a busy office. Nobody would ever know that just a few feet from where I am sitting is the desk of a missing person. The woman who left work one evening and never returned.

4

MANY YEARS EARLIER

'As a rule, we try to manage the behaviour of our pupils as best we can without getting anybody else involved. Calling parents into school is a last resort. I'm sure you understand that, but after lengthy discussions between ourselves, we felt it best to consult you and keep you informed of what's been happening.'

Marcia feels George squeeze her hand. She reciprocates, manages a small smile before lowering her head and closing her eyes, wishing back the tears, forcing her dark thoughts into that small space in her head, the one reserved for difficult times, the times when she wishes she was somewhere else. Somebody else.

'So anyway, as I was saying, we've become concerned of late, about Sadie.' Paula Wilkins places her hands in her lap, her fingers interlocked, knuckles white. Beside her, Brenda Vipond, the school family support officer, sits, an expression on her face that Marcia can't quite place. Sympathy perhaps. Or nervousness. What has she got to feel nervous about? This is her job, isn't it? Supporting parents, helping families through tricky times. Not that they, as a family, are going through a tricky time. Their day-to-day existence is as it should be. No marital breakdown, no bereavements. No job losses or serious *illnesses. None of the usual traumas that can tip people's lives upside down. There is nothing in their everyday routine, nothing untoward going on in their background, that can explain away Sadie's odd behaviour. Her reasons for the way she is. For the things she does. How can two siblings be so very different? Rosa's face fills Marcia's mind, her confident ways, her warm, easy manner, juxtaposed to Sadie's protracted silences, her frowns, her inability to interact appropriately with everyone around her. Twins who shared the same space for nine months, came from the same womb, born of the same parents and yet are poles apart, their characteristics at opposite ends of the spectrum. And then there is Jenna, another self-assured individual, their firstborn. Always smiling. Always willing to do whatever is necessary to make everyone's life that little bit easier. A people-pleaser. That's what they always called her. Jenna, their little star. Jenna, the people-pleaser.*

'We've consulted our educational psychologist and she's suggested using talking therapy as a way of trying to get Sadie to communicate. We, as a school, are more than prepared to try that. We have some staff trained to deliver the programme. Before we go ahead with it, we just wanted to run through a few things with you, if that's okay?' More hand-wringing, more nervous twitches – a series of blinks, faraway glances, tapping of feet – from Brenda Vipond.

Marcia swallows. What exactly is going on here? Sadie is a quiet child, withdrawn and nervous. Prone to the occasional outburst. She isn't a psychopath. She doesn't need therapy or educational psychologists giving her guidance. Does she?

'What things?' George's voice is a sudden crash in the room. A whip cutting through the air close to where they all sit, faces hardened by the circumstances, shoulders hunched in anticipation. Marcia winces, keen to avoid any unnecessary confrontation. She should have come alone, not told him about this meeting until it was all over and the matter sorted. She should have handled it alone.

Much like Sadie, she prefers the quiet, the solitude that silence can bring. That's not such a bad thing, is it? Why vilify somebody who prefers their own company? But of course, it's not just that, is it? She is deluding herself here, pretending everything is fine with their daughter when it clearly isn't. That's why they're here. To discuss her welfare, her mental health. Her future. And George is now readying himself for a fight, his hands cupped over his knees, his body bowed forwards, eyes wide, alert and on the lookout for whatever it is these professionals are about to throw their way. George likes control. He isn't comfortable with being caught on the back foot. And he won't take kindly to being talked down to. Condescension is one of his pet hates. It riles him, ratcheting up his temper and lowering his tolerance levels. She watches him, hoping silently that they soften their approach. She doesn't want an argument, hasn't the energy for it.

God, this is awful. Stupid. She should have come here unaccompanied, left him in blissful ignorance. He could be sitting behind his desk crunching numbers but instead, he is sitting here beside her, his temper fraying, spoiling for a fight. Marcia once worked in a school; she understands the protocol. George is an accountant, unused to these procedures and formalities. The hoops that have to be jumped through before they can go ahead with whatever it is these staff have planned for their young daughter.

'Oh, it's nothing major!' Paula Wilkins' neck colours up, a cerise web that climbs up her collarbone, over her throat before coming to rest on her jawline. Her mouth trembles ever so slightly as she continues with her assurances, a barely noticeable slack-jawed look that evokes pity in Marcia. George can be a formidable force when roused. He isn't a violent man with unpredictable tendencies, but this situation is making him edgy, like a cornered animal, its prey stalking him, sniffing out his weaknesses. This is his daughter they are talking about. His baby girl. He has always had a soft spot for Sadie, seeing her as the quieter one in their house, the one who isn't naturally

charming and vivacious. He feels a need to protect her, to metaphorically place his big, strong arms around her and hold her close. Even after what happened. That incident didn't dampen his love for her. He put it down to an accident, a horrible mistake. He forgave her. He moved on.

Marcia clamps her teeth together, chews at the inside of her mouth until a spike of pain forces her to stop. Now isn't the time to be thinking those thoughts. It's all in the past. They're here to concentrate on Sadie's future, to help her move forward and be the best that she can be in readiness for adulthood. She is ten years old. Secondary school is only a year away. She will be a teenager before they know it. It's good that they are getting help for her now, an intervention that will help her transition from child to young woman. Marcia tries to think of it as a way of recalibrating her daughter; a simple reboot after a small glitch.

'We just wanted to let you know of her academic progress and the social aspect of her days here at Portland Primary. We think it's important to give you an overall view of Sadie. It will help you gain an understanding of what we will focus on once the sessions begin.'

Marcia feels the tension in the room begin to melt away. In her peripheral vision she sees George smile and nod. He leans back in his chair, his posture softer, more malleable. Less threatening. Sadie is a bright girl who has the ability to focus when others nearby become distracted and are inattentive. It's her defining feature, and one that has bypassed her sisters. Being quiet and an introvert has its upsides. While she gets her head down and works, Rosa and Jenna are prone to chattering, their vivacious and gregarious natures too big, too robust to ever compress and silence.

They spend the next fifteen minutes going over Sadie's grades, Marcia getting a warm glow every time she hears the words 'outstanding' and 'exemplary' and mentally blocking her ears when she hears the words 'solitary' and 'averse to socialising'. For now, she will focus on the academic accolades heaped upon her daughter and ignore the traits and abilities she obviously lacks in other areas. She is all too aware of her daughter's flaws, her many defects and failings. For now, she is enjoying basking in the glow of Sadie's cleverness, her ability to absorb information and knowledge and pass tests with ease. Everything else can wait – all that negativity and anxiety about her daughter's well-being. She wants to savour this moment, enjoy it before her bubble bursts and everything becomes irreparably damaged, back to how it was. How it almost always is.

'We'll let you know the progress of the therapy. We can pencil in another meeting now, or we can contact you in a few weeks once she has had a few sessions? These things take time and we don't want to get a false sense of how it's going before Sadie has had a chance to make any real improvement,' Brenda says, finally speaking up after sitting mute for so long.

'Perhaps we should wait,' George replies before Marcia has a chance to find her voice. 'As you say, these things take time. Rome wasn't built in a day, was it?'

They part, George and Marcia linking arms as they exit the school building and head towards their vehicle parked up in the postage-stamp-sized car park. She ponders over what to say to him, how to best broach the subject without things turning sour and, in the end, decides to remain quiet. Sometimes saying nothing is better than filling a silence with useless, erroneous words. They can be a loaded weapon when used at the wrong time in the wrong context. George has just started to unwind. Best not to crank him up again, give him reasons to feel upset and worried and miserable. Sadie is their daughter, their baby. Silence affords her the respect she deserves.

They open the car door and slide in. George starts the engine, turns up the radio and they travel home without uttering a single syllable.

5

DEBORAH

She's whimpering, the new captive. A dull and muffled groaning sound is coming from behind her gag as she sobs and moans like a small child. I want to tell her to stop, that it's pointless and won't help her get out of here but the gag tied around my own mouth is too tight. Breathing is an ordeal. Speaking is impossible. Instead, I shuffle forwards and lean down, placing my head against her arm to show her some comfort. To let her know that I mean her no harm, that we are in this together.

The dull crying stops, only for the briefest of moments, then it starts up again, a convulsive sob. Soft and rhythmic. A heart-rending weeping that tears at my soul, making me feel hopeless and lost in this terrible place. Two of us now destined for possible death. Two of us detained for reasons unknown. And yet it would appear we are linked by a common theme – our faces. My hair is matted, my face twisted with grief and fear, my mouth pulled wide by a strip of fabric that stops me from crying out for help. I am unrecognisable. She, however, is still the same woman she was when this monster kidnapped her, her usual features and facial qualities still intact, not filthy and contorted like mine. Not cut and swollen by the regular slaps and punches that she metes out before quietly and gently bathing my sores and then tying me back up again.

She is unfathomable, my captor. An enigma. Everything she does is a mystery to me. I had hoped to work her out by this point but it would appear that her unpredictable ways have got the better of me, her actions and thoughts always one step ahead of my thinking with her erratic behaviour and bizarre requests. I'm too tired to fight her. Instead, I will bide my time, wait for the right moment – if there ever is one – and make my move. I thought I knew her, had the measure of her when we were friends. I don't. Time and time again, I have tried to climb inside her head, figure out why she has done this thing to me, and come up with a big fat nothing.

I edge back from the crying female, careful to keep the noise to a minimum. Dust motes swirl in the dim light. A dry sensation fills my throat and I have to swallow and still my breathing to suppress the coughing fit I feel rising from my gut. The air up here is thick and musty. I long for a drink of water but know that I've had my daily allowance. Any more liquid and I will need to pee in the toilet in the corner. Not that I can reach it, tied up like this. I would have to bang on the floor and then she would arrive, flustered and infuriated, ripping down my jeans and watching me as I release a stream of urine. Or worse. I've yet to suffer that indignity. So far, I have been allowed to use the toilet on my own while she stands guard outside. So far. There are times when I feel sure she wants me to be stripped of what little self-respect I have left so she can sneer at my expense. Anyway, it doesn't really matter as I'm regularly left alone here for hours and hours. I've learned to control my bladder and bowels, waiting until she arrives, her duality of anger and tenderness enough to make anybody lose control of their bodily functions.

In the corner, the crying stops, morphing into fits of heavy muffled breathing. It's silly really, completely skewed and bizarre, but hearing it gives me a sense of ease, helping to quell my fear and loneliness. I'm not on my own any more. I have somebody else here with me, somebody to sit with. Somebody who is just like me. For so long now, I have viewed my captivity here as a weakness on my part, allowing myself to be caught and trapped in this lonely, awful place, but it would appear that my thinking has been askew. I'm not weak. Just unlucky. And now there are two of us. A pair of unfortunates stuck here together.

Our breathing synchronises as the new captive attempts to sit up and take in her surroundings. Through narrowed eyes, I can see that she is about the same build as me but slightly younger. Our faces, however, are almost identical. At least I think so. Her gag has covered the bottom half of her face, but her nose, her eyes, they are mine. Instantly recognisable. We could be sisters. Except we're not. What we are is prisoners, our fate unknown. Our futures fragile.

I watch her closely as she pushes herself into an upright position using her feet and knuckles, pressing down on the hard flooring and grunting until she is sitting up properly, her back resting against the brick wall. I wonder what she sees when she looks at me. I'm grubby, my hair dirty, my face streaked with tears and dust. I am not the woman I used to be. Does she know that? Or is she able to see beneath the grime and fear and get a snapshot of the real me? To see the essence of who I am, my once raging spirit and sense of adventure still present, or is the new me the only one who is visible? The downtrodden, desperate me. The woman who can see no end to this living hell.

Below us, I can hear movement – the shuffling of her feet, and somewhere in the distance, a low drone, perhaps an HGV lumbering past or an aeroplane overhead – sounds that remind me there is life out there, a world beyond these walls that imprison us.

Making the most of that noise, hoping it will deaden the sound of my movements, I attempt to move closer to my new acquaintance, using what little strength I have in my legs, pressing my backside hard on the floor and pushing with my feet against the floorboards to propel me forwards. The pain in my shoulder grows a hundredfold, waves of agony shooting through the top half of my body. It's broken. I'm sure of it. Not that it will make any difference to my circumstances. If my head was hanging off, I don't think it would alter the approach of my captor. She is able to ignore my pain, seeing it as a nuisance, an intrusion to her plans, and would simply carry on beating me, feeding me, trying to brush my hair before discarding me like an old, battered doll, a toy she has grown weary of. Until the next morning, when she would climb the ladder with my breakfast and tell me how she loves me more than life itself. And so it would continue. Love, feed, beat. Love, feed, beat ad nauseum. Until I am dead.

I have no idea what I am going to do now I am sitting next to my new cellmate. I just know that I feel a need to comfort her, to let her know that we are in this thing together. Whatever this thing is. We need friendship and solidarity. Strength in numbers. So far, I have failed in my attempts to reason with the woman who brought me here, the woman I felt sure I knew so well. I have failed to break free, to come anywhere near close to escaping from this room.

After I woke up and first found myself here, shock took hold and I was too numb, too fearful, to do anything, but then a steely determination and a will to survive took over and I tried everything humanly possible to free myself. I spat, fought, kicked, screamed, refused food, my mouth twisting, my body bucking and bending as it was spooned into my mouth, but every single time I was overpowered, unaware at that point that she was drugging me. Silencing me and stripping me of my strength. I soon realised that something was amiss when sleep enveloped me like a dark, heavy cloak after consuming the food. She didn't want me to fight back and that was her way of quietening me down, making me listless and defenceless. So I stopped with the aggression and resistance because the more I fought, the more she administered those energy-eroding drugs. I feared that one day I wouldn't wake up at all. There were times when I felt so woozy, so damn sick and exhausted I barely had enough strength to sit upright. In the end, I acquiesced, tried to clear my head, be my best self. My strongest self. I figured that food is energy and when I do finally make my move, I am going to need every last ounce of it to get out of here. Sometimes we need to play ball in order to win, even if the opposition cheats and lies and throws away the rule book, making up their own set of instructions as they go along. One day I will outmanoeuvre her. I just don't know when that day will be. This new arrival, however, has given me hope. Maybe we can do something together, come up with a plan. I daren't look too far ahead but sitting here doing nothing isn't an option. I want to live. I want to get out of this place and the sooner the better before her madness takes hold completely and we all end up dead.

6

YVONNE

It's been a long while since we have done this. Meeting in the pub on a Friday evening after work used to be a regular occurrence but since Deborah's disappearance, it has tailed off, everyone too downcast, too unwilling to socialise. Some too frightened perhaps. That's understandable. Everyone is nervous and jumpy, a feeling of vulnerability palpable at the thought of walking home alone in the dark.

'It still doesn't feel right, all of us being here without her.' Merriel picks up her straw, idly swirls it around the glass, her thin fingers clutching on to it before bending it in half and throwing it onto the table. It rolls across the wooden surface, coming to a halt next to a half-drunk pint of bitter.

'Gotta move on sometime.' Adrian's voice carries over from the other side of the table.

All heads turn to look at him. I feel my skin prickle, my scalp bristling as a look of indignation crosses his face. An awkward lingering hush follows his words. He dips his eyes, turns away briefly, his skin reddening as realisation dawns at his faux pas. Did he expect everyone to agree, to nod their heads and give him their approval?

'Sorry, just trying to lighten things up. My bad.'

I can see Allison as she clenches her fists. She keeps her silence, afraid, I suspect, of what may spill out of her mouth if she opens it. Afraid of the insults she might throw his way that, once said, can never be unsaid. He's young, inexperienced, lacking in enough social graces and niceties to understand how and when to use humour correctly. He'll learn. And if he doesn't, then there are people seated around this table who will be more than willing to teach him.

'We need to stick together. That's the key,' Allison says after a moment of stunned silence. She takes a glug of her lager, foam clinging to her top lip as she places the tall glass back down with a dull clunk. 'Work might be a real grind but we're still all friends and decent people and we shouldn't ever forget that.'

A collective murmur of agreement takes hold, people nodding, sipping at their beer, avoiding eye contact with one another as they mull over Allison's words, the intent behind them. She's right, I think to myself, about most of it. Work is a grind and most of them here seem like decent people, but at the end of the day, we're all just colleagues, not friends, and how well do any of us truly know the people that we work with? Our real lives are hidden, the office providing a different context for everyone's behaviour. It's a formal environment, people acting out their designated roles – office junior, manager, cleaner – everyone doing what is expected of them so they are able to keep their jobs and pay their bills. They could be anybody, these people sitting around this table. Anybody at all.

The conversation starts up again, low voices slowly finding a way into the talk, speaking about everything and anything and avoiding the subject of Deborah completely. Perhaps it's for the best. What can be gained from sitting here, morose and melancholic, our mood dragging in the gutter? There's a time and a place for talking about a missing person and this isn't it. We are meant to be socialising, having fun.

Having fun.

What a phrase. I almost laugh out loud. It is infantile in its simplicity. Fun is bouncy castles and ice cream and playing ball games in the park on sunny days. Or perhaps I am being too rigid and austere in my view of the world. Perhaps it's time for me to lighten up, let my hair down. Live a little.

'Bloody depressing, isn't it? All this bad stuff online and in the papers. It's enough to make you stop reading the news altogether.' Merriel is staring down at her phone, finger poised over the screen as she scrolls through whatever site she is on.

'So do it then. Stop reading. Put your phone away and get yourself another beer.' Adrian is staring at her, his voice rising as his confidence returns. No more the apologetic individual from just a few minutes ago. His sureness has returned, his tone cutting and sardonic. 'I don't know why you do it. I don't want to read about other people's troubles and misery. Got enough of my own.' He attempts a smile, takes a long slurp of his drink and lowers his eyes, his mood souring once again.

'Like what?' Allison is watching him, her gaze intense. Unavoidable. 'You're a young guy. You've got a half-decent job, a flat of your own, a car. What have you got to be miserable about?'

Another difficult and embarrassing silence. Seconds of interminable awkwardness. I swallow, suppress a deep sigh. This is getting tiresome. I long to go home. So much for living a little. That particular aspiration didn't last long.

'How about surviving a shitty childhood? Moving from

foster home to foster home before being turfed out into the big wide world with no guidance on how to live on my own. That's just for starters. Plenty more to tell if anybody wants to listen?'

Nobody replies. A rustle of clothing as Allison squirms in her seat. The sound of glasses clinking in the background. They boom in my head, an echoing reminder of how little we all know each other, of how tactless and rude people can be without even realising it. Even the most mundane conversations can end up with somebody having their chest hacked open and their beating heart plucked out and held aloft for all to see. It's humiliating. Undignified and uncalled for. Such things should happen only in the privacy of one's home. There's a time and a place for such revelations and disclosures, and this isn't it. That's why I remain silent, attending these functions and get-togethers with an air of impassiveness. I refuse to let anybody inside my head, to rummage and delve deep inside my soul. Better that way. And easier. For them and for me.

'Sorry about that, Adrian,' Allison whispers. 'I had no idea. Me and my big mouth, eh?'

'Yeah well. We've all got something, haven't we? It's just that we don't always talk about it.' Adrian smiles, his mouth twitching, his eyes riddled with anxiety. I can almost see the cogs whirring in his brain as he forces himself to wrestle with painful recollections of his damaged upbringing while out drinking with colleagues. Hardly an ideal situation in which to air your past and face up to your demons – sitting around a table with people who will forget about you as soon as you walk out of the door. I feel myself soften. He's just a young lad and he is so right – we all have something. I think of my own problems and bury those memories, pushing them back down where they belong. Back into the darkness, into that rarely ventured corner of my mind where misery lurks. I look around the table, wondering what the others here have in their past. Wondering who they really are. I know who I am, *what* I am. But who are these people, really?

I finish my drink, the need to leave this place suddenly so strong, so pressing that I have to resist the urge to push everybody out of the way so I can bolt for the door. I take a deep breath, consider perhaps ordering another glass of wine, doing the right thing and trying to relax. Why do the simplest of tasks sometimes feel like an uphill struggle? I think that maybe it's this pub, these people, even the drink, then I think that maybe it's just me and the way I am.

The talk around the table strikes up again, the mood lighter. Easier and lacking in the tension from earlier. I do my best to hide my discomfort, to focus on the conversation, join in and be sociable.

'Christ almighty. Fucking hell, not another one.'

Merriel's voice cuts through the noise, stopping everything.

'What? Not another what?' Allison glances at her colleague, eyes narrowed as she waits for a reply.

Merriel looks up from her phone. 'The news. It's on the local news. Here,' she says, her voice reaching a crescendo. She holds up her mobile, pointing to the screen with her index finger and tapping on it with her long, painted nail. 'Look. Read that headline. It's happened again. It's bloody well happened again. Another local woman has gone missing. What the fuck is going on around here?'

I watch as Allison lifts her hand to her head. She wobbles on her bar stool, her face suddenly flushed. There are murmurs, gasps. A small shriek. Another one. Another woman gone.

I rub at my eyes, suddenly exhausted. All I can think about is getting out of here. In the distance I spot the door, the patterned glass panel, the thick wooden frame. I fix my eyes on it and use it as a focal point, somewhere I can reach without stumbling and drawing attention to myself.

Waiting for the right moment and ignoring the voices around me, I slip off my seat, take a deep breath and head towards the exit, Deborah's voice prior to her disappearance rumbling around my head.

Don't trust any of them, Yvonne. The people we work with are strange. A disturbed, disparate lot. Keep them all at arm's length.

And she was right.

The cold air is a welcome reprieve from the cloistered environment of the pub. The breeze laps around my face, travels down to my lungs as I take a deep breath and lean back on the exterior of the building.

It occurs to me that we are all vulnerable and exposed, every passing stranger a possible threat. They don't know me. I don't know them. All together and yet all of us, very much alone.

The clip of my heels on the pavement echoes through the growing darkness as I make my way to the train station. Autumn is close by, the nights drawing in. Soon the evenings will be pitch-black, the weather inclement. The roar of traffic on the overhead bypass filters into my thoughts. I pick up my pace, slip my hands in my pockets, lower my eyes to the pavement away from the glare of the ochre street lights.

It's louder than the noise of the nearby traffic, the buzzing that fills my head, when I feel a hand grab at my shoulder, fingers pulling at me, the force of it causing me to stumble. My legs give way under the weight of my terrified body. Above, the sky revolves, stars rotating and spinning. The ground is cold and hard as I fall backwards, my head hitting the pavement with a crack.

7

ADRIAN

And here we are again, me being portrayed as the bad guy while they all stand around with sanctimonious looks on their stupid fucking faces. We *do* need to move on and if not now, then when? I apologised anyway. It seemed like the only thing to do to shift the attention away from me, to get them to stop staring at me with their mouths open like a load of dying fucking fish. I shouldn't have told them really, about my background and my shit upbringing, but I needed to say something to get them back on my side or I risked spending the remainder of the night looking like the uncaring arsehole and I wasn't prepared to do that. I'm reminded of that old proverb – he that has an ill name is already half-hanged. Me telling them about my past also pulled Allison up short, made her stop and think. Not all of us come from a nice home with a decent family to fall back on when things get tough. She needs to know that. They all do. Maybe I spoke out of turn. Maybe I'd had a terrible day and had had a gutful of listening to everyone talking about Deborah and what might have happened to her. I was rash. I admit it. Thoughtless even. But I don't regret it.

The beer cools my gullet as I swallow, landing in my stomach with a welcome kick. I should slow it down really, take my time or I'll end up worse for wear and will then have to navigate my way back home on the last train – not a particularly appealing option. The last train seems to attract the dregs of society, the worst of them gravitating towards me while I sit keeping my head down, trying to mind my own business. Maybe we are like animal breeds, the damaged and the downtrodden. We seem to have an innate ability to recognise our own, people who are just like us. Look at me and Beth. No matter how hard I try, I cannot cut her out of my life. God knows I've tried. We are both spoiled by our twisted existence, dented and broken, Beth apparently irreparably whereas I have managed to more or less shake off the shackles of my past, refusing to allow them to own me completely. Most of the time, anyway. Maybe we belong together, two ill-fitting pieces of a jigsaw jammed together for all eternity. The thought of it makes me shudder. A lifetime of Beth. A lifetime of her impulsive, volatile ways and her need to suck all the enthusiasm and energy out of me in order to keep herself steady and balanced. I don't think I have it in me. But then, what choice do I have? Wherever I go, she will find me. It's just how it is.

I finish my beer and order another, happy to sit back, to be surrounded by the milieu rather than join in with it. The sound of voices, the clinking of glasses and the general hubbub of the place helps calm me, take my mind off what took place yesterday, the telephone conversation with Beth. Just when I think she cannot shock me any more, she always manages to find a new low, a different and unique way of getting into my guts and twisting and twisting until I feel sure my innards are about to explode.

Red-cheeked drinkers lean over the bar, their bellies

engorged with pints of ale and greasy food from the nearby takeaway. A fug of warm, stale air swirls about the densely packed pub, giving it a homely feel. I've always believed that people make places and the individuals in this particular building are unassuming, happy folk. It has a welcoming ambience to it despite it being in a less than salubrious area. No pretensions, no expectations. Just people being themselves and for that I'm grateful. I don't have the energy to perform, to be somebody else in order to impress those around me. I can kick back, relax. Just be me. Exactly what I need after such a difficult week.

Early evening turns into night-time, people filtering off around me, exhaustion and the lure of home picking them off one by one until I am left with only Ruth for company. That's not such a bad thing. I can think of worse people to spend time with. Inoffensive and practical. Those are the words I would use to describe her if asked. An inoffensive and practical lady who can also, as an aside, hold her beer as well as any bloke I've ever known.

'Sorry to hear about your childhood.' She takes a long slug of her lager, her eyes roaming about the place before landing back on me.

I shrug, down the remainder of my pint and shove my hands deep in my pockets. 'S'nothing really. Not even sure why I mentioned it.' It isn't nothing. I pretend it's nothing when, in fact, it's everything. It's always there, lingering, threatening to expose the real me. The child inside me. That lonely, terrified boy who grew up in the constant shadow of violence.

'It's good that you did mention it. Sometimes it's better to be upfront about these things than try to hide them away.'

I edge my way off the bar stool, the beer now doing its thing, making me dizzy and disorientated. 'I'm in better shape than

Beth,' I murmur. 'I'll never be as fucking mad as she is. Proper off her rocker, that one.'

'Beth?'

Despite my drunken state, I can see that Ruth is now all ears, her curiosity piqued. I almost laugh out loud. Deep down, they're all the same, these women – nosy bitches with nothing better to do than poke around in other people's lives. Even Ruth with her quiet, harmless persona is just like them. They can't resist a bit of gossip. A bit of dirt.

'My sister,' I manage to say, my words sounding slurred in my own ears. 'Not my sister really. Well, sort of, in a way, I suppose. She's a fucking psycho.'

I slip on a pool of something wet and sticky, my feet sliding as if on ice. Ruth's hand grabs at me, pulling me upright. I laugh. It sounds like a shriek, tiredness and tension fusing together in a miasma of near hysteria. It's time for me to leave here before I make my innermost fears an outer experience for those around me.

Before I can stop her, Ruth is by my side, her hand guiding me through the crowds, our feet shuffling along through the densely packed pub, elbows banging against passers-by, bodies colliding, drinks splashing our clothes, until at last, we are outside, the fresh, clean air filling our lungs, helping to sober me up.

'A complete nutjob,' I say again, Beth still filling my mind, her words eating at me as Ruth and I walk together to the station.

'Why do you say that?' She is leaning closer to me now, her small body almost holding me up.

'She didn't manage like I did,' I slur. 'It all got to her in the end. She couldn't hack it, the shit we had to put up with. It tipped her over the edge.' I hiccough, stumble a little and right myself. 'Tipped her right over that fucking edge, sent her crashing to the bottom. And now she's broken. Snapped in half like a bloody rag doll.'

The vomit follows my final words, rushing up my throat and splashing at my feet. I stand, dry-heaving once my stomach is empty. Ruth doesn't move, doesn't attempt to step away from my filth and my drunken ramblings, standing instead, stalwart-like, watching me. Waiting patiently.

'With me to the bitter end, eh?' I say, standing up and wiping at my mouth with my sleeve. The sour aftertaste of bile washes around my gums, sticking to the back of my throat. 'Sorry.' A sudden pang of embarrassment and regret weighs me down, the gravitational pull of the ground too great a force to fight.

I slump onto the pavement, my knees pulled up to my chest. I rest my chin on my kneecaps and wrap my arms around my lower legs, a sea of emotions running through me. I shouldn't drink so much. I'm not so much of a lush that I don't recognise my own failings. After tonight, I will rein it in, be the better version of me that I know is in there somewhere, fighting to get out.

'Come on,' Ruth says softly, hoisting me to my feet with a surprising amount of strength for someone so slight. 'Let's get you on that train and get you home, shall we? Before you end up asleep in the gutter.'

'I can think of worse places to be,' I whisper, hot tears of humiliation threatening to spill out. 'Maybe it's where I belong. Where I've always belonged.'

'Not tonight.' She laughs. 'Not here and not on my watch.'

She places her arm though mine and we half amble, half stagger through the narrow streets together like old friends.

8

DEBORAH

She's in shock, her body frozen, her sobs regular and rhythmic. I want to tell her to stop, to shut up and conserve her energy and that crying is pointless but I can't. My gag is too tight, cutting into the lower half of my face, the fabric tied tightly at the back of my head. The monster who has us imprisoned here doesn't understand fear and misery and the sense of helplessness that we feel. She's impervious to it all, locked in her own world of insanity and cruelty. Those are the things that drive her. I know that now. If only I had known it before, when we used to laugh and chat together. When we were friends. If only I had picked up on it – her growing anger and lunacy. Maybe then, I could have avoided this.

My backside aches as I shuffle backwards over to one of the beams that stretch across the roof and slope down to the floor. The pain in my shoulder screams at me, every movement sending a jolt of agony down my arm and across my collarbone. I try to ignore it, my eyes misting over, my breath catching in my throat until I feel the hardness of the timber behind me, and stop, my breathing a grunting sound, my chest heaving with the effort of my endeavours.

For the past few days, I have shuffled around this place, looking for a suitably worn and rugged piece of wood and just yesterday (at least I think it was yesterday, as time in here has lost all meaning) I found one.

It's going to hurt. I've resigned myself to that fact, but this is something I need to do. Every day that I do nothing is a step closer towards my own demise, so I have made the decision to use what I have around me to try to get out of this place. I can't sit here waiting to die. I won't.

The crying opposite me stops. My cellmate's eyes follow me as I lean back, my fingers fumbling for that sharp splinter of wood that is jutting out from the low beam, the one I saw yesterday. The one that offers me a route out of here. Us. Offers *us* a route out of here. I can't just leave her here and yet, if she doesn't calm down, pull herself round and start thinking clearly, then my new friend is going to be a burden rather than a help. And an added burden I can do without.

I take a deep breath and brace myself for the expected pain that will inevitably ensue once I start dragging my wrists over the length of wood, then begin the process, slowly at first, my arms and shoulders gyrating as I attempt to tear at the fabric on my wrists with the serrated edges of the beam. It's a slow and painful process and within seconds, I am sweating and panting, the added problem of my aching shoulder and arm bringing tears to my eyes. A pain takes hold in my abdomen, my breathing suddenly laboured. I stop, take a few seconds to prepare myself, then start again. Rubbing and dragging. Rubbing and dragging. My fingers catch against the rough wood, my nails tearing, my fingertips burning as splinters get lodged under my skin. It doesn't stop me. I have to keep going, to free myself of this material. I have to get out of here.

The searing ache in my shoulder is crippling. I let out a muffled groan, tears escaping and rolling down my face. Opposite me, all is quiet. I glance over, see her stupefied, frightened gaze and look away again, concentrating only on my movements, putting all my efforts into making sure I snap this stupid piece of fabric that is causing me so much heartache and pain. The monster has already given me my daily rations of food and drink. She won't be back up here for hours and hours. This gives me plenty of time to untie myself and work out what to do next. I didn't plan on escaping tonight, but with an extra person to help me, we could overpower her and get out of this place. It's not a perfect plan, rough around the edges and lacking in any detail and real semblance of order, but it's the best plan I've had so far and I'm going to take it, regardless of its risks.

Downstairs it is silent. I wonder how she manages it, what she does down there to deaden the sounds of her movements. Apart from the occasional rumble of a distant engine or the crows and hoots of birds flying overhead, this place is soundless, like living in a vacuum. Perhaps she does nothing, lying on a bed in a darkened room, biding her time until morning comes and it's time to visit us again. Maybe we are her life, the only thing that's keeping her going. That thought is enough to make me want to vomit.

My hands and fingers are wet. Sweat and blood probably. My shirt is damp, my face streaming with tears and perspiration and snot but I don't stop. I won't. Not until I'm free. And then it happens. I feel it and let out a rasping sound. A loosening of the fabric on my wrists, a slackening that tells me it is fraying and coming apart. I increase my momentum, moans and cries of desperation spilling out of me. I try to stop them, to bite down on the filthy gag that is covering my mouth, but they still find a way out. It's a sense of euphoria. I am close, so fucking close to freeing myself and it feels so good. Just a few more seconds, that's all I need. A few more seconds and I can untie us both.

And then I hear it – that instantly recognisable *clump clump* of her feet on the wooden stairs that lead to this loft space. I freeze, try to regulate my breathing, to show no outward signs of my efforts. I look down at my heaving chest, think about how filthy and sweaty I must look. I think of my blood-covered hands tied behind my back, and wonder if I can pretend to be asleep when she appears through the doorway. If I'm lucky, she will focus all her attention on this new person. Because if she sees what I've tried to do – well, I am done for. She will administer a solid beating using both her fists and her feet. More bruises, perhaps a few broken bones. Who knows how she will react? It all depends what day it is, which way the wind is blowing. The rules are that there are no rules. It's all a wild guessing game minus any of the fun that usually accompanies such activities.

The door is pushed open, slowly at first, giving me time to back farther up into the corner, then a broad spillage of light as it hits the wall with a bang. And there she stands, silhouetted in the doorway, her slim frame broadened, her presence giving off an ominous vibe.

She steps into the room and I feel a rush of blood as it pulses through my veins, pounding and throbbing in my neck, moving up through my head. Across from me, I see the new person flinch, hear her muffled shrieks, the scuffle of her limbs as she tries to back away. It's pointless. I want to tell her as much, that it's all a waste of time and energy, and if I manage to remove this gag, I will. It'll be a steep learning curve for her, knowing when to remain quiet, to be a docile rag doll in this monster's presence. It's the best way. The only way if she wants to live and remain sane.

'Food.' The figure steps into the room, a plate balanced in her left hand. 'Sit up. Here, let me take off your gag. And don't try anything. Shouting is pointless. Nobody will hear so don't bother wasting your breath.'

She's right. I've tried it. I have no idea where we are, but we clearly don't have any neighbours nor are we in a built-up area. We're completely isolated. But one day, we will get out of here, perhaps sooner than I ever hoped. We will free ourselves of the ties and gags and will plot and make plans. We will whisper our ideas into one another's ears. One day soon, we will get out of here, perhaps even sooner than I ever hoped.

I visualise myself standing up and charging into the monster, knocking the plate out of her hand, kicking her in the ribs and running down the stairs and out of the front door. But of course, I can't. My feet are bound together, my hands still tied. I was so close, so very, very close to freeing myself. And then she walked in. Impeccable timing on her behalf. Anybody would think she knew what I was up to. She doesn't. There are no cameras in this place. She knows that she doesn't need them. It's too dim, too empty and we are too constrained to do anything. Or we were. Not long now. Not long until my wrists are untied and I can free us both.

'Oh, you are so like her. I'm glad you've come home. It's been a long time since we've all been together. Now,' she says as pulls off the woman's gag and squats beside her crumpled body, 'I hope you like lasagne. I cooked it specially for you.'

I watch as the piece of soiled fabric is removed and the new captive spits in her face. Behind my own gag, I smile. She is feisty, my new accomplice. Not quite as soft and frightened as I first thought. This is good. I need somebody with courage, somebody who can think on her feet, not be a hindrance when we make a bolt for it out of here.

'Bitch!' I hear the slap, the unmistakable sound of flesh meeting flesh, see the monster's hand as it smacks into the side of the woman's face, knocking her sideways onto the dusty floor. 'I said not to try anything, didn't I? And now look what you've done. What you've made me do.' She takes out an old rag from the pocket of her jeans and wipes it over her own chin, then leans down and dabs at the new woman's face, gently wiping away the thin stream of blood that has started to trickle out of her nose. 'Please, co-operate. Everything is going to be perfect if you do as I say. Everything will be back to how it was. Back to when we were younger. You'll see,' she says, her voice suddenly soft and childlike. 'I'm going to make everything just perfect. Now sit up and open wide.'

9

It's dark out. Sadie sits up in bed, pulls the curtains aside and peers out into the garden. She wishes she could be out there, not up here, in this bedroom, in this house.

Next to her lies her twin sister, asleep in her own bed. Sadie drops her hand from the fabric, twists around to stare at the sleeping figure, at her slightly open mouth and tousled hair. Everybody says they're identical but Sadie doesn't think they look alike at all. Her hair is slightly longer than her sister's. She has more freckles and Rosa isn't as quiet as Sadie is. Everybody knows that. They have completely different personalities. People mention it all the time. She thinks it's funny how they stop and talk about you when you're a twin. They speak as if she and Rosa are objects in a museum, making comments about their appearance and comparing their mannerisms, always telling Sadie she should be more like her sister, be outgoing and chatty and how she should smile more.

'You look a lot prettier when you smile, you do know that, don't you?' her mum had said only last week, as if smiling was that simple. As if smiling comes easily to her.

They say things like that all the time.

'Chin up.'

'Has the cat got your tongue?'

'Why can't you be more like your sister...'

They say those words because they don't know. They don't know about Sadie and they don't know about Rosa. Why do adults feel as if they have the upper hand when it comes to assessing and judging children? Nobody can see inside their heads. And even if they could, they wouldn't want to. It's dark in there. Dark with lots of hidden corners for thoughts to lurk and hide.

Sadie smiles, lies back on the pillow and looks up, making shapes out of the shadows that scud across the ceiling. She can see a horse up there. It gallops across the bedroom and disappears into the darkness, melting away out of sight. She has always wanted a horse. Dad says they're too expensive and having kids is pricey enough. Mum says animals are too much like hard work and besides, doesn't she have enough to deal with, what with Sadie and all her problems at school?

A car moves across the room, a grey outline above her. It too vanishes with the shifting light of the moon. Then she spots it. She blinks, shuts her eyes tight, tries to make it go away but it won't move. It's still there when she opens her eyes again – a knife-shaped shadow. Sadie grips on to the edge of the mattress, digs her nails into the bedcovers and slips further down beneath the sheets. She would disappear altogether if she could. Out of this room, out of this house. Out of this life. She stares up at the shape and imagines the knife is real. She pictures herself grasping at it, plucking it off the ceiling and using it on Rosa's sleeping body, slicing and stabbing at her, cutting her into tiny little pieces until there is nothing left of her perfect twin sister.

Her eyes are drawn to the snoring figure in the next bed, envy and hatred rippling through her. Everything her sister does happens with such ease – speaking, singing, dancing. Theirs is an asymmetrical relationship. She knows what that word means. She heard her teacher speak to another member of staff about her and Rosa, saying they were asymmetrical and, although they looked alike, they acted very differently. Sadie looked up the word afterwards. It didn't take too long to find it although she already had a good idea what it meant. She isn't stupid. She's far cleverer than her twin, even cleverer than Jenna who is two years older. She's good at spelling too, good at all of her schoolwork. There are a lot of things she excels at. It's just that being happy and kind and smiling all the time isn't one of them.

She thought about that word all day in class and at home that night while she was eating her tea and watching telly. Most twins have a special bond, a lifetime attachment to one another, but not her and Rosa. That's because of their asymmetry. They are as different as can be. Sadie is quiet, withdrawn, and Rosa is the rest of her plus some extra bits.

Tiredness begins to creep in, the silence and the darkness engulfing her. One day, she will tell everybody about her life, about what goes on in her head. What goes on when nobody is looking. Despite being top of the class at school, it's difficult to find the right words, but she's working on it. And if the words won't come, then she'll just have to find another way.

10

YVONNE

'Jesus, Yvonne, I am so sorry!' Merriel looms over me, eyes wide, expression stricken. Her mouth is agape as she attempts to bend down into a squatting position next to where I lie sprawled on the pavement.

I close my eyes, take a long, shuddering breath and swallow repeatedly to stem the vomit that is rising. A tight band of pain is wrapped around my head, a wave of sickness travelling through my abdomen, up my throat. I reach up to touch my forehead and feel smoothness there. No blood, just a coating of perspiration. I feel hot and cold at the same time and shiver, my teeth chattering together.

'I thought I'd upset you so I followed you out to make sure you were okay. Here,' she says, placing an arm around my waist and pulling me into a sitting position, 'let me help you. I shouldn't have mentioned about another woman going missing. It was stupid and clumsy of me.'

The asphalt is cold and hard beneath my backside. I scramble to get up, my legs weak and watery. All I want is to stand, to get away from this place, from this situation, as quickly as possible but I don't quite trust my own limbs, fearing they will wilt and buckle under the weight of my body if I attempt to right myself too quickly. So instead, I remain on the pavement, legs splayed, hands pressed against my head.

'Can you manage to get up? Here,' she says softly, more gently than I have ever heard her speak before, 'let me give you a hand.'

And before I can protest, Merriel is hauling me up into a standing position. I stumble, still slightly dizzy, and lean against the wall for balance. Everything swims, the sky a medley of twinkling silver stars, the ground a swirling carousel. I'm usually stronger than this, fit and healthy. She caught me unawares and now I feel like a helpless old lady, unable to walk unaided. Stupid Merriel for pushing me over and stupid me for getting caught out and falling.

'I've got my car over there. I'll give you a lift home. Link my arm. It's only a minute's walk away.'

I want to tell her that I am perfectly fine, that I am more than capable of getting the train home on my own and that I just need a minute to right myself after she knocked me to the ground, but I can't seem to summon up the strength to speak coherently, shock and pain still rippling through me, so find myself being helped along the path by a colleague that I barely know and couldn't care less about.

Merriel's grip is strong, her fingers clasped tightly around my upper arm as we stride along the walkway. I'm desperate to shake her off, to tell her to get away from me but, instead, I acquiesce, be the biddable, quiet person she wants me to be. People pass by, their voices disappearing into the distance. They don't notice us. We are simply two friends out together after a night out in town, one of us slightly drunk, being helped along by the other one. Nothing to see here. Nothing sinister going on.

By the time we reach the car, the sickness has begun to abate, the pain in my head dissipating. I am helped into the passenger seat by Merriel who is talking incessantly, her voice booming in my ears, filling my head. No way to escape this woman. No way to shake her off. She continues talking. The words float around the space between us, empty and meaningless. I am too tired to concentrate, to join in with the conversation. All I can think about is getting home. Getting home and climbing into a hot bath then slipping between the cool sheets of my bed and sleeping for a hundred years. I hate being helpless like this. And right now, I hate Merriel. I have things to do when I get in, jobs to be getting on with. She has thwarted my plans for the evening with her stupid words and clumsy ways.

'So, as I was saying, I'm certain these two disappearances can't be connected so there's no need for you to worry.' Her words cut into my thoughts, the background buzz of her voice beginning to take shape in my mind, everything now slotting into place. She is trying to distance herself from her previous statement, to put some space between her words and the responsibility she feels for my rapid exit from the pub and subsequent bump to the head. She is convinced that her statement unnerved me. I am convinced she is a troublemaker who relishes spreading bad news and dissecting other people's lives.

'Are you sure they're not connected? This is a small town in the north-east of England. One person going missing is big news. Two is unheard of. People don't just vanish.' I wait for her to reply, eager to see what her response is going to be. Eager to see if she clings on to my question and allows herself to be drawn into a conversation that she knows nothing about.

The quiet that descends is a thick veil, impenetrable and heavy. I turn away, staring out into the murky night sky.

'Perhaps,' she murmurs, plainly aware she is being tested here. 'Or maybe not. Who knows, eh? Anyway,' Merriel says, suddenly keen to change the subject, 'I'm glad that we're going back to the pub on a Friday after work. It brings a bit of normality back, doesn't it?'

'Normality?' That one word, my tone, the look on my face is enough to stop Merriel in her tracks. I say it softly, slowly. Just loud enough to let her know how callous it sounds. I'm actually enjoying this, seeing her stumble about, having to watch every word that comes out of her mouth. Wondering what I'm going to say next. How many faults I will find with her trite phrases and inept and ill-thought-out axioms and platitudes. She doesn't reply, her mouth zipped into a tight, thin line.

The drive takes no more than ten minutes, Merriel occasionally humming along to the bland music on the radio while I stare out of the window at the passing traffic wishing the red lights we stop at would turn green at twice the speed. Being here in this car so close to the woman who irritates me beyond reason, is making my teeth itch with anxiety.

'I can come in with you if you like once we get there? Make sure you're okay and you don't get sick or feel faint. You have to be careful with head injuries, don't you?'

I feel Merriel's eyes flick over to me, assessing me, waiting for my reaction before turning her attention back to the road ahead. I don't want her in my house. Being here in this car is about as near as I ever want to get to her. She thinks she knows everything there is to know about me, about Deborah, about the other colleagues we work with. She knows nothing. Not a damn thing.

'I'm fine, thank you. I feel much better now. No lasting

effects. It was just the shock more than anything. I didn't hear you come after me and thought I was alone. Feeling somebody grab you from behind in a near-deserted street is enough to make anybody collapse in a heap.' I attempt a laugh, doing my best to lighten the situation, to disguise the contempt I feel for her. 'Although I have to say, the whole incident scared the living daylights out of me. Feeling that hand on my shoulder turned my stomach inside out. I thought that maybe I was going to be the next victim. I felt certain I was about to be bundled off somewhere and possibly killed.'

In my peripheral vision, I see Merriel's hands grip the steering wheel, her knuckles white under the glare of the nearby street lights. Her voice is a whisper as she speaks. 'Well, as long as you're sure you're okay and don't need any help getting inside. Anyway, here we are. Home safe and sound.' The grating noise of the handbrake being pulled on is the most welcome sound I have heard all day.

Pulling at the door, I all but stumble out of her car, my feet twisting beneath me. Before I can slam it shut, I see Merriel's face appear, highlighted by the inner glow of the vehicle. Her neck is craned to one side as she stares up at me, her cheeks sallow, her mouth slightly open as if she is about to impart some piece of important knowledge. I wait, see her smile and nod before leaning back and once again placing her hands on the steering wheel, her gaze fixed straight ahead.

'Thanks for the lift.' I have no other words, nothing to say to this woman. I should try to like her, be pleasant, affable in her presence, I know that, but it feels so difficult. My mind is closed off to her odd traits and foibles. Maybe we're just too different, two opposing people, our interests angled in opposite directions.

The door closes with a metallic clunk, echoing into the stillness of the night. The road is empty and silent save for the sound of a tinny alarm going off somewhere in the distance. I like this area. I feel safe here. Close to all amenities but also next to the countryside. A row of houses perched at the edge of a sprawling and scrubby, yet ruggedly beautiful, landscape that consists of a handful of dilapidated barns and an old farmhouse. And the neighbours are friendly too; children play without too much noise or rancour and dog walkers pick up their dogs' shit. These are the benchmarks of a half-decent area. It's good enough for me.

Rummaging in my bag for my keys, I watch as Merriel's car pulls away, the low growl of her engine setting off a relief valve somewhere deep in my abdomen. I breathe out and briefly close my eyes before unlocking my front door and stepping inside.

It's dark. A chill creeps over my skin. I lean forward, turn up the thermostat and head into the living room, the dim bulb affording me the smallest amount of light. Walking around, I switch on more lamps, giving the place a more ambient feel. More welcoming, less threatening.

It's only as I kick off my shoes and slump down onto the sofa that it hits me, the realisation of what has just taken place. The sudden sickening dawning that at no point did I give Merriel my address, and yet she drove here expertly through the narrow, winding streets before getting to my home as if she knew exactly where she was going.

A fire starts up in my face, my skin suddenly hot and clammy, flames flickering just below the surface of my cheeks and neck. I rub at my head to alleviate the pressure that's building there, a heavy pulsing beneath the bone that makes me feel queasy and angry. I should have been more aware. That bang on the head has made me slack and drowsy, made me lose focus.

I need to do something to shake off these uncomfortable feelings, to rebalance myself and clear my head. Racing up into the bedroom, taking the stairs two at a time, I pull off my clothes and drag on my sports gear. A night-time run will do me good, help me shut out any negative thoughts and get me thinking clearly again. God knows I need that. With everything in my life so finely balanced, I can't afford to see things through a fog of confusion. I need clarity in my life. I need to get back to how I was before Merriel bowled into me like a clumsy child and knocked me to the ground.

It's as I'm heading back downstairs that the thought wrestles its way to the forefront of my mind, presenting itself like a huge obstacle that blocks out everything else. I should have thought of it straight away, not been side-tracked by my pain or my fury. I stop, place a cool palm across my forehead and squeeze my eyes shut, the sudden realisation a heavy weight bearing down on me.

Besides knowing where I live, why the hell was Merriel following me in the first place?

11

DEBORAH

My body is rigid. I sit, huddled against the beam, doing my best
to disappear off her radar. She is focused on this new female,
feeding her forkfuls of lasagne, the cooing sounds she makes as
she shovels it into the poor woman's mouth turning my stomach. I am completely revolted by her. Everything she says and
does makes me want to retch. It hasn't always been this way.
That night after leaving work, that's when everything changed.
My memories of it are still hazy. God knows I've tried to piece it
all together, to ask myself why she would do such a thing. *How*
she did what she did. It's as if her iron will and bodily strength
increases day by day. It seems to fuel her resolve, seeing us
helpless. I just wish I knew why. I've gone over it again and
again and come up with nothing. I've tried asking, Christ
almighty, I have tried and tried and tried, but to no avail. In the
end I gave up. All it did was rile her all the more and that was
something I could do without. Keeping her pleasant and unruffled became my goal. Still is. She is less prone to temper
outbursts if I play the docile victim and after so many beatings

and mind games, I don't have the energy to continue confronting her.

The pain in my shoulder is shrieking at me. I need to move, to get into a more comfortable position but know for sure that she will notice every little movement I make; every single rustle of clothing will be accentuated as I try to adjust my posture and that means she will turn her attentions to me. Then my near-escape antics will become apparent. I can't let that happen so instead I sit, doing my damnedest to remain still and quiet and be completely unobtrusive. She is fixated on her new project. Maybe she will now forget about me. Maybe this new lady will be my chance to make a dash for freedom. I think about leaving her behind and whether or not such a move is something my conscience will stand and then remember that once I'm out of here, I can lead the police back to this godforsaken place.

By which time she could be dead.

I swallow down my misgivings, bat them away out of sight. I can't save everyone, but I can save myself. It's all about self-preservation at this point.

'Come on now. Just one more mouthful. There, that's it. Well done. We're all finished.' Her voice is saccharine sweet, her body, her face, so close to this other woman that they are almost kissing. Except they can't. Not as long as she is wearing that dark, tight mask to disguise her face. Stupid really. She thinks that it's hiding her real identity. It isn't. She has a voice. I know it, recognise it. I know her gait, that distinctive walk, her mannerisms. I know exactly who she is. The one time I called her by her real name I ended up with a broken nose. Blood spattered across the floor as she smashed her fist into my face. She had to spend the next day scrubbing at it to remove the stains. I had had to spend the night sleeping on it, like an animal in an abattoir awaiting its imminent death.

I've not done it since. It isn't worth it. Goading her simply results in me getting beaten, suffering broken bones, bruises, blood loss, so now I sit and watch her, working out ways in which I can get out of here. But she knows that I know who she really is and, for now, that is enough. Despite her attempts to alter her voice, changing its timbre and pitch, I know exactly who she is. I say her name over and over in my head. I go over a lot of things in my head. It keeps me sane. I've learnt the art of survival, mastered it well since being held captive in this stinking hole.

Sometimes, I can hardly believe what is actually happening here. That it's happening to me. Or that *she* is the one doing it. None of it makes any sense. A thick mist obscures many of the facts of that night but I do recall leaving the office and making my way home. It had been a really good day. Apart from the slight headache that had started to settle in, that is, as I collected my things and left. I could never in a million years have guessed what lay ahead.

'There we go. Another sip of water.'

I try to blot out the sound of her voice, thinking of other things – *anything* – to stop it infiltrating my thoughts. The less I have of her in my mind, the better I feel.

'Fuck off, you demented bitch.'

I wince, waiting for the noise of her hand meeting this other woman's face.

One, two.

And there it is. I didn't have to wait long. A slap, perhaps a punch, followed by a deep, drawn-out groan and the sound of a body as it slumps to the floor. The clunk of a skull hitting bare floorboards. The sudden silence of an unconscious female, blood possibly pooling beneath her head.

She'll have to learn and adapt, this newcomer. She will have to learn to conserve her energy, not expend every waking moment of her time on insults and hatred. She needs it to think, to survive. To get out of here alive.

'And what about you, sitting there quietly in the corner? What do you think of our new family member, eh?'

She is not my family. You are not my family. Stop speaking in that vulgar fake voice and leave me alone.

She's used this line on me before, calling me her sister, telling me we're related. I ignored her then and will ignore her now. Easier that way. Safer. When I once asked her why she called me her sister, she retaliated with a slap, telling me to shut up and that I always ruined everything, causing family arguments and spoiling her life, so I stopped asking.

The sound of her clumping towards me makes my skin prickle. If she decides to spin me around, I am done for. She will see that I've almost managed to cut through the ties on my wrists and then all hell will break loose. I can't let that happen, so I nod, try to smile behind my gag, be as biddable as I can be. This seems to stop her. She stands there, looking down at me before squatting next to where I'm sitting. I can smell her breath, warm and fetid, close to my face. My instinct is to move back, to scramble as far away from her as I can, but I know that would be a foolish move. A painful one for sure. So I stay still, try to soften my posture, not show her that I'm afraid or furious. I won't display any of the emotions that enrage her, sending her into a frenzy where her fists and temper dictate the outcome. It seems to do the trick. She backs away, her eyes flicking between me and the crumpled heap on the floor across from where I am sitting.

Suspicion and an ever-present latent anger emanate from

her, oozing out of her pores. Before being held here, I used to be good at reading people, often pre-empting them before they had a chance to speak or do anything, but this one is different, her moods oscillating from one day to the next, one hour to the next. One minute to the next even. This isn't the person I thought I knew. She has another life. One that nobody knows about. Not her friends or family or colleagues. I guess that's how most psychopaths operate. They aren't immediately identifiable by their bizarre appearance and quirky, unpredictable behaviour. They are sly and devious; they live two lives, have two different sets of rules. One set for the normal life, the mask they wear every day and another for their underworld, the rotten, evil universe they inhabit when they think nobody is watching. I think about Ted Bundy, John Wayne Gacy, Harold Shipman. All those purportedly trustworthy pillars of society with secret horrific lives. She is like them, her devious, unpalatable secret pastime kept separate from her ordinary life. Nobody would ever guess. I certainly didn't.

'I'll be back in the morning. Do you need a pee before I go?'

I shake my head, lower my eyes, do my best to appear submissive. She prefers it that way, but I mustn't overdo it. She is an astute one and would spot faux compliance. It's all about balance. I've learnt that much while being imprisoned here. Keeping the equilibrium just right has kept me alive thus far.

My bladder is screaming at me but I refuse to be accompanied to the toilet in the corner like a small child while she stands and watches. I've had enough of it. Once her back is turned and my hands are free, I will go to the toilet on my own. It will seem like a special treat. That's how it is these days. I'm overly grateful for the smallest of mercies.

Then after that, I can free us both and think about what I'm going to do next.

She waits for a couple of seconds, my heart thrumming like a bass drum beneath my sweater. I can feel her watching me, am able to sense her eyes as they sweep over my body, across my face, her gaze lingering and critical. Then she backs away, turns and heads out of the door.

I listen for the clump of her feet on the wooden stairs and am almost dragged under the wave of relief that washes over me when I realise she has gone.

By the time her footsteps have faded away I'm almost gasping, my chin quivering, my hands trembling. I give myself a couple of seconds to gather my thoughts and allow my pulse rate to slow down before continuing with my small bid for freedom. Just a couple more rubs against the roughly hewn wood and this material will snap and fall away from my wrists, fluttering to the floor like soft tissue paper.

Excitement balloons in my chest as I feel the break and gradual loosening of that final thread that is keeping my wrists bound together. I can hardly breathe. A pain shoots up my forearm and into my shoulder when I try to bring my left arm from behind my back. It's been stuck in that position for so long that any movement is torture, my joints locked firmly into position. That and the kicking she gave it when I dared to question why she was keeping me here, why the person I thought I knew had suddenly turned into a monster. I tried to count the number of times she drove her boot into my shoulder and the top of my spine as I lay whimpering, praying to die that night. The pain was excruciating, like nothing I have ever experienced. I begged, cried for her to stop and eventually passed out, an explosion of stars filling my head before blackness descended. When I awoke the next morning, she was laid beside me, stroking my face, staring into my eyes, telling me how sorry she was and assuring me that it would never happen again as long as I learned to behave properly. I will never forget that look in her eyes, the darkness there. The lack of compassion and empathy. The growing madness.

I knew then that begging and pleading and crying and sobbing would solve nothing. Escape was the only way out of this place. Either that or death.

And now it's here, an opportunity to get out of this makeshift prison. This is my chance, possibly my *only* chance. I have to get it right or my future is uncertain. She'll kill me. It may not be the result of a direct blow but eventually she will kill me. I'll rot in this place, be left to wither away and die.

The gag serves as something to bite on to help stem the pain as I move my left arm and flex my fingers. Bruising, possible broken bones and lack of movement all fuse together to make a flash of agony so strong it causes me to inhale sharply, for my eyes to water and my head to spin.

I take a couple of seconds to prepare myself and for the pain to subside, then reach up and with semi-dexterous fingers pick at the tight knot of my gag. It's not easy and I am just about to give up, to untie my new accomplice instead and get her to do it, when it goes slack. I pick at it frantically, excitement and terror pushing me on.

It finally flutters into my lap and I'm able to breathe properly, the warm, stale air in this small space feeling and tasting like liquid gold. I turn my face left and right, move it up and down, gulping in as much oxygen as I can. Everything suddenly seems right again. Getting out of here feels possible. No gag and no foul-tasting tepid food being shoved down my throat. I can actually breathe.

I'm caught up in the moment, so full of exhilaration for my newfound freedom, carried away on a ripple of euphoria. That's how I miss it – the look of terror in this new person's eyes as she lies sprawled and helpless on the floor, the subliminal signals she is trying to send me. I know before I spin around that she's behind me – the monster. I know then that all my hard work has been for nothing. I know then that she will possibly kill me.

I close my eyes, brace myself and wait for it to be over.

12

'Why, Sadie? Why would you do such a thing?' Marcia's voice is a near shriek.

The little girl stares at her mother, her mind a tangle of thoughts. She can't speak, isn't able to explain this situation. They wouldn't believe her anyway. They rarely do.

The scratch that stretches the full length of her sister's cheek begins to bleed. Tiny ruby rivulets run down Rosa's face. Sadie's twin sister begins to cry, a small hiccoughing weeping sound that soon develops into full-blown sobbing that could shatter glass.

Sadie watches as her mother pulls Rosa into her chest, her hands pressed against the back of her sister's head, the child's face buried into her mother's abdomen. Blood and tears and snot are smeared over Marcia's blouse, her favourite white one. Sadie bites at her lip. It'll be ruined, her mum's favourite item of clothing discoloured and unfit to wear any more and they will blame her for it. Another black mark against her name. Another reason to hate her.

The two other little girls stare from where they are standing in the corner of the garden. Friends from school over to play. And now everyone will know. They will go home and word will spread that *she is strange, her behaviour unpredictable. Not that they don't already know that.*

She takes a breath, stares up at the sky, trying to stem the tears that threaten to spill out. Her parents don't actually hate her, she knows that. They despair of her, are tired of her and that is just as bad. Are parents allowed to hate their own children? Maybe they are. Especially if they do bad things. Really bad things. She has read about children like her – children who get sent away to live in places far away from their home because they're too evil, too wicked to live with their real family. They don't deserve nice homes and loving mums and dads. Instead, they end up getting assessed, their behaviour recorded in medical journals, used as guinea pigs so that doctors can help diagnose other delinquents. She knows what that word means too. She knows lots of things. More than her family or teachers will ever realise.

She wants to explain what happened. A stream of words run through her head but they're disjointed and nonsensical and she can't get them to come out of her mouth properly. It's panic. That's what it is. Panic leaves her mute and unable to defend herself. If only she was more confident. More like Rosa or Jenna, the words gliding off her tongue effortlessly. Honey-coated sentences dripping with sincerity and joy. That's what her mum and dad say – that Rosa and Jenna are a joy to be around, that people warm to them. That they are both honest and easy. Natural. Full of tenderness. And then there is Sadie. Sadie with her sullen looks and lack of charm. Sadie with her wicked, wicked ways.

Last week at piano lessons, their teacher had commented on how unalike they were, the three sisters. She had said that Jenna and Rosa were more like twins than she and Sadie. And then she gave Sadie a sweetie when she saw how unhappy that comment made her feel. It was a marshmallow. She doesn't really like marshmallows but felt obliged to eat it anyway and then while Miss Pendergrass wasn't watching, she took it out of her mouth and stuck it behind the sheet music. That was the same kind of panic that often got her into trouble both at home and in school; a sudden decision born out of a lack of time and knowledge of what to do in the given circumstances. She got chastised for it, Miss Pendergrass shouting that she was a filthy child and hadn't she been taught any manners?

'Your sister would never do such a thing,' she had said, and Sadie had closed her eyes and then she had begun to hum. A delicate light tune that she had heard Miss Pendergrass play on the piano from time to time when they first started attending lessons in her house. She thought it might stop her from being so angry. She hoped it would calm her down. It didn't. She shouted all the more, shrieking at Sadie that she was being rude and disrespectful, that her strange ways were unacceptable. That it was about time she learned to behave normally, to be normal like other people. Like her sister.

The hour lesson had dragged after that, every minute stretching out endlessly while she was forced to play the scales over and over before being given a sheet full of theory to fathom.

No matter how hard she tries, it seems that she cannot do the right thing. Ever. Sometimes she wonders if it's worth the effort. But of course, she knows deep down that it is. If she tries really hard then her parents might see what is actually going on here. They might see through the shroud of lies that constantly swirls about their family like a heavy, thick mist, everyone stumbling around in it thinking they're heading in the right direction when in actual fact they are all wandering toward a cliff edge.

'I didn't do it.' Her voice is lost amongst the cries of her twin sister as she continues to wail into her mother's bosom.

'You know, Sadie, you really need to start thinking before you act. This can't continue. It really can't.'

She watches as her mother bustles her way inside the house, Rosa still pressed close to her chest, the shrieks an assault on her ears.

This is just like last time, that awful day when their dad took ill. The day when he ate his sandwich and was really sick afterwards. Really, really sick. Holly berries. That was what had caused it. Her mum found them in the remains of the bread afterwards, pushed deep into the thick, doughy slices of his ham and cheese sandwich.

One day, she thinks as she squats down on the lawn and plucks idly at daisies, she will get her own back. She will tell everybody about this family, about what goes on in this house. As soon as she is able, Sadie Milburn will rise up and show them who she really is. And then they will know. They will all know and wish that they didn't.

13

YVONNE

I sip at my coffee, Merriel still in the forefront of my thoughts. Last night, that drive home with her, it has left me feeling weakened, tired and out of kilter and I don't like it. Not one bit. Still, it's the weekend now. Time to switch off, not think about work. Or Merriel. I have other things planned, another life outside of the office and yet last night, the memory of her hand grabbing me, the car journey home – it is still tapping away at my brain. It doesn't sit comfortably with me. I don't want Merriel knowing where I live. She is a colleague, not a friend. I don't trust her. Something about that woman makes my skin pucker with disdain.

My fingers instinctively reach up to trail across the lump on the back of my head that formed after the fall. Was it a fall? Or was I pushed? Dragged to the floor perhaps? No. That's a ridiculous notion. Merriel may be an irritant, lacking in people skills, but she isn't violent. At least I don't think she is. Again, how well do we really know each other? And yet, she does know where I live...

I take another sip of the hot liquid, waiting for the caffeine to kick in, to help frogmarch me into the day after another long week in the office.

Anger begins to well up inside me. I've always tried to keep my work life and home life separate, so how *did* Merriel know my address? I have no memory of ever telling her, no recollections of it cropping up in conversation. It's not the type of thing I would ever randomly drop into a dialogue. It's not how I operate. I've only been employed at Haswell & Sons for just under a year and in that time I have managed to tread the fine line of being friendly and sociable without having to endure the agonising ritual of becoming close pals with everyone around me. They're colleagues, nothing more, nothing less. They don't know me and I don't know them. I don't *want* to know them. I have my own life, my own interests and pastimes. A life outside of work that doesn't involve the drudgery of being forced to talk about what happened to Sandra from accounts or how the photocopier needs upgrading or why our working week is being extended and our pensions slowly but surely eroded at the same time. None of it is of any interest to me. I only attend the Friday night drink in the pub after work because I am pestered and badgered into it. Not going would make me conspicuous by my absence, so I go along, sit and listen to their inane talk, make my excuses after a couple of drinks, and leave. That suits me just fine. Or it did up to last night when Merriel decided to follow me and knock me over then insist she bring me home without having to ask for my address. I don't like it, her knowing where I live – the fact that, at some point, she went out of her way to find out my address.

I open up my laptop, log on to my social media accounts – the ones I carefully anonymise for privacy – and search for Merriel. She's easy enough to find. Such an unusual name with no attempts to change or alter it in order to keep unwanted friend requests at bay. Perhaps she has nothing to hide, lives a simple life and I'm clutching at straws here. I try to think back. Did I once mention in passing where I live and my imagination is going into overdrive? Or does Merriel have an alternative agenda?

A montage of photographs fills the screen, Merriel in a variety of poses – with friends at a bar, at a wedding in a long cream dress, standing by a river in jeans and an old sweater, grinning inanely. All the usual things that people get up to in their everyday lives. Nothing amiss. Nothing sinister. An ordinary woman leading an ordinary life.

I continue scrolling, searching, trying to assess her lifestyle until my eyes become blurred and gritty. I rub at them with closed fists, snap the lid closed and push the laptop away, disappointment swelling in my chest. What was I expecting? Photographs of dead bodies? Maybe the odd picture of Merriel being cruel to a small child or torturing an innocent animal? Merriel posting pictures of my front gate as she stands outside waiting for me to emerge like a stalker, watching me, assessing my lifestyle and habits? I close my eyes, shut out those unsavoury thoughts.

Outside, the sun hangs heavily in the sky. I watch it, squinting against its auburn glare. This is ridiculous. I have to stop with this line of reasoning. It's childish and pointless. No good can ever come of it. Come Monday, I will thank Merriel for her help and the ride home and make the comment that I didn't remember giving her my address and she will reply that I mentioned it once in passing and that will be that.

Of course, it will be a lie. I didn't mention it in passing. I wouldn't. I haven't. I know this for certain.

A sharp pain gripes at my bottom lip as I bite at it, grinding at my own flesh with my teeth. Perhaps I should start giving

Merriel some slack, be nicer to her, more trusting of her unorthodox ways. Maybe she's lonely, in need of a friend, although she seems to have enough of those judging by her social media photographs and I certainly don't need another friend adding into my life, especially Merriel.

I sigh, take another glug of coffee. I'm being overprotective of my private life. I'm making too big a deal of it. Merriel is no threat to me. That bump on the head seems to have drained me of all common sense. She's just somebody I work with who accidentally pushed me over.

The memory of her last week nudges its way into my mind – Merriel hunched over her computer, looking shifty. Looking over at me. By the time I made some lame excuse to move around to her side of the desk, she had already closed whatever site she was on and did her best to look otherwise occupied.

And the number of times she twists the conversation around to Deborah's disappearance is astonishing, alarming even. She appears to have some sort of fascination with Deborah, always raking over the night she vanished in minute detail. I remember seeing Merriel watch Deborah from afar on more than one occasion prior to her going missing, staring at her when she thought she wasn't looking, assessing her movements. Scrutinising her when she thought nobody was looking. Why would she do that? Or maybe I'm imagining it. We're all on edge, our usual lives and routines shifted and warped, all bent out of shape.

A jarring thought suddenly pops into my head, a memory from a few weeks ago that I had forgotten about. The figure in the distance. How they turned away when they saw me watching them from my window. I thought little of it at the time, brushed it aside but now, with recent events, I feel the need to give it greater scrutiny. Could it have been Merriel, hanging about, watching me?

My heart taps out a solid beat, erratic and uncomfortable. I stand up, tell myself to stop this – this worrying and insatiable need that I have for probing and delving into things that are best left untouched.

I shove Merriel and her knowledge of my home and her interest in Deborah out of my mind. Today, I have to go into town, get a few essentials and then get on with the rest of my day. At some point I'd like to go running, clear the swirling mist that's blotting out all logic in my head. It's my way of keeping myself together, nudging away my demons. We all have our own ways of remaining sane, don't we? Mine is running, shedding my worries like layers of dead skin.

Outside, dark clouds gather. Distant trees are buffeted by a growing breeze, their long, crooked limbs swaying like arthritic gnarled fingers. I've always loved this view, ever since buying the place. It calms me, being able to see a sprawling landscape, to drink in the swathe of sky. It's good for the soul, living so close to the countryside. Being hemmed in on all sides by concrete and mortar isn't a natural way to live. I was lucky to be able to buy this place. After Aunt Deirdre died, I was left a sum of money, not a huge amount, but enough to live comfortably. I paid cash for this house and some of the land around it. I've always wanted somewhere with lots of space, somewhere I could wander freely, breathe easily and now here I am, spoiling what should be a happy time by fretting about things that aren't important to me. Things that have no impact on my lifestyle or the choices I make. Merriel is a peripheral to my life, a fly I should swat away. A nobody.

I sit in the dining room, elbows perched on the table, my gaze roving over the nearby sprawling fields. A breeze picks up, the high grass swaying, a sea of variegated green. Birds flit and swoop in and out of the hedgerows. Their tiny wings are spread wide as they coast on the thermals, their sleek bodies exposed and trusting of the elements. Once I've finished my coffee, I'll go for a walk over that way, breathe in the clean air, purge myself of last night's events. Do what I have to do to forget about work, to forget about Merriel.

I stand up, do some stretching exercises, try to regain my strength and vow that never again will I allow someone like Merriel to get the better of me. Being strong and fit and independent is important to me. I live alone, have no support network to fall back on should times turn rough. I need to be the best I can be to survive. I finish my coffee, throw the remnants down the sink and steady myself for whatever the day may bring.

14

ADRIAN

Sobriety. That's the first word that pops into my head as I wake up, my throat as dry as sand, my limbs, my torso, my entire body feeling like I've been kicked by a horse. A sense of panic zigzags through me at the realisation that my life has become a cliché, that I'm following the same path as my father, my drinking spiralling out of control. Misery settles in the pit of my stomach at the inevitability of it all, that it was always only ever going to be a matter of time before history repeated itself. A weight presses down on me, an opaque shroud of guilt and anxiety. That's another part of my character that has been formed by either genetics or my upbringing – the bouts of darkness that regularly engulf me. Maybe it's both. Maybe nature and nurture are both to blame for the shadows that litter my mind, blocking out all the light.

I recall those times as a child, the nights when my mother, beaten down by the poverty and my dad's drinking, would take to her bed for days at a time, leaving me to fend for myself. Dark times. Torrid times. Times I would sooner forget. This is what alcohol does, it flattens me both physically and mentally. I have no idea why I do it, why I allow those memories to resurface after a particularly gruelling drinking session. And yet here they are, niggling at me, refusing to budge. Reminding me how shit my life is, how close I am to another meltdown. I kid myself that I've managed to live my life as a normal well-balanced person who had a blissfully happy upbringing, when Beth hasn't, her craziness apparent for all to see, but the truth is, there are many days when I teeter on the brink. Work helps. It gives my life meaning and structure. Keeps me half sane and stops me from tipping over into that deep, dark abyss, but it's always there, that threat, those memories. A reminder that at any given moment, everything I've worked hard to achieve could come crashing down around me, shattering my fragile existence. If only people realised how lasting the effects of a damaged childhood are, maybe they would understand. Maybe they would give us fragmented, delicate people more chances to prove our worth.

The foster homes I was put in after being removed from my parents weren't much better, although my final placement was as stable an environment as I had ever known. The foster mother was kind, thoughtful. The girl I was placed with not so much. We did bond, after a while, but not until I had proved myself, shown her that I wasn't someone who could be fooled, a boy whose feelings were easily dented. I had grown a second skin by that point, protected myself with an invisible suit of armour, albeit subconsciously. It's what blighted, frightened children do, they display characteristics that to those around them appear abrasive, often arousing suspicion and abhorrence. And sometimes the people who experience and observe those emotions are right to feel that way. But not always.

I tried to be the best I could be and left my final foster home with a small feeling of hope that things might just turn out to be just fine. Finding myself an occupation with no idea of what was required of me or how I was supposed to function in a working environment was difficult and I went through a few jobs before landing my current position with a half-decent salary. I thought everything was beginning to turn out okay.

But then, of course, there was Beth to contend with. *Beth, Beth, Beth.*

Even now, all these years on, everything is still always about Beth.

I sit up and check my phone. Only two missed calls from her. That's not so bad. No texts and no desperate messages left in the middle of the night. No more hanging around outside the office every evening. Yesterday, I was able to leave without the embarrassment of Beth being seen alongside me, her sunken features and erratic behaviour making her impossible to miss.

My stomach clenches as I think about what she has done, how I should react to her news. I try to not think about it too much. After all, it's not my problem, is it? Not really.

Except it is.

Now she has told me, I am duty bound to do something. Beth tells lies, however. She isn't a reliable source. For anything. Maybe this is one big fabrication, a figment of her imagination. At least I hope it is. The alternative doesn't bear thinking about.

I sigh, run my hands through my hair, realising I need a shower. My mouth is still gritty, my head aching from the dehydration of the alcohol and the vomiting. God, I need to sort myself out, grow up and stop drinking. I also need to apologise to Ruth first thing Monday morning. Shame and disgust ripple through me, an undulating feeling of disquiet that will stay with me all weekend, preying on my mind until I can meet up with her and tell her face to face how sorry I am. And I am. It's not just empty words. I am thoroughly ashamed of my behaviour. Ashamed and embarrassed.

My stomach rumbles. I'm running on empty and need breakfast but not before I clean myself up. I swing my legs out of bed, perch on the edge of the mattress, the room still spinning slightly, and stand up, vowing to never drink again. Ever. I've said it before, half-hearted promises whispered to myself the morning after the night before. This time, however, I mean it. This time is the time when I put my sorry, stupid ways behind me.

Pulling back the curtains a fraction, I peer outside. Condensation sits like tiny snow slopes at the corner of the window. It looks cold out there – bright, but cold. In the small courtyard below, the last of this year's foxgloves are barely standing to attention, their long stems growing crisp and turning brown, wilting as summer bids its farewell and autumn beckons.

I let the curtain drop back into place, ignoring the continual beeping of my phone as I turn on the shower and step into the hot water, vigorously lathering myself down, keen to remove the stench of vomit and shed the indignity of acting like a fifteen-year-old after their first taste of beer. Today is going to be the first day of the rest of my life. The only reminder of my past will be Beth.

Once again, even with a renewed set of vows to turn my life around, Beth is still there. I wonder for the hundredth time this week – will she ever leave?

15

DEBORAH

I hear her before I see her – her stealth-like movements, the sound of her breathing, the rustle of her clothing as she approaches. My blood freezes, my scalp prickles, needles of ice jabbing into my skin.

She says nothing and I don't know which is worse – her silence or her anger. A beating is a clear-cut thing, something tangible that I can cling on to. At least when she uses her fists against me, I know what sort of mood she is in, but this – this is torture, sitting here waiting, wondering, steeling myself for what may come next. A slap. A punch? A kick or maybe another sickening display of faux concern where she attempts to pull me close to her chest and rock me to sleep whilst whispering in my ear how much she loves me. There is no telling, no way of knowing or predicting her behaviour.

The bones in my neck creak and groan as I turn to see her standing there, like a vision of death. I am suddenly overcome with fury, my fear leaking out of me now that I have had a taste of freedom. Now that I know escape is within my reach. I keep it contained, my anger. I'm not so stupid as to think I can win this particular battle. My feet are still bound and I can see that she is holding something behind her back. I visualise a claw hammer or an axe. Anything is possible where this woman is concerned. Anything at all. Only recently she attempted to undress me. I fought and kicked and resisted until she eventually gave up, murmuring that it wasn't sexual, she simply wanted to bathe me and put me to bed because that's what families do for one another. I tried to ask her what sort of families continually beat each other for fun but all she heard were my muffled screams and protestations from behind my gag.

'Here,' she says softly, her voice low and menacing in the near darkness, 'let me help you. You seem to have lost something.'

She bends down beside me, her breath hot and sour, her eyes glistening like marbles, set deep in their sockets, and stares at the discarded piece of rag in my lap.

'We can't have you not dressed properly, can we? Especially when there's a family party coming up.' She brings her hands from behind her back and places something beside me – a grainy photograph of a group of children sitting at a table, a small birthday cake placed in the middle. I turn away, make a point of not looking at it.

'Look,' she says, pushing it closer to me. 'This will be us at our little party.' I wince, a deliberate grimace so she is able to see my reaction to her statement, her warped words that are laced with a brooding menace.

'Don't worry,' she continues, her voice suddenly going up a full octave until it's almost sing-song in its lilt and delivery, childlike even, 'you don't have long to wait. Just one more day. Are you excited?' Her head swivels to look at the new addition to our freak show. 'You're invited too!'

'And you're a sick fucking psychopath.' I can't help it. The words are out before I can stop them. 'I'm not your family and there will be no fucking party.'

Once again, I wait, my body tensed, ready for the blows that will rain down on me after I've insulted and riled her. Nothing happens. Rather than mete out any physical blows, she picks up my gag, wraps it around my face, stuffing it into my mouth and tying it tightly at the back of my head. My hair is caught up in the knot and I let out a small shriek that goes unnoticed as she continues pulling and tightening, pulling and tightening, until she is satisfied that I won't be able to speak.

Then come the ties around my wrists. I inhale sharply, ready for the pain that will follow as she grapples with my arms and twists them behind my back. It's bearable. Just. I don't cry out again. This time, I refuse to give her the satisfaction of knowing she's hurting me. Were it not for my bound feet, I would use this opportunity to wrestle her to the floor, take my chances and try to overpower her. As it is, I give in; my body is limp, offering no resistance. When I do make my move, I want to do it properly, be fully able to free myself, not some half-hearted attempt that will end up failing and resulting in me getting beaten again. My body has had about as much as it can take. I need to choose my future battles carefully, make sure I can win them. I haven't the energy for any more losses, any more pain. I'm limiting my exposure to her violent outbursts. It's how I hope to survive.

'There we are, all sorted. No real harm done, eh?' She scoops up the photograph, stands up and steps away from me, her eyes sizing me up, sweeping over my body, my legs, as if she is seeing me for the first time. 'Now,' she says, taking a deep breath. 'Time for the good news. I've got you both a new outfit for the party. I can't have my two girls looking shabby now, can I?'

I all but vomit. My eyes bulge. I have no idea what she has in mind for us but know for certain from past experience that it won't be pleasant. How can the two sides of this woman be so different? A cool, composed female to the outside world and a psychopathic monster behind closed doors. I wonder if at some point she will crack, her other self slowly starting to bleed into her normal everyday life. I hope so. I hope that people around her begin to see the gaps in her sanity, spotting the festering darkness that lies beneath her shiny, flawless veneer. Maybe if I keep resisting her and ignoring her demands then the pressure will become too much and she will be knocked off balance. Or maybe she will simply kill me. Maybe she will take a hammer to my head and batter me to death without breaking a sweat.

'They're matching outfits so there won't be any arguments. You always look so cute when you have the same dresses on.'

Her words cut into my thoughts, her efforts at disguising her voice a humiliating attempt at severing any ties we had in the outside world. I can't work out whether she is serious or whether there is something else to follow. She is always so good at blindsiding me, catching me off guard. I can feel the new captive's eyes watching me. She has no idea what is happening. I don't either, but I do have the advantage of knowing how perilously close to the edge this woman is and what she is capable of, the lengths she will go to, to get exactly what she wants. The depth of her madness. It's a bottomless pit. A vast well of darkness.

'I'm going to leave you now to let you both have a nap. Beauty sleep is very important when you have to look your best for a special occasion.' She laughs, her voice light, uncharacteristically delicate, in complete contrast to our grim surroundings. She sounds like a child, an excitable, precocious child, her voice once again unrecognisable to its usual pitch, as if she is going through some awful transformation in her head, transporting herself back to her childhood. I know nothing of when she was little. Our conversations when we spent time together didn't cover that aspect of our lives. We stuck to superficial subjects – work, the weather, my useless boyfriend, the one I was going to break up with in the next few days. That didn't happen. I ended up here, stuck in this place with no sign of ever breaking free.

I stare down at the old sleeping bag she placed here all that time ago when I was first brought to this stinking hole, and feel myself shrivel. The thought of spending another night in this place drags my self-esteem and hope for survival so far down into the dirt, I feel as if I am choking on it, clumps of filthy air and grime blocking my airways, killing me much faster than she ever could.

Once again, I try to visualise my own death: my emaciated, broken body found many years down the line by somebody who stumbles across this place – wherever this place is – and reports their skeletal find to the police. Two skeletons. Perhaps even three or more.

'Either of you need a pee?'

The new lady makes a muffled groaning sound. I see her nod her head and want to stop her, to tell her to wait, that we could both manage after the monster has gone. At least that way, what little dignity she has left remains intact. I can remove these ties again, then free her of the gag and rope tied around her wrists. We could help each other.

'Right,' the monster says brightly, as if we are all old friends, as if this whole scenario isn't the most disturbing thing any of us will ever experience. 'Let's get you sorted then.'

I close my eyes, turn my head away so I don't have to watch as she helps this poor woman over to the filthy old toilet in the corner of the room. There is a wall but no door and the toilet itself faces where I am slumped on the floor. No discretion. No escape from our most basic, fundamental human needs.

The sound of her zip being pulled down and the stream of urine hitting the porcelain makes my skin crawl. Such a private moment exposed for all to see. This is how the monster satisfies her weird and depraved cravings, by using us as her playthings, doing with us as she sees fit. The violence is just a small part of it, like a child throwing a tantrum and tossing her favourite dolly across the room because things aren't going her way. We see the full range of her twisted, damaged emotions and are subjected to them daily. That's when it hits me – the idea that we should play along with her little game, not fight it. It may have an effect, it may not, but what I do know is this: if we do nothing, we will die here.

I wait until my new cellmate has been helped back to her place on the floor and we are alone before once more attempting to free myself. I refuse to do nothing. To do nothing is to give in to certain death. I am going to get out of here before we are forced to endure this party, whatever the fuck that is. This much I do know – I am not planning on hanging around long enough to find out.

16

YVONNE

The weekend is over, time losing itself in myriad mishaps and events. I went for a couple of runs, caught up with many jobs at home, and now I'm back here, sitting at my desk, counting down the days until Friday comes around once more and I can be free of these people and spend my time as I choose. With whomever I choose.

I can sense her close by. Even without looking, I know that she is standing next to me, her hip adjacent to my shoulder. I carry on typing, keen to get on with my workload. Keen to fill my day so the hours in this office pass by as quickly as the weekend.

'That was awkward, wasn't it?' she says quietly, her voice just loud enough to make sure I'm forced to take notice of her, to acknowledge her presence.

I spin around, trying to suppress my sigh and biting at the inside of my mouth, then stare up at Allison with heavy eyes. I refuse to become embroiled in more tittle-tattle and office gossip. Whatever it is she's got to say, I don't want to hear it.

'Hmm? Sorry, just trying to wade my way through this lot.' I point at my computer screen, willing her to pick up on my reluctance to speak, hoping she spots my body language, my stony expression, how I am angled away from her. She doesn't. She's oblivious to my words, to my deteriorating mood and clear lack of interest in her idle chit-chat.

'On Friday. What I said to Adrian. I hadn't realised he'd had such a shit upbringing.'

I shrug, unsure what it is she wants me to say. Why do I always feel as if certain answers are expected of me in conversations such as this one? That I am being put under pressure to say the right thing, show the correct expression when, in truth, I couldn't care less. About any of it. Why should I? I don't know these people and they sure as hell don't know me. I don't want them to. I'm a private person, happy with my own company. Work is work. It's not a social gathering.

'Oh, I'm sure it will all be forgotten about soon enough.' I try to sound charming. Helpful and concerned. Which I'm not. What I am is disinterested and busy.

'Maybe. Still, it's rotten, isn't it? Having a childhood like that.' She chews at a nail and spits it out on the floor next to my desk. I avert my eyes, a sickly sensation rising in my gut. Some people have no decorum, no idea of how to conduct themselves. 'I've been chatting to Ruth and, apparently, he survived it really well, unlike his sister who is properly damaged. A complete psycho by all accounts.'

My stomach flips. I swallow, rub at my eyes, fatigue gnawing at me. I'm already weary of this day and after only a few minutes of her company, I am definitely weary of Allison.

'Should she be telling you such things? Isn't stuff like that confidential?' I think of Ruth, our HR manager, and her slap-dash ways of managing everybody's files and the information contained within them. Surely disclosing this is worthy of a warning from her superiors? If she is passing information around on Adrian, then I have no doubts that she is speaking freely about the rest of our backgrounds and such talk should result in disciplinary action.

I think of my own childhood, my fractured upbringing, and feel a small part of me shrivel. Nobody knows about it. I have no next of kin, nobody to grieve for me should anything untoward happen. Sometimes being alone has its benefits and other times it is a crushing burden.

'Oh, don't worry,' Allison says, her eyes darting about, her body suddenly stiff with the realisation that her talk has crossed a boundary, leaving one of her colleagues susceptible to complaints, 'she only mentioned it in passing and, anyway, I sort of knew already.'

I suppress an eye roll. Allison clearly didn't know. None of us did. She just told me so herself only a matter of minutes ago but now that a possible reprimand is nudging closer to the person who told her, she is backtracking. I shrug, turn away, get on with my work, hoping she will do the same. The heat of her body bounces off me as she continues to stand, watching, waiting. Waiting for what, exactly?

'We all have our crosses to bear, don't we? I mean I know it's awful for Adrian, what he went through, but everyone has something going on in their lives. Including us.'

I have no idea what is meant by this comment, this throw-away remark she is using to salve her conscience, so I shrug rather than give her a concrete answer to an abstract remark that could mean anything but possibly means nothing. However, you never know. Not with Allison. Not here in this office where gossip is rife and loyalty is scarce.

'I mean, look at me and my history and I'm sure you have

things happening in your life that you would rather keep to yourself.'

She is relentless, I will give her that. Persistent and relentless if she thinks there is some gossip to be had.

'What about you and your life?' I ask, swerving the conversation back to Allison, determined to keep her interest in my background to a minimum. Memories of my childhood are reserved solely for me, never to be brought out into the open with these people. They wouldn't understand nor would they care. A child whose family perished in a terrible tragedy; it reeks of self-pity and somebody seeking sympathy and that, I can do without. It would be used for the purposes of gossip, to pass around the office as if I were some sort of freak to be pointed at and pitied. And it's not a competition as to who had the shittiest upbringing either. I refuse to partake in such ghastly talk. We are what we are and nobody can change that; no amount of clicking tongues and hollow platitudes will make any difference.

Her eyes dip to the floor, her lashes fluttering like the wings of an insect in flight. She sighs, bites at her lip, a stalling tactic I've seen her use in the past, before speaking. 'It's nothing really.' Another deep breath, a clearing of her throat. Either what she is about to tell me is monumental or she is formulating a story in her head at this very minute, allowing herself a couple of seconds to get it just right, for her lies and embellishments to be as accurate as they can possibly be.

'Nothing? Are you sure about that? I thought we all had something?' I keep my voice low, soft and unassuming. It's a fine balance. I don't want to insult Allison but nor do I want her to begin a soul-baring session and have her labour under the false notion that we are bonding and becoming close friends. We are not.

A few seconds pass in silence. In the distance, other people chatter, phones ring, the photocopier whirrs its usual clunky whine. I am about to turn away from her completely, focus my attentions on my workload, when she speaks again.

'I don't suppose it matters who knows but I'd rather you kept this to yourself. I know I can trust you, Yvonne. You're not the type to break confidences and get involved in office politics and pointless chatter.'

I swallow, wishing I hadn't prolonged this dialogue, wishing I had ignored her and watched Allison march back over to her own desk, but as it is, I am sitting here, being forced to listen to the ins and outs of a colleague's life, a colleague I don't particularly care for and one I hardly even know.

'My husband left me a few months back. He took the children with him.' She sighs, gazes out of the window and curls her hands into small fists. 'I developed mental health issues after my parents died in a car crash last year. My relationship with them was always a struggle but after they died it hit me really hard. And then one day—' She stops speaking, her voice breaking, eyes glistening with tears.

I'm unsure what to do next, whether I should intervene, offer her my seat. Hand her a tissue perhaps? Before I can do or say anything, she continues and, as I listen, I find myself wishing she hadn't, that she had remained silent and tearful instead.

'One day, I did something. I snapped, hurt one of the kids. I also hurt Jack, my husband.' She clears her throat, straightens her posture and blinks away the unshed tears. 'Ex-husband now. He's filing for divorce. I threw something at him, threatened to use the kitchen knife I was using at the time. Bad stuff. Really bad stuff.'

My lungs feel as if they have shrunk. My breathing is shallow, my skin suddenly cold and clammy. Why is this woman telling me these things about herself and her damaged life? We barely know each other. I have a vision in my head of telling her to leave, pushing her away, then I right myself and attempt a sympathetic smile, a tilt of the head, murmuring all the while about how sorry I am to hear of her troubles.

'Thank you, Yvonne. You're really kind. I knew I could open up to you. You've always had an understanding manner, always been the quiet, gentle one of this place. The sensible, astute one.'

I feel my face flush and this time I do turn away, her compliment catching me unawares. I wonder why she is saying such a thing when we are nothing more than acquaintances. She doesn't know me. Sometimes I feel as if I barely know myself. A memory of Aunt Deirdre pops into my mind, her voice filling my head, the feel of her arms wrapped around me when I was a child, comforting me as I sat on her sofa, glancing around at the unfamiliar rooms and furniture.

You can have your own room or you can sleep with me if you prefer. Don't be frightened. This is your new home now.

'It's my moods, you see,' Allison whispers, just when I think she has said all there is to say. 'Jack says I'm unpredictable. He's applying for full custody of the children.'

Why on earth is she telling me these things? I know that I should feel sympathy and pity for her but I am struggling to feel anything at all except annoyance. I'm not her counsellor or her priest. I'm not even her friend.

'Perhaps you should see a doctor? Ask for some sort of help?' I don't know what else to say. This isn't a normal conversation or a normal scenario and I am not an expert on such matters. I have no words of wisdom, no way of advising this lady. What if I say or do the wrong thing? Will she suddenly do something unpredictable or destructive? I think probably not but then she has never opened up about her home life before now. It could prove to be a catalyst for something entirely new. Something unpleasant.

'I'm fine. Really, I'm perfectly fine.' She sniffs, widens her eyes and smiles, her manner suddenly brighter. Chirpier and more upbeat. 'Sorry for burdening you with my problems.'

'Not a problem,' I lie. I don't add anything else; no words of assistance or assurances that she can cry on my shoulder anytime at all. I have enough of my own difficulties, enough to contend with in my own mind. I don't need Allison's problems as well. 'Anyway, these invoices won't pay themselves,' I murmur as I smile and push my face closer to the computer screen.

I hear the muffled pad of her feet as she heads away from me, and breathe out, relief unfurling in my chest.

17

It's dark. Her head hurts. She can't remember how she got here. Her knees are pushed up under her chin as she sits, squashed into the small space. Trying to move is pointless. Not enough room and every-thing spins, stars bursting behind her eyes if she tips her head or attempts to lift it up to orientate herself to her surroundings.

There is a whisper close by, the sibilant sound of a small voice floating towards her, penetrating through the solid surface that is keeping her imprisoned.

'Are you ready to come out now? Have you had enough?'

Visions fill her mind, memories, thoughts slotting together. She fell. Or perhaps she was pushed. She trails her fingers over her fore-head. A bump and some wetness there. Blood perhaps. Not tears. She is too stunned to cry. They'll come later, the tears, once she can recall how she got here. Once the shock has subsided and self-pity takes over.

A tapping on the wood, fingernails drumming out a dull beat. A voice. A hiss. Taunting and sickly sweet.

'Are you ready now? Are you ready now?'

It's her sister's voice. What time is it? The middle of the night perhaps. It's pitch black. No light coming from anywhere. No sound. Nothing at all.

She clears her throat, tries to speak but all that comes out is a thin trail of noise. A whimper, a strangulated attempt to reply. Something is stuck in there, stopping her from talking. She can only manage a faint squeak, weak and reedy, a disembodied sound that frightens her.

'Are you crying? You need to stop it. Only babies cry.' More whispering. Mean, callous words hissed at her. No compassion. No love at all. Just a huge vacuum where love should be.

She shoves her fist into her mouth to suppress any further noises then removes it and covers her ears to stop the sound of that voice from piercing her thoughts. Her fingers are cold, her knees trembling. Perhaps she should scream? Alert her parents. Get some help. And then she thinks of the repercussions that would follow. The protestations. And the lies. So many untruths and fabrications. An ocean of them. Their family is drowning in dishonesty and deceit, choking and spluttering their last as they sink to the bottom of the seabed. She thinks back to the scratch, all that blood. The pain and the aftermath of that incident.

An image appears in her mind. It was a push. Definitely a push. The memory of it suddenly rushes at her, penetrating through the fog swirling about in her brain. She was lying in bed, half asleep, heard a creak, a waft of air close by, then she was on the floor, her head catching the wooden bedpost as she fell, the sound of her body hitting the floor, muffled by the thick rug. Nobody heard her fall. Nobody came to help.

Her thoughts turn to Jenna, lying in bed in the room next to theirs. Will she wake, come to see what all the noise is about? Isn't that what older siblings are supposed to do – help younger family members? Stick up for them and protect them? She is so tired of this;

bearing the brunt of her twin sister's anger and poor judgement and impulsive behaviour. Enough is enough.

She squints, takes a deep breath. Her heart thuds in her chest like a drum banging against her ribcage. Suddenly she can move. The hard surface that is keeping her confined in this tiny space has been moved. She squints, looks around, tries to work out where she is. A tiny triangular sliver of pale light rests on her, highlighting her legs, her bloodied fingers. She's in the wardrobe, her body folded into the tiny space, arms wrapped protectively around her legs.

Through a crack in the blinds, a crescent moon sits high in the darkness, illuminating a fraction of the room. Before her stands her twin sister, face cracked into a half-smile, her features twisted with barely suppressed rage.

'Get out, and don't make a sound.'

She obeys, knowing the implications should she decide to flout the rules. Silent compliance is easier.

Her bed is still warm as she climbs back into it, fear rippling through her. It's the not knowing, being unable to see inside her sister's head, to work out what is going on in there and prepare herself. Every day brings something new, some small horror that creeps into her life.

Sleep comes slowly, her brain fogged up, her flesh still bruised and sore. She is tense, muscles rigid as she waits for the next nasty surprise. It doesn't happen. A reprieve. Instead, she drifts off, the darkness of her dreams her only escape from this madness.

18

DEBORAH

I wake up with a start, unaware I had actually fallen asleep. My head pounds, a grey heavy cloud of anger and anxiety marring my thoughts. Across from where I lay, I can see two eyes staring at me, a dim twinkling of terror amidst the gloom and the dust and the darkness. My back jars, pain shooting through my shoulder and down my arm as I reposition myself and sit up, my spine resting against the beam that has been my support for as long as I have been trapped here.

Fatigue swamps me. Despondency sits like a lead weight deep in my gut after my attempts to escape were curtailed. All that effort for nothing, and yet I know that I will do it again. Again and again and again if I have to because I am desperate to do something – *anything* – to get out of here, to know that even if I'm unsuccessful, I can at least say I tried.

Ignoring the aches and pains that needle me, ignoring the bone-aching tiredness that makes me feel a hundred years old, I start again with the arduous process of dragging my bound wrists against the splintered rough wood behind me. Up and down, up and down. Over and over and over until sweat courses down my face, running into my eyes, blinding me. My bladder is bursting. We both need to pee. I have to do this, to free myself of these ties around my wrists.

I grunt, then stop, take a breath, swallow down the exhaustion, frustration and terror that is coursing through me before continuing in silence. I have no idea if she is down there, lying below us, sleeping peacefully in her soft, warm bed, or if we are alone in this place – this desperately awful, filthy place – but either way, I carry on, making as little noise as possible, my hands and wrists see-sawing their way to freedom.

A soft noise filters through the sound of the splitting of fabric on wood and I look up to see my new accomplice quietly shuffling towards me, her body moving sideways in a crab-like motion. Our eyes lock and, in that moment, I know exactly what she is going to do. We are united in a need to flee this place, our minds geared towards the same goal.

I move away from the beam and spin around until our hands are touching, her fingers deftly picking at the fabric that is knotted tightly around my wrists as we sit back to back. She tugs and pulls, her nails catching my skin in a frantic scramble to untie me and ultimately free us both. It feels like an age to do it, every second a minute, each minute dragging on and on until, at last, I feel the material begin to give. It eventually drops from my hands and I slowly bring my arms to my sides, the pain in the top half of my body an unbearable ache. I feel certain that I'm lopsided, one half of me irreparably broken where she drove her feet and fists into my flesh and bones just because she could.

I am suddenly sobbing, my hot, sour breath filling the gag and making me retch. I reach up, pain screeching through my muscles and the sinews of my arms, and rip off the material that is stuffed in my mouth then turn my attentions to this other person who is now my accomplice. My ally.

Gasping in mouthfuls of musty air, I tear and rive at the ties that bind her, the remainder of my nails breaking and splitting in the process. My fingertips are sore. They ache and throb as I free her, the fabric dropping on the floor like a length of dead, decaying skin. Before I can reach over and untie her gag, she attempts to do it herself, her fingers swift and nimble and still dexterous after only being here for a short period of time, and soon succeeds, throwing the gag onto the floor before lowering her head into her hands and weeping.

I wait, aware that time is against us, but also cognisant of her need to release her fears and unleash the relief she feels at being untied and getting one step closer to safety. Except we're not there yet. I am hindered by my shoulder, we are both dehydrated and exhausted, and we have no idea where we are. We could be miles from anywhere and with no transport or phones to assist us; we may have a mammoth task ahead of us.

'Izzie,' she says breathlessly, her chin quivering as she speaks, her voice dry and husky. 'I'm Izzie.'

I nod, a moment of understanding passing between us that our resemblance to one another isn't a bizarre coincidence, that this is something much deeper, much more sinister and that we cannot waste too much time on unnecessary formalities.

'Deborah,' I whisper. 'We need to move quickly. Do you have any idea where we are?'

She shakes her head, tears still streaming, her face streaked with fresh dirt. I also have limited memories of getting here. I recall leaving the office feeling tired and groggy, turning left down Main Street to head to the train station. The area was more deserted than usual. I remember hearing footsteps behind me, the sound of clicking heels echoing into the emptiness of a nearby alleyway that I always avoided. I remember passing it, feeling a cold rush of air as it whistled through the narrow opening. Then nothing. I woke up here in this dark, dank place, terrified, gagged and bound, a terrible pain pulsing through my head. She must have hit me, knocked me out. How she managed to get me up here is anybody's guess. She has a car, that much I do know. Maybe it was parked around the corner? Maybe she had help. A wave of heat washes over my cold, limp body. An accomplice. Two of them. Christ, that thought has never entered my head until now. I suddenly feel sick at the very idea of it. Two psychopaths. Two people capable of keeping this horrible secret between them. Or maybe not. I've never seen anybody else, never heard anyone. Only her. Always her.

'Let's get these ties off our feet then we can work out what to do next.'

We pick at the fabric, our fingers working furiously at the material. It's tight. At one point, Izzie leans down whilst at the same time bringing up her feet, and tries to gnaw at the material with her teeth, the sound of snapping cotton a sharp reminder of our desperate predicament. These ties are the final thing holding us back, the final part of our route out of this desolate, godforsaken place.

I glance over at the door as we continue working at the fabric, wondering if it's locked. I have no memory of hearing a key being turned or a bolt pulled across. My heart sinks at the thought. I have never picked a lock before and wouldn't know where to begin; besides, what do we have here to do such a thing? Pieces of filthy rags and a stinking toilet in the corner of the room. We have nothing at our disposal to help us out of this room aside from our eyes, ears and what little strength we have in our weary, battered bodies. Izzie is probably in better shape than me but she is slightly smaller. That could work well for us if we have to squeeze through any narrow spaces, however. We need to utilise what few resources we have, pool our strength and work together to get out of this awful hellhole.

'Done,' Izzie says softly as the fabric falls from her ankles to the floor at her feet. 'Here, let me help you.' With her nails still unbroken and her skin not yet torn, she picks at the material tied tightly around my lower legs and in seconds it springs free. I almost cry with relief, a small, painful sob erupting out of my chest. 'Now what?' she says, an element of desperation creeping into her voice after the initial euphoria of untying ourselves has dissipated.

All of a sudden, it feels like an unsurmountable task, getting out of this place. We have no idea where we are or what sort of building we are in. I am guessing an attic space in an old derelict house but don't know that for certain. Getting through that possibly locked door suddenly feels like climbing a mountain. The thought that she could be on her way here right now, weapon in hand, her anger driving her on, is enough to catapult me out of my near-catatonic state. No time to waste. We have to leave this room and we have to do it now.

I spin around, looking for something – anything – we can use as a weapon, but see only dust and the pieces of rags we discarded from our hands, mouths and feet.

'The door,' Izzie whispers. 'Let's just take our chances and go.'

She's right. We need to get a move on. Tiptoeing over to it, I reach out and slowly twist the handle, my heart a battering ram against my ribcage. It's locked. Of course it is. What did I expect? An open door and a welcome banner along with a map and directions out of here?

'Shit.' My voice is hoarse, full of regret and fear and exasperation.

I spin around, squinting, trying to work out what to do next. We have nothing sharp, nothing heavy we could use to batter the door and help break the lock.

'What about that?' Izzie stares at me then turns to face the wall behind her.

'What?' I say, unable to keep the desperation out of my tone. 'What about what? I can't see anything!'

'There! That piece of plywood jammed up against the wall.'

'It's nailed in place. You can see the screws from here.' Everything suddenly feels utterly futile. I hate feeling this way but don't know how to turn this situation around and make good this rare moment we have forged for ourselves. We're on the cusp of getting out of here and now I feel flattened. So many locked doors. So many obstructions blocking our exit.

'So?' Izzie's voice is buoyant, her eyes bright, full of enthusiasm.

I feel obliged to follow suit, be positive, not fall at the first hurdle. This is my chance. *Our chance.* It might be the only one we ever get.

Nodding, I make my way over to the dark corner where a piece of wood sits flush against the wall. I've seen it before but have always known that removing it single-handedly was beyond my capabilities. It looks heavy, solid, jammed into place permanently. Telling myself that nothing is ever permanent, that being positive is what will get us out of here, I grasp one of the corners and attempt to pull it. No movement. Exactly as I expected. I stifle a scream, a ball of fury exploding in my head.

'Here!' Izzie points down at her feet. 'We can use my laces.'

I close my eyes and release a breath. I realise she is trying to appear confident and optimistic but at this moment in time

Izzie's suggestion, whatever it is going to be, feels pointless and ridiculous, like trying to hold back a tsunami. We are done for. The best we can hope for is a two-pronged attack against our captor the next time she pokes her head through that door and just pray that she doesn't have a hammer or a blunt instrument hidden behind her back. Or worse still, a knife. The thought that we could charge at her before she is even through the doorway, knocking her backwards down the stairs, begins to take shape in my mind. It's a glimmer of hope in a dark, desperate time.

'Like this,' she is saying as I turn again to look at her. 'If we can get a lace each behind the corner of the wooden panel and pull, we just might be able to drag it away from the wall. It's worth a try, don't you think?'

Izzie is holding a pair of thick laces from her trainers. In the dim light of the room, they appear to be remarkably sturdy. She's right. It's definitely worth a try. Better than doing nothing and wasting this chance that we've created for ourselves.

She hands one over to me and I slide the middle of the lace behind the corner of the thin plywood, grasping it tightly at both ends, my fists curled for extra strength. Already, with the minimum of effort, the wood begins to splinter, shards of it falling at my feet. Izzie does the same, sliding the lace as far behind the corner of the wood as she can for maximum effect and steeling herself, her back arched, the muscles in her upper arms, flexed and ready.

'Okay?' she says, nodding at me, and using both hands, we pull together, a joint effort to try and shake loose the large sheet of plywood. It begins to move, years of neglect and damp weakening its strength and rigidity.

Waves of heat billow from beneath my sweater as we

continue pulling, the sheet bending and groaning as it warps and shifts from its fixed position against the wall.

'The nails are hammered in in the middle,' Izzie says as she wipes a trickle of sweat away from her eyes.

She has barely finished speaking when a large section of the wood breaks off. We stop, now able to see what's behind it.

'A door. Jesus Christ, come on, let's move this thing,' I inadvertently let out a shriek, relief and hysteria driving me on. 'There's another fucking door in here.'

We spend the next few minutes pulling and grasping, our fingers jammed behind the wooden board as we heave and haul it away from the wall, the rusty nails holding it in place finally giving way and scattering across the floor. I am half tempted to pick them up, keep them for future use as a weapon.

The board is in pieces, warped and split, fragments of wood spread far and wide.

'Oh God, I daren't try it.' Izzie stares at me. 'Go on, you do it. See if it opens.'

My heart throbs and pulses arrhythmically; sweat courses down my back. The metal of the small handle is cold in my palm as I reach out and grasp it, my fingers curled around its tiny breadth. I swallow, wait for a second or two before twisting. It turns with ease. My scalp prickles with a combination of fear and excitement. I can hardly breathe. Blood pounds in my ears, rushing through my head as I pull at the door and feel it move.

It's unlocked. Dear God, it is actually unlocked. We are almost free. I brace myself, ready for an attack from behind as the door creaks and opens fully into a swathe of inky blackness.

'Be careful,' Izzie whispers, her voice a near croak.

My fingers reach out into the darkness, groping for a light switch, for a steady surface, for some sort of solidity – anything that will help me find a way out of here.

I step forward, my feet shuffling, hoping for a firm foothold, and find nothing. Quite literally nothing. My toes are hanging over the edge of a precipice and before I can do anything or warn Izzie or reach out to grab on to something, I find myself sailing through mid-air, my body plummeting, my fingers urgently groping for something to stop me from falling.

It's too late. I am tumbling downwards, my torso, my limbs, spinning and clutching at thin air. It's all too damn late. Terror, regret, horror, all travel through me. Everything is too late.

I scream, my voice a thin gurgle in the darkness. I feel my full bladder open, a stream of urine spreading over the lower half of my body. Then nothing.

19

ADRIAN

I fucking hate this kind of shit. Loathe it with a passion. It's a pointless exercise, created by psychologists who think it will bring us together and increase our productivity. All it does is make me detest my co-workers and managers even more, forcing me to take part in stupid games and activities that hold no interest for me when I could be sitting at my desk working my way through a backlog of overdue quotes and invoices. They tried something like this once before – organising a whole host of activities for staff to join in with on an evening after work, thus increasing our stress levels even more rather than simply treating us better and affording us a little more dignity while we're actually here.

Ruth is standing at the front of the office with Brian Digby, the MD of the company, a stupid smile plastered across her face, as if we've just collectively won the lottery. 'The team-building day will take place on Friday. Sorry for the short notice but the company we booked with got a cancellation and, luckily, were able to slot us in.'

I'm not sure whether to applaud or heckle so instead remain silent, my gaze downcast in case I catch anyone's eye and my negative thoughts become apparent, plastered across my face, irritation at this idea obvious in the black looks I cast about. This is a stupid and childish venture and, if I could, I would gladly sit it out but know that that particular option isn't up for grabs.

My shoes are dirty and in need of a polish; that's what I notice as I keep my eyes fixed firmly downwards. Ruth's words are just white noise in the background, my attention focused elsewhere, my mind shut off to her ideas as she addresses the entire office. I should be kinder to her really, more open to her ideas after she helped me out on Friday, getting me on the train and staying silent about the whole thing to the rest of the team. I saw her chatting to Allison earlier and she hasn't shown any interest in me or even looked my way so I'm assuming Ruth has kept it to herself. Or at least I hope so. Trust in her integrity is all I have. Not that it matters. The whole world could know about me and my problems and shortcomings and it wouldn't make any of it any worse. Or better. Only I can do that – improve my lot in life. Which is why I've decided to give up drinking and to tackle the issue of Beth. I'm going to call her tonight after work, speak with her and tell her that she needs to do the right thing and go to the police. She won't like it, and she will undoubtedly rail against the idea, shouting that I don't care about her and that I'm a grass and that I deserve to die, but that's fine. I'm prepared for it. I'm inured to it now after all these years. Water off a duck's back and all that.

'Some of it will take place outside in the grounds so don't forget to come prepared with suitable footwear and a fleece or a waterproof jacket. You know how unpredictable English weather is!'

A silence follows Ruth's lame attempt at camaraderie and humour. She's a nice lady but being a stand-up comic and an entertaining orator isn't one her strongest features. Her attempts at public speaking don't go down too well as people start to murmur and slowly begin to file away, already bored and distracted, her weak, insipid voice not enough to keep them interested.

'So don't forget – sensible shoes and a warm coat, everyone!' A flush creeps up her throat. She swallows and clutches at her neck, watching as everyone ambles back to their desks, the show of enthusiasm she was clearly hoping for painfully absent.

I give her a nod and a small wave before turning away, the discomfort of watching her flustered little body look up to Brian for affirmation that it went as well as could be expected, too much to stand.

Come Friday, I'll do my best to show willing, if only for Ruth. I will grit my teeth, join in with whatever shitshow they have planned for us, and get it over with. Like some sort of penance. Although for what, I don't quite know. Dealing with Beth is my penance for whatever sins I may have committed. An ongoing form of atonement for being a foster child and living with her, the pair of us muddling along together as best we could. Beth and me. Me and Beth, the two of us against the rest of the world.

Right on cue, my phone buzzes. I made a promise to myself that I would turn it off during office hours and haven't. Yet another failing on my part.

It's a text message from her. My stomach tightens as I read it.

I'm outside in the car park.

Shit!

I look around the office. Everyone is too busy doing their own thing, tapping at computers or talking on the phone, to notice me.

Why? Why the hell is she here? I've told her many times about coming to my place of work, explained that it's not the right thing to do. I can't even count the number of times she has done it in the past, hung around outside, loitering in doorways, waiting for me to emerge and escort her home. Chatting to my colleagues, making a show of herself and making me cringe as I watch them tolerate her, wondering who she is and what the fuck she is talking about.

My head pounds as I recall her recent revelation and how I will now need to convince her to go to the police. I block it out of my mind. It's probably a lie. Beth often cannot distinguish fantasy from reality. And yet if I don't speak to her about it and it turns out to be true...

Jesus Christ, why am I being lumbered with all of this? I'm willing to bet that other people around me don't have half as much to deal with in their lives. How can that be fair or just?

I stare over at Merriel and Yvonne, both of them concentrating on their work. How lovely it must be for them to go home every evening and be able to relax knowing that all's right in their prim and proper little worlds. And then there's Allison. I doubt she knows what it's like to struggle through life alone with no support or family around for assistance or guidance. Privileged lives, that's what they all have. Fucking marvellous, middle-class, privileged little lives. Even Ruth. They're all so fortunate and I'll bet they don't even realise it, taking all that they have for granted.

My fingers hover over my phone screen, my mind trying to

think of a reply to Beth. Whatever I say, it won't be enough to persuade her to leave. Stubbornness is one of her stronger traits. She is an immovable object. A leg iron.

If I don't go down there, speak to her, she will wait there all day, hanging about, embarrassing me in front of my workmates. I'm just delaying the inevitable. I push my seat back, stand up and head out of the office, hoping nobody notices my empty chair. At least the windows of our office don't overlook the car park. I can do this thing privately, tell Beth to go home and that I'll call her once I get in tonight. Which I will. I don't have any choice, do I?

* * *

'I hit her. She made me do it.' Beth gives me a crooked smile, her kohl-rimmed panda eyes glinting with excitement.

'Who did you hit, Beth?' I don't want to be having this conversation. Not here. Not ever, but this is how it is and now that I'm down here, there seems to be no escaping from her twisted story and facial features that are contorted with a sordid, unpalatable look of excitement that is almost bordering on euphoria.

If I show some interest, she might be more likely to leave me alone, to make a rapid exit and let me get on with my day. It's adulation and attention she craves. And lots of it. Even short bursts of it are often enough to satisfy her.

'Told you, a woman I found. She made me do it.'

Part of me wants to shout into the sky that I can't do this any more, that I need a break from this woman, and part of me wants to hear her out, see if there's any truth in her words. And if there is, if her story seems credible, well then, I will have no

other option other than to do something about it. I think of
Deborah and shut my eyes, fear making me dizzy. I want to hear
this. I don't want to hear it. I want to curl up into a tight ball and
have the ground swallow me up.

I take a long, shuddering breath and speak, my voice
distorted and disembodied. Detached from the godawfulness of
this unfolding situation. 'What happened? You need to tell me,
Beth. This is serious.' I am trying to keep the anger and exasperation out of my voice but it's so fucking difficult. It's like pulling
teeth, trying to converse with her. She lies, is selective about
what information she releases and her ideas jump about, her
timelines disjointed and fragmented.

'That woman from your office – she still missing then, is
she?'

I roll my eyes and clench my teeth together, no longer
caring if she sees and reacts. Acid crawls up my throat at
hearing her words, her questions about Deborah. 'Beth, just tell
me about this woman you attacked. Where is she now? *How* is
she? Did you injure her at all?' Stupid question. She will have
definitely injured her if she hit her. The two are inseparable.
The question is, how badly did she hurt this poor woman? I
visualise somebody lying unconscious somewhere, a back alley
or a country lane, where nobody will find her for days, or
perhaps even weeks. Or maybe it's one of Beth's associates – an
argument over money for the latest fix or bottle of cheap cider.
Maybe she gave as good as she got. I run my fingers through my
hair. Jesus, I'm starting to think like she does, justifying her
behaviour.

Or maybe it's Deborah.

I refuse to entertain that thought, do my best to block it out
of my brain completely.

When Beth and I were growing up together in foster care, the two of us flung together in the same home out of happenstance and fate, she used to do strange things: things that, as an impressionable teenage boy, I found both entertaining and scary. Things I myself would never dare to do. Once, while we were alone in the living room, our foster mother not there to supervise us, Beth set fire to the curtains. Another time, she jumped out of the bedroom window onto the garage roof in the middle of the night and broke her wrist after landing awkwardly. Rather than remain still until help came, she rolled off the garage roof and bolted down the street, hammering on neighbours' doors until the police were called and ended up having to restrain her. She was only thirteen at the time. And although her behaviour was odd and unpredictable, we sort of bonded, our relationship already established as a strange brother/sister connection. A year older than she was, I felt responsible for her, so we stuck together: two lonely souls groping about for stability and affection in an often cold and unwelcoming world.

Beth was desperate for a family of her own. Like me, her parents were a couple of feckless drunks and drug addicts. By the time she reached seventeen, she was pregnant, the idea of having her own child, her own little family, so appealing to her that she lost all sense of what was actually required to bring up a child single-handedly. After a miscarriage, her mental decline was rapid and she has never really recovered from it. She now lives in a run-down part of town in a squalid house, living hand to mouth on benefits.

She deserves better, I know that, but how can you help somebody who doesn't want to be helped? Somebody who isn't even aware that they have a problem? Every week there is a new trauma, a new dilemma to solve. And now this. An attack on another person. I don't know where to start, what to say to get the truth out of her, so I smile, rest my hand on hers and ask her again, who and where this woman is, and hope that this time she tells me the real story. Whether I want to hear it or not.

20

YVONNE

Well, I suppose it's a day away from my desk. Still, the thought of participating in childish games in order to bond with my workmates doesn't exactly fill me with glee. If I'm being honest, it actually fills me with a deep sense of gloom. I guess it's meant to increase our productivity or boost morale or some other silly goal dreamt up by teams of psychologists who charge the company a small fortune for their services. I'm never quite sure what is expected of us while we're here other than to complete the work given to us. We all do that with aplomb. What else are they expecting from everyone? We are all lumped together in this place because we have to be, not because we want to be. It's not a lifestyle choice, something we have all dreamt of doing since childhood. This is a job, not our entire lives. This place doesn't define us. It isn't a part of us. It certainly isn't a part of me. I have other facets to my life, to my character. Other things beyond these four walls that make me proud and happy and fulfilled. I don't feel a pressing need to play combat games or go paintballing with workmates or whatever it is they have planned for us to make me feel uplifted and content with my lot in life. It was bad enough being forced to listen to Allison tell me all about how her life is in freefall. Now I'm being forced to pretend we can all work and play together as one big corporate family.

Over in the corner of the office, I can see Adrian as he sneaks out. Again. I wonder if anybody else has spotted his frequent visits outside or to the toilet or wherever it is he disappears to on a regular basis. His head is dipped, shoulders hunched, hands slung deep in his pockets. A crease sits on his forehead, a pensive expression plastered across his face as he exits the doorway and slips out of sight. He'll be off to talk to that lady again, the one who sometimes stands outside waiting for him. I've seen her before. Maybe she's the one Allison spoke about, his sister. I once saw Deborah talk to her as only Deborah could, head tilted, listening intently. That's how she was. Affable and approachable. Everybody's friend.

My thoughts linger over Adrian, his purported torrid upbringing, and then contemplate my own formative years. The misery of them. The lasting memories early trauma can leave on the adult brain, certain events too deeply embedded to ever fully leave. Still, we're all grown-ups. We have to find ways through these things, combat the negativity with positive thoughts and experiences. That's how I managed it, how I survived those awful years and came out almost unscathed. Others might disagree, labelling me distant and aloof. That's self-preservation, a sure-fire way of keeping my sanity intact.

Being in touch with nature, thinking about Aunt Deirdre and my time spent with her – that's how I keep myself together. After the death of my family, living with her helped rebalance my fragile world. It wasn't perfect – far from it – but we rubbed along together nicely enough. I was hurt, upset at being moved to a place I didn't know. Deirdre did her best to care for me, having never had any children of her own and not being accustomed to their ways, and we learned as we went along, both of us trying to find firm footing on new and unsteady territory. But we got there. Everyone gets there in the end. All it takes is a little time and a lot of patience and foresight as to what the future can hold if you're prepared to work for it. I know that now. I just wish I'd known it before.

I shift my gaze away from the door, avoiding Deborah's empty desk. I'll bet that's why they are putting us through this ridiculous team-building business, to help restore some happiness back into the office after her disappearance. It's a preposterous notion that a few simple games will help reinstate a sense of equanimity amongst us, but it's their money and I guess they can do whatever they like with it. They have to be seen to be doing something, don't they? Simply going about our daily business screams lack of compassion and care, for Deborah and the rest of the staff. So come Friday we will be reduced to playing games of tig and seeing how much we can all pull together as a team to help boost morale. None of it will bring Deborah back. But to the outside world and its watching eyes, at least it looks like we're trying.

Merriel strides across the office, her long shadow obscuring the light next to my desk. I still haven't enquired as to how she knew my address. I've wracked my brains and can think of no conversation we have had where it has cropped up. It shouldn't bother me, her knowing where I live, and yet it does.

On impulse, I stand up and seize the moment, a need to know growing within me. I'll do it surreptitiously, slip it into the conversation as a matter of course, a natural meander to the subject of Merriel driving me home last week.

'I think it's broken again,' I say as I stand next to her at the printer. 'We're waiting for the technical guy to come and fix it.'

She rolls her eyes then smiles and angles her head towards mine conspiratorially. 'Between you and me, it's personal stuff I'm printing off so I guess I can't really complain, can I?'

She winks at me and I'm unsure how to react except to smile back and simply say, 'Oh.'

'It's my new CrossFit workout regime.'

Again, I have nothing to offer to this conversation. We may as well be from different planets, Merriel and I, so I nod and pretend I understand what it is she is saying to me.

'Never felt so fit and agile. I'm the healthiest and strongest I've ever been. That's got to be a good thing, hasn't it? I mean, take a look at these beauties.' She pulls up her sleeves and flexes her biceps. They bulge and grow as she clenches her fists repeatedly. 'Almost certain I'm as strong as any man in this place. I could throw you over my shoulder and run across the office and beyond without breaking a sweat. Mind you,' she continues, unaware she is dominating the entire conversation, 'you look as if you keep fairly fit yourself. What's your regime then?'

'I run,' I say quietly, wishing I had remained silent. I have visions of Merriel suddenly suggesting we join up for some sort of sporting session, the pair of us warming up on a roadside somewhere in leggings and leotards. I briefly shut my eyes and shudder.

'You're a runner?' Her eyebrows arch as she surveys me, her gaze critical. 'I never had you down as a jogger. Just goes to show,' she says breezily, 'you never can tell, can you? We think we know people and then they do or say something that takes everyone by surprise. Hidden depths, that's what we all have here in this office. Hidden depths.'

'I suppose we do.' I glance away, trying to work out how to steer this conversation around to our journey home last week.

Years of hurt have taught me to be cautious when opening up to people. I want to keep our dialogue limited, get straight to the point. 'I was just wondering,' I add brightly, deciding to go ahead and just say it, 'how you knew where I lived?'

Her eyes crinkle at the corners. Her mouth is crooked as she smiles at me. 'Hmm? Oh, you mean the lift home? You told me?'

'Did I?' I try to keep my voice smooth, light and jovial even, as if I am simply being curious, which, of course, I am. This is no more than idle curiosity, but it's niggling at me. An itch that needs to be scratched. 'Funny that, because I don't remember telling you.'

'Well, that's hardly surprising, is it? Given the bump you had to your bonce.' She tips her head sideways and smiles at me, her index finger resting against her forehead as she taps at it repeatedly.

She's lying. She knows it and I know it and, worse than that, I'm almost certain she knows that I know. The only question is why?

It's time to break this deadlock. I take a deep breath and speak.

'Well anyway,' I say lightly, aiming for maximum impact. 'No matter. That night,' I venture, thinking that if it's games we are playing here, then I may as well join in. 'The night that Deborah went missing,' I say quietly. 'I thought I saw you walking with her. Which is really confusing as I could have sworn you told the police and everyone here that you hadn't seen her after you both left the office.'

I feel vindicated as Merriel sways ever so slightly, the colour rapidly leaching from her face. I've hit the jackpot. She makes to lean against me then immediately rights herself, coughing and covering her mouth with a trembling hand. Many wouldn't spot it, her shock at my words, but I do. I see it all too clearly.

'I didn't see her that night. Not really. We walked together out of the main doors but then she went one way and I went the other. I'm not sure who or what you thought you saw but it definitely wasn't me.'

I nod, pretending I believe her, pretending that she has said enough to throw me off the scent, but she doesn't fool me. Not one little bit. Maybe they did part at some point after leaving here, but I did definitely see them together. I know that for certain because I wasn't far behind. I was going to meet somebody that night, somebody I hadn't seen for a long, long time. As Allison said earlier, we all have something going on in our lives that we keep secret, don't we? Even me.

21

DEBORAH

She is standing over me, the whites of her eyes cutting through the dimness of the murky surroundings. I blink, rub at my own eyes and realise I'm actually alone. For now. I'm just confused, seeing things that aren't there. My vision is blurred, my body aching, but at least I'm not dead. I'm alive. And I'm still here, not in a hospital bed, surrounded by doctors and nurses who are working tirelessly to resurrect my wasted body and get me back to full health. I am lying on the floor, battered and possibly broken after trying to escape. A part of me wishes I had actually died in the fall rather than this, waking up to realise that I'm still trapped here in this shitty, dank building with a psychopath who has lost her grip on reality. I'm also wet, the unmistakable odour of urine emanating from the lower half of my body. Shame consumes me. I thought the violence was bad and being fed like I'm a small child then led to the toilet to relieve myself while she waits outside but this is a new low.

I have no idea how long I have lain here, unconscious, sprawled out on the floor. Something saved me. I don't know the exact height of the door above me but I do know that I'm not seriously injured. I'm not bleeding but I am in a certain amount of pain. The base of my spine hurts as does my shoulder and hip bone. But I'm not dead.

I spread out my arms, my fingers trailing over the hard grittiness of the floor, and feel something softer beneath me, some sort of cushioned surface. I bring my hands to my sides and press down with my palms, feeling and groping about, and realise that I'm laid on a mattress. Is this a house we're in? If it is, it's definitely derelict, probably in the middle of nowhere where nobody can hear us or attempt to rescue us. A lump is wedged in my throat. My eyes mist over. We're completely alone. Any hope I had of getting out of here diminishes. A wasted, desiccated body left to rot, that's what I will become. Me and Izzie slumped together, a pile of dry, forgotten bones.

Attempting to lever myself up using my elbows, I can see dim shafts of light filtering in through broken, dirty windows. Doors hang from their frames; crumbling plaster has fallen from the walls, leaving exposed brickwork. It's cold and damp. Colder than upstairs where the heat travels and gathers. I shiver, try to orient myself to my surroundings. My damp clothes stick to my skin. Eventually they will dry but the shame will never leave me. I hate her for it. More than the violence, more than holding me captive. I hate her for stripping me of every bit of dignity I have, reducing me to this.

Beside me is a bottle of water, some blankets. And a mask. Her mask. She isn't wearing it. If she comes back now, I'll see her, be able to identify her. Not that I don't know who she is already. Oh, I know. She doesn't want me to, is in denial when I call her by her name, but I know who she is all right.

A shaft of light in the distance, a rustle of clothing, the

unmistakable clump of her footfall as she approaches where I lie, my body sprawled after the fall, my thoughts and reactions still hazy, scrambled and shaken about by the shock.

'Well, well, well. What do we have here, then?'

'Fuck off, you demented bitch.' I relish each and every word, firing them at her like poisoned darts, missiles designed to maim and kill. My brain function might be a bit hazy but I still have my wits about me, enough to see through her warped, banal attempts at humour and sarcasm. 'You're a fucking maniac and I hope you die a horrible, painful death, sooner rather than later.' I didn't plan on shooting so many insults her way. It just happened. They've been stored up inside me, waiting to wrestle their way out and I couldn't contain them any longer.

I want her to react. I want her to fly into a rage, to see some sign that she is human, that she is in possession of the same emotions as the rest of us and isn't completely invulnerable, resistant to insults and fear and threats. Nothing happens. Instead, she stands, body bowed, head tilted down as she stares at me, her eyes glinting like burning embers. For the first time since being held captive in this place, I am able to see her face, to scrutinise her hideous features that once held no fear for me. If she had retaliated to my insults, I could at least have made some effort to defend myself. Her previous temper tantrums happened while I was gagged and bound. Although I'm in pain, I'm not completely helpless. Maybe she knows that. Maybe that's why she hasn't responded. Maybe after all of her bravado and shows of aggression and controlling ways, she is just a filthy little coward.

'Come on,' she says, unmoved by my outburst, 'let's get you up and sorted, shall we?'

I feel the strength of her hands as she clasps them around my upper arms and drags me towards the wall. She's robust and solid, I'll give her that. My muscles have been inactive for so long now, I suspect some wastage has begun to set in, but that doesn't mean I'm completely helpless. I still have some fight left in me and intend to use it to the best of my ability. I will resist her attempts to move and restrain me until every last bit of energy has left my body. A wave of renewed positivity surges through me. I can do this. I can make an effort to save myself and I won't stop until I am out of here and both Izzie and I are free of this madwoman's clutches.

Just lashing out won't be enough. She will quickly over-power me and before I know it, I'll be back to square one, gagged and tied up again. Slumped in that squalid little space above us and left to rot. I need to think quickly, to formulate a plan. Izzie is up there somewhere and I need her to think on her feet, to do something to help us both before this crazy bitch realises that she too is untied and ready to make a bid for freedom.

'Tomorrow is the day of your party. You don't want to miss it, do you? We've got cake and balloons and prizes.' Her voice is almost a squeal. She's smiling and is giddy with excitement. As sickening as it is to listen to her childish squawks of enthusi-asm, I think that maybe I can use this chance to catch her unawares. She isn't her usual self, her focus shifted to this macabre gathering she has planned for us. This is her weak spot. This is our chance.

I nod at her, manage a watery smile and even a small, desperate laugh. It works. She leans in close, our faces almost touching, and holds up an object in front of me. I squint, try to get a clearer look at whatever it is, then feel my insides shrivel.

It's another photograph of a handful of children sitting around a table. This picture is clearer than the other one, more defined. The candles on the cake are lit up, the small, peering faces surrounding it highlighted by the amber flames. I recognise her immediately, see her sitting there, smiling as a child. Our captor. My colleague. A purported friend, somebody I thought I could trust. Somebody I once liked. She hasn't changed that much, her features, her eyes, the shape of her face, all still the same. The monster as a young girl. She is human after all; a deranged, unhinged individual, her perspectives and values skewed, but human all the same.

'You remember this? A birthday party at our house. Mum baked that cake. It was vanilla and buttercream with chocolate icing and frosted flowers around the edges. I loved it. Such happy times, weren't they? It was like nothing could ever harm us. We all lived in that house, safe in our protective little bubble. But of course, it didn't stay that way, did it? And can you remember what you did to the cake? Can you? *Can you*?' She is screaming at me now, her mood deteriorating second by second, her tenuous grasp of what is real and what isn't real rapidly slipping away. I have no idea where she is, what world or parallel universe she inhabits, but I do know that it isn't the same as mine.

'I don't remember what happened to the cake. I do know that I'm really sorry though. I never meant for it to happen. It was an accident.' I'm trying to play along. I have no idea if this will please or antagonise her but it's a chance I'm willing to take to try and soften her temper, to attempt to mould and placate her so I can exert some control over this situation rather than sit here, inert, inept and utterly helpless.

She stops when I speak, her eyes narrowed as she watches

me. I am rigid, waiting for something to happen. I can feel the warmth of her breath, am able to sense the thrashing of my heart as it leaps about my chest. Blood surges up my neck, pulses through my ears. I swallow, watching her every move. She shuffles closer to me like an animal hunting its next victim, her gaze boring into mine, tunnelling through to the very core of me.

It seems to take an age for the moment to present itself, for her to be close enough, for her temper to have cooled off. For me to be brave enough to do it. Steeling myself, I raise my hands and push my fingers into her eyes, the jelly-like feel of her eyeballs against my fingertips making me retch. It does the trick and she screams and tips backwards. I'm aware that I have now set things in motion and that there'll be no going back from this moment. No forgiveness and, if Izzie and I don't succeed, no means of escape ever again. Death may even be a distinct possibility, sooner than either of us ever anticipated. She is sick and twisted enough to do it. And angry enough now that I've hurt her. Up to this point, she has always had control. She won't take kindly to me suddenly turning on her. Bullies don't like being bullied.

I scramble to my feet, my eyes scanning the area for anything I can use as a weapon. Propped up against the far wall is a spade. If I don't grab it and use it against her, she will defi-nitely use it against me and she's stronger that I am. One swing from that will be enough to kill me.

It's overwhelming, the gravitational pull of the ground as I stumble to my feet and force my body forwards, my head angled upwards, my gaze fixed on that spade, the one thing that can save me and get me out of this hideous place and away from this crazy fucking woman. I manage to resist its clutches, the almost overwhelming pull of the earth on my exhausted broken body as I pelt forwards on liquid legs. I need that spade, it's all I can think about, fear and desperation driving me on. Adrenaline masks most of my pain as it starts up its trajectory and shoots around my system. I don't stop to look at her, to see where she is. Not enough time. Every second counts and every second I stop to search for her is a wasted one. She could be right behind me or she could be lying in a crumpled heap in the corner. I don't care either way. I need a weapon, something to protect me. Something that will bring her crashing to the ground.

My arm reaches out for the shovel, my fingers almost touching it as I feel the weight of her pushing me to the wall. I hear her manic shriek, am unable to do anything as she knocks me to the floor and straddles me, pinning me in place, her legs like lead weights on my spine. I have an image in my mind of her reaching for that heavy implement, raising it up above her head before bringing it down on the back of my skull over and over until I am no more. Just a splattering of blood and bone spread far and wide.

But that doesn't happen. Her screams die down and I listen to her low gasps and pants as she catches her breath and whispers in my ear, her soft voice causing my skin to ripple with dread and disgust.

'Why did you do that? You know we have to stay together, don't you? You *know* it, my darling. You will never escape. Ever. So don't bother trying.'

She must have somehow managed to get down, jumping onto the old mattress without injuring herself, because I see her shadow, Izzie's small frame, the spread of grey before me and am not sure whether to laugh with relief at her presence or cry because she will soon be overpowered. Izzie is no match for this creature. I know that now. But she does have the spade. She is holding a weapon. She has the upper hand.

Seconds drag by. I wait, hold my breath, then hear her soft voice, a few quiet words, prayers perhaps, for fortitude and strength, feel the weight pressing down on me shift slightly as Izzie swings the spade and brings it all to an end.

22

ADRIAN

I'm surprised and secretly delighted that she has remembered and turned up. Beth's grasp of time has never been one of her stronger points. She floats from day to day with no notion or understanding of how other people need to stick to a timetable in order to get to work and earn a living and yet here she is, standing at my door looking composed and, dare I say it, clean and attractive? Her hair has been washed and shines under the dim light of the outdoor lamp. She's wearing a long pale blue dress and navy ankle boots. In her hand is a box of chocolates. I have no idea where she got them from and don't want to think too long and hard about it so instead take them and thank her, then step aside to let her in.

'You look great,' I say quietly, keen to keep things low-key, not overwhelm her with compliments – something both Beth and I find hard to accept after so many years of neglect and abuse. I once read about pit ponies, who, mistreated and neglected after years of working underground in the grisliest of conditions, when brought back out into the light, became confused and upset and tried to go back down the mine because it was all they had ever known. That's Beth and me. We have spent our lives searching for happiness and thoughtfulness and compassion but when it finally finds us, we shrug it off like a heavy uncomfortable shroud because we have no emotional tools or internal compass to show us how to deal with it.

'Thanks. I do scrub up well if I try hard enough.'

I stop and nod, relief ballooning in my chest. She sounds sober. She looks sober and is acting as though this morning's conversation never happened. I pray it was all a fabrication, that she hasn't attacked anybody. I can but hope. During this morning's dialogue, when I mentioned calling around mine for a meal this evening, she didn't respond. I didn't for one minute expect her to actually arrive, but here she is and now I will have to magic up some food which, if I'm being honest, won't be too arduous a task. I'm a fairly competent cook and have plenty of ingredients in. I actually feel rather buoyed up at the thought of it. Better than yet another night sitting in front of the TV watching mind-numbing shows that wash over me, leaving no lasting impression. What could possibly go wrong?

'Tea? Coffee? Lemonade?' I keep my voice light and jovial. We're treading on delicate ground here. After my last shitshow of a performance with Ruth, I threw away every bit of alcohol I had in the flat and have resisted the urge to go out and buy more.

If Beth is annoyed or disappointed by the lack of drinks on offer, she doesn't show it, her expression remaining bright and breezy.

'Lemonade sounds good, thanks.'

We head into the living room and sit on chairs facing one another.

'I've been lying to you, Ade.'

The skin on my skull shrivels, puckering and tingling with relief and anticipation. She didn't attack anybody. I was right. It was all one big fat fib. It took place in Beth's imaginary world where nothing and nobody makes any sense, where there is no structure and there are no rules. Thank fuck. I almost laugh out loud. My face remains impassive as I wait, biting at the insides of my mouth.

'About my family. It's all lies. Every single bit of it.'

Oh God. My stomach twists. *Shit, shit, shit.*

I dig my nails into my knees; my spine is ramrod straight. I inhale, store the breath deep in my chest and wait. My gaze bores into Beth as her face changes. Her eyes darken, her demeanour alters, becoming jittery, her body twitching, adrenaline firing up her senses. She will be craving a drink or maybe the drugs she pumps into her body on a regular basis. She has clearly done her best to clean up her act tonight but I'm under no illusions that this is a new and changed Beth. She is what she is and this shiny, clean version of her is a brief and temporary one. Soon the darkness will return, her demons subdued for too little a period of time. There's little or no respite from them. They nip and claw at her constantly. It's exhausting watching it. Her body and mind must be a wreck, having to deal with them day in, day out.

I wanted her to tell me she was lying about the attack. Maybe she was. Maybe I should ask her right now, now that she is seeing things through clearer eyes. They are rare, these moments of clarity. I need to make the most of it, get as much out of her as I can but, of course, I still have to be careful, not make her feel cornered, or I risk scaring her away. It's such a fucking minefield, tiptoeing around the explosive contents of Beth's life, picking my way through the shrapnel without getting injured.

'I'm not sure what you mean?' It's a lame response but I don't know what else to say. To be honest, I'm bewildered by her statement. For years now, Beth has insisted that her parents were alcoholics, that they neglected and abused her. I cannot begin to imagine what she is going to come up with so play it safe with bland questions and a neutral expression.

'I told you they were drunks, my mum and dad, that they were weird and unbalanced. They weren't. I came from a normal family. I'm the weird one. I was always the odd one out.'

I shrug, as if what she is telling me doesn't matter. Which it doesn't really. It was all such a long time ago. I mean, what difference does it make to the Beth of now? I suppress a sigh. Deep down, I know that I'm lying to myself. It matters a lot. Our formative years shape who we are and what we become. And if Beth hasn't been shaped and moulded into the damaged, unpredictable woman that she is now by a neglectful, uncaring family, then I have to ask myself, why is she the way she is?

'I miss them, that's the thing. I'd like to see them again.'

Disappointment spears me. I hide it, conceal my discontent with a nod and a polite smile. I thought I was Beth's family. We might not be related by blood but we've weathered a few storms together and that has to count for something, and now here she is telling me that there are others out there who mean more to her than I do. Beth has been a nuisance in my life for so long that I've forgotten how to love her. There are days when I don't even like her, but we have always thought of one another as brother and sister. Except we're not. And now, apparently, there are other people she misses. People she hasn't seen for years and years. So where does that leave me? If, indeed, what she is telling me is true. Who knows the intricacies and shadowy, crooked corners of Beth's mind? I doubt she knows them herself, stumbling from catastrophe to catastrophe on a weekly basis with me as her safety net to catch her when she falls.

'Tell me about them. I'd like to hear.' My teeth are gritted. I try to keep the growing anger and resentment out of my voice but it's not easy. I feel let down, deflated and pushed aside. I'm Beth's unpaid carer. And if she doesn't want me, then who will?

'They were lovely, my parents. Quiet, gentle people. I miss my sisters too. After I left you today, I wandered around town and realised what a fucking waste my life has been, how I've pissed everything up the wall.' She nibbles at her broken nails, her teeth working furiously at a piece of loose skin. 'I've been a fucking idiot, I know that. Today I saw a woman with a newborn baby and knew then that it had to stop. I had to stop all this shit.'

I remain silent. I have no idea what to think, whether or not to believe her. Tomorrow morning, she could revert back to form, start drinking again, injecting fuck knows what into her veins or shoving it up her nose or rubbing it into her gums or whatever the hell it is she does to get those much-needed highs in order to escape those demons that sit on her shoulders, taunting her on a daily basis. This is Beth talking. Anything is possible. I've heard some real corkers come out of her mouth over the years. This could just be another massive lie.

The slapping sound as I hit my hands on my knees like a jovial Santa Claus character reverberates around the room. 'Right, tell you what, let me make some food and we can talk some more as we eat.' I stand up, simply because I don't know what else to do or say, and head into the kitchen, my head spinning at Beth's latest revelation.

It occurs to me while standing next to the cooker, wondering what I can rustle up in record time, that this is what Beth does. She turns up, chucks a hand grenade into my life and expects me to smile and be supportive of her latest crisis, never once thinking of the impact her actions have on me or the hurt and wounds I sustain in the process.

I spend the next ten minutes stir-frying noodles and vegetables, mulling over Beth's words, calling through to her, telling her idle bits of gossip about the latest happenings at work, and every time am greeted with silence. It's no more than I expect. It's how Beth is – who she is. Erratic and unfathomable, her world the epicentre of everyone else's. It's the only thing that matters to her – her issues, her problems. Her life.

Deciding that eating on our laps is more informal and saves me the hassle of setting the table, I dish up the food and carry it through to the living room, half expecting her to be browsing through my bookshelf or possibly even curled up asleep on the sofa. What I didn't expect, or perhaps if I'm being open and honest about it, I actually did expect, was for her to be gone, a small piece of paper with a scribbled note on it laid on the coffee table, the only thing to suggest she was ever here.

I turn around, Beth's plate clutched tightly between my fingers, and head back into the kitchen before scraping the contents into the bin. I should have known it wouldn't last, that small snatch of normality. So why do I feel so disappointed, rejection like an arrow lodged deep in my veins? I knew this would happen. I fucking *knew* it.

It's only as I sit down to eat, my stomach suddenly feeling full and bloated before I've had one mouthful, that I realise why I am so bothered by this latest occurrence. Beth is a drifter, a nobody, a borderline miscreant, and if I'm suddenly not good enough for her, then how useless and pointless is my existence?

I chase pieces of food around my plate, my appetite waning second by second, before placing my cutlery down, putting the plate on the floor, curling up on the sofa and closing my eyes.

23

'Why, Sadie? Why?' Marcia's eyes are brimming with tears.

She covers her face with her hands, peering out between splayed fingers at the disaster before her, staring in disbelief at the spread of ruined food she spent hours and hours baking, at the buttercream that is smeared over the tablecloth, the layers of crumbled sponge, smashed and split beyond recognition, the sandwiches torn and shredded by tiny, angry fingers.

The child says nothing, gaze fixed ahead, expression cold and unseeing. Her face is pale, hands hanging limply at her sides. Marcia shuts her eyes, bats away images she has of slapping her daughter, hitting her repeatedly until her palm is sore and Sadie cries out in pain for her to stop.

Her breathing is a staccato rhythm, her vision misted and blurred. Marcia rushes around the other side of the table, grabbing at her daughter's hand before yanking her upwards to view the calamity that only a few hours ago was their party table, the food waiting to be eaten while the children played games in the living room.

'Look at it, Sadie. Just look at it! You've ruined your special day. Why would you do such a thing? What the hell is wrong with you?'

She stops, puts her daughter back down and steps away, her head pounding, her heart thrashing around her chest. She feels woozy. Woozy and sick. This is too much. At what point, she thinks miserably, does this family finally fall apart? They are only capable of taking so much pressure before their lives implode. And all because their young daughter cannot behave in a normal fashion. How did it get like this? Did something happen to turn her into the devious, miserable child that she now is? Or was she born that way? Nature or nurture. Did she do something to warp this child's mind or, and this is the thing that sickens and worries her more than anything, did she give birth to a child who has a seemingly unlimited capacity for causing untold hurt to everything and everyone around her?

Marcia stands, waiting for the pain in her head to subside, for the bashing of her heart to slow down, for her legs to regain their usual strength. She waits for those awful images in her mind of attacking her young daughter to disappear. It isn't normal for a parent to ever imagine doing those things to their child. She swallows hard, tries to steady her breathing, her dark thoughts, doing her utmost to quash them, push them back into that barely ventured space inside her head. At the end of the day, it's only a cake. Nobody has been hurt or injured. The world will continue to turn, regardless. Perspective. That's what she needs to do right now – to put this minor misdemeanour into perspective. It can't be easy for Sadie, constantly spending her life being pushed into the shadows, deprived of light and attention, her sisters always taking centre stage with their confidence and charisma. Maybe this is her way of trying to get noticed, to let everyone know that she's here and she matters, even if it is an act of destruction.

Her hand moves across, touching the child's head, brushing lightly over her hair, gently stroking the ribbons that sit on the top of *her ringlets. Pink ribbons chosen specifically by Sadie for this special day. Rosa chose red polka dots. Jenna declined, stating quite clearly that she was now far too old for ribbons and ringlets.*

Marcia smiles, the sensation alien to her amidst the carnage of the party table. It's not that bad. Now that she is over the shock, she can see that it doesn't matter. It's just food after all. It tastes the same no matter how it looks. We don't eat with our eyes, do we?

She leans across, deftly putting sponge butterfly wings back on broken cakes, pressing them together into the buttercream to disguise the damage. More spare sandwiches are brought in from the kitchen, Sadie's trembling fingers helping to lay them out. Napkins are strategically placed over smears and stains that litter the white tablecloth. Marcia smiles and steps back, surveying the freshly made and repaired food.

'There we are. Not so bad after all, eh?'

The child stares up at her mother, mouth half open, poised to speak. Small dark irises glint in the afternoon sunlight, her pupils tiny pinpricks. She watches. She waits. And then she finally utters a few words.

'I didn't do it, Mummy. It wasn't me. It's never been me.'

But Marcia is too fixated on ensuring everything is as acceptable and as presentable as it can be to hear what her daughter is saying, the child's words floating over her head, swallowed up into the ether.

Sadie turns and stares out of the window, her small, pallid face devoid of all emotion. 'None of it was me.'

24

DEBORAH

Except it doesn't bring it to an end. Far from it. Izzie brings up the spade and lets out a shriek like a warning signal, announcing her presence. She misses her intended target, a weight sliding off me as our captor dodges the hit, the metal of the huge implement slamming into the wall instead.

I scramble to one side, desperately scanning the vicinity for something to use against her but can see nothing that would be of any use. I can only hope that Izzie has kept hold of that spade, otherwise we are done for. It'll be used against us and then everything will definitely come to an end, just not the one we planned or hoped for. There's no turning back now. We've angered her, made her look stupid and weak by breaking out of our gags and ties. She won't like it and will want revenge.

She prowls around the room, legs bent, head dipped, animalistic grunts emanating from her throat. I haven't a clue what to do next and hope that Izzie has some sort of strategy set out in her head. In theory, we should be able to run at her, two of us against one, and pin her to the ground, but I'm aware of her almost superhuman strength, seen how fit and agile she is, and it scares me. I'm not sure we are any sort of match for her abilities. Izzie is small. I am feeble and probably malnourished, my muscles weakened by lack of natural daylight and inactivity.

'Don't. Don't even think about it.'

She is staring at Izzie who is edging closer to the spade laid close to her feet. She too is bent over, poised, ready for battle. She looks nimble and sprightly. Whether or not she has enough muscle and power to beat this woman is another matter. I know that our captor is a fitness freak, that she does workouts to keep herself strong and trim. How else could she possibly drag us here and do what she does? This is the side of her I didn't know existed; her secret life. Her warped hidden existence.

I say her name over and over in my head, doing my best to stop it spilling out of my mouth, knowing how it enrages her. Knowing how she wants to remain anonymous, as if who she is now is detached from her other self. She isn't. They aren't. They are the same person. What she is, is a good actress, keeping it all tucked away, concealed from everybody around her. I wonder if at some point she will come undone, all of her madness spilling out for everyone to see.

'And you, crouching there all wide-eyed and innocent. This is all your fault!' She is watching me now, her gaze flitting between the two of us. 'If you had just stayed where you were, done as you were told, then I wouldn't have to do what I'm going to do next. You were always the same – even as a kid. An annoying little bitch is what you are and were. Nothing has changed. I was going to make it all so lovely for you here and look how you've repaid me. Just look at what you've done!'

I don't have time to react. She pounces at me, feline-like, her back arched, arms outstretched. Her hands land on my throat, fingers clasped tightly around my windpipe, her long nails digging into my flesh. I am clearly stronger than I realise because, somehow, I manage to shake her off. She lands next to me, rolling onto her back, seemingly unhurt. We both scramble to far corners of the empty, dilapidated room. Izzie stands, fear now rendering her helpless. She is trembling, her eyes bulging with terror. I want to tell her to move, to get that shovel, but don't want to startle her so instead we all stand, trying to work out who will move first. Who will grab that spade and wield it, bringing it down with so much force that it kills the victim with one heavy blow.

My head is pounding, my stomach tied into knots. I can't allow my fear to stop me. Not now we've made it this far. This is our chance, our moment. No time to waste. I refuse to die today. It's not my time. I'm not ready. I won't leave this life without a fight.

I take a step forward. So does she. I take another, edging and shuffling across the floor. So does she. I prepare to lunge but she is too quick for me and before I can grab it, she picks it up, raises her arms and holds the spade aloft. Purely for effect she swishes it about, the noise a sickening sound as it cuts through the air. I envision it smashing against Izzie's skull, her tiny body collapsing, her heart stopping and her body dropping to the floor with a thud, leaving me here alone. Again. Nausea wells up in me. I can't let that happen. Not again. Izzie is my chance to escape this house of horrors and I am hers. If we don't make a break for it now, then we are both doomed.

My heart thuds, a pain threads itself across the base of my skull as I dip my body, ready for battle. I will call out her name and throw myself at her abdomen, hoping to knock the spade out of her hands. If I can catch her unawares, knock her off balance by pushing my full body weight into her solar plexus, then I may stand a chance.

It works. She stops prowling as I scream her name out loud and run at her head on.

I hear a deep gargling sound, feel her resistance waning and then we are wrestling on the floor, our limbs locked in battle as we thrash around for that weapon. I can see it in my peripheral vision, the glint of the metal close to her hand.

My mind races while I try to hold her steady, to keep her writhing limbs and strong body from getting up again. Where the fuck is Izzie? What the hell is she doing?

Then I hear it, the unmistakable metallic scrape as the spade is dragged upwards across the concrete floor. It vanishes out of my limited view. I hear a deep, rasping breath, feel the movement of air nearby, then the swish of a heavy object being swung through the air.

I suck in my breath and wait.

Then nothing.

* * *

It's dark. And silent. I'm floating. Yet I'm not. The numbness begins to fade, replaced by a feeling of heaviness. The floor is cold and hard beneath me. Oh God, I'm still here. After all that planning, the fighting, the spent energy, I am still here. Despondency sits like bitumen in my gut. I can't go through this again. I just can't. I have nothing left to give, nothing in reserve. I'm an empty husk. I may as well be dead. I would rather be a rotting carcass than spend another day in this terrible, awful place.

I move my legs, feel a weight there that wasn't present before. My hands land in something sticky. I recoil, my body wracked with pain as I move. A deep, searing ache travels up my spine, the likes of which I have never felt before.

A voice cries out, a tinny echo that bounces off the walls. I think perhaps that it's coming from me but then realise that I'm in too much pain to whimper, let alone shout. I shuffle into a sitting position and am able to see Izzie on the other side of the room. She is half lying, half sitting, her face streaked with tears.

My eyes take some time to adjust. I blink to clear my vision and turn my head to see the smear of blood next to me, a sticky ruby coagulation incongruous against the wooden floorboards.

'Your head,' Izzie says, her voice echoing in the emptiness around us. 'Oh God, I am so sorry, Deborah. I tried to hit her and missed. It was so heavy. The metal end of the shovel caught you on your back. You fell and banged your head on the floor.'

She starts to cry. Not a loud wailing and sobbing, more of a soft weeping full of regret and fear and resignation at our plight. I would join in but fear that once I start, I won't be able to stop. It will be the undoing of me, stripping me of what little energy I have left.

'Don't cry,' I say, my eyes roving around the place, trying to assess our situation. 'We'll get out of here. I'm certain of it.' I'm not certain at all. Of anything. I have no idea what the future holds for us. My voice is a lonely echo, bouncing off crumbling, damp walls. A sensation sits in my stomach, a feeling that we may never get out of here alive.

I look down at my feet. They're roughly tied together as are my hands but they are nowhere near as tight as they were when we were up there in that attic space. That's another thing – she hasn't hauled us back up there. We stand a greater chance of escaping from here. I look around at the small broken windows and closed doors. Maybe they lead straight out on to a path? A path that could help us get out of this place.

'I tried to fight her off but after you were knocked out, she tied me up with some bits of rags she had in her pocket and then went upstairs and got more rope to tie you up as well.' She shakes her head despairingly. 'Stupid. So stupid of me. I had a chance and I blew it.' Izzie wipes at her eyes and sniffs. 'She is so strong. I don't know how we'll ever get out of here. It feels like there's no end to this hell. And I have no idea what we've done to deserve this. I mean, why us?'

Even as Izzie is talking, I am already trying to loosen the roughly tied rags that are wrapped around my hands and feet. A wave of pain shoots up and down my back, spreading across my bones like boiling molten metal, covering every inch of me. I wonder how many broken bones I've sustained while being held here and think about whether or not they will ever properly heal or whether I'll be permanently disfigured, my lopsided gait an ongoing reminder of what I've endured.

'Our faces,' I murmur. 'It's because of our faces.'

'Because we look alike? But that's just plain crazy! It makes no sense.'

'Not just our faces,' I say, pulling at the ties that bind me. 'She thinks we're her sisters, her long-dead family.'

My words are met with a lingering silence. I can guess what's coming next, can almost hear her thinking it, the words rolling around her head like huge boulders searching for an escape route.

'She told you this?' Izzie says eventually, disbelief edging into her voice.

I sigh, stop what I'm doing and peer through the dimness to where she is sitting on the far side of the room. 'I know it.' My voice cracks as I speak. 'I know *her.*'

Izzie is a vague outline, her features too distant to see properly, but I can imagine the look on her face as my words register in her brain, the shocked expression, the wide-eyed look of horror and fear that I am possibly part of this warped plan.

'You know her?' Izzie's voice is a high-pitched shriek. 'I

mean, what the actual fuck?' She lets out a rumbling cough and tries to stand up. 'Are you related to her? Christ almighty, what the hell is going on here?'

'No!' I am shouting now, exasperation and a desperation to disassociate myself from this situation present in my voice. 'I know her from work. We're definitely not related. I work in an engineering office in town and know her from there.'

'So how the fuck...?'

'Did I end up here?' I stop what I'm doing, raise my eyes to the ceiling to stop the tears from falling. 'I wish I knew that, I really do. I've asked myself the very same question many times over and all I can think of is that I look like one of her sisters.'

'Who is?'

'I have absolutely no idea. I only know the bits she has whispered to me while I've been here. I'm as mystified as you.'

I watch as Izzie slides back down to the floor, her back pressed against the wall, a definite air of mistrust evident in her body language, the way she turns away from me.

'I know this all sounds completely deranged and unfeasible but I promise you, it will come to an end,' I say, surprised at the strength of my voice, how confident and assured I sound. I don't feel confident and assured. I feel exhausted, desperate. Yet my will to live is still strong. An overriding emotion bubbling up in the centre of me. It hasn't died yet, the determination and the steely resolve I have to survive.

We sit in silence for the next few minutes. I try to concentrate on my pain, working out how I can ignore it and forge ahead with our escape plan. I won't let any number of injuries stop me. If I have to hobble out of here or even crawl out on my hands and knees, then so be it. That's exactly what I will do.

'So, she thinks we're her sisters. What is she planning on doing with us?' Izzie's voice is melancholic. She is losing it –

that will to live. She sounds husky, dispirited, as if all the life has been sucked out of her.

'I honestly don't know but I can tell you this much – we are not going to hang around long enough to find out.'

The rope around my ankles loosens. I give it one last pull and let out a trembling sigh as it drops away to the floor.

'Okay,' I say quietly, the fear that she may be on her way back or even outside listening suddenly weighing heavily on me. 'I'll come over there and unpick you, then we can work out what to do next.'

I stand up, the usual reflex of walking now an onerous, painful task, and make my way over to the shrivelled, tiny husk that is Izzie, slumped on the floor.

'Come on,' I say, trying to sound positive. 'Let's get you untied and we can both get out of here before she gets back.'

25

ADRIAN

Christ almighty, this is going to be fucking awful. Worse than I imagined. I stare at the email, my insides churning with dread. This stupid bloody team-building day has now been extended into an overnight stay at a local hotel. How long do they want to drag this thing out for?

'I'll be speaking to Ruth about this. I can't possibly go. I have other commitments.' Merriel is standing behind me, peering down at my computer screen. I turn to look at her, taken aback by the look of anger and horror that is etched into her features. I'm thoroughly pissed off at this new turn of events but Merriel's sentiments are on another level. 'There is no bloody way they can make us go. It's our time and, besides, we're not getting paid for it. I can't go. I won't. This is completely out of order!'

'I agree.' I keep my voice low, keen to defuse the situation, not draw attention to Merriel's escalating anger.

'I have things to do at home! What if they say we have to go? How do we get out of it?'

I watch, both mystified and curious as she tenses her jaw,

the muscles at the side of her face twitching and pulsing when she grinds her teeth together. I don't want to go to this thing, every sinew in my body straining against it, but find myself wondering what Merriel has going on in her life that makes her so dead set against it? A secret child perhaps? A controlling boyfriend who doesn't trust her to stay away even for just one night? I smile at the idea that she has another life that none of us know about. I envisage her as a member of some clandestine mafia group and have to suppress a smile. Maybe she goes out on an evening, stalking unsuspecting victims, robbing them or, worse still, bashing them over the head and kidnapping them. I almost laugh at the thought of it.

'What sort of things?' I shouldn't be asking but then, she brought this subject up. She was the one who mentioned her inability to stay away from home even just for one night.

Her head spins around, her eyes dark slits as she stares at me, anger and mistrust oozing out of her like thick tar.

'What do you mean?'

I shrug, try to appear unruffled by her outburst. 'You said you had things to do at home. I was just wondering what sort of things?'

She doesn't answer, instead shaking her head as if I have just asked the most unreasonable question imaginable.

'A boyfriend? Or maybe a girlfriend who you don't want to be parted from even for just one night?'

She rounds on me, eyes full of fire, skin reddening. 'What the hell are you on about, Adrian? For fuck's sake!' Her voice is a near shriek, her words hitting me like bullets.

I hold up my hands in mock surrender and smile. 'Hey, hey! Don't forget, you were the one who started this conversation. All I did was ask why you're so dead set against going!' I'm laughing now. I can't help it. Such a disproportionate response to a simple question. I'm always staggered by people who do this – throw comments out there to pique everyone's interest, then go into hiding when the queries and requests for follow-up information start. Isn't that what they want by mentioning it in the first place? To garner support and faux sympathy for their purported plight? Or maybe it was me mentioning that she might have a girlfriend as opposed to a boyfriend. I was trying to be helpful, not box her into a corner and make her feel threatened. 'If you didn't want me to ask, then why mention it in the first place?'

Merriel shrugs, closes her eyes briefly and slumps down in the empty chair next to mine. 'Sorry. I'm just feeling a bit fragile today. I had a bit of a run-in with some people I thought I could trust. I genuinely thought they were on my side, that we could work towards the same goal, but it appears not. They've let me down and I feel a bit betrayed, that's all.'

'You want to talk about it?' I lower my voice, shuffle closer to her. Merriel isn't exactly the most approachable of people nor is she the warmest, but I do feel some sympathy for her. We're all susceptible to being hurt. I know that as well as anyone. My often brusque exterior masks a multitude of emotions that many would find surprising. I'm as breakable as the next person but at least I've learned some coping strategies to deal with the stuff that spins around in my head. Beth's sudden departure left me reeling. I'm her safety net and for all it has irritated me always having to be there for her all these years, I felt rudderless once she left, like a mother mourning her child after they flee the nest and forge their own way in life. If Beth no longer needs me then who am I? What is my purpose in life? I come here every day, earn a half-decent living and go home again. Like Merriel, I feel let down. Let down and, if I am being perfectly honest, very much alone.

She shakes her head. 'Not really. Talking and soul baring isn't my thing. I know people in this place think I'm a bit of a loudmouth but it's just an act. I like my own space as much as the next person.'

I'm taken aback to see that she is close to tears. There's a nasty little scratch under her eye and I begin to wonder if she has an abusive partner, somebody who regularly beats the shit out of her. She doesn't look as if she would kowtow to anybody but then you never can tell, can you? None of us really know what goes on behind closed doors. We all have things we would rather keep secret, our private lives that nobody knows about. Beaten partners don't go around declaring it to the world; they put on an act, keep it all hidden away as if it's something to be ashamed of.

'If you change your mind and need a shoulder to cry on, I'm here.' I say it knowing she won't open up. Us damaged souls can't do that – talk about our inner feelings, our deepest, darkest emotions. The ones that fester in our minds, waiting to appear unbidden, declaring themselves and demanding our attention when we least expect them to.

I never thought I would think it, but maybe Merriel and I have more in common than we will ever realise. Maybe this office is a place full of dark secrets and blighted beings. Like magnets we attract each other. I look around at everybody else – Allison with her bright and breezy outlook; what's her real story? And Ruth with her chirpy, friendly ways and nervous disposition; what is really going on in her life that we don't get to see or know about? She rarely, if ever, speaks about her home life, where she goes to once the computer screens turn black and the lights are flicked off in this office. And then there's Yvonne with her sensible, practical ways and austere manner whenever a dirty joke is cracked. Does she have a partner at home? What are her hobbies? Like Merriel, she looks as if she keeps herself fit but I have no idea what her regime is, whether she visits a gym or does kick-boxing or runs the London Marathon every year. I know nothing about any of these people. Not a damn thing.

A shift in temperature, a slight movement of air as Merriel moves away, her confidences still buried deep within herself. Perhaps she will eventually open up, recognising how alike we actually are. Or perhaps not. We're just colleagues after all. Not friends.

I check my phone, see if there are any messages from Beth, and feel a stab of disappointment to see my inbox and text messages are empty. I wonder what she is currently doing, where she is. Who she is with. I think of her revelation about hurting another person. We didn't get to speak about it; that is, if it ever happened at all. And then I think of Deborah.

Stop it!

'So, what are your thoughts on it then, Ade?' Ruth is beside me, her face pale, eyes wide. Her hand flutters up to her neck, small fingers tapping away at her collarbone.

I don't have to ask what she's referring to. She's probably approaching everyone, trying to gauge their reaction to her email. I don't have any other commitments, nobody at home who relies on me. There's nothing to stop me from attending. Apart from, that is, a deep-seated desire to not go. It simply isn't my thing, climbing up high ropes or solving stupid fucking simulated murder mystery games. Heights definitely aren't my thing anyway and it's not something I will ever work to overcome. I can't. I won't. I don't have it in me to even attempt to do such a thing. I've read about these team-building antics before now. They're childish and undignified and totally unnecessary.

I sigh before speaking. I don't want to upset Ruth but I also don't want to lie to her. I try to find a balance, choosing my words with precision and care.

'To be honest, it doesn't bother me either way, whether we stay over or make it a day session, but there are others here who might have other commitments. I'm not sure it's fair to expect them to stay away from home for longer than is necessary.'

Ruth smiles, fiddles with her collar and tries to appear unperturbed by my words. 'It's a five-star hotel. Everything paid for. Free food and alcohol. Surely that's an attraction?'

Not to me it isn't. I've given up drinking. Not that I'm about to share that nugget of information with her. I like Ruth but she's not my confidante or some sort of counsellor. My business is my business and not for other people's ears, so instead I shrug and try to act nonchalant.

'All I'm saying is, you can't expect people to give up their personal time for something work related.'

'Well, if they were going on a course, they would have to stay overnight if it wasn't local. Some of them have done it before now.' She is clutching at straws here, but does actually have a point.

In the past, Merriel has been uppity about others going to London on accountancy courses and staying in plush hotels while she is stuck here in the office with a cup of lukewarm coffee and a pot noodle and now, here she is complaining about being asked to do the very thing of which she was once jealous.

'What if they have family or other commitments; people who depend on them for assistance?'

'Then we'll have to rethink. We only have a couple of days to change our plans. I thought everyone would have jumped at the chance but it appears we have some resistance in the ranks.'

Ruth smiles resignedly and starts to walk away, her head dipped slightly. Part of me feels sorry for her. Damned if she does and damned if she doesn't. She also has management to deal with, has to take on board their ideas and feed them back to us. Piggy in the middle is what she is.

'I'm up for it, Ruth.' The words are out of my mouth before I can stop them, born out of a sense of sympathy for this woman who helped me when I was at my weakest. I watch her shoulders lift, see her smile as she turns to give me a wave of gratitude and a thumbs up before heading back into her office and closing the door behind her.

26

YVONNE

It's quiet in the staffroom. So few people eat in here nowadays. They go into town or sit at their desks nibbling at sandwiches and flicking through magazines, or staring at their phones, eyes glazed over as they switch off from customers and invoices for an hour, revelling in the fact that for a short period of time they don't have to listen to suppliers barking down the phone at them, shouting and demanding that payments be made before they release the goods.

The room is clinical. I understand why hardly anybody visits the place. With white walls, plastic chairs and a tiny window, it's hardly conducive to rest and relaxation. More like a prison cell. My office chair is more comfortable and a lot easier on my back, plus the view in there is better, with a sweeping vista of the town, unlike this one that affords people a grim outlook over the car park with its graffitied walls and then the railway tracks beyond, the screech of metal as trains slow down to rumble their way into the station a constant background noise.

I think about the email we all received this morning and

whether or not it sits well with me. I don't have to think about it for too long. It doesn't suit me at all. I have things that I need to do, plans to be carried out. People here in this office may not know a great deal about my private life but that doesn't mean I don't have one. This weekend is the anniversary of Aunt Deirdre's death. I always visit her grave, take some flowers, say a little prayer and a thank you to her for all the things she did for me. I can't miss it. It's unthinkable that I won't be there for her. I've never missed one yet and I don't intend to start now because of some silly team-building exercise to help salve the conscience of a company who simply carried on as if nothing was awry after one of their employees vanished into thin air one evening after leaving this office.

Besides, I also have other things going on in my life; there are people I haven't seen for many years who I met up with recently that I want to spend some time with. All of these things are more important to me than mingling with colleagues in an upmarket hotel in town that is only a stone's throw away from where we actually live and work. It seems like such a silly and pointless endeavour and an expensive one too.

I glance at my watch, relieved that I'm only doing half a day today. This is my morning break. Lunchtime can't come soon enough. I'll be leaving here as soon as the clock hits 12 p.m. I've brought my car today. I need to get home as soon as possible. There are things I need to be getting on with but before I leave, I have to speak with Ruth about this team-building nonsense. I want to give her my views, tell her that under no circumstances will I be staying overnight in a hotel, regardless of how swanky and expensive it is. Deirdre means more to me than all of my colleagues combined. Deborah's absence is with us every day. We don't need to group together and go abseiling or make paper bridges out of cereal boxes to prove how much she is missed. It's childish nonsense and no more than a box-ticking exercise to show everyone how much we care.

My mind is fixated on getting out of here, going home, getting on with the things that I need to do once I'm there. I also need to buy some flowers for the weekend visit to the cemetery. Lilies and Michaelmas daisies: they were her favourites. I take them every year, place them on her grave and sit contemplating anything and everything while I'm there. A hundred tasks race through my head while I sip at my coffee and bite into my cereal bar.

It's the bang of the door that startles me, not Merriel's appearance in the room. She stalks in here, her face creased with concern. I try to look sympathetic even though I don't know what the problem is and nor do I care.

Conversation between us is stilted, both Merriel and I finding it difficult to break down the barriers that sit between us. Eventually I decide to come straight out and say it.

'What's happened to your eye?'

She blinks repeatedly and half turns away as if embarrassed by my noticing her recent injury.

'It's nothing,' she says quietly, her voice muffled and distant. 'What happened to your hand?'

She is staring at my bruised knuckles, the red welts that sit across the flesh on the back of my hand.

'Like you, it's nothing,' I murmur, shoving my curled fist deep into my pocket. 'I fell while jogging.'

'Fell onto your knuckles? Wouldn't normal people put out the flat of their hand to save themselves?'

I don't reply, my gaze still drawn to the bruise and small laceration just above her cheekbone. 'Must have been a hell of a fight. What was it then, welterweight or heavyweight?' I smile as I say it to lessen the impact of my words but keep my eyes locked with hers. She won't get the better of me.

She doesn't smile in return nor does she reply so I continue with my line of questioning. In for a penny and all that. 'I never did find out how you knew where I lived. Remind me again?'

If Merriel is shocked by my sudden change of direction, she doesn't show it, her face remaining impassive. Unreadable.

Her eyes are glassy when she speaks, her voice flat and monotone. 'Okay, hands up. I saw it on the front of your payslip last year when I was standing next to your desk before it all went digital, and just remembered it.'

A buzzing sound fills my head. Our eyes lock, the two of us caught in the moment. Ready to do battle. My voice is croaky when I do eventually find the right words. 'Why?' I say quietly, a hint of menace, and possibly exasperation, in my tone. 'Why would you keep my address in your head?'

'Why not?'

I refuse to accept that answer so try again, my voice louder this time, more forceful. 'Come on, Merriel, you can do better than that. Why did you memorise my address? It's not a difficult question now, is it?' Our eyes are still locked. I refuse to look away, to be the first to capitulate and glance elsewhere. Never break eye contact: the first rule of winning a silent encounter.

The quiet seems to go on for an age even though it's only a matter of seconds before she finally replies. It's the things we aren't saying that mean the most, the invisible daggers pointed at one another. An invisible skirmish, that's what this is. A quiet combative moment. I don't lose. Merriel needs to know that. I never ever lose.

'I thought I knew you from somewhere else so I made a point of trying to find out where you lived to see if you were the person I thought you were.' Her voice is flat, resigned to being caught out, having to own up to something that feels akin to stalking. This is a humiliating moment for her, being held to account. I think back to that shadowy figure loitering outside my house and suppress a scream.

'Why not just ask if you knew me? Why all the deceit?'

She sighs, rubs at her face, eyelashes fluttering, eyes narrowed. She looks over at me, her gaze boring deep into my soul. More seconds pass. I hold my breath and wait.

When she does speak, it feels as if all the air has been sucked out of the room. My blood begins to heat up, bubbling like hot oil in my veins while my skin grows cold and clammy.

'When I was a child, my brother was murdered by somebody we grew up with, another child. It was the girl who lived next door to us who did it and she looked a lot like you. Or at least how I expect her to look as an adult. Same shaped face, same features, same colour hair. I thought you might have been her. I heard she was back living with her parents somewhere locally and so visited your house to see if I could see them. They wouldn't have changed that much so if I could get a good look at them, I would know for sure. Then I found out that I was wrong, had got hold of the wrong end of the stick and knew then that you couldn't have been her but of course your address sort of stuck in my head.' Merriel chews at the inside of her mouth, her teeth grinding and grinding as she struggles to find the right words. 'I'm sorry, Yvonne. I didn't want to tell you all this but you backed me into a corner.'

She's right. I did back her into a corner. I caught her out because she made a mistake, wasn't quite devious enough to cover her tracks and now we are here, caught in this mortifying situation. Two colleagues trapped together by a past that should never have been brought out into the open. However, I'm not to blame for any of this and I had a right to know why she knew where I lived. And now I do know, there is little else for us to say. I can hardly throw any anger her way so, instead, I change the subject, swerve it around to something more current. Something that shows we have common ground, Merriel and I, even though we don't. I'm nothing like her. She is nothing like me. We've been flung together and have to make to most of it, make the best of a bad job.

'What do you think about this latest idea for the team-building day? All of us holed up together in a hotel for the night?'

'I think it's a load of old shit. How about you?' She almost smiles as she says it, realising that we're now on safer ground, the previous conversation safely behind us.

'Same here. Couldn't agree more. I have things to do at home.'

'Me too! I'm so glad I'm not the only one with plans and commitments and I'll be saying as much to Ruth when I get to speak to her. She might not have a life outside of these four walls but I bloody well do.' Merriel's voice has risen almost a full octave, her cheeks and neck flushed with anger and frustration. 'I've got relatives staying over with me. I can't just up and leave them, can I?'

I shake my head. 'No, that definitely doesn't seem fair or right. How about we all speak to Ruth together? Strength in numbers and all that jazz? Maybe we can get Allison and Adrian to join us?'

Her shoulders bunch together as she shrugs listlessly. 'Wouldn't bank on Adrian joining us. He didn't seem bothered either way about it but Allison might speak up against it if we ask her?'

'I'm off this afternoon but feel free to note my concerns. I certainly don't want to go. I'll refuse.'

Her smile lights up the room, the crimson web that covered her face suddenly dissipating. 'I'll do that. Thanks.'

My coffee is barely lukewarm. I swig it back regardless and stand up. 'See you shortly,' I say quietly as I exit the room. All of a sudden, we are almost friends. Except we're not. We're just not enemies any more.

I push the door ajar and head towards my desk, the warmth of the room making me dizzy and light-headed, the noise of the photocopier whirring around me like a flock of angry birds. I sit down at my chair, lower my eyes to my keyboard and begin to type.

27

He won't move. She shakes him, calling out to him, her voice a thin, distressed ribbon of noise. 'Daddy, Daddy, Daddy!'

A slight stirring followed by a snore. It's pitch-black but she can see his mouth as it shifts and wobbles about, the snore escaping and disappearing into the silence and darkness of the room.

The carpet is soft under her feet, her toes curling against the fringe of the pale blue rug at the side of their bed. She moves around to the other edge of the mattress, her hands reaching to touch her mother. She paws at the bed sheets, is able to feel her mother's body beneath the covers. It looks snuggly warm in there; she would love to climb in, cuddle up, tell them that something is wrong, but knows that she is too big for that sort of thing now. Not enough room. Her legs are too gangly, her body too long and bony. Soon, she will be at big school and girls at big school can't climb in bed with their parents when they're scared. And she is really, really scared. Because something is happening. Something bad. And it's taking place in their house.

A painful lump is lodged in her throat. It feels like a big rock is stuck in there. Or a spoonful of sand. Her mouth feels dry. She stifles a cough. It hurts too much and she is sure that once she starts, she won't be able to stop. Water. She needs a drink of water but needs to wake her mother first. She shouldn't really go downstairs on her own. It's too dark and it's far too late.

'Mum, wake up. I think Daddy left the fire on.'

That's what it must be. The smell is really strong and it's getting worse. Both of her sisters are still sleeping. At least she thinks they are. She didn't check. She raced out of bed as soon as the smell woke her.

Tiptoeing out of her parents' bedroom, she peers into Jenna's room. It's really, really dark in there. Too dark to see properly. She has blackout blinds in her room because of the light from the lamp post outside that keeps her awake at night.

Backing out onto the landing, she heads towards her own bedroom, eyes wide as she searches for her twin sister. She pats at the bed but feels nothing but cool sheets. She isn't there. Maybe she's in the bathroom.

The smell is stronger nearer the bathroom. She opens the door, steps inside, finds it empty. Where is she? The thought that her twin may be downstairs stoking up their open fire sets her heart racing, makes her stomach shrivel. It's dangerous. They're only allowed to do it if their parents are in the room watching them. Never when they're on their own. Ever. They were all given a stern talking to the time Jenna took it upon herself to add more logs to it without asking. She remembers the look of horror and anger on their dad's face, how his forehead creased like crêpe paper and how his mouth trembled as he spoke to them. He did his best to look calm but they could all see that he was on the verge of being properly angry.

Turning to look down the stairs, she switches on the light, stops, blinks and lets out a small cry. Smoke. There is smoke coming up the stairs, seeping out from under the living room door. Great curling grey tendrils billowing out from under it.

She runs back to her parents' bedroom, calling out to them to get up.

'Wake up! Wake up! There's smoke. Fire. There's a fire!'

He mother wakes first, mouth puckered, lips thin and angry at such an abrupt awakening. She pulls at her mum's hands, tries to drag her out of the bed, then leans over and pummels at her father's slowly rousing body, dragging at his limbs, pushing at his back.

'Come on! Get up! We need to stop the fire! Get up, get up, get up!'

A thump of feet on the rug as her mother stands up and sniffs at the air. Then more shouting as her mum pulls off the bed sheets and pushes at her husband's body. He sits up, eyes white in the murkiness of the room, voice low and croaky.

'What? What the hell is going on?'

And then he knows. It takes only seconds for the unfolding situation to hit him, for the acrid smell to curl its way into his throat, into his lungs. Burning his chest. Choking him.

He grabs at his wife and daughter, pulls them towards the window and rattles at it. It's locked. No key. Stupid. So stupid. He hid it away, didn't want the children opening the windows upstairs and falling out.

'Downstairs! I'll grab your sisters, you two go downstairs, unlock the front door and get outside.'

They follow his instructions, him behind them as they all stumble on to the landing but it's too smoky, too hot, the fumes rising rapidly, obstructing their airways, scorching their skin. Clouds of grey billow around them, stinging their eyes. They stand at the top of the stairs looking down but escape seems impossible. Nowhere to turn. No way out.

Behind them, the sound of a girl gasping for breath, her hacking cough and croaking voice filters through their shouts and cries as she staggers towards them, still groggy from sleep. Then a man shouting, his bellowing loud and insistent. Powerful, yet also brimming with fear.

'She's not here! Where the hell is she? She isn't here, for God's sake!'

* * *

Outside, a child sits alone, eyes raised to the sky. She stares at the blanket of stars overhead, is mesmerised by the way they twinkle and shine. They remind her of a kaleidoscope, all those sparkling, glittery dots; the way they form a pattern above her is almost magical. She likes patterns, pretty twinkly patterns. She imagines herself up there, hopping from star to star, each one a stepping stone to somewhere else, each one forming a route away from here.

Her hands feel sore. She sighs, holds them out, tries to inspect them, her vision marred by the darkness. It was tricky, getting the fire to start. Not half as easy as she imagined. People think that you just pile things up and take a match to them and poof! But it doesn't always work like that. You also need air circulation. She read about it in a book at school. So she tried and tried again, rearranging the logs, shifting them about until eventually a spark took hold and the flames began to rise. Then came the tricky part. Using the tongs, she lifted out one of the logs and laid it on the rug in front of the fire. She expected the orange glow to die down, for the flames to flicker to nothing. But they didn't. Small embers fell onto the rug, glistening and glowing like a tiny little volcano erupting before her very eyes. She stifled her giggle, not wanting to wake anybody, and stood up, stepping back to watch it happen.

The rug soon began to smoulder, but it wasn't enough. She wanted a bigger pattern and was almost ready to add another log when suddenly, whoosh! A big flame danced in front of her, rising up, the heat and ferocity of it making her dizzy with glee. Orange, flecked *with pale blue, swayed and pirouetted, holding her captive to its beauty. It grew and grew until she realised that it was time to leave. Pretty patterns were beautiful but this one was hot and the smoke was catching in the back of her throat.*

As quietly as she could, she tiptoed out to the hallway and turned the key that was hanging in the door lock, then stepped outside and shut the door behind her.

And now here she sits, waiting for everything to begin. For the fire engines to arrive, for everyone to see how clever she is for managing to escape unhurt. For them all to see how silly it is to not have a fireguard in place. Her mother had said for years that logs could drop out at any time and that it was a health and safety hazard. After lighting it, she placed the matches back on the shelf so people wouldn't suspect anything. It was just an accident after all. A horrible, horrible accident. Fires are dangerous. Everybody knows that but Daddy kept on saying how cosy it was and how sensible his girls were, that nobody would ever mess with it because they were all so careful, weren't they? He had stared at them all in turn when he had said it, a stern look on his face, and all three of them had nodded and looked suitably worried. Except her. She had done her best to look aware and pretended to listen hard to his words of wisdom, but her mind had floated off elsewhere, small sparks of ideas already forming in her mind. The fire didn't worry or frighten her because she had read all about it in school and it's a good job she did because it was now raging behind her, the windows aglow with russet and golden flames, smoke building behind the glass, billowing and building, fighting to be out.

She shivers. It's cold out here. She wishes the fire engines would hurry up and arrive, for somebody to come and get the rescue mission underway. For everyone to see what a clever hero she is for getting out of there.

Her body is twisted towards the house, her small frame half hidden amongst the shrubbery, shielded by the garden shed as she watches the beautiful formations coming from inside the house; the grey and black that contrasts against the golden ochre flames. It's such an attractive sight. Fire is an angry thing, just like her. It also controls everything. She likes control too, knows what it is and how to use it. Just like the flames currently raging through her house, she is the one in control here and it feels good. Her own warm glow settles inside her, blossoming and unfurling, filling her full of goodness. That's how she envisages it, like a flower in summer, coming into its own. Having everyone notice it because of how strong and beautiful it is.

A distant siren pierces her thoughts. She sits upright, ready for them. Ready to tell them her story, how she tried to wake the others before running downstairs and unlocking the front door. And then they will gather round her, awestruck by her bravery, telling her how wonderful and clever she is for doing that. Because she is. She created this situation, tried to save everybody, and people will love her for it, hailing her as a hero. Or a heroine. Because she is, after all, only a little girl, and girls are always heroines, aren't they? Especially her.

28

DEBORAH

The bump on my head must be far worse than I realised. I'm dizzy, a feeling of nausea rising in my gut as I stand staring out of the window at the vast pale sky, peering between the grime and zigzags of broken glass. We're still upstairs. What did I expect? It's obvious to me now. We were in the loft and we dropped down a level. This building clearly isn't a bungalow. We still need to get down to the ground floor before we can escape. We are both untied and able to get out of this place and now we're faced with yet another hurdle. Barrier after barrier after barrier. Is there no end to it?

I can feel blood, warm and sticky as it oozes down my face. I wipe it away, furious with myself for getting caught out like this. A schoolboy error. I was convinced we were on the ground floor, that we could clamber through one of these broken windows and make a run for it. We can't. Not unless we both want broken legs and shattered kneecaps. Life isn't like a movie, where we can jump from an upstairs window and sustain no injuries before pelting off into the wilderness where an army of police are waiting for us.

I punch at the broken glass, pulling shards of it free of the frame, and peer outside. We're pretty high up. I lean farther out and catch sight of a drainpipe. It looks rickety but it just might be our route out of here.

'I'm going to give it a go,' I say to Izzie and, without giving her time to tell me that it's a bad idea, I lean out and grab hold of the old black drainpipe.

I drape the upper half of my body around it and attempt to drag my legs out of the window frame, my wet trousers causing some resistance.

'Help me, Izzie! Lift up my legs and swing me round.'

She does as I ask but before I'm fully outside the drainpipe pulls away from the wall, the bolts holding it in place shearing and the pipe swinging free in my hands. I feel Izzie clutch on to my lower legs and let out a scream of frustration as the pipe topples to the floor with a crash.

'Shit!'

I hear Izzie behind me, panting and mumbling while she hoists me back in. I slump onto the floor and shake my head. 'It's too high to jump. If we try, we'll land on a concrete path that runs around the perimeter of the building. Christ almighty, we're doomed. We're going to die here, Izzie. We're going to fucking die in the shithole!'

'No,' she says quietly, 'we're not. We're going to escape, you and me. We're going to get out of here.'

'How, Izzie? How did she get out from here? We need to use the same way in and out that she did.' My voice is loud, wild with frustration and fury. One step forward, two steps back. My words echo around us, my anger evident.

'There.' She is pointing to a door in the corner of the large room. 'She went through that door over there.'

I take a shaky breath. It looks solid. Locked perhaps? I pray it isn't but know how she operates. With precision and malice. She won't be caught out without a fight. My cuts and bruises and aching bones are testament to that fact.

Izzie and I both march over towards it, my heart beating so fast I think I may pass out. Her hand grasps at it before mine, fingers curled around the old brass handle. She pulls hard. It's no surprise that it's locked. She continues to pull and rattle at it, frustration and sheer rage forcing her on.

'Shit, shit shit!'

I take a deep breath, try to still my thrashing heart telling myself we can do this. We can get out of here. I push away the negative thoughts that are doing their best to consume me. 'This isn't the end,' I say, my voice sounding relaxed and a damn sight calmer than I actually feel. 'It's an old door. We can shoulder barge it, the pair of us. Knock it off its hinges.'

Izzie taps at it with her knuckles, shakes her head despondently. 'You sure about that? It looks like solid oak to me.'

'This place is derelict. Has been for years. It's old and damp. The wood is probably rotten. Two of us can do this.' I look around, my eyes resting on a broken brick at the far side of the room. That's all we have. She's taken the shovel with her. She's a cold, calculating psychopath who has meticulously planned this whole thing – she isn't an idiot. 'Here,' I say, marching over and grasping at it with two hands. 'Try this. We'll be able to hack a hole in it with this in no time at all.'

The brick is cold and heavy and sharp as I lift it and batter it against the wooden panel of the door.

'See, told you,' Izzie murmurs, fresh tears springing into her eyes. 'Not a dent. Nothing at all. It's hopeless.'

I lean in closer for a better look. 'It isn't hopeless. We can't just sit here and do nothing! Look,' I say, pointing to the edge of the wood. 'I can see some scratches where I've hit it. Go and find something heavy and we'll both keep at it.'

She spins around, sniffing and rubbing at her eyes before bending down to pick up a sharp-looking stone as big as her fist.

'That's it!' I shout, no longer caring if anybody can hear us. No longer caring whether or not *she* can hear us. If she were to march through this door at this very moment, I would likely club her to death with this brick and smile while I did it. I am beyond following any laws or rules. Beyond any niceties and morals. I just want to go home.

Tears of frustration and weariness spill out of me as we both pummel the door with our small, heavy implements. I place the brick at my feet and charge at the door with my one working shoulder, letting out a roar as I hit it again and again and again. Nothing. Not a damn thing. No movement. Not even a creak or a splinter.

'What the hell is this?' I cry. 'An entire fucking tree blocking our path? Jesus Christ. This can't be happening!'

I want to slide down the door onto the floorboards, place my head in my hands and weep for an age, but I can't do that. I don't want Izzie to see me crack. She is looking to me for strength and a way out of here. I won't allow my determination and resolve to slip through the gaps in my veneer, leaking out of me and leaving me listless and weary. Good for nothing. A prisoner stuck here in this stinking hovel for evermore.

'We could try the windows again,' I suggest, already knowing that we're too high up and a leap would result in us breaking something, possibly even death.

Izzie steps away, my suggestion sailing over her head. She turns and runs at the door, kicking at it with her trainers. I watch for any kind of shifting or movement from it. Anything at all. I'm not sure if I imagined it but I could swear that I saw a crack of light at the bottom as she hit and kicked at it with her feet.

I join in, running and kicking, using the brick, my shoulder, anything at all to move this fucking huge door and get out of here. There is definitely something: some sort of give at the other side.

'What if we manage to move this one and then there's another padlocked one downstairs? What then?' Izzie says, her voice thick with tears and exhaustion.

'Then we do the unthinkable and climb out of the window. We punch out the glass, pray for our lives and we get the hell out of here!' I mean every word. I don't care if I snag and tear at my own flesh. I don't care if I end up with lifelong scars and stitches and limbs that are so permanently damaged, they won't work properly any more. I am leaving this place far behind me, never to return. This isn't who I am. I won't let this episode of my life own me any more. I am Deborah Wilton. Not a prisoner. Not a captive. Not a person stuck in this place waiting for death to arrive. I *will* get out of here. Maybe not today, but I will do it with Izzie by my side, the pair of us making a dash for freedom from this unimaginable pit of hell.

_____

29

She is surrounded, faces all around her, voices placating, soothing and assuring her that everything is going to be just fine. Which it is. She knows that. She is still alive. Everything is better than fine.

The house is gone. Nobody has told her as much but she is able to see by its blackened windows and charred bricks that nothing remains of it. It's gutted. Her childhood home, gone up in smoke. Turned to a pile of ash. The stink is overwhelming, filling her nostrils, her throat, causing her eyes to sting and her flesh to itch. It clings to her clothes, making her smell like a bonfire. Like the one they had at Brownies when they went camping that time last summer. She had been fascinated by fire back then too, how the flames flickered and spat, how they made everyone just that little bit fearful and cautious, their eyes darting about whenever anybody got too close to the blaze. She didn't feel fearful. She was captivated by it, enamoured by its power and ferocity, enthralled by its potential. It stuck with her, that day, that bonfire, the feelings that popped and fizzed in her veins as she sat and watched it while all the other children grew bored and wandered off to play childish games that held no interest for her. It was a sensation that took hold deep in her belly. It grew and grew until she couldn't hold it off any longer. She had to do it. She had to scratch that itch. To set that spark going and watch it burn and burn, eating and destroying everything in its path.

And now it has. Fire always conquers everything. She knew it would happen. There is an unexpected emotion present in her bones, settling there like thick black tar. She can't quite pin it down or put a name to it. It's only later when she is taken to hospital and settled in a lovely warm bed in a room of her own that it comes to her, what it is that she is feeling, this lovely sensation that she couldn't quite name – satisfaction. That's what it is. Satisfaction and a feeling of happiness that swirls around her in an invisible mist. All this attention, all these people wanting to talk to her. It's fun. No. More than that. It's pleasurable. Delightful. It makes her feel warm inside, her own little furnace roaring away beneath her ribcage, firing up her senses, travelling up her spine until it explodes in her brain, stars bursting, glitter spreading through her limbs, making her feel special and wanted and important. She's never felt anything like it before and wants it to continue, for it to never ever stop.

The hospital is busy, nurses chattering away, trolleys rattling past full of metal and plastic things that bounce and shake about. The noise never seems to end, but she doesn't mind that. Every so often, somebody will peer into her room, checking she's okay, asking her if she wants anything. She has all she needs right here – warmth, attention, a constant stream of strange visitors checking everything is just fine with her.

Outside, a long blur of orange and yellow pierces the darkness, lines of street lights snaking through the murkiness, petering out as they reach the hills in the distance. Sirens blare, ambulances transporting the injured and dying to hospital. They come and go all night long. It sets her pulse racing. She is in the heart of it here. This is where it's all happening. All these people, these figures of authority, showering her with attention and care and kindness. She cannot get enough of it.

There's another lady as well who has been talking to her. A social worker. She has no idea what one of those is, but they have given her one and she likes the idea of that too. Everyone is here for her, telling her that they're going to help take care of her. All because of the fire. They haven't mentioned how brave she is yet, but they will. She can sense it. They need to check she's okay first, not hurt or injured. Then the praise and adulation will come. And when it does, her life will be as perfect as it can possibly be.

30

YVONNE

The morning dragged past, every second a minute, every minute an hour. Concentration was hard for me, something I usually excel at. Things rattled around my brain. Things I couldn't seem to shake. The team-building issue preyed on my mind. I had to get out of it, this pathetic evening palaver. My time is precious and I refuse to hand it over to near strangers without a fight.

But now I'm away from it, out of the office, a feeling of freedom at being absent from my desk slowly unfolds in my chest, blooming beneath my skin. I gave Ruth my opinion of her silly idea before I left, telling her it was akin to bullying, forcing people to spend time away from their homes and families when they had other commitments. Her face flushed a deep shade of crimson, a mesh of humiliation spreading over her chest and up her neck.

'I'll give it some serious thought,' she said as I moved away.

'Please do,' I half shouted. 'Otherwise you might just find yourself with a whole host of vacant hotel rooms and a hefty bill for something that isn't getting used. Because I certainly won't be there and neither will half the people in this office.'

I could hear her gasp of embarrassment and anxiety as I hurried past, grabbed at my coat and slipped it on before dashing out of the door and down the stairs.

The traffic in town is a never-ending stream. All of these people on their way to somewhere else, hindering my progress when all I want to do is get home. Each car, each bus, each large, cumbersome van that obstructs my view ahead, is an obstacle, all of them stopping me, doing their utmost to slow me down.

The bouquet of flowers on the passenger seat rolls about as I take a corner too sharply. Water drips onto the floor in tiny spherical splashes. I lean over and place the flowers in an upright position towards the back of the seat, their stems pressed up against the headrest. They need to be perfect for when I take them to Deirdre, not a mushed-up mess of petals and wet stems. She wouldn't like that at all. Aunt Deirdre was all about perfection, keeping things neat and tidy. A place for everything and everything in its place. Nothing like me. I learnt to adapt as time went on. But it wasn't always easy. Being pristine has never been one of my fortes but I was always ready to try, to be the best I could be for her. She deserved that much after taking me in. Being orphaned at such a young age and uprooted to a new home with somebody I barely knew was bound to have an effect on me. I think I've turned out pretty well given the circumstances. Things could have been a whole lot worse. I could have ended up in a foster home or a children's home, somewhere totally alien where I felt like an unwanted addition, a person that didn't belong, but I didn't. I ended up with Deirdre. She cared for me, did her best.

I gnaw at my bottom lip, my teeth grinding at my own flesh.

There were times, however, when even that didn't feel good enough. There was a hole in my life that she wasn't capable of filling. A family-sized hole.

I shake away those thoughts, focus on the road ahead and set my mind to the things that I've got planned for when I get home. Delving into the past isn't always the best idea. Not today. Perhaps not any day.

The lights change to red and the car stalls before I'm able to drive through. I curse under my breath, feel my temper begin to flare; people in vehicles, passers-by, even inanimate objects are all working against me. My fingers are heavy on the steering wheel as I tap out a dull rhythm. This is meant to be an easy afternoon. No work. And yet the day is now beginning to feel heavy, the sensation of near happiness that was blossoming within me rapidly dying and rotting away, like blooms in autumn, ruined by their harsh environment, perishing because of a lack of light. I try to push away the darkness that has started to envelop me but it's always hard to shake them off, these moments of fathomless despair. These white-hot flashes of fury. Anger presses down on me, rushes up and down my spine, brushes against my skin, creeps and slithers its way through my pores beneath my flesh and into the marrow of my bones.

Behind me a horn blares, then another one. And then another. The lights have turned to green. People are waiting for me to move. I should put my foot down, drive away as fast as I can. But I don't. The nearby noise intensifies my mood, thickening it. The beeping of horns, the shouting, the frantic gesticulating from other drivers forces me out of my car and onto the pavement. Blood roars in my ears, thumps against my skull. I glance around, fists furled, eyes narrowed as curious pedestrians stop to observe the unfolding drama. I give them

what they want, upping my anger levels so it's obvious for all
to see.

'Had a good look, have you?' I bark at a middle-aged man
who is standing close by, a bulbous carrier bag clutched
between his white bony fingers. He shakes his head and walks
away.

I march to the car behind me and bang on the driver's side.
A young guy winds down the window, his thin, wiry goatee
beard reminding me of a teenage boy attempting to look like a
grown man. He's slim, his skin a deep shade of sunbed orange.
He's wearing cream chinos and a too-tight pale blue T-shirt.
The sight of him sitting there with a half-smile on his face irritates me beyond reason. An image of me driving my fist into his
face loiters in my mind, blood spattering over his perfect
clothes and the pristine interior of his vehicle, small splashes of
red everywhere.

'The lights are on green now. You need to move your arse,
missus.' He's holding his palm over the horn like some sort of
threat and he is grinning, a row of gleaming white teeth just
visible behind his thick, rubbery lips.

I feel the red mist begin to lower even further, try to stop it,
and fail miserably. It drops down, trapping me. I'm unstoppable
now, all reasoning evaporated.

'Driving your dad's car, are you? You stupid little prick.' The
words are out before I can stop them, a long line of expletives
that should have stayed in my head. I can't seem to help it, my
untethered anger driving me on. 'Maybe if stupid fucking idiots
like you weren't allowed to drive, then the roads would be a far
more pleasant place to be. As it is, we have to put up with arse-
holes like you, driving everywhere as if they own the frigging
road!'

I take a step back, lift up my foot and slam it into the side of his door. Not once but twice. 'Now why don't you take your stupid fucking car and shove it up your arse!'

Without waiting to see the look on his face or hear his reply, I open the door of my own vehicle, slide in, slip it into gear and drive off at speed. Behind me, in my rear-view mirror, I can see him as he gets out to inspect the bodywork for any damage, his eyebrows arched, his shoulders hunched. There won't be anything to see. No scratches, no dents. Nothing at all. I'm wearing rubber-soled boots, not steel toecaps. He's lucky the only thing I hit was his car. He's lucky I didn't smash my fist into the side of his face and break his perfect little teeth. Today is his lucky day. He got off lightly.

My temper doesn't diminish on the drive home. If anything, it increases, a wave of fury clamping itself around my temple, thudding away at my brain like a gavel hitting solid stone. By the time I reach my driveway, I can barely think straight, so many thoughts whirling around my head, banging and colliding as they all vie for my attention.

I glance at the clock on the dashboard. Time – it is always against me, snatching away great chunks of my life and leaving me restless and jittery. I need to get these flowers in some water. I need to do lots of things this afternoon but before I do any of them, there is something that is nagging at me, an urge rippling just beneath the surface of my skin.

Inside the house, I place my bag, boots and coat at the bottom of the stairs, drop the bouquet in the sink and fill it with water, then head upstairs where I throw off my clothes and pull on my running gear. This is what I need to shake off these feelings of anger and hurt and frustration. Why are some people so determined to go against me? They seem hell-bent on stopping any progress I try to make, throwing hurdles in my way, making my life more difficult than it needs to be.

I tie up my hair, pick up a few extra items and head outside where the air suddenly feels fresh and welcoming, a stark contrast to the stuffy atmosphere of the office and the recirculated exhaust fumes I pull into my lungs when driving. This is bracing, a break from the rat race, a break from the outside world.

The grass sways in a soothing and majestic rhythm, long waves of pale green moving like a line of dancers as I set off, the reassuring heft of my backpack a solid reminder that the world isn't always a threatening place to be. A reminder that I am the one in control of my own destiny. I have the power to make or break my future. All I need to do is keep my head, not let my temper leak out over trivial situations and spoil everything.

Up ahead, I see it, my route, the familiar territory that calls out to me, pulling me on, helping me to feel alive. A place where I am able to throw off the shackles and drudgery of my day-to-day existence and be the real me, the one who is glad to be alive.

31

ADRIAN

It's off. They've cancelled the night at the hotel. I stare at the email and have mixed emotions. For all I don't want to take part in this stupid idea or spend the night in a plush hotel that reeks of money, seeing something that was promised snatched away before I've had a chance to fully dismiss it feels like an insult. After all, and it pains me deeply to even think this let alone admit it to anybody else, I have nothing else going on in my sad little life. Pathetic, that's what I am. A pathetic little nobody. All my friends over the years have fallen away. Alcohol was the only thing that bound us together. Pals from the pub who weren't really pals at all. They were drinking buddies, people who happened to prop up the same bar that I did night after night, that's all they were. We had nothing else in common. Most of them didn't even know where I lived. All they knew about me was what sort of beer I drank, which football team I supported and the fact that I was single and lived alone. That's it. A shallow existence full of 2D acquaintances. Even Beth has seen through me and my pointless life. The damaged girl from damaged town has sprouted wings and flown away. I'm alone now. Alone and perhaps even lonely.

Jesus. Talk about fucking melancholic. I take a swig of hot coffee and swallow it down, enjoying the burning sensation as it sears my gullet, landing in my stomach, the spread of boiling liquid helping to kick away the feelings of misery. I need to stop this. Fancy getting so bloody morose over a cancelled work commitment.

'I thought that with the backlash, it was for the best.' Ruth is walking towards me, her face devoid of emotion.

She's looking to me for support, some sort of reassurance that she hasn't pissed off half the workforce. I'm not really in the mood for bolstering somebody else's feelings today. Ruth probably earns more than me. She's a big girl, she can handle this on her own.

'You're probably right. Best keep it as a day thing, eh? Then nobody has to make extra plans or tell their other half they'll be away for the night, living it up while their partners are stuck at home watching crap TV with a bag of crisps and a cheap bottle of wine for company.'

Ruth doesn't react, her feelings well hidden behind a mask of impassivity.

'I need to ask you a favour, Ade.' She is almost whispering, her body language furtive as she swings her head around to see if anybody else is listening in.

My skin prickles with apprehension. What now? And why me? Do I look like the sort of guy who enjoys having to shoulder the troubles of everybody around them?

Ruth doesn't wait for me to reply or agree, carrying on as if this thing is a fait accompli. As if I will agree wholeheartedly without putting any real thought into it. Is this because I backed her idea earlier? Does she now consider us allies?

'This thing tomorrow – will you try to make sure everybody enjoys it? I know I shouldn't be asking, but I'm under a lot of pressure to raise morale in the office since Deborah's disappearance. I realise this isn't going to bring her back but the least we can do is try to stick together and act as a team, don't you agree?'

I find myself nodding, not because I agree with her but because, like the coward I am, I don't know what else to say or do in return. I wonder if she's asking others to do the same or has singled me out because I initially backed her idea of the hotel business. Not that it matters because we both know that I'll do as she asks, blindly following her request. Ruth would never approach Allison or Merriel to do this, both of them too confident and mouthy to go along with it. She probably wouldn't approach Yvonne, who is too reserved to be the type to gee everyone else on. Which leaves me. I should feel flattered really. And yet I don't. What I feel is pressured. The others think me young and inexperienced. Like they're going to take notice of anything I say anyway.

'That's great,' she says, already moving away now I've bowed to her pressure. 'Thank you. I think this thing is going to turn out just fine after all.'

And with that, she is gone, bustling back to her office, closing the door behind her with the gentlest of clicks. Typical Ruth, managing to appear timid and unassuming while also managing to offload all of her burdens and tasks onto somebody else. Passive-aggressive, that's what she is. And I'm her useless, cowardly partner, too unassuming and stupid to refuse her demands.

In my pocket, I feel my phone begin to buzz. I slip it out, the weight of disappointment at my own ineptitude and cowardice a heavy force that is pressing down on me. It's there, glowing at me – Beth's name. A message. She's finally made contact. The dread that usually sits in the base of my stomach at the sight of her name isn't there. I feel something that I never thought I would feel at the thought of communicating with her – happiness and joy. She's back in my life and what upsets and pleases me in equal measure is the fact that I am actually experiencing those feelings. This is how far my life has fallen. How far *I* have fallen. I've become the person who looks to the local loser for friendship and support.

Sorry, Ade. Been off on one doing a bit of thinking. Fancy meeting up at the weekend?

I reply straight away, aware of how sad and pitiful that looks, telling her that I'll call round and pick her up on Saturday and we'll take a walk into town.

Cool. See you then. Lots to tell you. Beth x

And that's it. My mood has already lightened. I can't work out whether I'm a sad old twat or just easily pleased, but either way, Beth is back in my life and I'm hoping that this time she will manage to hold herself together.

I turn back to my computer screen, everything that little bit easier to bear. Even the dreaded team-building day doesn't feel like such an onerous undertaking. Outside, the sun makes an unexpected appearance, peering out from behind a gathering of clouds the colour of gunmetal. Warm amber rays spread over my desk, a small blanket of contentment in what was, up until now, a dull and joyless day.

Even this ridiculous event tomorrow doesn't faze me. Beth is back, and regardless of how difficult or overbearing she is, regardless of how much energy she sucks out of me, I'm glad of it.

'See you tomorrow.' Merriel passes me, a look on her face that I can't quite define.

'Tomorrow? Where you off to so early?' I'm tempted to make a joke about her suddenly being part-time but something about her mood, her body language, stops me. Now doesn't feel like the right moment for frivolous sarcastic comments.

She stops, turning to glance at me before letting out a long, tremulous sigh. 'Problems at home. Need to get back to sort it out.'

'Oh. Anything I can help with?' I would like to help if I could but, if I'm being honest, I'm also curious. We all know so little about each other. Maybe I was right and Merriel does have some issues with a violent partner. I really hope not. Merriel and I may not be the best of friends but nobody deserves to live with someone who beats them to a pulp on a regular basis.

'Not really.' She sits down beside me and lowers her voice to a whisper. 'I've not told Ruth so please keep it to yourself. I've got family staying over and they're causing me loads of problems.'

'Is it anything to do with your eye?'

She nods and looks away. 'I've got two sisters and things are... difficult at the minute. I thought it would all be okay but it turns out that they're more selfish than I ever realised.'

'I'm sorry to hear that.' And I am. Families can be a horrible burden. Forget the families that ooze love and happiness and long-standing commitment to each other, there are those, like mine, that ooze toxicity and violence and the other many endless problems that substance abuse and addiction can bring. 'If you need to talk, you know where I am.'

Merriel nods and moves away, her features and body all angular and defensive. I hope she works it out, I really do. We all deserve some peace in our lives. Even Merriel.

I turn back to my computer, open the folder that contains the latest quotes from our main supplier and get back to work.

32

DEBORAH

She's on her way over here. I can see her through the grime and dust that clings to the window, pockets of visibility amidst the years of accumulated filth. The same window that may as well have bars at it for all the use it is. We're just too damn high to risk jumping. A fractured skull, broken legs or death. They would be probable if we attempted it.

I stare down at her, knowing she wouldn't stay away for too long. She's like an addict and we are her fix, her ability to remain parted from us for long periods of time, an impossible task. I wonder what she plans on doing when she gets here? This could be our chance. We're untied and there are two of us against one. I might be weak and weary but I've still got plenty of fight left in me, and Izzie, although scared, is a force to be reckoned with. I feel stronger, both mentally and physically, now we're no longer tied up in that attic. I can see daylight and although I still have no idea where we are, just being able to view the sky and nearby fields has given my morale a much-needed boost. We're almost there, Izzie and me. We're so close to getting out of here. I can feel it in my bones, a sudden surge of strength and positivity that is pulsing through me. We also have the brick and the rock. If we are to use them, we'd have to make sure she didn't get her hands on them, using them against us.

'She's coming back!' Izzie is standing next to me, fear springing from her, her body braced for what is coming next.

She needs to be stronger than this, more resilient and as tough as she can be if we're to get out of here. Her weaknesses and terror will be spotted almost immediately and used against her. She will be manipulated and preyed upon and I cannot let that happen. I have to get to her first, bolster her and make her see that she is a capable woman and as strong as the one who is holding us here against our will.

'Right, this is what we're going to do,' I say, surprised at the power in my tone, the strength of my voice and words as if I know what we are actually going to do, which I don't. I'm making it up as I go along, hoping inspiration and a sprinkling of good luck will help me with what we're about to be faced with.

Izzie is suddenly watching me intently, her eyes fixed on mine, a glimmer of hope evident in her penetrative gaze. I pray for some sort of assistance because we really need it. Outside, I can see that she is carrying something. A stash of weapons perhaps? Something she can use to overpower the pair of us? My head begins to pound, my heart thrashes and squirms around my chest, knocking at my ribcage like a battering ram. I take a few deep breaths and try to steady myself.

'We're going to wait until she unlocks the door and then we're going to charge at her and knock her down the stairs. One huge push and she will easily topple backwards. Two of us and only one of her. We can do this, yes?'

I don't know that we can do this, am riddled with doubt, but

I am doing my best to sound positive, as if I know exactly how this is going to play out. It's what Izzie needs to hear. It's what *I* need to hear.

'Yes,' she says, her voice a whisper, her face furrowed with trepidation.

She's frightened. I get that. I'm frightened too but my need to get out of here is greater than my fear. She is, after all, just a woman like us. She's not a superhero with magnificent powers. She is just another ordinary person.

'We can do this, Izzie. We really can. In a couple of minutes, we could be pelting across those fields and heading towards the nearest place that will help us. We'll scream and shout and tell the world what she's done, and all the while she'll be laid on the floor concussed, hopefully even half-dead with blood pouring from her head.'

I am holding Izzie's hand. Her flesh is cold and soft. I watch as a lone tear rolls out of her eye and travels down her cheek, coming to rest on her jawbone.

She nods and exhales, a trembling sigh escaping from her throat before smiling and letting out a small laugh of relief. 'You're right. I'm just so tired. I can't see any end to this. Do you really think we'll get out of here? Is it actually going to happen?'

'I know it is, Izzie. I fucking know it is.'

'I hate her, y'know. I mean, I really fucking hate her with every fibre of my being. I'd gladly see her hang.'

'Me too,' I reply, my mind still focused on how we will manage to overpower her. I don't want to get bogged down with any thoughts or emotions that don't involve getting out of here.

I look again outside to see she has disappeared out of sight. 'Quick,' I whisper. 'We haven't got much time. She's on her way up here.'

Dragging Izzie by the hand, we tiptoe to the locked door

and stand to one side of it, our backs flush against the bare brick wall. I place my finger to my lips to quieten Izzie's muffled breaths and squeeze her hand. As if in slow motion, the door opens inwards just a few inches. I steel myself, ready to hurl my entire body at her. A huge metronome thunders away in my chest, the noise filling my head, making me dizzy. There is a low shuffling sound and before either of us can do anything the door is pulled closed again. I shriek, grab at the handle and twist it but already I can hear the loud click of the lock from the other side.

'What the fuck?' My voice is a shrill echo.

'Look,' Izzie says quietly, her eyes lowered to the floor. 'Down there.' She is pointing, her outstretched finger shaking.

A small package sits at our feet. Fuck! We were both so focused on looking straight ahead, preparing ourselves, readying our bodies for the final big push that we didn't even think to lower our gazes and work out what was being surreptitiously slid inside.

I fight back tears. Crying is pointless. A waste of time and energy, something that is in short supply around here.

I lean towards one of the broken windows and scream out into the open space around us. 'Bitch! You fucking maniac!'

There's nobody around. A row of tiny houses in the distance but, apart from that, nothing at all. Not a soul around to hear us. The ground looks so far away. The more I consider it, the more likely it is we would die if we attempted to jump.

'It's food,' Izzie says, squatting beside the small parcel wrapped in muslin cloth. 'And a bottle of water.' She picks it up, screws the top off and holds it out for me to drink. 'Here,' she says, eyes suddenly full of hope. 'We're going to need something to keep us going.'

'No!' I snatch the water out of her hands and glare at her.

'Don't you see what she's doing? This food, the water, it's full of drugs. That's how she got us here in the first place. Don't touch any of it! One sip of this or a bite of that sandwich and we'll be flat out in no time and then she'll be back up here to tie us up again.'

Izzie lets out a small shriek, her hand fluttering up to her neck, her fingers tapping against her throat. 'God, I'm such an idiot. Such a fucking stupid klutz. I didn't even think...'

'It's fine,' I say a little too sharply. 'It's fine, really. I just need a little bit of time to think.'

There isn't any way out of here other than jumping from these upstairs windows and risking smashing both of our legs or breaking our necks. And yet, I can't see a different route out.

'Next time she comes back, I guess she'll be expecting to find us flat out after eating and drinking this lot then?' Izzie is holding up a ham sandwich and staring at it as if it's a lab specimen. 'I guess we'll have to drink out of that toilet upstairs then?'

The thought of it makes me shudder. How long can a person go without fluid? I seem to remember reading somewhere that three to four days is the limit. Without fluid, our brains begin to shrink. We suffer headaches and eventually our organs shut down. Just three or four short days is very probably all it takes for a lack of water to kill us. I'm not going to let it happen. Not here and not like that. But what are we going to do to survive? Jesus Christ, what has happened to my life? What the hell have I become?

Outside, clouds begin to gather. I don't know what day it is or what time it is. I wish I was more practical, able to work out which direction the sun is facing, whether it is rising or setting. I'm tired, disorientated and lacking in any kind of Boy Scout skills that will enable me to work out whether the day has begun or whether it will soon draw to a close. I stand in silence, watching. Waiting. Seconds pass, turning into a minute or possibly even two. I blink and realise that it's starting to get dark out there. An incremental change to the amount of light with greyness slowly edging in. Regardless of angry rain clouds that mask any natural daylight, I know that it's actually dusk which means that soon it will be pitch-black.

A tension of opposites sits within me: a clawing need to get out of here versus a sense of hopelessness so deep it has no end. Continually thinking about it is exhausting.

I turn away, doing my damnedest to hide my stricken expression and the tears that are threatening to spill out. I don't want Izzie to see me like this. I'm meant to be the strong one around here, the one who props her up when it all gets to be too much for her. And now I'm on a downward spiral, everything spinning out of control. And I'm not sure I will ever be able to get any of it back.

* * *

I wake up, a noise dragging me out of my torpor. It's dark. Izzie and I are laid next to one another on the mattress. We talked and talked after the food package was left and decided to wait until it was light before we made any more attempts to get out of here. I've not slept particularly well, always on edge in case I woke up to find her standing over me, rope in hand, and we ended up back where we were, bound and gagged. Back to square one.

My head thumps as I sit up, groping around until I orient myself and am able to see through the murkiness to the far end of the room. Something has been placed next to the door. Another food package? I wish I had a watch, something to give me an idea of what time it is.

I scramble over there and tear open the brown paper wrapper to be faced with the same thing – more food wrapped in muslin. Peppered with drugs, no doubt. It all looks so tempting. My stomach is hollow and I am incredibly thirsty. We need to get out of here today. A few more days without water and we're dead.

Why did she not come in, presuming we had eaten and drunk the other little picnic she left for us? She saw us laid out, silent. Why didn't she creep in and gag us again? What exactly is her plan now?

I lean back against the wall, a dizzy spell forcing me backwards, the ache of my bones an intense pain that has no end. We're so close to getting out of here. So close and yet still so very far away. I ask myself the same question over and over, whispering it to myself under my breath as Izzie continues to sleep on.

What is she going to do next?

33

YVONNE

It's dark out, the world shrouded in a blackness that swallows everything. I pull off my running head torch and stop by the fence that borders the perimeter of the woods, my breath curling into little tendrils in the bleak autumnal air. I love it here. I love its rugged beauty and the rough terrain and even its ambience of mild peril at this hour of the morning when there's nobody around to assist should anything untoward happen. Dog walkers rarely take this route, the risk of falling over broken branches and piles of stones too great for them. They tend to stick to the main path when it's dark which suits me just fine. I did used to bump into another jogger round these parts. We would give one another an affable nod and a knowing smile, as if we were in some sort of fraternity. She no longer takes this route but I have continued on with it, its familiarity affording me some comfort, allowing me the headspace to think clearly.

Laying the flowers at Deirdre's grave yesterday unnerved me. It always does, memories bubbling up to the surface and knocking me off-kilter as I stand there saying a silent prayer to the woman who tried her best for a child who couldn't always comprehend the world around her. For all it comforts me, that annual ritual of visiting her graveside, it also leaves me feeling out of sorts, my past a constant reminder that sometimes our innate emotions and attributes won't ever leave us. They linger, like the cold fingers of death, always waiting to drag us back to those dark places that scare us. I didn't wait until the weekend to do it. I have other things to do.

It's as if her death brings all those recollections back – the way she died doing something she loved – that day, that walk up in the hills along a stony ridge. That terrible fall.

I bat away my misgivings and regrets, lift the flask to my lips, take a swig of water, put my head torch back on and turn to the rough path that will lead me back home. The sky ahead is gradually lightening, a small purplish hue just visible above the spread of the North Yorkshire hills. Roseberry Topping is a pimple at this distance. This is why I run and this is why I take this route. Close to home but isolated enough to let me do my thing, for me to be alone and gather my thoughts into a manageable bundle before the rest of the world wakes up and goes about their day. A hot shower beckons before I prepare myself for what lies ahead.

* * *

Here we go. It's finally here. The show of making out that we care about each other in Deborah's absence, pushing forward the notion that we're working as a team and her disappearance has pulled us all closer together. Which it hasn't. Nothing has changed around here. Why would it? We're still the same people with the same issues and problems. Somebody hasn't suddenly waved a magic wand over the office and relieved us of all our worries and anxieties even though Ruth would have everyone believe that. It's the same team, working alongside each other in the same office doing the same tasks day after day after day. Except for today. Today, we're visiting a conference room in a large hotel in town and we're going to play stupid games with each other. One day and all our problems and past issues will be solved. We'll return to the office on Monday as changed people, our work output vastly improved, any friction between us a thing of the past. How wonderful. How politically correct. How ridiculously naïve.

Getting here this morning proved more difficult than I would have liked. I had to move heaven and earth and leave extra early to get a parking spot in town and to avoid the dense traffic. I didn't want to get embroiled in another altercation with another driver. I hadn't the stomach for it. Not today. And I couldn't face public transport, being forced to sit alongside an army of strangers, everyone scrambling for a seat, each of us avoiding eye contact, our gazes cast downward as the world speeds by.

It was still extraordinarily early when I set off. I hate fumbling about in the darkness, that cloying sensation of doing half a job because it's too dim to see properly. It makes me jittery, leaves me feeling on edge. There were so many things I wanted to do before I left, tasks left undone that I considered important. Too late now. I'm here. Whether I want to be or not.

I lock up my car and head across the car park towards the main entrance, my trainers squeaking against the tarmac. Allison and Adrian are already inside, their indistinct figures a dark blur through the frosted glass. I glance around, see nobody else I know – no Merriel, no Ruth – and decide to head into the reception area, perhaps grab a coffee before this charade kicks off.

'Morning. How was your drive in?' Allison winks at me and for a minute I feel sure she knows about my previous quarrel with the other driver. Did somebody see me? Has word got around that I suffer from road rage and now everyone is having a giggle at my expense?

'Fine,' I reply, my manner starch-like, my expression and voice frosty.

She turns away and I am sure I hear her say the words, *suit yourself*, but can't be entirely certain, so instead walk to the vending machine at the far side of the room and dip my hand into my pocket for loose change.

'Sorry, it's out of order.'

The voice echoes across the reception area. A young woman who looks as if she is barely out of school is watching me, her glossy blonde hair impossibly straight, her face so pale and heavily made-up it appears to be chiselled out of alabaster, her foundation applied with a trowel and smoothed out with a paintbrush.

'Out of order? There's no sign saying that?' I try to sound unruffled but my temper is fraying, bits of me coming undone.

'It's only just stopped working. A technician is on his way but he won't be here until later this morning.' She is smiling at me, her teeth glaring like tiny little spears, white and incongruous against her glossy scarlet mouth.

I visualise myself running over to her and slamming her head against the marble desk, hearing it crack, seeing those teeth fly out from between her perfectly painted lips, then stop myself. I have to keep this under control, the cracks and splinters in my character. This isn't me. It's not what people expect to see from me. I'm a calm person, a reasonable individual with a strong moral compass. What have I become?

Tears bite at the back of my eyelids. I blink them away, the need to readjust myself suddenly an all-important task.

'It's not a problem,' I reply, my mouth forming a rictus. 'I'm sure there'll be plenty available once we get in there.'

'Oh, you're with the Haswell & Sons group? I think your morning break is at 10.30 a.m. That's when the refreshments are booked for.' She runs her finger over the small iPad propped up on the desk in front of her, a low hum coming from between her pursed lips as she concentrates, her eyes sluggishly scooting over the screen. 'Yes, there you are. Definitely 10.30 for coffee. Biscuits as well,' she says breezily, as if this small nugget of information will ease my immediate burning need for caffeine.

'But there's nothing before then? No more vending machines? No staff around to serve coffee?'

'There's a café over the road.' Her long red talons point towards the automatic doors and over the traffic-congested road to a tiny sliver of a place jammed in between two old, large buildings that practically swallow it whole. 'I'm sure they open up early and do takeaway coffee. Maybe you could try there?'

I want to shake some sense into her, to tell her that the customer is always right and that the very least she can do is get me and my colleagues a cup of damn coffee, that my company is helping to pay her wages. But I don't. I smile benignly, give her a cursory nod and walk away but not before I hear her call after me, her young voice a thin strand of venom designed to catch me off guard. 'Of course, you're all going to be craving that coffee once you've reached the top of the climbing wall. I saw them setting it up earlier and all I can say is good luck, because you're going to need it.'

I swear I see her grinning as she turns her back to me and slips through an archway into a back room and out of sight.

34

ADRIAN

'You've got to be kidding, right? This has got to be one big fucking joke?'

I stare up at the immense simulated wall of rock in front of me, my stomach sinking to my boots. The footholds are an array of multicoloured pegs jutting out from the plastic grey rock face. It's meant to look harmless, appealing and fun. It looks like hell. I can't do this. I won't. All my latent fears scramble to the surface, bubbling within me like boiling oil.

'Oh, come on, Ade. Don't tell me you're scared? I thought a young lad like you would be right into this climbing malarkey. I booked this with you in mind!'

I can't bring myself to look at Ruth, at her expectant gaze and faux jovial manner. What the fuck was she thinking, expecting us all to take part in something as taxing and, quite frankly, as juvenile as this? I'm a buyer in an engineering firm, not a bloody athlete. Merriel is probably clapping her hands with glee at the sight of it. Even Yvonne looks fit enough to scale it without missing a beat, but me? I'd rather dig out my own eyeballs with a blunt spoon than set foot on this fucking great monstrosity. And now, I have to risk losing face by refusing to take part. Either that, or I face my greatest fear, get myself hooked up to the harness and climb up there. Today is going to be one big bloody nightmare. I can just sense it. Every bone in my body is screaming at me to turn around and leave, every muscle and sinew straining to walk away from this place. Yet I can't. I'm here and, whether I like it or not, I have to take part.

My eyes sweep across the room. Allison is looking up at the wall, her face blank and expressionless. I wonder if she is some sort of fitness freak with hidden strengths who will scale it in seconds, or is she, like me, staring up at it, her stomach a mass of hot swirling liquid at the thought of having to go up there? And then there's Yvonne who looks as if she is ready to slap somebody, her face flushed, her eyes dark and angry-looking. Merriel seems to be the only one who is sizing it up, ready to head up there without breaking a sweat, although even she looks on edge, her eyes darting around the room like a cornered animal ready to lash out and pounce before looking back to the cartoon-like rock face, her neck craning upwards at the sheer scale of it.

'Scared of heights, then?' Ruth has inched closer to me, is nudging me affably, her eyes twinkling with good humour. I want to push her away, to tell her to fuck right off and that maybe she should set a good example by going first. But not before I loosen her harness and watch her fall. I swat that thought away. Cruel and unnecessary. Yet the sight of Ruth sailing through the air, limbs flailing, eyes bulging with terror, lingers in my mind. The sound her body makes as she hits the floor, her spine breaking in half, like the crack of a whip.

'Yes and no.' I'm not prepared to reveal my dread, to show everyone my innermost fears. 'Probably as much as the next person.' My voice is husky. I can't look at her. I won't give her the satisfaction of seeing through the cracks in my armour to the soft, frightened boy underneath. To the soft, frightened boy who was held upside down over a bridge by his drunken brute of a father. I remember it as if it were yesterday – the blackness beneath me, the cold wind lapping around my face, the sudden rush of blood to my head. The absolute unutterable terror that he would let go and I would be enveloped by that dark, icy water, the swell of the current carrying me downstream as I gurgled and struggled to breathe before succumbing to the inevitable, death taking me before my rightful time.

'I'm looking forward to seeing you scaling it like a feral cat,' she says, thinking her words are droll and amusing. Expecting me to join in with her unsophisticated wit and rough-edged attempts at humour. She's about as funny as a dose of the clap.

'We can hold hands on the way up, Ruth. You and me scaling this thing together, eh? The pair of us setting an example and all that? After all,' I say, trying to keep the animosity I feel for her out of my voice, 'you need to show us all how it's done since this was your idea. I mean, you can't expect other people to do something that you would never do yourself, can you?'

I enjoy watching the colour leach from her face, am delighted to see a tremble take hold on her bottom lip as she replies.

'Ordinarily I would jump at the chance but I'm here today to organise and facilitate this whole thing. Somebody needs to be in charge here, Adrian. We can't all join in with the fun, you know!'

At this moment in time, I would gladly push her to the floor. For all I like Ruth, and I do, right now I find her condescending manner both irritating and downright insulting. Who does she think we are – a class of blank-minded schoolchildren awaiting her instructions before we're allowed to go about our next set of tasks? Can she not see by our scowling faces that each and every one of us is here under duress?

'I know I can count on you for a bit of support though. I mean, you were the one who said you wouldn't have minded staying overnight to extend the session.' She is smiling up at me, her small eyes twinkling with hope. 'And you also agreed to chivvy everyone else along, didn't you? We're in this together, Ade. You and me. We're a team, right?'

Stupid me. Stupid, stupid Adrian for trying to be the peacemaker and keep everyone happy. It's what I do. Avoid conflict after a childhood riddled with it. I've witnessed enough fights and arguments to fill an entire lifetime and have no desire to see any more. And yet, there is an anger building up inside of me at the thought of being forced to scale this fucking huge wall. Risking my life on one of these things isn't on my radar and never will be. Let those who've had an easy, sedentary life take all the risks. I've had more than my fair share. Enough for everybody in the room.

'You do know that you'll be clipped on to a safety harness, don't you?' She leans in and taps me on the arm affectionately. 'I mean, after all, we don't want to lose our best members of staff, do we?'

Her giggle is a shrill childish squawk that makes my flesh crawl. I want to run at her and smack her in the face, pull at her hair, make her cry. Anything to vent my anger. To release my deepest fears.

'Right, everybody,' she says loudly, moving away from me and striding towards the middle of the room. 'We just need to run through a few housekeeping rules before I let our hosts take over. Ron and Dave here who run the climbing wall company will talk you through our first task and show you the ropes.' A pause as she waits for her joke to be applauded. An awkward silence ensues, a toe-curling moment that makes me squirm with embarrassment on Ruth's behalf. 'So,' she says, quickly skirting around the moment with a clap of her hands, 'let's get the day started with me telling you that a fire alarm isn't planned for today, so if you do hear it go off, then we need to evacuate through the fire doors at the far end. The toilets are situated out on the corridor through the other double doors. We'll take a comfort break at ten thirty-ish so if you can hang on until then, it will be very much appreciated. We want everyone to have a go at the climbing wall so no sneaking off to the bathroom in the hope of missing your turn!'

She is playfully wagging her finger and chuckling. I have a strong urge to slap the smirk off her face, to haul her out of the room and tell her to stop playing mind games with everyone, messing with their heads and dragging out horribly painful, long-buried memories. Ruth with her perfectly groomed little life, her cherubic little face and squeaky-clean childhood. An image of my father's face lodges in my head – his twisted features, his hollow demonic laugh as he dangled me over that water, threatening to drop me if I didn't stop crying and being such a baby. When he did finally stand me back up, I got a beating for not acting like a man, for being frightened of the water and that deep drop below me instead of laughing and braving it out. I was six years old.

We're all forced to listen to a whole host of safety instructions before being asked to line up like a group of errant primary school pupils, Dave and Ron talking in an overly jocular manner at us as if we're all old buddies at some kind of reunion party.

Merriel is first to be harnessed up. She looks calm and collected, if a little discombobulated. The scratch under her eye is healing well but the bruising around it looks like an angry welt, a dark purple smudge in stark contrast to her pale skin. With a startling amount of aplomb, she scales the wall, her arms and legs moving with such ease that it is actually soothing to watch, a therapy of sorts for those of us terrified of heights. It gives me a modicum of confidence observing her agility and speed. It can't be all that difficult, can it? I'm not super-fit and certainly not as supple and strong as Merriel but neither am I a couch potato. Giving up the alcohol must stand for something, ridding my body of all those toxins. If I can just shut out my fears, silence the part of my brain that is screaming at me that the world will stop spinning if I try to climb that wall, then everything will be perfectly fine.

I won't fall, I won't fall, I won't fall.

I'll be harnessed up. Even if I do slip, then everything will be okay. I'll simply spin and swing in mid-air.

Like being dangled from a bridge by my ankles by a drunken psychopath.

Bile rises up my gullet, burning at my oesophagus. I swallow, coughing hard to clear my throat, and stare up at Merriel as she rings the bell to indicate she has reached the top. It's high. Jesus, it is so fucking high up there. And that stupid fucking bell, hanging there like the bloody sword of Damocles. A big fucking reminder that those who don't reach it have failed in front of everyone in the room.

'Okay, if we can have Adrian next, along with Yvonne, see if we can get a bit of healthy competition going here, eh?' Dave slaps his thigh. He throws his head back and lets out a hearty chuckle. A few people join in, Ruth's laugh an embarrassing guffaw. 'How about a race to the top, guys?'

In my peripheral vision, I see Yvonne step forward, her features deadly serious, eyes dark with some emotion that I can't work out. Simmering fury, perhaps? I know so little about her. She could have any number of things going on in her life that are rumbling around in her brain making her anxious and out of sorts. Maybe she is also scared of heights? Terrified that she will make a spectacle of herself in front of all our work-mates. Maybe it's not just me that's scared shitless.

My legs are blocks of wood as I hobble forwards, trying to appear nonchalant while my innards are squirming like a nest of vipers, coiling and twisting in my gut.

I stand motionless, refusing to look up above me and step into the harness, all my attention focused on this piece of fabric that stands between keeping me safe at a great height and certain death if it fails. I watch, transfixed as it is tightened and attached to a metal clip and a length of rope. My eyes scan it for frays or signs of wear and tear.

'Right, you're good to go. Don't forget to ring that bell when you get to the top.'

Ron slaps me on the shoulder as if we are old buddies. I suppress an urge to turn around and punch him square in the face. Is he doing this on purpose? Sensing my fear and exploiting it for comic effect and gain?

My palms are slippery. I don't know how I'll ever grip on to those holds, how I will ever get down if I do manage to get up there. This whole thing is beyond the pale. A stupid fucking idea put in place by a moronic woman who is standing there with a clipboard and an idiotic smile plastered across her face. She thinks this is bringing us together as colleagues and friends. She is wrong.

I step forward, do my best to swallow down my fears and start to climb.

35

YVONNE

Adrian is white, his skin drained of all colour. He looks as if he's about to pass out.

'Not keen on heights?' I say as I lean forward and place my foot on one of the lower brightly coloured footholds.

He doesn't reply and I don't push it. I haven't the energy for other people's problems and worries. None of us want to be here. It's something we just have to get through so we can say we've done it. A box-ticking exercise. It's bugger all to do with team building, that much I do know. Bugger all to do with boosting morale or bringing us all closer together and bugger all to do with caring about Deborah.

I don't dither or hang about. I'm not scared of heights but neither do I want to stand around here harnessed up like a child about to embark on a particularly frenetic fairground ride, while people stand around and watch, applauding like sea lions when I reach up to ding that bloody stupid bell.

It only takes me a couple of minutes to reach the top. My early-morning and late-night runs have paid off. Below, people are cheering Adrian on. I turn and am able to hear him huffing and puffing, stopping halfway up to catch his breath. Beneath the straps of his helmet, I can see his face, his pallid complexion now ruddy and shiny, reddened by the effort of climbing up here. For one second, I almost lower myself down and give him a helping hand but am aware of the embarrassment that could cause him. The last thing I want to do is emasculate him in front of everybody, so rather than assist, I wait, pretend to be catching my breath and finding a more comfortable foothold as he struggles up to meet me, his breathing a raucous gasp.

'Everything okay?' I keep my voice down. This isn't exactly the ideal place to start an argument or to insult somebody unintentionally. I run the risk of humiliating him, the little woman having to help the proud man down in front of a full audience.

'Not really but I'll manage.' He leans in and rests his face against the wall. 'I'll be fine. You get yourself down. Don't wait for me.'

'I don't mind waiting. We can pretend you're helping me. I'll let out a whimper if you like – shout down to everybody that I've hurt my ankle. I'm good at lying. Nobody will ever know.' I try to inject some humour into my tone. Poor Adrian. This was a stupid idea. He's an office worker; he sits at a desk all day. He isn't a serious climber. I'm fitter and possibly stronger than him thanks to my jogging. I'm not like Merriel, some fitness freak who blindly follows the latest bodybuilding trend, but I do have a certain amount of resilience although not everyone is aware of that. I could easily feign terror or an injury. Like I said, I'm quite the liar. I could fool them all, turn on the tears and the faux terror to save Adrian's dignity and I would get away with it too.

'I'm fine. Really.' His teeth are gritted, his eyes raised upwards. At least he's not foolish enough to look down. 'I'll just hang around here and think of a hundred different ways to kill Ruth once this is all over.' He manages a watery laugh.

I also let out a low chuckle, both of us up here, grinning at the inane and absurd woman below us who is responsible for our current predicament. There is a sharp movement from him, an unexpected shift in his position and, all of a sudden, Adrian is swinging freely, his hands desperately pawing at thin air, his expression stricken. He's terrified, a small, dry shriek escaping from the back of his throat.

I reach out, our fingers almost touching. 'Swing close to me. I can grab you.'

Below us, there's a collective gasp from the onlookers, Dave and Ron shouting up that he will be fine and that they'll lower him down.

'I've got you,' I say as he swings back towards me, his own body weight propelling him closer and closer to me until I am able to grasp at his arm and hold him still, to the cheers of everyone below me.

'Fuck's sake!' Adrian's face is crimson, a line of perspiration trickling down the side of his temple and onto his cheek. 'I'm fine! I'm perfectly fine. Stop treating me like a fucking baby.'

He shakes me off but I manage to hold on to him, moving my body behind his and hooking my arms around his middle. His manner stings but I refuse to leave him. He's self-conscious and feels humiliated at being rescued by a woman, that's all it is.

'What are you doing?' He struggles to be free but I hold him tight, hands clasped around his midriff, my strength clearly greater than his. I hook my fingers through his harness and lean in to speak to him.

'I'm helping you down. Come on,' I say coarsely. 'Hang on and we'll make the descent together.'

But by now, he is now furious, fear and mortification at his predicament blurring his judgement and decision-making. With one swift movement, he nudges me aside, pushing himself away from me. My fingers slip free, and I am suddenly the one who is swinging in mid-air, my feet dangling, arms wrapped around the rope above me. Except I'm not scared. I'm not Adrian. I'm the tough one, the person who has weathered many storms. Adrian isn't the only one who has suffered. It's about time he snapped out of it, held his head up and forged ahead instead of continually looking back. That's what I've done. I've worked hard to replace what I lost. Maybe it's about time he did the same instead of continually playing the victim.

I feel myself being lowered and look up to see Adrian clinging once again to the holds, his hands white as he presses his body up against the wall, his feet lodged in the crevices. He is panting, hyperventilating even, panic locking him in position.

Dave shouts up that he's going to lower him down but once again Adrian refuses, his head shaking violently, a small desperate moan trickling down to the gathering crowd below him, his guttural whimper absorbed by their murmurs and shouts of encouragement.

My feet hit the floor with a thud and I turn to see Allison standing behind me. 'I'm next. I'll go up there, see if I can help talk him down.'

Before I can protest or say anything in return, I am elbowed aside, Dave unhooking me and loosening my harness, his rough hands jostling with the buckles. It drops to the floor and I step out of it, humiliation at being rejected burning at my face. I could have talked him down if he'd let me. What makes Allison so sure she is able to do it, to succeed where I failed? All I needed was a little more time. I could have calmed him down, guided his descent. But he wouldn't let me. He took umbrage at my well-intentioned intervention. And now Allison is on the case, good old Allison with her mental health issues and borderline violent tendencies. I wonder if these fine people here know about her history, about how she has abused her family and is being divorced by her husband. I'm guessing not.

I look up, watching as she scales the wall like a feral cat, arms and legs pumping furiously until she reaches Adrian who is still clinging on for dear life. They lean in together, helmets touching. She is talking to him, saying something into his ear and he is nodding, a small smile starting to form, his body relaxing into her. She wraps her arms around his midriff, her hands locked around his stomach. They stay like that for a few seconds until she turns and nods at Ron who begins to feed the rope through at his end. Adrian lets go of the holds, his body now dangling in mid-air. He is moved lower and is almost halfway down when it happens. He begins to spin, another panic attack gripping him. His face is frozen with dread, his body tipped backwards as he tries to clamber up the rope. Ron shouts up to him that he's getting him down and to remain still but Adrian is caught up in the moment, his fear rendering him deaf to any shouts of encouragement. The rope gets lowered again inch by inch. Adrian leans up, his body tipped backwards. And then it happens.

He is falling, his limbs flapping, his screams filling the room, the rope that was attached to his harness dangling freely. It happens in the blink of an eye and yet is also so painfully slow to watch, his fall a jarring thing to observe. Nobody has time to do anything. That's not entirely true. Dave rushes over to the place where they expect him to fall, both he and Merriel forming a chain with their hands to try and catch him. It's not enough. They're too slow. Everything is pointless. He hits the floor with a thud, the soft mats beneath him deadening the sound of his bones clattering and breaking as he hits the floor.

Screams. I'm surrounded by screams that he is dead, that we need an ambulance.

'Now!' Merriel hollers, her eyes bulging, her face ashen. 'Fucking now!'

Then Ruth drops that damn clipboard that has been practically superglued to her hands all morning as she scrambles in her pocket for her phone.

People rush around, voices raised; doors open and more people arrive; there's a rustle of determined movements, pale faces, more screaming that he's alive, that he is speaking. That he's not dead. He can move. He can't stand up, but is awake and is responding to questions.

I stand, blood pounding in my ears, my veins bursting with it as it soars through me. He's not dead. Adrian is still here. He is still alive. He survived that fall. So far.

Myriad thoughts circle and swim around my head, fear and logic colliding – Adrian and Allison up that rope together, her arms wrapped around his waist, her fingers fumbling at his harness as she made a show of calming and reassuring him. Allison's violent and unpredictable ways.

I swallow, make my way over to Ruth who is now kneeling beside Adrian, talking to him, and squat down next to her.

'How is he?' It's a stupid question. I wish I hadn't spoken, had remained silent and kept my thoughts to myself.

Ruth turns and glares at me; there's something in her eyes that wounds me, makes me feels scared and vulnerable.

'He's able to speak, to tell me what took place up there.' Acid drips from her words, poison directed at me.

'What do you mean, what took place? What on earth are

you talking about?' My face feels hot, fire flickering beneath the surface of my skin.

'I think you know exactly what I mean, Yvonne. Do I really need to spell it out?'

The heat in my face grows, a furnace scorching my flesh, my muscles, working its way deep into my bones. 'I think that perhaps you do need to spell it out.' I'm almost gasping now, my usual poise and reserve abandoning me.

Behind me, a team of medics spill into the room, their uniforms and hi-vis jackets a flare of luminous yellow and green. They bustle their way in and kneel beside Adrian as we are pushed to one side out of the way.

Ruth grabs at my arm, pulling me closer to her. We stagger to the far corner of the room, away from the rest of the crowd. I stumble back, lose my balance and right myself. This isn't the Ruth I know, the quiet timid Ruth of old. Her face is creased with anger, her mouth a tight, unforgiving line. 'The clip, Yvonne. He told me about the clip on his harness being undone.'

I shake my head to display my ignorance at her words. They sound like an accusation. An accusation directed at me.

'He told me, Yvonne. He told me what you did.' She is hissing at me, her teeth bared, glistening like small splinters.

I am aghast, words pouring out of me in a desperate rush. 'Ruth, this is nonsense! He's clearly upset. I wasn't the only one up there with him, was I? We need to look at all the options. I mean' – I lean closer to her, my words a low whisper in her ear – 'Allison has lots of problems at home. You probably already know that, and I don't want to cast any aspersions but maybe she unfastened his clip?'

Ruth pushes me away, both hands flat against my chest. I

fall back into the wall, the heat of her anger, her white-hot fury, a force to be reckoned with.

'No! He is completely compos mentis and he told me what you did. He said he didn't realise at first but remembers you fiddling with something. He had no idea at the time and thought you were actually tightening it to try and help him but as soon as he came loose, he realised what you had done. And I believe him. I believe what he told me, Yvonne. What I want to know is, why? Why would you do such a thing?'

I don't reply. That's because I don't have an answer. The walls feel as if they are closing in on me, the floor tipping and swaying. Ideas drain out of my head like water down a plughole. Her face, Ruth's dark-eyed stare, the look of unadulterated malice – I can't stand it. She hates me and soon they will all hear what she is saying and they'll hate me too. They'll believe Adrian. People always believe the victim, don't they? Pity will ooze out of them, all directed towards the man currently lying on the floor, his body twisted and wracked with pain. They will all believe him.

There isn't any time for thinking, for trying to defend myself with well thought-out words and phrases, so I decide to do the right thing. The only thing. The only option left open to me.

I fix my gaze on the doors out of this place, push Ruth to the floor and do the one thing that I know I am good at. I run.

36

ADRIAN

The pain. Christ, the pain is like nothing I've ever experienced before. Everywhere. Flaring through my bones. Racing up and down my spine, a searing spear-like pain. Even breathing hurts. But at least I can feel everything. My arms, my legs, fingers and toes, I can feel them all. No numbness. I'm not paralysed. Not yet anyway. Maybe that'll come later. I can't even think about that, losing the use of my legs, spending the rest of my life in a wheelchair. I wouldn't cope. Some people manage it but I'm not some people. I've been through enough, had more than my fair share of misery. I don't have the headspace or patience for any more.

At first, I couldn't think straight, couldn't put it all together in my head, the terror and agony of the fall marring my thinking, blurring everything. But then it came to me, a sudden rush of realisation, what happened up there. I should have been more prepared, had more control over my fears. I thought I would've managed it better than I did. I'm a coward. Such a stupid, pathetic fucking coward.

Tears sting at my eyes. I blink them away. No crying. A baby

as well as a coward, that's me. Little saddo Adrian with his
whining and crying because he had to climb up a children's
fucking playground apparatus. The others did it without
missing a beat, but me? Too scared, too full of my own fears.
That's how I let it slip, my concentration. That's how I missed it.
It took a while for it to slot into place in my head, for everything
to come back into focus but now it has, I'm almost certain I
know what happened up there. I can remember what she did.
What I don't know is why.

'Adrian.' Ruth is kneeling beside me again. She places her
tiny cool hand over mine and more tears threaten to come at
her small acts of kindness and her unobtrusive, thoughtful
ways. 'Are you absolutely sure it was Yvonne who undid your
clip?'

I see the doubt in her eyes, her wavering expression. This is
a big accusation I'm making here. Huge.

She leans closer to me, whispering into my ear. A medic
tries to get her to step aside. Ruth uncharacteristically bumps
him away with her hip, her voice stern. 'Allison was up there
with you afterwards, wasn't she? Are you absolutely certain of
what you're saying, Adrian?'

And all of a sudden, I'm not. I thought I was but now
everything has become vague and hazy again, those few
seconds cloudy and distorted in my mind. God, what have I
done? I've said something terrible and now I can't unsay it.
Was it Yvonne, or was it Allison? Or in my anger and confusion, did I do something to the clip? I was clawing at the
ropes in panic, my body swinging wildly. Maybe I did this to
myself?

'I-I don't know. I could have sworn she was mad at me
because I pushed her away, wouldn't accept her help. I was
embarrassed. I wanted to manage on my own. God, Ruth,

maybe it wasn't Yvonne. Maybe I did it myself without realising it?'

'Or maybe the person who was up there after Yvonne did it? Come on, Ade, think!'

She is patting my hand now as if trying to shake the memory into my mind, sifting out the unwanted stuff until we get to the nub of the matter.

'I don't remember, Ruth. I'm sorry. I thought I knew but now it all seems so foggy and unclear.'

A tiredness washes over me as a cannula is placed into the back of my hand and a mask covers my face. Ruth is a speck in the distance, a misty circle of unfamiliar faces surrounding me, their voices soothing, a jumble of words floating around the air above me. The pain begins to ease slightly. At least I'm not paralysed. At least I'm not dead. At least I didn't see Yvonne unclip me while I was up there. Or maybe I did. Surely not? Why would she do such a thing? Could it have been Allison? Or did I accidentally do it myself? No. I was frozen with fear. Can't have been me. I think of Yvonne's face as the allegation is fired at her, her features dropping, melting like hot candle wax. I think about what I have done, those words I said to Ruth. I close my eyes and pray for sleep to take me. Maybe after this is all over, death will seem like the easier option. Maybe I will end up wishing I had hit the deck and died, my spine snapping in two, my brain turning to mush.

I feel myself being moved, straps holding me in place, tight and reassuring. No more falling. I don't want to fall again. Please don't let me fall again.

Everything feels so far away, the voices shouting that she has run off and that somebody needs to go after her. Then Merriel is shouting that she will go and find her.

I think of Yvonne. I think of Allison. I think of Ruth. I think about the words that fell out of my mouth too easily, those accusatory words, and wonder what I've started, what can of worms I've opened. My eyes stay shut, my mouth zipped into a tight strip of anxiety. I want to stay like this, the way I did when I was little, and think the same thoughts, that if I can't see any of it happening, then it might just all go away. Except, it didn't. And it won't. No matter how hard I wished, how tightly closed my eyes were, everything was still there when I opened them again and it will be this time. The bad stuff never leaves. It hangs around like a bad smell, poisoning everyone and everything in its wake.

It's the quiet that gets to her. The endless hush of each and every room in the house, the deafening silence of it all. No rumbles of laughter, no background noise that accompanies the radio or the television. They are rarely switched on anyway, their usage limited to the News at Six and Panorama. Boring programmes for grown-ups, full of doom and gloom.

'Full of nonsense. Far better to read a book and broaden your intellect than be dumbed down by the coarse TV shows and soaps shown on that contraption.'

She has it barked at her every time she asks to switch it on.

'And as for those pop-music programmes – thinly disguised pornography is what they are.'

She doesn't know what pornography is but gathers by the timbre of her aunt's voice that it's a bad thing. And so the television stays off and the house remains cloaked in a blanket of nothingness. A vacuum where only two people exist, the sound of their voices and movements echoing around her. It's so hard to get used to, a difficult adjustment to make for a young girl. She needs something to do, craves stimulation and entertainment. She has an active mind, enjoys being occu-

pied. This isn't how she thought it would be. She hoped for a happy, vibrant place, being surrounded by people who thought her heroic and wonderful and witty. She didn't for one second imagine this – a quiet house in a quiet street with a quiet woman who rarely speaks or smiles. She wanted more and got a whole lot less. Not what she had planned. Not exactly the house or family of her dreams.

'Why don't you play out in the garden? The roses are beautiful at this time of year. You can take your book out there, sit in the shade and relax.' The older lady is standing over her, gaze lowered as she watches the child closely.

'I might.' The young girl picks at the hem of her dress, pulling at a loose piece of thread. It begins to unravel, to come apart. Just like her, she thinks. Just like her life. Like her mind. Everything always comes apart in the end, she thinks miserably. Everything always splits and shatters around her.

* * *

The sun is hot on the back of her neck as she sits, her eyes locked on to the page, the words blurring, losing all meaning. She can't concentrate. It's boring here. No friends, nothing to do except read and walk and walk and read. And yet, she has to try, has to make a go of it here. Nowhere else to go. Nobody else around to take care of her.

She doesn't miss them, her family, not really. It's the buzz she misses, the noise and the fun. The quiet here is crushing. No life in the place. Days drag, minutes feeling like hours. She would rather have gone to a children's home than live here. There are nice bits of it. Of course there are. Nothing is ever completely bad. They have tea together in the park sometimes, a picnic with egg sandwiches and crisps and fizzy drinks.

'But not too many. We don't want you losing those lovely teeth of yours, do we?'

She hears that line a lot. Her aunt seems to have a thing about teeth. Teeth and tidiness and walking. Usually, after they've been to the park for the picnic, they go for a walk up the hills.

'Always nice to walk off the food, isn't it?' she says. 'We can't have too much stodge sitting in our stomachs now, can we?'

This always baffles the girl, how egg sandwiches or a gulp of orange juice can be described as stodge. She imagines stodge as something horrible and dirty, like a pile of rotting meat or melting lard.

'Another hour and we're going for a trek on the moors.' The voice cuts into her thoughts, an adult-sized shadow obscuring her view as her aunt strides across the lawn, hands on hips, voice disembodied as it's carried on the thermals towards her.

More walking. Up on the blustery barren North Yorkshire moors where the sky is big, the wind strong and the clouds aplenty. Always grey, scudding across that vast pale sky, great bubbling, ominous shapes disappearing and reappearing. That's how she remembers it every time they visit. Cold and windy. A place for proper well-equipped ramblers, that's what her aunt always says. Not a place for token walkers. An area set apart for people who take their hikes seriously.

'A place where you can empty your mind of your troubles and think clearly.' The same old line each time they load up the car and set off. The same repeated brusque phrases, the same old walk. The same woman doing her best to whip a young girl into shape, doing her best to mend her broken bits, shove them back into place so that nobody sees the cracks and damage.

She wonders if her aunt actually has any troubles. She has a nice house and an easy job working from home. Something to do with rewriting other people's books to make them better before they get sold in shops. Why the people who write them can't get it right the first time around seems a bit strange but what would she know? At school, the teacher corrects her work but that's to be expected as she's *only a child whereas adults should know better and shouldn't need another person to tell them where they are going wrong. But they clearly do. Maybe her aunt needs telling? Maybe somebody should tell her that young children get bored and that she is sick of doing everything that her aunt wants her to do and fed up of not being able to do anything that she herself wants to do. Or maybe her aunt knows it and the problem is that she simply doesn't care.*

She places her book down on the ground, stares up at the hot sun and thinks that perhaps things need to change around here. The rules need shuffling and reshaping, more attention given to her needs, more of what she wants given without question. She can make that happen, can't she? She did it previously and she feels sure she can do it again. And as far as she is concerned, the sooner the better before she goes out of her mind with boredom, her cravings and the darkness that loiters in the shadowy corners of her thoughts once again directing her movements, forcing her to do things. Because when that happens, she simply cannot be held responsible for her actions.

38

YVONNE

I see her as she takes off after me, probably sent by Ruth to bring me back, make me explain what happened up there. I don't need to explain anything. To anybody. Ever. Least of all to Ruth. And definitely not to Merriel.

The brick wall of the alleyway is cold and damp against my back, the cragginess of the bricks rough against the palms of my hands as I stand here, giving myself some time to think, to work out what just took place in there. I wait a little longer until Merriel is a speck in the distance and then step out into the daylight again. Who exactly is it she's following? Somebody she thinks is me? Or is she herself running away from something? We all have things we would rather keep hidden, secrets we salt away from the rest of the world. We are none of us perfect. Even Merriel. Especially Merriel. She told me of her background, her secrets and who she thought I was. Her damaged childhood. I'm not the only one around here who is cracked and splintered, my outward veneer a thin coating that disguises a shattered individual beneath. I tell myself daily that I'm strong, that I can withstand anything. I say it because the more you convince yourself of something, the more of a possibility it becomes. But it's not who I really am. I'm weak. Jealous and mean and weak. That's the real me. I wish it wasn't so but it is and there isn't anything I can do to change that fact. Everything is too deeply embedded in me to ever shed it and start again.

Only when I think she has disappeared do I start to walk into town. My car can stay where it is. The place will be flooded with blue lights. Too risky to think about going back. I'll find another way home, another way out of this godforsaken mess of a place and back to where I need to be. Back to a place where nobody will think of looking for me. A place where there are people who do actually truly care about me.

I wonder where Merriel is thinking of going to search for me? Perhaps a stroll through town or maybe over to the office. And then I remember that she knows where I live. Perspiration breaks out on my forehead. I'm not going there anyway. She can stand outside and hammer on the door all she likes; she won't get an answer. I'm not so stupid as to sit and wait for her to call. I have other places I can go to, even if it's just for a short time while the furore dies down.

The queue at the cashpoint feels excruciatingly long as I stand in line, my legs itching to run, to escape the confines of this town. An old lady ahead of me forgets her PIN and we have to wait while she stands, face tipped up to the sky, finger poised on her chin as she racks her brains to remember. Another attempt and then another until the machine keeps her card and she eventually turns to me with a gasp, all glassy eyed, and stares at me, hoping for some sort of assistance.

I walk away. There are plenty of other machines dotted around town and plenty of other people in the queue behind me who can give her the help she needs. I'll go elsewhere, get a wad of cash and take a taxi back home. The longer I hang around here, the greater the chances are that Ruth will do something stupid and unforgivable like send a team of police officers out to search for me. I mean, would they really do that? Use up their scarce resources to go searching for somebody as helpless and innocuous as me? Probably not but I'm not prepared to take that chance.

I head up Morton Road, my mind focused on the ATM that I know is definitely there. I've used it before. Opposite is a taxi rank. I can grab the money, hop in the back of the cab and be where I want to be in fifteen minutes. I make it sound so easy, so effortless and all the while my heart is pounding, a crushing feeling hanging over me that everything is about to implode, my tiny little world spinning off its axis and rotating into oblivion.

The machine is free and I take out as much cash as I can, up to my daily limit, and stuff it in my pocket, then turn and hail down a cab that is about to park up.

I climb in, rest my head against the headrest and give him my address, hoping I make it home before Merriel does. I'll pick up a few things and disappear. Just a few minutes is all I need to prepare before she comes poking around, trying to find me.

The drive takes an age, other vehicles, pedestrians, red lights all working against us. The story of my life, a repeating pattern – people and inanimate objects causing me distress, impeding my progress. Everything is a blur in my peripheral vision as we pick up speed and take a right turn a little too quickly, the tyres screeching, drawing attention to us.

'Sorry, love. Clipped the kerb there trying to make up some lost time 'cause of the traffic.' The taxi driver's voice is an affable sound, soft and inoffensive. Not the usual coarse, inane banter that some of them spew out, telling me about how well their kids are doing in school or how rubbish the government is or how their missus spends more than they can earn. I don't care about any of it. But not this one. He sounds okay. A normal guy. It doesn't make me feel any better though. I have other things on my mind.

'Right, here we are,' he says as we pull up outside my house. 'That'll be £14.50.'

My opinion of him plummets. I want to scream at him that his prices need readjusting, that rather than help my plight, he has added to it with his erratic driving and scandalous prices, but I don't. I slap a twenty-pound note in his hand and tell him to keep the change. I don't have time for more chat and to wait while he roots around for the right coins.

Without waiting to see his reaction, I climb out and head up the path, my fingers fumbling for my keys. I shove them in and shut the door, leaning back on it for a few seconds to recalibrate myself before racing around the house, gathering up the things that I need.

I'm just about to leave when I see her running up the road, Merriel, her face lined with anxiety, eyes darting about. She looks furtive. Shifty. Did she follow me in the taxi, staying a couple of cars behind? I shake that notion away. No, she can't have. I watched her vanish into the distance, heading in the opposite direction.

Shit!

She is moving at a lick, her pace steady and authoritative. I need to get out of here as quickly as possible. I won't lower myself to speaking to her. She is nobody to me and certainly not a person I hold in high esteem. Who does she even think she is, following me here? I doubt she has done this to help me out, knowing her character, what sort of a person she is. She'll be here to stir up trouble, to cause a fracas and point the finger at me. She thinks I'm guilty. They all do. Adrian has made his accusation and now there is no unsaying it. They will all gladly see me cornered like a snared animal. Well not today. Not any day. They'll have a long wait if they think I'm about to capitulate and bend to their allegations, hanging my head in shame and admitting to something I didn't do.

I shove my arms through my backpack and hoist it up over my shoulders, then lock the front door before slipping out the back way, sliding the key in my pocket and zipping it up for safekeeping.

The back gate closes with a clang. I wince, eager to get away unnoticed, my retreating figure invisible to Merriel and her prying eyes. She won't know where I'm going, will have no idea of my secret retreat.

My feet slip on the old cobbles, recent rain making them slick and difficult to navigate. It doesn't matter. I can creep to the corner of the alleyway, poke my head out, see if the coast is clear and make a dash for the fields beyond, my running territory, the place I know and trust.

'Everything okay, lovey?'

Her voice makes me jump, my concentration honed in on Merriel and my imminent escape.

I turn to see Agnes, the little old lady from three doors down, leaning over her back gate, watching me intently. Her small, bony fingers are hooked over the black wrought-iron pattern, an intricate design that makes me think of a spider's web. Her eyes look dark, as if she is able to see inside my head.

'Everything's fine, thank you, Agnes.' I nod at her, turning away to indicate that I don't want to get drawn into a dialogue with her, that this conversation is over before it's even begun.

'Off for another run, are we? Mind yer step. We had a right downpour earlier, we did. Those cobbles are lethal when wet.'

She continues to stare at me, holding my gaze, her eyes narrow and inquisitive.

I have no idea what it is she wants me to say, whether or not I'm supposed to thank her for her advice and turn away or whether a nod will suffice without causing some deep unexplainable offence to an old lady who simply wants to make conversation because her days are drab and grey, the only splash of colour being the talk she makes with passers-by and neighbours.

'Thanks for the advice, Agnes. I'll watch how I go.' I hope this is enough. I need to move, to get away from here. Away from Merriel and whatever it is she has come here to say.

'And mind the police cordon at the end of the street, as well. They set it up a couple of minutes ago. Watched them from the upstairs window, I did. Blue lights flashing all over the place. Surprised you didn't hear them when they pulled up with a screech. Never go about their business quietly, do they, these policemen? No wonder the burglars and murderers always get away, one step ahead and as quiet as the grave while t'police arrive all guns blazing.'

I freeze, Agnes' loud cackle an eerie echo in my head.

'Anyways, don't tek any notice of me and mind how you go, lovey. Them cobbles are wet and you'll come a cropper if you don't watch your step on 'em.'

I spin around and start to run, Agnes still calling after me, her words, the pitch of her voice, turning my blood to ice.

'Oh, and I saw yer friend a few minutes ago as well, the one that sometimes runs t'same way as you do, the one that's hung around outside yer house on occasion.'

My limbs turn to stone, my thoughts suddenly sludgy and out of focus. 'My friend?' I try to keep the panic out of my voice, keep my tone neutral. I'm making a polite enquiry, that's all it is.

A polite enquiry asking Agnes to clarify her statement. I'm not panicked or knocked off balance. Even though I am. Very much so. Merriel has been following me?

'Aye. The tall one. Looks a bit like you, an athletic type. She set off at a right lick she did, off towards the big fields over yonder.'

I nod, try to keep the smile on my face even though my jaw is twitching involuntarily, blood rushing through my ears, my head, making everything before me soft and unsteady.

'That's okay,' I say, my voice suddenly hoarse and croaky. 'Thanks, Agnes, I'll see if I can catch her up.'

I manage another tight smile, take a quick glance around me, pull on my gloves for warmth, and begin to run.

39

DEBORAH

The crimson pool on the floor by my feet is growing, the cut on my arm bleeding profusely and dripping onto it, a constant trickle of red liquid spreading and slowly congealing. It's not a main artery. I'd be dead by now if that were the case, but it's deep, folds of pink jelly-like flesh surrounding the wound. And it's painful, a stinging, throbbing sensation that is making my eyes water. Just another injury to add to my ever-growing list. Another thing to slow me down when we finally make a run for it out of here.

My second attempt at climbing through the broken window was soon thwarted by a gouge from an unseen shard of glass as I reached out with my right arm to search for more drainpipes or lengths of guttering that would help us escape. It was point-less. There was nothing, only the old decayed one that had fallen away after my earlier attempts to climb it. It is now lying in pieces on the concrete path below.

I had let out a scream as the glass pierced my skin. And then came the blood. And the delayed wave of pain up and down my arm that sent me crashing to the floor with a shriek. The gloopy crimson blood. So much of it. It's hard to believe it will ever stop.

'Here,' Izzie says, pulling off her fleece, 'we can use this instead.'

She kicks away the lengths of blood-soaked muslin that did nothing to stem the bleeding and squats beside me. Wrapping the thickest part around the gaping wound, she uses the arms of the fleece to tie it.

'As tight as you can,' I say. 'Like a tourniquet to help stop the bleeding.'

'Is that okay?' She is staring up at me, pity and fear in her expression. Fear at our current predicament and my injury, but more than that, fear at the fact we may never get out of here. It's evident in her face: the way her eyes flick about, her body language, the weakness in her voice. I can see it in her, how she is beginning to fold under the pressure, her resilience and anger waning, replaced by a sense of hopelessness. She looks tiny, as if she has shrunk to half her usual size. Already slightly built, she now appears to be a slip of a thing. A helpless child.

'I met her one day while I was out running,' she says, her voice taking me by surprise. 'We got chatting. It only happened once or twice. She said that she didn't usually take the route I was on and that it was nice to meet somebody.'

Shock renders me silent. I nod, willing her to continue. I want to hear this. I *need* to hear it, to find out how we both ended up here, being held against our will. To discover that I wasn't the only one caught out by her manipulative, wily ways, that I'm not the mug I thought I was for falling for it.

'She seemed really nice. I didn't realise it was her at first, when I woke up here. With the mask and everything, and then the shock, it took a little while for me to piece it all together in my head, but I'm certain of it now. As soon as she stopped trying to disguise her voice, I knew. I just knew…'

Tears spill out onto her face, a stream of them dripping down her cheeks, dripping onto her T-shirt. She sniffs and laughs, wiping them away with the back of her hand. 'That's why I'm wearing these.' She points down to her Lycra trousers and top. 'But I suppose that at least my fleece has come in handy, hasn't it?'

I should laugh and manage to force a smile. I think I've forgotten how to be happy, how the sound of laughter feels in my throat, the noise it makes as it emerges out of my mouth unbidden, a reflex action to a humorous event or sentence.

'The last thing I remember is me and her talking near the fence in the woods. She offered me a drink, told me it was the latest sports drink and would help combat my exhaustion. I'm new to running and believed her. Stupid of me. So stupid…'

'And she drugged you.' My voice is full of resignation and anger because I fell for it too. 'Same here. We worked together in the same office. By the time I left work, I was already feeling a bit tired and woozy. She must have followed me, waited till I was ready to collapse, and then – well you know the rest.'

Izzie nods and I want to tell her not to be so hard on herself, that I thought I knew her, could count on her, that I'm fairly streetwise and even I succumbed to her nasty, scheming little tricks.

'Maybe it's true, what they tell you on the television,' Izzie whispers reflectively, 'that most crimes are committed by people we know. It's not strangers on the street who do these kinds of things, it's the people we think we can trust. They're the ones we should be scared of.'

I stare at the recently applied fabric on my arm, praying it's enough to stop the flow of blood. 'She is a master manipulator.

That's how she got us here. Not because we're stupid and she is more intelligent. It happened because we trusted her and she took advantage of that fact.'

We sit for a few seconds, digesting all this information, my mind wondering if I have the strength to cope with the idea of my own demise in this rotten place. I'm incredibly thirsty. I'm tired and hungry and I am also in a great deal of pain, but most of all, worse than all of those things, I am feeling stripped of my earlier feelings of optimism.

I think of my family, my mum and dad. Even Brett, for all of his faults. I've wondered if the police have questioned him over my disappearance, whether he has thought about me as much as I've thought about him. The boyfriend is almost always the first obvious suspect. I hope the police went easy on him. He's a philanderer not a kidnapper or potential murderer.

I wonder if they are still out there, searching for me. For us. Surely Izzie going missing has sparked a bigger investigation. Or have they given up on us? Wherever they will have looked in my life, a work colleague is probably the last person they would expect to be involved.

'My head really hurts.' Izzie is leaning forward, her forehead resting against her open palm.

'You're dehydrated.' My voice is flat and monotone. I don't even try to dress up my anguish. No need for any pretence and no energy for it either. Maybe this is it – the end. Maybe my mind is shutting down, my expiry date imminent. Maybe I've come to accept my fate. No fight left in me, my resistance tapering off into nothing.

'Fresh air,' she says, her voice a thin whisper. 'I need to get some fresh air.'

I watch her stand and move towards the window. She leans

her head downwards, her nose poking through a small gap in the splintered glass. And then I hear the gasp.

My head thumps, my entire body throbbing with pain as I try to stand up to join her to see what she can see.

'Down there!' Izzie says, her voice cracking, raw emotion filtering through. 'She's down there. Can you see?'

I crane my neck and see a figure in the distance, still an unrecognisable hazy blur but it's definitely a person and they're heading this way, their arms pumping furiously at their sides. I slump down out of sight, pulling Izzie down with me, a million ideas and questions whirring around in my brain. My back is pressed up against the wall, the feel of the cold brick kicking some life into my weary bones.

'This is it, Izzie. We have to get it right this time. This is our last chance. Mess it up now and we'll be dead in a couple of days if we don't get any fluid into our bodies, maybe even sooner.'

Her eyes are wide, her mouth and jaw quivering as she listens to me. 'I'm really scared. What the hell are we going to do?'

'We watch and wait until she opens that door and as soon as a crack of light appears, we pull it open completely and push her down the stairs. No hesitating this time, we just go for it.' I'm hissing at her now, desperation spilling out.

I don't know if it'll work but it's all we've got and I'm prepared to give it a go. I'm beyond attempting to cover up my fear to try and embolden Izzie. We're in this together. Whatever we manage to do will be a joint effort. I'm going to give it my all and pray that Izzie is too.

'But what about your arm?' She is staring down at the blue fleece that is rapidly turning a dark, dirty shade of red as blood continues to leak through it.

'I'll worry about my arm,' I say, my voice suddenly steady and calm at the thought of what comes next, the possibility that at last, this could finally be it. 'You just concentrate on yourself and getting out of here.'

We creep towards the door, a definite shudder taking hold in my limbs, my guts swirling like a tidal wave crashing against the lining of my stomach. I tell myself to stop it, that we're at rock bottom and have nothing to lose. Except our freedom. I shut it out, that negative whispering voice that is echoing around my brain. We're currently at rock bottom. The next rung down this particular ladder is certain death and I will fight that option until the dark hooded spectre drags me away kicking and screaming.

Together, we crouch behind the door, breaths suspended, arms, bodies poised for action. A noise outside. Somebody getting closer, their footsteps becoming louder, heading up the stairs, the graceless clump of their footfall a reminder that it's almost at an end. We can do this. Together, we can do this. I tell myself this over and over, a mantra on repeat in my head. No room for failure. Freedom is a hair's breadth away. Just a hair's breadth is all it is.

The sound of a key turning. A twist of the handle, a deep groan as the door moves a fraction. I eye Izzie and nod, our bodies arched, hands outstretched, legs bent and ready to run and push her backwards down those stairs.

One, two, three.

We move together, our hands hitting the silhouetted figure in the chest with full force as we run and push. She topples backwards, her body bouncing off the walls, limbs flailing. The sound of a deep groan as she lands at the bottom with a crash. Then nothing.

And suddenly, the jumbled clatter of our feet as we half

throw ourselves down the stairs, my legs weak and unsteady. Whether it's the shock or dehydration or blood loss or perhaps a combination of all three things, I feel horribly sick and dizzy and have to stop to catch my breath, my hand resting against the wall for balance.

'Deborah?' Izzie is watching me, her hand reaching out to hold me up.

I willingly take it, wrapping my fingers around hers to keep myself upright. With my foot, I nudge at the body lying near my feet, pushing at it until it turns over and I can see their features clearly.

Merriel's eyes are closed, a trickle of blood coming out from one of her nostrils.

'Look! Over there.' Izzie is pointing out of the open door that leads out on to the field.

Yvonne is running over towards us, her slim shape edging closer and closer. I keep hold of Izzie's hand and step out into the daylight.

40

ADRIAN

A fractured pelvis. That's what they think I've got. A fractured pelvis and probably a fractured collarbone. I'm also having an X-ray done on my leg later today. Fractured doesn't suggest as much pain as a break and yet all I know is it hurts like hell. Every slight movement, every little breath, is making me gasp in agony.

Lucky to be alive. That's the phrase they keep coming out with. Every nurse and doctor who has leaned over me, assessing my condition, has smiled and told me I'm lucky to be here at all. They're actually a lovely bunch. I suppose I am lucky in many ways although I don't feel it right now. I feel tired and desperate and let down and anxious. I also feel confused. The more I try to remember, the fuzzier it all becomes, being up there, trying to work out how that clip came loose.

My initial reaction was to blame Yvonne. I don't know why I did that, it just seemed right at the time, those wild, untethered words falling out of my mouth before being scooped up by Ruth who ran away with the idea, accusing her before I had time to change my mind and take it all back. Maybe it was panic that made me do it. Or maybe I said it because it's true. I once read that our first instincts are usually accurate. It's only when we take time to scrutinise the facts after the event that doubt sets in. And yet, Yvonne? And then there's Allison to consider. She was up there with me as well, her hands wrapped tightly around my waist. But similarly to Yvonne, I have to ask myself, Allison? Really?

I lean back, close my eyes and try to forget. I will wait until the hospital tests and examinations are over before I delve further into it. My hands creep over the side of the bed, feeling for my phone, a warm sensation ballooning in my abdomen. The text from Beth, those words – they were enough to help ease my pain, to block out all those negative thoughts about the fall.

I pick up my phone, read her message again, savouring each and every word, ruminating over how well she appears to be doing. How far she has come. It's been a long and difficult climb but hopefully the end is in sight. I smile at my poor analogy given my circumstances.

I've done it, Ade. I've taken my social worker's advice and joined AA. Feels good to see things clearly at long last. Won't be easy but I'll give it a go. What a fucking mess I've made of everything eh?

My fingers are thick and clumsy as I type in my reply and click send.

Glad to hear it. Behind you all the way. You go girl x

It takes only a matter of seconds for her to reply, my phone pinging and lighting up in my hands.

Whatever I told you in the last few weeks, just ignore. I was out of my skull and talking shit. Long rocky road ahead but got to be better than the one I've left behind. Speak soon. Xx

I leave it at that. No point or sense in probing any further. She'll tell me in her own good time anything that needs to be said. We can separate the facts from the fiction at some point in the future. For now, we need to focus on Beth turning her life around. She's giving it a go at getting clean and that's good enough for me. I don't want to spoil the moment by asking awkward questions, making her uncomfortable. Giving her a chance to change her mind and reach for the nearest bottle. The truth is a hard thing to face when doing it with a clear head. Chances are, she won't remember half the things she has said anyway. Better to harness our collective energies and help her move forward rather than looking back at her mistakes, raking over them again and again. Reminding her of how bad it got, rubbing salt into the wound and watching her writhe and wince in pain.

'I'd ask if you're comfortable but that would be a daft question, wouldn't it?' Fiona, the healthcare assistant, is standing at the foot of my bed watching me. 'I've come to ask if you need anything for your pain?'

'A new pelvis and maybe a new shoulder?' I say, managing a low laugh without it feeling as if my body is about to break in two from the effort.

'I'll see what I can do for you, shall I?' She shuffles off, calling over her shoulder that she'll be back soon with a cup of tea for me.

A cup of tea. Always a good healer. The best medicine money can buy. I may be laid up and incapacitated with the thought that I have to face Ruth and Yvonne and explain away that accusation once I'm well enough to be up and out of this place, but after reading Beth's text, at this moment in time, a cup of tea sounds just about perfect.

I close my eyes, listen to the rattle and clank of nearby trolleys and the wail of sirens from outside my window and think that, despite my current circumstance, maybe things are finally looking up.

41

She can't recall the day it came to her, the idea for what should come next. Maybe it had always been there, a seed planted many years ago in her mind that has taken root and sprouted shoots. There is a life outside these four walls, the four walls that have held her prisoner day after day for so long now, and she wants to be a part of it. She's seventeen, ready to be independent, be her own person, not be constantly chaperoned by a woman who has begun to see behind her disguise, the mask she wears every day to the watching world. It's become tiresome being under constant scrutiny. She wants more. Deserves more.

After a recent altercation, college has decided she is better suited elsewhere. They didn't say where but she definitely isn't wanted on their premises any more. Not after the last debacle. It was a simple misunderstanding. It has also been the ruin of her, putting an end to any hopes she had of making it to university. Still, it was worth it, that flare-up. That deep scratch. Ruby Winter suited her scar. It reminded her of that time all those years ago, the one where her mother was overwrought thinking that the facial scar that was inflicted would be permanent. It wasn't. She made sure of it, had

practised it many, many times until she had perfected the art of snag-
ging skin to make it look worse than it actually was. There is a knack
to drawing blood without leaving any lasting long-term damage.

There were no bystanders or onlookers at college when this latest
quarrel took place. Nobody to verify her story, to check the veracity of
both of their stories. But the college principal didn't want the bad
publicity or the hassle and chose to believe Ruby. Ruby whose
parents threatened to go to the local papers if something wasn't done.
So it was. It was all done and dusted without consulting her. She was
removed. Thrown out on her ear. A small scuffle, that's all it was. A
couple of teenagers falling out and, all of a sudden, everyone thinks
her unhinged. Incapable of continuing with her education.

'A brisk outing is what we need.' The voice penetrates her
musings, shaking her back to the present. Reminding her of what
needs to be done.

Without any preamble or complaint, she gets herself ready, mind
sharp and fixated on the task that lies ahead. What she must do to
free herself and get her life back. For so long now, she has capitulated
to other people, allowed them to bend and shape her, turn her into
somebody she doesn't want to be. But not any more. Today it comes to
an end. Today she takes back control of her life. The control she felt
sure she would gain after the fire. It didn't happen, everything
turning to ash, her life controlled by a matriarch, somebody far
sharper and more rigid than her parents ever were.

The drive up there is strained, the atmosphere tense.

'You know, you really need to lighten up a little, let people get
close to you. You can be wonderful company when the mood takes
you, but after the carry-on at college, I do feel that things have taken
a downward turn. You can't let what happened to you as a child
define who you are or who you might become. It's time to move on.'

The young woman checks her phone. It is indeed time to move on.
That much is correct. She's got something right. Four bars – a decent

enough signal considering their remoteness. Here's hoping it stays that way.

She slips it into her pocket and sits silently as they park up at Clay Bank. She is blind to the sweeping vista of Teesside and North Yorkshire, the rolling hills and vast pale blue sky. Today is the day everything changes. No room for romantic notions of breathtaking views. No room for anything except meticulous planning of her long-overdue task.

'Right. Good to see you've got your proper walking boots on. I'll grab the rucksack. Let's see if we can shake off those cobwebs, eh?'

Deirdre opens the door and both women step out into the bracing breeze, their hair tousled by the strength of the wind, their faces cold and reddened within minutes.

It doesn't take long for them to reach the point that has filled her head of late. The sheer height of it, the jagged rocks beneath. The opportunity.

'Come on, Deirdre. I'll take a photo of you. Strike a pose.'

The older lady leans forward over the precipice, face raised to the sky, chin jutting out, arms outstretched as she takes in the spectacular views. The younger woman watches as her aunt breathes deeply, sucking in the cold, her face the picture of contentment as a sharp gust of wind washes over her, a small sigh springing from her throat, barely audible above the sound of the gathering breeze.

She moves closer, knows that her aunt can feel the movement of air behind her, is able to hear the crunch of small stones underfoot, a distinctive sound that cannot be deadened. Her approach is sensed. It's obvious in her body language: a slight stiffening of her backbone, the rucking of skin on her forearms. The younger woman knows that she will move aside for her, insist that they take in the view together, re-establish their relationship that has faltered in the past few months, bond once more as family members thrown together in the most terrible of circumstances. Her aunt may have lost a brother but *she at least gained a substitute daughter. She has heard it all before, the old tropes about family bonds and blood being thicker than water and every other facile, glib cliché she can think of about love and relationships and how they should stick together. Blah, blah, blah. She is bored of it all, exhausted by the adages that are constantly thrown her way in a bid to change her.*

She places her arm over her aunt's shoulder, steps forward, her hand suddenly sliding down the ridges of the older woman's spine until it comes to rest in the small of her back.

The older woman turns, tries to say something but is stopped by a gust of wind so strong it takes the words from her, carries them away into the ether. She looks into her niece's face, sees that all too familiar darkness there and shudders, trying to move back away from the pressure of her carefully placed fingers. She feels the push, and knows with a sickening sense of realisation what is happening but by then it's too late. The pressure is too heavy, the weight behind her too great to stop the fall. Everything rushes past, all the things she loves – nature in all its raw and rugged beauty spins around her, the sky, the grass, the soft white clouds kaleidoscoping and rotating until at last she reaches the bottom, feels solidity, her head crashing into a large boulder. Then nothing.

The scream sounds natural. She's practised it in her head many times over but is still pleasantly surprised at how rich and powerful it is, way beyond anything she expected or hoped for. She's a better actress than she ever knew. She thought perhaps that Deirdre's austere ways had ironed out all her quirky creases, robbed her of who she used to be, how she used to be, but apparently not. She's still there, that devious, wayward child, still itching to be free. Still capable of so many things.

Nobody hears her or comes running. She supposes that's a good thing. No reaction means no witnesses. She has the picture as proof as well. Proof that her aunt leaned too far towards the edge. Always the risk-taker. Each week pushing herself further and further, walking higher and higher for longer and longer. She was an accident waiting to happen.

She slumps down onto the ground, her heart remarkably still and rhythmic, and stares at her phone before pressing the button for emergency services, her voice ready to shriek down the handset that she needs help and she needs it now.

Quickly! *she will scream as the tears begin to fall.* Come quickly and help me. I think she might be dead. She leaned too far over the edge and fell. I tried to help her but couldn't hold on. Oh God, please send somebody straight away. I think she might be dead! *Then a smile, her mouth trembling as she stares out over the sprawling landscape, wondering what comes next.*

42

DEBORAH

I try to push Izzie back inside but she bustles her way past me down the dark hallway, her touch remarkably strong for one so small. I can't bring myself to look down at Merriel, to see what we have done. We need to garner our strength, Izzie and me. We need to pull together and finish this thing.

Behind us, I hear a groan, a rustle of clothing against the concrete floor as poor Merriel stirs. Later. We'll deal with that later. The here and now is what we need to concentrate on.

The small figure in the distance grows larger, her features coming into focus, the scowl on her face, the fire in her eyes. That look. That dark, menacing look that seems to have taken over her entire self. I know it well, recognise it for what it is – pure evil.

'Move her inside. Get her out of sight. The pair of you, move. Now!' She is shouting, her usual poise diminishing, her finger pointing down at Merriel. She is losing it, that control she has wielded over us. Her grip is weakening and she knows it.

Izzie nudges closer to me, our bodies melded together as one, the heat from her tiny frame filling me with hope that we can do this. We can stop her doing whatever it is she has planned. Yvonne continues running, almost reaching us, a combination of anger and desperation written all over her face. This is a new look for her. No more the powerful one, she is now reduced to this – an equal. Less than equal. No drugs to keep us quiet and placid, no weapons to use against us, no utensils handy to bind us and hold us captive. One against one. An equal footing. I can't count on Izzie in this battle. Unassuming, diminutive Izzie who is scared witless. It's just me and Yvonne. She has the advantage, I know that. She's stronger, fitter, in better shape with no broken bones and gaping wounds. I just have to hope Izzie steps in should things go terribly awry.

'No.' I keep my tone even. No raging fury or resentment, no signs at all that I'm scared of her. No signs either that I'm about to blindly follow her command. No more of that. Today is the day I stand up to her, give as good as I get.

'I said move her!' She has dipped a full octave, shock at my refusal showing in her face. Her eyes are screwed up, her jaw twitching as she continues striding towards us.

I almost laugh, suppressing the spontaneous burst of amusement by biting down on my bottom lip. It's heartening seeing her like this – a lonely-looking, desperate creature who is losing it.

'And I said no.' My throat feels sore, my head is throbbing, a painful ache is twisting at the muscle and sinews in my upper arm and shoulder. I'm the weaker one here but I won't be beaten. Not any more. The time has come for me to rise. For us to rise, Izzie and me. And Merriel. I have no idea why she is here, how she got the key to open the door, what made her dash across to this derelict old building in the first place, but I do know that I won't let this monster do to her what she did to us. Enough is enough. The balance of power is finally shifting.

Time to knock Yvonne off her pedestal, let her know that her lowly prisoners are finally rebelling.

She stops, softening her face, her posture, and sits down on the grass, her legs crossed. I try to not look shocked. This is a ploy, an act to make us lose focus, make us think she's given in.

'What the hell are you—'

I hold out my hand to quieten Izzie, my fingers bent in a silent plea for her to remain quiet. It works. She stops, her shoulders slumping, her face staring up at me, eyes quizzical.

Yvonne pats the grass next to where she is sitting. 'Come on. Come and join me. We can chat about the old times. Come on, Jenna, come and talk to me.'

'I'm not Jenna.' My reply is firm, my voice flat but powerful. I won't be pulled into one of her silly little tricks, the imaginary world she inhabits where we are all one big happy family. I pray that Izzie doesn't fall for it, get sucked into that warped fantasy that Yvonne has going on in her head. I move even closer to her, try to give her a look that says, *don't do anything!*

'Oh, don't be like that! We're sisters, aren't we? It doesn't matter what happened in the past. We need to stick together.' Her smile is fading, a look I can't quite fathom beginning to take hold in her eyes. A look that I don't care for. When she's in this sort of mood, her strength seems to grow a hundredfold. When the madness takes hold of her. It's an endless pit of nothingness in those eyes of hers. Dead shark eyes. No emotion. No kindness or empathy. It's like somebody flicks a switch somewhere inside her head and suddenly she has gone, the normal Yvonne, somebody else occupying the space in her brain where she used to be. A small strand of insanity that grows and multiplies before taking over completely.

She scrambles to her feet and starts to move even closer to us. My heart starts up. I'm furious at myself for feeling frightened. She's just like me – another woman. We're equally matched. Except we're not. I know that. She is super fit. I'm badly injured. Izzie is tiny and dehydrated. Merriel is unconscious. For all I know she could be dying. A frisson of terror pulses through me. I did that to her. I may have killed an innocent woman. My head thumps, a vibrating realisation running through me. Except I can't think about that now, those consequences, Merriel's pain and fear. No time for anything but honing in on Yvonne's next move. Being prepared for her. Ready to protect us and stay alive.

She is now only a few feet away from me, her eyes glinting, her smile a crooked split across her face. I gulp, a rush of bile burning my gullet. I tighten my hands into fists and stare at her, refusing to break eye contact. She's almost upon us, so close I can smell her putrid breath, feel the heat of her insanity and rage as it gathers momentum, increasing exponentially with every passing second.

What now? What the fuck am I going to do now? Behind me, I hear a low moan. Beside me, I feel Izzie flinch, her body tensed, ready for that fight-or-flight moment, her adrenaline surging. I push out my chest, arch my back slightly, give myself a better, firmer footing should Yvonne decide to run at me. She doesn't. She creeps closer, her jaw jutting out, teeth bared.

'You stupid cow. You'll wish you'd taken more notice of me when we were younger.'

I block out her words. They're meaningless, hollow phrases designed to distract and topple me.

'Nobody had any idea, did they? Not a fucking clue. They all thought they knew but they didn't. All those educational psychologists and support workers. They were completely fooled by our family, weren't they?'

Again, no reaction from either me or Izzie.

'Say something!' A shriek now, spittle flying out from her mouth, drool running down her chin, glistening in the sunlight.

It repulses me, the wetness on her skin, the small rivulets gathering beneath her bottom lip. Still, I don't look away. That's all it would take – one second, one infinitesimal lapse of concentration and she will have me knocked flat, her fists pummelling my already enfeebled body, knocking what little strength I have left out of me. And then it will all be over. Even with Izzie fighting for me, it wouldn't be enough. We need a head start. I'm still bleeding. I'm exhausted. Whatever we do, it'll have to be swift, catching her on the back foot.

'Say it! Admit that we're related.'

'No. I am not your sister. We are not related. Now why don't you just turn around and fuck off!' I don't intend for it to come out as a roar but it has an effect, causing her to stagger slightly. She soon rights herself, moving even closer to us, seemingly growing in stature, her anger causing her to rise like some sort of monstrous being. Ugly and unstoppable.

'Yes, you are. You're one of them. Just like me. We're meant be together. Now say it. Say it!' She tips her head to one side, smirks and spits on the ground.

My stomach roils. I do nothing, say nothing. It irks her, I can see that, her face twitching in annoyance. She needs that response, craves it like a druggie in need of their next fix.

'I left the key in the door, that's how she got in.' She juts out her bottom lip in fake sympathy. 'Silly of me, wasn't it? As you know, I'm usually very precise, in control of everything. I was in a rush, you see. Under pressure and feeling slightly out of kilter. Still, she hasn't come out of it that well, has she? Serves her right, wouldn't you say?' Her eyes drop to Merriel's slumped figure behind us. 'She followed me apparently. Thought I was somebody else and stalked me and now she knows where I live, where you live, the pair of you.' She laughs, a low tinkling sound, soft and gentle in its pitch, a noise that belies the depth of her madness. 'Funny, isn't it? And you thought I was the only insane one around here, yet here she was, spending her time following little old me, thinking I had something to hide when all it was, was a small family get-together. A long-overdue reunion. Nothing to see here, eh?' She winks and smiles.

Her words echo around us, empty and meaningless. Just a continuous stream of bile. If it's a reaction she's after, then she's speaking to the wrong person. I say nothing, my silence my only weapon, fists furled up tight as I watch her, waiting, working out what her next move is going to be. Her talk is just a cover, a way of distracting me. It won't work. I'm impervious to it now; I learnt the hard way not to get sucked into any dialogue with her, thinking I can win her round, get her to soften her approach. She doesn't have the capacity for warmth or any understanding of the suffering of others. If anything, she thrives on it. It empowers her. I'm guessing it's all she's got.

More groans from behind me, a dull shuffling, then fingers clasped around my ankle. I freeze, sweat breaking out under my arms, on my scalp. Running down my back. It's then that it happens, the moment of change. The turning point. The catalyst that aids our escape.

I see Izzie take a step back, squat down and pick up the object that Merriel has pushed our way, all the while never taking her eyes off Yvonne. If there is one thing poor Izzie has learnt while being held here, it's to never trust her. Don't allow her any space or she'll turn on you, pounce, and take back control. It's what she does, what she's good at.

Izzie holds up the phone, her gaze still locked on Yvonne's face, and punches in a number. 'I think you can guess who I'm calling, can't you?'

'Your word against mine,' Yvonne says, a definite growl of resentment creeping into her tone. Anxiety is there. I can hear it, her nuanced timbre, the tightening of her jaw. She's close to being caught. Close to losing everything. Like she hasn't lost it already. It's all slipping away, everything she ever wanted, rapidly turning to dust.

'Whatever, but we all know who they'll believe, don't we?'

'Do we? Are you sure about that?' Her mouth is set into a snarl, lip curled upwards, aggression always bubbling just beneath the surface.

She takes another step towards us and, exhausted as I am, I brace myself. I have no idea what she thinks she is going to achieve by yet another onslaught. Izzie has called the emergency services. They're probably already on their way here.

'It's the losing I don't like,' she says, as if she can see inside my mind, is able to read my every thought. 'I've always been the same. Don't you remember when we were little? I had to win, had to be in control. It's just the way I am. You should know that about me.'

I'm not sure if it's the light illuminating her features or the angle of her head, but I swear that I see tears glistening on her face. She sees me watching her and straightens her posture, a sudden rigidity to her spine.

Even though I've steeled myself for whatever she is going to do next, she still takes me by surprise, launching herself at me, fists and feet pumping furiously, jaw tensed as she delivers blow after blow. Next to me I hear Izzie's screams, Merriel's deathly moans and for a brief period I think that this is it, that we have come this far and failed in the dying moments. All that effort, all the hurt and pain we've endured and still we will lose. I hear Izzie screaming at Yvonne and feel the weight of her tiny body as she attempts to pull Yvonne away from me, her nails clawing at bare flesh, her voice shrieking that it's all over.

And soon it will be. Soon they will be above us, around us, the screech of sirens piercing the air. I will see a flash of blue in my peripheral vision. But before that happens, she stops, a cessation of the punches and scratches. A slackening of her limbs locked around my body. I drop to the floor, pain and fatigue pulling me downwards. I look up into Yvonne's face, stare deep into her eyes. And see nothing. No compassion, no guilt, no fear. Just emptiness.

'This could have all been so different,' she says, a mournful lilt to her voice. 'Why did you make it so hard for me? We could have had a good life together, you and I.' She glances at Izzie then back at me. 'All three of us. We would have been so happy together but as always, you ruined it.'

Izzie stares at her, phone in hand. 'They're on their way. A couple of minutes and they'll be here. Ambulances, police. They're all on their way.'

Yvonne stands up, brushes down her clothes, straightening out creases with her long, slim fingers. She cups her hand over her eyes, stares off over the field and shakes her head. Nothing for a few seconds. No movement, no words spoken. And then she is gone.

It's rapid, her exit. She bolts across the field like an animal diving for cover from a hunter, her slim frame soon a speck in the distance before disappearing altogether.

'The battery's dead,' Izzie murmurs. 'But she was never going to know that, was she?'

For the first time in a long while, I giggle, peals of laughter bellowing out of me as hysteria and shock and relief all merge together in one huge miasma, Izzie joining in, her voice an edifying sound to my jaded ears.

43

YVONNE

I see them everywhere, my family, my sisters, Deirdre. The ghosts of their faces haunting me. Telling me how wrong I've been. How soon it will all begin to unravel, everything unspooling and spilling out for the watching world to see. They always knew it would end like this. I imagine they're happy about it, delighted even, thinking that this is their retribution. My penance for what I did to them. They're wrong. Life doesn't work like that. There's no such thing as yin and yang, no karma or getting even. No everlasting hell for one's sins. But there is such a thing as escape. Escape from the past, from the thoughts that bite at me, the incessant silent judgements directed my way every time I look at Deirdre's old photographs, see the faces of my family gazing out at me, those accusatory stares that say, *Look at what you did.* I can at least escape from that. I'm not a monster. Many will think me so when the truth comes out, when my sins are revealed and held aloft for all to see, but I'm not. I've done monstrous things but I am not a monster. Misunderstood, wired up differently, a loner perhaps, maybe even lonely. But definitely not a monster.

There's nobody around as I unlock the door and let myself in. No Agnes, no nosy neighbours. No police cordon. It was a car accident, the heavy police presence earlier on. I almost laugh out loud. I thought they had come for me. How stupid. Egocentric really. Not everything is about me. If only it were. Maybe everything would have turned out very differently. Maybe then I wouldn't be doing what I'm about to do.

Funny, isn't it? We are conceived, born, have no say over our identity, what family we live with, how our lives will turn out. I never chose to be a twin. It just happened. The splitting of an egg. Another half of me growing alongside me, taking what should have been mine. Pushing me out of the way. Shadowing my life. Ruining it.

They'll be on their way here shortly, the police. I know the score, know what comes next. I'm not an idiot. They will have told them everything. It's all over. I know that now. I put up a solid battle. I tried and failed. But at least I tried. Nobody can ever say I forgot about my family completely. I didn't. I tried to recreate what we had, pay homage to our lives, but it only went so far, my attempts falling at the final hurdle. I had no idea how it would all pan out, my family reunion. I had no endpoint in mind. I just knew that I wanted them, my replacement sisters, had to have them. And now I've lost them. Again. Both of them slipping away, trickling through my fingers like water, the remnants of my dreams leaking away and evaporating.

I haven't decided which way to play it yet, my grand finale. I need to get a move on if I want to get it right. Standing up, I head into the kitchen, open the cupboard door that contains my little bag of tricks and empty everything onto the counter. This small pile of drugs has served me well over the past few months. My permanent angst and insomnia, coupled with paying to see a doctor privately, somebody who questioned rarely, means I've managed to accrue enough muscle-relaxing drugs to fell a whole family of elephants. Flunitrazepam. Otherwise known as Rohypnol, the date-rape drug. Those visits for the medication happened a while ago, before the media publicised its side effects. I hung on to them. Just in case. And my *just in case* theory served me well.

In the beginning, the medication helped me to sleep, but then it stopped working and other things took hold. Wild imaginings and impulses I couldn't control. I wasn't impaired enough to not understand what was going on. I knew that I was having paradoxical reactions to the drug. It was meant to cure my severe insomnia but I became jittery and anxious. Driven by a need to do things. Things that filled a hole in my life.

Deborah and I were friends. Colleagues at first and then a friendship began to blossom. She trusted me. It was her mannerisms that drew me to her. There wasn't really a strong family resemblance as such. But then I began to see traits in her, little idiosyncrasies that I recognised from my past and I knew then that I had to do it. I had to take her, make her mine. I needed her to fill that gap.

And as for Izzie – sweet, unassuming little Izzie trying her hardest to do the right thing, to follow the advice of her family and friends and take up jogging in a bid to keep fit. She knew so little. I knew a lot. We met one morning when the sun was still low in the sky, an orange blur on the horizon, pushing its way up over the hills. She was struggling, I could see that, her body bent double as she gasped for breath.

'Take it slow and steady,' I had said, my hand resting on the top of her spine, a solid, reassuring weight. The hand of somebody older, more experienced. 'And these energy drinks really help. If you meet me here same time tomorrow morning, I can give you one. They make the world of difference. We can maybe run together? I can show you a safer route. Fewer crooked paths, more light.'

Sweet, dippy little Izzie with her hidden zest, tucked away beneath layers of helplessness and vulnerability. A little feisty thing itching to be out. It didn't take long for the drugs to kick in. She initially set off at a lick and for a minute I thought perhaps it wasn't going to work, but then I watched her falter, staggering through the woods, her legs suddenly weak, her head thick and fuzzy. She was unable to navigate her way out on to the nearby track. So I helped her. Just like I helped Deborah. The three of us working together as a team. A family.

She made it so easy for me it was embarrassing. Like taking candy from a baby. And the resemblance to Deborah was uncanny. I had to have her. There was no way I was going to let her go. One way or another I would make it happen. And I did. But now it's at an end, everything crumbling away. I'm losing my family all over again.

I don't remember much about the fire all those years ago. It was the patterns I adored; the heat and the colours. It sent me off into another dimension where nothing and nobody mattered. It was always about the patterns. And the control. I've always liked to do things my way. We all have our own strange little ways, don't we? Control is mine. To lose it is to lose everything. I won't let myself be at the mercy of others. It isn't right and it isn't me; it's not who I am.

I run my hands over the collection of pillboxes. It never ceases to amaze me, how much trust doctors have in their patients, prescribing powerful medication and hoping they use it as directed, not stash it away for other purposes. Sinister purposes. Which, of course, is exactly what I did. It was easy, slipping it into Deborah's coffee, following her and waiting until she stopped, drowsy and weak, before placing my arm around her waist and guiding her to my car. I had watched Merriel accompany her out of the office and prayed that they would part and go their own ways, which they did. That was when I stepped in. Luck smiled on me that evening. I'm not sure what would have happened had they continued on their journey together. I guess I would have had to bide my time, wait for another opportunity. But I didn't. She was finally alone. She was mine for the taking.

I had watched her for so long prior to that night, mesmerised by her. That was when I knew that I had to do it. And I'm glad I did. No regrets. It was a compulsion, a need to have her close to me. To atone for my sins. Except it wasn't always like the image I had in my head. She resisted my attempts to love her, to care for her. She made it difficult. Almost impossible at times. Towards the end she started to back down, acquiescing to keep the peace. That wasn't what I wanted either. It enraged me, made me do things I didn't want to do. It wasn't natural, her quiet, dim-witted ways, her lack of spirit. So I tried to wake her up a little, knock some fight back into her. In the end, I had forgotten what my true intentions actually were. It all became very blurred and confusing. Difficult to separate my anger from my aspirations.

And now look at me, sitting here ruminating over what I had. What I've lost. I suppose I've come full circle. I wonder what they'll say about me when the story breaks? Will I be portrayed as a maniacal woman, a crazy despot who kidnapped two women and held them captive or will I be painted as a sad female, a loner who had mental health problems? The desperate twin. The media like to do that, put their own slant on it. Anything to sell papers. Anything to get people poring over their words, greedily gobbling up chunks of misinformation without stopping to think about the human aspect of the story. The people who made mistakes and were denied access to things that mattered to them. Deborah mattered to me, and now I've lost her. Izzie was just a bonus, a wonderful addition to our secret little family. And now I've lost her too. I've lost everything. I have nothing. Nothing at all. Nothing to live for.

My fingers come to rest on the remaining packets of tablets, the medication that held such promise for me. I know what I have to do. It's only a matter of timing, getting everything just right. I'm a stickler for that. Getting everything exactly how I want it, but then I guess you already know that about me, don't you?

44

DEBORAH

It seems to take forever. I'm on my haunches, squatting down next to Merriel, my hand covering hers. She feels cold, her skin losing heat with every passing second. I rub back and forth, her slim hand between my palms as I try to force some warmth back into her pale, icy flesh.

Izzie is tramping over the field, her small, weak legs carrying her towards civilisation. She is so tired, her body almost bent in two. I want to shout at her to hurry up, to bang on every door she passes in case Yvonne comes back and does the unthinkable. Something deep down tells me she won't but I don't know that for certain. If there's one thing I've learnt from this whole awful episode of my life, it's that people cannot be trusted. I thought I knew her. I didn't. We used to sit opposite one another in the office, chat about anything and everything. She was always reserved but I didn't mind that. I felt comfortable talking to her about my concerns about Brett, my philandering partner. Unlike many of my other friends and colleagues, I knew she wouldn't betray my confidence and go off gossiping, letting others know my most personal and private worries and woes. I know now that it was a ruse, a way of getting to know me. A way of luring me into her trap. She's clever, I'll give her that. Clever, devious and manipulative. While the rest of us spend our days thinking about work and paying bills and relationships with family and friends, she uses her time to scheme and plan and work out ways in which she can hurt people. All that energy and intelligence used to wreak so much havoc and destruction. I don't want to know why. I don't want to spend any more time than I have to, thinking about her, trying to work out what is going on inside her head. She is nothing to me. A nobody. A person I will choose to erase from my mind. She doesn't deserve my time or anything else from me. It'll all come out anyway, her possible motivations, her demented behaviour, the reasons behind it. Let everyone else pick through the scraps of her life, feasting on it like wild animals. I'm going to move on with my own life, be reunited with my family. I'm finally free.

I place my fingers over Merriel's forehead. Cold and clammy. I check for a pulse. It's there. Faint but definitely there.

Please don't die, Merriel. Please don't die!

She loved this latest turn of events, seeing Merriel lying here injured, unconscious. The more bodies the better. That's how she thinks. Let them pile high. Death, damage. It flicks a switch inside her head, gives her a buzz. All the more reason to make sure Merriel lives.

All the more reason for Izzie to hurry up, to get the police and an ambulance here before anything dreadful happens.

Please hurry up!

My thoughts are muddled, my emotions tangled, everything focused on making sure Merriel lives. That's how I miss it. The figure in the distance. I see it at the edge of my vision, a lithe, willowy outline coming towards us. A running streak of black, stark and eye-catching against the pale green landscape. Field after field after field, the houses no more than a row of grey rooflines in the distance. My heart leaps, my blood fizzing and popping through my veins. She's coming back. Yvonne is doing the one thing I never expected her to do and she is coming back to finish us off.

I stand up, the world a sickly blur around me. I'm still bleeding. What use am I going to be against her? Tears spring to my eyes. A lump is wedged in my throat. I allow myself to cry, great big fat sobs heaving out of me. Not again. I can't go through it again. I've nothing left to give, no energy left in my tank, all stores depleted. I thought I was free. I was wrong.

Beside me, Merriel lets out a groan. I have to do something to save her. I'm the one who did this to her. I can't let it happen again. I have a duty of care to this woman. Her life is in my hands.

My legs are liquid as I step over her and head out into the daylight, the bright glare of the sun an assault on my eyes after being cooped up in the darkness for so long. I shield my eyes with my cupped hand, my fingers trembling, my arm throbbing and aching as if I'm having to hold the weight of a hundred men.

Her approaching figure fills me with trepidation but I'm not about to back down. This is my final hurrah, my way of showing her that she no longer scares me, even though she does. She's unpredictable, strong and psychotic, but my strength is from the belief I have in myself that I can stand face to face with her and brazen it out.

I can see as she gets closer that there's something different about her, something in her gait that is less threatening and menacing. She isn't radiating hostility but instead is smiling, her features softer. As if all the hatred and malice that has lived in her for so long has suddenly melted away.

Experience tells me to treat this new turn of events with caution. I step back into the relative safety of the derelict house, the old run-down farmhouse that has been my home for what feels like an age, and try to puff out my body, tensing my muscles, like a wild beast trying to scare off its opponent.

'Here, I brought you this. Look at it later, when I'm gone. Or throw it away. Whatever. Just don't give it to the papers. This one is only for you from me.' I'm not sure if I'm imagining it but her speech sounds different: there's a slur to it, each syllable merging into the next one.

She places the white envelope down at her feet, turns away from me and then she is gone, her body suddenly loose and floppy. She runs, her frame moving unsteadily until she is no more than a dot on the horizon.

I pick up the envelope, stuff it in my pocket. Later. I'm not about to be brought down by any more of her tricks. I'll hand it over to the relevant authorities. If and when they arrive. I won't keep it to myself. She doesn't deserve my trust and I don't want to hear any more of her lies or dark, unfathomable secrets.

Another moan from Merriel's unmoving body.

Oh God, please hurry up! Please, please, please!

I count the minutes, my fingers tracing a delicate line over Merriel's wrist, saying a small prayer for her, telling God how sorry I am for every little misdemeanour I have ever committed both as an adult and as a child, asking him for help, swearing on my life that I will do everything I can to help other people and make the world a better place if he can just make that ambulance hurry up and get us both out of here. If he can just let Merriel live.

And then I hear it, the low wail of a siren, somewhere out there, a ghostly echo.

Here! We're over here!

I let go of Merriel's hand and run outside to an overgrown gravel track, waist-high weeds towering on both sides of the road that leads to where I'm standing. I don't know how she did it, Izzie, directing them to this place that is so close to the rest of the world and yet at the same time, so very, very far away and yet she has. She has saved me. Saved us.

'This way!' I scream as the ambulance and police car screech to a halt beside me, their tyres making a loud cracking sound against the pebbles. 'Around the back. She's around the back. Please help her.'

I feel myself slipping, the world falling away around me, everything melting and oozing until there's nothing left, just a jumble of thoughts and a pain so deep it pushes me to the ground.

I think that I cry out but can't be certain. It may have come from elsewhere. From Izzie or Merriel. Except that as I fall to the ground, hitting the gravel with a sharp crack, I know for sure that it came from me, the jolt of the fall slotting everything back into place in my head.

'Please,' I say, the sky spinning above me, white clouds swirling and revolving in a chalk-white bulbous mass. 'Please take me home.'

45

ADRIAN

Did I dream it? Maybe it was the drugs. These painkillers have been giving me the weirdest nightmares and hallucinations. I've been trying to wean myself off them, trying to not press the button for that morphine pump but it's so tempting to keep at it for some relief from the pain that is screeching up and down my spine, flaring into the lower half of my body like a flamethrower being taken to my flesh and dragged up and down repeatedly.

Apparently, I also had a broken leg which required an operation. God knows how long I'm going to be laid up for. It already feels like I've been lying in this bed for an eternity, the world going about its business while I lie here totally incapacitated and separated from everyone and everything.

Was Ruth really here a few hours ago? I'm almost certain she was but am too doped up to trust my own instincts. I could have sworn she told me that they've found Deborah. It all seems completely surreal, a thick scribble of peculiar images running through my mind. God, I hope it's true, that they've found her and she's safe and well, not badly injured and close to death. I want to reach over for my phone but think that the battery has died. If they have found her, then where has she been all this time? Maybe she did take herself off somewhere, took some time to sort out any problems she had going on in her life. Or maybe something awful happened to her, somebody snatching her off the street before bundling her into a car and hiding her. Doing terrible, unspeakable things to her. I shut out that thought, turn away from it and stare outside to the overflowing car park and stream of visitors coming and going.

A wave of drowsiness washes over me, threatening to pull me under into that world of darkness that now fills me with dread. I try to resist but the morphine does its thing and drags me away. I slide under, my fight to stay awake a futile battle.

* * *

'It's true. They've both been found. Press coverage is in overdrive. They haven't said exactly where they were found but they've hinted that it was somewhere local. Good news for a change, eh?' The nurse standing at the bottom of my bed is nodding at me and smiling. She pulls out a watch from her chest pocket and checks it before pushing it back in and shuffling off out of sight.

I rest my head back on the pillow and smile. I hope Deborah's okay, not harmed in any way. She's alive at least. Deborah is alive. Not another name on a police statistic chart somewhere that keeps a tally of the number of dead bodies found every year in the UK.

I've never been one for crying. Letting the dam burst has never solved any problems for me in the past so I've always made sure to hold it back. But not today. These are tears of relief and happiness. I let them flow, embrace them even. At one point I actually wondered if Beth had something to do with Deborah's disappearance, linking her bizarre texts and messages with Deborah's vanishing, but it would seem not.

Beth visited me earlier. She had a lapse yesterday, succumbed to her urges and demons and drank herself into a stupor. Probably took drugs too. At least she was brave enough to admit it to me, not pretend that everything's going swimmingly when it clearly isn't. It's going to be a long haul, getting her back on the straight and narrow. I only hope she sticks to it and these lapses become less frequent.

I try to sit up and wipe my face with the back of my hand, tears and snot smearing everywhere. A pain ricochets though me, pinballing up and down my leg. I suck in a deep breath, waiting for it to pass. I'm going to be okay. Deborah's hopefully going to be okay. We still have no idea what happened to my climbing clip but maybe that's something I'll have to put on hold until I feel fully fit again. To be honest, I'm going to shove it away to the back of my mind, wait until I'm ready to think about it. Ruth and the rest of management have decided that they don't want the police getting involved anyway. Bad for business to have the company name dragged through the gutter by the press and, for once, I agree with them. Far better to think of it as an unfortunate accident. Easier for the hotel too. The saying that any publicity is good publicity doesn't lend itself to matters of safety and individuals coming close to losing their lives. It scares people away, can even be the undoing of a decent business.

Thinking about it is exhausting. I have shed so many tears lately that I'm awash with them. Why is crying so tiring? I won't need any morphine to knock me out after this marathon sobbing session. I feel tired already, as if I could sleep for the next decade and still wake up exhausted.

I turn on the television by my bed, using the card that Ruth kindly paid for, and scroll through the channels, looking for the local news. It doesn't take long for the headlines to start flashing up about the discovery of a number of women at a derelict farmhouse. Details of their injuries are yet to be released but it's believed that as many as three females have been taken to hospital.

The pain in my pelvis jars as I attempt to lever myself up. Three? Jesus, this person is a madman. A total psycho. *Three fucking women?*

I hope Deborah is okay, not too scarred by what has taken place. I know as well as the next person how deep those memories can become lodged, how difficult it is to shake them off once they have burrowed far down into our bones. I also know how hard it is to stop them from resurfacing every day, stopping us from getting on with our lives, the minutiae of our existences making no allowances for the damaged or the frightened.

When I finally get out of here, I'll do my best to connect with Deborah, atone for my stupid words in the pub that evening. They've stuck with me. Even after all of this carry-on, I still think about what I said. How it sounded. How it made me look. It was a stupid throwaway comment, a mistake. And at some point, I'm going to have to forgive myself for it because we all make mistakes, don't we? All of us.

46

YVONNE

To whoever may find this,

I've done what I had to do, the only thing left to do. That's the irony of all of this. I was only trying to do the right thing by my sisters, to make amends, but as is always the case, it ended up going horribly wrong and there didn't seem to be any way of getting it back, undoing the damage I had done.

People wouldn't understand anyway. They rarely do. That's why I said nothing for all those years, wore another face to the outside world. What would any of them know about it? The abuse I endured at the hands of that man. Everyone thought him blameless, the perfect father. And he was – to other members of our family. But I was singled out. Pulled aside and mistreated. My sisters were loved, but me? I was shown a different kind of love. A love I didn't want or ask for. And I was angry at them for it, for failing to notice what was going on right in front of their eyes.

That's why Rosa did what she did for all those years, punishing me because she felt left out. Had she known what

was happening she may not have felt so envious of my
special status. May not have felt a need to get back at me
and hurt me. I'd been hurt enough and spent so long
wanting to lash out and do the same to others. It's taken me
a long time to recognise what happened to me, why I don't
think the same way other people do, why I'm wired up the
way I am.

My head thumps as I screw up the letter and throw it in the bin. Nonsense. It just seems to spew forth out of me. I can't help it. It's who I am. Who I've always been. Deborah was right all those times she screamed and spat at me. I am a psychopath. A maniac. Psychotic. It doesn't bother me, those insults and accusations. That's the oxymoron in all of this. Nothing bothers me. No fear or racing pulse as I set fire to the house all those years ago and watched my family perish. No anxiety or terror as I pushed Deirdre over the edge of the cliff. Just a sense of fulfilment and contentment. A job well done.

I try again, writing a simple note, slipping it into a plain white envelope and pushing it into my pocket before setting off to see Deborah one last time.

* * *

I didn't stay for long. What was the point? Besides, I had to get back here before the police arrive and ruin everything. I would at least like to do something right. For once in my life, I am determined to do something properly, for everyone to see who I really am. What I am.

It doesn't take long for the fire to take hold. Everything is tidy, spick and span. At least I can say that Deirdre taught me something. When the vultures do pick through the remnants of my life, they can do so with ease. When they wait for the flames to die down, for the smoke to clear, then they can find out about my life. What I did. Who I hurt.

I hope they find what they're looking for. I hope they stumble across things that make them repulsed by who and what I am. I hope they feast on it and fight over the carcass of my life, stepping on each other for the biggest scoop. They won't, however. No matter how hard they look, they will soon realise that there's nothing here for them. All my life, I've discarded things, kept only the absolute essentials. Easier to travel light. When your soul is as dark and heavy as mine, only hand luggage is required.

Except for Deborah's letter; that is, if she shows it to them, allows the world to see who I really am. Why I did what I did. All I have is trust that she does as I asked and it stays between the two of us. Us twins.

Because at the end of the day, all we have ever had is each other.

47

DEBORAH

They've let me come across to this ward to see her. I'm walking down the corridor, like a real person, not a prisoner. A normal person free to do whatever they please, to go wherever they please. No more gags or ties. No more ropes cutting into my wrists. I'm here, on my own, strolling at a leisurely pace. God, it feels too good to be true, like all my Christmases have come at once. There were so many times I was convinced I was going to die in there, so many times when freedom and being able to stare up at the sky felt like an impossible ask. Yet here I am, doing just that. All that time, that pain, those bleak, bleak days. They're all behind me now. Never to be repeated.

It's hard to believe it but I sustained no broken bones whatsoever. A deep cut on my arm, a frozen shoulder from my hands being held behind my back for so long, and deep tissue damage on various points throughout my body, but no fractures or breaks. It's a miracle. In many ways, I'm a very lucky girl.

Izzie has been discharged, her statement taken, and is currently being driven home to her small cottage in Little Ayton by her brother. We've exchanged details and promised to keep in touch, our imprisonment forming a strong bond between us. I feel a need to talk about our time together holed up in that place, a way of healing my internal wounds. Izzie is the only one who will truly understand my experience and I'm the only one who will ever understand hers.

Merriel is sitting up in bed as I open the door to her side room. A woman I guess to be her sister is sitting on a plastic chair next to her bed. Their features are strikingly similar, their hair colour the only thing that sets them apart. Same high cheekbones, same green eyes.

Her head is resting back on the pillow, hair splayed out behind her. I smile, unsure how she'll react to seeing me. It's been explained to her, what happened. The police have been, taken her statement as they did from me and Izzie. And now it's my turn to speak with her, to apologise, work out how she feels about me and what I did to her; see if we can still be friends in the future.

It's difficult to gauge her reaction to my unannounced visit, with her bruised eyes and swollen mouth masking her facial expressions – injuries she sustained by the push I gave her that sent her hurtling down a set of stairs. She could have died. I thought she had. Relief doesn't begin to cover the feelings I have about the fact she survived.

My stomach tightens, my heart begins to race as I walk up to the bed and look down at her. 'Merriel… I'm…'

Without missing a beat, her sister stands up, pats the seat for me to sit down and then holds out her hand for me to take. We shake, her fingers warm, clasped around mine. I shiver, glad of the show of affection, the sincerity of her smile. I didn't expect this. I envisaged coldness, resentment. Hatred even. This is more than I hoped for. Perhaps more than I deserve. I should have waited to see who was behind that door. I didn't and now Merriel is lying here, battered and broken.

'Come in. Please sit down. Merriel was hoping you would call in.' She bends down, picks up her bag and slings it over her shoulder. 'Listen, I'm going to head off now. I need to get home, sort out a few things.' She bends down, kisses Merriel on the forehead. 'See you later, sis. Good to have you back in the land of the living. We'll have you home in no time at all.'

And with that, she is gone, leaving nothing except a scent of musky-smelling perfume in her wake.

I'm not sure what to say, how to break the ice, let her know how sorry I am. Turns out I don't have to say anything at all. She is there before me, her voice croaky, a faint whisper that I have to strain to hear.

'Good to see you. We've both lived to tell the tale. What a time to be alive, eh?' She manages a sly wink through her puffy eye.

Our laughter is synchronised, both of us struggling with our injuries as we titter like a pair of errant schoolchildren. My ribs ache and my shoulder still feels like I've been kicked by a very large horse, but the release of happiness feels so good. I've been like a taut bowstring for so long now, keeping everything tucked away, that I can't seem to stop the laughter. It pours out of me, filling the room until at last, we stop, both of us panting for breath.

I dip my head, a quiet taking hold as I struggle for the right words. 'I didn't know,' I finally say after the silence becomes too much to bear. 'I honestly thought—'

Merriel interrupts me, her hand reaching out for mine. 'I know. You don't have to say anything. I know.'

I nod, blinking back tears. So many highs and lows, a smorgasbord of emotions hidden within me.

'The police have told me bits, but not everything. I was just wondering...?' I say softly.

'How I knew where you were?' She sighs, her poor swollen eyes flickering. 'It's a long story if you've got time to spare?'

I look around and spread my hands. 'I'm not going anywhere. I've got the time if you have?'

She sighs, her chest rising and falling rhythmically, and tells me everything I need to know.

* * *

'My life at home hasn't been easy the past few months. That was my sister, Tina, who was here when you came in, although I'm sure you guessed that, didn't you? Everyone says we look alike. Anyway, since our dad has been ill, I've tried to look after him. Tina works long shifts as a nurse and my other sister, Michelle, lives down south so I've been coping with him on my own. He's got dementia and last week he attacked me, hence the cut on my eye.' She points to her face and laughs. 'Not that you can see it now, of course, with these two beauties. I was really pissed off as I felt like my two siblings had let me down and left me to cope on my own. Since this has happened, they've come together to talk and we've now got a rota going. Michelle is going to have Dad stay with her for a few weeks down in Essex to give me a break. Her and her partner, Sarah, are going to come up here and collect Dad then drive back down to Essex with him. God knows how that's going to pan out but at least I'll have a few weeks to myself to recuperate.'

I feel my face flush with shame and feel a desperate need to apologise once again.

'Anyway, I digress. That doesn't really answer your question as to how I knew where you were being held. The real answer is

that I didn't know. I went there looking for Yvonne.' Merriel
sighs, closes her eyes briefly and waits a few seconds before
speaking again. Every blink, every swallow, every slight movement she makes looking like agony. I shudder, clench my fists
until my ragged nails dig into my palms, rough edges nipping
and tearing at flesh. I wince at the pain then stop myself,
thinking that it's nothing compared to what I've endured. What
we have all endured – me, Izzie and Merriel. A simple flash of
pain, a transient thing. Fleeting and bearable. We've all been
transformed into resilient individuals now. It didn't kill us. *She*
didn't kill us. She inadvertently made us stronger. I wonder if
she knows that? What she would make of it.

'When I first started working at the company, I felt sure I
recognised her from somewhere,' Merriel continues. 'So, after a
while, quite a long while actually, I started following her to see
where she lived, see if I could work out whether or not it was
really her. I needed something concrete to confirm my
suspicions.'

'But why didn't you just ask her if she was who you thought
she was?' I narrow my eyes, my curiosity piqued, unsure
whether or not I actually want to hear the next part of this story.
Something doesn't quite fit. I suddenly feel uncomfortable, my
senses attuned to something that hasn't yet been voiced.

Merriel lifts her hand, an act that clearly causes her pain.
She drops it back onto the bed and shakes her head, a lone tear
escaping and rolling down her swollen cheek, a watery streak
incongruous against the purplish hue of her damaged flesh.

'I couldn't. If she was who I thought she was, then she would
have possibly fled. I was also quite scared. It took me quite a
while to muster up the courage to do anything. Months and
months actually. I know everyone thinks I'm brimming with

confidence but that's just an act. Inside, I'm like everybody else, an unsure individual who is as worried about things as much as the next person. I took my time, thought about what I was going to do, how I would discover if she was who I thought she was and stalked her instead, watching her leave her home to go jogging, disappearing into that old building from time to time. And then she found out that I knew her address and kept questioning me, asking me how I knew. So I lied, made up a tale about thinking she was the person who was responsible for the death of my brother when we were kids. I knew she wasn't. The person who killed my brother is long since dead, drank herself to death at the ripe old age of twenty, but she caught me on the back foot so I had to think of something and that's what I told her, along with a load of other lies to try and throw her off the scent.'

There's something big coming next. I can just feel it. The police have given me snippets but not enough for me to put it all together on my own. Yvonne isn't who we all thought she is, that much I do know.

'That's the weird thing, something I should have picked up on but didn't.' Merriel sighs, her breathing ragged. 'When I told her that I thought she was the person who murdered my little brother, she didn't flicker. No sharp intake of breath or a shriek or even an irritated *how dare you mistake me for a child killer*. Nothing at all. If it was me, I'd have been bloody livid, but she didn't bat an eyelid.'

I can believe that. I don't say anything to Merriel though. Instead, I nod and murmur that it is indeed an odd reaction to a deeply unusual statement. Not the sort of thing that gets said every day. But then, Yvonne isn't your everyday person. She's different. Off-kilter. Way, way off balance. Too far off balance to ever be righted again.

'I suppose you've heard about the fire?' Merriel says and I nod.

'Police said they've found a body and are in the process of recovering it for identification. That's the thing,' I say, a sudden thought piercing me. 'She never once mentioned any relatives or friends. I don't actually think she had anybody at all—'

'She didn't,' Merriel cuts in. 'I'm almost certain I was right when I thought I knew her. I'll have to wait for the formal identification process to prove my suspicions but I'm pretty sure I knew her when I was a child. We grew up together, lived a few roads away from each other.'

'And?' I say after a short silence, the need to know the real Yvonne gnawing at me.

Merriel shakes her head, a small act that obviously causes her pain. She closes her eyes and takes a long breath. 'It's a long and grisly tale, I'm afraid.'

I look up at the clock and smile. 'So how about I go to the machine and get us both a coffee? If there's one thing I've got a lot of right now, it's time.'

48

MERRIEL

I wish I'd never recognised her. I wish I had let it go, ignored my nagging intuition that something was amiss with that woman and just got on with my life instead. But I didn't. I dug and probed and followed and stalked. And now look at me. Bruised and battered, lying in a hospital bed with journalists waiting outside, hoping to get a picture of either me or Deborah once we're discharged. We're the latest news story; today's scoop, next week's chip-shop paper.

I guess I understand the interest and intrigue. It's an odd story, although the full truth probably won't come out until the inquest has been completed.

'Here you go.' Deborah places a plastic cup down on the tray next to my bed. 'Can you sit up? Here, let me help you. Easy does it now.'

She places her hands under my armpits and slowly shuffles me into a sitting position. It hurts, but not as much as it did a couple of days ago. Every day is a step closer to getting better. I'm counting down the days to a full recovery. Two cracked vertebrae and a fractured arm. Not as bad as it could have been.

Maybe my brutal fitness regime helped keep me alive, strengthening my body. Here's hoping it will aid a swift recovery as well.

Deborah passes me the coffee, her long fingers clasped around the rim as she carefully passes it to me. 'Can you manage?'

I nod, blow on it and take a sip. 'Caffeine. Thank God.'

'So?' she says softly, her eyes finding mine.

'So,' I say in return. 'Time to talk, eh?'

I take another sip, let the scalding hot liquid do its thing, the caffeine finding a route into my system, and start to speak. 'Yvonne is, *was* a twin.'

Deborah nods, as if she already knew this. 'She had a sister or sisters, that much I do know, just from her ramblings.'

'Yeah, two sisters. They both died. Her two sisters and both of her parents, they all perished in a fire. She was found outside, sitting near a patch of undergrowth, not a scar or burn on her. Somehow, she managed to get out of the house unscathed. At the time, everybody called her a miracle child, the local girl who survived a horrific fire. She was sent to live with an aunt. I can't remember where, but I do recall what happened to the aunt quite a few years later.'

I take a rest, shut my eyes for a second or so before continuing. Who would have ever thought that speaking could be so exhausting?

'So, what *did* happen to the aunt?' Deborah's voice is a whisper, a look of expectation evident in her expression. She knows what's coming. I hardly need to say it but I do anyway.

'She died. Fell over the edge of a high rock while out walking. With her niece. The same niece who survived a fire that killed the rest of her family.'

Deborah swallows, the lump in her throat bobbing up and down.

'You think she was responsible for both incidents?'

I try to shrug, pain and dressings making it difficult for me to move properly. 'Some people had their suspicions after her aunt died but nothing was ever done about it. It was years later. Many felt sorry for her, thought she'd had a tough life, told the ones who suspected her to stop with all the talk. I'd not seen her for years. After the fire she moved away. Her aunt lived closer to North Yorkshire but we heard about her death through the grapevine and I have to admit, it made my skin prickle.'

'I take it the police didn't suspect her then?'

'No. Only local people who found it all a bit strange. You have to remember she was just a kid when the fire happened. Nobody would ever think to accuse a child of murdering their entire family, would they? But there was talk after her aunt died. She had always been a strange one as a child, really precocious and overly confident, and it all felt a bit – I don't know – a bit coincidental.' I lean my head back on the pillow, a crippling sense of fatigue suddenly hitting me. It's a struggle to keep my eyes open – my sore, swollen, bloodied eyes. They're as heavy as lead, gravity forcing them downwards. I blink, take a long sip of coffee, hoping it will wake me up. It's these painkillers. They send me into a death-like exhaustion, knocking me out for hours at a time.

'I guess we'll never know now, will we?' Deborah's voice snaps me out of my reverie.

I nod, my voice raspy. 'I guess we won't but I had my own suspicions and then after you went missing, it got me thinking that if she was who I thought she was, that yet again something untoward had happened when she was around. And after the accident with Adrian, when she ran, I felt compelled to follow her. I knew then that something was up. I just wasn't sure what. It was all instinct and supposition.'

'Strange. Isn't it?' Deborah says. 'How she went the same way as the rest of her family. I wonder if that's why she did it? Her final way of admitting her guilt?'

'Possibly. I suppose we'll just have to wait and see what the police say after they complete their investigation. From what I've been told, her body was found on the sofa. She made no attempt to leave the house.'

Deborah closes her eyes for a second, lowers her head then looks up at me. 'I get it now. That makes sense.'

'What makes sense? I don't understand?'

'The drugs she gave me and Izzie. I'm willing to bet she took them. When she came back to see me one last time, I noticed that she was unsteady on her feet, her speech slurred. I'll bet she was knocked out or maybe even dead before the fire got to her.'

We sit in silence for a short while, our breathing synchronised. I'm not sure what else there is to say so we say nothing for what feels like the longest time until Deborah stands up, reaches into her pocket, and brings out a small white envelope. She pulls out the piece of paper from inside it and hands it to me.

'I can't,' I say quietly. 'Too painful with these swollen eyes. You read it to me.'

So she does.

Dear Deborah,

I'm sorry for everything. It didn't turn out as planned, our time together, and for that, I apologise. I wish things could have been different, our final hours more genial, less trying and hostile but like lots of things in my life, I cannot change them. They are what they are. I hope you realise that I was trying to make up for what I did to you, for what I did to our

little family. I didn't mean to, it just happened. Life has a way
of dragging me downwards. Seems it's the only direction I
know.

Take care of yourself and stay safe. You always were the
blessed one.

Love Sadie.

'No.' I try to sit up, shock jarring at me like dozens of tiny electrical pulses.

'No what?' Deborah stuffs the letter back in her pocket, a small line of anxiety forming between her eyes. She sits down and takes my hand between hers. 'No what, Merriel? I'm not sure what you mean?'

'No, that's not her,' I whisper, phlegm catching the back of my throat, forcing me into a painful coughing fit that seems to go on for an age.

Deborah rubs at my back and looks around for assistance.

'I'm fine. It's fine. I don't need anybody. Just a drink of water, please.'

She hands me the glass and I take a couple of sips to alleviate the dry ache at the back of my throat.

Another protracted silence. And then, 'What do you mean, that's not her?'

I sigh, place the glass back in Deborah's outstretched hand and speak. 'Yvonne is Rosa Milburn. Sadie, her twin, died in the fire. I remember it well. Even visited her grave with a couple of other friends when we were older, placed some flowers beneath her headstone. I've no idea why she has called herself Sadie but she definitely isn't her. *Wasn't* her. Yvonne changed her name from Rosa Milburn.'

The fatigue creeps up on me again and this time it's pointless fighting it. Better to sleep and let my body rest and heal.

The sooner I heal, the sooner I can get out of here and back home to my own family, my own sisters. And my dad. That particular aspect of my life will be a hurdle I have to leap but leap it I will. He's my father, my close family, and he needs me now more than ever.

I close my eyes and within seconds feel myself being carried away to another place where pain is non-existent and possibilities for a stress-free existence endless. I embrace it, my exhaustion a cavernous pit I'm powerless to fight. When I wake up, everything will be better, my body a step closer to being fit once again. I'm alive. Yvonne isn't, and I'm good with that. It's how things should be. How they should have always been.

49

DEBORAH

Six Months Later

'Adrian, you are such a forgiving soul, you really are. I'd be suing this company if I were you, but that's just me.' Merriel picks up the flask and pours herself a coffee, the sound of her slurping no longer the irritating noise it used to be when we worked alongside one another.

I decided after my period of captivity to look for another job and after taking a few months off to rest and heal, made the decision to retrain and become a teacher. I'm taking my PGCE and this time next year I'll be standing in front of a class of pupils. The thought of it is both exhilarating and terrifying. But not as terrifying as my recent ordeal. I survived that so I'm damn sure I can survive spending all day with a group of ten-year-olds.

'She's already serving a sentence of sorts. What's the point?' Adrian shrugs and smiles, and at that point, I want to hug him.

He's come a long way, taken a rough and rugged path through life but here he is, a gentle, thoughtful man, willing to forgive and forget an act that could have so easily left him permanently disabled or even taken his life.

'Hardly a punishment though, is it? A nice comfy bed at the local mental health unit with access to a widescreen TV and a canteen that serves hot food. Better than your average Travelodge if you ask me.'

I say nothing. No matter how comfortable Allison's surroundings are, nothing will make up for her losing her family and friends and her liberty. The mind is a complex thing, that much I do know. After her surprise admission about unfastening Adrian's harness, she went missing and was found over a week later, dehydrated, bedraggled and unrecognisable, her mind fragmented, her spirit broken. Allison is a tortured woman and is clearly suffering. She was sectioned after she tried to harm herself and is now hopefully receiving the proper care she deserves. Adrian understands suffering. Merriel, for all she is a friend, is a little less magnanimous and that is fine as well. We all have our own ways of dealing with trauma. There is no one perfect way of getting through difficult times.

I have told Brett to find somebody else who is willing to put up with his philandering ways and am ridiculously excited about my future career as a teacher. Merriel is still working at Haswell & Sons as are Ruth and Adrian. Merriel's dad is now in a care home, his own needs too great for Merriel to deal with alone. We have all moved on in one way or another.

The story of our kidnapping made national news. Izzie contacted me in a complete frenzy, terrified at the army of journalists that were camped out on her front lawn. I told her to ignore them, to hunker down and gorge herself with daytime TV until they all got bored and left. Which they did. We're no longer the main headline, reporters now more tied up with stories of a global pandemic that seemingly has no end.

'Same time next month?' Adrian stands up, packs away his flask and hauls his rucksack over his shoulders.

Merriel and I nod. 'I still think we should invite Ruth next time,' Merriel says, eyeing Adrian cautiously.

He juts out his bottom lip, thinks awhile and smiles. 'Yeah, why not? Maybe once this is all over, we could even consider having a get-together indoors. Still,' he says, staring off into the distance, 'as long as this weather holds, being outside is fine by me.'

Nearby, a small group of teenagers mill about by the children's playground, their chatter carried our way by the soft summer breeze.

I close my eyes, feel the heat of the evening summer sun on my face and sigh. Today is another step towards the rest of my life and I will treasure it always.

'Come on,' Merriel says with a laugh. 'Race you to the swings. Last one there's a rotten egg.'

We stand up, our once damaged bodies now fit and repaired, and we run.

ACKNOWLEDGMENTS

Acknowledgements are often harder to write than the actual book itself, the fear of missing anybody out so great, it makes make me lose sleep at night, but here goes!

First and foremost, a big thank you to Boldwood Books for taking me on and allowing me free rein with my idea. It took a while to take shape but with the help of Emily Ruston, we got there in the end, so a big thank you to Emily for her supportive words and guidance. Emily, you were so right – the introduction of Adrian brought the book to life!

A big thank you to Anita Waller and Valerie Keogh for keeping me going with our (almost) daily chats. You ladies are brilliant and I'd be lost without you.

Without readers, online book clubs and book bloggers, authors would be nothing, so a huge thank you to anybody who takes the time to read my book and review it. I'm honoured you chose my story over the thousands of others out there.

A big thank you to my family and friends who support me every single day with their kind words and patience when I'm slumped over my computer and having to break yet another engagement to finish my latest manuscript.

Finally, gratitude and love to my husband, Richard, who keeps me supplied with endless rounds of coffee and cake. This latest story was brought to you, dear reader, by a shedload of sugar and caffeine. I hope you like it...

I am always available to chat on social media and can be found at:

www.facebook.com/thewriterjude
www.twitter.com/thewriterjude
www.instagram.com/jabakerauthor

ABOUT THE AUTHOR

J. A. Baker is a successful psychological thriller writer of numerous books. Born and brought up in Middlesbrough, she still lives in the North East, which inspires the settings for her books.

Sign up to J.A. Baker's mailing list for news, competitions and updates on future books.

Follow J. A. Baker on social media here:

facebook.com/thewriterjude

twitter.com/thewriterjude

instagram.com/jabakerauthor

tiktok.com/@jabaker41

ALSO BY J. A. BAKER

THE

Murder

LIST

THE MURDER LIST IS A NEWSLETTER DEDICATED TO SPINE-CHILLING FICTION AND GRIPPING PAGE-TURNERS!

SIGN UP TO MAKE SURE YOU'RE ON OUR HIT LIST FOR EXCLUSIVE DEALS, AUTHOR CONTENT, AND COMPETITIONS.

SIGN UP TO OUR NEWSLETTER

BIT.LY/THEMURDERLISTNEWS

Boldwood

Boldwood Books is an award-winning fiction publishing company seeking out the best stories from around the world.

Find out more at www.boldwoodbooks.com

Join our reader community for brilliant books, competitions and offers!

Follow us
@BoldwoodBooks
@TheBoldBookClub

Sign up to our weekly deals newsletter

https://bit.ly/BoldwoodBNewsletter